LEAVES NO LONGER GREEN

Praise for *Leaves No Longer Green*

'A tribute to the story of tea, to *Camellia sinensis* and tea estate dynamics, Arup Dutta's book is an epic narrative blending history, memory, identity. A compelling work by a versatile and pioneering internationally recognized master storyteller.'

—**Mamang Dai**, poet and novelist, Pasighat, Arunachal Pradesh.

'*Leaves No Longer Green* has transformed cold, tea-plantation facts into a deeply moving story. Its enduring value lies in its illumination of the awful evil of colonialism, pointing our thoughts to its equally evil new avatar in contemporary neocolonialism and apartheid, colonial systems. Epical in scope, this is historical fiction at its most alluring!'

—**Kynpham Sing Nongkynrih**, poet and novelist, Sohra, Meghalaya.

'In telling the story of an epoch that is also the account of individuals caught in the throes of an evolving society, Arup Kumar Dutta's novel takes us on a journey unlike any other where Assam's cultural markers find history's etchings brought forth in remarkable relief. This is a book not to be missed. A real gem.'

—**Dr Bibhash Choudhury**. Literary critic, Guwahati, Assam.

LEAVES NO LONGER GREEN

a novel

ARUP KUMAR DUTTA

HarperCollins *Publishers* India

First published in India by HarperCollins *Publishers* 2026
HarperCollins *Publishers* India, Cyber City,
Building 10-A, Gurugram, Haryana – 122002, India
www.harpercollins.co.in

2 4 6 8 10 9 7 5 3 1

P-ISBN: 978-93-7307-572-3
E-ISBN: 978-93-7307-021-6

Typeset in 10.5 pt/13.5 Adobe Garamond Pro
by HarperCollins *Publishers* India Pvt. Ltd

Printed and bound at
Manipal Technologies Limited, Manipal

This book is produced from independently certified FSC® paper to ensure responsible forest management.

HarperCollins *Publishers*, Macken House, 39/40 Mayor Street Upper, Dublin 1, D01 C9W8, Ireland

For my wife, Rupa

'Many of the adventurers who came hither from Europe are the greatest profligates the sun ever saw; men whom nothing but despotism can manage, and who, unless they are really under a despotic rule, would insult, beat and plunder the natives without shame or pity.'

—Bishop Heber, the first head of the Diocese of Calcutta, 1824

PROLOGUE

'First, we had the wild rush, the mad fever, when every man thought that to own a few tea bushes was to realize wealth. In those days, existing plantations were bought at eight or ten times their value; nominal areas of five hundred acres were paid for which, on subsequent measurement, proved to be under one hundred; new gardens were commenced on impossible sites and by men as managers who not only did not know a tea plant from a cabbage, but who were equally ignorant of the commonest rules of agriculture ...'

—Edward Money, writing about the 'Tea Mania' of the 1860s

In the third decade of the nineteenth century, the British East India Company began experimenting with the cultivation of *Camellia sinensis*, or tea, in the newly annexed territory of Assam to cater to the rapidly enlarging 'home market' while reducing dependence on China for supply of the brew.

In 1839, the first Indian tea company called the Assam Company was established, followed by the Jorehaut Tea Company. The success of these two companies, as well as a few proprietorial planters, led in the 1860s to what has aptly been called 'tea mania' among European speculators. Europeans of all shapes and shades made a beeline for Assam and a mad scramble ensued among them to grab as much land as possible and start planting.

The search for easy money attracted the scum of European society to Assam. Cheating and treachery were the watchwords of the speculators. Many simply cleared small portions of their land holdings, stuck a few mature bushes on them and sold them off at extravagant prices to gullible buyers as full-fledged tea gardens. The worst aspects of imperialism: avarice, amorality, exploitation and hypocrisy, held sway.

And at this virulent altar of laissez faire were sacrificed thousands of coolies*, conscripted by ruthless coolie-catchers and transported like cattle on steamers, flats and country-boats, to slave and rot and die in distant plantations, to turn red, with their blood, the green leaves of Camellia!

* The word 'coolie' today is considered to be a pejorative and, therefore, is avoided. However, during the period in which the novel is set, the term was commonly used to denote a manual labourer.

BOOK ONE

THE RIVER

'On the last trip of the steamer some 80 coolies were brought up for the Assam Company, and as I came up from Gowhatty on the steamer, I had a good opportunity of observing the habits of the coolies, their accommodation and treatment, and I am of the opinion that much may be done by better arrangement to mitigate the misery and consequent mortality on the passage. The most obvious inconveniences were: first, insufficient cooking accommodation causing undue delay in the preparation of their meals, and as each individual or family had their rations served out to them in a raw state, those who were the latest to cook, rather than wait, satisfied the cravings of nature with uncooked food. Secondly, no private conveniences for relieving the calls of nature, nothing but the ship's side, in the most public manner, the candidate for relief requiring another person to hold on by the hands; if a woman, this was a source of positive terror to the female emigrant, several of whom are dumped overboard each trip. Thirdly, wet decks, and the inability of the sick to be on their legs until the decks dried, which is a very slow process in wet weather … At Tezpore, damp raw weather set in and with it cholera made its first appearance … the young, the sick and the weakly falling the first victims.'

—Report of Superintendent, Jorehaut Tea Company, to his Managing Director on 21 September 1860

Calcutta. 7 September 1861.

Chandpal ghat clung, a scabby cicatrice, to the river Hoogli's swirling belly.

That early in the autumnal morning the sun, unable to burst out of its chrysalis of fleece and river mist, daubed the ghat with a matt, opaque, aqueous light, giving it the time-ravaged looks of a courtesan long past her prime. The wooden pier, first built in 1774, mildewed, reflected neglect; the supporting tree trunks rising from the river bed were furry with lush, dark-green moss. At places, the heat and the damp had so cracked and blistered the wood that fading layers of paint could not hide the wrinkled smears age had etched upon its features.

Yet this dilapidated cenotaph to an obscure grocer who had lent it his name had been touched by the timeless fingers of history. The decrepit courtesan had been a charmer once, used and abused, vivacious, vibrant with sound, life and laughter. Before the landing steps of incoming ships had been hauled away to the upstart Outram ghat, named in honour of Sir James Outram, all sea-going vessels had made it their port of call. Those days, the skyline of the Hoogli river at that point bristled with the masts of arrogant East Indiamen, poised to depart with the exotic wares of the orient; swift, sleek, elegant clippers which brought in English goods, news from 'Home' and the latest in European fashions; heavy-armed gunboats and troopers manned by haughty, bearded men resplendent in scarlet, blue and white; quaint Chinese crafts with eyes painted on their sides so they could see their way across oceans; merchant ships of all the maritime nations of the world; ships from America, lean and sprightly, their holds laden with huge blocks of ice; dugout canoes; ungainly native boats which swarmed around the bigger vessels like flies around treacle; and river barges of all shapes and sizes. The ghat too had been an impassive spectator to the death of the East Indiamen and the clippers, and the advent of the *Smellpots*, those graceless, unromantic, ugly steamships, the first of which had left Falmouth in August, 1825, touching Calcutta in December that year.

With the passage of the years, however, the fortunes of the ghat took a fall. The Indian subcontinent was rapidly emerging as Imperial Britain's prized possession, the refulgent jewel in Regina Victoria's crown, a milch cow to be milked dry to feed the ravenous machines of the Industrial Revolution. Calcutta was gradually growing in stature to become the commercial hub of an Empire upon which the sun never set, replacing such Far East bases as Amoy, Canton or Macao. Chandpal ghat could no longer cope with the increase in trade and traffic; a new ghat was built to handle the bigger, sea-going vessels; and the aged crone left to decay.

Now, apart from native tradingboats, the ghat handled only the inland water transport—the ferries which plied the Ganges and the Brahmaputra. One of them, the Indian General Navigation Steam Company's paddle-steamer, the *Ultaganga*, with the flat *Shaitan* in tow, chafed at her moorage this morning.

She had been scheduled to steam off on her voyage to Assam, the remote eastern corner of Britannia's vast Indian Empire, at 6 a.m. It was past seven now, and she was still at the pier.

The huge and hideous hulk of the steamer lay in enforced quiescence, its engine cold, stacks smokeless. Though groups of passengers stood on the upper deck, there was not much movement. Even the more boisterous of the upper stern deck passengers, all natives and quite a few in number, tired out by the delay, had given up hopes of ever leaving and sunk into solemn stupor.

Scattered clusters of people, mostly Hindustanis, loitered indolently upon the wooden platform which jutted out into the waters. The goods shed at the other end of the pier was somnolent, the officials having completed their morning chores. Beyond it, half a dozen gharries—one-horse buggies—flanked the strand in a neat row, while behind them sat the palanquin-bearers, big, black and hefty men who puffed on a chillum they passed from one to another.

The ceaseless bustle on the adjacent bank was in sharp contrast to the static immobility of the pier. Scores of natives carried out their morning ablutions there; bhistis filled goatskin water carriers and slung them on their backs; dhobis washed clothes, whirling them expertly in the air before bringing them sharply down on flat stones. A line of barbers squatted on their haunches, like vultures on a simul tree, face to face with their customers in a stance of indecipherable intimacy. Bare-torsoed Brahmins, sacred threads pegged to ears and foreheads vermillioned, stood half-submerged in the sluggish currents, invoking the sun-god, chanting Sanskrit shlokas. Demure Hindustani women, head and face shaded with their sari ends, stepped lightly down the bank to collect pitchers of water which they carried on their heads, backs ramrod straight. Cows and horses, buffaloes and goats, mingled undisturbed with the bathers and the bhistis, guzzling deep from the river, the precious source of life.

On the strand itself, the white sahibs and memsahibs took their morning ride, stiff-backed and proud, staring straight ahead, not condescending to notice the babbling hoi polloi on the river bank. The maidan rolling away from the strand like a velvet carpet was cluttered with European couples, their children and dogs, and native retainers who perpetually scurried after the sahiblog. It being early, the buildings of Calcutta at the far edge of the maidan were hazy shadows yet.

On the forward, upper saloon deck of the *Ultaganga*, an exclusive preserve of Europeans, David and Cordelia Esscombe were bidding their hosts in Calcutta, the Swinnerton-Dyers, a protracted farewell.

Quill in hand, with just a shirt to his back, Alexander Swinnerton-Dyer had set out for Hindustan four decades back, raw and gangling, yet shrewd, calculating, eminently avaricious and scorchingly ambitious. The prosaic mantle of petty clerkdom ill-fitted him; but he had to endure its weight for a decade before he could sever the umbilicus binding him to the British East India Company. Then he had struck out on his own, predatory instincts unshackled and made good.

Penny by penny, pice by pice, he had risen on the material and social scale till he grew rich and respectable. Now, in his early sixties, tall, silver-haired, grave-miened and bewhiskered, he was unassailably perched on his plateau of prosperity and respectability.

His friend and compatriot from the East India Company days, Henry David Esscombe, had not had Alex's luck. Esscombe had never been able to concentrate on a specific enterprise for a prolonged period and make a success of it—he had flitted from one venture to another; whatever capital gains his rare successes accrued and made possible his commercial adventurisms were finally wiped out four years back, when he and his family were caught in the thick of the sepoy uprising. They had, mercifully, escaped with their lives, but lost the greater part of their worldly assets.

That was the grim price he had paid for ignoring his friend's advice and shifting his base of operations from Calcutta to distant Delhi. But now, he was tucked away in the interiors of the inhospitable terra incognita known as Assam, growing tea plants! And, by the looks of it, he was gravely ill. If the malady had not been of a severe nature, Esscombe, who loved his two children more than anything else in the world, would not have summoned them to that miserable, God-forsaken place.

Three summers back, Esscombe had suddenly resurfaced in Calcutta, unheralded, to seek out his crony. Swinnerton-Dyer had been startled at the change in the man. The old, immaculate Esscombe had disappeared, that perennial optimist with the booming, infectious laughter, and in his place had come a being who moved heavily, powerful shoulders drooping, and talked sombrely of fate and predestination and the futility of human endeavour. Swinnerton-Dyer discovered to his dismay that Esscombe had become, like most Orientals, a fatalist!

They sat at the opposite ends of the rectangular, mahogany dining table; two Englishmen, one wrapped in the benign glow of success, the other, failure deeply graven in each facial contour. Esscombe had caught his friend alone, the mistress of the house having set off a month back on the annual migration to a cooler clime. Normally, the husband accompanied his aged spouse on these mandatory pilgrimages to Darjeeling or Shimla, for Calcutta was oppressively hot and humid during the summer months. Urgent affairs requiring personal supervision, however, had kept Swinnerton-Dyer back.

The two men talked very little as they ate. The merchant, shrewd and worldly-wise, suspected that his friend's visit could not be unmotivated. Despite this, when Esscombe finally offered enlightenment with a deceptive nonchalance over an after-dinner brandy in his host's study, the merchant was caught off guard.

'I'm going to Assam, Alex.'

Swinnerton-Dyer was appalled. His instincts, honed to razor sharpness by years of dealing with native traders, cautioned him he was about to be drawn into something he would regret.

'Another of your get-rich-quick schemes, Henry?'

'On the contrary, dear chap, the scheme I have in mind will take years to bear fruit. A proper play on words, eh?'

The merchant did not respond to the smile. 'I fail to get your point,' he said warily. 'Let alone your pun!'

'Not fruits, old man. Just leaves! I'm off to Assam to try my hand at tea. But you'll have to help. That's precisely why I've come to you.'

'All I have is yours, you know that, Henry. But there's no future in tea.'

'You can't be more wrong!' Esscombe asserted with vehemence. 'The age of Indian tea has finally arrived. A few of our blokes have even opened up private tea gardens. Mark my words, now's the time to get into tea!'

'Have you any knowledge of the finance involved? Astronomical, Henry, astronomical! Do you have that kind of money?'

Esscombe slumped down into his chair, closed his eyes, and drifted into meditation. Silence like a bird of the night swept in on shadowy wings and settled in the room—a strained silence, taut as a sitar string. But absolute silence in an Indian summer night was impossible. Sibilants punctuated the dark; yet these deepened rather than disrupted the all-pervasive silence. A self-effacing punkah-puller, wraith-like, had followed his master into the study and the apparatus hissed softly overhead. A big dung-beetle, unwieldy in flight, emitted a drone; a gecko, eyes unblinking, gazed at it with ill-concealed greed, ticking at intervals. Through the open windows came the chorus of cicadas and, suddenly, the metallic clang of a gong being struck somewhere to announce the hour of eight.

When he finally broke the silence, Esscombe's voice was harsh, his anger barely controlled. 'Wouldn't be here, would I … if I'd that kind of money? But I too have done my homework. I know exactly how much we require. Mind you, we're talking about opening out a single plantation, not a dozen!'

'I see,' remarked the merchant dryly. 'You've shifted from the first-person singular to the first-person plural with remarkable facility!'

The man before him guffawed in a reversal of mood. 'My dear fellow,' he said. 'It has to be we! At this moment I'm worth a thousand pounds or two. You, I conjecture, are worth a hundred times more.'

'Ah, Henry, even if I were interested in such a risky proposition as tea, I've not the slightest desire to go for anything new at my age.'

'Not even for a friend? You owe me, Alex! You owe me!'

The ruthless businessman in Swinnerton-Dyer was determined not to allow his acumen to be swayed by emotional impulses. Placing his goblet firmly on the felt-topped escritoire, he balmed his words with a layer of gentleness and said, 'Yes, I owe you. But no more than what you owe me. I value your friendship. I'm prepared to help you, but on my own terms.

Come back to Calcutta, bring your children here. I'll let you in as my trading partner. You aren't growing any younger, Henry. This is no age for you to go to a remote, plague-ridden, frontier outpost like Assam.'

'Your terms, old man? Don't presume to offer me alms, Alex, least of all to my children!'

'You misunderstand me, Henry,' Swinnerton-Dyer said hastily.

'No Alex, it's you who misunderstand me. I've come to you seeking help, not handouts. I need the finance which you're in a position to provide. It'll be on a basis of mutuality … I shall do the dog's work; we share the profit. You get to keep your money, I my selfrespect.'

The words were incandescent, the heat genuine and uncontrived. This made denial easier, more acceptable to the merchant. Relieved, Swinnerton-Dyer said, 'I'm sorry, Henry, I'm not prepared to accept your terms.'

To the merchant's astonishment, Esscombe suddenly smiled and emitted a long-drawn sigh. 'What must be, must be,' he intoned. 'To tell you the truth, I did anticipate your refusal … I didn't really want to come all the way to Calcutta. But I was encouraged to do so by a native soothsayer.'

'Good heavens!' the merchant exploded, genuinely startled. 'Do you, an Englishman, allow your actions to be guided by a native charlatan?'

Esscombe remained unperturbed. 'Oh, he was a venerable Mussulman from Delhi with whom David and Cordi struck up acquaintance. He took no reward for his pains, so he was no charlatan. "You have a friend in far-off Calcutta," he told me. "One who is a rich and respectable merchant. It is wrltten on your palm that you'll live out your last years further east, in some desolate wilderness. Your friend will help you get there." That's what put the idea of going to Assam into my head and to seek your assistance.'

'Your venerable Mussulman was wrong,' Swinnerton-Dyer cried out. 'I shan't assist you in this mad scheme!'

Esscombe held up his hand. 'Wait. The soothesayer sent a message for you also. "Your friend may not wish to help you." he said. "But warn him that I, Allauddin, see great danger for him if he does not do so."

So that was it! Such a childish essay! 'Come Henry,' said Swinnerton-Dyer, chortling dryly. 'I'm too much of a rationalist to fall for such superstitious claptrap …'

'Let me finish!' Esscombe interrupted, his voice hard. 'Allauddin further said, "The danger comes from a dark-skinned beauty, one who sings and dances, a charmer! Just tell your friend that, and he'll help you."'

Swinnerton-Dyer started, features paling in the lamplight. The hand holding the brandy goblet was no longer steady.

Summoning up a ruthlessness alien to his nature, Esscombe pounced. 'Tell me, Alex, have you been dallying with some native siren? A nautch girl from Sonagachi, perhaps? Or a whore from Karaya Lane? Hasn't the narrow escape some five and thirty years ago from the clutches of that Bengalee harlot taught you anything, you who prize your respectability so much! On that occasion you stood to lose just the Company's job and the risk of being deported to Britain. But now you stand to lose far more!'

Swinnerton-Dyer drained the contents of his goblet at a gulp, placed it heavily on the escritoire and flung himself out of his chair.

'All right, I'll finance you just this once, and no more.' His voice was strained, the words forced out of him. 'For heaven's sake, don't tell Patricia about this soothsayer and his wild foreboding! Nor anyone else, for that matter!'

Then more brusquely, almost offensively. 'Come, out with it. How much will you need?'

'About ten thousand pounds should do to set up a new plantation.'

'My role, if I am to understand you correctly, is limited to just financing this venture?'

'For the time being, yes. But in the third year, when the seeds mature into adult tea plants, plucking and manufacturing shall start, then, old man, it'll be up to you to handle affairs at this end. Getting the tea chests onto a steamship and despatching them to the London Auctions. We must have an office at Calcutta, of course, which you'll manage.'

'Will you be staying in Calcutta for a while, Henry?'

'I leave in a day or two for Delhi. Must apprise David and Cordi of my decision to set out for Assam. But I'll be back soon.'

'Excellent!' the merchant said. 'We can work out the details when you're back.' He pulled the bell-cord, and a menial appeared to refill the goblets.

'What says you, Alex? Shall we down a toast to our new partnership?'

The two friends touched glasses in a travesty of a toast. What must be, must be ... Esscombe's favourite phrase echoed and re-echoed weirdly through the caverns of the merchant's mind as he asked, 'Tell me, Henry. Do you know anything about growing and manufacturing tea? For that matter, have you, so far, seen a tea plant?'

His companion's laughter was an uncharacteristic tinkle, like that of tiny jhumkas on the ankles of a nautch girl. 'No, my dear Alex! But have I ever allowed such trifling considerations to come in my way ...?'

Three years ago, almost to the day, on such a September morning, Swinnerton-Dyer had seen Esscombe off on his way to Assam. His friend had met with unexpected success—Swinnerton-Dyer had no cause to regret having invested his money. Esscombe communicated his progress through a series of letters: 'Have you ever had your private vision of hell, Alex?' he wrote in one of his missives. 'Hell is the mud hovel where I subsist now, surrounded on all sides by evil, stinking marshland; the infernal jungle which grows and grows. Mosquitoes and malaria, leeches and slimy hamadryads—it's an endless list of hellish tormentors! But more than the place, hell is this incredible loneliness—I cannot speak my own tongue, but a patois of broken English, Hindustani and Assamese; for months on, I see no one of my own kind. I have decayed in body, mind and spirit. A stock of liquor is my only friend and companion. But I shall persevere ... it is my destiny, to spend the twilight years of my life cut off from my own, and I shall see it to the very end ...'

Dhanboa (meaning rice-sowing in the local Assamese language), the spot where Esscombe had staked his land-claim, was some nine miles away from the large market-village of Jorehaut in Upper Assam; three miles less from the Cinnamora plantation of the newly formed Jorehaut Tea Company. The claim had been for eight hundred acres of densely wooded jungle land; he was awarded five hundred. In the first couple of years, he suceeded in clearing close to a hundred acres and planted seeds and seedlings procured from various sources. The first of the plantation's yield had arrived at Calcutta early August this year—not much, just thirty chests of a hundred pounds each—which Swinnerton-Dyer, in his new role of handling agent, had despatched to London on the S.S. *Nile*. The results of the auction would be available only towards the end of next year but, thanks to Esscombe, Swinnerton-Dyer had become the part owner of a yielding tea plantation which was not a bad thing at all, considering he had initially written off his ten thousand as a dead loss!

But, in the relentless quest to open out a plantation single-handedly, Esscombe had given everything away. While the garden gradually took shape, his letters grew gloomier and more pessimistic; ominous portents of looming disaster seemed to darken each word. 'Physically I am a living corpse. My mind has shrivelled along with my body. My wasted frame is wracked by fits of shivers; lately I have spewed blood with my vomit. There is no medical assistance to be had—native quacks are worse than useless. So, I have to be my own physician. Yet I am without regrets, for I have done what I have for Cordi and David. They had little love from their poor mother. I must leave them something to remember me by. This tea garden will be their anchor and my memorial …'

Though, this morning, David and Cordelia, and not Henry, stood before him, yet Swinnerton-Dyer could not rid himself of the eerie sensation of reliving an episode of the past, for David was the spitting image of his father. By his side stood Cordelia, the youthful manifestation of a mother she never really had.

Brother and sister made a handsome pair. If Swinnerton-Dyer envied Henry anything, it was his fine off-spring, his own marriage being childless. They were a study in contrast, in appearance as well as character. David, in his twenty-second year, not only possessed the rugged, handsome looks of his father, but also his exuberance. Cordelia, two years younger, had inherited her mother's delicate, sensual features—the same blue eyes, lush, auburn hair and her quiet seriousness. She was almost as tall as David, a pretty girl in the process of flowering into a woman.

'It's such a pity, Cordi dear …' Lady Patricia said for the hundredth time, '… that you too have to go on this trip. So wicked of Henry, summoning you to Assam! The climate's terrible there! As for the inhabitants, uncivilized brutes, and some of them head-hunters too! David might suffer them all right, but why you, Cordi dear?'

'I told you, Aunt Patricia. Papa wanted only David to go. I was asked to stay wtih you for a while. But he's desperately ill, so I can't stay behind, can I?'

'Oh, Henry will come out of it all right! Nothing but a touch of malaria, I suspect. The Calcutta season's about to begin … I'd hoped to be able to take you out to the dinner and ball at the Government House. You would have created such a flutter, with your looks and figure!'

Swinnerton-Dyer plucked his chronometer out of his topcoat pocket and glanced at it. 'Good Heavens!' he cried. 'It's crossed half past seven! Delayed by an hour and a half, and no explanations forthcoming! Where the devil is the captain?'

As if on cue, a figure popped up at the top of the companion-way leading to the nether world—a tiny Scotsman, skin tanned and wrinkled like old leather, attired in a navy-blue shirt and white drills, his legs encased in a pair of Kolhapuri chappals. A cap dangled at a jaunty angle upon his cranium while his pipe let forth foul-smelling fumes every two minutes or so. The Scotsman dragged his left leg a little as he walked. He was such a comical little fellow that the sight of him brought an involuntary smile to Cordelia's lips.

'You owe us an explanation, Captain,' Swinnerton-Dyer said without the least attempt at politeness. 'As well as an apology.'

The Scotsman stopped in his tracks, blew out a plume of smoke and squinted at the merchant. 'I don't owe anyone anything, sir, least of all an apology. As fer an explanation … the catchers are late with the cargo.'

On that cryptic note the captain flicked his cap off, bowed gallantly to the ladies, blew another cloud of smoke directly into Swinnerton-Dyer's face, and limped away.

'The catchers, Uncle?' David asked.

'The coolie-catchers, son. This steamer is taking along a cargo of coolies. So that's why the flat is empty.'

'Oh dear!' bubbled Lady Patricia. 'Heaven only knows when the catchers will arrive! We can't wait any longer. Another half hour and you can bake biscuits on the streets!'

'She's right, David,' said the merchant. 'I'm afraid we shall have to depart.'

Lady Patricia hugged Cordelia and pecked her on both cheeks. 'Take care, love,' she said with genuine regret.

'By the way, David,' Swinnerton-Dyer said, 'there's something I'd wanted to ask you, but so far it has slipped my mind. How's your friend, Allauddin, the soothsayer?'

His answer was scrawled on the blank features of the two youngsters before him. David's face screwed up as he sought to stir his memory. 'Allauddin? We don't know anyone by that name.'

'I see. Must have been someone else Henry talked about.' The merchant's visage remained impassive, though his soul recoiled at the suspicion that he had been the victim of monstrous perfidy. He avoided his wife's puzzled stare, and said heartily, 'Well, well, goodbye. Keep us posted about your arrival. Give our best to Henry.'

With more goodbyes and take-cares and don't-forget-to-writes, the twain departed, David and Cordelia following them with their eyes, across the pier and into their phaeton.

'You'd better go to your cabin, sis,' David told Cordelia affectionately. 'Time to unpack your things and settle down.'

'In a while, David.'

'Lucky sis, having a cabin all to yourself! I have to share mine with some other bloke. Haven't met the chap yet. Time I do so. See you later, sis.'

Cordelia gazed fondly at his retreating back. In many ways David was a boy at heart, she the more mature of the two. She knew how devastated he had been when the summons arrived from Papa; not only because Papa was ill, but also because he had dreams of his own and these were threatened with disruption by the need to go to Assam. 'Growing bushes in some ruddy rat hole isn't exactly my cup of tea, sis. I tried to dissuade Papa … he wouldn't listen.' But he had borne what he deemed to be a temporary setback to his personal plans with stoic cheerfulness.

She herself had not got over her trepidations. Deep inside, she was afraid, not really because of all the bad things she had heard about Assam, but for what it had done to dear Papa. His letters to them, routed through Uncle Alex, had always glowed with cheerful optimism, even the final one admitting he was ill and bidding David to dispose of their assets in Delhi and set out for Assam. Only when Uncle Alex showed them Papa's letters to him did they fully appreciate the chilling horror and hell their father had undergone. A terrible ache had settled down in a permanent niche within her heart.

How she longed to see dear Papa again—to listen to his voice, to revel in his laughter, to nurse him back to health! Papa, in his last letter, had insisted she stay with the Swinnerton-Dyers till alternative arrangements could be made. But she mutinied at the suggestion, whining and whittling away at David's defences till he capitulated and agreed to take her along. She had always been wildly in love with dear Papa! Yet, as a kind of foil to the intense longing to be with him again, was the consciousness that they were cutting themselves off from familiar roots. David's disposal of their mansion at Delhi and winding up all their business interests had the air of a ritual about it, an irrevocably symbolic severance with the past. Now, the Swinnerton-Dyers—their remaining link with familiarity—too had departed and Cordelia was overcome with an indefinable sadness born of the irrational prescience that she was heading for doom and destruction and would never set foot on the soil of Calcutta again.

But she was no stranger to terror; not after those horrendous summer days of May 1857 when hordes of demented Hindustani sepoys had poured into Delhi from nearby Meerut, and gone on a rampage, killing and looting—raping every white-skinned woman they could lay their hands on, not with their sexual organs, but burning sticks or red-hot iron rods. The three sepoy regiments stationed at Delhi had joined the marauders from Meerut and for days on end Delhi was the scene of indescribable savagery, the white firanghees being the targets.

Had it not been for Khan, a huge Pathan from the North-west Frontier who her father had befriended, and Tulsi, their house bearer, they too might have been killed. But their saviours, in the dead of the night, even as flames engulfed the European quarters and mutilated and charred bodies of white-skinned men and women lay sprawled in the gutters of Delhi, had taken the Esscombes, disguised, to the native quarters at Chandni Chowk, at a close vantage to the Lal Qila, which the mutineers had made their headquarters, where Europeans were least to be expected.

While the aged Bahadur Shah, last of the Mughals, was declared Shahensha-e-Hindustan and violence raged through the subcontinent, the Esscombes stayed in hiding in a small ill-ventilated attic in the thick of it all, for a week, before their escape to neighbouring Ambala, where British troops' presence was strong. At the gravest risk to their lives, for their own people would have skinned them alive had they come to know, Khan and Tulsi smuggled the Esscombes out of Delhi in a bullock cart with a hollow, false bottom.

That ghastly ordeal, the horror stories they heard of brutalities inflicted on the firanghees by the savage sepoys, the torture of European men and rape of women; of white children being thrown alive in blazing bonfires; the rumour-ridden fears and uncertainties of the days spent in the confines of the Ambala cantonment; their eventual return to Delhi to discover their gutted house; the loss of everything, including friends—all these could have left scars and an abiding hatred for the natives in their hearts, as it had done in those of most Europeans. Was it their youth which insulated them against futile animosity, the desire for vengeance? Neither Cordelia nor David could summon up the antipathy which had irreversibly estranged the white rulers from the native populace. That they were no expatriates shipped out from the cold climes of England, but had been born and brought up in this land, amongst these very people, could have been an added reason. They too were aware of the compelling truth—if the Hindustani sepoys had gone berserk, they had been sufficiently provoked into doing so; if they had behaved barbarously, the British had behaved no better.

Above all, there were individuals like Khan, Tulsi and Putlibai, the ayah, serene and ageless, who had been with the Esscombes ever since Cordelia's poor mother died, and who had practically brought her and David up from infancy. These were the ones who gave them their love and loyalty without asking for anything in return. At a very tender age, Cordelia had discovered the incontrovertible truth—the barriers existing between the whites and the blacks, the ruler and the ruled, were rigid, but not impermeable. If one stayed within one's side of the barriers, one was treated with fear, respect and, occasionally, admiration; but if one simply slipped through and reached out, one earned something infinitely more precious, love and loyalty.

The malady with most of her kind was that they refused to reach out, complacently cocooned within the layers of their monstrous egos, equating the paleness of their hides with physical and mental superiority. It was this persistent endeavour to keep the barriers intact, the innate, incongruous terror that familiarity might breed contempt, which had warped their sensibilities, imbuing a capacity for barbarism in men and women who were, with their own breed, perfectly decent and civilized.

That, Cordelia reflected bitterly, was no excuse, for the British had come to Hindustan of their own accord, mastered and lorded over these people for their own self-seeking interests. It was merely an explanation—this was what made Englishmen away from their tiny island such vile, abhorrent and dangerous creatures; individuals, who in their native villages had been warm and amiable beings suddenly, on being shipped out, metamorphosed into loathsome caricatures, inordinately insistent of their genetic superiority and their God-given right to rule over others.

Thus the terrible vindictiveness her countrymen, with few exceptions, had displayed after the sepoys had been suppressed and British suzerainty reestablished over the subcontinent, was no temporary aberration; rather, it was an extreme manifestation of the deep-rooted malaise infecting the aliens. Even now, when the passing years should have blunted the sharp edges of memory, diluted the fear and pain of those terrible days, the barriers continued to remain. The memsahibs—the most vocally vituperous in their aversion to natives—continued their self-righteous, whining plaints of the stupidity and rapacity of wretched Hindustani menials over cups of afternoon chatterbroth; the sahibs to exchange puerile jokes about the damned *Pandies*!

Cordelia had little objection to inconsequential high tea chatter or insipid, wine-inspired jokes. But the continued, shameless exploitation of the country and its inhabitants, treated no better than cattle, was not. The fact that after the sepoy uprising the omnipotent East India Company had been wound up and Her Majesty's Government directly assumed the mantle of Imperial Authority, had changed things little. Everywhere she went, Cordelia was constantly reminded of how deep-rooted the antagonism in the British mind against natives was.

In contrast, she herself loved the country with a passion she could not, dared not explain, not even to herself, least to others—its vigour, vitality and variety—to such an extent that England, in some subtle way, had become a foreign country for her. Papa was a man of strong attachments, of an almost puritanic disposition. His dead wife had been the one *grand passion* in his life, though he had met her but a week before the marriage, on his first visit to England fifteen years after he had left its shores. When she died, he never set eyes on another woman again, transferring his affections to his children, especially Cordelia. His daughter had been the sun of his existence, as he of hers. She understood him as no one else did, not even David. He was unlike any Englishman she knew; scrupulously fair and honest, just and humane, with a genuine affection for this land and its people—the very antithesis of the archetypal English expatriate—thus fated to failure! That he was a failure she could not deny, though such an insight in no way lessened her love and longing for him.

Over the last few years, after the debacle of 1857, Papa had changed. The consciousness of having failed must have finally seeped into him, subduing his optimism—his age began to show on his features, actions and attitudes. Though he attempted to conceal the moods of hopeless melancholy devouring his soul, leaning upon the bottle to provide him strength and false cheer, Cordelia knew, and ached for him.

When Papa had told them of his plans to go to Assam to grow tea, David had opposed them. If they were to begin afresh, it was the son rather than the sire who should shoulder the burden, he said. But Cordelia encouraged her father to make the final attempt; with feminine instincts, semi-maternal, she sensed that unless he had something to work towards, he would decay and crumble, his failure heavy on him. In a way, she had been right; for a while Papa's success with the plantation had spiritually rejuvenated him. But he was ill now; had she, in her desire to give him renewed life, encouraged him to a lonely death?

Cordelia shook her head as if to drive away the gloomy thoughts. Overhead the sun abruptly exploded into view; it grew fiercely hot; the gharris and the palanquins disappeared; the stretch of the riverbank beside the pier, the stone steps leading to the waters, which all morning had seen a procession of natives coming and going, was now almost deserted.

On the horizon, across the strand and the maidan, the great city of Calcutta seethed in a blaze of whiteness, the green shutters of the huge, palatial buildings melting into the unrelieved whiteness of the walls. She could identify the dome of the Post Office, rising majestically over the other buildings and, further off, the Government House. The Auckland Park, or Eden Gardens as it was called nowadays, was devoid of humanity now—the picturesquely ugly pagoda, which had been transported piece by piece from Burma, she could see, and the artificial lake fronting it, its glistening waters a solitary jewel inlaid on a cushion of green. Further up the river, obscured somewhat by the heavy grills separating the stern, could be sighted masts of the taller ships, their colourful pennants aflame in the brilliant sunshine.

A whiff of acrid odour plucked her out of her self-induced trance. She whirled around and looked down at the wizened face of Captain McClintock.

'The heat hasn't driven ye indoors?' the captain asked in a kindly voice.

'Oh, not yet, Captain ...?'

'McClintock, m'dear, John McClintock. And ye, if the rolls be correct, are Cordelia Esscombe, passenger from Calcutta to Kokilamukh ghat in Upper Assam?'

Cordelia bowed her head in acknowledgement and smiled at Captain McClintock.

'A pleasure to have ye aboard, Miss Esscombe. But Assam's no place fer young and bonny lassies. What's taking ye there?'

'Papa is a tea planter. Henry David Esscombe of the Dhanboa Tea Plantation. Perhaps you've heard of him?'

'Aye, yes. Met him once too, during a trip late last year. He'd come down to Kokilamukh ghat to purchase supplies off me ship.'

'How did he look to you? Did he seem tired and ailing?'

'He looked well enough,' the old man replied, taken by surprise at the intensity of her tone. 'Why, what's the matter? Be he ill? I'm sorry, m'dear. But I'm sure he'll get well.'

As if to change the depressing conversaton and give it a new direction, Captain McClintock screwed up his eyes, gazed through the refulgent air at the deserted strand, and mused aloud, 'I wonder what's keeping young Buckingham. Met the lad at the Great Eastern Hotel only last evening. Told me the cargo's arrived at Calcutta safely. Should've been here hours ago.'

'Is he a coolie-catcher, Captain?'

'Nay, he isn't. Young Buckingham's a manager in one of Assam Company's tea gardens. But he'll be herding a catch of coolies the catchers've caught.'

'Why do you call them cargo, Captain? The coolies are human beings, aren't they?'

'Aye, yes. Ye can call them human beings, I suppose. But in me ship's manifest they're listed as cargo!'

The smile wilted on Cordelia's lips.

'You aim to put the coolies in that empty flat, don't you? That's what my godfather said.'

'Aye, yes. The flat belongs to the Assam Company. It's their coolies, by the way, who me ship'll be carrying.'

'But the flat looks so awfully small and uncomfortable!'

'Ah, twenty-five feet by fifteen, and dashed comfortable. It'll be quite a squash, though. The manifest lists four dozen men and women to be transported.'

Cordelia stared aghast at the diminutive old man. 'You can't be serious, sir.' she cried out. 'Forty-eight souls to be cramped into that confined space! It's … It's inhuman, sir!'

'That's the company's lookout, not me own.' the captain replied, avoiding her shocked gaze. 'To be fair to them they sent *Shaitan* and his mate on this trip … another flat called the *Yama*. If ye know yer Hindustani, m'dear, Shaitan means the devil and Yama the Lord of Death. But as ill luck would have it, Yama with a cache of tea chests struck a sand reef on the way and capsized!'

'So, the poor devils will be sent to hell on the back of Beelzebub! Appropriate, sir, isn't it?'

Cordelia turned to face the intruding voice behind her. The man was short, barely five feet four, but, unlike the captain, squat and thick set. His beard fell half the length of his chest. He wore a pair of horn-rimmed bifocals; the eyes peering through them brimmed with good humour and tolerance. Though dressed ordinarily in a light-blue cotton shirt and thick, baggy trousers, feet encased in a pair of deer-hide sandals, he appeared not to be a trader, or a planter, for he carried an ivory crucifix threaded around the neck. She was, however, not left guessing long, McClintock providing immediate enlightenment.

'Ah, the one and only padre, me ship's own man of God!' he cried out, his voice lacking its earlier warmth. 'M'dear, this is Brother Garry Swanson, of the American Baptist Mission at Sivasagar in Assam.'

Cordelia was surprised, but recovered quickly and extended a gloved hand. 'Good morning, Father,' she said, inclining her head. 'I'm Cordelia Esscombe.'

'How do you do, ma'am,' the padre acknowledged, shaking lightly her outstretched hand. He could not have been over forty, yet his tired visage and greying hair made him look much older. His voice was deep and stentorian, the voice of the pulpit, but softened by compassion. Cordelia, instinctive in her preferences, took an instant liking to the man.

Brother Swanson had caught the astonished look in her eyes and said with a smile, 'I don't match your conception of a priest, do I now, ma'am? You're used to seeing your Catholic or Anglican priests … black frockcoat, white collar et al. Praise the Lord, the American Baptist Church does not require its ministers to don such formal habits. Black frockcoat and white collar in this terrible heat … perish the thought! In fact, it was the heat which drove me out of my cabin. Overheard you, lady. You seem perturbed that our good Captain's going to cram forty-eight souls into the *Shaitan*?'

The Scotsman, cut to the quick, rose to his own defence. 'We discussed this before, Swanson. The original arrangement was fer two flats.'

'Oh, come off it, Captain! You don't have to explain to me! I've been on your steamer before. I was about to tell Miss Esscombe that it's quite customary to tow four dozen souls in a small flat on a month-long journey. She shouldn't spare those wretches a second thought. She has, after all, a snug little cabin all to her own!'

Cordelia flushed; yet, curiously enough, was not offended, though the biting mockery of the words was not lost on her. 'If a flat's been destroyed, Captain, can't you refuse to carry the coolies?' she hastily intruded. 'Or leave half of them behind for the next trip?'

'That's easier said than done,' the old man said gruffly. 'There's a tea boom on, don't ye ken? Labour in the plantations is in desperate short supply. If I refuse to carry the coolies, young Buckingham's liable to crucify me. I might as well chop me head off and offer it to me directors on a platter.'

'But sir, it's shameful! Forty-eight men and women loaded on that tiny flat in this terrible heat! It's … it's wicked!'

'I have a job to do,' the captain said heavily, anger no longer audible in his words, just weariness. 'I merely run this ship, lassie. I'm not responsible fer who's put aboard.'

'The winds of expediency snuff out the flame of conscience,' the padre exclaimed, and Cordelia was startled at the bitterness in his tone. 'You used the word wicked, lady. Well, there's so much wickedness all around. But that's to be expected, for wickedness is the foundation upon which imperialistic structures are erected … a lesson in history we, who ourselves are a part of that history, conveniently tend to forget.'

His gaze once more shifted towards the captain, eyes bitter and challenging. 'Oh yes, in Hindustan today you can characterize your white men by the attitude they adopt towards the rampant wickedness. Most do not recognize it as such, blinded as they are with a false sense of their own superiority. Some do recognize the wickedness, but condone it because imperialist interests necessitate it. The coolies must go, or the plantations will wither!'

Swanson fixed the diminutive old man with a glance of contempt. 'The tragedy is of the third category … those who possess the sensibility and humanity to recognize this all-devouring wickedness, and abhor it, but turn a blind eye because they do not wish to get involved, or dare not oppose it. Your honourable Captain belongs to that category, dear lady!'

The padre's words, stinging like a whiplash, bit into her soul. And what about her? To which category did she belong? Every moment, at every step, she had been a witness to ugly cruelty and indignity heaped upon the natives but had said nothing, done nothing. She too had chosen to wear blinkers which in reality implied compliant acceptance of her countryman's right to inflict indignities, just as the natives themselves, especially after 1857, had accepted subservience as their lot. She had been repelled, no doubt; but repulsion was a flimsy substitute for action. Had she ever raised her voice in protest?

She looked quickly at the captain. McClintock's features had turned a fiery red once again, but the padre, wilfully oblivious of the old man's wrath, continued his recriminations.

'When the British first became the masters of Hindustan, you only exploited the wealth of this land. But, as the consciousness of your power over the Hindustanis blunted your sensibilities and hardened your hearts, you carried on the exploitation to the human level. Lady, the tea plantations in Assam are extreme illustrations of this. They reflect the savagely naked, ugly face of British imperialism. You'll see it for yourself when you get there.'

The padre's voice drilled into her consciousness, the words wrapping themselves like wet rags around her heart.

'In 1843, less than two decades ago, you abolished slavery in Assam, sir. Another instance of British hypocrisy, for you created a new class of slaves. True, it was all legal and overboard; you British created the laws which could institutionalize slavery in a decent, civilized, legitimate way. Your catchers could lure, kidnap, coerce or blackmail coolies, ship them off to distant Assam in a most brutal manner, there to drudge away and die or taste the whip of the omnipotent planter. Indeed, all legal and overboard, sir! But sir, morality is law's spouse; you have divorced morality from law … that is the most heinous aspect of imperialist hypocrisy. These coolies are slaves. Call them slaves, for you, after all, are the masters of this country. Why varnish stark truths with the gloss of legality, and give cold comfort to your conscience?'

Cordelia, benumbed, looked at the captain, as if he could provide respite. The old man could take no more. There was fire and rage in his eyes.

'Do ye presume I'm a slaver, sir?' he roared.

The padre was unruffled. The captain's anger, he sensed, was directed inward. 'You pack those coolies into the flat, Captain, and I'll have no option to presume otherwise,' he said. Then, in a softer voice, 'You've been long on this route, sir. Haven't you ever counted how many of these poor beasts have perished on their journey to Assam to man the tea plantations there? Don't you remember the very first attempt, Captain, in the forties? Six hundred human animals shipped to Assam! Over half of them died of cholera aboard and the rest took to their heels and were never heard of again. Since then, the passage to Assam has witnessed the death of thousands of coolies. The reason for this astounding mortality is obvious, isn't it? Yes sir, Captain, pack those coolies in the flat and I'll presume what I wish of you.'

A watery film settled over the eyes of the old man, quenching the blaze in them. 'All right, m'dear,' he spoke to Cordelia, deliberately turning his back upon the padre. 'I don't promise ye anything, mind ye. But I'll see what I can do. Let young Buckingham arrive with his human beings! I shall talk to him.'

Instantly, Cordelia felt lighter; something hard and heavy, oppressive with the weight of lead, had been lifted. Such was the vehemence of her exultation that she impulsively hugged the captain and planted a kiss on his cheek, which the years in open air had dried and wrinkled into parchment.

The old mariner flushed with pleasure and tried unsuccessfully to conceal it. 'I don't see why I've to fight the coolies' battle fer them,' he growled with false gruffness. He turned towards the padre, about to hack into his victorious stance, when a movement and a yell from the direction of the pier forestalled him.

Moments later, the steamer's bells pealed out, loud and discordant, and the static pier came alive. There was a dull, throbbing keen, a piercing whistle and a staccato phut … phut … phut as the engine was fired. The *Ultaganga*, thus far an inanimate hunk of wood and iron, suddenly became a creature alive, vibrating slightly as it warmed up for the imminent journey. Nearby, an adjutant stork, unnerved by the sound, flapped its wings and flew away ungainly.

The forward upper saloon deck began to fill as the passengers left their cabins to satisfy their curiosity. David came up in the company of a young, handsome man, who walked erect as armymen do. Cordelia did not see them, or the other travellers. Her eyes were fixed upon the strand in a hypnotized gaze as a strange caravan rolled lethargically up to the pier and creaked to a halt.

A gharri arrived first, followed by a number of covered bullock-carts, backs curtained. Four men, tall and big-bodied, all Hindustanis, hopped quickly down from the end wagon. One of them held a rifle in his hand; another wielded a long-barrelled *zezail*, while the remaining two carried short, leather whips. The four stood beside the bullock-carts, in the explicit stance of guardsmen, as the side doors of the gharri opened and two figures stepped out.

Cordelia leaned further forward, gaze nailed onto the taller man, oblivious of the other, short and portly, who waddled by his side.

'That's young Buckingham, m'dear,' Captain McClintock said. 'The fat fellow is William Gordon, doctor of the Assam Company.'

The two newcomers looked up, saw the captain, and waved. Minutes later they emerged on the upper deck and Cordelia gazed upon one of the handsomest men she had ever seen.

Fair skin bronzed by the sun, a face perfectly moulded, eyebrows thin, delicately etched on a forehead that belonged more to a woman than a man. The long, dark-brown hair, unkempt and unbrushed, yet with natural symmetry, gave to the face a reckless, dissolute look, as did the eyes, also dark-brown, heavy-lidded. The nose and the mouth too were delicate and feminine; full, sensuous lips signifying a capacity for unreined passion. Unlike the hair, his beard was short and carefully clipped, and sideburns virtually non-existent.

He moved easily, his body disturbingly masculine, rippling with muscles which told of strength and athleticism. Buckingham was simply dressed in a half-sleeve shirt unbuttoned at the top, dark trousers, black socks and shoes. But the simplicity did not distract from the man's personality; instead, in conjunction with the casualness of his gait, his smile, self-assured and contemptuous, the virile manliness he so effortlessly exuded, gave him an image of recklessness and dare-devilry, of one who feared or cared for nothing and no one.

For one brief instant his eyes met hers. There was the slightest flicker of astonishment in acknowledgement of her beauty, a deliberate appraisal as his glance travelled down her body. Cordelia looked away, afraid that those piercing eyes would penetrate into the inmost recesses of her being and discover the tempest surging within her. But, try as she might, she could not coerce her eyes away for long. They returned once more. Now, however, he was looking at Captain McClintock, who had advanced a few steps to meet the newcomers.

'Our sincere apologies, Captain McClintock,' Buckingham replied, though the arrogance of the words did not convey contrition. 'We had a spot of trouble. Two of the buggers attempted escape late last night.'

'Escaped, did they?' another voice spoke out from the wings.

'Ah, Elwin old chap, you here? How's the chest? Improving?'

'The river trip did wonders for him,' said the woman who had been clinging to the arms of a thin, elderly man. She was dried and desiccated, features anaemic and grim, a scrawny frame and sawdust voice.

'But go on, Christopher. They escaped, did they? Were the contracts signed?' Elwin Winterbotham asked.

'Oh yes, signed and sealed, their thumbprints on the documents. They didn't get far, though. We caught them. Taught them a lesson they won't soon forget.'

'Educated them, eh?' the captain said testily. 'Are they fit enough to travel?'

The question caught Buckingham by surprise. His eyes narrowed and Cordelia, watching, saw the face transformed—the easy charm erased, the edges of the lips tautened into viciousness.

'Our doctor would be the best judge of that, McClintock.'

'Fit enough, fit enough,' said the stout man by his side, tugging self-consciously at his beard with fat fingers.

'Yes, he's the best judge! Tell me, my good doctor, how much do you collect per head for getting the coolies to their destination?'

The words were spoken by Brother Garry Swanson. They crept like smoke from a wood-burning chula into the atmosphere and intensified the tension. Christopher Buckingham's face grew rigid. There could be no doubt that he recognized the voice. He did not take his eyes off the captain, choosing to express his disdain by ignoring the intrusion.

'Enough time has been wasted, McClintock,' he said. 'Do I have permission to load the flat?'

'I have a problem too, Buckingham. Yer Company sent two small flats down. The *Yama* capsized on the way.'

'I'm aware of that.'

'The original scheme was to take yer coolies in two flats. I doubt if the *Shaitan* by itself can carry the entire load.'

Cordelia watched Buckingham's eyes narrow, the heavy lids drooping till the eyes were mere slits. There was something reptilian in the gaze he fixed upon the captain—the terrifying, beady stare of the cobra as it eyed the snake charmer's flute.

'I met you at the Great Eastern yesterday, McClintock. You said nothing about this ... gave no hint.'

'Today, Buckingham, is another day. Fer God's sake, lad, ye're loading the flat with human beings, not chests of tea. The journey's long and difficult. Squash them into the flat like that and ye'll have them dead before ye get halfway to yer garden!'

'Leave that to my conscience, McClintock. The flat's mine … the coolies are mine. If some of them perish on the way, the loss will be mine.'

'But I'm responsible fer the lives of all me passengers, be they coolies or otherwise.'

Suddenly a voice spoke up from behind the ring of onlookers and a tall, imposing figure threaded his way to Captain McClintock. 'May I put in a word, Captain?' he said. Such was the authority of his tone that the words, couched in the guise of a request, emerged as a command.

'But of course, Major Gosselin,' answered the old man with a sharp nod of his head.

'What are your instructions from the Company, sir? Are these coolies listed in your manifest? Has Buckingham brought more than originally booked?'

'No, I haven't,' Buckingham, and not the captain, replied.

'That should settle matters then, Captain. Since they are booked, you're legally bound to carry the coolies. Come, we are delayed already. Let us be on our way.'

'I've stated me position, Major Gosselin. Two flats were meant to carry the coolies. One of them's been destroyed.'

'And whose fault is that? Surely not Buckingham's! I ask you again, what're your instructions from the Company? Have they cancelled the bookings?'

The captain hesitated perceptibly before replying, 'Nay, they haven't.'

'Then you have no cause to delay us further. If you baulk at carrying the coolies, Buckingham has every right to prosecute you. In that case, your Company is liable to lose its licence to ply this route. You have no desire to be an instrument of your Company's misfortune, I presume?'

The unmistakable threat in the words was not lost on the captain. The old mariner glowered at the padre, the causal core of his discomfiture, and turned to Buckingham.

'All right, lad. Go and load the *Shaitan* with yer human beings!'

Cordelia took an involuntary step forward, consternation writ upon her beautiful features. She wanted to shout aloud her protests at the captain's abject surrender, but the words were missing. Her conversion to a crusader required stronger impulses, she thought ruefully, as she watched the Scotsman limp haughtily away, followed by Buckingham and Doctor Gordon.

Garry Swanson came and stood by her side.

'I wasn't much of a help, Father, was I?' she said apologetically.

'Wouldn't have made the least difference, ma'am,' the padre said in a consoling voice. 'Even our indomitable Captain can't stand up to Major Richard De V. Gosselin! Being a senior covenanted officer of Her Majesty's Government, the Major spouts legalities just as the devil quotes the scriptures!'

'Is he an army officer, Father?'

'He was once, but now he has been inducted into the civil services. He's the Personal Assistant to the Commissioner for Assam, for the Sivasagar disrict, and wields enormous power. In fact, the Civil Judge, Superintendent of Police, Executive Engineer, Education Officer and Post Master, all rolled into one.'

'You seem to know everyone aboard.'

'Not the newcomers, surely. But the rest I do know. None of them like me, however. They look upon me as an articulate mirror reflecting their secret guilts. But look, here comes the cargo!'

Cordelia's eyes turned to the pier. Buckingham and Gordon stood at its centre. The men with the whips cracked them in the air as they shepherded the coolies—a motley assemblage of men, women, children and babies—into lines for the final head count. Then, still maintaining the straggling columns, they shuffled slowly towards the *Shaitan*.

'Note, my dear lady,' the padre pointed out. 'There are forty-eight adults in that group. Add the toddlers and babies, and the final count would be nearer sixty!'

The coolies filed past the *Ultaganga*, heads bent, eyes downcast, submissive; two of them, in all likelihood the unsuccessful escapees whom Buckingham had mentioned, had their wrists bound behind them with ropes, but the others were unfettered; yet they seemed to shuffle slowly along as if carrying the heavy weight of chains around their feet. The children exhibited no trace of cheer; the suckling babes in their mothers' arms did not cry. The men, dressed in short knee-length dhotis, looked as if they had sold their souls, which indeed they had; the women, their bodies draped in saris and hair untied as if in mourning, carried small bundles on their heads, these head-loads being all their earthly possessions. Each of the coolies, without exception, had semi-starved looks on their faces and bodies. If they had put their thumbprints onto the documents which had condemned them to a lifetime of servitude, it was hunger and poverty that had driven them to it.

'Buckingham's got himself a prize catch this time,' said a voice nearby. Cordelia recognized the nasal accent of Elwin Winterbotham.

'Looks a sorry lot to me, Mr Winterbotham,' a new voice piped up. Cordelia turned her head a little, seeking its source—a fresh-faced youth, in his late teens, scarcely a hair upon his chin.

'Spoken like a true griffin!' laughed Winterbotham. 'But Jeremy, they'll perk up once they get a whiff of the river breeze. I myself am hard pressed for labour in my garden. Wish I could've traded a dozen off Buckingham.'

At the pier the last of the coolies straggled past and disappeared into the devil's innards. From where she stood, she could not see the *Shaitan*, the heavily grilled partition separating the stern from the forward deck. But, in her mind's eye, she could visualize them, herded like cattle on to the hard, cold, inhospitable floor of the iron flat, carving out bits of space for themselves, where they would squat, with the stoic stolidity only an Oriental could manage, for the greater length of the month-long journey.

The lascars began unloading large sacks from the bullock carts, carried these upto the steamer, and stored them.

'Provision for the coolies,' Swanson, unsought, explained.

'Just two cartloads?' Cordelia asked. 'Isn't that inadequate for so long a journey?'

'Not really. His cargo would be depleted on the way ... Buckingham knows that well enough. He'll consider himself lucky if he can land at Kokilamukh ghat half of what he has brought.'

The girl stared at the man of God, unbelieving. Swanson smiled—a harsh, bitter grimace. 'They don't eat much, these coolies, on the journey. And, if he's luckier than he deserves, Buckingham can always buy rice and atta from the captain.'

Prompted by a desire to escape the dreary conversation, Cordelia turned around and looked at the deck. The passengers were clustered together in small groups, like bunches of lychees. She could see the griffin in one such cluster, listening enraptured to the expostulations of Major Richard De V. Gosselin. There was another gentleman in the group, a giant of a man, with a face like the full moon save that it was bearded, wide shoulders and limbs thick as plantain stems. She looked to the Reverend for enlightenment.

The padre, in pursuit of her gaze, said at once, 'Stuart Hutchinson, famed explorer and big-game hunter. The terror of bipeds and quadrapeds! It's rumoured he uses elephant tusks as toothpicks!'

David was at some paces away to her left, in the company of the same young man of military bearing. As Cordelia's eyes shifted to him, he waved, turned and said something to his companion, and the two advanced to where she and the padre stood.

'Sis, this is Lieutenant Michael Bailin, formerly of the 9th Bengal Infantry. We're to bunk in the same cabin.'

'At your service, madam,' the Lieutenant bowed, exaggeratedly stiff and formal, his firm grip as he shook her hand conveying inner strength and tenacity. Clearly, he was older to David by two or three years, though both were of the same height and build. He possessed the features of a boy whom life had matured too quickly into an adult. The blue eyes were hardened with experience, but they were neutral, unable or unwilling to reflect his secret thoughts and passions.

The padre was introduced to the newcomers and he asked, 'A Lieutenant, Mr Bailin? Did you resign your commission?'

'Yes,' answered the Lieutenant shortly. Did Cordelia sense a flicker of hesitation before he replied, or was it just her imagination?

'Michael has recently bought a tea plantation in Assam.' David spoke out, compensating for his companion's taciturnity. 'One of those newly opened ones. Chahpuli, isn't that the name, Michael? Guess what sis, his garden too is near Jorehaut. We might be neighbours yet, eh?'

'I sincerely hope so,' the Lieutenant said with a smile.

'Chahpuli?' the padre enquired, visibly perplexed. 'Where exactly is this garden located?'

'I can't say for certain. But the map with the location is in my cabin.'

'When was this purchase made?' asked the padre with increasing agitation.

'A few months ago. At Calcutta.'

'Why, what's the matter, Father?' Cordelia asked, puzzled by the missionary's perturbation. It seemed for a moment that the padre wanted to speak out more, but he abruptly changed his mind.

'Nothing,' he muttered. 'Nothing, at all.'

The steamer's siren blared an abrupt warning, a cracked, nerve-racking, ear-shattering screech, drowning out all thoughts, riveting attention once more to the pier. Buckingham and Doctor Gordon did not tarry for the caravan's departure, and boarded the *Ultaganga*. A man rushed across to undo the mooring ropes, while a band of lascars heaved the gangplanks aboard. The siren coughed out its ultimate warning, the lascar who had undone the ropes took a flying leap onto the lower deck and the *Ultaganga*, relieved of its tethers, moved away from Chandpal ghat, as the few native crafts around it hastily scampered away towards safety.

The sound of the *Ultaganga*'s engine gradually deepened, the paddles whirled faster and faster and the steamer, turning portward, picked up speed. From somewhere came the recurrent refrain of the leadsman as he wailed out in a singsong voice, '*Ek bahm, mila nahin, do bahm, mila nahin, teen bahm ...*'

David, eyes aglow with excitement, slapped Michael on the back. 'Hurrah! We're off at last!' he cried. Michael Bailin, ever phlegmatic, held himself erect, but his flushed face betrayed his thrill. Gosselin, Hutchinson and the griffin came up to the railings to watch the city of Calcutta dissolve slowly into the distance. 'Assam, here we come!' the griffin yelled, waving his hands vigorously at a sola toupee-wielding official still valiantly manning his post.

The passengers started to walk off to the dining chamber in response to the breakfast call. 'I'm famished,' David said. 'Coming for breakfast, sis?'

'You go ahead. I don't feel too hungry.'

Once again, she was alone on the deck. Crushed by the weight of the solitude and emptiness which seemed to stretch out its tentacles till the furthest edges of vision, Cordelia felt renewed fear and sadness wash over her. She coerced the spectres down, redirecting her musings away from herself and, like a man drowning, the elastic fingers of her consciousness thrust out for something else to cling to. The coolies! What were they doing now? Had the thrill of sailing out to meet their destiny rubbed onto them too and put sparks of brightness in those lustreless eyes? Or were they still squatting with resignation on their squares of hard iron, their glances yearningly fixed upon the distant, circling kitehawks?

A compulsive desire to see the coolies overtook Cordelia. They had been effectively shut out of her conscience by the grilled partition. Now she padded up the narrow corridor running along the starboard, inexplicably guilt-ridden, as if she were about to commit a crime, caught the grilling with her right hand and a railing with her left, and leaned out as far as she dared. From that angle she could see only a small portion of the *Shaitan* as it was towed along by hawsers at the steamer's rear. But the limited glimpse was enough.

A coolie woman was defecating. She dangled from the outer side of the *Shaitan*, simian and terrified, legs on the metal flange which ran around the flat, hands desperately clutching the solitary protective railing. Her sari was pulled up to her waist; she had her back to the steamer and Cordelia could see her thin, black legs and naked buttocks thrust in her direction. Abruptly the folds of the buttocks parted and before Cordelia's horrified eyes a jet of slimy, yellow excreta squirted out to fall into the glistening waters.

Her stomach churned and bile rose to her throat. Yet Cordelia could not tear her eyes away from the defecating woman. A pair of masculine hands was gripping the woman's wrists, lending her strength to subdue the very real terror of toppling into a watery grave. One of those hands now loosened its hold to pour water over an outstretched palm. She rubbed her buttocks vigorously to scrape away the faecal remains, and then was hauled into the flat, her intimate parts covered once again by her sari.

Cordelia reeled back and closed her eyes. But the image of that coolie woman with her sari pulled up lingered—an image of utmost degradation, a ruthless erasure of the distinctions which separated men from beasts. Somehow, she shared the woman's humiliation, as though she herself had performed the act! Suddenly in her consciousness what had so far been an abstraction, sympathy for the coolies' suffering roused by the padre's words, assumed a new and sinister reality—a woman forced by circumstances to perform an intimate act in view of others—the coolies, herded onto that narrow flat, and left to wallow in their own excreta!

Once again, the vision of the woman's buttocks parting to defecate rose before her eyes. She could contain herself no longer. She leaned over the railings and vomited. Waves of nausea wracked her body; her insides heaved to spew out the frothy bile. She retched, gagging, and then retched again. Giddy and spent, she straightened, sucking in lungfuls of air, desperately striving to get a hold on herself. She set off across the empty deck in a blind stagger, rolling and holding onto the cabin walls like a drunken sailor till, she knew not how, she reached her cabin, legs almost giving way. With a final effort she flung open the cabin door, stumbled inside, managing to close and bolt the door before throwing herself onto the bed.

As she lay on the linen-covered mattress, her face buried into the cotton pillow, the sensation that world was revolving around her subsided, the trembling of her body ceased. And then she began to cry, in great bursts which emanated from the very depths of her soul—hot, salty tears, laden with all the anxiety and fear she had felt ever since receiving the last letter from Papa, and the pain and aches of her suddenly disturbed world, poured out of her eyes. She gasped out, calling aloud Papa's name, and fell back, exhausted. Soon her body could cry no more and she slid into uneasy slumber.

She emerged from the dark void, hearing renewed tapping on the door of the cabin and a voice hammering insistently into her consciousness. David was at the door, anxious, enquiring. 'Are you all right, sis? Open the door.'

'In a moment, David. I'd fallen asleep. Let me tidy up and freshen myself.'

'Right. Come to the deck when you're ready. We'll be waiting there for you.'

Cordelia gargled away the vomit from her mouth, changed her dress and emerged from her cabin. Though it was late afternoon, the light beyond the corridor leading to the deck was bright. Chairs and tables had been placed on the deck; David was in one, in the company of Lieutenant Bailin and the Reverend Swanson.

She waved to the seated men, about to join them when, all of a sudden, her eyes travelled to her right. She gasped aloud with astonishment, ran to the steamer's railings and gazed fascinated at the awesome aspect unfolding before her.

The Hoogli at the point was a giant python-head, grotesque mouth split wide open, swallowing the gargantuan monstrosity of sand and rocks that was the Ganga Saugor Island. The triangular, arid tract rolled away into the horizon, every dune, each undulation sharply shaded by the slanting rays of the late afternoon sun. The *Ultaganga* was on the eastern inosculation, moored to the river island's side. Far away to the west the waters of the upper channel glimmered darkly and beyond that was barren emptiness, a ribbed morass of sand and marsh.

Cordelia, who had traced the route along with David on the printed pages of a map in the hall of the Royal Geographical Society at Calcutta, knew that the Bay of Bengal was not very far away. She could almost hear the roar of foamy breakers dashing against the rock-strewn shore.

'Daunting, isn't it?'David came up and stood beside her. Cordelia nodded mutely, her astonishment and awe precluding speech.

A slight river breeze sprang up, bringing with it a babble of sounds. She looked towards the rear of the *Ultaganga* and her face broke into a smile. The coolies had been allowed to disembark and taken to a distance so as not to disturb the sahiblog. Their temporary reprieve had infused new life into them and the sandy stretch bustled with activity. Cordelia could make out the two men who had attempted escape at Calcutta. They stood together, a little apart from the rest of the conscripts, their hands no longer bound.

'Come, sis,' David said, gently pulling her away from the railings. 'Tea's being served.'

Lieutenant Michael Bailin stood up at their approach, Swanson remained seated. Cordelia favoured both with a bright smile and settled into a large, comfortably cushioned, cane deck-chair. A uniformed bearer, dashingly smart in red pugree, crimson tunic with brass buttons and white pyjamas, stood at her side, pouring tea into cups. On the wicker-table before her lay a generous spread—toasted bread stuffed with Gruyere cheese, an assortment of pastries, Huntley and Palmers's cream biscuits, and a jar of orange marmalade. Cordelia suddenly discovered how hungry she was.

'Skipped your lunch, sis? Come to think of it, I didn't see you at breakfast either.'

'A touch of mel-de-mer, perhaps?' Michael Bailin ventured.

'Oh, come on, my dear fellow! We're on a river, not in the middle of the Indian Ocean! It was the beastly heat, sis. You spent far too long on the deck this morning.'

Cordelia, saying nothing, picked up the cup of libation which the bearer offered with exaggerated courtesy, sipped it, and sighed. Swanson broke the silence. 'I envy you English folk,' he said. 'You do not allow your surroundings to dictate your moods or change the rituals of your race. Put an Englishman amidst the thick jungles of Assam, and he'll still insist on his afternoon cuppa!'

'Not at all, I assure you,' David rejoined laughingly. 'Feel dashed awkward, I do … drinking tea and indulging in chit chat in these circumstances! Should we put patches on our eyes and drink rum instead, Father?'

'An apt metaphor!' observed Swanson, with humour, sans malice.

'Father, you aren't doing too badly with the tea and biscuits yourself!' Bailin remarked lightheartedly.

'Touché!' cried David, smacking the sides of his chair.

'Ha ha,' chuckled the padre, looking all the more lovable in Cordelia's eyes. 'But I react to what I see, and that's more than what can be said of the average Englishman. When you get to Assam, you're sure to encounter a quaint animal there … the *Rhinoceros unicornis*. When I think of an Englishman I think of the rhinoceros. Both have very thick hides and myopic eyes.'

'Does it drink tea, Father?' Cordelia asked with a mischievous smile. David burst into exuberant laughter and the padre's lips parted in a vastly amused grin.

But Bailin said earnestly, 'I've been with you but for a little while, Father. Too brief a time, perhaps, to make judgement. Yet you seem to me to be a man obsessed.'

'You're perceptive, Michael. Have I, Brother Garry Swanson of Brendon, Vermont, not been for close to twenty years a castrated witness to such sorrow, misery and suffering here, so much greed and bigotry, exploitation and shameless flaunting of power? Garry Swanson, the bearded eunuch … a role thrust upon me, one I intensely abhor. So, I get my own back by needling you all. That's a salve to my wounded conscience, my favourite pastime, in fact, my sole recreation.'

'No, Father,' the Lieutenant spoke with utmost seriousness. 'It's unjust of you to put all Englishmen in the same basket. There are those who react and feel, even amongst us.'

Cordelia shot Michael Bailin a look of quickened interest, as if seeing him for the first time. The Lieutenant's lips sported a deceptive half smile, but it did not carry to his eyes.

'They wear blinkers, my friend, like those ill-fed nags which draw Victorias in the Eden Garden. They see and do not see. They react but do not act. I've nothing else but contempt for them.'

Bailin coloured, face constricting with some inner anguish. 'The consequences of action are too frightful, Father. Only God knows how frightful!' He leaned back and closed his eyes. Cordelia, amazed, saw the face twisted with barely concealed grief. The padre's words had touched a hidden chord in the Lieutenant, and struck a note of despair.

David, unconscious of the darkened mood now touching his companions, said, 'Have you noticed something, Michael? Our Captain has moored his steamer in the middle of the river. He's to be congratulated for this. Berth the *Ultaganga* on the banks, and mosquitoes, green aphids and God only knows what would've made our life miserable.'

'That, however, is not the captain's chief consideration,' the padre said. 'You forget our cargo, David. They possess legs, each of them without exception, and can be expected to make a break for it, unless a river is placed between them and freedom.'

David's face screwed up in a mock grimace. 'Oh come, Father, you're putting me on! Marshy wastelands and mangrove swamps? An absconder wouldn't last an hour in them.'

'Go tell that to the coolies, son! A few nights on the flat makes any alternative welcome. Our traders in human flesh have learnt it from past experience. Every trip has its quota of runaways. So, our good Captain will moor in the middle of the river all through the journey. Also, the coolies are too precious to be left on the river island at night. After they've finished their meals, Buckingham's watchdogs would shepherd them back into the flat, there to spend the night under the watchful eyes of the sentinels.'

'But surely,' protested David, 'the coolies knew what they were getting into when they put their marks on the contracts?'

'Contracts, David? A contract is made between equals; not between an illiterate, starving wretch, and a wily, heartless recruiting agent. Not without reason are these agents called coolie-catchers! They use the most blatantly unethical and brutal means to collect coolies to be transported to tea plantations in Assam. Planters call them pimps … an entirely apt and self-explanatory appellation!'

'Get paid by the head, do they?'

'Yes, David. Trust me, coolie-catching is a lucrative business! The famine-stricken regions of Lower Bengal and Chotanagpur in the Bihar province are the favoured hunting grounds of these pimps. They scour these spots, painting a rosy picture of tea garden life … light work, good pay. Advance money is waved in the air to bait the trap. There's no length to which they will not go … kidnapping, blackmail and what else, to collect their cargo. Existing laws side with these pimps and planters. The workman's Breach of Contract Act of 1859, for instance, renders a coolie liable to prosecution for any breach of contract, no matter what fraudulent means was adopted to have him put his thumbprint on his contract. The Act gives him no protection from his employer, thus de facto reducing him to a contracted slave. So, Buckingham's coolies haven't come of their own volition. You heard what the planter said this morning … two of the conscripts, apparently unmarried, made a bid for freedom in Calcutta itself. That, dear David, is why they recruit entire families as far as possible. A married man would think twice before running away.'

'I don't disbelieve you, Father.' David, inspite of himself, was persuaded by the padre's earnestness. 'But would it not be more worthwhile to take the case to the authorities? A petition to the Viceroy, detailing the existing conditions, should do the trick.'

'The blinkers Your Majesty's Government wears are even more blinding, David. You have a sampling of authority on this steamer, the high and mighty Major Richard De V. Gosselin. Whose side did he take this morning? Bureaucrats are realists. They know of the scarcity of labour in the fledgling tea industry, so they turn a blind eye when laws are infringed. Even then your government, after decades of indifference, has at last roused itself. Early this year the Government of Bengal appointed a Commission of Enquiry to go into the matter.'

'But you don't think anything will come out of it, do you?' Michael Bailin spoke up.

'Oh, a new act or two might even hatch out of this Commission's labours. But laws by themselves are not enough to change the system. It needs individuals to do that … individuals of conscience who will fight tooth and nail against that which goes against humanity and Christianity. Michael, David, it is young people like you who can change the system. But be warned! If you can't change the system, the system will change you! It will swallow you up till, a couple of years from now, you not be able to recognize yourself.'

'We'll see about that,' David replied with the confidence of the young. 'What about you, Father? Has the system changed you?'

'Yes, immeasurably. Not merely in terms or greying hair and lined features … my objectives and values too have changed. When, in 1840, I first went to join the Baptist Mission at Sivasagar in Assam. I'd come straight from my native town in America. To the Church it is a challenge to bring waiting millions the knowledge of Jesus Christ, I was told! It needed but a few years to rob me of my proselytizing zeal. I discovered it was Europeans, not the natives, who needed to be civilized with our Lord's teachings.' Swanson chuckled; a joyless sound pregnant with cynical disillusionment.

'This morning, Father,' Cordelia said. 'You couldn't stop the coolies from being boarded. Another failure, wasn't it?'

'Not my first,' replied the padre wryly. 'Nor my last, I guess. Two decades have I spent in the hinterlands of Assam. Twenty long years of futility, pitting myself against wickedness and injustice … not a single brick of the citadel of imperialism have I been able to dislodge.'

'Then why struggle at all?' Bailin asked angrily. 'Why not bend the way the wind blows?'

'Because that, Michael, is our justification for existing, yours and mine. Perpetual struggle against wickedness and injustice … that is our sole pathway to salvation. The moment we cease our struggle, we are nullified, we become nothing.'

The padre gazed far away into the horizon, as though seeking an answer to his failures there. His companions fell into a thoughtful silence. The heat around them lessened, the light dimmed perceptibly and a cool evening breeze, laden with brine, blew in from the Bay of Bengal.

'I've this awful knack of bringing conversation to a standstill,' Swanson laughed. 'David, Michael, how about a walk up the island? The sands should have cooled by now. Care to stretch your legs, Cordelia?'

'Yes,' the girl said, standing up.

A man came up the stairs from the lower deck, a tall bearded native, bare bodied, his lower parts wrapped in a green lungi, a fez on his head. Approaching the group he brought his right hand, palm up, to his forehead in a salaam, and said in chaste Hindustani, 'The gracious Captain presents his compliments, sahibs and memsahib. He is hosting a dinner this evening. He entreats your presence on the occasion.'

'This is Salim Ali,' Garry Swanson said. 'First mate of the *Ultaganga*.'

'We'll be happy to attend the captain's dinner,' David said.

Salim Ali bowed gravely and walked away, his eyes probing the deck for the other passengers.

'Oh Ali, we're going for a walk on Saugor Island,' Swanson called out. 'Tell your gracious Captain to wait for our return before he sails away, will you!'

The first mate stopped, a puzzled frown on his forehead. Then he understood and smiled, white teeth flashing against the ebony face. Once again, he bowed gravely and shuffled away.

Swanson led the others down the steep and narrow staircase. The lower deck, warm and stuffy, was cluttered with men, stores and machinery. Brown faces in the shadows, rodent eyes unblinking, stared at them as they pushed past in a single file across the small passage leading to the starboard exit, and Cordelia, vaguely uncomfortable, felt relieved to be out in the open once more. But the feeling of relief was momentary for, with a wild beat of her heart, she saw Buckingham at the far end of the gangway, waiting for them to cross over.

The planter pointedly ignored the three of them, choosing instead to address the padre. 'Gathering converts, I see, Swanson.'

'Unfortunately, not. These gentlemen are potential tea planters, thus irretractably heathenish!'

'Ah, our tribe's increasing! Could you favour me with introductions, Swanson?'

'Certainly. This is David Esscombe. He's off to Dhanboa plantation to relieve his ailing father. David, Christopher James Buckingham, the reputed scourge of coolies.'

'Hullo, Henry's son, are you? Dhanboa's a stone's throw away from Bihguri, where I work.' Although he could not have been much older to

David, his manners were patronizing, those of an elderly man towards a youngster.

'This, Buckingham, is Lieutenant Michael Bailin. He has recently bought a tea garden called Chahpuli.'

'Chahpuli?' Buckingham's face was blank. 'Didn't know there was a tea plantation by that name in Assam! Know anything about the tea planting business, old chap?'

The Lieutenant's face was impassive, but Cordelia could sense he was irritated by Buckingham's brusqueness.

'Not much, I'm afraid,' he replied, civilly enough.

'That's just the trouble. Too much planting and too little experience. The bubble's sure to burst one day.' Buckingham turned towards Cordelia, and the girl, in close proximity, felt the full force of the dangerous charm of the man.

'Cordelia Esscombe, David's sister,' the padre said. Cordelia did not offer her hand, fearful that physical contact would expose her, that the man would somehow know of the violent beatings of her heart and the wild yearning coursing through every fibre of her body.

'Your servant, madam.' Buckingham bowed, then raised his head and looked her straight in the face. Her eyes met his. There was a sudden flicker of enlightenment in those heavy-lidded eyes, like the brief spark of a tinderbox snuffed out by the wind; the edges of his lips curled into an arrogant, omniscient smile, and Cordelia knew her secret was a secret no longer. She felt strangely demeaned, as if he had violated her with that glance. She wanted to cry something savage to wipe away the supercilious look upon his handsome face. Yet, though at that moment she hated him more than anything else in the world, her tongue was frozen. Fortunately, Buckingham turned to face the padre, and Cordelia was saved further humiliation.

'Stay away from my coolies, Swanson! I've enough trouble as it is.' Buckingham bowed again and moved lithely up the gangway.

'Bloody cheek!' Michael Bailin burst out.

'Yes, Buckingham's insufferable,' the padre said.

He offered Cordelia his arm and, flanked by David and Michael, they moved across the sandy, barren stretch. They progressed in silence, the stark harshness of the surrounding nature's handiwork directing their thoughts inward. The landscape loomed forbidding viewed from ground, without the false shield of invincibility provided by the mammoth steamer. The sun, sinking slowly on the horizon towards their right, poised momentarily at the point where earth met sky. But the prismatic hues flecking the firmament could not lighten the menace-filled gloom of the atmosphere, nor bring colour to their thoughts. Without a word they turned back, each enwrapped in inscrutable reflections.

Reaching the *Ultaganga* brought unaccountable relief, as though they had been dogged by unseen presences. The Reverend parted their company on the upper deck, but her brother and the Lieutenant escorted her to the door of her cabin.

'David, call for me in an hour. We'll go into dinner together.'

'Leaving me to fend for myself, Miss Esscombe?' Bailin cried out. Cordelia started, guiltily. She had almost forgotten his presence, so immersed had she been in her own thoughts.

'Please do come along, Lieutenant Bailin.'

He bowed gallantly as she turned to enter her cabin. But the face that hovered in her consciousness when she pushed open the door was not that of Michael Bailin. It was Christopher James Buckingham's face, mocking and reckless, which stared back at her from the room's lamp-lit depths.

Cordelia washed herself with the rose-petal odoured water in the small, rectangular, cast-iron tub, and dressed with care for the evening's dinner. David's summons soon arrived. Lowering the flame of the lamp, she opened the door.

'By Jove, sis, you look gorgeous!'

The cabin's half light heightened the allurement of her transformation and Bailin, standing stiffly a couple of yards away, was visibly affected. He gazed at her with yearning in his eyes but Cordelia, her attention directed elsewhere, was unconscious of it.

She gave her arm to her brother and the trio emerged into the open. The passengers slowly filtered through the doorway to the dining cabin, the captain shaking their hands and offering formal greetings. His foul briar, the girl noted with amusement, was nowhere to be seen.

Lamps and outsize tapers brilliantly illuminated the small dining chamber. The tables, ordinarily placed separately, had been joined together to form a wide rectangle, and chairs lined on either side. She felt her spirits lift as the sparkling ambience of the dining chamber, decked up for this special occasion, enveloped her. Salim Ali, garbed in white kurta and pyjama, gravely bowed her and her escorts to their appointed chairs at the centre of the table. Gosselin sat on the host's right, Stuart Hutchinson, the explorer, on the left. The chair beside Gosselin was empty, but the next two chairs were occupied by the Winterbotham couple, then Doctor Gordon and the padre at the end. The chair between Cordelia and Hutchinson too was unoccupied; on her immediate left sat Bailin, David and Jeremy, the griffin.

A little later Buckingham entered, dashingly handsome in a shirt of satin open at the neck, billowy sleeves and lace-rimmed, buttoned-up cuffs. The lack of coat and tie heightened the aura of reckless unconventionality, underlining his total unconcern for what others might think of him. He advanced into the room, bowed to the company and, with a, 'The coolies, McClintock, had to be fed,' took the chair next to Cordelia.

Favouring the diners opposite to him with nods, Buckingham turned towards Hutchinson, speaking in a low voice. If he was conscious of Cordelia, of her creamy bare shoulders, the cleft of her breasts or the perfume warmed by her body heat, he gave no indication. But she herself sensed his overpowering puissance; the animal masculinity which poured out of him flooded her consciousness. Was he aware of the effect that the proximity of his presence was having on her? Was that the reason for his shutting her off, almost offensively, from the circumference of his attention?

The chair beside Gosselin remained empty. 'Dropped somebody overboard, McClintock?' Hutchinson's facetiousness drew attention to the fact.

'We have a native passenger aboard,' said McClintock. Though he continued to smile, his voice was a trifle wary. 'Me intimate friend, Gokuldeva Barua. Should be here any moment now.'

'So, we're to be kept waiting by a damned wog,' exploded Buckingham. 'I know the blighter! Seditious bastard!'

'That was totally uncalled for, Buckingham!' The objection, surprisingly, came from Gosselin. 'Gokuldeva Barua has emerged indispensable to the

British administration in Assam. Her Majesty's Government has been pleased to put on record the splendid service rendered by this native gentleman.'

'A sly old fox, all the same!' retorted Buckingham. 'He's opened out a tea plantation, as you very well know. Has the audacity to compete with us!'

'Nevertheless, he has been of great help to us,' Gosselin said. 'He's widely respected among his people. His assistance, especially during the uprising of 1857, was invaluable.'

'I'm personally indebted to him, Buckingham, m'lad,' Captain McClintock, asserted forcefully. 'When I first sailed to Assam as a trader, it was Barua *dangoriya* who lent me a helping hand. He was then a close confidante of Purander Singha, the last of the Ahom kings of Assam.'

'But that hardly gives him the licence to keep us waiting,' whined Dorothy Winterbotham petulantly.

'The fault, madam, is entirely me own. Barua dangoriya had no mind to attend me dinner. But I convinced him he must attend.'

'You could've invited a few of the coolies too,' said Elwin, making explicit his objection.

Cordelia felt indefinably abased. The brightness and sparkle of the dining chamber were false; the facade of sophistication conjured up by the white linen and glittering cutlery, the uniformed *khidmatgars* and finely dressed diners, fraudulent. These were petty men, sans gentility or breeding, whom circumstances had elevated and magnified.

Salim Ali, near the door, announced the entry of Gokuldeva Barua. Conversation at the table ceased, heads simultaneously turned towards the doorway. An aged native gentleman approached the head of the table, bowed politely to the diners, shook the offered hand of the captain who had risen to greet him, and was escorted to his chair. Gokuldeva Barua was a stocky man of medium height, with short-cropped, cottony white hair which floated in a halo over the dusky features and the dark suit he wore. His eyes swept the table quickly and then veered towards Gosselin, to whom he spoke in a low voice.

The wine glasses were filled. Cordelia stole a glance to her right, not surprised that Buckingham preferred whisky to wine. Not once had the man turned to her or displayed the modicum of courtesy. It did not trouble her any; on the contrary she was thankful for his indifference, secretly dreading any attention from him. The Lieutenant, on her left, did not prove adept at small talk; her presence seemed to induce in him discomfiture similar to the effect Buckingham was having on her. If her role this evening was to be of a passive onlooker rather than an active participant, Cordelia thought contentedly, it would suit her only too well!

Captain McClintock now stood up, wine glass in hand, and proposed the first toast of the evening. 'To Her Royal Excellency, Queen Victoria, Commander of the British Empire,' he cried, voice suitably sonorous. 'And her consort, Prince Albert. May their magnificence never lose its lustre!' Glasses were raised, assenting voices subscribed to the sentiments expressed. Cordelia saw that the native gentleman too raised his glass—although his was filled with water, he being a teetotaler. Then the food arrived; an uncommon fare was on offer this evening, as perhaps befitted the singular nature of the journey—turtle-egg soup, filletted fish in mustard to go with prawn biryani, and, as the piece de resistance, venison kebabs dipped in garlic sauce. For a while conversation languished as the food was tucked into.

Despite the presence of the native gentleman, it was the Reverend Swanson who appeared the odd man out in the company, for the padre studiously ignored the toasts proposed with patriotic fervour between each course. By her side Buckingham continued to ignore her—she attempted a matching indifference, but her glance every now and again did stray in his direction and she was amazed at the prodigious amount of whisky the planter could consume. A salad of fruit in rich, thick cream rounded up the repast and as each guest finally laid aside his or her serviette, conversation reached its former pitch.

Cordelia noticed that Gokuldeva Barua spoke excellent English, though with a pronounced accent. She felt oddly pleased that the old fellow was not at all discomfited by the fact that he was the sole brown skin among the diners. On the contrary, he carried himself with assured dignity which bespoke nobility of birth.

The dessert plates were cleared. Coffee and brandy were served, though the gentlemen refrained from smoking cheroots in deference to the presence of the ladies and the smallness of the room. Then the Captain stood up once more—a little unsteadily this time, for the mariner had been imbibing wine and whisky freely—and raised his glass for a final toast. 'To the glory of our Celestial Empire and to its permanence!' he said.

All, except Garry Swanson, raised glasses and drank.

'An admirable sentiment,' the padre's voice boomed out from his end of the table, making others look sharply towards him. 'But improbable. History is against you, Captain.'

'Oh, for heaven's sake, Swanson! Leave your preaching to your rice and curry Christians!' Buckingham retorted with contempt.

'Let the man speak,' Gosselin intruded authoritatively. 'Come Swanson, I'm with appetite for an argument.'

'Permanence, Major, is a deceitful word. There's a reassuring fluidity about the universe … a constant flux in its functioning, which denies permanency to human efforts and achievements. Thus, when you aspire to the permanence of the Celestial Empire your moralistic queen rules over, what you actually aim at is a transient illusion of permanence.'

'A semantic falsity, eh, padre?' Gosselin said tolerantly. 'All right, I shan't split hairs with you on that. But what prevents our Empire from assuming permanence, even if it be an illusory one?'

'The very nature of imperialism, Major. Imperialism is like the serpent which feeds on itself. The attributes which enable a race to erect an Empire also help bring it down … a fate which, without doubt, awaits your Celestial Empire. As an administrator of experience and wisdom, you at least ought to know that.'

'That's a seditious speech if I've heard one!' exploded Buckingham, the furious temper, skin deep in the man, prodded by the whisky. Cordelia quailed at the planter's crudity and was simultaneously pleased that the Reverend had pricked his mask of contemptuous nonchalance.

'Don't be asinine, Buckingham,' Gosselin rebuked. Curiously enough, the planter did not react as strongly to the Major's reprimand as Cordelia expected him to do, but pulled down again the veil of indifference over his features and assumed a couldn't-care-less attitude.

'My dear padre,' Gosselin said, reverting to Swanson. 'You talk in abstractions. You have to be more precise if you're to make a convert of me.'

Much to Cordelia's discomfort, the Reverend, instead of a direct reply, chose to address her, thereby drawing her into the discussion. 'Miss Esscombe,' he said, 'if you'll recall, only this afternoon I'd pointed out to you that the British do not allow their surroundings to change the rituals of their race. Instead, they mould the surroundings to their own needs … a trait indicative of extreme egoism. It is this egoistic trait in your race which has helped you build your Empire. It is this same trait which will pull it down.'

Gosselin chuckled. 'You have a queer way of looking at things, Swanson. We British haven't won an Empire in a game of dice, have we? Like that chap in the *Mahabharat*! Our grit and resolution … sense of adventure and enterprise … has time and again won the day for us. Such admirable traits you contemptuously dismiss with one word … egoism. But our good Captain's hospitality has made me indulgent this evening. Right, I grant you that egoism gives the thrust to Empire building. But how does it help to bring it down?'

'By perpetually widening the gulf between the ruler and the ruled, Major Gosselin. The wise emperor knows that if he's to lend an aura of permanence to his domain, he must keep the welfare of his subjects in mind. There have been other empires at other times. Study them closely, Major, and what do you see? Whenever the ruling class sought closer rapport with the masses, the illusion persisted for quite a while. When they didn't, heads literally rolled!'

'Let's call a spade a spade, damn it!' Elwin Winterbotham cried out. 'We didn't come here to mollycoddle the bloody Hindustanis!'

'I couldn't have phrased it better myself,' the Reverend said with a chuckle. 'You didn't come here to mollycoddle the bloody niggers … you came here to enrich yourself! This is the very reason permanence would be denied to your Empire. It's a vicious cycle, Major Gosselin. Whenever a small group wrests power in any society … a group motivated solely by egoistic avarice … it invariably moulds the system to facilitate exploitative enrichment, thus alienating itself further from the multitude and bringing about its own destruction. A recurrent historical pattern which you British have chosen to ignore. So, continue to rape the land, and I give your empire another five decades or so.'

'Surely you oversimplify, Swanson,' Gosselin said, cool and unruffled. 'You fail to take into account the innate superiority, both of character and arms, of Europeans over Hindustanis. You overlook the weakness and cowardice of the people we rule. As long as we enjoy our advantages, we shall hold sway over the multitude.'

'My dear Major!' Gokuldeva Barua intruded with surprising strength and authority. 'Never underestimate the people. They possess hidden strength which might catch you unawares.'

'Fiddlesticks!' scoffed Hutchinson. 'I have travelled all over the globe. A more submissive lot I am yet to come across.'

'That's a matter of opinion,' said the padre. 'But granted that the Hindustanis are submissive, persecution can drive even the worms to turn. History is nothing but a reiteration of this truth.'

'Recent history, Father!' interposed Bailin. Could Cordelia catch a note of anguish in the words? 'The Hindustani sepoys, whom we used to conquer this land, turned against us. And how savagely did they turn! For a while it seemed all was lost. You're right, Father. Insulation and exploitation do not make for permanence.'

'You've bought a tea garden, Bailin?' Buckingham shot the query as if launching an attack. 'That's what you told me this afternoon.'

'Yes, I have,' the Lieutenant answered, not attempting to mask his displeasure at the intimidatory tone adopted by the planter.

'Then I pity you, old chap. Approach your coolies with such a liberal attitude, and you're done for as a planter!'

'You don't pamper your coolies, do you, Buckingham?' the padre observed acidly. 'That's the grand secret of your success?'

'Yo're damned right, I don't!' Buckingham cried. 'The language of the whip is all they understand. Ill treat them, Bailin, do you hear? Drive them like pack mules if you want to get a pice worth of work out of them.'

The blood rushed into the Lieutenant's face. For a moment it seemed he would respond to Buckingham's effrontery with anger. But he controlled himself with difficulty—in deference to her presence she was sure—and willed himself into a stiff, wooden silence.

Cordelia, suddenly apprehensive, looked across at David, who had sensibly remained silent, and tried to catch his eye. But her brother was looking at the padre, who now said, 'Major Gosselin, you spoke of superiority of character. Well, Christopher James Buckingham here is an example of British "superiority" of character! I've always held that unmitigated power, in any form or guise, is a disintegrating force before which character crumbles.'

'Why, you impudent, sanctimonious swine!' shouted Buckingham, rising from his chair with a violence which sent it crashing on to the ground. The half-filled whisky glass before him tumbled, spilling its contents onto Cordelia's gown.

Hutchinson was on his feet, restraining the inebriated planter. 'For God's sake, Buckingham!' Gosselin called out. 'Rein yourself in! There're ladies present!'

Cordelia, visibly disturbed, had scraped her chair back as the whisky glass spilt. The planter lost his aggressiveness and laughed aloud. 'You're right, Major. Our man of God can be infuriating sometimes, can't he?' He turned towards Cordelia, picked up a napkin and, uncaring of Dorothy Winterbotham's reproach-filled look, dabbed at the speckled spots on her gown. 'I'm sorry, Miss Esscombe,' he said, his voice slurred, hands just a little unsteady.

Cordelia felt limp, suddenly drained of all energy, as the powerful figure hunched over her. 'It's ... it's all right,' she blurted, pushing away his hand. 'I'll clean up in my room.' She stood up, conscious of the embarassed silence as anxious eyes probed her countenance, and walked upto Captain McClintock. 'Thank you for the wonderful dinner,' she strengthened herself to say.

The old man rose, took her hands and said inebriatedly, 'Good night, lassie.' David too had stood up, but she waved him down. With a slight bow to the diners, she turned on her heels and stepped out of the door Salim Ali held open for her.

The air outside was crisp and cool. The landscape too had suffered a sea change; a new and insubstantial menace had intruded into the moon-inspired melancholia; the sound of far-off breakers was clearly audiable now, snarling and petulant. The mist was rising from the river, rolling across the sand dunes, curling phantom-like against small rocks, creating spectral shapes which disintegrated with the river breeze to re-form as soon as the breeze died down.

With a start of guilt Cordelia remembered the coolies, and looked for their fires among the sand.

The captain's dinner had momentarily evicted them from her consciousness, though she could not understand why that should induce a feeling of guilt in her. Their fires were out now, the *Shaitan* sheltering them in its lap. Cordelia craned her neck for a glimpse of the flat. The gangplanks had been removed and a guardsman squatted on the sand, a rifle cradled in his arm. Even among this uninhabited wilderness Buckingham was taking no chances with his cargo.

She heard a swishing sound behind her—feet moving over the deck. Startled, she whipped around and saw the spindly, wraith-like figure of Dorothy Winterbotham. In the semi-darkness of the covered deck her gaunt features, death-pale skin stretched tight over bony cheeks, lips that life had curved into a sour, unsmiling expression, looked weirdly skeletal. Only the eyes were filled with life and suffering.

'I gave you a start, didn't I, Miss Esscombe?' her voice was a shrill whine. 'Sorry about that. I left just after you. Tell me, Miss Esscombe, why are you going to Assam?'

'To join my father in his tea garden. He's ill, and has summoned us.'

'Just like my Elwin. He almost died. I was terribly afraid he would die! He's all I've left, Miss Esscombe. I took care of him day and night. If I hadn't been by his side, he'd have perished.'

Cordelia had a sudden vision of her father on his sick bed, all alone, holding on to the remnants of his strength so he could see his son and daughter again. She could share the fear of this dried up woman.

'It's a man's world out there, Miss Esscombe. No place for women. You see me now as I am. But I was not like this always. Fifteen years in that place has destroyed me.'

She caught Cordelia's hand in her bony grasp and brought it to her cheek. The skin felt hard and rubbery. Repelled, Cordelia drew back her hand from that talon-like grip.

'Why're you telling me all this, Mrs Winterbotham?'

'To caution you, Miss Esscombe. Go and nurse your father back to health. Then leave that place, do you understand? Put it forever behind you, unless you want your firm flesh to rot and your soft skin to wither.'

The woman touched Cordelia once, gave a low, hysterical cackle, and melted away into the darkness. Cordelia fled to the lamp-lit warmth of her cabin.

She woke up early, to the knocking of the native steward, who brought in *chota hazri*. Having washed her face, she began unpacking her things. David dropped in towards the end of the unpacking, looking more boyish and sprightlier as ever. If he had had a late night, there was no trace of it on his face.

'A ruddy disgrace, really, sis!' he kept up the conversation as he watched her put her things away. 'The way you had to leave last night's dinner! Mrs Winterbotham, the native bloke and the padre left soon after you. Michael wanted to leave too, but I persuaded him to stay on.'

'Seems you had a nice time, David?'

'Marvellous. Simply marvellous. That new chappie, Jeremy Arbuckle, has a terrific voice. Sang of Old Blighty and had the captain and the explorer bloke weeping on each other's shoulders.'

'I can well imagine that!' said Cordelia happily.

'The captain was tight as an owl, sis. Gosselin too, once he's had a few, shrugged off his officious air and became quite amiable. But Buckingham's the one I can't make out. He's too aggressive for my liking. Drink brings out the devil in him.'

'He's insufferable,' said Cordelia, and David grew abruptly wary, catching the note of hostility so uncharacteristic of his sister. But he thought he knew the cause.

'The way he ignored you last night was downright insolent,' he said with some heat. 'He had a few swipes at the native bloke too. Forced the poor chap to leave the company. Michael hates his guts; I can feel it. But Michael's a gentleman.'

'Perhaps the only one.'

'Oh, come off it, sis!' David said reproachfully.

'Do you know why I left so early, David? The stained gown was a mere pretext. I couldn't tolerate their coarseness anymore, their pretence at gentility when they're so crude and uncouth. There were Hindustani menials all round. What they must be thinking I can well imagine!'

'You do them an injustice, sis,' David replied placatingly. 'They are a different breed of men, that's all. Different from what we're used to.'

'You're righter than you think. So far, on this steamer, I've seen nothing but vulgarity. Only Reverend Swanson is different. He's ... he's more humane.'

'Sis, you don't understand! These men are all adventurers!' There was a note of admiration in her brother's voice. 'They've led the kind of life I wish I had. Captain McClintock, for instance, has experienced more of life than you or I would ever do.'

'He's a dear old man. But an impostor, like the rest.'

'And Hutchinson, sis! He's been all over the globe. Now he's on a trading expedition to China. Told us about it. Exotic places, sis, with such romantic names. How I wish I could go with him!'

David's eyes were fixed on some distant place, his mind far away. Cordelia saw her brother's face recede to a distance and an invisible wall shut him out from the ambit of her affection. She shook herself, striving at control, and gripped David tightly by his shoulders.

'Don't be silly, David!' she said with a nervous laugh. 'This is no adventure for us. Papa is ill. We're going to him.'

David was contrite. 'Awfully sorry. Got carried away. You're right. Papa must get well and I suppose I'll have to learn the tea business. But one can have one's dreams, can't one?'

'But David, this'll be a kind of adventure! A new life!'

'Of course, yes. But having met blokes like McClintock and Hutchinson … even Buckingham, for that matter … being stuck to a readymade garden suddenly seems too tame.'

Cordelia's face fell and David, seeing the apprehension shadowing her features, willed his usual high spirits to return. 'They're serving breakfast on the deck,' he said jauntily. 'If you're ready, let's go join them.'

The deck was awash with bright sunshine; most of the passengers were already there. Gosselin, Hutchinson, the Winterbotham couple and the griffin sat at a table on the portside, while Lieutenant Bailin and the padre occupied another some distance away. David and Cordelia joined them.

The *Ultaganga*, early that morning, had entered the Sunderban Delta, a vast, swampy slough encompassing hundreds of square miles, where the two giant rivers, Ganges and Brahmaputra, poured jointly into the Bay of Bengal through a myriad inosculation.

Breakfast over, they sat on the cane-chairs, gazing lazily at the shifting vista. Suddenly two figures appeared at the end of the corridor leading to the cabins. Buckingham and the doctor. To Cordelia's consternation they made their way up to their table and asked if they could join them.

'Our pleasure,' David replied uncertainly, and the two sat down.

'Hullo! *Koi hai*? Garo ... Garo Munda?' Buckingham called out.

A native came scurrying from the shadows of a corridor, salaamed to the company and remained frozen in that stance—a short, squat, powerful fellow of uncertain age and dark, unsmiling features. He was not in livery but bare-bodied, with a short, knee-length dhoti wrapped around his waist; so, in all probability, the planter's personal servant.

'*Ki laage, huzoor*?'

'Beer. *Aru gilash. Memsahibar baabe* sherry.' He turned to his companions with a charming smile. 'I've my personal stock of liquor. Some good Solan beer. No ice, though. The ship's stock must've melted by now. Molino sherry for you, Miss Esscombe?'

Cordelia, beyond speech, nodded mutely.

'I'm not averse to a drop of beer,' the padre said, which made David return the planter's smile and air his assent, but the Lieutenant maintained a stony silence. Garo Munda arrived with a tray containing the bottles and glasses, placed it on the cane table and stood aside for further instructions. Buckingham dismissed him with a wave of his hand, filled the glasses and handed them individually to the others.

'This is my way of making amends for last night's behaviour,' he said, his beaming eyes fixed on Cordelia's face. 'The only excuse I can make is that I was a trifle tipsy.'

'It's not necessary, Mr Buckingham,' Cordelia managed to blurt out.

The padre, apparently, presumed otherwise. 'But it is necessary!' he said. 'My dear Cordelia, I congratulate you. Not everyone can wring an apology from Christopher James Buckingham!'

For one brief instant a flash of anger was visible in Buckingham's eyes as they swivelled towards the padre. But the spark vanished and the planter laughed pleasantly.

'No, Swanson. You'll not get me to quarrel with my prospective neighbours. A tea planter's life is lonely as it is. And dashed difficult too! I wouldn't recommend it as a way of earning one's living. That brings me to you, Bailin, old chap. You were, as you informed me yesterday, a Lieutenant in the army, but resigned your commission. One would have expected you to join the civil services as most ex-army men do. Tea planting is a poor substitute for an army commission, even if you're the owner of a garden, and not a salaried slave, as yours truly. What made you turn to tea, Lieutenant?'

A cloud passed over the young Lieutenant's face and he hesitated. Cordelia, once again, was filled with puzzlement at Bailin's reaction. The eyes, a candid blue ordinarily, had suddenly grown inscrutable; instead of being windows to his soul, they seemed to be barred doors that kept locked his innermost thoughts and emotions.

'I had some money of my own,' Bailin said guardedly. 'After a stint in the army I had no appetite for the services. A salaried slave … wasn't that the phrase you used? I wished to be my own master.'

It was a riposte worthy of Garry Swanson. Buckingham was stung to the quick, though he maintained his pleasant exterior. 'So, you bought a garden? Chahpuli, was it, old chap? Well, I've been over eight years in Assam. Have yet to come across a garden called Chahpuli.'

'Perhaps because Chahpuli's a newly opened one. I've studied carefully the map I was given by the man I made the purchase from. Dhanboa's on it, as well as your plantation … Bihguri. Chahpuli lies at a distance away, near a village called Titabar.'

'Well, I hope you knew what you were doing when you made that purchase, dear fellow,' Buckingham said. 'Now that the tea industry is picking up, lots of fraudulent transactions are being carried out. Blokes wheedling out land claims, planting a few saplings and then reselling at preposterous prices as full-fledged tea gardens. I would hardly wish such a fate to befall you.' But his negligent voice and could-not-care-less attitude belied his words.

'I'm certain the Lieutenant's capable of looking after his own interests,' the padre, sensing Bailin's rising anger, interposed hastily.

'No doubt, no doubt,' the planter said, shrugging his shoulders, He quickly shifted his attention to the brother and sister, favouring them with his smile.

Buckingham, thought Cordelia, would dominate any company he chose to grace—even one in which the Reverend was present. His overbearing personality, complemented by an assured self-centredness, made that inevitable. But there was a studied air to his nonchalance, a disconcerting theatricality in each word and gesture, as if in real life too he were playing out a role. Now, seated in close proximity to him, she was more than ever conscious of this streak of thespian in the man. The smile which became him so devilishly was an artifice—that she knew. Yet she allowed it to hit her like a breaker overwhelming an unwary bather, her soul gasping and short of breath.

'David, old chap,' Buckingham was asking, his words directed at her brother, but consciously embracing her in their ambit. 'Your Papa was ailing, you'd said.'

'He appears to be in a bad way, Mr Buckingham. Frequent bouts of fever, loss of weight and vomiting. Occasionally, there's blood in his vomit. He never wrote any of this to us. Only to our godfather, Alexander Swinnerton-Dyer.'

The planter's eyes cocked a query at the doctor. 'Can't say offhand, Chris,' the portly man of medicine replied. 'Must examine the patient before pronouncing judgement.'

'Yes, you must do that, Bill, the minute we get back. Ah, but of course, if David and Miss Esscombe permit it.'

Cordelia's plea, involuntarily, came tumbling out of her mouth. 'Oh, Dr Gordon, you must come and examine Papa as soon as you can!' She checked herself abruptly, her face reddening.

Buckingham pretended not to notice the girl's confused embarrassment. 'David, old chap,' he said. 'You would be wondering why I'm so ignorant of your Papa's condition. After all, my garden adjoins Dhanboa. But the fault lies not with me.'

'I'm sure it doesn't, Mr Buckingham,' David said quickly.

Cordelia's eyes and ears were unabashedly concentrated on the planter now—all thoughts blanked out from her mind save those of Papa and whatever news of him Buckingham could offer. The man, conscious of this, switched his attention onto her.

'Your Papa's a reclusive man, Miss Esscombe,' he said with an air of intimacy. 'I was already at Bihguri when he arrived to open out Dhanboa. He made no effort to get in touch with me.'

Cordelia continued to look at the planter, but said nothing.

'So, instead, I paid a visit to Dhanboa … offered him all assistance as a good neighbour should, but he made a flat refusal. It was almost as if he were determined to carve out his plantation all on his own, and sought no outside help.'

'I ... I understand, Mr Buckingham,' Cordelia said, nodding.

'I went to Dhanboa a couple of more times. But he never paid me a visit at Bihguri … no, not once in these three years.'

'Dhanboa's an obsession with him, Mr Buckingham,' David said with a hint of apology. 'I hope you'll recognize that.'

'I do now, David, old chap. But it rankled somewhat at that point of time. My visits to your Papa's garden grew infrequent, and then stopped altogether. How I wish I'd kept in touch with him? Bill here is a rare commodity in Assam … a qualified European physician. He visits Bihguri every now and again, although I do my own doctoring in the garden. If only your father could've had the benefit of Bill's advice, things may not have come to such a sorry pass.'

'Please do not blame yourself, Mr Buckingham,' Cordelia said with earnest gratitude. 'I'll be bringing Papa away while David takes charge of Dhanboa. But Doctor Gordon must examine him before that and administer the proper medicines.'

'You'll be leaving Dhanboa soon then, Miss Esscombe?' Buckingham asked and then sighed. 'But, of course, it's imperative he be taken to Calcutta for proper medical attention. And you must accompany him. What about afterwards, Miss Esscombe? Do you propose to return to Dhanboa after your Papa has recovered?'

'I don't really know. We haven't charted out our plans that far in time. Our concern for the moment is Papa's health.'

'Certainly. And David old chap, you'll have to handle Dhanboa's affairs. I doubt if you know much about the tea business, do you now?'

'Absolutely nothing, Mr Buckingham,' David said with a laugh. 'To tell you the truth, getting into tea was never a part of my plans. Cordi knows that well enough. It's only because of Papa I'm here at all.'

'You'll have to learn, old chap,' the planer spoke reassuringly. 'But never fear, I'm an experienced hand at the tea business. Teach you all there's to know. Give you every assistance. What are neighbours for, eh?'

He waved away the youngster's effusive thanks with a gesture of boundless magnanimity, clapped loudly and called out to Garo to replenish the glasses. Only the Lieutenant, who had been sitting in glum silence all through, declined the offer of another round. The planter ignored him, as well as the padre, and continued his conversation with the brother and sister, smugly aware that he held them spellbound. He spoke of the travails faced by the path-breaking tea pioneers—a born story-teller, one who could imbue the most prosaic incident with an element of drama, till even Bailin, after a while, was forced to shed his indifference and listen enwrapt. As for Cordelia, she drank in each word, like a child listening to grandmother's tales, oblivious of passing time. Upon her mental screen she had supplanted Buckingham with her father; the images his words conjured up concretized the blurry imaginings in her mind, till his experiences loomed as those of Papa, his exhausted loneliness Papa's own.

She could have listened on for eternity, but suddenly Salim Ali arrived, with summons for the planter from the captain. Buckingham, with ill-concealed regret, stood up, as did Doctor Gordon. He favoured brother and sister with a parting smile, turned on his heels, and strode away, with the portly doctor hurrying to catch up.

The morning of 9 September saw the *Ultaganga* make its way up the Bhadra. More to pass the time than anything else, the Reverend Swanson began teaching the rudiments of the Assamese language to Cordelia, David and Bailin.

'For instance,' he began, 'the name of your Papa's plantation is composed of two common words: dhan and boa. Dhan means rice and boa means to sow. Then we have Chahpuli. Chah is the local word for tea, puli means seedling. So Chahpuli literally stands for tea seedling. Even more appropriate and picturesque is our friend Christopher James Buckingham's Garden ... Bihguri! Bih is the vernacular for poison and guri for ground powder. So, Buckingham's domain is literally poison-powder, ha, ha!'

'Speak of the devil and there he is!' Bailin said sourly.

Cordelia looked towards the cabin corridor. Sure enough, Buckingham was there, without his portly companion this morning. She caught the padre peering closely at her, and made an unsuccessful try at an air of negligence. But she saw what she assumed to be a knowing rebuke in his glance and reddened; his subsequent words, though wrapped in humour, appeared to her as a subtle warning.

'Something has drawn our reptile out of its hole again this morning, Michael ... some unheard melody filling the air, from the flute of some unseen charmer!'

Cordelia lowered her eyes and thus did not catch the spark of anger in Bailin's.

Buckingham tarried a while with the other group, exchanging pleasantries with Gosselin and he rest, thereby arousing hopes, which, however, were dashed in no time, for he bowed, turned around and strode purposefully up to them.

'Good day, Swanson,' he said, his features exuding bonhomie. Unlike the previous morning, he did not ask if he could join them, but proceeded to do so, seating himself in a chair and calling out with a loud clap of the hands, 'Hullo! *Koi hai?* Garo ... Garo Munda?'

The menial arrived and was ordered to fetch beer and sherry. Hutchinson came up to where they sat, bowed to the company, and addressed the planter,

'Hardly three days out, Buckingham, and we're already afflicted with ennui. How about a stint of shooting to liven up things?' His glance took in David and Bailin. 'You too, gentlemen, if you know how to handle a gun.'

Bailin stood up, bowed his head slightly to acknowledge the invitation while Buckingham laughed out loud and said with supreme confidence, 'Certainly, Hutchinson. Ten pounds to anyone who can get the better of me.'

David said, 'I'm not too good with a gun, Michael. But Cordi and I will cheer you on.'

The Lieutenant departed for his cabin to get his rifle, while Buckingham summoned Garo Munda to fetch his. The company moved starboard where the other group was already collected.

There were four contestants, each with his personal weapon. Different targets on the bank were selected and several rounds were fired. Bailin scored perfectly in each round. Clearly, notwithstanding Buckingham's arrogance, the Lieutenant far outshone him with a gun!

An involuntary cry of delight emerged from Cordelia's throat. Buckingham looked quickly at her with surprise, his face reddening, and then turned as quickly away. David sprang forward and pumped his friend's hand with, 'That was terrific, Michael.'

Buckingham, his face flushed, took out his money pouch, but Bailin said, 'Keep your money, Buckingham.'

'It was fairly won,' the planter said. 'I insist on paying you.'

'Then use it to feed your coolies,' Bailing retorted brusquely. Cordelia saw Buckingham recoil as if he had been stung.

'As you wish,' he said, no longer attempting to be pleasant. He walked off towards his cabin to return his firearm. David escorted Cordelia back to their table. Bailin and the padre followed. The reverend suggested that the Lieutenant teach the siblings the basics of shooting firearms, to which the latter readily agreed.

The arrival of Buckingham cut short their conversation. The planter had regained his good spirits as he took his chair, oblivious of the sudden chill which crept into the atmosphere on his return. He picked up his half-full tumbler and drank its contents in one gulp. Seeing that the other glasses were empty, he asked, 'Some more of the stuff for you, gentlemen?'

'Thank you, Mr Buckingham, but no more. We've imposed enough on your hospitality,' David said.

'Not me, David,' Bailin interposed with heavy sarcasm. 'You noticed I didn't touch his stuff! Unsolicited hospitality fills me with suspicion.'

The planter's face hardened. But, as quickly as the tense muscles relaxed, the cold gleam in the eyes was cloaked over by the disarming smile. He clapped his hands loudly and Garo Munda came running up.

'*Ei bilak loi ja*,' he ordered. Ignoring the Lieutenant and the padre, he turned to Cordelia and David and said, 'Miss Esscombe? David? Assam's a pretty dangerous spot. It would be useful if you knew how to handle a gun. I would be happy to be of service to you in this matter.'

Cordelia remained silent, but David, needlessly apologetic, said, 'Thank you again, Mr Buckingham. But Michael has already taken upon himself to teach us.'

'Oh, I see,' Buckingham's voice lost its pleasant edge. He stood up from his chair. 'Well, I must be off now. These damned coolies ... they take up a great deal of my time. Good day, Miss Esscombe. Good day, David.' Warming Cordelia with a direct glance, he walked arrogantly away towards the shadows of the cabin corridor.

Swanson looked at the retreating back and said, 'Buckingham's been behaving mighty peculiar the past couple of days. The apology, the beer, the enchantment of manners. Could it be, my dear Cordelia, that our snake has been captivated by a charmer?'

Bailin looked up sharply at the girl and Cordelia flushed. Confused, he turned his face away, and reached for his rifle, as if handling it gave him comfort.

'I wonder,' the padre spoke again, with greater volume, when his words failed to elicit a reply. 'Oh yes, I very much wonder.'

Khulna was that night's stop for the *Ultaganga*. Cordelia spent the evening at the railings, watching the coolies prepare their meals, ate an early dinner, and leaving her brother to chat on with the Reverend and the Lieutenant, retired to her cabin.

As she lay on the bed a cool breeze continually swept in though the open porthole to fan her cheeks and caress her body, now draped in a nightgown of diaphanous silk. Ordinarily the soft touch of the breeze would have acted as a tactile lullaby, and she should have gently drifted off into slumber. But, tonight, the zephyr seemed to stir her mind as it stirred the leaves of trees, and a wave of perplexing thoughts drove away sleep.

What was it the Reverend Garry Swanson had said in that laconic, slightly mocking tone of his? The snake charmed by the charmer? Or was it the other way round? Had those scaly coils twirled around the flute, and the deadly fangs cut into the charmer's soul?

If not, why then the contradictory pulls of her mind and her body? The sudden hot flush in her as he approached, when she had closed the gates of her mind against his entry? Even now, as the blurry image of the man formed in her consciousness, she felt strange sensations coursing through her. How could her shameless flesh react this way, when all she harboured for the man was uncompromising antipathy?

Buckingham, she knew, was a dangerous man. He too was the manifestation of all she abhorred in her own kind, egoistic, mercenary and heartless, without any of the benevolent sympathies and emotions which soften a human being. She had used the word insufferable to describe him. Yet she had suffered him all right, the past two mornings; had, in fact, felt secret pleasure at his presence! And he too had knowingly unleashed all his charms on her.

Couched within the depths of her psyche was the awareness that men like Buckingham spelt nothing but disaster. Yes, she must steel herself against Christopher James Buckingham—ever since the morning when she had first beheld him jumping down from the gharri he had occupied her thoughts. But now she must coerce her body to correspond with the insights of the mind.

In the days that followed, however, Cordelia grew to realize that ice-hard resolutions made in the dark of the night dissolved at the touch of daylight's reality. Within the limited confines of the steamer escape was not possible, unless she chose to bolt herself reclusively away in her cabin. The gentleness of her disposition made impossible an open and blunt endeavour to fend him off; even the insulating presence of the padre and the Lieutenant could not help her distance herself from the planter. Yet, there was nothing offensive in the way he comported himself; with her he was now at his suave best; the jagged insensitivity integral to his mental makeup and which lay skin-deep in the man was adroitly camouflaged by what the Reverend had termed his enchantment of manners. Despite her resolve Cordelia could not help but be moved by his effortless witchery.

Effortless it certainly was, for the man emanated an animal magnetism which constantly threatened to overwhelm her. The beauty of his outward shell; the picture of male virility that he made standing by the railings; his flawless profile outlined against the vast blue sky; his, long, silken hair flailed by the breeze; the smile, mysterious and taunting; the easy fluidity of his movements and his air of wanton recklessness; all this was designed to sweep a young, impressionable girl off her feet. If she had been devoid of intelligence, or, perhaps, if the circumstances had been different, she may have succumbed to his allurement. But her own perceptions were acute and the fortuitous presence of others on board ensured that these were not blanked out by the tyranny of the senses. She had seen through the essential shallowness of the man that night in the captain's dinner; his crudity had oozed out like smelly sweat through the membrane of his charm. Also, the capacity for deep passion innate in her precluded transient shipboard flirtation, inconsequential and effervescent; her observation of the planter made her suspect that he lacked the capacity for absolute commitment which she herself possessed. Above all was the concern for Papa's health, which remained like an old ache in some hidden cranny of her heart, reminding her with a twinge every time she looked at David.

Then, of course, there were the coolies. Buckingham's coolies! The image of a woman defecating! Of those wretched, bedraggled creatures swarming around their captors at feeding time! And the Reverend Garry Swanson, the articulate mirror of her secret guilt, always at hand to reinforce those images in case they sought to retreat to the peripheries of her consciousness and get lost there for ever. And last, yet not least, was the constant presence of Lieutenant Michael Bailin, the perfect foil to the tantalizement of Buckingham—taciturn and inarticulate, yet in many ways solid and comforting, stodgy, unable to inspire anything but affection, incapable of arousing the passionate flame that the wily Buckingham, at a different time and in different circumstances, possibly might have.

In fact, even more than the padre, it was the Lieutenant who aided Cordelia's combatment of Buckingham's overtures. There was no love lost between the two; this friction served continually to bring out the viciousness lying submerged in the planter. Paradoxically, it could have been Bailin, Cordelia suspected, who may have been instrumental in the erasure of Buckingham's simulated indifference and his head on approach. Woman that she was, she could grasp that the Lieutenant harboured deeper emotions towards her than his phlegmatic exterior permitted to reveal. This was not to be seen in his actions or his manners towards her—he was the perfect embodiment of rectitude. Rather, it was sometimes to be seen in his eyes, as he looked at her; and in his voice and gestures. That he aroused no kindred sensations in her he may have known, yet the knowledge in no way led him into incivility or induced in him a desire to remove himself from the company.

But was Buckingham aware of her indifference towards his adversary? She could gauge how the planter's mind may have worked. He had seen the desire in her eyes; had thought her an easy conquest; had initially assumed a haughty, indifferent air, confident that she would mindlessly and on her own flutter into his web. But, instead, Bailin had loomed as a potential rival! Had the Lieutenant brought out latent insecurities in the man, coercing him to reformulate his stratagem, and make a direct approach? Had she been transformed into an object of contention?

Whenever the two were together Cordelia could physically feel the waves of hostility emanating from them towards each other. The very air tautened and the tension threatened each time to snap into violence. Bailin no longer hesitated to be openly offensive. Buckingham's initial response had been one of displeased tolerance; the facade of gallantry which he sought to present to Cordelia went ill with verbal squabbles. But he had approached the girl with confidence, for had he not seen desperate cravings in her eyes? As he discovered that his objective was not as easily attainable as he had thought, he began reacting belligerently to Bailin's affronts.

Though conscious of the friction building up between the planter and the Lieutenant, Cordelia had not apprehended that sparks would fly. Thus, when the climax arrived with soul-shattering violence, she was not prepared for it, as were not the others. And, to her dismay, she herself was indirectly responsible for the incident.

The *Ultaganga* had been steaming steadily for the past days, up the Bhadra, making night stops at Kacha and Barisal. They entered the Meghna inosculation in the afternoon of the 12th, moored on a large island of sand at the point where the Ganges, called the Padma there, and the Meghna met. The night of the 13th was spent at Arialkhan. The next evening, they were scheduled to reach the large village port of Goalundo, where the *Ultaganga* was to replenish her depleted supplies.

Early in the morning of the 14th she departed from Arialkhan on her way to Goalundo. A mood of ennui had settled over the passengers who were, as usual, congregated on the deck. Gosselin, Hutchinson, Elwin and Arbuckle were seated at a table engaged in a game of cards. Dorothy Winterbotham sat upon a chair beside the group, her gaze resting on a volume of poetry.

Cordelia, David and Michael stood by the starboard railings, the latter teaching the siblings how to handle small arms. Captain McClintock too appeared on deck, limped towards the card players, exchanged a few words and then shuffled towards them. He nodded pleasantly at the trio, took a chair at the table where Reverend Swanson sat, and puffed away at his pipe.

All at once there was a frightened yell and sounds of a scuffle. A cabin door crashed open and the enraged voice of Buckingham was heard. An instant later a native came rushing through the corridor onto the deck—Buckingham's khidmatgar, Garo Munda. The man's eyes bulged in their sockets; the muscles on his face and neck were tight with half-crazed terror. His master was at his heels, a long, supple cane in his hand, blind rage distorting his features.

In his desperation to get away, the unfortunate menial stumbled on the polished deck and fell. Like a beast of prey Buckingham was upon him. As the native cowered on the floor and covered his face with his hands, Buckingham slashed savagely at his bare back. The cane pierced the skin and a thin line of blood appeared on the dark hide of the quarry.

'Chor! Badmash! Son of Shaitan! Filch my whisky, will you?' the cane flashed again and again, leaving the bare back a welted, gory mass. The victim's first shrill cries of pain gave way to whimpers; the sable skin peeled away from his back to reveal bare white flesh.

Those on the deck were traumatized by the sudden disruption to the sluggish morning. Each pair of eyes turned towards the master and his slave, but no one made a move. Cordelia, in the first horror-filled moments tongue-tied, suddenly found voice, and shrieked, 'Oh, my God! Somebody, stop him, for heaven's sake!'

In response to her plea the diminutive captain jerked upright, a strident command about to issue from his throat. But, before he could do so, there was a click and the bang of a pistol and Buckingham's upraised cane was instantly split in two.

The planter's fury gave way to incredulity as he looked at the broken cane in his hand. The passengers were paralysed with shock and disbelief. Only the fumes from Bailin's pistol rose languidly in the air as the warm, rusty, acrid odour of gunpowder filled the deck.

Then the tableaux moved. 'Bravo!' shouted the captain, while the padre burst into spontaneous applause. Cordelia's hand was at her mouth, stifling the exclamation of relief which sought to escape from it. Bailin, calm and unflustered, began reloading his pistol.

Flat on the deck, Garo Munda sensed a change in the atmosphere. Hidden strength, born of desperation, enabled him to raise himself to his knees. Bleary, pain-filled eyes surveyed the situation. Sudden comprehension dawned on the native and he half crawled, half scampered to where Bailin stood and threw himself at his feet.

'Excellent! Bravely done!' The words, emerging from Buckingham's mouth, far from being eulogistic, were pregnant with venom. The planter's face had grown devoid of the anger it had reflected just moments ago. In fact, he was smiling, a contemptuous, diabolic smile which chilled Cordelia's blood.

He flung the broken cane away and strode up to Bailin. 'All right, Garo, get back to the cabin. I'll deal with you later.'

'*Nai, nai, najao*!' the khidmatgar muttered in a fearful voice, shaking his head and grasping Bailin's legs in a fierce grip.

'Go, damn you!' Buckingham roared as the blood once more rushed to his face. He delivered a brutal kick on the cowering man.

'That's enough, Buckingham,' the captain's voice rang out commandingly. 'The man's been sufficiently punished. Get Doctor Gordon here to treat his back.'

Buckingham ignored the captain. He fixed Bailin with a curious stare. 'So, Garo's found a godfather, has he?' he spat out the words.

'I'll buy him off you,' said Bailin in a conciliatory tone.

'No. You can have him free. I have no further use for him. But Bailin, old chap, you'll have to answer me first.'

'Certainly, Buckingham.' The Lieutenant's face was neutral. 'Only I must know the nature of your question.'

'This evening. At Goalundo. We'll have it out!'

The others had come up meanwhile and stood around the combatants. On the deck Garo Munda lay supine, clutching Bailin's legs like a drowning man grasping a log of wood.

'May I remind you, gentlemen, that the 1844 Articles of war forbid duelling,' Gosselin spoke out with authority.

'I'll not allow any such thing on me ship, Buckingham,' Captain McClintock growled.

'Ah, duelling yes,' the planter, without taking his eyes off Bailin, said. 'With guns, rapiers and kindred weapons, isn't it so, Major?'

'Yes, that is so,' the officer replied.

'Also, I as the aggrieved party have the right to the choice of a weapon?'

'That's true. But since ...'

'Then, Bailin, I challenge you to a fight with bare fists. That should satisfy you, Major?'

For once in his life the officer failed to find a suitable reply. Buckingham turned to McClintock. 'Not on board your ship, Captain. This evening. At Goalundo. Upon a sandbank. I shall expect you there, Bailin.'

He swivelled sharply on his heels and strode back to his cabin.

For a while no one spoke. Then Gosselin said, 'You needn't pick up his gauntlet, Lieutenant, if you don't wish to.'

'No,' Bailin answered shortly. 'I'm game.'

'David, m'lad, go and rouse up Doctor Gordon and fetch him here. This fellow's wounds need tending,' Captain McClintock said.

'You can put him for a while in our cabin,' Bailin offered. He turned towards Cordelia, but before he could speak, the girl said in a voice which yet held the residues of shock and fear, 'I am sorry, Michael.'

A warm smile came to the Lieutenant's lips, not because of her needless apology, but the fact that, for the first time and spontaneously, she had called him by his first name. Yet something within prevented him from uttering hers as he said, 'That's perfectly all right, Miss Esscombe. The fault was not yours. I did what I had to do.'

Her glance fell squarely on his eyes. For the span of a moment those blue orbs became passages to his soul. Cordelia, frightened by what she saw, turned and walked away to the insular womb of her cabin.

The village port of Goalundo nestled at the junction of two mighty rivers, the Brahmaputra, or Jamuna as it was called hereabouts, and the Ganges, or Padma. The distance from Arialkhan to Goalundo being quite short, the steamer reached the pier much ahead of sunset. Before touching it, however, she stopped for while on a gigantic sandbank to offload the coolies. Then she went to the pier to heave aboard supplies of fuel, potable water, fresh fruits and vegetables.

These operations took quite some time and dusk was falling when the *Ultaganga* headed once more to the sandbank. The passengers, all except Buckingham and Bailin, took an early dinner; their mood was sombre, their thoughts clouded by the impending fight.

Hutchinson was unanimously elected to oversee it. Doctor Gordon and the griffin would act as Buckingham's seconds, while David and Swanson would do duty for Bailin. The time was to be 8 p.m., well after the coolies had fed and returned to the flat—three rounds, lasting three minutes each, with a minute's gap in between.

Everyone, including Bailin, pleaded with Cordelia to stay back on board, but she was unrelenting. She had taken upon herself the blame for the situation in which the Lieutenant found himself, and was determined to render every assistance. Her womanly instincts alerted her that her presence would inspire him as nothing else could.

After dinner their group sat in the cabin which the Lieutenant shared with her brother, conversing in low voices. Around 7 p.m. the griffin popped his head in and breathlessly informed them that his party was leaving for the arena. 'Come,' said Bailin, after the griffin left. 'It's time we moved.'

Just past the gangplanks a figure left the shadows cast by the vessel and scurried after them—Garo Munda, the swath of white bandage around his torso and the white dhoti he wore gave him a spectral look. 'He says he will go with Bailin sahib,' Swanson informed them. 'He has pledged his life to Bailin sahib and will never leave his side, no matter what the circumstances are.'

'Thanks, Garo,' said Bailin with feeling. They had to traverse the entire sandbank before they saw the other group, grimly awaiting their arrival. Hutchinson had traced a large square on the sand. 'You two must stay inside this ring,' he cautioned. 'No one else apart from me can set foot within it.'

At a signal from the explorer the two men stripped. Buckingham stepped into the ring first, his body naked except for the skin-hugging, knee-length tights. The masculine virility which he exuded when fully draped, his animal sexuality, was now even more pronounced. The moonbeams melted into his skin, gave it a bronze sheen, obliterating the contrast between cloth and flesh, so that he seemed voluptuously naked. The muscles rippled on his flawless body at each graceful movement. The man seemed utterly oblivious of Cordelia's presence; yet her presence seemed to accentuate his aura of maleness. Desperately, she endeavoured to control the concupiscent stirrings in her body, but she could not tear her eyes off him; his beauty took her breath away; the sexuality emanating from him like slow rising river mist wrapped her till she thought she would swoon.

Then Bailin stepped in and the spell was broken. Although a tall and well-built man, his physical endowments seemed commonplace measured against Buckingham's magnificence. Cordelia vainly struggled to get a hold on herself, summoned up inner strength to see the contest through, as Hutchinson asked the two gentlemen to shake hands and the first round commenced.

Each of the onlookers was gripped by the bizarre quality of the ambience as the two combatants warily circled each other—the moonlit vista, the silver sands rolling away from them in every direction, the dark hulk of the *Ultaganga* framed like a painting by the gleaming waters, the ill-lit port of Goalundo and the mud and thatch hutments of the village further off. Buckingham struck, his right fist streaking, quick as the striking fangs of a cobra, hitting the Lieutenant a hard, painful blow on the left of his face. Bailin closed in with a flurry of punches, but his adversary back-stepped away on nimble feet. That first blow was an indication of things to come and Cordelia, with a flash of insight, suddenly saw through the diabolic trap into which Bailin had allowed himself to be lured.

Buckingham was all around Bailin, a quarry rather than an opponent, fast, agile and graceful, repeatedly striking with hard, stinging blows and then neatly retreating so that the countering punches of the other man pounded empty air. Compared to his speed and agility Bailin appeared lethargic. The planter was toying with his adversary, laughing tauntingly each time his blows landed. Something in the Lieutenant seemed suddenly to snap and he rushed headlong at his enemy, guards down, intent only on smashing his way through the other's defences. But Buckingham was ready for him. He parried the charge and then caught Bailin in a clinch. The two clutched each other in a lover's embrace till Hutchinson, a powerful man, stepped in and separated them. 'Round one over,' he shouted. 'Retreat to your corners.'

The second round was even more brutal. Again, and again, Buckingham's fist slammed into Bailin's body and face. He himself remained relatively untouched as he teased and taunted his opponent. Bailin moved heavily and ineffectively; whenever he sought to close in on his fleet-footed antagonist, by sheer will-power rather than skill, Buckingham kept him at bay with straight rights, or clinching holds. Bailin's lips were spilt, a cut had appeared on the corner of his right eye, and his face was a gory mess. As Hutchinson sounded the end of the round and Bailin slumped at his corner, David bent over him, swabbing away the blood with a wetted napkin, and said, 'You've had enough, Michael! It's time we put an end to this nonsense.'

'No,' said Bailin through cracked lips. 'I must go through with it.'

He pushed himself up and entered the ring for the third time, a dogged gleam in his eyes. Buckingham smiled, a raffish, mocking grin, and said, 'I've saved my best for the last, old chap.' He flitted lightly around the other, moving in with quick, hurting jabs, dancing round and round, the ruthless smile never off his face. The Lieutenant's nose spouted blood, red-stained sweat entered his eyes and he could not see. Buckingham feinted with a left to the face, followed by a power-packed punch to the belly. Bailin emitted an audible whoosh as the air was knocked out of him. His guard dropped; he staggered blindly on wobbly feet. Buckingham was all over him in a trice, ignoring Hutchinson's commands to stop fighting, savagely mauling the battered and unsteady Lieutenant. The victim's face was a ghastly mask of red as Buckingham swivelled on his left foot and swung his right first in a final, hammer-like blow to Bailin's unguarded chin. The Lieutenant's feet gave way and he crumpled senseless onto the gritty sands.

'Get back, Buckingham, you devil!' Hutchinson yelled when it seemed that the planter was enraged enough to kick the life out of his fallen adversary. Doctor Gordon and Jeremy Arbuckle rushed forward to pull him away. David and the padre ran to Bailin's side. Swanson, unmindful of the drops of blood staining his shirtfront, lifted the unconscious man's head on to his lap, while David wiped away the blood with the napkin and laid a wet compress to his forehead.

Cordelia stood where she was, transfixed by what she had just witnessed, unable to move or utter a sound. 'Patch him up, Bill,' Buckingham said brusquely. 'Come, Jeremy. Pick up my clothes and let's go.'

The griffin, too overawed to demur, collected the clothes and set off after the planter. Gordon came and knelt beside the fallen Lieutenant. He prised open the closed eyelids, peered into them and said, 'Doesn't look too good to me, Hutchinson. We must get him aboard as soon as possible. You, Swanson, don't let the sand get into his wounds.'

Minutes later Garo Munda arrived, with three other natives, a stretcher between them. Bailin was carefully lifted onto it and the party proceeded to the *Ultaganga*.

'Mind helping me?' the portly man of medicine asked Cordelia as the stretcher bearers transferred the unconscious man to the bed.

'Of course not, Doctor Gordon,' Cordelia said eagerly.

Already the cabin was overcrowded. 'You must give me room,' the doctor wailed. 'I'll be obliged if all of you, except Miss Esscombe, step outsides. Swanson, ask Garo to fetch a bucket of boiling water.'

The young Lieutenant lay on the narrow bunk, his features waxy pale as if in death, the lamplight accentuating the cadaverous lifelessness. His lips were swelling, the clotted blood disfigured the face. The area around the eyes was blackened; blue-black patches of bruising marred the fairness of the skin on his bare torso. Cordelia gazed down at the battered frame and her heart was suffused with pity and affection, mixed with admiration at his undeniable courage.

Garo arrived with a pail of steaming hot water. Gordon emptied a pungent-smelling lotion into it, dipped a wad of cotton-wool, and scrubbed away the grit and blood from Bailin's wounds, his hands gentle. The Lieutenant stirred as the medicine bit into the raw flesh, groaned once or twice, but the eyes remained closed

'That's all I can do for him at present,' Gordon said with a final swab. 'The nasal bone, unfortunately, seems to be broken. There may be dislocation of the jaw, though I can't be sure right now. Buckingham's a powerful man.'

'He'll be all right, won't he, doctor?' Cordelia asked anxiously.

The doctor's flabby countenance turned towards her, his small, weasel-like eyes probing her countenance. 'He should be recovered in a day or two, Miss Esscombe. But I suspect a fever's coming on. Prepare a wet compress for his forehead and fan his head.'

He talked earnestly and in low voice to the group at the door and waddled away. Cordelia went to the bathroom, wet a fresh towel, squeezing it till the excess water drained off, and laid it on Bailin's forehead. She sat at the edge of the bunk, picked up a palm-leaf punkah and began fanning his head.

Meanwhile David, the padre and Captain McClintock had entered and were sitting silently on the other bed. For a long time, no one moved, not a word was uttered. Then Captain McClintock stood up and said, 'I've me ship to run, lassie, so I must leave. But don't fail to summon me if the need be pressing.'

He had directed to words at Cordelia alone, as though she were in charge, and the girl coloured a little at the implication. But David said, 'You had better go now, sis. The Reverend and I'll take up the night's vigil.'

'No, I'll stay,' Cordelia said simply.

Swanson came up and laid a palm on Bailin's cheek. 'He's running a fever. But it'll pass. His body's reaction to the violence done to it, that's all.' He spoke to David. 'We'll allow your sister to sit for a while, David. Garo, by the way, is stretched out on the corridor outside. If you need anything, my dear, just wake him up.'

The hours passed. Cordelia sat with unmoving stoicism, her hand mechanically wielding the punkah. All the while Bailin had lain prone, the regular up and down movement of his chest the only indication he was yet alive. The fever raged in him; his face was flushed, the heat radiating from him seemed to warm the entire cabin. Suddenly he stirred uneasily, the cracked and swollen lips opened and the shadow of some unknown anger and sorrow passed over his features. Cordelia bent low to catch the words which tumbled out of his throat.

'I'll not do it,' Bailin murmured deliriously. 'I'll not be a party to murder!' Then, after a stretch of silence, again, 'Be damned all of you. I'll not do it!' His body had grown rigid, his fists were clenched, the chords of his neck muscles distended till each sinew stood rock-hard and visible. But his eyes were closed. 'Do your worst!' he cried. 'I'm ready for the consequences.'

'Michael, Michael!' Cordelia whispered, but the eyes remained shut. It was clear that in his delirious state the Lieutenant was reliving a painful experience of his past. The body remained rigid, the fever raged. Panic stricken, Cordelia was about to awaken her brother when abruptly Bailin relaxed; the tense, screwed up face softened into a smile, and the words stopped erupting. He began to perspire heavily, beads of sweat oozed out of his skin and joined together to form drops which trickled down his body onto the bed linen. Cordelia found another towel to soak away the sweat from his chest and neck. The fever was lessening in intensity. Suddenly his eyes flickered open. They were unfocussed, dulled by pain and fever. 'Water! I am parched!' he muttered hoarsely. Cordelia bounded up and brought him a tumblerful of water. She knelt by his side, helped him with one hand to raise his head, while the other held the tumbler to his lips.

He drank thirstily, draining the tumbler to the last drop, and fell back exhausted on the pillow. The eyes settled on the contours of her face, sharpened with recognition, and a wondering look came into them, replacing the dullness and ache. 'Thank you, Miss Esscombe,' he said.

'Go back to sleep, Michael. You'll feel better in the morning.'

His eyes closed and a long-drawn sigh escaped his throat. Soon his breathing became regular. Once more she touched his cheeks. They were cool and moist.

As quietly as she could she stole to where the padre slept in the single chair in the cabin, and shook him awake. 'He's no longer feverish, Father,' she whispered. 'I'm going to my cabin.'

She was startled to discover that the darkness of deep night had lifted and, as she came out onto the deck, saw the first fingers of dawn tracing the horizon. Weariness settled over her as she opened her cabin door. Without taking off her clothes, she fell onto her bed and slid into exhausted sleep.

She woke up late, washed and dressed quickly and repaired to Michael's cabin. David was inside, as was the padre. The Lieutenant was fully conscious; the light of the day to a large extent had diminished the marks of violence on his visage; the swellings had subsided, while the fresh nightgown he wore hid the bruises on his body.

'You nursed me throughout the night,' he said as soon as she entered. He spoke with less difficulty and his voice sounded stronger. 'I'm deeply indebted to you, Miss Esscombe.'

Cordelia was at a loss for words. 'I'm sorry, Michael,' was all she could say.

'I would have done it over and over again,' Bailin said, his eyes fixed on hers. Suddenly the other two no longer seemed to exist. Uncomfortable with that gaze, Cordelia turned her face away and looked towards the padre.

'Has Doctor Gordon examined Michael again, Father?'

'Yes. And he had good news to offer. Our champion has taken heavy punishment, no doubt, but there's no permanent physical damage. Michael should be up and about in a day or two.'

'Captain McClintock popped in this morning, sis,' her brother added. 'So did the others. And guess what, sis? The native bloke too was here! In fact, everyone seems most anxious for dear Michael. Buckingham's the sole exception.'

'Naturally!' Cordelia said shortly.

'Had your breakfast, sis?'

'No, not yet, David.'

'Oh, then we must fetch you some.' He pulled the bell cord to summon a steward but, as if he had been anxiously waiting for the summons, it was Garo Munda who entered the cabin.

He had removed the bandages around his body; the crisscross welts on his back, snarling, angry red, were visible. He left after finding out what was required, and the Reverend said, 'Garo is sticking to Michael, did you know that, Cordelia? His former master is not at all bothered with what Garo does. Appears to have chucked him out of his life.'

'Poor fellow,' Cordelia said in sympathy. 'That back of his must be hurting terribly.'

'I think it's admirable of Garo to stick to Michael,' David intruded approvingly. 'We all heard Buckingham publicly state he had no further use for the man. Michael need not feel bad taking him on. He will be of considerable help, especially in Assam, knowing as he does the local language. So, some good might yet come out of this rotten business, eh, Michael?'

'Out of evil shall spring forth good!' the padre intoned oracularly. 'The supreme irony of Providence! But you were a fool to have taken up Buckingham's challenge. You realize that now, don't you, Michael. He lured you into a trap.'

'I must disagree with you, Father,' David said with some warmth. 'Michael's a gentleman. He couldn't have acted otherwise. Buckingham issued a challenge. Michael had to take it up.'

'Ah, but he must recall what he himself said some days back. The consequences of action are fearful! If you choose to react to what you see in this benighted age, you must be prepared to face the consequences.'

'I'm not complaining, am I, Father?' Bailin said, endeavouring to be facetious.

'Father,' Cordelia asked, 'are you implying Michael should not have saved that poor creature from being half killed?'

'You misunderstand me, dear child. One must certainly fight injustice, using every weapon at one's command. But the consequences need not be harsh, if you only act with subtlety.'

'Meaning?' David asked.

'I'm teaching you all the art of survival, David. Draw a lesson from a tiger. You must have its strength as well as its stealth if you're to survive in this social jungle. Just look at me! Don't you think my priestly calling makes a good camouflage?'

'You're no predator, Father!' David said laughingly.

'But I'm a subversive, David! Perhaps not in your eyes, nor in Michael's or Cordelia's. But the Gosselins and Buckinghams of this world would term me one, for I endeavour continually to pull down the devilish structure they've erected. Had I not been a priest, do you imagine I would have lasted half as long as I have in this country? Unfortunately, none of you are armed with the immunity I possess. If you don't learn to swim with the tide, to behave as your brethren behave, to mould yourself as the system dictates, you'll loom as a threat to those who've erected this system. They're powerful, believe me! They'll squash you as little boys squash ants under their heels!'

Cordelia said, 'Is there no hope then, Father? Are those who fight for justice condemned to suffer?'

'That's what I'm trying to put across, dear girl! Why must stealth and guile be the sole prerogative of the wicked? No Cordelia, to survive in this jungle of corruption and greed, goodness must pretend to be one with the wicked and, shielded by camouflage, go hammer and tongs at them. Take Michael's case, for instance. If only he had insisted on a duel with firearms instead of fists, Buckingham would have retreated with his tail between his legs!'

'But duelling with firearms is banned by law!' David protested.

'So there would have been no duel! And none of this. All Buckingham could've done was to nurse his grudge, leaving you free to go which way you please.'

'Saving my face was not the foremost in my thoughts then, Father,' Bailin said.

'You are a misfit in the milieu in which you find yourself, Michael. In your country words like gentleman, honour, chivalry and so on may have validity but not in British-ruled Hindustan. Here only thugs and thieves prosper, though they have nothing to recommend them but the whiteness of their skins. Innocence like yours is ruthlessly destroyed.'

Cordelia had a passing glimpse of her father in her mind's eye. She saw him, destroyed by his own innocence. How right the padre was, how perceptive! Her gaze fell on the Lieutenant's face. There was pain in his eyes; not the physical pain of the body, but an anguish of the soul, as if the padre's words had rekindled hurtful memories.

At that moment Garo appeared, carrying Cordelia's breakfast tray, accompanied by a liveried steward who brought tea and biscuits for the others. For a while conversation languished, the silence lasting till the girl completed her breakfast, and Garo cleared the trays.

All the while the Lieutenant had reclined with eyes closed, appearing to have turned inward into deep reflection. Suddenly he opened them, looked determinedly at the padre as though he had arrived at a hard decision, and spoke.

'It's not always possible to combat evil with guile, Father,' he said. 'Sometimes circumstances thrust a clear choice before you, when subterfuge becomes meaningless.'

'You've confronted such a situation, Michael?' the padre's voice held a ring of compassion.

'Yes, Father. I've not told you the truth about myself. I have a confession to make. I did not resign voluntarily from the army. I was dishonourably dismissed. For not carrying out orders.'

Dead silence reigned in the room. David felt the shock most keenly. His face was suffused with colour and there was the anger of betrayal in his eyes.

'I pride myself on being a good judge of character. If you had disobeyed orders, you must have had good reasons for doing so.' Swanson, aware of David's anger, said in conciliatory tones.

'Yes, Father. I couldn't have acted otherwise. I was compelled by circumstances. David, listen to my story, and judge whether another choice existed before me.'

Lieutenant Michael Bailin was born into an old, landed family which held an estate near Ipswich, Suffolk. Four generations of the family had served with distinction in the British army; his father, Colonel Douglas Bailin, had seen action both in China and India. It was expected that Michael would maintain the family's military links when he grew up. Sure enough, after his seventeenth birthday, the youngster sat for the East India Company's recruitment examinations, assiduously cramming his Greek and Latin to cross this hurdle, and succeeding fairly easily. Having opted for the Company's military wing he was forthwith despatched for training at the Company's military college at Addiscombe, where in due time he received his commission.

The newly commissioned young man, in December 1854, sailed off for India on the P & O's *S. S. Euphrates.* On arrival he was attached to the 17th Native Artillery of the Bengal Army, and saw action almost immediately in the Punjab. For almost the whole of the year 1855 he was involved in the Afghan campaign till early 1856, when his regiment was withdrawn and rested at Ambala.

Then came the events of May 1857 that plunged Hindustan into nightmare. Within weeks after the capture of Delhi by the insurgent sepoys, a series of uprisings broke out in major centres of North and Central India. More than half of the Company's sepoy strength of 2,32,000 rose in revolt against the British superiors. In Oudh, Rohilkhand, Bundelkhand, Bihar, Rajasthan and the Central Provinces the insurrection of the sepoys was transformed into a mass upheaval as the civil population was released from fear of British authority and joined hands with the mutineers. The rebellion took on the shape of a bitter and bloody war. For a while the British administration disappeared entirely from many parts of India as hundreds of firanghees were massacred.

Bailin's regiment was pressed into service almost as soon as the revolt broke out. It took part in the battle for the recapture of Delhi in September 1857, and entered the imperial city on the twenty-eighth of that month.

The long-drawn campaign to restore British authority on violence-torn Hindustan spilled over to the first half of 1858—a brutal, bloody conflict which brought out the worst in men, both white and black. Bailin saw and experienced it firsthand, and quailed inwardly at the savagery his brother officers were capable of. He sensed the change in them as they heard of the massacre of European women, children and babies; witnessed the vengeful, barbaric slaughter of Hindustani women, children and babies, no less innocent. All they had learnt of British justice and fair play had been thrown to the winds; he watched with horror natives hanged without allowing them the rites of purification. Whenever they camped near deserted villages,

European officers moved into the jungles and paddy fields in search of natives hiding there, and shot them on the run.

Bailin had tried to keep aloof from all the barbarism, telling himself he was a soldier and not a killer. But as the brutality raged on unabated, he could tolerate no more and spoke out against it. That had been his undoing!

Word of his 'treacherous' behaviour was gradually brought to the notice of Major Landon, their Commanding Officer. Landon had served under General Neill, the Butcher of Cawnpur, and during the period of mutiny earned notoriety akin to his mentor's. Bailin's background and the fact that he had fought with unquestionable gallantry during the campaign against the rebellious sepoys saved him for a long time, for the Major had at first baulked at taking punitive action. But the complaining barks had grown in intensity. Soon things reached such a state that Major Landon had no option but to bring his subordinate to book.

The fait accompli came one wet morning in June 1858. They were under the Generalship of Sir Colin Campbell, fighting against that wily Maratha chief, Tantia Tope, who was waging guerilla warfare against the British troops. One of Tope's allies, Feroze Shah, had been a thorn in the flesh of the British for quite a while. But three days previously that feudal lord had been captured, betrayed by one of his allies who had been bought over. He had been put in chains and was under the custody of Major Landon.

Their depleted regiment had bivouacked near a large, deserted village, about five miles from one of Feroze Shah's fortresses. It had been a miserable morning. A thin, incessant drizzle rendered the ground muddy and made things slushy and uncomfortable. Bailin was cleaning his weapons and protecting them from the damp when the summons came from Major Landon.

The Major greeted Bailin cheerily and while the Lieutenant stood at attention, told him that he had a job for him.

'Come with me, Lieutenant,' Landon said. They emerged from the Major's tent and walked some distance away to a small clearing. A brass cannon stood at its centre. A Hindustani sepoy was stuffing it with powder, unmindful of the drizzle. Another sepo*y* stood close by, an unlit torch in his hand.

Major Landon barked out a command at an underling, who hurried to a heavily guarded tent and spoke to one of the sentries. Minutes later a man was brought out, pushed on from behind by a European Captain. It was Feroze Shah. All at once Bailin, with failing heart, knew of what was to come and his role in the drama to be enacted.

The prisoner was a tall and powerfully built man, head turbaned, face heavily bearded, robes in tatters. The burn-marks on his arms and face bore evidence that he had been tortured. His wrists and ankles were shackled and the link-chain was suspended round his neck; his left leg dragged as he walked and he was in obvious pain. Yet the man moved proudly, head held high, and the state of his clothes or his battered frame were unable to conceal the essential aristocracy of his character.

The captain prodded the limping, chain-bound figure with the back of his rifle to the centre of the clearing, beside the canon. Two sepoys tied the unresisting prisoner to the mouth of the cannon. Feroze Shah was absolutely unafraid though he knew of his fate. Instead, when they were binding him to the cannon's mouth, he raised two chained hands as high as he could in the air, and shouted defiantly, '*Tantia Tope ki jai*! Victory to Tantia Tope!'

The captain hit him on the head to silence him, but the blow was too hard and Feroze Shah, knocked unconscious, slumped forward, held to the cannon-mouth by the ropes. Major Landon berated the captain for his stupidity, for the overzealous officer had done the prisoner a favour by rendering him senseless just before his execution. He ordered a pail of water to be fetched and the prisoner brought back to consciousness.

The debasement of the prisoner was complete. He spluttered into consciousness and shook his shaggy head like a dog after a bath. Landon must have now seen the humour of the situation, though not with the grimness which had darkened Bailin's perception, for he chuckled and, turning to the Lieutenant, said, 'We must make an example of any one who dares wage war against Her Majesty's domain. You should deem it a privilege that I ask you to go and fire the cannon.'

Observing Bailin's lack of response, the Major barked once more, 'Go and fire the cannon, Lieutenant! That's an order!'

Bailin found his voice. 'Has there been a trial, Major Landon, sir?'

Landon's temper flared. 'A trial, Lieutenant? For this brigand? This nigger assassin? Go, damn you, and blow him to smithereens!'

The tension drained out of the Lieutenant. Suddenly he was composed, the beating of his heart stilled. 'I'll not do it,' he said with dignity. 'I'll not be a party to murder!'

An angry muttering broke out among the officers at the Lieutenant's refusal. One of them called out, 'Let me do it, sir, if Bailin won't. I'll finish this bastard!'

'No,' Landon said in a voice steeped in menace. 'It must be Lieutenant Bailin and no one else.'

The blood rose in Bailin too as he surveyed the gloating faces of his compatriots—men who had shared his mess, fought and won or lost together. They looked like a pack of vultures waiting for an animal to give up its breath.

Violent anger made his voice incoherent as he shouted, 'Be damned, all of you! I'll not do it!'

Major Landon recoiled as if he had been slapped. 'Are you aware of the consequences of your disobedience?' he demanded.

'Do your worst!' Bailin cried out.

'I'll break you, Bailin!' the Major spat out the words. He turned to the other Europeans. 'Have this man arrested. Detail some men to guard his tent.'

Willing hands grabbed the Lieutenant and divested him of the holster and ammunition belt. As he stood between two guards, Major Landon stepped up to the cannon onto which Feroze Shah was strapped. The chieftain had just enough time to look up to the heavens and cry '*Allah ho Akbar*,' before Landon grabbed the lighted flare and touched it to the powder.

There was an ear-shattering explosion as the unfortunate victim's body was smashed into hundreds of bits of bloody flesh. Major Landon's face and uniform were spattered with blood.

'Throw the remains outside camp area,' the Major shouted. The jackals, hyenas and other scavengers which had been stealthily following the regiment ever since the campaign began, would feast upon them that night.

Bailin looked at the faces around him. The Hindustani sepoys, without exception, had been struck dumb with terror. But the Europeans wore hard, smug, satisfied looks. He could detect no sympathy for the valiant fighter who had been but no longer was.

The Lieutenant was sent under guard back to Ambala to await court martial. This was a long-drawn affair and it was almost February 1859, before the trial could be held. For the unfortunate Lieutenant these seven months of incarceration were pure hell. Despised and shunned by all, he had spent the time wracked with anger and anguish at the injustice of the predicament in which he found himself, and filled with dread at the type of punishment awaiting him at the end.

What added to his agony was the letter he received from his father. Colonel Douglas Bailin had been so shocked when the news reached him that he had collapsed. His missive, in fact, was an ultimatum. If Michael could not come out of the whole affair with his own reputation as well as that of the family restored, his father had rather consider him dead. The Lieutenant tore up the letter, not condescending to a reply.

The trial was short and swift. The Lieutenant was to be dismissed, decommissioned and disgraced, from the army and left to wallow in a limbo of his own creation.

In the months following his ignominious dismissal Bailin was a man adrift, a leper shunned by his fellow mortals. Disgraced as he was in the eyes of his father, there could be no question of a return to England. He tried to lose himself amidst the vastness that was the Indian subcontinent, search out some hidden nook, and efface himself into anonymity therein. But he soon discovered that his attempts to remain outside the European pockets were fraught with pitfalls; a solitary white amongst the browns elicited attention. On the other hand, the residents of the European enclaves, whether in the cool heights of Shimla or the hot and dusty Deccan plateau, were a tight-knit clan, and gossip travelled inexorably. The stain of his ignominy was a blob of ink in a pail of water, spreading and spreading till each aqueous particle was tainted with the tinge. Wherever he sought to take refuge someone was sure to be acquainted with the infamous 'Bailin case of Ambala', and it did not require much time for a bright spark to connect two and two, and point an accusing finger at the Lieutenant. At even the faintest whiff of suspicion that his past had caught up with him, Bailin, high-strung and sensitive, would immediately be on the run.

The winter of 1860 he spent at Calcutta; there, by coincidence, he had met a certain Mr Theodor Leach, a dapper, amiable and well-dressed individual who was on the lookout, or so he said, for a young man of adventurous disposition, as well as some money to invest. This Leach had been to Assam where he had laid claims to a large area of land with the aim of opening out a tea plantation. Others were making huge fortunes in tea, Mr Leach had avowed, and there had been no reason why he could not have done the same. In fact, he had soon cleared well nigh a hundred acres of jungle land and opened out a tea plantation which was thriving. But Leach had not taken into account the deplorable climatic conditions of that place nor his own advancing years. Life in Assam was for the young and vigorous, Leach had asserted. The upshot of it all was that the gentlemen had returned to Calcutta to find a buyer for his tea garden. Since it was a distress sale, he was willing to let it go for a preposterously low sum.

Bailin had grasped the offer with alacrity. Purchasing a tea garden in Assam was the perfect way out for one in his situation. In the wilderness of Assam, where the European population was sparse, Bailin would find sanctuary. The transaction with Leach took a surprisingly short time, and almost all of his money. The man had simply transferred the proprietorship of Chahpuli Tea Plantation to Bailin's name, handed him the relevant land-deed, a map of the claim, a receipt for the sale as well as a letter to the Assamese babu who was looking after the property in his absence, and disappeared forever from the Lieutenant's life.

'Oh Michael, how you must have suffered!' Cordelia's words erupted spontaneously. David came up and clutched the Lieutenant's hands. 'Can you forgive me, Michael?' he said, filled with self-reproach. 'How could I ever have thought you could act like a cad!'

Bailin's response was a wan smile. 'I feel lighter now that's off my chest,' he muttered feebly. The reliving of the disastrous event of the past had visibly weakened him, but his eyes were shining like those of a man at peace with himself.

'I grieve for you, Michael,' Swanson said. 'I grieve not only for your past, but for your future and your innocence. Be brave, Michael, in the face of adversity. There is so much strength in you that you will come out unscathed, whatever the future might hold for you.'

The others continued to probe the padre's features, but Swanson fell into a dead silence and shut his eyes. Then Garo Munda arrived, bringing the ailing man's broth and double roti, and the opportunity for elucidation was gone.

The food seemed to revive Bailin further. He became another man altogether; the demons which had been eating away at his soul had decamped following his revelations; the blue eyes were no longer impassable shutters. Cordelia found herself exulting at Bailin's metamorphoses—all through the afternoon he was carefree and gay, unmindful of the aches which must have yet endured in his body, shedding his habitual reserve. His joie de vivre was infectious; it lit up the atmosphere of the cabin, and Cordelia was surprised how time flew. The transformation of Michael had buoyed her up too, lightening the feeling of guilt within her and she felt happier during these hours as she had not for a long while. The early dinner they took in the cabin itself. After the meal was over and the dinner trays cleared, Cordelia stood up to take leave for the night.

'David, I must go. Look after Michael, won't you?'

Once again, she was alone; the empty deck, the immense shadow-filled landscape of which she was the centre deepened the sensations of solitude. Yet she was alone and not alone, lonely yet no longer lonely. This night the cold beams of the moon did not wrap the scenery with the pale shroud of melancholy. It is the inner human eye which animates the inanimate, the colours of the soul which tinges the external world with its own hues. The moonbeams gambolled and frisked impishly on the constantly moving waters; the sands throbbed and pulsated with a life of their own. The tropical nights on the steamer, so far menacing and dispirited, had suddenly exploded before her eyes into breath-taking beauty. Cordelia felt her heart lift up. Her euphoria might be short-lived, but for tonight at least the thoughts and images which depressed her—of the coolies or her father—had been pushed to the peripheries of her consciousness.

The emotion in her heart was not born of pity, certainly; nor feminine compassion or maternal instinct. These could never be the foundation for passion. She introspected, probing into her psyche, searching for extraneous factors which may have influenced her judgement. No, it was not the natural reaction of a young, soft-hearted girl when confronted with a lonely sufferer. Rather, she was convinced, she was reacting that way because of the essential goodness of the man, what the Reverend had called his 'innocence'.

It had come all at once, this abrupt change of perceptions, the first stirrings of tenderness, while he lay on the bed, unburdening himself of the tale of his martyrdom, a confession, or so he thought. How foolish she had been, how utterly blind! What had been strength she had mistaken for stolidity! His goodness she had dismissed as prosaic dullness! Yet, though steeped in self-reproach, she could not conceal from herself the fact that it had been Buckingham's presence which had rendered her so undiscerning. Buckingham's superficial lustre had dazzled her, made her so uncomprehending and sightless. Even now, as the vision of that man, naked amidst the sands, came to her mind, her body was responding. But now she could stifle the shrieking of her senses, for Michael had lit a different flame in her heart, warm and abiding, not the fierce blaze which could raze her to cinders.

Michael, oh Michael! I saw the passion in your eyes and turned away. I had your silent pleas for comprehension and shut my ears. As she gazed on at the speckled sands and the shaded skyline, the certainty seeped into her heart that it was a beginning, not the end. At this thought her spirits lifted; she was so happy that she could weep. The past was no longer as attractive as it had seemed, the future no longer held the terrors of the past.

It was in a state of elation that Cordelia left the deck and retired to her cabin. The wick in the wall-lamp was turned low, so the interior was very dim. Cordelia walked up to it and turned the screw to increase the flame.

'I've waited for you, Cordelia.'

She sensed his presence even before he spoke, whirled around to face him, her eyes wide with shock and fear. He was sitting in the chair in the corner, silent and still as a predator, merged into the shadows so that she had not spotted him when she entered. Now he stood up and slipped out of the shadows, the lamplight falling on his features, accentuating their striking beauty. The two dark brown eyes held a weird phosphorescent iridescence. They seemed to glow in their sockets.

He stood there, his virility filling the room. Her senses were overwhelmed with the unalloyed sexuality which exuded from every pore, every muscle of this magically handsome creature. She smelt the animal odour he exuded, sensed her own pliant body respond. His burning eyes swept over her, deliberately provocative, stripping her with his glance, raping her without touching. His very proximity served to stimulate her senses; she fell back against the dressing table, weakened and helpless, her hands hugging her chest in a defensive gesture.

Then Buckingham advanced. The face was wreathed in an omniscient smile, intimate and audacious. She watched him approach, unable to utter words which might yet fend him off. He came up to her, his mocking, ironic glance caressing her all the while, supremely self-confident, cognizant of her helplessness when confronted with his blatant masculinity, for he had seen and known of those secret desires in her eyes. Cordelia could retreat no further; she could not move; could not speak. Nor could she still the violent beatings or her heart or cool the animal heat that her own, shameless body was radiating!

He took her hands and held them with surprising gentleness. His voice too was soft and tender as he said, 'I want you, Cordelia. I've desired you ever since the day I first saw you on the deck.' Yet the mocking light in his eyes contradicted the passionate intensity he sought to put into the words. They rang hollow, but such was the overpowering puissance of the man that she felt petrified with shock and the unsought yearnings of her flesh, incapable of resisting. He, conscious of the fever in her, mistook her inaction for compliance. His hands went around her, he pulled her close to him and his lips came down hot and wet upon hers.

He was all animal now as he held her in a tight embrace. Cordelia's world exploded; she ceased to exist; her mind went blank; her body was responding now of its own volition and her arms were around him. Still holding on to the kiss, chest, belly and thighs pressed against hers, his fingers unclasped the hooks at the back of her dress and pulled it away over her creamy shoulders.

There were sudden footsteps in the corridor outside, and a muted snatch of conversation. Buckingham's lips came away; he threw his head back and cocked his ears. 'The door! It must be locked!' he whispered in a hoarse voice. Breaking away, he moved to the door and drove home the bolt.

Abruptly the spell was broken. Cordelia turned around and saw herself in the mirror, looked at her eyes and beheld the shock and bewilderment and lust in them. A wave of revulsion washed over her as she hastily righted her gown. The blaze in her flesh was dying down, the heat dissipating itself as she turned once more to confront Buckingham.

The man was upon her again, predacious. But she was in total control of herself now, her sanity restored. As he reached for her, she side-stepped away.

'Please leave my cabin, Buckingham,' she said, awed by the hardness of her tone.

Buckingham laughed, his gaze resting on her tantalizingly as ever. 'Come, girl. Don't play the prude with me.' He reached out once more, confident of her submission. Her right hand streaked out and struck him full across the face.

The man retreated a single step and looked at her with incredulity. His eyes sparkled like a wood-fire when logs are shifted. For one moment it seemed he would hurl himself on Cordelia. Then the insane gleam disappeared and was replaced by a mocking light. He chuckled.

'Well, I thought you would be easy meat! I look for conquests, dear girl, not companions. If you want anything more, go to your Lieutenant. But be warned, he'll provide cold comfort in bed.'

'Get out,' Cordelia spat out the words. The grossness of her tone was a reaction to his crudity.

'There'll be another time, another place,' Buckingham said, laughing, and was gone.

There was a cold rage within her and its very unfamiliarity was daunting. She sat on the edge of the bed, angry yet frightened. Feeling infinitely demeaned by her abject surrender, she wanted to sob her heart out; but the fury fomenting in her heart would not allow her that luxury.

She continued to sit like that for a long, long time, rigid as a statue, gripped by a crushing sense of sin yet filled with a baffled fury. Then she knelt at the foot of the bed, closed her eyes and, placing her folded hands on the bed, bowed her head and prayed. It was a prayer without casuistry, with the simplicity of a child, pouring her heart out to God and begging His forgiveness.

Having prayed, she lay on the bed and dispassionately pondered over her dilemma. Should she tell the others of Buckingham's transgression? Yet, in the turbulent world she had suddenly found herself in, would that not be flinging fat into fire? Also, if she did complain, thereby inducing intractable hostility in the planter, would he not shy away from his pledge to send Doctor Gordon to Dhanboa to examine Papa?

The very moment the thought of Papa came to her mind all vacillations ceased. Papa, alone and ailing, and in dire need of medical attention! Oh God, the damage had already been done! By no action or word must she aggravate things further! She had irrevocably alienated Buckingham, but David was there. If she kept her lips sealed, not letting out the incident to anyone, not even the Reverend, her brother might yet succeed in bringing Doctor Gordon to Dhanboa!

That morning no one alluded to the fight, but there was a noticeable change of attitude on the part of the other passengers towards the Lieutenant. The punishment that Bailin had taken in the fight with the planter, his refusal to bow out when savagely mauled, had earned him respect. It was the universal opinion that Bailin had behaved as any Englishman was expected to behave, and so deserved to be applauded.

The *Ultaganga* touched Sirajgunge ahead of sundown, loaded and unloaded and retired to a sand-bank. Although the sun was already dipping across the horizon, there was a considerable period of daylight remaining. So, the padre suggested they take another walk across the sands. But the moment they emerged from their temporary dwelling, instead of cutting across the vast expanse of sand away from the *Shaitan*, Swanson directed them towards the flat. The coolies were at a distance—this evening they had been taken further than usual from the steamer.

As they neared the spot where the coolies had been herded for their evening meal, two musket-wielding men ran up to bar their way. Buckingham's watchdogs, tall and large-limbed, with stupid, intractable faces, loyal to such a degree that they would kill for their master.

'Buckingham sahib's *hukum*,' one of them said in Hindustani. 'No one's to be allowed near the coolies.'

Bailin plucked out his pistol from his waistband and pointed it at the man. 'Don't stand in our way, damn you, or I'll blow your head off!'

The two guardsmen retreated a few steps, uncertainty writ large on their stupid faces. They looked at each other, then at Bailin's pistol. It was apparent they did not relish a confrontation with the white sahibs, hukum or no hukum! Abruptly a gleam of cunning flickered in the eyes of one as he said in a plaintive whine, 'Don't go near them, sahibs, I implore you. Just look at them. See how weary and listless they are. It's a sign, huzoors. The dreaded scourge would be visiting them soon. Just wait and see, huzoors.'

Their eyes shifted to where the coolies rested. The guardsman was right. Even from this distance they could sense the listlessness. Cordelia recalled the sight of these same men, women and children the first evening, upon the dirty-grey, bramble filled sands of Saugor Island. Despite their day-long incarceration in the *Shaitan's* belly they then had bustled about with energy. The children had splashed and frolicked in the shallow waters; babies had crawled playfully on the sands; the elders had pursued their evening chores with a vigorous sense of purpose.

But the week-long confinement in the narrow flat had drained the coolies of whatever vitality they possessed. This evening too they were performing similar tasks. But the life was missing from their actions. The toddlers lolled about on the sands in apathetic exhaustion, men and women worked at cooking like zombies, movements sluggish.

'They don't look too good, do they?' Bailin, breaking the sudden hush, said.

David asked, 'The dreaded scourge? What's that?'

'Cholera! So far each and every consignment of coolies transported to the plantations has been afflicted.' Swanson's eyes scanned the coolies. 'But this lot doesn't seem stricken yet.'

The guardsman, though he did not understand a word of what was being discussed but guessed correctly, interposed, 'They are shitting out liquid stuff, huzoors. Whitish grey like water of cooked rice. Smells like a week-old carcass.'

'You exaggerate, you crafty old fox! Buckingham sahib will give you a hiding if you let us proceed, isn't it? But listen carefully and listen well. This sahib's pistol has the devil in it. He'll shoot your kneecaps off if you don't keep out of the way.'

Confusion gripped the two guardsmen. 'Come,' Swanson told the others and strode on ahead, unbarred. One of the guardsmen raced towards the steamer to inform his master of the happenings as the four of them strode briskly to a group around a burning fire.

It was a small coolie family—the husband, wife and a toddler who looked two years old, but was probably a year older. Taking extreme care to erase any trace of unfriendliness from his voice, Swanson asked, 'How are you feeling, my man? Any trace of nausea? Giddiness?'

Their eyes jerked up at them, a curious admixture of sullen fear and suspicion lighting up the vacant, lustreless pools. They looked pathetic; their bodies emaciated, rib-cases showing. The woman wrapped her sari top more firmly around her otherwise bare upper body in a wordless gesture of rebuke at this unwelcome invasion of their privacy. The man did not answer.

'Is anyone ill in your group?' Swanson tried again. 'Has the dreadful fever struck anyone yet?'

The man's lips parted. There was no rancour, no hatred in his voice when he spoke, only resignation. 'Go away, sahibs,' he said, so softly that the words were barely audible. 'No one can help us. Go away.'

'No use, Father,' Bailin said. 'They won't let out a thing.'

The padre looked around and his eyes alighted on a pair of men who squatted round a fire a little away from the main body of coolies. Cordelia, following his gaze, recognized them—the two who had attempted escape at Calcutta. The padre made a beeline for the duo, his companions at his heels.

The two coolies sat hunched around their fire, not deigning to look up although they sensed their presence. Cordelia, horrified, saw that their backs were welted and scarred like Garo Munda's. They were even worse, for they had not had medical attention and a few of the cuts appeared to have suppurated.

'*Tum log kaise ho*?' the padre repeated his questions. 'Is anybody showing symptoms of the scourge?'

The coolies ignored the insistent voice. The padre turned to the guardsman who had been following them, and asked, '*In dono ka naam kya hai*?'

The man took one nervous look at Bailin's pistol and replied with alacrity: 'The taller one's Bircha, huzoor. The shorter fellow is Meghu.' He spat on the ground in an emphatic show of contempt. '*Jungl*ee *hai,* huzoor. Needs to be tamed.'

The padre made one final attempt. 'Bircha-bhaiya?' he asked, addressing the taller coolie as brother. 'Is anybody ill in your group?'

The coolie named Meghu kept his eyes fixed on the cooking pot, but Bircha abruptly looked up. Cordelia took an involuntary step back. The fires of hell burned in those two eyes; they were smouldering pits of hatred; if looks could kill, the four of them would have been razed to the ground.

The coolie made no reply. He looked down again and shifted on his haunches so that his back was firmly towards them, an unmistakable gesture of dismissal.

For the first time Cordelia grew aware of a hundred impeaching eyes peering at them from every corner. Each face was turned towards them, silent voices clamouring for their departure. The tension coagulated and the unshorn hostility thickened so that it seemed to touch their skin. 'Let us leave, Father,' she said. 'They will not answer.'

'They are like beasts,' David sounded disgusted. Cordelia looked sharply at her brother, struck by the unfamiliar note of derision in his voice. But it was the padre who spoke.

'That's because they've been treated like beasts. Come. No use wasting time here anymore. And, if my eyes don't deceive me, there comes the welcome party.'

At a distance three individuals were emerging from the *Ultaganga* and walking rapidly to where they stood—Buckingham and his henchman, and the portly, waddling figure of Doctor Gordon. The trio met them halfway on their return trip.

'I thought I'd asked you to leave my coolies alone, Swanson!' the planter cried out.

Buckingham had addressed the padre. But Bailin, fixing the planter with a glance of scorn, very deliberately withdrew his pistol from his belt, cocked it and said, 'We'll go where we please, Buckingham. We'll talk to who we please.'

His tone was challenging; the firearm in his hand made his intentions crystal-clear. If the planter wanted an answer to his question, he would get it. But this time it would be on Bailin's terms.

Buckingham turned towards him with an imperious toss of the head, saw the gun in his hand and tensed. A derisive smile made those sensual lips part, but before he could don on his habitual mocking mask, Bailin detected the fear which showed fleetingly in those dark-brown eyes.

'The Lieutenant has spoken for us,' the padre said bitingly. 'We'll do as we please. Now, if you'll excuse us, we'll get back on board.' Without waiting for an answer he walked on ahead, his companions behind him.

They made their way to the upper deck. Settling down on the chairs, flushed with victory, Michael said laughingly, 'If you hadn't turned to the cloth, Father, you would have made a successful trader. You understand the human mind all too well.'

'A wolf in a priest's garb, am I?' the padre asked.

Though Cordelia understood what Bailin was hinting at, David could make nothing of it. 'I haven't the foggiest notion what you're talking about,' he said, somewhat peevishly.

'The Reverend instructed Michael to take his pistol with him when we went for our walk,' Cordelia explained. 'He certainly knew what he was doing!'

'Ah!' exclaimed David, enlightened. 'Just as well he did! Buckingham came at us like a fighting cock. The instant he saw Michael's weapon, he turned into a sparrow.'

'Learn to use such crutches in the future, Michael,' Swanson said. 'David, Cordelia, I've no fears for you. You'll retire to the safety of your father's plantation. My words are for you alone, Michael. When you find your defences down, when you discover that you are utterly alone, just remember that power is not in this two-legged thing that is born and dies. Power comes from sources other than the self.'

They heard footsteps come up the companion-way and moments later Captain McClintock hoved into view. He made directly for their table. Pulling up a chair, he deposited himself in it and turned disapprovingly towards the Baptist missionary.

'What's all this, Swanson? Young Buckingham tells me you've been at his coolies. He has sought me assistance in protection his cargo.'

'What exactly is the nature of his complaint?' Swanson asked.

'He claims when he caught ye amongst his coolies, inciting them to abscond, Bailin fended him off with a gun.'

Swanson emitted a loud guffaw. 'The man's got a vivid imagination!' he said. 'Yes, we did go near the coolies, Captain. Let me not deny that. Just to see how they were taking the journey. We asked a few questions, but the dumb beasts were too terrified to answer.'

'Mr Buckingham accosted us on our way back,' Cordelia said, recallment of her shame and humiliation lending a cutting edge to her tongue. 'His attitude was insolent and his intentions hostile. But when he saw Michael was armed, he quietly slunk away.'

'Now, now,' said the captain, the hand holding his pipe upraised placatingly. 'Don't get me wrong, m'dear. I hold no brief fer young

Buckingham, ner take his words as the gospel truth. But ye must admit it, padre. It was wrong of ye to take these young folks amongst the coolies. Ye ken as well as I as to why.'

'Afraid they'll catch the scourge?' Swanson asked with asperity.

'God forbid, Swanson! But cholera makes no distinction between whites and natives.'

'So, was it your concern for our welfare that has brought you to us?' Bailin asked.

'I must make yer welfare me concern, whether ye like it er not.'

'We should be of less bother to you, sir,' Bailin retorted vehemently. 'But do something for those poor blighters out there. Yes, we've seen them, seen what's cooking in their pots! Buckingham's starving them. Half-fed as they are, what with the heat and the exhausting journey, they are easy prey to pestilence.'

'The Lieutenant's right,' Swanson said. 'The scourge hasn't visited the coolies yet. But they've been reduced to such a sorry state that it's merely a matter of time.'

McClintock shrugged despairingly and said, 'I've no control over young Buckingham's cargo. It's hands off fer me … and fer ye too! Promise me, Swanson. Ye'll not visit the coolies again.'

'I can promise nothing,' the padre replied calmly.

'Then I'll make it an order, padre. I can't have ye endangering the lives of the passengers. If need be, Swanson, I'll take Gosselin's aid to enforce me diktat.'

The captain, genuinely angry, limped away. 'Well, that's that, I suppose.' the Reverend chuckled. 'We can't fight the entire ship, Cordelia. At least not with Gosselin on it!'

'But the Captain's absolutely right,' David spoke out. 'The coolies belong to Buckingham. We have no business with them. Nor should we jeopardize the passengers aboard just to have a look at a handful of coolies.'

'You have a point there, I suppose,' the padre nodded, although he did not seem very convinced. 'But come. It's time for dinner. The coolies have had theirs, and we must have ours. We all need strength to confront our destinies, don't we, Michael?'

It had grown to be a second nature with her, this post-dinner sojourn on the deck before the final retreat to her cabin. Tonight, too, the deck was deserted. The cool, undefiled river breeze was an ablution, cleansing and refreshing. At a distance the winking lights of Sirajgunge were being snuffed out one by one.

The onslaught on her sensibility the past few days, the constant shift of moods and attitudes, was making her more introspective. Things in reality did not always conform to their outward appearance. People too were changing, had changed, even those whom she could call her own. David was not reacting in the manner he should have reacted. As for Reverend Swanson, he seemed to be probing into his newly gathered acolytes to find out if they could be made instruments of some larger design. David, he had rejected; he had tarried with Cordelia, but she had failed, Michael had turned out to be the genuine apostle, Cordelia was sure. Yet the father used enigmatic innuendoes when looking into the Lieutenant's tomorrows. What knowledge did he possess—or, as he had put it, suspect—that made him fear for Michael's future?

The very moment the thought of Michael came to her all the doubts in her mind were swept away as if with a broom. Humility, the true companion of nascent love, washed over her as she thought of Michael and his crucifixion. She understood clearly that the vast emptiness felt in herself ever since they had left Calcutta's shores could only be filled with Michael's strength and his love.

Momentarily she closed her eyes and his face skipped into her imagination, the strongly defined features and the deep-blue eyes, now no longer inscrutable orbs of concealment but which ever since the unburdenment of his secret sorrows sparkled with humour and joy. Cordelia opened her eyes and the hazy outlines of his features which her fancy had created out of nothingness melted into that of the breathing self. Had her heart had been unknowingly beating out a necromantic abracadabra? Was his appearance the inevitable response to her incantations, her preoccupations muting his footfalls? The sudden sense of unreality, however, was dispelled by his voice, immeasurably tender and whispery, as he said,

'May I join you, Miss Esscombe?'

It was the softness of the tone, its furry, silky texture, which alerted her to the significance of his presence. There was nothing accidental about this; he had sought her out, choosing the moment and the place. Her body tensed eagerly, each sinew and nerve parched with expectation. The hush that had settled over the land and sky and water demanded communications of momentous import. She said nothing but smiled warmly at him, fearful of the fragility of the moment, which a false word or gesture might shatter, leaving words unsaid, feelings uncommunicated.

The setting was perfect—the vista's quietude, the silence of the nether world, the lonely upper deck, her smile of enquiry. And yet he hesitated. The sensations within him were unfamiliar; the words voicing them must be couched with care if they were to be safeguarded from the risks of banality. Or was it his ingrained reserve, the cardinal sin of individuals of deep passion; the inarticulateness of the habitually taciturn? He would dearly have loved to prolong the revelation with trivial chitchat, providing him time to mentally arrange his words into a meaningful pattern, impregnate them with the fierce emotions fomenting within him. But her soliciting silence denied him that opportunity.

'I have something to say to you, Miss Esscombe.'

Her smile lingered on her lips; her eyes remained enquiring. Facing her, his features were in the shadows. Yet she could feel his eyes afire with his passion and see the contortions of his mouth as he groped for the words. With feminine wilfulness she did nothing to alleviate his torment, was secretly amused and yet knew the very moment those words emerged from his mouth her surrender would be completed. She could not allow his triumph to be so easily achieved!

As he stood by her, breathlessly silent, she marvelled at the depth of her own feelings and the strength he had armed her with. He too emanated an aura of maleness in close proximity, not as powerful and all-pervasive as Buckingham's perhaps, yet sufficiently provocative to enkindle desire. But there was no lusting blaze in her; rather, she was enveloped by a gentle rapture, the snug sentience of a well-lit room in winter. A feeling of contentment wrapped her like a blanket; the warmth of his presence was not felt only in her flesh but penetrated into the deepest corner of her soul, and a boundless sense of peace and well-being settled over her.

But, unaware of her state of mind, he still struggled inwardly, remaining silent so long that Cordelia grew afraid he would falter. Then, abruptly, his body straightened and the words came tumbling out of his throat.

'Miss Esscombe, I have not spoken out so long only because I have not been able to catch you alone.' His formal tone would have sounded ludicrous had it not been for the fervour with which he uttered them. 'But ever since I first beheld you on the deck you've meant more to me than I am capable of ever expressing.'

Cordelia maintained her silence, though she longed to shout out how infuriating his diffidence was, how prim and alien his 'Miss Esscombe' sounded to her ears!

'I was aware, Miss Esscombe, that I was no more than a stranger to you and could make no claims to your affection. But the events of the past few days have changed my life. Believe me, Miss Esscombe, after being decommissioned, I had even considered taking my own life. It was only the cowardice of the act which had prevented me from putting a noose around my neck and jumping towards deliverance.'

His words effectively transmitted the anger and bitterness that for long had lain like a cesspool in the core of his being. Then his voice mellowed, as he said, 'And then you came into my life and all changed. Your presence was a gentle breeze which swept away the noxious exhalations poisoning the horizons of my mind. That night, as you sat fanning my head, it was not only the fever which had been cleansed from my body. You have healed the deep wound in my soul which was slowly killing me. You've given me new life, Miss Esscombe, and for that I'm deeply grateful.'

'Gratitude, Michael?' Cordelia said softly. 'Is that all you can express?'

He caught the inflection in her voice, understood its import, was startled into joy. But then he shook his head and said, 'No, Miss Esscombe. I am a man branded by my past. I can demand nothing more from you.'

'Oh Michael, you fool!' Cordelia cried out, half-laughing, half-angry. 'Would you let your past stand between the two of us? Only you matter, Michael. Only you!'

Impulsively he reached out for her hands, a wondering look in his eyes. 'Do you mean that?' he asked, his eyes probing hers in disbelief.

'Yes, Michael.'

'Oh, Cordelia!' he whispered as he pulled her to him and held her close. His lips came down upon hers and moved quickly away. There was the comforting feel of his arms holding her in a tight embrace. 'I love you, Cordelia,' he murmured continually. 'You mean more to me than I can ever say.'

For a long while they stood like that, two children in love, gazing rapt at the moonlit landscape. To her there seemed no need for words, yet all of a sudden, he released her, turned and took her hands in his own, and said, 'Promise me, darling, that you'll wait.'

'Wait?' she whispered back, bewildered. 'Wait for what?'

'For me to come to terms with my future.'

'I do not understand, Michael.'

'We're moving towards the unknown, my love,' he said with utmost seriousness. 'I have not yet seen my plantation. I know nothing about tea. I'll have to learn. That'll take time.'

'We'll build the garden together, Michael,' she said. 'It'll be our garden!'

His answer was a definitive shake of the head. 'No,' he said. 'That too will be a betrayal of my love for you … to place on your frail shoulders a load you otherwise wouldn't have to bear! But don't worry, Cordelia, my darling. I'll slave away at my garden to make it pay. Till then you'll wait. Promise me that.'

'I will, Michael, I will!' Cordelia cried out passionately. He gathered her once more into his arms for a final kiss.

'Thank you, my love,' he said, and was suddenly gone.

David was at her cabin early next morning, fervid with ingenuous excitement. 'Michael told me everything last night, sis,' he said. 'He lay awake till late in the night unburdening himself. I'm so happy for you. For him, too.'

Cordelia felt unaccountably shy, like a newly married bride. 'I'm glad you approve, David,' she said, mumbling.

'Approve? Of course, I approve, sis! What magic you've performed on Michael! He's a different chappie altogether.'

'He has passed through some difficult days. A great injustice has been done to him. He will need your friendship and support.'

'He'll get it from me in full measure,' David said with utter sincerity. 'But guess what, sis? For a while I thought you'd fallen for that blister, Buckingham! Well, we'll have some good news to take to Papa. I've jumped the gun a bit, sis. Already discussed it with Captain McClintock ... about a berth on the *Ultaganga* for Papa and you when it returns.'

'That was splendid of you, David. Yes, Papa must return to Calcutta.'

'But now I suppose I'll have to find someone else to accompany him.'

Cordelia smiled when she saw the worried frown on her brother's features. 'Don't be silly, David! I'll accompany Papa!'

'But will Michael permit it? It'll be months before you can come back to Assam, you know.'

'You're thinking of the wedding, aren't you?' she hastily clarified. 'That's a long while away, David. Michael must settle down before we can contemplate marriage. Right now, Papa must be my first concern. And you too, of course.'

Cordelia watched the wrinkles being erased from his forehead. How young and youthful he looked! But the thought of the mantle which awaited him in Assam was already maturing him as he mentally prepared to come to grips with his responsibilities. He was callow. Without his father's guiding hand, would he not be lost in the wilderness of Assam?

'Yes, yes,' David was saying. 'Michael spoke about it. How he must make himself worthy of your trust. But you know how capricious people who are madly in love can be!'

Cordelia laughed inwardly at his attempt to seem worldly wise. 'I won't be capricious, I promise you that, David. Michael must do his stint in the garden before we can marry. So, I'll be with you and Papa for quite some time.'

Cordelia's words assuaged the hidden concerns in her brother, for David brightened up. 'Well, only time will tell,' he intoned, still assuming his guise of maturity. 'Let's join the others at breakfast, shall we?'

The Lieutenant was an individual incapable of dissimulation, and his attitude towards her was apparent the moment she and David appeared on the deck. He bounded up on seeing them and came up to offer her his arm. There was a proprietorial air about his actions as he escorted her to a deck chair.

Cordelia stole a glance at the other group and was disconcerted to find that Buckingham was with them. The planter could not have failed to notice Bailin's manners towards her, nor the warmth of her response. But his face wore an indifferent look and gave away nothing. His eyes caught Cordelia's before she looked away. She felt her heart lurch violently, for those eyes, contradictions to the uncaring features, were so replete with feral yearnings that she involuntarily grasped Michael's arms tighter.

That afternoon, as the *Ultaganga* plodded towards Golabari, its day's destination, the Reverend told them about the incipient tea industry in Assam. 'It was in the middle fifties,' he said, 'after the success of the Assam Company, that the tea itch began to infect the British trading community. You should have seen the dregs of white-skinned humanity which crawled up the Brahmaputra to lay claim to land in Assam. Individuals like your father, David, were rare exceptions. Most were vermin spawned in some filthy English gutter, sans gentility, breeding or basic humanity. It was sheer greed which had driven them to Assam; any compunction or decency they may have possessed they threw away in one of the stench-ridden drains of Calcutta. You have seen one example of them, our inimitable Christopher James Buckingham.'

His audience of three, rendered speechless by the raw bitterness of the padre's voice, said nothing. The man of God continued.

'Michael. David. When you get to your plantations you will know what true power is … power over human beings! A planter in his garden is a law unto himself. He is a demigod whom no one can rebuke, nor chastise. The British administration, having created the environment where plantations could be established, adopted a hands-off policy. That left the planter free to do as he wished in his garden. The local people could not be coerced into working for the Europeans. So, they brought in coolies from far off … wretches like the ones now floating in the *Shaitan*. It is the same with exploitative societies everywhere, whether here or America. There slavers brought in Negroes from Africa to man cotton and sugarcane plantations. Here it is the coolies.'

'Does the administration wield no control over how they are treated?' Bailin asked.

'None at all! I have seen coolies being whipped raw. Sometimes the planter erects a gibbet and hangs some poor wretch by his wrists in the blistering summer sun. They set men on horses with dogs after absconders to hunt them down. I've been witness to acts of unimaginable barbarity. We brought such heinous acts to the attention of the authorities … to people like Major Gosselin. Oh, the bureaucracy harbours no affection for planters. In fact, they look down upon that breed. But they wouldn't interfere in the affairs of a plantation. British commerce, above everything else, must be protected!

'Just imagine, dear Cordelia, the very people who attend our church, those who call themselves Christians, have directly or indirectly assisted in these un-Christian acts. My attitude towards my chosen calling changed, as did my objectives. I lost all zeal for preaching. Instead, I silently resolved to declare war against imperialism, and fight it tooth and nail.

'It's my personal battle, my defence against debasement. The Hindus call this age Kaliyuga, the era of untruth, when false gods are worshipped. Corruption of the soul is inevitable in such a milieu, unless one wages incessant war against the corruptive principles which operate in it. I fight on not only for God and humanity, but to save myself from perdition! Cordelia, David, Michael! They think me to be an anarchist … how right they are! This priestly robe is the disguise of Garry Swanson, the subversive! No longer am I interested in taking the gospels to the heathens. My time, let me assure you, is practically devoted to taking Christianity to Christians.'

'But isn't this like attempting to loosen a rock with a breadknife, Father?' Cordelia cried. 'What can you achieve alone? How much can you alone do?'

'A man with convictions is a dangerous creature, dear girl. Imperialism may loom as a solid rock, but the foundation upon which it is built is fragile. I may not achieve much in my lifetime; just chip away a bit here and a bit there. But there will be others like me, nibbling away at the exploitative society. One day it will crumble and the entire edifice will come down.'

David gave a nervous laugh and said, 'You have two converts here, Father. I shall give my workers a fair deal and so will Michael, I daresay. That's quite a dent in your edifice!'

'Power does strange things to people, David! And one has not been given eyes by the good Lord to see into the future. So, remember. If you can't change the system, the system will change you!'

A chill crept into Cordelia's heart at this cautionary reiteration, she knew not why. Outside, the light had faded; the sun slid rapidly down the western horizon, daubing the sky and waters with blood-red streaks. Groups of bamboo and thatch hutments appeared on the hitherto empty bank, signalling the approach of Golabari.

For two weeks now the steamer had been crawling like a giant crustacean over a labyrinthine route down the Hoogli, across the Sunderbans and up the Brahmaputra. On 21 September, she turned the eastward bend of the river which, for the first time, took her into the territory of Assam. The next port was Dhubri.

The minds of the passengers seated as usual on the forward upper saloon deck were preoccupied with the disquieting rumour that a few of the youngsters amongst the coolies were showing symptoms of the scourge. To make matters worse, in the later part of the morning, the weather changed unexpectedly, dark clouds appeared in the sky, accompanied by a moisture-laden breeze. By the time the village port of Dhubri had been reached a slow drizzle started.

Cordelia was struck by the instant change the rains brought to the landscape. Grey, overhanging clouds muted the sun's rays and draped everything in a dull, gloomy light. Her heart went out to the coolies. How would they sleep tonight, with the wet breeze flailing them continually? The baby who was running a fever? How would its mother keep it dry and warm? With the rain pouring down, how would they light their fires, and cook?

Prompted by such questions, she left her cabin, and made her way to the open deck. Moments later she heard voices on her left. It was Buckingham! The doctor was standing by his side.

'The rain is the last nail in their coffin,' Buckingham was saying. 'After this, the chance of staving off the scourge is slim. The child is almost at an end, did you say, Bill?'

'Only a matter of time now! Our men have put in their report. The mother too seems stricken. Three or four others are showing symptoms.'

'Well, it has begun. We can merely wait and hope. How many do you think we'll lose?'

'The hardier ones will survive, but I doubt the toddlers will. Shall I put it at half the number?'

'I'll call myself fortunate if I can unload half of them at Kokilamukh! Is there enough firewood aboard? We can't leave unburned bodies behind and be accused of spreading pestilence.'

'Our Captain would know. If not, stock up at Chonari. But be assured, you'll need enough firewood before the journey's over, even if you put two or three of them upon a single pyre.'

Cordelia's world went blank. Cautiously she withdrew, but sleep eluded her that night. The next day, however, the weather lifted and there was bright sunshine again. Yet neither the sunshine nor the presence of her companions could sweep away the dark clouds in her heart and her mind.

She instinctively knew that in the days which would follow, the sands were to be the coolies' cremation ground.

Cordelia awoke, her senses on full alert. A pack of jackals were baying somewhere out there, a perpetual wah-wah-wahahha, rising and declining in a wave, muted by the cabin walls yet unmistakable. Jackals? But they were in the middle of a river, moored to a sandbank! There could be no jackals here!

With a sinking heart Cordelia realized what the sound was—the wail of grieving human beings. With grim determination she dressed and stepped out of her cabin. Michael was immediately by her side; David too, and the Reverend Swanson. The sandbank was cut off from view by mist and darkness—the wails seemed to emerge out of nowhere. Streaks of light darted out from the steamer: two flares borne by Buckingham's minions. They outlined the shapes of a group of lascars, each shouldering piles of firewood. They had obviously gone to stack up the funeral pyres.

After a while the lascars returned. The wailing increased in intensity. The flares reappeared, now borne by the coolies themselves, for on no account would Buckingham's guards or the ship's lascars take further part in the proceedings.

Two balls of fire grew visible, flowering into large, incandescent blossoms as the flames licked at the dry firewood, doused with quick-burning ghee.

'Three dead,' the padre called out. 'A baby, a child and a woman.'

As a spectacle it was out of the ordinary—and they had ringside seats! Apart from the flares, the two burning pyres were the only points of illumination in that vast hollow of darkness. They could clearly see the naked bodies, outlined against the licking flames, lying spreadeagled on the heaps of wood, the mother and her child on one, a boy of indeterminable age on the other. The light of the fire fell upon the coolies who were sitting on the sands—all men, perhaps the father and husband among them. They squatted, in the stance natives assume while defecating, and gazed at the burning piles of wood. One of them, armed with a pole, circled the pyres watchfully, his job being to ensure that the bodies were entirely consumed by the flames.

Within minutes the pyres were burning high, and the three corpses slung on them disappeared from sight. As the flames caught human flesh, the smoke became turgid and the peculiar odour of burning flesh wafted to the *Ultaganga*.

Cordelia felt faint, but Michael was by her side, arm around her, infusing strength into her limbs. 'There's no more to see, darling,' he murmured. 'Get back to your cabin. You'll catch a chill standing out here like this.'

This, again, was true! There was nothing more to see! The two pyres, having reached the peak of luminosity, were wilting, and would soon shrink into balls of embers. The cadavers had been consumed. The coolies around the fires were growing shadowy and would soon disappear. The weeping from the *Shaitan* was lessening and a few discordant whimpers were already breaking the even rise and ebb of the wailing. This too would sink into silence with the death of the pyres' flames.

The novelty of the scene had clearly worn off for the other passengers, who retreated in ones and twos to the privacy of their cabins, till only the four of them were left on the deck. 'That's the most sensible thing to do,' the padre urged. 'The performance is over! If you're fascinated by the sight of burning coolies, come back for a repeat performance tomorrow night!' Without waiting to bid the others good night he trotted off towards his cabin.

With a hasty 'Good night' David also departed, well knowing that Michael would want a moment alone with his sister. Bailin turned to sweep Cordelia into his arms, but she said, 'No, not here,' as if an embrace on the deck, in sight of those smouldering pyres on the sand, would be an affront. But at her cabin door she turned and clung to him. He kissed her passionately in an endeavour to lighten the sadness inside her. When they broke away, she looked straight at his face and said, 'Promise me, Michael, you won't change.' Surprisingly, before he could answer, she darted inside her cabin. He stood for some time outside the door, listening to her sobbing in the darkness, and his love strengthened with each sob.

The twin mounds of ash and cinders which stood out like black ulcers against the speckled sands were the only visible reminder of the previous night's happenings. But those on board had not forgotten. The smell of burning flesh seemed to permeate the atmosphere and cling to each nook and cranny of the posh, forward upper saloon deck. The passengers longed for the *Ultaganga* to be on the move again; perhaps only distance between themselves and the sandbank could sweep away the scorched odour from their nostrils.

But, for that day at least, there was to be no reprieve. One of the boilers had malfunctioned, and a day had to be squandered repairing it. Suddenly the deck seemed far smaller than it really was; nerves were in tatters, tempers were frayed. The truth, as Garry Swanson told his wards, was that everyone was afraid. With the cholera raging among the coolies, the clammy fingers of death could any moment reach out towards the steamer. Contact between the *Ultaganga* hands and the coolies had been strictly terminated. Precautions had been taken and cholera-pills distributed among the passengers by Doctor Gordon himself. Yet the spectre of a quick and painful death was on everyone's mind, the dramatic spectacle of the previous night having reinforced apprehensions.

This time the weeping started earlier, a little after it grew dark. There were four stacks that night, and seven corpses—two adults, a man and a woman, the rest children. It was a grander spectacle than the previous night—the pyres burned brighter, illuminating the entire sandbank with their fierce glow, the wailing was louder, and the passengers watched it from their lofty perch, drawn by primal compulsions.

Early next morning, even before the first light of dawn streaked across the misty sky, the damaged boiler having been repaired, Captain McClintock took the steamer away from that benighted island. But death stalked it for the next three days, ten at Chonari, six at Goalpara, and five at a night's halt between Goalpara and Kholabanda. By the 26th of September, when they reached Kholabanda, the scourge had had its fill, and there were no more deaths. Almost the entire child population upon the *Shaitan* had been wiped away. Ten female and eight males amongst the adult coolies had perished. Mercifully, the contagion did not spread to the steamer.

At Palasbari, which they reached on the 27th, Captain McClintock decided to let the steamer moor for an additional day in order to allow Buckingham's remaining coolies to recuperate. However, to placate his forward saloon deck passengers, the captain took the flat to a smaller sandbank a little further on and left the coolies there. With the coolies taken out of sight and thus out of mind, the passengers regained some of their joie de vivre. Jeremy Arbuckle's suggestion of a picnic luncheon was greeted with enthusiasm. Captain McClintock instructed Salim Ali to make the requisite arrangements and the steamer settled in for the night.

The next morning, after breakfast, the European passengers of the saloon deck were out on the sands. The stewards made sure everything needed for the outing was provided—parasols, beer, food, card games and the like. A parasol had been set up for Miss Esscombe and Lieutenant Bailin at some distance away from the rest to offer the two some privacy.

By the time luncheon was over, the energy which had gripped the passengers began to desert them and they lounged upon the darries and deck-chairs with half closed eyes. The languorous afternoon, however, was suddenly disrupted by the regular pht-pht of a steam engine, jolting everyone into renewed awareness. Moments later came the long-drawn wail of a siren and a steamer hove into view, chugging upstream towards the landing ghat on the opposite bank. There was a general scramble amongst the passengers towards the edge of the sandbank. The lettering on the side of the other vessel could clearly be seen—*The Lucknow*. Everyone waved; the griffin threw his hat in the air and, as was his wont, emitted a loud hurrah. *The Lucknow* hooted in acknowledgment, and, from its deck, a hundred khaki-clad, brown faces gazed, stolid and unsmiling, at the cheering throng on the sandbank.

'An army steamer,' Captain McClintock said, though to no one in particular.

'Carrying sepoy reinforcements,' Gosselin added. 'I fear there's trouble in Assam.'

Meanwhile *The Lucknow* had moored on the landing ghat. A while later two army officers appeared, aboard a small native canoe which made its way dexterously across the wide channel separating the sandreef from the river bank.

The sound of *The Lucknow's* engine had been enough to shift Cordelia and the Lieutenant from their chairs.

'Should we join the others, darling?' Cordelia asked.

Michael had tensed at the sight of the two military officers. There was an apprehensive quiver to his voice when he said, 'No, we'll stay where we are.'

The girl looked at him sharply. 'What's the matter, darling? Are they someone you know?'

'No,' he replied. 'Never laid eyes on those two before.' He smiled to reassure her and led her back to her chair.

On the island's edge the visitors disembarked. Captain McClintock and Major Gosselin stepped forward and introduced themselves. 'Glad to meet you, gentlemen,' he said. 'I am Lieutenant Colonel Timothy Saunders. Captain Hutton is with me.'

'We're honoured to have you with us, Colonel. Tea is about to be a served. Would you care to join us?'

'I would be delighted, Major. But you'd better be quick about it. Our steamer sets off in an hour. Major, would you favour me with introductions.'

The passengers were introduced, all except Cordelia and Bailin, for they were a distant apart, and had not caught the eyes of the self-assured Lt Colonel.

'I'm presuming,' Lieutenant Colonel Timothy Saunders said, 'that apart from the Major and Stuart Hutchinson, and our padre, the rest of you are tea planters. Ah, excepting, of course, Captain McClintock and our doctor.'

Elwin Winterbotham, avidly drinking in the words emerging from the Colonel's lips, nodded eagerly, like a child seeking praise. The griffin was beyond speech as he gazed adoringly at the great man. Buckingham too nodded. David was the odd man out, not knowing if he really fitted into the tea planter category. Seeing his lack of response, Saunders raised an eyebrow and asked, 'What about you, young man? You are a tea planter, aren't you?'

'Well, I really can't call myself one yet, sir. My father is a tea planter. I'm journeying out to Assam to join him in his garden.'

'His sister is with him on board,' put in Captain McClintock. Colonel Saunders glanced around, his eyes resting on Mrs Winterbotham, she being the sole woman in the company.

The lady coloured and said with a smile, 'Oh no, not me, Colonel Saunders! Miss Esscombe is … er … not here right now. She's with a gentleman. I believe they're engaged to be married.'

'May I ask who this fortunate gentleman is?'

'His name's Michael,' the padre intruded, a trifle too quickly. Christopher Buckingham's eyes whipped towards Swanson's face and then to David's, just catching the brief flicker of anxiety in the latter's eyes.

'His name's Lieutenant Michael Bailin,' the planter spoke out. 'It's a curious case, Colonel Saunders, but the fellow resigned his commission in the army and bought a tea garden.'

'Lieutenant Michael Bailin?' Saunders echoed musingly. 'Ah, but it can't be!'

'Can't be what, Colonel?' Buckingham persisted.

'Well, there was another Michael Bailin in the army. A Lieutenant too. Major Gosselin, surely, you've heard of the infamous "Bailin Trial" of Ambala?'

'No, I haven't. News from that far doesn't percolate to this remote region, you know.'

'A disgrace, really! In the early part of 1858, a certain young Lieutenant was court martialled in Ambala, charged with refusing to obey his superior's command. Dishonourably dismissed, he was. Never met the chap myself, though. Heard he later migrated to your country, padre.'

'Good for him!' said Swanson. 'Look, Colonel, *The Lucknow* is making ready to depart.'

Eyes turned towards the other steamer. All, except those of Buckingham. His gaze remained fixed on the ingenuous visage of David. The young man's face wore a troubled look. Then, at the padre's adroit bit of subterfuge, it relaxed.

'I don't see any signal,' said the bemused colonel.

'I thought I saw your Captain wave,' said Swanson in all innocence. 'Perhaps it was a trick of the light!'

'I daresay it was.' The Colonel brought out a chronometer from the pocket of his khaki tunic and took a quick look at it. 'Well, it was pleasant enough in your company. But I'm afraid I've to leave now. The call of duty, you know.'

He rose, as did Captain Hutton, shook hands all around and strode briskly towards the dugout. The duo sat at the prow and continued to wave till they reached *The Lucknow*.

Christopher James Buckingham stood a little apart from the throng. In his eyes was a savage gleam and a smile of triumph lit up his handsome features.

There was no comminatory intimation to the morning of September, the twenty ninth, as the *Ultaganga* paddled up the Brahamputra towards Gowhatty. When she left her cabin to join the Reverend and her brother, Cordelia found the deck draped in a pall of treacherous placidity.

'Michael will be here shortly, sis,' her brother said in response to her questioning glance. 'He's going through his garden papers.'

'Oh, go and fetch him, David,' Cordelia said with a touch of impatience. 'It's too beautiful a morning to squander away in the cabin.'

David left to do his sister's bidding and the two arrived soon, chatting and laughing like schoolboys sharing a private joke. The Lieutenant bent down to plant a decorous kiss on her cheek. 'Sorry, darling,' he apologized. 'I was doing homework. The closer we get to our destination the more nervous I grow. To face my garden babu not knowing a thing about tea would be quite a disaster!'

'Oh, it's perfectly all right, Michael,' Cordelia said. 'The morning's so lovely and I wanted you on the deck. I shan't trouble you this afternoon … and that's a promise!'

The Lieutenant turned towards the Reverend. 'Your lessons in Assamese have been a great help, Father. I've practiced it on Garo and can make myself understood. There's a lot he knows of tea. He's a terrific bloke, helpful and loyal to a fault. Buckingham did not deserve him.'

'Treat him well, Michael,' Swanson said.

'Like my own brother. He'll consider my garden as his own, he says. He'll consider my life as his own, he says.'

Breakfast arrived, zealously guarded by Garo, who waited in attendance along with the steward. Awhile later, after the trays were cleared, Bailin said, 'Father, I've begun to sense a duality in my life … a vague feeling of being reincarnated, Somehow, I seem to have disassociated from Michael Bailin the fugitive, the traitor to country and cause! The Michael Bailin who stepped aboard the *Ultaganga* belongs to the past. You see a new avatar before you, a being with no past, only a future!'

'Oh, come now, Michael! No matter what, you can't just pretend your past doesn't exist!'

'David, you're more veracious than you realize,' said the Reverend. 'Your so-called avatar is an illusion, Michael, wrought by the past's afflictions and the euphoria of the present. But do not take it to be the reality, for the past will brook no disaffirmation. It can be a whimsical imp, popping up at the most unsought moment and unforeseen manner.'

'Please, Father, I beg of you! If what I feel is an illusion, let it be!'

Cordelia's hand reached out and clasped the Lieutenant's. 'The past is dead and gone, Michael. Think only of the future.'

'No,' said the padre harshly, startling the three with the coldness of his tone. 'I'll not permit you the luxury of burying your past! Face it with dignity. You've done no wrong. Do not attempt to escape your past. Above all, do not allow that past to cloud your present judgement, or propel you towards irrational, impulsive actions.'

The Lieutenant's hold on Cordelia's hand tightened, his tension coursing through her veins. 'For three long years I've been running, Father! Where else is there to run? By heavens, I don't know what I'll do if the past catches up with me again! I think I'll go mad!'

'It won't catch up with you, Michael,' Cordelia said fiercely. 'You'll go to your garden and build it up. Nothing will come in the way of our happiness, darling.'

The padre spoke no more and fell into a secretive silence, his face stern. But his eyes were full of fatalistic sadness. Bailin let go of Cordelia's hand

and, turning to David, began comparing notes on their knowledge of the local language. Cordelia gazed fondly at him. How immensely he had changed! At their first meeting his deep-blue eyes had been shuttered and unrevealing, his manners those of a man who had erected inviolable barriers between himself and his fellow creatures.

But once he had unburdened his soul, purging it of violent passions, he regained his intrinsic gentleness and compassion. He was a good man in the truest sense of the term; a decent man, one for whom principles were more important than personal gains, much like Papa. And, like Papa, circumstances had been hostile to him, temporarily twisted his personality and wrapped it in alien garbs. But his innate goodness had lain like a miser's pearl cunningly cached in a plebeian cover. That she, along with the Reverend and David, had been instrumental in tearing away the layers to reveal his essential purity induced in her not only joy, but also a sense of achievement, of triumph almost.

She watched her lover with eyes of love. *Michael, I'll protect you, whatever the vagaries of our destiny might be. I'll be the shield to your past, screening you with my love from predacious memories. We shall build our own destinies, you with your goodness, I with my love.*

Captain McClintock emerged from the under-deck. He approached Gosselin's group and was seen engaged in discussions with it. Then he turned and limped towards them.

Cordelia saw the Reverend grow tense. He seemed to loom physically larger, like a mother hen puffing up her feathers when sensing danger to her chicks. She could not explain to herself why this filled her with nagging disquietude, for there was nothing remotely forbidding about the diminutive captain's approach.

Her brother and Michael stood up to greet the captain, resuming their seats only when the old man occupied his. McClintock said nothing for some time and sat puffing at his briar, his features puckered in a frown.

'A poor journey!' he burst out unexpectedly. 'We lost a flat and chests of tea on way to Calcutta. On way back, young Buckingham's lost near a third of his cargo.'

'As was to be expected,' said Swanson tersely.

'Now, now,' the captain said, pointing his briar at the padre. 'Let's not open that chapter again. The blighters are in fine fettle presently … young

Buckingham should be able to land the ones which survived the scourge. We touch Gowhatty this eve. Tomorrow, the thirtieth, we lie at that port. So ye all can step ashore and take in the sights.'

'The Reverend has taken charge of that. There's an American Baptist Mission at Gowhatty and a missionary school. He's promised to take us there.' This was from Cordelia.

The captain continued, 'Only two stops between Gowhatty and Kokilamukh … at Tezpore, the other midway to Kokilamukh, which we touch on the third. However, since we'll berth towards sunset, ye'll get to yer Papa only on the fourth of October. Will he come to receive ye, lassie?'

'We doubt it, sir. He's very ill, as you know.'

'Never ye mind, m'dear. I'm sure he'll send someone with a boat or an elephant to take ye to Dhanboa.'

The captain looked towards Bailin. 'What about ye, lad? What're yer plans?'

'He's first coming with us to meet Papa,' David said eagerly. 'Someone at Dhanboa can direct him to his garden.'

'How nigh be yer garden from Dhanboa, lad?'

'Looks pretty close on the map. But the Reverend here says there are no roads linking one to the other. Only impassable jungles in between.'

'Well, lad. I wish it had been as far as the poles. Far from Buckingham's Bihguri. Ye were unlucky to have crossed swords with young Buckingham! He's the very devil! Aye yes, I wish yer garden was located elsewhere.'

'I can take Buckingham on,' Bailin said grimly.

'Ye're a straight lad. But Buckingham's entrails are those of a viper. He's capable of a million schemes to harm ye. He's started already!'

Cordelia, dismayed, asked, 'Started what, captain?'

'Ah, spreading lies and canards about young Michael. He's been shooting his mouth off before the other passengers. Gosselin and the others've requested me to talk to ye. Clear matters up.'

'That's not necessary,' Swanson intruded. 'Michael, pay no heed to what Buckingham says! And Gosselin has no authority, legal or moral, to demand explanations. Say nothing, Michael!'

'No, Father,' the Lieutenant said fiercely. 'I must know! Captain, sir, what lies is this wretched planter spreading about me?'

'Ye ken, lad, the last noon at Palasbari, while we all were out on the sands, a Lt Colonel Saunders paid a visit. Ye and Miss Esscombe were apart from the company, so ye wouldn't ken what took place. Yer name was bandied and Saunders said that there was another Lieutenant Michael Bailin court martialled at Ambala. Buckingham's claiming ye're him!'

Cordelia froze, fear clutching her heart. David's features were a picture of consternation. Both looked at Michael. His face remained impassive. But Cordelia was watching his eyes. The shutters had come down once again!

The Lieutenant started to say something, but Swanson was quicker. 'Shut up, Michael,' he said, almost rudely. He turned to the old man. 'What kind of people are you, McClintock? You, Gosselin and your tribe? Who gave you the right to play inquisitors?'

'Look padre, I didn't say I believed Buckingham,' the captain protested defensively.

'You appear to conveniently forget what Saunders also said ... that our Michael Bailin cannot be that Lieutenant Michael Bailin!'

'I did hear Saunders say the disgraced officer had migrated to the New World.'

'Yet you come at Buckingham's bidding to interrogate Michael?'

'I didn't come on me own, Swanson. I'm here at Major Gosselin's behest. He wishes the air cleared. The Major can send a message to far off Ambala and get details of the case. And, if I ken Gosselin, he might well do so, unless the matter is satisfactorily resolved with him.'

Once again Bailin sought to say something but the padre brusquely silenced him. 'Go then, McClintock, and resolve matters with His Royal Highness! Our Michael has committed no action of which he should be ashamed before man or God!'

The captain looked relieved. He favoured Cordelia with a warm smile. 'Lassie, ye ken very well Michael's a lad after me own heart. I'd never be party to anything to ruin yer happiness.'

'Thank you, captain,' Cordelia spoke from her heart. McClintock stood up, nodded briefly to the four of them and hobbled off to the other group.

The icy chill lying at the pit of her stomach slowly thawed. But, as she reached out for Michael's hand, she found it unresponsive. His lips were compressed and facial muscles taut. Renewed fear engulfed her, making speech impossible. David too seemed dumbstruck by the turn of events.

'For the Lord's sake keep talking and smiling!' said the padre angrily. 'They're watching. Don't look as if the sky has fallen! Michael, you mustn't allow Buckingham's villainy to upset you.'

Bailin's expression did not change. His face was stony as if it had been hewed from marble and his eyes were cold. But David was quick to react to the padre's urgent appeal. He slapped his thighs and burst aloud in exuberant laughter.

The padre too laughed. 'The hyenas have lost a meal!' he said. 'You noticed, David, I did not utter a single untruth. I can yet meet my Maker without a blush on my face!'

On the other side of the deck the old captain, after a brief conversation with Gosselin and company, took leave and limped away. That group spared them another glance of curiosity and looked no more.

'Cheer up, Michael,' said David. 'No harm done.'

'Please, Michael,' Cordelia squeezed her lover's unresponsive hand. 'Don't look that way. It fills me with dread!'

At her words Bailin tried to regain his composure. When he spoke, his voice was tender. 'Sorry, my darling. I've had a shock! But I'm over it now. You were right, Father. Doors are forever getting closed ... there's no escape. You'll have to excuse me. I must get back to our cabin and reflect.'

His grip on Cordelia's hand tightened till it hurt. He leaned forward to touch her cheek with his lips. Then, as though he had made a decision of immeasurable magnitude, he rose with purpose, and quickly strode across the deck to his cabin, not sparing the other group a glance. They looked up and gazed unabashedly at him as he strode past.

Cordelia made a move to go after him, but the padre restrained her. 'Leave him be, my dear. He must be alone with himself for a while.'

The other group dispersed. The three of them continued to sit without any exchange of words, simply staring at the shifting landscape.

A fabulous sunset across the Brahmaputra, with low hills in the foreground, greeted the *Ultaganga* when it crawled wearily into Gowhatty ghat. David, Cordelia, and Reverend Swanson, along with other passengers, stood at the railings, watching the flurry of activities the arrival of the steamer had brought about.

The light gradually dimmed and the various activities on the pier slowly came to a standstill. 'Michael's still in his cabin,' David said. He had spent the afternoon with the padre, loath to disturb his companion.

'You'd better go and fetch him,' Cordelia said.

'It would be better if you yourself go, my dear,' the padre said.

Cordelia nodded and made her way to Michael's cabin. She tapped gently, once, twice and then, hearing no movement, pushed at the door. Bailin lay fully dressed on one of the beds, seemingly asleep, right arm thrown across his face like a shield. But at the sound of her voice, he stirred and sat up. The lamplight fell on his face and Cordelia, unprepared, gasped at what she saw.

His haggard features were of a soul in torment. He had lain on bed all afternoon grappling with spectres which permitted him no respite, not even in the lonely wilderness of Assam. He looked blankly at her, eyes unseeing, momentarily without recognition. Then the eyes focussed, and he raised his right hand—an ambivalent gesture, to ward her off, or to draw her to him.

Cordelia clasped the outstretched hand in her own, sat on the side of the bed and drew his head on to her lap. Her left hand kept stroking his hair while her right held his in a fiercely possessive grip. At the brush of her fingers he shuddered violently once and then relaxed. 'Oh Michael! Michael, my darling,' she continuously murmured as she stroked his hair. For a long while his head rested on her lap. But suddenly he sat up, swivelled towards her and grasped both her hands in his.

'I don't deserve you, my darling!'

'Hush,' she said. Releasing her palms from his grip, she caught the sides of his head and drew it towards her own. She kissed him hungrily full on the lips.

It was he who drew his lips away. Abruptly he stood up and turned his back towards her. 'Where is David? And the Reverend?'

'On the deck. I came to see how you were.'

He pulled her up by the arm and said, 'We'd better go and join them.'

Cordelia did not understand and was hurt by his attitude. They could have spent an eternity in the cabin; neither David nor the Reverend would have grudged them that. Yet Michael seemed almost fearful of the intimacy and was anxious to be gone. She said nothing, however, and followed him out. Her brother and the padre awaited them on the deck.

'Good evening, Father. David, sorry I behaved like an ass. The captain's revelations came as a thunderbolt ... you understand that, of course.'

Cordelia pricked up her ears; there was an uncaring joviality about the tone, one that was sharply in contrast to the mood she had found him in. Her perplexity deepened.

'You've got over it, apparently,' Reverend Swanson chuckled. 'I'm delighted. You had me worried for a while.'

'That's the spirit, Michael!' David laughed approvingly. 'Hell and damnation to Buckingham and his tribe! Now, shall we repair to the dining chamber for dinner?'

Bailin spoke abruptly, as if he had just recalled something. 'Oh, Father, you'll have to excuse me from tomorrow's trip to the Mission. This day's events have prevented me from doing my homework as I had planned in the morning.'

'You're sensible,' the padre nodded. 'And practical. All right, I shall excuse you from our trip. But a higher authority than I exist in this company. You'll have to convince her too.'

The girl said at once, 'Of course! I understand, darling. David and I'll go with the Reverend. You can read on undisturbed through the day.'

She awoke early, disturbed by the firing of the steamer's engine as it was brought back to the pier, carried out her ablutions speedily, and was on the deck before the others. They arrived soon afterwards, had an early breakfast and made their way to the pier.

Having crossed the gangway onto the dust-filled bank they stopped. The Lieutenant shook hands with David and the Reverend, kissed Cordelia lightly on her cheek and said, 'Goodbye, my darling. May God bless you always.' Without another word he turned his back upon them and strode towards the *Ultaganga*, his shoulders squared and tread firm.

When they returned to the steamer from the day's excursion, a shock awaited them. Lieutenant Michael Bailin, along with his man-servant Garo Munda, were gone!

It was David who conveyed the information.

'Gone? Gone where?' Cordelia, puzzled, asked.

David's eyes were filled with pity and anger. 'God alone knows, sis! But his stuff's no longer in the cabin. And he's left this for you.'

He held out a slim envelope. *To Miss Cordelia Esscombe.* She recognized Michael's handwriting.

'I must inform the Reverend. The captain too, if he doesn't know already.' David left hurriedly.

Cordelia sat down on the edge of the bed. Her fingers shook as she tore open the envelope and extracted the sheet of paper. The letters sprang up before her eyes, hazily at first, and then with a preternatural clarity. 'Cordelia, my darling,' Michael had written:

> I know it will hurt you to read these words, as much as it has hurt me to pen them—my action will cause you the deepest anguish, I am sensible of that—I cannot demand your forgiveness—the pain I have inflicted on you is beyond forgivenes—but I must explain–must endeavour to make you understand—I care not what others might think—might insinuate—there is only one individual in the whole world from whom I desire understanding—and that is you, my darling.
>
> The past hours have been all a charade—you must have realized that by now–last evening itself I had made up my mind to disembark–to cut myself off from you all—in fact, the very moment I learnt that Buckingham suspected–however I or you might dissemble, today's suspicion will become tomorrow's certainty—especially since Gosselin knows—he can find out—he has the resources and a sensibility petty enough to delve into petty matters.
>
> The Reverend was right—one cannot escape the consequences of one's past actions—I have tried but failed—the past is an obdurate stalker—it will dog me for ever—I am destined to remain branded as Lieutenant Michael Bailin the traitor—the renegade—Michael Bailin of the infamous Ambala case.
>
> Face it with dignity—wasn't that what the Reverend had said—I am game for that, my darling—I have faced it in the past—I will face it in the future—but there must be no sacrifice of innocents—if it had been me alone, I would not have made a run for it as I am doing now—you can be certain of that, my darling.
>
> You are more precious to me than I can describe—when my soul lay dead you had breathed new life into it—you are my life, my darling—you are my soul—you are my very breath.

How can I willfully injure someone so precious to me—debase and degrade a being whom I so tenderly cherish—I am an untouchable, my darling—an outcast—a pariah—I am the leper who infects others by his touch—my very presence will contaminate you—your purity, your goodness—you will have to wear a badge of ignominy like siblings of low-born Hindus.

I cannot—will not—allow that to happen—I shall not pull you down into the whirlpool of despair I find myself in—go back to Calcutta, my darling—when your father is well again marry someone who will love and cherish you as I had done—someone with an irreproachable past—tear me away from your memory, my darling, as I shall you from mine.

Mine is no act of betrayal—rather, it is an act of love—I do not ask for forgiveness—only for understanding—your unfortunate Michael.

She sat for a while stroking the papers with her fingers, and then, like a miracle, from some hidden recess within herself emerged a strange, uncanny strength, a strength which she never imagined she possessed. It steeled her to face the reality of Michael's departure. She stood up, bolted the door, and took a bath. She dressed carefully; a shirt of fine muslin, pale-yellow in colour and a skirt to match; she spent an inordinately long time over her makeup, combing her eyebrows and lashes but not shadowing them, powdering her face to obliterate any trace of paleness. A touch of colour to her lips and she was ready to confront the deck.

The padre and David were there, along with the captain. The old man was not angry, although it transpired that Bailin had left ship without intimating him. He reached out to take Cordelia's hands, held them in his crinkled palms, and said, 'Take heart, m'dear. We'll find him yet.'

But the hours passed, the sun set, the other passengers who had gone out for the day returned one by one, yet there was no trace of Lieutenant Michael Bailin. The search for him was given up when it grew dark.

Soon the other European passengers came to know of Bailin's jumping ship, and the *Ultaganga* buzzed with rumours, the universal refrain being that Buckingham's suspicions regarding the Lieutenant had been well founded. In a matter of minutes, the good opinion which the Lieutenant had earned lay trampled on the floor of the deck. Hutchinson had all along held 'little opinion of him', while Elwin Winterbotham, from the very first, had suspected there was something rummy in the fellow's behaviour. Even the griffin chipped in with derogatory comments, while Gosselin promised to send for details of the Ambala trial. But, in deference to Cordelia's presence at the other end of the deck, they did not voice their denunciations too loudly, for the evening breeze had a pernicious habit of carrying sound.

However, Dorothy Winterbotham did walk up, her otherwise dull eyes afire with expectation, to where Cordelia sat. As she later said to her Elwin, she was surprised to find the girl remarkably composed, considering the situation. She had gone to her all set to offer consolation, to show her the rosier side of the catastrophe that had befallen her, that it would free her from matrimonial obligations to a tea planter—not that, of course, she herself had any regrets, or Elwin had been anything but the best of husbands. But the girl was far from inconsolable; nay she seemed positively gay and carefree, as if she had never cared for the Lieutenant at all. Yet it was just a week ago she had talked of the Lieutenant to the girl and she could have sworn she was totally infatuated with him. It made you think, it did, as to what these girls were coming to nowadays!

'Well, the lad's not to be found,' the captain finally told their group. 'Can wait no more for him, m'dear. Have to take me ship off the pier.'

'Thank you, Captain, for trying to locate Michael,' Cordelia said gratefully. 'If he has any dues outstanding, David will settle them on his behalf.'

'Never ye mind dues outstanding, m'dear. But we've to leave at daybreak on the morrow.'

The captain having made his departure, Cordelia insisted they eat their dinner at the dining chamber along with the other passengers. Throughout the meal she sat with her chin up, braving the surreptitious glances flung at her with quiet equanimity. Her only moment of discomfort came with the abrupt entry of Buckingham. Her eyes had accidentally met his; she caught the triumphant gleam in those heavy-lidded eyes, and her mask almost slipped off her features. Unaccountably, the planter withdrew as abruptly as he had entered, followed by the doctor, and the duo did not reappear while they were at their meal.

Afterwards the three of them stood at the deck and Cordelia said, 'Father, I've a request.'

'Name it, my child.'

'Can you disembark at Kokilamukh ghat and accompany us to Dhanboa? And stay with us for the night? Please, Father. I am filled with strange fears … presentiments of disaster. More than ever, we need the strength your presence affords. Just for a day, Father. Till we meet Papa and make future plans with him.'

David sensed the hopeless sadness in his sister's voice and suddenly his perplexity disappeared. He put his right arm around her shoulders. 'Yes, Father, you must come with us. I pledge on my life I'll see you to your Mission afterwards.'

Swanson nodded. 'All right, my dear. I'll disembark at Kokilamukh.'

'Thank you, Father,' Cordelia spoke with feeling.

'My child, you have more strength than I imagined. Be brave and strong. Never give in to despair; put your faith in the Lord and draw upon your inner strength. Derive strength from David too, and that of your Papa. But sometimes there come moments in one's life when there are no crutches to lean on; when one is left starkly alone to confront despair. If, the good Lord forbid, such a moment falls to your lot, draw on all your inner strength and triumph.'

David squeezed his sister's shoulders. 'Don't worry, Father. I'll take good care of her. If only Michael had not played the fool like this!'

'Cheer up, David. Michael's departure is temporary. He'll be back, I feel it in my bones. Come, my dear, we'll escort you to your cabin and repair to our own.'

She bade them good night and entered her cabin. The moment she bolted the door, the tenuous veil she had worn the whole evening slipped off her features. She had kept her emotions in tight rein, now they welled up inside her, wave upon wave, till her face grew grotesquely distorted with the force of her grief. She did not bother to turn up the cabin lamp. She took off her clothes but did not slip on her night gown. Instead, she flung herself naked on to the bed and buried her face into the pillow to stifle the fierce screams issuing from her bowel, threatening to rend the night's silence, much as the howling of the grief-stricken coolies had done.

Yet the tears did not come. Perhaps she had held them back too long. Perhaps they had become frozen and hung like icicles in the chambers of her heart. She crouched in the foetal position and hugged the pillow with all her might. Utter desolation washed over her, her body radiated heat and went into violent spams as though with tropical fever. And all the while the screams inside her, denied outlet, hammered against her brain and eyes and eardrums till she thought she would go mad.

For a long time she lay in the foetal crouch, asleep yet semi-awake, steeped in despair yet uncrying, her mind awhirl with thoughts yet incapable of thinking. Where was the strength which had kept her head up the whole of that evening, the strength the Reverend had imagined he perceived in her? No, that strength too had been derived from Michael, from the hope they would find him and he would return, that strength had been a part of the dissimulation. But he had not returned; confronting that reality she felt debilitated, naked and vulnerable. How could she come to grips with the future without Michael's love and strength?

She remembered the days prior to their departure from Assam—the anxiety-ridden hours at the thought of Papa ill at his garden; the terrible ache at their gradual awareness of what he had undergone for his children's sake; the terror of cutting herself off from familiarity and sailing towards the unknown; and the coolies, the human cargo, who had lacerated her conscience; all these had been made bearable because of Michael. His presence had diluted the pain and fear; he had exorcised the guilt from her soul. But now that he was no longer there, leaving her alone and without strength, the floodgates reopened, the aches and the fears came rushing in. They tormented her throughout the long night, flagellating her mind and draining away her vitality till, weak and exhausted, she fell into troubled sleep.

The *Ultaganga* steamed off at first light, with the *Shaitan* in tow. Two stoppages later, on 3 October, she touched the river port of Kokilamukh. After mooring the flat *Shaitan* on a sandbank, the steamer slid off towards another, there to rest for the night.

The firing of the *Ultaganga's* engine at first light, as it pushed itself and the *Shaitan* to the jetty, was sufficient to stir Cordelia into wakefulness. The native steward who served chota hazri found her packed and dressed and ready to leave. Soon she emerged from her cabin and joined her brother and the Reverend at the rails.

'Hasn't anyone come for us?' she asked.

David shook his head, and the Reverend answered, 'I'm afraid not. But there's time yet. At least two hours before the captain can finish dealing with all those people and sail away.'

The ghat, indeed, was reassuringly crowded with men, horses and elephants. They were mostly merchants from Jorehaut, or kinsmen of native passengers come to receive them. Two Europeans, both young men, stood amidst the throng, their fair skin and pallid hair in marked contrast against the brown of the natives. They wore riding habits, long boots putteed at the ankles, and sola toupees to protect them against the sun.

'The taller one's Nicholls,' the Reverend said, referring to the Europeans. 'He's an assistant at Cinnamora, one of the prized gardens of the Jorehaut Tea Company. Been at this place for over a year now. His companion is Captain Ralph Hewitt, Major Gosselin's deputy at Jorehaut.'

After breakfast, two stewards carried their trunks and other belongings to the shade of a huge hilikha tree which stood a little beyond the river's edge. A steward kept guard over the baggage while the trio bade farewell to the other passengers. Gosselin, due to disembark at Dikhowmukh, the next port, invited the Esscombes to visit him at Sivasagar some time. The Winterbothams, Hutchinson and Jeremy, bound for Dibrugarh, the steamer's final destination, too extended a similar invitation.

Then, without further ceremony, they departed from the *Ultaganga*, relieved the steward of his charge, and waited patiently under the cool shade of the tree. A while later, the two Europeans, Nicholls and Hewitt, approached and introduced themselves. Nicholls, tall and gangly, was still in his teens. He was already infatuated with Cordelia, which made him awkward and tongue-tied. Captain Hewitt was not only older, but more mature and spoke with a deference which was music to David's ears. The officer graciously offered to hire a boat on their behalf but the padre rejected his offer. Meanwhile the merchants and other visitors from Jorehaut, having concluded business with the captain, were all set to leave en masse. The two Englishmen called for their horses, mounted them and trotted off, after expressing hopes that they could visit the Esscombes at Dhanboa soon.

The strange caravan, comprising of elephants, horses, *palkis*, *dolas* and men on foot, set off at a brisk pace and soon disappeared from sight, leaving the ghat practically deserted. Captain McClintock now appeared on the gangway and slowly hobbled towards them. He was genuinely pleased that they had not left without bidding him goodbye. 'I shall be back in a couple of weeks,' he told Cordelia. 'Bring yer Papa along to me ship. Ye shall journey back to Calcutta with me, m' dear.'

'We'll do that,' assured David.

The old mariner's eyes were sad. 'I like ye both, lassie, ye and yer brother. Wish that young fool hadn't left ship like that!' Saying so, he walked back to the steamer.

Buckingham and Doctor Gordon, both dressed in Jodhpurs and riding boots, sola toupees on heads, came out of the *Ultaganga*. The planter was met at the end of the gangway by the three henchmen who had travelled with him and four others from his garden who had come to receive him. Buckingham mounted his horse in one agile movement; the portly doctor, however, had to be helped on to the saddle.

Wooden planks were laid on the *Shaitan's* side, and the coolies shuffled out. The line was far shorter than what it had been when Cordelia had first seen them board at Chandpal ghat. No longer did the women who survived the scourge carry babies in their arms; no father led a toddler by the hand. The youngsters she had seen that evening at Ganga Saugor Isle, splashing about in the waters and emitting unrestrained squeals of laughter—nothing remained of them, except perhaps piles of ashes on some forgotten sandbank.

'Pachan? Gangi? Sombari? Lalmoya?' Cordelia heard their names being called out by Buckingham from a list he held in his hands. She saw the tall figure of Bircha and, just behind him, Meghu. The journey had emasculated them too, for they exhibited the same lassitude as their brethren. The rollcall over, the coolies were ordered to embark. They shuffled slowly forward, stupefaction writ over faces, neither understanding nor caring about what had happened to them. Yet, as they plodded past, her eyes met those of Bircha and abruptly her heart beat faster. Those eyes contradicted the slouch of his body, for the same fires of hell she had seen once before continued to blaze in them.

There was a sudden commotion as the line of coolies reached the part of the bank where the boats waited to transport them to their garden. A woman, the one just ahead of Bircha, stumbled and fell. She lay unmoving on the ground, paralysed by fear or weakness, unable to rise. The coolies ahead of her continued to move, but those behind her came to a stop.

'*Utho*! Get up, you vixen!' screamed an escort, kicking at the woman. Bircha was at him in an instant, fingers reaching for the throat. The man toppled with the coolie on top of him. So quick had been Bircha's action that the others had no time to react. The coolie would have throttled the life out of his tormentor had not Meghu, just behind him, pulled him away.

The fallen man picked himself dazedly up, while his comrades, fists and musket-butts upraised, converged on Bircha, teeth bared in fury. The other coolies, except Meghu, stood immobile, too terror-struck to come to Bircha's aid.

'Stop, you bloody fools!' Buckingham's voice cut through the air like a whiplash. His minions halted in their tracks and turned baffled faces towards him.

The planter jumped down from his horse. 'We haven't brought them so far to provide meat for you mongrels!' he shouted, slashing the air with the riding crop in his hand. His men, like scavengers at a kill when the tiger approached, retreated a few paces.

'Tie those two up.' Buckingham said again, indicating Bircha and Meghu. He pulled out a small flask from his belt, uncapped it, bent down and, holding the fallen woman by her hair, poured some liquid down her throat. The woman stirred, he pulled her up by the hair on to her feet. It seemed she would fall again the very moment he released his grip, but the pain and the restorative had the desired effect and she moved unsteadily forward on her own.

The hands of the two coolies were bound with ropes and they were roughly shoved ahead. One by one, Buckingham's cargo climbed aboard the native crafts and sat there in sullen silence, their meagre belongings by their sides. Though three boats had come for the coolies, two sufficed. Buckingham remounted his pony and rode off, along with Doctor Gordon.

'Look, David!' the padre cried out. 'I believe your welcoming party has arrived!'

At a distance, powering its way upstream, was visible a large boat, with half a dozen men on it. It come to a stop at the point where Buckingham's crafts had been previously moored. One man remained aboard while the rest, eyes probing and voices raised in excited jabber, led by a dhoti-clad, toupee-wearing individual, dashed up the slight incline towards where they stood.

'Good morning, good morning, good morning, good morning,' said the dhoti-clad apparition, bowing to them in turn, the reiteration of his 'good morning' being necessitated by the fact that there were four recipients for them. Apart from his sola toupee, dhoti and sandals, he also wore a shirt which had seen better days, and an ill-fitting half-coat, which presumably was an insignia of his office, for he wore it even in the heat. The half-coat, a hand-me-down from some unknown source, was frayed at the collar and had all its buttons torn off.

His specifically directed 'good mornings' made it imperative that each of them in his or her turn make suitable reply. Satisfied, the man, in English which needed liberal deciphering, spoke again; with a start of delight Cordelia recognized Papa's accent in his voice.

'Forgive us, Your Excellencies, for we know not what we do. We're dangerously late. Huh, you find funny I know the English? Esscombe sahib bery fine teacher. I peruse the books … peruse your Shakethespear and such like. Speak much English. I, Bapukan Hazarika, bormohori. You like Esscombe sahib, I know Your Excellency, dear David sahib. You beautiful, Cordelia memsahib. Esscombe sahib speak much much for you. I delight meeting you, I, Bapukan Hazarika, bormohori. Call me Bapu babu. You with crossed neck, Your Excellency, I know you not. I, Bapukan Hazarika, bormohori.'

The apparition paused for breath and Cordelia quickly asked, 'How is Papa?' The man's features twisted as he made a frantic effort to dredge the word from memory. 'How is Esscombe sahib?' the padre clarified.

'Papa!' spoke Bapu babu, vastly relieved. 'That a good word. New word I speak English every day. Papa is bery, bery bad. He evil. That damn fellow, *Yama* … bless his soul … he sitting on doorstep like damned foxes and vixens. Papa Esscombe sahib speaks me every day. Why not dear David sahib come? Why not darling Cordelia memsahib come? He get letter from

Calcutta and he speaks me every minute. But I come, Your Excellencies. I, Bapukan Hazarika, bormohori. I come take you Dhanboa and Papa Esscombe sahib. I bring boat and men. Come and go to Papa Esscombe sahib.'

He signalled and the four men with him standing some yards away came hurrying up. 'What, these your chests?' Bapu babu asked, indicating their baggage. 'Come and go, you mountains of laziness, shove damn chests on boat. *Khor kor*! *Utha*! Easy does it, you fat big leeches, you jackals after big fat eat.'

'Papa's men seem well fed. That's a relief.' Cordelia said.

'They're not imported coolies but local men,' the padre said, 'The bormohori is caste Hindu, but the men with him are local tribals, most likely Kacharis. Very strong and hard working. Loyal too. Your father's fortunate to have them. They don't work for all and sundry.'

'What's a bormohori, Father?' David enquired.

'Burra Muharrer, or head clerk. An important functionary in the garden, in his own way. Our Bapu babu seems to have your father's trust.'

Meanwhile that worthy, having got the loading process started, came and stood by them. David made an attempt to practise his Assamese on him. '*Deri kiyo hol*? He asked, wanting an explanation for the delay in his arrival.

The bormohori looked thunderstruck. For one moment it seemed that David's unexpected phrase had bunged a cork into the fellow's loquacity. But then he got his larynx working again and the words poured out. 'Huh, you speak my tongue?' A good-natured grin spread on his face. 'Huh, goodness of my gracious, Your Excellency speak the Assamese as I speak the English! That bery, bery good. I practice the English; you practise the Assamese. That bery, bery funny, no?' The man burst out into loud laughter, his delighted surprise natural and spontaneous.

'David, we should leave now,' Cordelia said. 'Our stuff's on the boat.'

They sat upon the transverse beams beneath the thatch *soi*, as the boat traversed an interlinked maze of streams and rivulets—four hours of crawling progress and they were at their destination, the tiny private jetty of Dhanboa Tea Plantation. Sensing they had arrived, the three passengers stood up in readiness to disembark but Bapu babu waved them down. He spoke rapidly to the padre in his native tongue, explaining the situation.

The Reverend passed it on to David. 'He says that this is our first visit to Dhanboa. We are honoured guests. We should be welcomed in a manner befitting our stature.'

So they continued to sit on the boat, amidst the cool, shaded gloom, the silence couching them like peas in a pod till it was split with dramatic suddenness by the clash of cymbals and beat of drums. A babble of high-pitched voices added to the noise and minutes later a weird procession emerged over the path to the riverbank. It comprised of villagers from the bormohiri's village, and the coolies of the garden; the latter a composite crowd, some Assamese tribals like the boatmen, skin the shade of pale-brown ochre, flat mongoloid featured and with almond-shaped eyes. These stood out in sharp contrast to the imported coolies who were as swarthy as the ones they had seen on the *Shaitan*. However, despite their physiognomic disparities each individual in that throng, young or old, had one feature in common—every face was wreathed in a welcoming smile.

Having ceremonially welcomed their guests and showered traditional blessings upon them, the boisterous procession led the newcomers over narrow paths into the tea garden. Cordelia reached out for David's hand and cried out in elation, 'It's home, David! We've reached home at last!'

David too was visibly moved. Two crude signboards, in English as well as the vernacular, had been strung up on bamboo poles beside a nongola, or bamboo gate. 'Dhanboa', one said. 'Private Property, Keep Out', warned the other.

Cordelia and David had their first view of tea plants. These grew in uneven, bushy rows on either side of a mud-brown garden track, acres upon acres of them, rolling away like a verdant sea, not a single tall tree in between to break the uniformity. Turning a bend, the bushes petered out and they saw the rude cottage which stood in a clearing amidst the tea bushes. The hut was set upon a terrace of clay, about three or four feet above the ground—the walls were of closely woven, spliced bamboo plastered with mud, the roof of thatch. At the front was an open verandah shaded at the top, and a little flower garden. An easy-chair, of woven cane, stood on the verandah. A man reclined upon the chair.

About fifty feet from the cottage the procession came to a halt; it would proceed no further. Bapu babu said, 'Come now, dear David sahib and darling Cordelia memsahib. Papa Esscombe sahib he sits for you.'

Cordelia, perplexed, advanced a few steps, as did David. She could clearly see the figure, swathed in a blanket despite the afternoon heat, as it reclined on the easy-chair. But Papa, where was Papa? Surely that skeletal creature with the gaunt, haggard, bearded face, head matted with long, uncut hair the colour of sooty snow—surely that could not be Papa? Papa had been tall and strong with a voice which could shake mangoes off a tree and a laughter which rumbled like thunder among the clouds! True, he had been ailing; but no ailment could reduce a man of Papa's physique to the thin, shrivelled caricature that sat weak and impotent upon the chair!

'Cordi. David. Come to me.' The voice floated feebly to them, and she could cheat herself no longer. She set off in a half-run, half-stagger, a wild shriek forming in her brain but not rising in her throat, the flower garlands flailing maniacally upon her breasts. Stumbling over the few steps leading to the verandah, she fell to her knees and hugged the frail body with all her might.

'Oh Papa, what have you done to yourself?' she cried, and buried her face in his blanketed lap. Petals from the garlands, torn by the strength of her hug, lay scattered on the floor and his lap. Their fragrance could not waft away the strong stench of urine and pus that his body emitted.

He raised a bony, nerveless hand and stroked her hair. David, face contorted with grief and bewilderment, gathered the other hand into his own and stood mute and helpless by his side.

Then the tears that lay congealed behind her eyes and in the caverns of her skull, the tears that would not come the other day in the cabin of the *Ultaganga*, thawed and melted like icicles in the sun. The drops came pouring out, incessant like a tropical drizzle, wetting the coarse, woollen blanket to mingle with the flower petals strewn upon his lap.

At mid-noon the pagal ghanta sounded at Bihguri, Buckingham's tea garden. The pagal ghanta, or 'mad bell', was a brass gong rung only when some imminent disaster, such as a rampaging herd of wild elephants, threatened the garden and its inmates. But today the clang of the gong signified disaster of another kind to the coolies, for they all knew it signalled the arrival of the lord and master of the plantation, Christopher James Buckingham.

Naked fear, rising like river mist, slithered through the dingy lanes and bylanes of the sprawling coolie basti. Coolie men and women, working in various sections of the garden, stopped whatever they were doing and cocked their ears at the ominous signal. Mothers hushed wailing infants, toddlers frolicking in the dust stopped their play and slunk like guilt-ridden shadows to their elders.

Half an hour later Buckingham rode into Bihguri, in the company of Doctor William Gordon. A huge man, tall and well-built for a coolie, awaited them on the patch of lawn fronting Buckingham's bungalow. He gripped the reins of the ponies and led them away after the riders dismounted. 'Give them a good scrub, Luthra,' Buckingham called out in Hindustani. 'Then come and meet me in the bungalow.'

The two riders walked up the steps, threw their toupees on the wicker-table and flung themselves into the chairs. Bath and lunch later, they were at the front verandah once more. Luthra was waiting for them at the foot of the steps.

'Everything all right in the garden while I was away?' Buckingham asked the coolie sirdar.

'*Haan, sahib. Sab theek thaak tha.* No problem.'

'Good. I shall inspect the tea sections tomorrow. The pruning had better be done to my satisfaction, or they all suffer pay cuts.'

'They've done a good job. They know what happens if they don't.'

'We open up another fifty acres in my personal holdings this winter. Get in touch with the Naga contractors.'

'Fifty acres, sahib?' A worried frown creased Luthra's forehead.

'That's right. Fifty goddamned acres! Puts spiders in your belly, Luthra?'

'No, no, huzoor. But Naga workers getting scarce day by day, sahib. They become very proudy, demand much money. Too many gardens opening all over.'

'Well, if you can't hire Nagas, have the garden coolies do the job. Fifty acres. I'll not have an inch less, do you hear?'

Luthra's stupid face betrayed no emotion. '*Ji huzoor,*' he said.

'I've brought back a batch of recruits. They should be here any moment. Put them in the sheds for new arrivals. A week's rest for them, then they shall be put to work. Two of them must be kept apart. Bircha and Meghu. Unbind their wrists, but put chains on their feet.'

A gleam of joy lit up Luthra's face. 'Trouble makers, sahib?'

'That's right. Been nothing but trouble, those two. Tried to escape at Calcutta. Almost throttled Budhu this morning. They must be kept apart. It's the dog-house for them.'

'You wish them tamed, sahib?'

'Yes. I don't care how you do it, but I want the fire out of them.'

Doctor Gordon, who had been sitting quietly, looked surprised. 'You'd better tell your sirdar to take it easy on those two. A maimed coolie won't be of any earthly use to you.'

'Leave that to my judgement, will you, Bill? You know the human body, but you know nothing of the human mind. I have the biggest work force around these parts, except perhaps Cinnamora. A sacrifice or two helps to keep the work force in control.'

'Have you considered an alternative, Chris?'

'There's none. Just imagine, Bill. I'm alone for months together amongst my two hundred odd coolies. What prevents them from rising up as one man and cutting me down? Fear, Bill. Not merely physical fear, but stark, naked terror of the mind. That's my only weapon.'

Buckingham turned to Luthra. 'I've brought a cache of *vilayati paani* for you, Puran, Budhu and Gandru. Better than the muck you brew in the basti. Share it among yourselves.'

Luthra grinned happily. Buckingham was about to dismiss him with a wave of his hands when Gordon intruded. 'You've forgotten one thing, Chris.'

Buckingham laughed. 'Oh yes, of course! Luthra, Gordon sahib needs someone to console him through the hot and humid night! Can you suggest someone?'

Luthra's grin widened. 'There's one. Lachmi … Sanatan's wife. She's good at consoling. You know her well, sahib.'

'Do I? Oh yes, I suppose so. Send her to the bungalow at seven. But have her take a good bath before that. Give her a new cake of soap. You can get one from Chotu.'

The planter and the doctor retreated into the bungalow for their afternoon siesta. Luthra too left to carry out his chores.

'The light hurts my eyes,' Papa said in the voice of a tired child. 'Carry me to my bed.'

Cordelia raised her head from his lap, her eyes watery. Willing herself into greater resolve, she set about making his bed, to which David gently carried him. Asking him to leave the room, she undressed the stricken man and cleaned him up as best she could. When David and the Reverend entered the room, they found that the planter had drifted off to sleep.

David said, 'We've been discussing it, the Reverend and I. Papa needs a doctor urgently.'

'Doctor Gordon is at Bihguri,' the padre spoke in measured tones, wary of her response. 'If you recall, my child, Buckingham had offered to send him to examine your Papa.'

'Bapu babu informs us it's half-hour by elephant to Bihguri … if we take the short cut from Dhanboa. We can be there and back much before sundown,' David said.

Cordelia caught her brother's arm. 'There's not a moment to waste, David,' she cried. 'Go and fetch Doctor Gordon.'

'No,' said the padre. 'Let David remain by your side. I'll go with Bapu babu.'

'Sit with Papa for a bit, will you, David, while I prepare some broth for him.' She turned to the coolie boy who, apparently, was Papa's helper. '*Tumhara naam kya hein*?'

'Mongla,' the boy replied.

'*Mere saath ao*.' She emerged from the room, harvested some vegetables from the small vegetable patch at the back of the hut, and made a vegetable broth.

'He has to eat, you know!' she told Mongla, for no apparent reason.

'Yes, yes,' the boy said eagerly. 'Sahib eats too little. Only drinks *vilayati paani*. Morn and eve sahib drinks *vilayati paani*!'

The boy's words pierced her soul like a rapier, but her face remained emotionless. 'We'll have to change that, won't we, Mongla? But get going about your tasks, while I take a look around.'

She skirted around the cattle-shed to peek at what lay behind it, and reeled back as if a fist had been thrust at her face. A huge pile of empty whisky bottles glittered in the afternoon sunshine.

The sun was on the verge of setting when Garry Swanson, accompanied by Buckingham and Gordon, reached Dhanboa. The doctor examined the patient with painstaking thoroughness. David and Cordelia stood by the bedside, hope and fear alternating on their features.

Christopher James Buckingham was also in the room, standing close beside Cordelia, a layer of anxious solicitude impasted upon his handsome face. But the girl was oblivious of his presence. She was blind to everything else but her Papa, her dazed eyes following each move the doctor made. At last, the physician concluded his examination. However, he said nothing about the patient's condition.

'Prepare some broth for him, my dear,' he told Cordelia.

'I've already done that, Doctor Gordon.'

'Excellent. Feed him with a spoon … as slowly as possible. If you administer it too quickly, he might throw up.'

'I understand, doctor.'

'I shall prescribe no medicine. What he requires now is careful nursing. And nourishment. I shall come again tomorrow.'

With no further elucidation the man of medicine waddled quickly out of the room. Cordelia remained by her father's side, while the three men followed the doctor out. They paused on the front lawn where the elephant and the sirdar waited.

'Your father is in very bad shape, David,' Doctor Gordon told the young man. 'His pulse is very feeble, his heart-beats irregular. He is emaciated almost beyond recovery.'

'Is there no hope at all?' David cried out in anguish.

'It would be unjust of me to raise false expectations. Only a miracle can save your father now, David. All you can do is pray for such a miracle.'

The young man held himself in control with great difficulty. 'Thank you, Doctor Gordon, for coming to examine Papa. And thank you too, Mr Buckingham.'

'Well, what are neighbours for?' Buckingham said, as he and the doctor bid the young man goodbye, with a renewed pledge to come again the following morning.

They mounted their elephant and set off for Bihguri.

'Esscombe looked a dead man to me,' Buckingham said as they passed out of earshot.

'He is,' said Gordon. 'A wonder he's survived this long! He was a dead man weeks ago!'

'Perhaps the hope of seeing his children kept him alive?'

'The human will, Chris, can be strangely obstinate. Esscombe had kept himself alive by sheer strength of mind.'

'But now that hope has been fulfilled!' the planter said, his voice ruminative.

'I'm afraid so. I give him less then twenty-four hours! Nothing that I could do, of course.'

'The boy looked absolutely stupefied. He hadn't expected to see his father in such a bad state.'

'The girl even more so! Your magnanimous posture of good neighbourliness was wasted, old boy! I doubt she even noticed you were there.'

'There's time enough for that. A dead father … a whelp for a brother! On yes, there's time enough for that!'

'You're being perverse now, Chris!' said Gordon, not in rebuke, but with a dry chortle. 'That aborted shipboard romance rankles yet, I see. Her father is on his deathbed and you are already contemplating the role of a suitor for yourself!'

'A suitor? Not I! You needn't worry on that score.' Buckingham's voice was harsh with suppressed anger. 'I shall be the eternal spider, Bill old chap, weaving an eternal web.'

Dinner was ready by the time they got back. After the meal they sat for a while on the verandah, smoking cheroots and discussing affairs of the garden. Then Doctor Gordon bid the planter good night and retired to his bedroom.

A tantalizing fragrance touched Gordon's nostrils the minute he entered, bringing goose pimples to his skin and fire to his loins. Gordon shut the door and placed the bar in its socket. He paused for a moment to let his eyes adjust and then called out softly, 'Lachmi?'

She had been squatting patiently on the floor amongst the shadows. She now rose languidly and floated towards him. Lachmi was naked. Her clothes lay strewn on the floor. The yellow light of the lantern fell on her body and gave it a supernatural lustre, as if her limbs and heavy breasts and the flat belly were moulded of gold. Gordon smelt the heady fragrance she emitted and the fire in him exploded into white lust. Then, when he too was naked, she slithered her arms around his blubbery frame, pressing her own naked body to his, stoking his lust to a pitch when he could no longer contain himself. Like a wrestler Gordon's pudgy arms went around her waist, he pulled her down onto the mud-backed floor and threw himself upon her.

The floor was hard and cold under her, but the mass of flesh above her was hot and quivering. Her body too was cold and hard as the mud floor, but the frenzied man who puffed and panted seemed unmindful of that. All the time, at the back of her mind, were Luthra's vicious words, hurled at her along with the fresh cake of soap and phial of vilayati perfume. 'Sahib's guest needs warming. So warm him, you bitch! If he complains to the sahib tomorrow, I'll take it out on Sanatan!'

So she dug her fingers into his spongy buttocks, moaning and making yearning sounds as he entered her, her simulated passion surpassing his. Abruptly the man emitted a series of throaty grunts and lay limp and exhausted on top of her, his body heavy on her own. She uncurled her legs and lay spreadeagled on the floor till the man slid off her, pulled her onto her feet and led her to the narrow bed set against a wall.

Thrice more that night she aroused him, Luthra's mocking face urging her on. Then, when he lay satiated and snoring on the bed she arose, put on her clothes, and glided noiselessly out of the bedroom. Leaving the bungalow by the backdoor, she slid ghost-like into the night and the light from the half-moon guided her way. All around her rose the baying of jackals interspersed with the barking of pariah mongrels in the coolie basti. At last, she reached the tumbledown hovel she could claim as her home. She stripped and bathed her defiled body, scrubbing it with the soap Luthra had given her. She could wash clean the mucus from her loins but the stains of defilement lay unwashed in her heart.

Re-wrapping herself in her clothes she tiptoed into the single-roomed hut where her family cooked, ate and slept. On the tattered sheet of hessian spread across the floor lay Sanatan, her husband, and her two children, a boy and a girl, five and two years old. Taking care not to wake them she lay down alongside, keeping the children between herself and her husband. But Sanatan was awake and called out softly, with gentleness and love, 'Lachmi, is that you?'

He received no reply. But the sibilant sounds of her stifled sobs, emerging from the very depth of her being, floated clearly in the night's silence.

With Mongla's assistance Cordelia wrapped a gamocha around her father's throat and poured a spoonful of the thick, tepid liquid into his mouth. The sick man's throat constricted as he struggled to swallow the spoonful; he gagged and retched; and the broth, mixed with his own spittle, oozed out of the corners of his lips. Patiently, with a touch that was feathery soft, she wiped away the slimy expectorate and fed him again, half a spoonful this time. But try as she might the broth would not travel down his throat.

Then the convulsions started. A slight tremble at first; the eyes of the sick man thrust wide open and the eyeballs rolled back till only the whites were visible. The mouth too was a big, hollow well, with the tongue curled back out of sight. The spasms became progressively violent—the frail, fleshless body thrashed and jerked. Cordelia, unprepared for such a grisly sight, lost whatever control she had and screamed in terror. David too was petrified. Only Garry Swanson moved; grabbing some blankets he piled them upon the convulsing man and flung himself on him, holding the bony frame in a vise-like grip to halt the violent tremblings.

At the very first signs of convulsion Mongla had raced out of the room. He was back in a matter of moments, carrying a bottle of brandy from some secret cache. 'Sahib tells me to give him vilayati paani when this happens,' he said, thrusting the half-filled bottle at Swanson. The padre uncorked the bottle and, holding the rolling head firmly with his left hand, poured a little of it down the man's gaping mouth.

Curiously, the very throat which had rejected the broth accepted this libation willingly, almost greedily. The tongue moved to lap up the brandy as Swanson poured a little more, and sought even more. But the Reverend re-corked the bottle and handed it to Mongla and continued to hold the trembling body in his arms.

Slowly, as the brandy took effect, the spasms wracking the body eased. The dying man began to perspire freely. A transient flush crept onto his cheeks and erased the sallowness. His eyes opened, swept across Cordelia's face, then David's, and finally came to rest upon the padre's hirsute visage; they widened a little, as if he were seeing the man of God for the first time.

'No time … no time.' He spoke in a voice that was remarkably strong. 'Father, you've come as an angel of hope … must speak to you … alone … no time … no time.'

Swanson glanced towards Cordelia. She nodded and guided David out. Mongla followed them, leaving the padre with the dying man.

'I've sinned, Father,' Esscombe said. 'I must make confession … ready myself to face my Maker.'

'You may speak, my son.' The man of God took Esscombe's limp hands in his own and bent low to catch the words.

Esscombe spoke. He took the padre back the span of three years to distant Calcutta, to a merchant named Alexander Swinnerton-Dyer, to a time when Dhanboa did not exist. The padre listened, nodding every once in a while, but not intruding, silently piecing together the disjoined tale.

Henry David Esscombe's life had been a series of commercial disasters climaxed by the calamity which struck them during the 1857 Sepoy Uprising and, in effect, had virtually reduced him to a pauper.

'You must understand, Father … I was getting no younger … my concern for David and Cordi made me desperate … a cynical disillusionment overshadowed all my actions … blunted my moral sensibility … a sensibility which had sustained me throughout my life …' Esscombe's eyes pleaded for comprehension.

The padre nodded. 'I understand. Go on, my son.'

Unless Esscombe did something drastic he and his dear children faced the prospect of impoverishment. No help was to be had at Delhi; so, early in the year 1858, although British military action had not yet ceased in isolated pockets of sepoy resistance, and conditions were not settled enough to be deemed safe, he risked a journey to Calcutta, arriving there towards the end of April. He could have availed himself of the hospitality of his old acquaintances in the city; but, instead, he took up rooms in a boarding establishment at Chowringhee.

The metropolitan trading circle at the time was abuzz with talk of the commercial opportunities the Assam Company's success in cultivating and manufacturing tea in Assam had opened up for European entrepreneurs. Esscombe had frequented the bar of the Great Eastern Hotel, conversed with strangers and discovered in them an obsession with the brew, and chauvinistic pride at the prospect of establishing a British Tea Empire in Hindustan, thereby bringing down the haughty pride of imperial Cathay.

As he talked and listened, probed and learnt, his own imagination was fired, and a plan gradually took shape. He would fling himself into the last act of the fading drama that was his life, go to Assam and start a tea plantation.

What Esscombe lacked was finance; with a cunning alien to his character, he schemed to make good the lacuna. The target was to be his close colleague from the East India Company days, Alexander Swinnerton-Dyer. He knew that no amount of convincing would persuade his colleague to invest in his planned enterprise. Alex would have to be coerced into lightening his purse. For this, his life would have to be scrutinized with a magnifying glass in the hope of discovering a chink in the armour of his solid respectability.

For a month Esscombe dogged Alex's footsteps—in adequate disguise—and discovered his Achilles' heel, an old failing in the merchant for naked, dusky bodies. The ageing Patricia, who had been passably beautiful in her youth, had grown fat and querulous and could no longer quench the flames yet raging in the merchant's loins. So, he had taken to visiting Karaya Lane, the infamous whore-street which provided solace to lonely Europeans. On four occasions Esscombe had followed the respectable merchant, seen him alight from his phaeton and enter a dingy, ill-lit tenement. That had been enough.

'Just a hint, Father … the soothsayer Allauddin and his warning … a transparent piece of subterfuge … blackmail … wouldn't have worked if Alex had not been so infernally conscious of his respectability …' The dying man's voice faltered and the shame, guilt and agony of his act burst forth from deep-sunk eyes.

'I understand,' the padre said. 'But who amongst men of clay can claim to be without sin? We're all sinners, my son, conscious or unconscious. But the good Lord has shown us a way out … the path of repentance … you have chosen that path. The Lord's all merciful, my son. He has felt the agony in your heart as though it were his own. He will forgive you, my son.'

At the padre's words the face of the dying man underwent a wondrous transformation. The dark despair befogging it was blown away by the gentle breeze of hope. The contours of the face changed, the bony edges softened. 'The Lord will forgive me, Father?'

'Yes, my son, He will. But we must all pray together.'

David and Cordelia re-entered at his summons. The trio knelt beside the bed, clasped their palms and closed eyes in an attitude of devout prayer. Though the dying man had spent the remnant of his strength in pouring out his confession, yet he mustered up enough from some hidden reserve to clasp the nerveless fingers of his hands together. Mongla, who too had come into the room, imitated the sahiblog, fell to his knees and adopted an attitude of worship.

They prayed for almost an hour. The padre's voice, as he recited passages of the Bible from memory—spacing the words so that David and Cordelia could repeat after him—emerged hollow and sepulchral within the closed space of the mud-walled, ceilingless room. The dying man attempted to utter the words but his strength soon failed him, and he lay supine, listening to the others. Lulled by the hypnotic reiteration of their voices, he slowly drifted into sleep.

Long after the prayer session was over the three of them continued to squat on murrahs beside the bed, silent, each wrapt in unvoiced reflections. The young native menial stretched himself on the floor and slept.

Cordelia's gaze was fixed on Papa's face. An unearthly serenity overspread the attenuated features. She no longer harboured any illusions; she knew that Papa was dying. Yet the tranquillity layering his features now, in marked contrast to the haggard, haunted look that had been there before he had opened his soul to the Reverend, filled her with a strange sense of repose, even of joy. She was no longer the little girl who could demand immortality of her father—he would be dead soon, and she must rejoice at the serenity that glowed softly on his face.

Then the darkness began to melt, the light of the taper dimmed in intensity, the shadows within the room slowly dissolved. Somewhere a cock crowed.

The dying man spoke with great difficulty, 'Cordi, David, come closer.' The daughter and son moved up and sat at the edge of the bed, each holding one of their father's hands.

'I hung on till you came,' their father spoke again, the voice barely a whisper. 'I can hang on no longer. I'm sorry Cordi. David.'

'Hush, Papa. You mustn't talk,' Cordelia said.

'Dhanboa's your home, David. Cherish this garden as you would cherish my memory. Deal gently with the coolies. Their whims might infuriate you, but be patient. Show compassion. Bapu babu will teach you all you'll need of tea. He's a good man. Treat him as a brother.'

David, too overcome to speak, dipped his head. 'You'll find a box in one of the trunks. Contains money, what remains of the sum given by your Uncle Alex. I've been thrifty. There's enough there to see you though the next two seasons. Deal fairly with your godfather. Cordi, my darling, take good care of David. Tell the Reverend. I see a brilliant light in the distance, and hear your mother call out. Goodbye, Cordi. Good bye, David.'

Once again, his body contorted in spasms, he gasped out the name of God and was abruptly still, eyes wide open as if startled into immobility. Henry David Esscombe was dead.

For one incredulous, unbelieving moment Cordelia stared at the death-still body. She shook the limp form, calling out 'Papa! Papa!' Frantically she scoured for the brandy bottle, found it, and tried to pour some into his mouth. The liquor dribbled down the dead man's throat, its fumes filled the air. Cordelia shrieked, a wail that emanated from the very depth of her soul, and flung her head onto his chest, her body shaking violently with her sobs.

David too wept openly. Mongla, awakened by the shriek, and realizing that Esscombe sahib was dead, set up a wail. Bapu babu, who had spent the night in the dispensing room, came rushing in. 'Esscombe sahib is dead!' the padre told him.

Bapu babu ran out as fast as his dhoti-clad legs could carry him. Minutes later the pagal ghanta sounded in a mournful toll for the dead. The coolies, alerted by the sound, came pouring out of their hutments and hurried towards the sahib's cottage. They squatted at some distance from the tiny bungalow and commenced a piteous wail which fell with a strange familiarity on Cordelia's ears, carrying her back to a sandbank and blazing pyres.

Never before in her life had Cordelia felt a more intimate rapport with any human beings as she did now with the coolies. They mourned her father with a grief that equalled her own and imbued her with vitality by taking on some of her load of despair. She pulled herself away from her father's dead body, dried her tears and made a supreme endeavour at self-composure. David put his arm around her shoulders and lent her some of his own strength.

'There must be a quick burial,' the Reverend said. 'Without the services of an undertaker a body decomposes quickly in this heat and humidity.'

'We'll need a coffin, Father,' David said.

Bapu babu, who stood close by, heard this. 'Coffin?' he asked. 'But Papa Esscombe sahib make coffin many moons behind! He show our village *kaath mistri* and he make. It lives in chang-bungalow he make for you.'

'Please fetch it, Bapu babu,' said David.

'A very thoughtful man, your Papa,' the Reverend remarked. 'He didn't burden you much in life. Nor does he burden you in death.'

The wailing outside, which had diminished in pitch, reached a crescendo when the coffin emerged. Cordelia, David and the others sat on the grass beside the wooden casket, as the mourning coolies filed past to bid a final farewell to Esscombe sahib. Many of them carried bunches of wild flowers and fragrant orchids, which they reverentially placed on the body. Meanwhile, Doctor Gordon and Buckingham arrived. They expressed no surprise that Esscombe was dead, but assisted the padre in having a deep pit dug in the middle of the garden by some coolies, and fashioning a rudimentary cross from the branches of a tree. Sometime later grave-faced rustics from Bapu babu's village came to pay their last respects. And then, amidst silence punctuated only by the stentorian voice of Reverend Garry Swanson as he read out from his pocket Bible, the coffin was lowered into the pit; clods of earth were shoveled in to cover the casket, and the cross fixed upright at the head of the grave.

It happened so quickly that Cordelia, benumbed with grief, could not yet reconcile herself to the reality that Papa, the one person who could have armed her with the resilience to rebuild her shattered life, lay buried under six feet of earth. Someone thrust a bunch of flowers into her hands. Eyes blinded by tears, she moved in slow motion to the grave, placed the flowers and kissed the ground in a gesture which marked irrevocable parting, and then half-walked and half-ran into Papa's cottage. She stumbled into the bedroom and collapsed in one corner.

While the rest of the new batch of Buckingham's coolies were lodged in a shed, Bircha and Meghu had been shoved into what Buckingham called his doghouse. It was an apt sobriquet, actually resembling a kennel, a four-by-four-by-four feet wooden structure, without any outlets save a low door through which one had to crawl inside, and which could be bolted from outside.

The hands of the two coolies had been unfettered but their legs were manacled, so they could not run but hobble about in an ungainly fashion. Two days and a night they had spent in the fetid air of the doghouse; had it not been for the minute gaps between the planks they would have suffocated to death.

'Arrey Bircha-bhaiya,' said Meghu, his cramped body racked in pain. 'They mean to starve us to death.'

'Don't worry, brother,' said his companion. 'These madarchods won't kill us. They paid us an advance, don't you remember?'

'You're too hot-headed, Bircha-bhaiya. They'd have battered us to death at the ghat itself, had not that white bastard stopped them.'

'And whose fault is it that we were on board at all, Meghu-bhaiya? Who accepted that fellow's invitation for a bite to eat and a bottle to drink?'

'Yes, I'd been a fool. But Bircha-bhaiya, we have to think of survival now.'

'So, what do you think we should do?' his companion asked.

'Act meek as mice, brother. Call them mai-baap. Grease your words with mustard oil, Bircha-bhaiya, if you want to live. And once the mother-rapers are convinced they've broken us and call off the monkeys who, I am ashamed to say, are of our kind, we'll run like the cheetah through these jungles, and go where our kismet takes us.'

'You're right. I'll tremble before them like a frog that has seen the snake's eyes! But let me tell you, one day I'll put my hands round their necks and throttle the life out of them.'

'Hush, I hear footsteps! Maybe they're coming to let us out. Remember, act as if they've broken your balls.'

Meghu was right. They, meaning Luthra, Puran, Budhu and Gandru, had indeed come for them. The sirdars had been drinking the vilayati paani Buckingham sahib had gifted. Like their master the whisky brought the shaitan into them. They had put the troublesome coolies into the doghouse as their master had ordered. They had starved the two. And now, fired by the whisky and the bestial streak which had always been in them, they had come to tame the wild dogs!

Luthra unbolted the door. The two coolies crawled out, surprised to find it dark, for they had lost all sense of day and night. But the half-moon provided enough light for them to see the vicious smiles on their captors' faces. They had risen unsteadily to their feet; but once they sensed the atmosphere of aggressive violence they dropped to the ground and grabbed Luthra's legs.

'Huzoor, mai-baap,' Meghu whined, clutching Luthra's legs. 'We've had enough! I swear in the name of my mother that we'll be like slaves to you, sahib.'

'Huh!' said the surprised Luthra. 'You hear that, Puran? He called me sahib!'

'You're our mai-baap,' Bircha desperately chipped in. 'We'll give no more trouble.'

'The wild dogs have been tamed, I see,' said Puran.

Luthra seemed pleased. 'What says you, Puran? Have they been tamed enough?'

But it was Budhu who answered. He was the sirdar whom Bircha had assaulted on the riverbank. He was not to be deprived of his revenge.

'The bastards need more taming, Luthra,' he said. 'What would Buckingham sahib say if he saw them unscarred? What would the other bastards in the basti think? That we've lost our testicles?'

Budhu delivered a brutal kick on the unsuspecting Bircha. That kick seemed to be contagious, for no further deliberations took place. The inebriated sirdars began kicking and pummelling the helpless duo, battering them in senseless fury till their bodies went limp. Then they dragged them into the shed housing the new arrivals and flung them into an unoccupied corner.

'Let's hope we haven't killed them,' Luthra said. 'Otherwise, Buckingham sahib will eat our livers raw tomorrow.'

Henry David Esscombe had spent three dreadful years sequestered in his tiny mud hovel, a bamboo platform for a bed, wooden chest for a table.

But such had been his love and concern for his children that he had built for them a new bungalow before they arrived at Dhanboa.

By no stretch of the imagination could this bungalow be called a grand structure but, in contrast to the rude hut occupied by their father, it looked to them as magnificent as a Mughal palace. The entire edifice stood six feet above the ground upon trunks of teak—three rows of four each. The doors and windows too were made out of wood. The bungalow possessed a confidence-inspiring solidity.

A four-feet wide verandah, balustraded, ran along the entire outer edge of the bungalow; a small corridor bisected the structure into two unequal halves, the smaller having three rooms, the larger five, including the dining chamber and a spare bedroom. It was almost as if Papa had set apart the smaller, isolated section for his daughter. Cordelia could believe he had prognostications of his own death but how could he have known she would tag along with David, or of her present fierce resolve to make Dhanboa her home? Such a certainty had been born of the closeness of their love, an insight engendered by the perfect understanding between a father and a daughter.

Brother Garry Swanson's fortuitous presence at Dhanboa had helped her retain her sanity. He had infused in her fortitude to bear up to the twin assaults—Michael's departure and Papa's death. David too had been invigorated by his presence and repeatedly turned to him for advice and guidance. The siblings were two orphaned waifs in an alien world. The Reverend was aware of their helplessness and, despite the urgent need to return to his mission, had deferred his departure by a couple of days.

But he could not be expected to postpone it any longer, and thus it was that, early on the third morning after they had buried Papa, the Reverend, David and she sat on the verandah of the new bungalow, the padre due to leave within the hour.

'The last few days have been a revelation,' the Reverend said. 'A week back, if you'd asked me, I would have denied that a tea plantation like Dhanboa really existed. One in which the coolies are not half-crazed with fear … where coolie men wear smiles on their faces, coolie women flowers in their hair! They held your father in affectionate respect. Tells you a lot about him, doesn't it?'

Cordelia's heart warmed at the padre's words but David, too full of his own anxieties, took no comfort. 'I feel utterly lost without him,' he confessed. 'Frankly, Father, I don't know what to do. Opening Dhanboa had been Papa's idea, not mine. Had it not been for his last words, I'd be tempted to sell off this garden.'

'You can still do that, David,' the padre said. 'Your Papa wouldn't have wanted to saddle you with something you had no liking for.'

'No,' David said, squaring his shoulders. 'I am bound by a sacred obligation. I cannot go back on my pledge. I'm stuck with Dhanoa but sis must return. This is no place for her.'

'I shan't be going back,' Cordelia said firmly. 'My place is here ... by your side, David.'

'I understand, sis. It's because Michael is around somewhere, isn't it? But you harbour false hopes. Michael belongs to the past.'

'You do me an injustice, David!' Cordelia cried out. 'It's you, and you alone, who keep me at Dhanboa. Oh David, with Papa gone, who do we have but each other?'

David saw the hurt in her eyes and was contrite. 'But there's hardly a thing to occupy you at Dhanboa. I'll be up to my neck in work. Won't be much of a companion, I'm afraid.'

'You're wrong, David. I shan't have the least problem keeping myself occupied. Papa did the doctoring in the garden, I'll take his place ... run the dispensary ... that will be a load off you. Papa has a medical manual by Doctor Goodeve. I can read that. Then there are the coolies; I must work for their welfare. Keep the bungalow spick and span, care for the poultry and the cows, maintain the kitchen garden ... Why, David, there are a thousand and one things at Dhanboa to occupy me. And, of course, there's looking after you.'

She had spoken more than she intended to, and with greater vehemence. Her earnestness brought a smile to David's face and he said, 'Now, now, sis! I'm not going to force you to go! But the novelty will wear off after a while, you know. Perhaps the loneliness and lack of society might make you regret your decision then.'

'Dhanboa's my home, David,' Cordelia said with finality. 'I shan't ever regret my decision.'

David was about to say something but the Reverend intruded. 'She can be of immense help to you, David. And of immense help to herself. Isn't that so, my child?'

Cordelia nodded. How perceptive the Reverend was!

'Well, in that case I'd better find a niche for your dispensary. Papa's cottage is an eyesore. We'll have to pull it down.'

Cordelia was aghast. 'Pull it down, David? You must be out of your mind! It's one object which will keep Papa alive in our hearts. Leave the cottage be. The medicine-room must stay where Papa had it.'

'But sis, it's in a shambles, really! To repair and maintain it would be so much money down the drain.'

'Nothing's too expensive to keep Papa's memory alive! I'll take care of the cottage … and Papa's grave, and the garden around it.'

The padre agreed with her. 'It's essential to keep your Papa's memory alive, David,' he said. 'His memory would be a lantern lighting your way … and, of course, the inspiration for you to deal with your coolies with justice and humanity.'

'On no account will I let Papa down! I had looked to him to guide me … My grief at his death was tinged with anger. I had permitted only my grief to find expression but over the last few nights, whenever I have been alone, I have had bitter thoughts.'

'That's quite normal, my son, for a heavy burden has been thrust upon you. You know nothing of growing tea … You are overwhelmed with inadequacy … but such feelings will be erased by the passage of time. As you learn more of tea-craft, you will be filled with inner strength to carry out the pledge you gave your father.'

'Yes, I suppose so,' the young man said haltingly. 'You know, Father, the other day, after we buried Papa, Buckingham renewed his offer to teach me about tea. He's asked me to drop in at Bihguri as often as I can.'

'You can't do that, David' Cordelia said anxiously. 'You can't go to Bihguri! It was Papa's wish that you learn about tea from Bapu babu.'

'Oh, come on now, sis! Buckingham's an experienced planter. He'll prove a far better teacher than Bapu babu, who's so devilishly incomprehensible most of the time.'

'But Papa's wishes must be respected,' Cordelia said obdurately. 'He wished that you learn about tea from Bapu babu. You'll not go against what Papa wanted, will you?'

Her brother, having no answer, looked helplessly at the Reverend. 'Why not give Bapu babu a try?' the padre suggested tactfully. 'He might prove to be better teacher than you think.'

'All right, I'll do that,' David said, not pressing the issue. 'I shall start this very day. To tell you the truth, sis, I'm glad you'll be around. If you take care of the house and the dispensary, I'll be free to concentrate on the garden.'

'That's the spirit, David,' the padre said. 'Ah, but I think I hear Bapu babu at the stairs.'

The padre warmly clasped David and Cordelia's hands. 'Goodbye, Cordelia. Goodbye, David. It'll be quite some time before I can pay another visit to Dhanboa. But do keep writing to me. I shall anxiously await news from you.'

The brother and sister duo saw him off at the Dhanboa ghat. The boatmen pushed off, and the large craft slid swiftly downstream, leaving David and Cordelia with the curious sensation of having suffered another bereavement.

On the morning of 21 October, a large country-boat, laden with sacks of pulses, atta and potatoes, approached Kokilamukh. On its prow sat Lieutenant Michael Bailin, Garo Munda stood by his side. The three weeks since his unobserved departure from the *Ultaganga* had witnessed a terrible loss of weight in him. His lineaments were lean and unshaven, his eyes were blood-shot and black patches had formed round the sockets. This was as much due to the inability to sleep he had been experiencing from the time he had left the steamer, as to his excessive intake of mod—the fermented liquor the boatmen had provided to assist him in overcoming the bouts of insomnia.

Bailin and Garo's stealthy escape from the steamer had been adroitly effected upon a country-craft about to depart from Gowhatty. The boat had set off a little after they had embarked, the *Ultaganga* passing it the next day, with Bailin and Garo concealed under the soi till it disappeared from sight.

Reverend Garry Swanson had pencilled a line on the map he had been given by Leach to denote a rough route from Kokilamukh to Chahpuli—up the Disoi and across a network of tiny streams to the vicinity of the village of Titabar. The more Garo looked at the map the more certain he grew that he could lead his master to Chahpuli. He had been to Titabar and knew that one native passenger on the steamer, Gokuldeva Barua, lived in that village and had a mansion there, a giant of a building made of brick and mortar, with roofing of corrugated iron and a large compound. Barua's small plantation lay a mile from Titabar in the direction in which Chahpuli was.

Bailin told him, in halting Assamese, all that the other sahib called Leach who had opened out Chahpuli had informed him about that tea plantation. It was a large garden, a land claim of seven hundred and odd acres according to the papers, although only a hundred acres had been cleared and planted upon. The population of workers numbered around sixty; their wages had been paid till December that year so he did not need to worry about that. There were two sirdars; Leach had even given their names, Gobordhan and Phuchua, and in Leach's absence a native clerk by the name of Saikia babu was managing the property.

Within half an hour of touching Kokilamukh, Bailin and Garo were once more on their way—despite the Lieutenant sensing the onset of a fever—first on a light canoe with three boatmen guiding it and, afterwards, when Garo judged they were close to his master's garden, on foot across the thickly-shrubbed land. Hours of slow progress later, on the last reserves of their energy, the native gave a yell of discovery. Bailin forced his legs to move faster and the two of them reached the clearing, set like an oasis amidst the surrounding jungle. It was square in shape, a bare ten acres or so of unfenced, open area, overgrown with vegetation! There was a single man-made structure in the entire area, a dilapidated bamboo and thatch hutment, with gaping holes in the roof so that bars of bamboo showed through the thatch. Much of the clearing was occupied by straggling rows of waist-high bushes.

'A chah plant, sahib!' Garo said with undisguised perplexity. 'But a dead one!'

With a growing sense of urgency Bailin pulled up a tea bush, then another and yet another. No tea plants grew in that small clearing. All were cut branches planted in the ground to give the appearance of a tea garden. It was as if some prankster had wilfully erected a stage in which to play a monstrous practical joke!

A sinking feeling gnawed at Bailin's entrails and he cried out, 'For heaven's sake, Garo, search! Seek something … anything … that will give us a clue to this place!'

As it turned out, they did not have to search for long. One step into the mud-floor of the tumbledown hutment and the answer they sought was provided—on a wooden signboard, ant-eaten at the edges, the only object in the empty shack, 'Chahpuli Tea Plantation, Prop. Theodore Leach,' tauntingly painted upon it.

There was no Saikia babu, no Gobardhan and Phuchua. They were all phantoms conjured up by an evil wizard in Calcutta. There was no coolie basti, no tea house. There was only the emptiness in the heart and demented hammering on the brain. The walls and roof of the hutment moved round and round with increasing pace; a half-human, half-animal cry of despair and desolation emerged from Bailin's throat and he plunged to the ground in a dead faint.

BOOK TWO

THE VALLEY

Sirdar bole, kaam-kaam,
Babu bole, dhore-aan,
Sahib bole, lib pither chaam,
Hai re nithur Shyam,
Phaki maari anaili Assam ...

The sirdar says, work, work,
The babu says, catch and bring him here,
The sahib says, whip the skin off his back,
Oh, you heartless God,
You betrayed when you brought us to Assam ...

—Assam tea-plucker's song

Dear Aunt Patricia,

David and I arrived at Dhanboa on the afternoon of the fourth of October. Papa died at night on that very day. It was only his fierce desire to see us before he died that had made his mind will his body to stay alive. Once we were with him and he had thrust Dhanboa's responsibilities upon David, that strength of mind gave way .

We had to bury Papa quickly—the damp, heat and insects not permitting otherwise—in a simple grave, with a rudely constructed cross to it. But, dear aunt, we must have something more permanent, a headstone with his name and an epigraph upon it, to keep his memory alive. I write to you with a request that you dispatch the same by the earliest steamer.

David wished I return to Calcutta. You and Uncle Alex must be desirous of the same. But I cannot return to Calcutta with my heart empty and my mind in pain; I will wilt in the heat and dust of Calcutta, with nothing to fill up the emptiness. Here I have David as well as Dhanboa which Papa built up bush by bush. David's welfare would be my primary concern.

There is another compelling reason that must bind my future inexorably to Dhanboa ... The *Ultaganga* had a flat in tow; five dozen coolies, men, women and children, were transported on it and landed at Kokilamukh. Not all, for cholera stuck midway and half of them perished enroute. There were babies and toddlers in that group of coolies! Not one of them survived! That night, when I saw those dead bodies burning on the sandbank, what had till then been a vague desire inside me firmed into a resolve. I would have, perhaps, taken up the coolies' cause even if Papa had been hale and alive and not dead and buried.

That, dear aunt, is also what keeps me tied to Dhanboa. Papa was an exception as he had been throughout his life. The coolies in Dhanboa lead a better life than their brethren in other plantations. But a lot still remains to be done; with Papa gone I shall be his instrument to make Dhanboa a better place for the coolies!

Papa had built a bungalow for me and David; a quaint little house on stilts of a kind you must never have seen. Papa's hutment lay empty. I have since then converted it into a dispensary, with a medicine-room and two beds for patients. I have persuaded a young man in Bapu babu's village, a relative of his by the name of Kamal, to work in my little dispensary as an assistant at a salary of fifteen rupees a month. We have an adequate stock of medicines; it appears that Papa had laid the utmost stress upon keeping his medicine cabinet full, because every coolie life is precious to Dhanboa, and the death of one means a depletion of the workforce. That was the paradox in the final years of his life; he thought of what was best for us, he took care of the health of his coolies, but denied the same thought and care to himself.

I've been studying Dr Goodeve's medical manual as best I can and discussing the matter with Bapu babu and the coolies, attempting to separate ailments most rife in this region, and preparing myself to recognize and treat them. This is the dry season, supposedly a healthier period for the population, when they are spared severer maladies such as kala-azar and cholera, which invariably break out in epidemic form in this province during the rains. Incidences of malaria are also less in these dry months; however, David and I continue to take the prescribed precautions, a daily dose of quinine. It is impossible to give this medicine daily to the coolies, for that would be prohibitively expensive so they get it only after they are actually stricken by a malarial attack. But the perennial disorders suffered by the unfortunate coolies, whether it be summer or winter, are those related to the water that they drink; diseases like dysentery and diarrhoea. Almost all the coolies, especially the children, are infested with worms, which render them vulnerable to the more pernicious ailments. David and I have taken our worm preventive, 80 minims of carbon tetrachloride; and I have personally administered the same to each and every member of the garden—in two doses for the coolies, for their constitution cannot cope with a single heavy dose. So, dear aunt, you can see that I haven't been idle. David approves thoroughly of what I am trying to do, for he too realizes that the prosperity of Dhanboa depends upon the coolies' health. But one affliction that no medicine can cure and makes me utterly helpless is snake bite; snakes proliferate everywhere, not only in the planted areas, but in the jungles, coolie basti, shallow pools of water. The most beautiful of these, the banded krait, its body striped with yellow and black, is also the deadliest; but it is a sluggish creature, as slow as the python, which though of huge length and ferocious looking, is relatively harmless. Not so the ordinary cobra, perhaps the most prolific among hamadryads, six-seven feet long—and the fearsome king cobra, which I have no yet seen, but which the coolies tell me is fourteen–sixteen feet in length and very fast and aggressive, a terrifying sight when it rears up to strike with its huge hood unfurled. The coolies, however, fear the bamboo snake more—it derives its name from appearance, thin as a whiplash, of pale, yellowish green, and extremely venomous—it has the deadly habit of remaining coiled unseen in tea bushes, and striking at pluckers of tea leaves …

One complaint against the coolies on every planter's lip aboard the steamer was that they were a lazy and indolent lot, and the whip had to be applied thick and fast if a day's work was to be got out of them. Dear aunt, for myself I have discovered that it is their physical condition, as well as the climate, and not their natural disposition that makes them so. These coolies are semi-starved and poverty-stricken when initially conscripted; the long journey debilitates them even further so that when they are landed in Assam, they are physically most unsuited to work in this damp and hot climate, and require far better nourishment. No wonder they are listless and indifferent towards their assigned tasks, and endeavour to shirk duty whenever the opportunity is offered. This is regarded as indiscipline and the planter's answer to that is the whip …

… But when treated more humanely, when it is acknowledged that they are creatures of flesh and blood and not dumb beasts for work, they impose touching trust in you and consider the plantation as their own. Dhanboa's an astonishing illustration of this. They had looked up to Papa as a kind of God—that is the image planters have sought to instill in their minds—but usually it is a god of malevolence, one that hits back with wrathful vengeance at the slightest misdemeanour. In Papa's case the image was benevolent; the coolies here really consider Dhanboa their home, and Papa was their mai-baap—a parental figure. They are a simple-minded lot, totally illiterate, ignorant and filled with superstitions; but very human in their unquestioning trust and easily content if their basic needs are met. They are not paid fixed wages, but according to the hours of work they do. Most planters take advantage of their ignorance and their inability to calculate to cheat them of their dues. If a coolie falls ill and cannot work, he or she is not paid. Thus, many coolies do not report if they are sick, and work in the hot sun even though fevered, to fall unconscious and perish. The planters can deduct from their meagre earnings for continued laziness—since the planter is the judge and the jury, he deprives the poor wretches their just dues on mere pretexts. It is all chicanery and thievery here, dear aunt —can you then wonder why I've taken up the coolies' cause?

We are trying to maintain Papa's tradition at Dhanboa—I've persuaded David to pay each coolie adult fixed monthly payment of four rupees—that is the average amount they can earn if they work an entire month. That way they are assured of a fixed income even if they fall ill or have a mishap, or are not allotted work for one reason or the other … Papa had left us an amount of money, and David has his own stock from disposal of our mansion and other things at Delhi; if these sums are utilized for bettering the coolies' lives, Dhanboa would be the ultimate gainer …

I have taken to visiting the coolie basti—it is incredible how unclean and unhealthy their living habits are, but that is because they haven't been shown a better and more hygienic way. But they are receptive to my ideas and carry them out. With the jungles around them they do not lack in firewood—I've told them to boil the water which they drink; to store the boiled water in clean earthen kolohs, which are matkas in Hindustani. I've set them to dig a chain of nullahs around the basti, so that stagnant water drains away, and to answer their calls of nature away from their hutments, in pits dug for the purpose. Such steps are but drops in the ocean—a lot more remains to be done, dear aunt, but I aim to carry them though.

The pattern in our new life has already been established. The paucity of fuel for lighting makes daylight precious. We get up with the first light, so that the whole day lies before us. Mongla, our houseboy, serves chota hazri at five, which we take along with our daily dose of quinine. Then David leaves for the garden, while I repair to my dispensary. We breakfast late at eleven a.m.; an hour or two of siesta, and David is at the garden again, while I busy myself with household chores, work with Mongla at the kitchen garden, cattle shed or the murgi coop. Supper is at half past five, while there is light enough to see by, and the insects do not rise from the grass—but I suppose as the days shorten, we will have to go in for candle-lit suppers. Then David and I sit on the verandah of our chang-bungalow talking about the garden's affairs. That is the best part of our routine, dear aunt, those few intimate moments in the evening on the verandah—alas, too brief—the insects, even in the cooler season, are sufficiently proliferate to make longer sojourns impossible. By seven we are in bed. Sometimes the coolies, in the evening, indulge in music; lilting melodies and throbbing drumbeats float up to our bungalow; but their moments of joy too are brief, for by six the basti also falls silent.

All too humdrum, isn't it, dear aunt? But it's a life which has filled me with satisfaction and helped salve the wound Papa's death had opened. There's not the least doubt in my mind that this is the only kind of life which will enable me to face a future without Papa … you must understand how vital it is for me to stay on in Dhanboa. Papa's garden is my home, dear aunt. I've something to do here; it is Dhanboa which has given a meaning to my existence.

David has written separately to Uncle Alex about the affairs of the garden. I look forward to your reply. Write quickly, for you and Uncle Alex are our sole links with the world outside. Convey my affectionate regards to Uncle Alex—yours obedient daughter, Cordi. (Dhanboa, 21 October).

Post script: The dak doesn't come to Dhanboa, but must be collected from Captain Hewitt's office at Jorehaut. But you need not worry; someone or the other from Dhanboa makes weekly trips to Jorehaut for supplies, and will collect any mail for us.

Post script: It would help me greatly if you could purchase a few medicinal volumes, such as Doctor Graham's Domestic Medicine, and send them to me.

Garo watched his master drop, aghast. Bailin lay spread-eagled on the floor. Garo bent over him and touched his forehead. It was burning with the heat of a chula. A putrid odour of decaying eggs emanated from the sahib. Garo the native reeled back and scampered towards the door. The unforgettable stench of cholera! The stench of certain death! Blind panic took hold of Garo. Images, deep buried in his consciousness, tumbled out: the scourge ravaging the coolie bastis unfailingly every monsoon, rows of rotting corpses, sacks thrown in heaps on a blazing pyre. Garo paused at the door for one final look. Then he fled.

He ran on and on till, after a while, he abruptly stopped, his mind bewildered, chest heaving. Squatting on the ground, he held his head in his hands and moaned aloud at the conflict racking his brain. Then he stood, his features resolute, and retraced his steps through the gathering darkness to the mock tea garden that was Chahpuli and the ramshackle shed where his master lay. He threw himself in one corner of the hutment, curled his arms around his legs, and slept.

Waking up the next dawn, Garo wasted little time. Unless he could get help and have his master conveyed to where he received proper treatment and nourishing sustenance, the white man was as good as dead, no matter his constitution was far stronger than that of a coolie. He must go to Titabar, seek out Gokuldeva Barua, and plead for his help.

He came out and bathed in the stream, soaping and scrubbing himself thoroughly. He put on a fresh dhoti. Spreading Bailin's map on the ground, he studied it. If he was right about Chahpuli's location on the map, the village of Titabar could not be far away. A narrow road called Na-ali linked Titabar to Jorehaut. By cutting across the jungle in a southerly direction he was sure to hit Na-ali, and thence he could walk to Titabar.

Having looked up at the newly risen sun to fix his direction, Garo entered the jungle, dao in hand. Half hour later he hit Na-ali, a wide, kutcha track through the forests; the jungle thinned out to be replaced by paddy fields, with farmers at work. Soon he was at the well-populated village of Titabar, making his way to Gokuldeva Barua's mansion. He told the gate-man that he had a message for Barua dangoriya from Bailin sahib, whom the former had met aboard the steamer while journeying from Calcutta. Soon he was allowed entry for an audience with Barua dangoriya.

Gokuldeva Barua was seated upon an elaborately ornamented chair. He was not alone; quite a few people were seated on the verandah but they sat on low, wooden pirrahs in two rows before him. Garo waited with his hands folded before him, head bowed.

The native nobleman called out to him to come up. Approaching closer, Garo fell on to his knees, touched his forehead to the floor and, still on his knees, said, '*Devata ishwar*, I come from Bailin sahib. He needs your help.'

Gokuldeva now recognized Garo. He listened impassively to the menial's tale. When Garo ended his recital he said, 'I'll have Bailin brought to Titabar. He'll have to be kept isolated for a while. But I have just the place. Now go and eat while I have men and elephants readied.'

The sun was climbing in the sky when a party of men on three elephants, led by Garo, reached Chahpuli. Taking care not to come in direct contact with the stricken man, they strapped him on a stretcher which was placed on an elephant's back, recovered his personal effects, and returned to Barua's estate. Bailin was taken to an outhouse, luxuriously furnished, with a wooden bed and adequate furniture and a bathroom and kitchen attached. As Garo watched his master being laid gently down on the wooden bed in the hut, he felt as if a huge weight had been taken off his shoulders.

Christopher James Buckingham had been recruited by the Assam Company in May 1852, at the age of twenty-five, as a probationer assistant for its tea plantations in Assam, one of the earliest direct recruits from England. He sailed for Hindustan in July on the S. S. Marlborough, and set foot in Calcutta in November, 1852. In February 1853, he left for Assam and joined the Hukanpukri plantation as an assistant.

Buckingham took to tea planting as fish to water; inbuilt traits in his character, amorality and instinct for dominance, enabled him to find self-fulfillment in the profession thrust upon him. In the lawless environment of a tea plantation, what might have been considered weaknesses elsewhere emerged as positive qualities, and Buckingham shone. He proved himself an efficient taskmaster and impressed his superiors by the way he utilized his workforce to secure optimum results. For the Board, the ends always justified the means. The members lived within the comfortable ambience of Calcutta and were none too sensitive about what was going on in the plantations as long as the balance sheet of the company showed continuous and growing profits.

Within three years of his joining the company Buckingham was given independent charge of Bihguri plantation. In Bihguri Christopher James Buckingham's life reached its consummation; the plantation satisfied the contradictory inner urges of his psyche, twisted by circumstances of birth and upbringing. Bihguri endowed his existence with a semblance of stability; ensconced in the garden, with a bungalow he could call his own, his personal horse and servant, his salary deposited with unfailing regularity in his own account by the company, he could appreciate the insecurity that had troubled him in his childhood and adolescence.

Yet none who knew him could sense the profound dependence that tied the man to his company—the sardonic banter which marked his conversation was often directed at the very institution which sustained him. Nor was he deluded with the faithfulness of the blind—the innate cunningness of his character perverted that, as witnessed by his endeavour of feather his private nest by planting on his own account.

But the one thing in Bihguri which brought him genuine satisfaction was the joy yielded by total, unchallenged ascendancy over a group of human beings. Never in his life could Buckingham forget a childhood spectacle; a play enacted by the senior boys at school, called *Tamburlaine*, written by some seventeenth-century dramatist whose name he had long forgotten. The enactment had been universally castigated as an unmitigated flop. It was, Buckingham recalled, a drama centred around a single character, a world conqueror, filled with ornate, high-sounding rhetoric which fell flat on the ears of the youthful scholars. Only young Buckingham had been perceptive enough to diagnose the true cause of the play's failure—the boy who had been selected to play the role of the world conqueror had not been able to feel himself to be one! If Buckingham had been given that role, he would have raised the roof in it, not only confounding his compatriots into thunderous applause, but also waking up those black-robed, pedantic bastards entrusted with the task of educating them. Young Christopher had decided if the play was ever enacted in the school again, he himself would volunteer for the lead role. Unfortunately, the failure of that attempt ensured it was never tried again, and Buckingham had to convert his yearning into childhood fantasy.

Yet, the very moment he reached the shores of Hindustan, the prospect of playing that role appeared a distinct possibility; not the vicarious one in a school-hall, but on the more exciting stage of real life. The young planter was gratified to discover that though he remained callow and unimportant in the eyes of fellow Britons, the natives treated him with a deference incompatible with his age and social status. The abject subservience of the natives to the white-skinned masters of the land fed Buckingham's famished ego; by the time he arrived in Assam he, like Tamburlaine, had invested himself with godhood. Though Hukanpukri, his first billet, where he was a mere assistant, cramped his style, Bihguri, where he was accountable to no one, witnessed the flowering of his histrionic genius!

At Bihguri the make-believe of the world of drama finally blended into the world of reality. A stage, spanning seven hundred acres, across which he could strut, mouthing flowery rhetoric; a script written by himself, a cast of characters over which he commanded absolute, despotic control. His rifle, his horse, even the sirdars were nothing but stage-props designed to support his stellar portrayal; his insistence that each coolie raise the palm to his or her forehead in salaam at his approach was as essential to the script as the sirdars furling their umbrellas when he was around. The fact that it was no make-believe but stark reality lent added verisimilitude to the enactment and offered deeper satisfaction to the central player.

Pain and suffering, disease and death, beatings and floggings, were essential elements in this twilight world of real-life drama. Fear had been the key to dominance, physical pain the key to fear. There was none in Bihguri to question his divine right to rule his minuscule kingdom; he was its undisputed Lord and Master, passing judgements, meeting out punishment, bestowing rewards, demanding obeisance, playing God.

No doubt his ego was occasionally buffeted in the larger world; he was intelligent enough to concede there were others in that world who wielded greater potency and he must pander to these egos by subduing his own. But that was all the concession he was willing to make. On no account would he allow an equal or an inferior to challenge his ascendancy.

On board the *Ultaganga* a renegade traitor had posed such a challenge, only to feel the venomous backlash of the serpent's tail! There had been another, whose beauteous face had held deceptive yearnings, the sting of whose slap Buckingham could still feel on his soul. But she had seen the eyes of the snake, there could be no escape for one who had seen the eyes of the snake! For her, too, there was no escape—enthroned in his own domain, endowed with certitude born of power, Christopher James Buckingham bided his time, as sure of that reality as he was that night was night and day was day.

'Bapu babu is impossible!' David said, half-laughing, half-angry.

'What on earth do you mean?' Cordelia, surprised at this sudden outburst, asked. The two of them were on the verandah, seated on wicker-chairs.

'He talks and talks and says nothing,' David continued in the same half-laughing vein. 'I don't blame him, though. He tries hard to explain things, but his English is not up to it. Nor my Assamese, I daresay. We're well into November, and I'm still to get the hang of it. Must know the ropes, mustn't I, sis, if I'm to make Dhanboa pay?'

'Of course, you must, David!'

'But not through Bapu babu. He learnt his stuff from Papa, who was way behind the times. He learnt what he learnt at the beginning and stuck to it. Techniques are fast changing, sis!'

Cordelia suddenly understood what David was driving at. She stood up quickly and said, 'Bapu babu has done an admirable job running the garden since Papa's death. He's loyal, trustworthy and knows his job.' She bent over to touch his head in a goodnight kiss, but his words came up like an assassin's knife to pierce her ears, and she froze.

'I'm visiting Bihguri early tomorrow morning, sis.'

Cordelia straightened sharply, walked back to the cane-chair and sat wearily down.

'I thought we'd discussed this before, David,' she said reproachfully.

'Oh, I had a bash at Bapu babu, didn't I, sis? It's no use. Either I go at it by trial and error, or get knowledge from another source. Buckingham's the right choice whichever way I look at it.'

'Buckingham is despicable!' Cordelia said, her voice hard and cold as ice.

'He's that and more … I won't argue the point with you. But I can't allow my personal likes and dislikes to come in the way of what's good for Dhanboa. Papa wouldn't have wished it otherwise.'

'Please don't bring Papa into it, David,' Cordelia interrupted with the same hardness of voice. 'For Papa, means were as important as ends. All through his stay he didn't visit Buckingham even once … he must have had his reasons for it.'

'And Dhanboa's suffered for that!' David said. Cordelia could not see the expression on her brother's face, but she could feel the pent-up frustration in him. 'Papa was a poor businessman, let's not cheat ourselves. If you imagine Dhanboa's in ideal shape, you're mistaken. Talk to Bapu babu about it. He'll tell you.'

Cordelia remained mute, rendered silent, despite herself, by the intensity in David's voice. 'I've run through Papa's accounts, sis,' David continued. 'A considerable amount was spent on opening out Dhanboa. But the money invested and the results obtained are not at all commensurate. He sent his first dispatch in July this year … three thousand pounds of made tea. At two or three shillings a pound that would fetch a maximum of three hundred and odd pounds at London. A poor return, considering that almost eight thousand pounds have already been spent on Dhanboa.'

'It must be, if you think so,' Cordelia said, marvelling at the maturity which had overtaken her brother in such a short span of time.

'Something's intrinsically wrong with Dhanboa, sis! I've questioned Bapu babu minutely, but the poor blighter has no answer. To my inexperienced eye the tea bushes seem all right; but the bormohori tells me, as things stand, we can at best expect to double the yield next season. That's not good enough. Like it or not, I must go to Bihguri. Buckingham might be able to provide the answer.'

Cordelia felt the stirrings of her own anger, made more pronounced because David's reasoning was infallible. If something indeed was wrong with Dhanboa, the man to approach was Buckingham, with his years of experience and thorough knowledge of tea craft. Moreover, Buckingham himself had offered to help. Yet deep inside her lay the certainty that for an individual like Buckingham selfless help was impossible. His offer was sure to be wrapped in insidious designs. She tried to keep the growing anger out of her voice as she said, 'Oh, David, have you forgotten what he did to Michael?' But the anger and the bitterness could not be kept out of her words. 'Have you forgotten what havoc he has wrought in our lives? Buckingham will not prove to be Dhanboa's saviour, take my word for it. Buckingham's pure poison, David!'

Unlike in the past her anger and hurt did not make her brother retreat. Instead, he said, 'I know what Buckingham is. But I'll sup with the Devil if it'll make Dhanboa profitable!'

Her anger ebbed. Suddenly she was afraid. 'No, you mustn't say that, David! If I can't convince you, at least recall what the Reverend had advised.'

'It's all very well for you to remind me,' David burst out. 'But the responsibility falls on me. I've given it deep thought, believe me, sis. Buckingham has done you and Michael incalculable harm. But personal considerations must be kept out of commerce … that's a business principle Papa unfortunately never learned. I gave my pledge to Papa … I aim to carry out the pledge. Dhanboa under my stewardship shall be a profitable concern, that's my sole objective!'

Cordelia had no words against her brother's outburst. David took her silence to be acquiescence.

'Buckingham's changed for the better,' he continued. 'When Papa lay dying, he had the civility to call on us. The manner in which you treated him on the steamer could have made him stay put in his own plantation. Instead, he came with Doctor Gordon and was decent enough to be present at the funeral.'

Cordelia could not believe her ears. 'The way I treated him, David? But … but …!'

'Yes,' David said. 'And sis, during his visits here you ignored him in the most marked manner. Yet he has gone out of his way to offer me help. I'm determined to accept it. Look sis, I have gone that extra mile to keep you happy. Fixed wages for the coolies, cheaper rations and medicines … whatever you asked for. But on this issue, I'll not be guided by you. I'm going to Buckingham tomorrow morning … let's leave it at that, shall we?'

Cordelia felt the tears spring to her eyes.

'You're not being fair, David,' she said, no longer concerned about stifling her anger. 'It's not I who treated Buckingham badly on the *Ultaganga*. There was another shameful incident which I kept back from you, Michael and the Reverend, in fear that it will lead to greater conflict. Now I wish I had exposed Buckingham for the villain he is.'

'Buckingham's no saint! I don't deny it!'

'That's an understatement, David. You can't imagine how low he can stoop! Listen, David … that evening on the *Ultaganga*, at Sohagpur. I'd left you and Michael in your cabin and entered my own. Buckingham was in the cabin, waiting. He pressed his affections upon me and spoke the most undesirable words! I … I … had to strike him in the face to ward him off!'

David laughed. Cordelia had not known how he would react to the revelation—but the hollow laughter was an unexpected blow, as were his subsequent words.

'Oh, come sis! You're making this up, aren't you? A spur of the moment fantasy to stop me from going to Bihguri? It doesn't become you, sis!'

Cordelia was shocked. 'Are you accusing me of lying, David?' she cried out.

David caught the genuineness of her surprise and lost his levity.

'No, no, sis. You're very much like Papa … you won't lie even to save your neck … for that matter, mine either! Buckingham's a cad, but you must make allowances for him. If he did press himself upon you on the steamer, it was sheer jealousy … an overwhelming desire to replace Michael in your heart. Take it as a compliment and let it pass.'

'Knowing of it now, you'll yet go to Bihguri?'

'Of course, sis. Doesn't change a thing. I simply want information out of Buckingham. You're not involved in this in any way. *I* will be going to Bihguri … Buckingham won't come to Dhanboa! And, if it's of satisfaction to you, after using him, I will discard him. But I must learn what's wrong with Dhanboa!'

With an involuntary expression of anger Cordelia bounded out of her chair. 'You're stupid, David! One day you'll realize that!' She rushed across the verandah, entered her room, lit by a solitary candle, and flung herself onto the bed.

She lay there, watching the shadows thrown on the wall by the candlelight, waiting for David to knock softly on her door, for his voice to say how sorry he was. But David did not come. He continued to sit on the dark verandah for a long while. She left the candle lit waiting for David to come; saw its gradual destruction, the molten tallow drip down the sides to collect on the saucer below. Then she heard the creaking of the cane-chair as David rose, heard his footsteps vibrate on the wooden floor. But, instead of gaining in depth and volume, the sound of footsteps diminished. She heard the closing of a door and then there was utter silence.

Recumbent on that soft bed, surrounded by wavering shadows and the deep silence, Cordelia felt the whipcord of solitude bite into her soul. The momentary anger in her had long dwindled away like the candle, to be replaced by naked fear. The walls of the room dissolved before her eyes; darkness, unrelieved by the mellow light of the moon, rushed in from all sides; the darkness stretched out, unbounded by the walls, so that her little bed was set in the very core of a dark, unlit and lonely universe. Then the darkness thickened palpably, pressed down on her with the weight of a gigantic piston, till she could not breathe, could not move. Coils of terror slithered around her mind and her body. She gasped aloud, calling out for Michael and for David. Buckingham's reptilian shadow had already fallen between herself and Michael! If fell between her and David, there would be no one left!

With a desperate effort Cordelia sprang up from the bed, re-lit the candle and pussyfooted down the verandah. She knocked on David's bedroom.

'David? Are you awake, David?'

She heard the sounds as he got out of bed and unbolted the door. The candlelight fell on his concerned features. 'Sis, what's the matter? You look as if you've seen a ghost!'

'I'm sorry, David. I lost my temper.' She reached out for his hand and caught it in a fierce, possessive grip. 'Promise me, David … you'll ... you'll never allow Buckingham to come between the two of us!'

'Of course, I won't, silly!' David said with a chuckle. He leaned over and kissed her on the forehead. 'Now go back to sleep. Come, I'll take you to your bedroom.'

Hand in hand, like two children, they traversed the short distance to her bedroom. He kissed her again and said, 'It'll take more than a Buckingham to take me away from you.'

'You have come to me seeking knowledge,' Christopher James Buckingham said in a tone steeped in magnanimity. 'Well, I shall be your guru.'

'I shall be most obliged, Mr Buckingham.'

'Come off it, old chap! Drop the Mr Buckingham stuff!' The planter slapped David on the shoulders. 'I'm Chris to you. Neighbours, after all!'

'Well, thanks a lot, Chris,' David said, his dislike of the man slowly evaporating before his undeniable charm.

'You said you had a problem. Care to tell me about it?'

David related his suspicions about Dhanboa. Buckingham screwed up his eyes in a gesture of disbelief. 'But that's preposterous, old chap! Three thousand pounds of made tea! Your Papa must've committed an awful blunder somewhere! How much planting did you say there is?'

'A little over ninety acres, as I judge it. Papa cleared a hundred, but the coolie basti and tea houses occupy the rest of the space.'

'What are your total land holdings?'

'Five hundred.'

'And these ninety acres are all planted? No vacancies?'

'Vacancies?' David asked with a puzzled frown.

'You have a lot to learn! Vacancies … meaning vacant spaces between tea bushes.'

'I'm not too sure,' David said, feeling more and more like a schoolboy being lectured to by a tutor. 'Bapu babu didn't mention any.'

'Oh, confound Bapu babu! That's the first lesson in tea planting, old chap. Never acknowledge that you are learning things from a native. As it is, what can a damn native teach you, eh? But don't worry. Two–three visits to Bihguri and you'll get to learn all there's to know.'

'Are you convinced something's wrong with Dhanboa?' David said, anxious to change the tenor or the conversation.

'No doubt about it. Two hundred pounds per acre, that's the amount I get. I also have a private land holding … around two hundred acres, contiguous to Bihguri. The plantings there are almost as old as those of

Dhanboa. In the season just ended, I sent twelve thousand pounds of made tea on my private account. Your Papa should have been able to get at least six thousand pounds last season.'

David's face fell. 'I smelt a rat somewhere,' he said gloomily.

'I have my own suspicions as to what's wrong with Dhanboa. But I shall have to make sure. Spend some time there inspecting your plantings.'

David hesitated. The planter caught the shadow of anxiety on the young man's features and laughed. 'Tied to our sister's corset, are we, old chap?' The mocking tone was back in his voice. 'Does Dhanboa have two managers?'

'No, no,' David muttered aloud, confused and angry. 'Sis has nothing to do with it!'

'Entirely up to you, old chap. A physician must examine the patient if he's to diagnose the disease. So must I visit Dhanboa if I'm to discover what's wrong with it. Logical what, old chap?'

'You are most welcome at Dhanboa, Chris,' David said haltingly. 'I was just thinking of the time such a visit would consume. You've your own work cut out for you, I daresay.'

'You needn't worry about that! Neighbours after all, eh! White skin and all that! I go to Dhanboa on the morrow.'

'Tomorrow?' David said in a low voice.

'Lost your voice, eh?' said Buckingham, still in that infuriating tone. David contemplated a display of anger and quick departure, but controlled himself. Dhanboa's future was too important.

'Sooner the better, I suppose,' he said.

'So, it's settled then. Dhanboa at daybreak. Lunch at your place.'

Luthra had come to the bungalow with two horses. They cantered across the sprawling expanse of Bihguri tea plantation. Buckingham took David to the seedbarrie, where they allowed tea plants to grow into trees so as to collect the seeds. Next, he took his visitor to the nursery where saplings were first raised from seeds before being taken to the main garden for replanting.

They set off on a survey of the plantation, Buckingham talking all the while, pointing out things, offering illuminating answers to David's questions. The more David saw and heard the more conscious he grew that he had much to learn. They traversed the entire plantation till they reached its western extremity. 'My own little acre,' the planter called out. 'You can hear the hullabaloo.'

Like Bihguri, it was neatly laid out, a rolling expanse packed from one end to another with tea bushes. Unlike Bihguri, however, there were no bungalow, hutment or tea house; it was all planting—so, obviously, Buckingham made his teas at Bihguri.

'Just look at the bushes, old chap. Healthy, what?' Buckingham shouted over the din.

The same, however, could not be said of Buckingham's coolies, and David was uncomfortably made aware of the disparity with those of his own plantation. Even from a distance the emaciated, underfed appearance of the toilers could be gauged. From their numbers it was apparent that Buckingham had pressed almost all his workforce against that patch of jungle land, as well as the three elephants Bihguri possessed. Egged on by their sirdars, one of whom carried a rifle and the other whips, drenched with sweat from their exertions, grimy and insect-bitten, the coolies threw themselves against the jungle in a continuous wave.

The sirdars were doing a good job, giving the bonded slaves no respite, slashing at any who stopped to steal a moment of rest, bawling at the women and children if they displayed signs of flagging. The coolies themselves were shouting at each other, or at nothing in particular, which induced in them a loss of much required energy; yet, at the same time, the clamour acted as a measure of safety, driving away as it did any menacing presence in the jungle.

A sirdar caught sight of the master and pointed him out to the others. Suddenly the shouts and curses ceased and a hush fell over the work-gang. The coolies dropped whatever they carried and stood at attention, their hands to their foreheads, even the children and women. The sirdars had shaded themselves against the sun with unfurled umbrellas—a privilege of their position. Now they brought them down. The mahouts dug the spiked ends of their iron dhoms onto the hide of their mounts to bring them to a stop, and then slid down to stand on the ground, and put their right hands to their foreheads in salaam.

A thrill of awe mingled with admiration shot through David as he beheld Buckingham's ragtag army, each soldier transfixed in an attitude of homage! Beside him the planter seemed to grow in stature and radiate waves of raw energy that could paralyze into unmoving stone all who came within their sphere. Never in his young life had he met a being who could, by his mere presence, wield such a hypnotic spell over creatures of flesh and blood. The wonder was that this was no army; these dark creatures with spindly limbs and vacant eyes and dressed in tatters were no soldiers. This was no army encampment, it was a tea plantation in the middle of nowhere. Buckingham was no proud General inspecting his troops; he was merely a white-skinned intruder in an alien setting, surrounded by a band of black-skinned creatures who bowed to his will.

Buckingham urged his mount into motion. David followed, involuntarily straightening his back just a shade, attempting to emulate the nonchalance of his mentor. He was suffused with an unaccustomed feeling of ascendant power, heightened by the supple strength and mobility provided by the steed. It was a feeling not altogether unpleasant, satiating as it did one's ego; David allowed it to exhilarate him and bring a haughtiness to his gaze as he, with Buckingham, surveyed the rows of faces before him.

The planter spoke no word; it was all a language of the eye and the body as his gaze took in the achievement of the morning. Suddenly he wheeled his horse around to face the rifle-wielding sirdar. 'Get them back to work, Gandru. Then come and see me.' Without another word the planter rode away; he made no sign to David—by now the young man's slot in the universal scheme of things had been established and he was destined to follow.

He stopped a hundred yards away and wheeled once more to face his troops. At a curt command from the sirdar the coolies were back at their toil, but now in absolute silence now. For some unfathomable reason David's exhilaration waned at the sight, to be replaced by subdued dread.

Gandru lumbered up through the young tea bushes.

'Bircha aur Meghu yahan hai?' Buckingham asked

'Ji, huzoor.'

'Jao, use le ao.' He smiled with secret triumph at David. 'Thought I would surprise you, old chap. Wait and see.'

Gandru ran back to the coolies, barked out instructions, and two figures stepped out of the front line. Puran and Budhu gripped them by the arms and marched towards the waiting horsemen. David recognized the delinquents, first from the wharf of Chandpal ghat and, later, from the river-island. But somewhere along the way a metamorphosis, both of mien and manner, had occurred—one of the coolies had a broken jaw; the other came limping, continually grimacing as if in severe pain.

But more remarkable than the physical change was the transformation in attitude; on the sandbank David had seen hate and fury in the eyes of these two, especially the one that came limping. There was no hate in the eyes now; it had burned itself out, leaving the eyeballs finely glazed like porcelain, the orbs dull with pain. Submissiveness had replaced defiance in the gait of both—as they reached Buckingham, they broke free of their captors' grip and flung themselves fully on the ground. There they lay prostrate, faces in the dust, awaiting their fate.

Buckingham looked at David with flashing eyes of triumph, aware that the visitor had recognized the duo. 'An exercise in managing these apologies for human beings, old chap!' he crowed. 'I've perfected the art! They won't give further trouble. Just watch.' He shouted out in Hindustani at the supplicants beneath him. '*Aare Meghu aur Bircha, mein kaun hoo?* Who am I?'

'*Hamara mai-baap, huzoor.*'

'Your mother and father, am I? Thought you were bastards! *Aur tum kaun ho*?'

'*Hum kutta hain, huzoor. Aap ka paltu kutta.*'

The planter laughed uproariously. 'My pet dogs, did you hear that, old chap? It's highly unlikely I would keep these mongrels for pets! But watch ... another demonstration!'

David gaped in amazement, for when the planter spoke again, his voice was kindly, magnanimous.

'*Utho, Meghu. Bircha. Hum tum dono se khush hai. Tum achche aadmi ho. Hum tumhe inaam denge! Aaj se tum dono duffadar ho.* Gandru, *een ko kaam batao ...* section *do.*'

He called out to David. 'Bloody buggers can't believe their luck. Made 'duffadars' ... and not two months in the garden! But let's push on, old chap. Back to the bungalow. Chotu has laid out quite a meal and I have some superb wines for us to drown it in.'

Cordelia sat alone on the verandah of the bungalow, her eyes fixed upon the path to Dhanboa by which David must return. It was not even five in the evening; the light was strong yet she could not rid herself of the anxiety which had kept her brows furrowed for the past hour. Surely her brother should have been back well before now?

It had been practically an idle day. She had breakfasted alone, her first at Dhanboa without David's company. She had sought to busy herself with routine chores but her heart was not in them. Finally, she had given it up as a futile endeavour and chose to sit on the wicker-chair, awaiting David's return.

At quarter past five Mongla came up to enquire if she would have dinner. She asked him to ready the table and leave the food there and retire for the evening. She was determined not to have another meal without David—a supper, even if it be cold, in his company was infinitely more sustaining than one taken alone.

Finally, when the plantation grew filled with deep shadows, David came. The mahout brought the elephant up to the bungalow and positioned it in such a way that the sahib could step onto its floor directly from its back. She smiled with genuine pleasure and rushed towards her brother to hold him in a fiercely protective embrace. He reeled back, wanting to avoid her proximity.

'You're drunk, David!' She cried out, surprised and a little hurt.

He said nothing but turned unsteadily and stumbled towards the door of his bedroom. Cordelia made as if to follow, but he shooed her off. He halted at the door.

'Chrish ish coming tomorrow morning.'

'Chrish?' she echoed.

'Oh, Chrishtopher Jamesh goddamn Buckingham! Comesh to Dhanboa at daybreak. I wash right, shish. Shomething'sh wrong with Dhanboa. Good night.' David disappeared through the door.

Their dinner lay uneaten on the table. She no longer felt hungry. For a long while she sat on the verandah, alone with her thoughts and fears, watching the darkness engulf the plantation.

The sun was poised to set on the western horizon when Gandru called an end to the clearing activities of the day. Despite the general exhaustion, for the next half hour the basti bustled with activity as the workers bathed, treated their leech and insect bites, lit fires and cooked their simple meals. While the women and the chokris fed the children, the male adults and chokras brought out their kolohs of home-brewed mod or chillums of opium and drank and smoked. The womenfolk soon joined them for a brief span of respite after the children were fed and asleep. Few words were spoken—then they had their food and went to sleep. By nightfall the basti was as silent as a graveyard.

Buckingham's sirdars, however, were a class apart, and had their meals cooked for them by Chotu, the sahib's houseboy cum khansama, at the management's expense. Their master too kept them supplied with phatika, which was distilled spirit far better and more expensive than the mod brewed in the basti. Their huts were, however, in the basti—all except Luthra's. The head sirdar had a room beside Chotu's hutment adjacent to the sahib's bungalow.

In selecting his sirdars Buckingham chose younger men, unmarried and unencumbered by family ties, and by investing them with absolute power over the coolies, as well as by throwing bones at them in the form of free meals and hooch, converted them into terrible instruments of his own designs. The sirdars had a free hand to keep order among the coolies and get the utmost work out of them; no one dared complain. A sirdar also had power over the female coolies—he could, with impunity, summon any of them to comfort him at any time he desired. No husband could claim absolute possession of his wife's body, for, if a sirdar lusted after her, she must be shared; no parents could see their daughters grow into womanhood a virgin, for the shaitans—either the white sahib or his guests, or the accursed sirdars—were there to deflower her when hardly past puberty.

This night, while the basti slept, the sirdars of Bihguri drank phatika in the sahib's kitchen and joked and spat.

Two of the coolies too were awake. They huddled in a corner of the tiny shed which they shared, and passed a koloh of mod to each other.

'What a shit life!' Bircha said. 'Aarey Meghu-bhaiya, had it not been for your caution, I would have made a bolt for it many moons ago!'

'Patience, bhaiya, patience! My scheme is yielding fruit. The *sahib* promoted us to duffadars. That'll make them less watchful. Getting out will be easier.'

'So, when do we move, Meghu-bhaiya?'

'I've talked to Sanatan.'

'Lachmi's man? They summon her almost every night. If that wet rag had any manhood in him, he would have knifed each and every bastard. Hanging would be worth it! But anyway, Meghu-bhaiya, what did Sanatan say?'

'I told him we wanted to bolt.'

'You told him what?' Bircha cried.

'Keep your voice down, you ass! I know what I'm doing. Sanatan hates them as much as you or I. He won't say a thing.'

'What did he say?'

'He advises us to wait. This is not the right season for it. Now no rains. Roads are dry, rivers calm. How far do you think we'll get if we bolt now? The sahibs have men in khaki everywhere. They can move like the wind and grab us wherever we are.'

Bircha saw sense in Sanatan's advice, but persisted in his queries. 'And, Meghu-bhaiya, what happens when the rains come?'

'Sanatan says it rains heavy and long in these parts. The rivers grow fat and swollen, the roads sticky with mud. The jungles grow fast. The sahib cannot venture out of the garden; everything's cut off. Also, that is the time they make chai, which keeps the sahib and everyone busy day and night. They won't have the time to search for us.'

'It is indeed wise advice Sanatan gives,' Bircha conceded. 'But, Meghu-bhaiya, when do the rains come?'

'They'll come someday; don't you fret. Till then keep your temper in check and play your role. You limp well, you crafty jackal!'

Bircha laughed, a sound fraught with menace. 'All right, I'll wait for the rains. And limp for all I'm worth! But Meghu-bhaiya, I can't promise you that if Gandru taunts me again, I'll not wring the bastard's throat!'

Cordelia awoke the following morning to the sound of horses' hoof-beats. David, apparently, was up and ready, for she heard him hail the visitor and descend the bungalow stairs. Hoof-beats sounded again and they were gone.

Buckingham had brought both the ponies. The two men moved over the narrow garden-paths in a slow trot. The experienced planter scanned the tea bushes with an expert eye but said nothing. A couple of times he stopped, dismounted, and peered closely at the tea bushes and then, remounting, rode on in silence. Only when they reached the outskirts where the jungle impeded further progress did he ask, 'Where the devil are your coolies?'

David's boyish features flushed at the implications of the tone, but he kept his voice even as he replied, 'It's too early for them to be out, Chris. Off season, you know?'

Buckingham smiled, the characteristic omniscient smile of the man. 'Ah, I see. Saving on wages?'

'Oh no, not really! We pay fixed wages, not by the amount of work they do.'

His visitor raised delicate eyebrows in simulated astonishment. 'Fixed wages, eh? Keep that close to your chest. Planters hereabouts would draw and quarter you otherwise! Do I see your sister's hand in this?'

'Keep Cordi out of this, will you, Chris,' David said sullenly.

'Three thousand pounds of made tea! Doesn't really go with coolie pampering, does it?'

David flinched at the mockery and the flush on his face deepened.

'Get the buggers out by first light,' Buckingham continued unmindfully, a domineering sharpness in his voice. 'This is the coolest part of the day, when you can get the utmost work out of them. If you wish to be soft on them, leave it for the afternoon, the hottest part of the day. Let me tell you another thing, old chap. Tea planting is man's business. So, keep your plantation insulated from women and their whimsies if you want to make profit!' There was a venomous quality to the words which made David look up with surprise. But Buckingham's heavy-lidded eyes were neutral.

'You're determined to be offensive, aren't you, Chris?' David said.

'Plain speaking isn't rudeness, old chap,' Buckingham said with studied belligerence. 'Yesterday you came to Bihguri to find out what is wrong with Dhanboa. I've discovered the fatal flaw. Now let me tell you some home-truths. With things as they stand, Dhanboa will never break even.'

The anger drained out of David and was replaced by fear. The planter wasn't lying! The young man's shoulders slumped in a gesture of submission to a stronger will.

'So, tell me, old chap. Do I indulge in plain speaking?'

David laughed, a nervous, ingratiating titter. 'Oh, drop it, Chris! I certainly wish to know what's wrong with Dhanboa. That, I'd supposed, was the objective of your visit.'

'Was it? Oh, of course it was.' Buckingham laughed, as if recollecting a secret joke, known to himself and none other. He dismounted, signalling to David to do the same. 'All right, you wait here with the horses while I collect the evidence.'

Handing over the reins to David he disappeared among the tea bushes. Fifteen minutes later he emerged. In his right palm he held three leaves. He held his left palm flat and rigid and, with his right hand, placed the tea leaves side by side upon it. Even an inexperienced person could judge that the length of the three leaves were not equal, nor their hues similar. The planter picked up the largest of these and held it up before David. The leaf was elliptical in shape, about eight inches in length and two inches broad at its centre, glossy, with distinct bullations.

'This is the Assam jat—strain—of tea leaves. Grew wild in this region ... hill tribes hereabouts concocted a drink from it. Commercially the finest tea species for Assam ... Being a native, it is hardy, resists pests and diseases and flushes profusely.'

Buckingham was clearly relishing the role of David's tutor, half playing the conjuror too, to add a trace of drama to his revelation. Slowly, with intended deliberateness, he replaced the Assam jat leaf and picked up another from his palm. This too was elliptical in shape, but far smaller than the one previously displayed, barely an inch long and half inch wide, sharply serrated, matt, smooth and unbullated.

'This too is a tea leaf, but of the China variety. Difficult to imagine that it is a cousin of the Assam jat, isn't it? Now, when the British authorities first sought to start experimental planting in Assam, they chose this China plant, although they knew of the existence of the native jat. Considered the China plant to be a commercial crop, the Assam jat to be a degraded species. That was a proper bloomer, for the China jat doesn't grow too well in the soil of Assam, yields far less and is prone to pests and diseases.'

'And Papa planted these too, is it?' David asked.

'Wait,' said Buckingham. 'Worse is still to come!' He replaced the China leaf and picked up the third. This leaf resembled the China jat in size and the absence of bullation, but the sharp serration was missing and it had a debilitated, sapless look about it.

'When the China plants were imported into Assam and planted here,' Buckingham explained, 'cross-pollination between these and the Assam jat took place. The result was a hybrid ... an absolute commercial disaster! This third leaf here is from a hybrid plant growing in your garden. It was this damned hybrid which delayed the success of the Assam Company's tea operations in Assam. Sorry, old chap. I don't know where your Papa acquired his seeds from, but I have scanned your garden. Dhanboa's mostly planted with unprofitable China plants and this beastly hybrid.'

David looked utterly crestfallen. 'What's to be done?' he cried.

'Only one course is open to you, old chap,' Buckingham said, after some reflection. 'Root out the hybrids and replant the area.'

'But they look just like the China plant!' David cried out. 'How can I tell them apart?'

'You're right,' Buckingham said, turning his head so that his smile was hidden from view. 'That makes it even more difficult! You'll have to root out the China plants too, I'm afraid. From what I can make out, almost two-thirds of your clearing has to be planted again. Rather fortunate, that! Your Papa raised some native bushes, at least!'

'Is there no alternative?' David asked in a desperate voice.

The note of banter crept into Buckingham's words again. 'Oh yes, there is! Dhanboa, as you no doubt know, translates into rice sowing. Well, my lad, you can start sowing rice and convert it into paddy fields!'

'This is not the moment for facetiousness, Chris!'

'Oh, perk up, David my boy,' Buckingham said. 'It's not the end of the ruddy world! Couple of years at most and things will be right once more. But leave them as they are, Dhanboa's yield will never be worth the expense.'

'But we don't have a nursery,' David pointed out. 'Procuring such large numbers of saplings would be a bloody task!'

'Not to worry, old chap,' Buckingham said lightly. 'I have enough saplings in my nursery for both of us. What are neighbours for, eh? Provide you seeds too to raise a nursery. But get your coolies out of their holes and set them to work.'

They set off on another reconnaissance of the garden. 'Well, there's not much to be seen any more,' the planter finally said. 'I have earned my breakfast this morning, eh? Shall we ride towards it?'

The breakfast table had been set for two. 'Isn't Miss Esscombe joining us?' Buckingham asked, carefully nonchalant.

David hesitated for a second before replying. 'I don't know. But let's ask her, shall we?'

He sent Mongla to inform Cordelia. The houseboy returned soon, with the answer that memsahib had her hands all tied up at the dispensary and would not be able to join David at breakfast this morning.

The meal over, Buckingham took his leave. 'I'm sincerely indebted to you, Chris,' David said. 'Quite a shock you gave me there … the inferior plantings, I mean. But I guess I can pull through … with your help, of course.'

'I give my help freely.' Buckingham's voice was frigid, as were his eyes. 'But on one condition: the gates of Dhanboa must forever be shut to Michael Bailin!'

'Dash it, Chris! That's hitting below the belt!' David said feebly.

'Entirely up to you, old chap … take my offer, or leave it. I shall help you with seeds and saplings and not charge you one pice for it. The knowledge and experience I've garnered shall be yours. Raising a nursery, replanting, mulching, pruning … there is a lot to learn. Come the rains, and I shall show you how to wither, roll and fire the green tea leaves. I shall assist you in building up Dhanboa as an ideal tea plantation. A single condition is all I stipulate in exchange.'

'We haven't heard from him thus far. Perhaps he's gone out of our lives forever. But what if he appears again? What if he pays a visit to Dhanboa?'

'Then fend him off, dear boy,' Buckingham said, unrelenting. 'Make it clear to him you no longer desire his acquaintanceship. The choice is entirely up to you. If you value the companionship of a traitor to Queen and country more than you value my offer of friendship and aid, you merely have to say so.'

Even as the man before him spoke, David's mind was awhirl with thoughts. Dhanboa needed Buckingham's seeds and saplings. Papa's garden needed the planter's knowledge and expertise—especially when the rains came and the leaves had to be converted into tea. He had to go to Bihguri then to learn the latest in manufacturing techniques. Once he had done that, once Dhanboa reached the threshold of relative safety, he could bid Buckingham farewell. If only Michael would stay away till then; till the seeds and saplings arrived, till he had learnt enough about tea craft to be able to stand upon his own feet!

He quickly said, 'No, no, Chris. You mustn't say that! I value your friendship greatly. You have my word.'

Buckingham nodded with satisfaction. 'Some more home-truths, old chap?' he asked.

'Certainly. If it'll help Dhanboa.'

'Since we planters live in a hostile environment, our superiority must be emphasized in our actions and way of life. That's vital to our survival. You know why I always use a horse in the plantation? Improves mobility, no doubt, but, at the same time, it puts me at a higher vantage than the coolies.'

'I can manage one, I suppose,' David said. 'You said you know a trader?'

'I'll send him to you. Then again, old chap, see this riding crop? I'm rarely without it, or a rifle. Even when I'm on foot, amongst the coolies, I carry it, or a leather thong. These are small things, but they serve immensely to maintain control over my workers.'

'I think I'm getting your point, Chris.'

'Then act upon it, old chap. I intentionally showed those two buggers to you yesterday. They were pretty wild at the outset. But by now they have been housebroken and will give no trouble. Rather, they'll prove to be invaluable workers. It mustn't be the stick always. Sometimes you have to offer a carrot or two. You saw their eyes light up, didn't you, when I told them they were made duffadars? Lay a wager with you, old chap, within another month they'll grow to be my blue-eyed boys … conspiring with me against their own kind!'

'Like Luthra? He looks pretty savage to me.'

'He's not the only one. I have others … Puran, Gandru, Budhu and their ilk. That's the trick. Use some of them to do your dirty work for you. I don't flog the coolies myself, I have a sirdar do it for me. That way, all the antipathy is directed at the sirdar. Pretty neat, what?'

'Papa brought us up with different beliefs,' David said, a trifle pompously.

'Ah, but not in Assam, old chap! If he'd brought you up here, he would have taught you a different tune. Here, in Assam, you've no place to run! Take Dhanboa or Bihguri, miles from anywhere! You have to stand on your own feet in a crisis, old chap. It's your image amongst the coolies, the amount of dread you can instill into them, that's your protective armour.'

Buckingham laughed again, a disagreeable cackle, replete with arrogance. 'Study your coolies, old chap. They're feckless creatures, without a mind of their own. A rotten egg or two amongst them can sway their moods and make them capable of breaking out against their white masters. You have been to Bihguri and seen for yourself the kind of respect and awe I inspire in my men. Your coolies are having it too easy. They'll sit on your shoulders one day if you don't watch out.'

David would have preferred a change of subject, but Buckingham would permit no respite. 'Lesson one, old chap. Never allow the buggers to sit while you're around. Lesson two. Never permit them to intermix with local villagers, or even to leave the garden perimeters. Except select sirdars, to carry out assigned tasks, with your permission. The day your Papa died, I saw local villagers mingling with your coolies.'

'They were from Bapu babu's village,' David explained lamely.

'Yes, your Papa left you a problem in the shape of that bormohori. Why don't you impress on the chap the need to keep the coolies insulated? Trust me, there are coolie poachers around! Tell him not to bring his relatives into the garden. Or better still, get rid of him on some pretext or the other and run the garden all by yourself.'

'That'll pose some problems, Chris,' David said, unable to look Buckingham in the eye.

'Your sister again, is it?'

'I keep telling you … Cordi has no say how Dhanboa is run! Bapu babu was with Papa since Dhanboa's inception. Knows every inch of this garden. I'd be lost without him.'

'No, you won't,' Buckingham said, rising from his chair. 'As long as I'm behind you! The more you learn and experience, the greater your confidence. You won't have to depend on a ruddy coolie then, eh!'

'I suppose so,' David said, allowing his visitor's confidence to rub on to himself.

'You have your work cut out for you for the next few weeks. Quite a big job, uprooting and replanting. Tighten up things, will you? Make the bastards slog or you'll never complete the job in time.'

Buckingham, along with Luthra, rode away. Cordelia was standing in front of the dispensary, talking with a coolie woman. The planter halted, saw her face turn towards him, and lifted his sola toupee.

What should have been a gesture of courtesy was, in fact, one of supreme insolence. The girl retreated to the hutment, but not before she caught the glint of haughty triumph in the planter's eyes.

It was as if Buckingham's visit had erected a diaphanous screen between brother and sister; they saw each other but could not reach out. That evening they sat in uneasy silence on the verandah, each fearful of the other's reaction if the fragile quietude was to suddenly shatter. Cordelia sensed David was deeply troubled; he sat hunched in his chair wearing such a vulnerable look that she wanted to reach out and cradle him in her arms. But the experience of the other night had made her diffident. Thus, fearful of widening the gulf that threatened the easy and natural relationship which always existed between herself and David, she kept quiet. Finally, rising from her chair earlier than usual, she bid him goodnight, and fled to her room.

The next day, however, a panic-stricken Bapu babu had a long chat with her, and Cordelia could no longer remain silent. That evening she said to David, 'Bapu babu came to me today.'

The moment she said the words she regretted them. David's features tautened into an irate grimace as he said, 'So he went whining to you?'

'No, David. He came to me not to complain, but to voice his fears. It appears you've plans for Dhanboa which he doesn't like.'

'He'll have to carry them out whether he likes them or not! Look, sis, I've had to take hard decisions. It's not been pleasant taking them. Things are bad enough without the blasted bormohori making them worse!'

He quickly told her of Buckingham's diagnosis of what ailed Dhanboa and the cure he suggested. 'Bapu babu doesn't like the idea of three-year old bushes being uprooted. I concede that's quite natural. But sis, two-thirds of Dhanboa consists of unproductive plantings. The garden will never make a profit no matter how much we work on it. We have to plant these acres anew while there's still time.'

'But David, those bushes were planted by Papa!'

'Now, sis, try to be logical, not emotional. If Papa chose the wrong type of tea plants, they must be uprooted. It'll do Dhanboa good in the long run.'

'I'm sure you're right, David,' Cordelia said. 'However, Bapu babu's suggestion is not without merit. You should give some thought to it.'

'Do you imagine that native fool's capable of giving sensible suggestions?'

'Well, I thought it was. Let the bushes be, as he suggests … they'll at least yield some tea, even if it be little. Instead open out more jungle and plant it with quality seeds. That way the yield of Dhanboa will not decline disastrously the next season.'

'That man's an ass! Clearing the jungle is no easy task, sis. How many acres can we clear in so short a time? Ten acres? Twenty acres? But here we have almost seventy acres of cleared land which can be planted anew with the Assam strain. They'll yield a great many times more than what the China plants will.'

'You trust Buckingham, David?' Cordelia asked with unexpected abruptness.

'In matters relating to tea, certainly. His knowledge is deep, his judgement sound. Seriously sis, I wish you would let me do things my way.'

A shadow passed over Cordelia's features. 'God knows I've been trying to, David,' she said. 'But I have overpowering presentiments of disaster. Ever since that man's visit a dark cloud seems to hang over Dhanboa.'

David laughed nervously. 'Come on, sis! I'd imagined you were here to infuse confidence, not to fill me with doubts and hesitations! Now, don't worry. I know what I'm doing. Two, three years hence the outcome will be before you. Then you'll realize had I not acted, Papa's garden would have been destroyed, taking us down with it.'

The next few weeks witnessed sweeping changes in Dhanboa as David set about in earnest to repair the 'damages' caused by 'Papa's ignorance and lack of commercial foresight.' When asked to uproot the bushes they had planted and tended all these years the coolies, at first, raised vocal protests. David had to assert himself repeatedly to make them carry out the assigned tasks. Bapu babu too did as he was told, but with a reluctance he made no attempt to conceal.

With gathering anxiety Cordelia watched David change his pattern of management. Previously the bormohori communicated the sahib's instructions to the coolies, and had been responsible for getting specific jobs done. But now David chose Harua, a coolie youth, barely out of his teens and yet unmarried to be the head sirdar. The choice of a stripling caused dissatisfaction and anger amongst the elder coolies, but since it was the sahib's hukum, all they could do was accept it. The Kachari labourers too did not take kindly to an immigrant coolie being placed over them, but with characteristic taciturnity said nothing.

To add salt to the elder coolies' wounds, David made two other unmarried —Ajam and Robiya—sirdars, to work under Harua. The head sirdar was to take orders directly from David and to ensure that, with the help of his two lieutenants, each day's work was completed to the sahib's satisfaction. Bapu babu was thus effectively sidelined from the field work; he was entrusted with keeping the plantation's accounts—exiled to a little cubicle in one of the tea houses, provided with a table and chair and a ledger to record his figures and quill and ink to write them down with.

David threw himself into his work like a man possessed, personally supervising the uprooting operations. He put his entire workforce to the job; the coolies were made to work in two shifts; from five in the morning till twelve noon, and then from two in the afternoon till five in the evening. Thankfully they, despite the fact that the young sahib was making greater demands on them than his father, did not complain, but worked hard at it, so that for a while there was remarkable progress till suddenly an unforeseen setback upset David's calculations.

Bapu babu had not forewarned him. He came to know of it only when, with two days remaining for November to end, Ganesh, the eldest among the tribal Kachari labourers, came to the bungalow with a couple of others one evening after the day's work had been done. Ganesh's request was a straightforward one—the annual contract with the tribals ended on the 31st of November. If the sahib wanted to retain their services, he must draw up fresh contracts and pay advance, as was the custom.

The sahib, so said David, would be damned glad to retain their services! He would ask Bapu babu to have their contracts ready at the earliest. And, of course, the advance would be paid.

'Please have the contracts ready by tomorrow, sahib,' Ganesh said. 'We leave day after tomorrow morning.'

'Leave? What the devil do you mean?' his amazement made David burst out into English. The tribals stared at him in incomprehension.

'Jaabi? Kiyo jaabi? Koloi jaabi?' David asked, correcting himself.

'Don't you know, sahib? Back to our villages across the Brahmaputra where our families are. It is the custom. We go every year.'

'But you can't go now! What will happen to the uprooting? *Tohot jabo noaro*!'

'We must go, sahib.' With a sinking heart David saw the flat, mongoloid features harden with obduracy. 'It is the custom.' Ganesh raised his palm to his forehead in a salaam and, gesturing to the other two, went down the stairs.

David sat in the wicker-chair, stunned by the bad news.

'Consult Bapu babu,' Cordelia advised. 'He gets along well with the tribal coolies ... he might persuade them to change their minds.'

'I can't do that,' David said, shaking his head.

'But why not?'

David hesitated. 'It will be a loss of face, sis,' he finally said. 'I have declared my independence from him. If I run to him for help at the very first crisis, what will he assume?'

The hint of mockery in Cordelia's words was almost unconscious, a spontaneous offshoot of deep-rooted hurt. 'But David, you yourself said that one's personal likes and dislikes must not be allowed to intrude into Dhanboa's affairs! And, anyway, I don't believe Bapu babu can nurse a grudge.'

David conferred with the bormohori early next morning. 'Call a durbar, dear David sahib,' Bapu babu advised. 'Get all the Kachari fellows here.'

The tribals were summoned and a durbar was held on the open ground fronting the bungalow. For almost ten minutes Bapu babu spoke, imploring them to postpone their departure by two weeks. so that the uprooting and mulching could be advanced. But his pleas had no effect on the coolies. When Bapu babu finished, Ganesh stood up. Their womenfolk might wait, but the ripening rice grains in the paddy fields would not. They must go on the morrow. However, they would return after the crop had been reaped and the harvest festival celebrated. They assured their loyalty to David sahib as they had done to Esscombe sahib.

Perhaps it was the weight of inadequacy which disturbed David's judgement for he made a grievous error. The infuriatingly pleading tenor of Bapu babu's speech had given rise to anger, and that was evident when he suddenly spoke. 'Listen coolielog, and listen well. The bormohori has civilly requested you not to leave Dhanboa when your services are required. You have refused. I am a sahib. I make no requests. If you leave Dhanboa now your contracts will be terminated. But those who leave after two weeks get their contracts renewed as well as advance. So, think well. I want all of you in the fields tomorrow morning. I make no request like the bormohori. I make no idle threats either.'

Without waiting for their response David turned and walked stiffly away.

The next morning no tribal coolies came to the fields. David sent Ajam and Robiya to the hutments where they lived. The huts were deserted. The tribals had decamped!

'Bit of a muck-up, what, old chap?' Buckingham said, when David apprised him of the problem. 'I'm afraid you didn't handle the situation too well. Loss of twenty tribals is irreplaceable.'

'I had hoped that the threat of losing their advance money would deter them.'

'Well, you found out the hard way it didn't! But you still have sixty odd coolies left. If you drive them hard, you should be able to manage with the number.'

This ultimately proved to be the case, for the imported coolies, with nowhere to run, had to toil on despite the depletion in the workforce. David, however, had chosen his sirdars well. Harua, Ajam and Robiya proved equal to the requirements of their elevated status; for, by dint of much threats and abuses, they succeeded in making one coolie do the work of two, and satisfactory progress continued to be made.

It suddenly rained on the first of December. Not a heavy downpour, but a nagging, steady drizzle which continued for two days. Standing at the railings of the verandah Cordelia watched the raindrops fall. The thatched roof of the bungalow soaked away the sound of the rain so that the drops descended in silence.

Her eyes focussed on the brown, grassless strip just beneath the bungalow, and she stiffened. A rippling slither had caught her eyes. Now she saw it clearly: a black streak like a long, thick, leather whip gliding sinuously over the rain-spattered earth. With rising horror, she recognized the false eyes on the head—the dreaded cobra! And then she saw its quarry, a toad the size of a child's fist, brought out from some hidden niche by the smell of rain.

The snake's tongue flickered out again and again as it closed in. The cobra stopped a foot away from the prey; the toad squatted transfixed, unable or unwilling to attempt escape. For five frozen minutes the hunter and the hunted eyed each other, without movement. Prompted by impulses which contradicted the laws of nature Cordelia wanted to cry aloud, throw something at the toad to break its trance. But she found herself paralysed, as if she and not the toad were the hunted. She had seen the cobra's eyes and her own skin had grown cold and clammy and was covered with goose pimples. Abruptly the cobra's entire body straightened and darted out like an arrow, its mouth opened wide, and the deadly fangs sank into its prey.

Though the rain had cooled and soothed the landscape, Cordelia discovered that she was drenched with sweat.

With the passing of the days Michael Bailin underwent a change for the better. True, there was sadness in his heart at the manner in which Cordelia had been wrested from him. There was hatred, too, against Buckingham, who had coerced him into fleeing the *Ultaganga*, and Leach, who had sold him a mock-garden.

Yet, the demented desire for annihilation was no longer there. It was as if, having set a tentative foot at death's doorstep, he had suddenly seen the preciousness of life despite its inherent suffering and anger.

Cordelia, of course, had gone out of his life forever. She must be in Calcutta, nursing her ailing father back to health. Her brother must be in charge of Dhanboa; but Bailin knew in the heart of his heart he could no more face David than he could Cordelia. It was better to leave them buried, like mementos in a dusty attic.

His own concern must be to build up Chahpuli and lose himself within its finite bounds. Leach had perpetrated an awful fraud, Chahpuli was a mere mirage, but the land grant was no mirage! Bailin may not have a ready-made garden but he had the land—over seven hundred acres of virgin jungle which a man with a new found zest for living could convert into a plantation. And, in the process, amidst the jungles, perhaps he would be able to flee for ever from the spectres haunting his life, and find, in its reclusive solitude, the peace of mind that had been long denied to him.

Only when his guest had, according to the physician, recovered fully, did Gokuldeva invite Bailin to meet him in the main house, sending a dola as a conveyance. 'Good evening, Lieutenant Bailin. I trust you're sufficiently recovered now,' he said, after his guest was seated comfortably in a chair before him.

'Yes, sir,' Bailin replied. 'I have been delivered from death's door, thanks to you.'

'It's not me you've got to thank, Lieutenant. It's Garo, your man'

'I am cognizant of that, sir. Garo senses my gratitude.'

'He's paid you a tribute too by his devotion. You must be an extraordinary white man to have inspired such loyalty in a native!'

'I can hardly a comment on that,' Bailin said with a half-laugh.

'I have no love for the white man, Lieutenant, having suffered enough humiliation at their hands! But then I saw the desperate plea for help in Garo's eyes. Such desperation springs from fierce love and loyalty. That made me curious, and I decided to have you transported to my house.'

The nobleman's swarthy features were unsmiling. 'I do not deny that I have been of service to the British Raj,' he continued. 'But that was a compulsion foisted upon me. I'm a survivor, Lieutenant. Time and again I'd come to the assistance of Major Gosselin and his kind. So, I've survived. I'll continue to survive as long as I'm of use to them. The moment my usefulness ends, I'm finished. So, I try to remain useful. But it doesn't mean I have to love the white men.'

'Yet you came to my help,' Bailin said softly.

'I'm not a man without sentiment, Lieutenant. There're things you do from the heart. I told you I was curious ... To command such loyalty from a native, it was unusual. Moreover, Lieutenant, our paths aboard the steamer may not have crossed much, but it didn't mean I knew nothing about you. Even at that point of time I understood you were different from your breed. To come to the aid of a native! Cross swords with a scoundrel and get beaten up for it! Not many Englishmen would do that. I learnt about your affair with Miss Esscombe too … believe me, I was happy.'

Gokuldeva saw his guest's face stiffen into granite hardness but it did not dissuade him from continuing his probe.

'And then I learnt that you were a man disgraced before the eyes of fellow Englishmen. You bolted like a frightened deer when that came out. But it all fitted into my mental image of you. Someone whom his own kind abhors can't be bad, I said to myself. That's the reason for my help, Lieutenant. Perhaps you would care to tell me the circumstances of your disgrace. I'm sure I'll approve of your actions.'

Bailin briefly narrated the events leading to his dishonourable discharge from the army.

'You are a decent man, Lieutenant Bailin,' Gokuldeva said with feeling. 'You deserve a much better fate than has been your lot so far. May I call you Michael?'

Bailin smiled, and nodded.

'To tell you the truth, Michael, the poor white man in Hindustan is to be pitied than censured! A degenerative environment, is it not so, Michael? Every white man is a nawab in Hindustan, no matter that he had been a humble stablehand or a wheelwright or a clerk back in England. It's the colour of his skin which invests him with divinity, not his intelligence, education or family background. No man can live up to such ego-pampering! It becomes an opiate; the more the ego feeds upon the fawning, the more it craves.'

Bailin sensed that his host was trying to engage him in a verbal duel. He remained silent, for the truth in the words brooked no contradiction.

'So used is one to sycophancy and subservience that one expects similar subservience from every native, even those who are superior by virtue of intelligence or birth. The absence of such servitude breeds anger in lesser minds. But the truly cultured man would recognize his equal when he sees one. I told you I'm yet to meet a truly cultured individual among the white men. Someone who could lessen my contempt for the kind. But I believe my search has ended this evening. In you I've finally found an individual whom I can respect.'

'I'm thankful, Barua dangoriya,' Bailin said, unable to hide his pleasure. 'My feelings towards you, sir, are those of gratitude.'

'My dear Michael, I harbour deep suspicions of British gratitude, you will surely understand that! You too will understand my sense of insecurity. Who knows, the noose fashioned by British gratitude will be around my neck someday!'

'God forbid, sir, that such a thing should come to pass! However, since I myself have had a taste of British justice, I cannot with assurance claim it might not come to that!'

'Especially now, for I have thrown them the gauntlet. It might interest you to know that I have opened out a small tea garden.'

'I'm aware of it, sir. Buckingham mentioned it aboard the steamer. He seemed none too happy at what he termed your effrontery!'

'My audacity has raised the heckles of British planters, no doubt. But Major Gosselin is aware of my influence among my own people. So he graciously permits me my little tea garden. In return I help him administer his domain.'

'Does your plantation have a name?'

'Yes … Mohoniya. It means enchanting. Tea is an enchanting brew, isn't it?'

Long into the night they talked, the aged native and the young Englishman. Bailin poured his heart out as he had never done before. Much later Gokuldeva said, 'Your personal life is your very own. I shall not venture to advise you on that. But as far as Chahpuli is concerned I'll extend to you all possible help. You say that you are all eager to start your career as a planter?'

'Yes. I and Garo will carve out a tea plantation even if we have to sweat out the last drop of our blood.'

'You know nothing about tea planting?'

'Unfortunately, not.'

'A minor obstacle. You'll learn the techniques of tea in my plantation. I shall also help you with money.'

'No,' said Bailin, his voice flat in refusal. 'I'll not take money. I'm in no hurry. I and Garo will open out Chahpuli acre by acre, with the little money I have left.'

'You rise in my estimation every minute! However, you'll need seeds and saplings. And men and elephants. I can provide those, at least.'

'Not men and elephants. As I said, I and Garo will work in the garden by ourselves. We will, of course, take Mohoniya's seeds and saplings, but only if you allow me to pay for them. You talk of friendship, Barua dangoriya. Too much imposition can destroy a friendship. It cannot be that you remain forever the giver and I the receiver.'

'Oh, but you've already given me something precious, Michael! You have acknowledged I am worthy of your friendship and trust, as I have of yours. You are different from others. They are mercenary, avaricious, grabbing. If I'd made them the offer I have to you, they would have eaten me from home and hearth!'

'I'm anxious to start as early as possible.'

'But you've overlooked an important aspect. That's because you're so trusting. Me, I'm forever suspicious. And cynical. But enough of that! Now tell me, what makes you sure that you are in possession of a vast land grant?'

Bailin blanched. 'I've the papers with me …' he began, but Gokuldeva cut him short.

'My dear Michael, don't be naive! The man who sold you Chahpuli was a scoundrel. There's no guarantee the papers he provided you are not false. You'd better check their veracity. Go to Sivasagar. Meet Major Gosselin. I'll make the necessary arrangements for the journey. If the land claim is not genuine, problems will crop up in the future.'

'I suppose you're right,' Bailin said after some reflection.

'A single encounter with the Major, Michael. Get the papers verified. Lodge a complaint against Leach. Then you can show your back to Gosselin and his ilk and go about your business.'

Bailin nodded. 'When can I start?'

'Tomorrow evening, after dinner. I'll provide you with a boat. My man, Phukan, will go with you and Garo. He knows the way to the *kechari* … the courthouse … where Gosselin sits. Now come. We'll walk down to the cottage.'

Outside it was still drizzling. Unmindful of the rain Gokuldeva stepped out, Bailin by his side. Two men carrying lanterns lighted their way. At the door of the cottage the nobleman stopped and held out his hands to Bailin.

'Remember what I told you on the steamer—justice is always on the side of the righteous. You have nothing to fear, Michael. Good night.'

The old man stepped out once more into the rain.

The outcome of the Lieutenant's trip to Sivasagar to meet Major Richard De V. Gosselin in his office were mixed. The officer was openly contemptuous of the Lieutenant, but being a man who adhered strictly to the code of conduct demanded by his position, had his staff seek out and furnish Bailin with the required information. The supplicant, indeed, had been cheated by the conman named Theodore Leach. However, rather than no land grant at all, the Lieutenant had one of exactly 147 acres!

Studying the records, the astute officer also ventured the speculation that Leach's original intention was to actually attempt tea planting, but something had made him give up.

'I'm grateful to you, Major Gosselin,' Bailin said as he rose to depart. 'I won't lose sleep over whether Leach attempted tea planting or not. I aim to set up a plantation, small though it might be.' He held out his hand but the officer ignored it.

'Don't test me again, Lieutenant!' Gosselin said. 'I abhor individuals like you. You bring no credit to Her Majesty's domain. I have sent a dispatch to my superiors in Calcutta asking for details of the Bailin case of Ambala. You haven't heard the last of me.'

Bailin turned around and, with the map and papers safely in his hand, marched out of the building.

Reverend Garry Swanson awaited him on the path just outside the courthouse. Much to the surprise of his two companions, Bailin emitted a wild hoop and clasped the missionary in a fervent embrace.

Swanson held him by the shoulders at an arm's length and looked fondly at him. 'Praise be the Lord you're safe, Michael. It's good to see you again.'

So elated had the Lieutenant been at this unexpected encounter with the padre that he could make no answer. But he soon regained his composure and related to Swanson all that had happened to him.

'I've managed to salvage something at least,' Bailin sighed, and said: 'The land claim, though much truncated, has proved valid. A bit of land,

Father … not much … but more than enough to fill up the void and give a definitive direction to my existence.'

'Yes, Michael. The Lord had taken you towards death, and then plucked you to safety. Truly a miracle! Be worthy of this miracle, Michael. Go back to Chahpuli. Piece together the fragments and build your life anew.'

'Those moments aboard the *Ultaganga* with you and the others were the most beautiful ones of my life. I'm hoarding them, to hold close when loneliness grips me like a vise.'

'It's I and the others now, is it? Aren't you curious to learn where Cordelia is now? What she is doing?'

Bailin said nothing. The padre continued speaking with intensity. 'Listen to me, Michael. To fritter away the brief moments of one's life in self-pity … that is nothing but foolishness! Who are these Buckinghams and Gosselins? Why should you allow such people to stand between you and your happiness?'

The euphoria of his triumph, and the joy of meeting the Reverend, swept out of the Lieutenant. His eyes darkened again with despair.

'Try and understand, Father!' he cried out. 'If it had been me alone, I wouldn't have spared them a second thought. But I can't pull others down with me.'

'That's precisely the point, Michael. You'll not be pulling anyone down … you have committed no crime. Cordelia knows and approves of what you did.'

'But she must be in Calcutta by now!'

'Oh, of course, you wouldn't know! Cordelia's father is dead. He died the very day she reached the garden. She's stayed back at Dhanboa itself.'

The news, clearly, came as a severe shock to the Lieutenant. 'Poor girl!' he cried out. 'How she must have suffered!'

'Yes. She's suffered greatly, but she's determined to make Dhanboa her home. She hopes to derive comfort by working for the upliftment of the coolies, and looking after David. Two simultaneous blows on her tender sensibility … your disappearance and her father's death. Yet she has shown more grit than you have. Unlike you she has not tried to escape from realities. Rather, she's attempting to come to grips with them and remoulding her life as best as she can. Michael, my son, would you not go to Cordelia now? Would you not give her the strength and love she so desperately needs?'

'Yes, I'll do that,' the Lieutenant said with sudden determination. 'Yes, I must do that.'

The Reverend smiled broadly, the smile dancing in his eyes. 'You were a fool, Michael, to have cut off so abruptly the thread of love. You are a great one for self-inflicted punishment but you must go now. Pick up the thread and wrap it around your heart. And, if a missionary might be allowed to reiterate use such words … to hell with the Buckinghams and Gosselins of this world!'

The padre stayed back on the hillock but his eyes followed the Lieutenant all the way to the boat that would take him back to Titabar.

Back at Titabar, Gokuldeva Barua took Bailin's setback stoically. 'One hundred and forty-seven acres?' he exclaimed. 'As we say in Assamese, *Nai momaitke kona momai bhal* … a blind uncle is better than no uncle at all! What do you propose to do now?'

'I fear I shall have to impose upon you further. But I must learn something of tea before I can strike out on my own.'

'It's no imposition, Michael. You can stay on for as long as you wish. My tea garden, Mohoniya, is very close by; a mere half-hour journey upon an elephant. You can spend your days at the garden, your nights here.'

'Is there anyone who can tutor me?'

'I'll depute Phukan. He runs Mohoniya on my behalf. I also have a few Chinese tea makers brought from Calcutta. They'll teach you the rudiments of making tea.'

'Thank you, Barua dangoriya. Another thing … could you please spare a boat for a day? I wish to send Garo to Dhanboa.'

The Assamese nobleman nodded understandingly. 'So, you've decided to renew ties with Miss Esscombe? But why send Garo? Why don't you yourself go?'

'I must first test the waters. I played a petty, mean and thoughtless trick on David and Miss Esscombe. The Reverend Swanson believes Miss Esscombe's regards towards me have not suffered as a consequence. But I have to make sure. Will you spare a boat?'

'I shall, certainly. You know, Michael, you're an obstinate creature in your own way. And tenacious. Duped as you have been, others in your shoes might have thrown in the towel and gone back to Calcutta.'

'A misjudgement on your part, Barua dangoriya,' the Lieutenant said with a laugh. 'Not tenacity, but compulsion, makes me stick it out.'

First the tribal coolies. Then the rains. And now Cordelia. The whole bloody universe appeared to be conspiring against him!

David sat on the verandah of the bungalow full of petulant anger. Damn Cordi! How he wished she was back in Calcutta with the Swinnerton-Dyers, amongst people she really belonged. Yet, the very moment such a thought crept into his mind it leapt back, like fingers from a hot poker, and the awareness of her love came flowing in. He was at the centre of his sister's existence; there was no denying that. In the absence of Papa and Michael who else did she have to call her own? For that matter, who else did he have to call his own? They had only each other, through thick and thin.

But such emotional proximity could also be a burden impeding progress. Why the devil could Cordi not appreciate the kind of pressures he was working under? He did not want to end up as Papa did, reduced to the skeletal mockery of a man, gasping for breath in a stink-filled hovel. Nor did he wish to play out his entire life within the prosaic circumventions of a tea garden, waking with the dawn, yelling at the coolies, planting seeds, tending plants, plucking leaves, turning them into bits of twisted, black threads, day after monotonous day, hour after monotonous hour.

David had loved Papa, and was loyal to him with equal ferocity. Papa's letters had revealed how proud he was of Dhanboa. The garden was, so he had imagined, the elusive symbol of success he had pursued all his life. That had been a lie, for had Papa not died, and David not arrived, Dhanboa with its unproductive bushes would have turned out to be just one more of his many failures. But Dhanboa must not be allowed to fail; that would be disloyal to Papa's memory. Yes, he would build up the garden into a triumphant memorial to Papa. As he had told Cordi, if need be, he would sup with the devil himself to ensure that!

These were the compulsions which drove him. He had reconciled the compulsions to his dreams—had fashioned his very own crystal ball and gazed into a future of his own making. How long would it take to liberate himself from a father's legacy? To throw away an unsought burden but untainted by the guilt of betrayal? Five years? Eight years? Ten years?

Dhanboa would be a prosperous garden then, five hundred acres of Assam jat bushes; thousand upon thousand pounds of made tea. They would have a manager just as moneyed companies. And then David would be unburdened of compulsions and free to embark in quest of his own holy grail!

Cordi did not understand his desperation—perversely illogical, she refused to condone the fact that he was trespassing on what she considered to be alien grounds in order to make Dhanboa succeed. She wanted him to act as Papa had acted, behave as Papa had behaved. She did not know that was a prescription for disaster! She too had worshipped the very ground Papa walked on. But unlike his, hers was the devotion of the blind, a faith without insight, sans reason and perception. She had not analysed the root cause of Papa's failure; in fact, he very much doubted if she was aware at all Papa had failed! So, she constantly measured him against Papa; wanted to guide him over paths Papa had traversed, little knowing that those paths led to a tumbledown cottage, a racked body covered with purulent abscesses, and a lonely death.

After the very first outburst against his decision to be tutored by Buckingham about teacraft she had made no further remonstrations; had borne with stony acceptance Buckingham's later visits to Dhanboa. But often uncomplaining silence was greater reproof than vociferous complaints, especially to minds filled with guilt and self-reproach. That had made the decision even more painful for him.

No, he could not expect her to see Buckingham, as he himself did, as Dhanboa's saviour. But this was the reality. Without Buckingham's knowledge, expertise and experience, and his guidance, Dhanboa would be Papa's final failure and David's first. The planter's offer to supply tea saplings free of cost had made his role in shaping Dhanboa's future indispensable. Bihguri's proximity made Buckingham's offer a godsend—how do you explain that to one who had mulishly pulled down the shutters of her mind?

By no action must he give offence to Buckingham; he must check his own impulses, for his abhorrence of the planter occasionally threatened to seep out at the fellow's insolent, omniscient postures. He had begun work on the nursery, with seeds supplied by Buckingham—the replanting of the uprooted area would begin soon with saplings supplied by Buckingham—

let all these be completed. When the rains came and manufacturing started, he would make the final visits to Bihguri, to learn the latest technique of making tea. Then, with Dhanboa rendered self-sufficient and his own knowledge complete, he would withdraw from Buckingham's shadow. Only a matter of months! Cordi would then understand means were not important in commerce as long as the desired end was reached; something Papa could never comprehend.

He would not buckle to Cordi on the issue of Buckingham—but, as far as the coolies were concerned, he had always met her halfway. Here she was on firmer grounds; it was good business logic to keep the coolies as healthy and happy as possible. But she had been making too many demands on him lately, as if the welfare of these creatures were of greater importance than Dhanboa's future. Papa had made the same mistake; he had spoon-fed them to an extent that they had become incapable of rising to the occasion when the crisis came. But he himself had shown his mettle in a moment of crisis; driven his coolies beyond their capacities and succeeded in keeping to schedule.

The inevitable happened; the lazy bastards, pampered by Papa, began to fake illnesses, and swarmed to his sympathetic sister and her dispensary. A litany of fabricated complaints—nausea, headache, stomach ache, diarrhoea; they had kept Cordi busy, all right! She was incapable of seeing through their game. And then she had begun to pour forth in his ears her own litany. 'You're driving them too hard, David. Over-exhaustion breeds illnesses, it's but natural.' 'Oh, come on, sis. I'm working as hard as any of them. I've not fallen ill, have I?' 'But you're different, David. Their constitutions are not as strong as yours. And anyway, I'm worried about you too.' He had tried to explain, but she simply wouldn't listen. It was always Papa did this, Papa did that!

The well-being of the coolies lay in the well-being of Dhanboa—he had not been able to get that message through because of her pigheadedness. Lately, she had been at him for making his workforce toil throughout the week without a break. 'But Sunday is the day of Sabbath, David … the day of rest. Papa never made them work on Sundays.'

'It's only for a short while, Cordi. Then they can have their Sundays off again.' But Cordi could not be put off with logic! And this Sunday morning she had adroitly preempted him. At the crack of dawn, even before he had arisen from bed, she was at the coolie basti, on a 'sanitary inspection', that's what she had said. The sirdar trio—Harua, Ajam and Robiya—had come to the bungalow and sheepishly informed him that the coolies would not be coming to work today. Memsahib's hukum. She was on a 'sanitary inspection'!

David was furious. With the three sirdars in tow, he had marched into the coolie basti, determined to wrest his workers from Cordi's grasp, and take them to the fields. At the open square beside the coolie basti, where the coolies danced the jhumur during festival days, and youngsters played guli-danda and catch-me-if-you-can, he came upon a unique sight. A table had been laid; Bapu babu sat on a chair taking down comments uttered by Cordi. She herself, as well as that pipsqueak Assamese assistant of hers—what was his name, Kamal—stood by the table, physically examining, one by one, each and every coolie man, woman and child. They stood in a line, silent and obedient, subjecting themselves to her scrutiny without qualm or complaint. Cordi was apparently preparing a medical dossier on each of the coolies!

A pang of admiration—even a streak of jealousy—ran through David. How these creatures adored Cordi! She had a hold on them he could never aspire to. The same hold that Buckingham had upon his coolies—but how different! David admitted defeat. He returned to the bungalow, there to cool his heels for the rest of the day.

He sat on the verandah, sipping his tea, readying himself to take her on when she returned. Suddenly Mongla came running up. '*Sahib, ek aadmi aya hai,*' he said '*Naam hai* Garo. He has a letter from Bailin sahib.'

Mongla's words so startled David that the hot tea in his hand spilled on to his shirt and trousers. 'Garo? Bailin sahib?' he foolishly repeated the names as his mind strove to come to terms with this development.

He willed himself to act. 'Bring him up,' he said.

The native, whom he had last seen on board the *Ultaganga*, was led up. The fellow had a presumptuous grin on his face. He salaamed neatly and asked, 'How are you, David sahib? How is Cordelia memsahib?'

'We're fine, Garo,' David said, forcing a smile on to his face. 'My man tells me you've brought a letter from Bailin sahib?'

Garo offered David the missive.

'Dear David,' Michael had written:

Years seem to have lapsed since we last saw each other. The Reverend Swanson informed me of the passing away of your father. Words are inadequate to convey how deeply I grieve your loss.

I owe you both an apology. My leaving the *Ultaganga* was an act of unpardonable cowardice. I cannot forgive myself for the hurt I caused you. But I hope both of you will find it in your hearts to forgive me.

A great deal has happened to me since I last saw you. I'll not fill up these pages with a narration. I'd rather tell you about it myself.

If it is convenient to you, I propose to pay a visit to Dhanboa and renew a bond I so thoughtlessly severed. Right now, I am at Titabar, as a guest of Gokuldeva Barua. You recollect the name, don't you? He was the native nobleman who sailed on the *Ultaganga* with us. This gentleman has been very kind to me. Now I'm engaged in learning about growing tea in his plantation. I shall be with him for another week or so before moving on to Chahpuli.

I plan to visit Dhanboa prior to that. Do let me know through Garo if that would be convenient. We've so much to talk about. Please accept my condolences once more. And my apologies. I shall offer them in person when I'm at Dhanboa.

Michael

A cold funk rose up in David even as his eyes pored over the letter but, conscious of Garo standing before him with anticipating eyes, he fought it down and tried to sound normal as he said, 'Thank you, Garo. You may wait, while I write out a reply.'

He went quickly to his room, his mind racing. Michael must be prevented from coming to Dhanboa, or all was lost! The taunting features of Buckingham rose before him. Hurry, hurry, his nerves shrieked. Cordi might return any minute now. Garo must be sent packing before she arrived!

He shoved Michael's letter beneath some papers, momentarily out of sight. He sat at the writing table and with shaking hands penned the reply.

Dear Michael,

Received your note. We accept your condolences. There is no need to apologize. Your departure from the *Ultaganga* was entirely your personal concern. Both Cordi and I are unanimous on that point.

It will not be convenient for us to have you at Dhanboa in the immediate future. Papa's death has disrupted all our plans. We are still trying to recover from the blow and reorganize our lives. Perhaps after a few months, when the manufacturing season ends, and we are in a proper frame of mind to play the host to you.

David

In a state of blind panic by now, David searched for an envelope, found one, and pushed the note into it. He hastened outside and thrust it at the perplexed Garo.

'Give this to Bailin sahib.'

But the idiot did not move. Instead, he asked, 'I would like to meet Cordelia memsahib. Can I not wait?'

'No,' said David. It needed all his efforts not to shout at the man. 'Cordelia memsahib has gone to Jorehaut. She'll be back tomorrow. Now, for heaven's sake, go!'

Garo looked away. He knows I am lying, David thought. But the man before him turned and walked down the stairs, moving with dignity. David followed him with his eyes as he walked over the path leading to the entry gate.

He called out loudly for the houseboy. 'Mongla, keep this man's visit a secret. Don't tell anyone, not even the memsahib, about it. If she gets to know, I'll skin you alive!'

Now that the immediate danger was over, the panic subsided, and a self-congratulatory euphoria settled in him. He had accomplished everything none too soon, for fifteen minutes after Garo's departure Cordi arrived, grimy and dishevelled, and very tired. He greeted her with a nervous smile.

'Must've been utterly exhausting, this medical checkup, sis?'

'But worth it, David.' Cordelia was surprised and pleased at the mildness of his tone. 'I was really anxious, you know, when they began to flock in droves to the dispensary. But I've good news for you. They are all in reasonably sound health.'

'They are all fakers, sis! Give them some real work and they troop to your dispensary! When will you ever learn?'

Cordelia refused to be baited. 'Must clean myself up, David,' she said, looking fondly at him. 'You sit right there till I'm back.'

David allowed the tension in him to dissipate slowly, like warmth from a cup of tea. No, he would not allow guilt to enter his heart! For the time being Papa's garden was everything. The rest did not matter.

The following morning, Garo kept his eye fixed on his master's face as he read the letter. 'Well, that's that, Garo,' he finally said. 'It seems the Reverend was wrong. Chahpuli must be a hole for the vermin!'

His master asked no questions. Nothing about Dhanboa or David sahib. Nothing about the memsahib who had once been so close to him but seemed was no longer.

The week which followed was spent in preparing for the imminent shift to their mock-garden. Gokuldeva's pigtailed Chinamen were good teachers, as was Phukan. They taught him all he needed to know about preparing the ground for tea planting. Local villagers had been engaged by the nobleman to build a small hutment in Chahpuli in which he and Garo could live.,

Although Gokuldeva knew of Garo's Dhanboa visit, he had not spoken on the subject, but on that last evening, after dinner was over and plates cleared, he asked, 'Did Garo return disappointed from Dhanboa? Could he not meet Miss Esscombe?'

'Garo brought a letter from David.' He fetched the letter from a side-table and gave it to Gokuldeva who glanced quickly through the contents.

'The letter says it all, Barua dangoriya!'

'Something's the matter here, Michael. The letter does not sound quite right. Did you ask Garo what transpired during his visit? Did Garo see Miss Esscombe?'

'I didn't ask.'

'Why not ask him now?' Gokuldeva called Garo and questioned him. The truth was out. David sahib had been greatly perturbed when he read the Lieutenant's note. He had lied about Cordelia memsahib.

'So, all is not what appears on the surface, isn't that so, Michael? If Miss Esscombe had been there, things might have been different. David, apparently, wanted to keep her away from Garo.'

'But why on earth?' Bailin cried out in bewilderment.

'I would need a third eye to tell you that. But I can guess. Remember, the blackguard called Buckingham is their neighbour. David is a callow, inexperienced youth. His father is dead. Might he not fall prey to Buckingham's machinations?'

'That's preposterous, Barua dangoriya. No, my reading of the letter was correct. I thoughtlessly deserted them … my concern was only for myself. I didn't consider the shame and humiliation my actions could cause David and Miss Esscombe. They have every reason to loathe my very name.'

'Read the letter again, Michael. It contains unuttered hints. If they abhorred you for what you'd done, David would have forever barred your entry to Dhanboa. But his inconvenience lasts only till the end of the manufacturing season. That speaks volumes!'

'So, you think Buckingham's behind all this, do you?' Bailin was not entirely convinced.

'That rogue's capable of anything!'

'You hate him as much as I do?'

Gokuldeva's reply caught him by surprise. Not the words but the venom with which they were uttered. 'Let me put it this way, Michael. If tomorrow someone, somewhere, offers to get rid of Buckingham, I would lend him all assistance!'

Winters in Assam were far different from those of Delhi. There the chill crept in slowly, with forewarning. Here it abruptly stole upon an unsuspecting earth—a few days of incessant drizzle and the temperature dropped steeply, giving people barely enough time to unpack and air the woollens, put quilts and blankets out in the sun. In Delhi the winters had been dry, dusty and windswept; here it was far milder and moist. At night a thick, foggy blanket covered the earth, reducing visibility. The sun could not be seen till late in the morning but when the mist finally thinned and the sunrays burst forth, they dazzled off the myriad dewdrops on the leaves and the grass. For a few flitting moments those were not tea bushes which grew in Dhanboa, but magical plants sprouting diamonds and pearls and emeralds!

Barely a few days were left before Christmas. In Delhi these days would have been ones of frenetic activity. Invitations would have poured in, there would be gifts to be wrapped, parties to be planned, constant shuttling between home and the emporiums, shopping for presents, jostling in the native bazaars haggling for all one was worth, innumerable visits to the darzi for fittings for the evening dresses which would welcome the new year in. Here it was life as usual, or the unusual which had become the usual. The only Christmas invitation had been one from Buckingham, which David, with uncharacteristic self-restraint, had politely refused with the plea that he and Cordi would spend a quiet Christmas at Dhanboa.

The only party Cordelia planned was the feast she was giving in the coolie basti on Christmas Eve, and a small dinner she was having at home, for David, herself, Bapu babu, Kamal and Mongla. A turkey could not be had for love or money, but David had been appalled by the thought of a roast murgi on Christmas Eve. The bormohori came to the rescue. with his suggestion that since 'the famous and noble bird, the turkey' could not be procured, they could roast 'the humble duck' instead. He had a whole 'cackle of ducklings, all very well domesticated,' in his village home, and would choose a young, tender and plump one. Oh, he wouldn't accept money for the 'duckling;' it was a signal honour for him to be invited to dine with dear David sahib and darling Cordelia memsahib, so he must do his bit to make the 'Christmas bhoj' a success, mustn't he?

Three days prior to Christmas Cordelia had dispatched Bapu babu to Jorehaut with a list of things to be purchased, including some wine and tinned provisions, if available, from a 'European shop' in the market village. He was also to enquire at Captain Hewitt's office for mail. They had already spent over two months at Dhanboa and had not received a single letter. The bormohori had another chore. Some time ago a Mohameddan trader from Jorehaut, sent by Buckingham, had visited Dhanboa. He could procure two Walers for the sahib and the memsahib, he had said, but could not tell off-hand when they might arrive. The sahib must pay half the money as advance; he must also enquire at Jorehaut in a fortnight for a specific time when the animals would arrive. So, Bapu babu on this trip to Jorehaut must drop in at the trader's establishment and learn the date from him.

Cordelia had expected David to react angrily to her plans to give the coolies a feast on Christmas Day, and to her intimation that Bapu babu and Kamal would grace their table on Christmas Eve, and spend the night in the bungalow, being unable to return to their village at so late an hour. David had changed, oh how he had changed! The change in him had become more marked ever since Buckingham pointed out Papa's faulty planting and he had had to uproot a greater part of the plantation. Cordelia had watched with alarm as her brother made his workforce slog till many of the coolies almost dropped with exhaustion. Unknown facets to David's character opened out for her during the uprooting. The intense love for him had blurred that discernment; she had sought to make the excuses he himself had never offered. But the transformation had been far too severe for prolonged self-deception—the terrifying obsession to succeed without counting the costs, the haughtiness that had crept into him; even his features had changed, and his eyes. Sadly, she had discovered that she now had to fight him every inch of the way. Papa's name was no longer a magical key—David too was armed with understanding of Papa's character, but it was the awareness of the weaknesses in Papa which seemed to motivate him into acting otherwise, rather than Papa's big-heartedness and strengths.

Yes, she had had to wrest each concession from him, till she had felt herself an intruder at Dhanboa. That had induced a change in her too, making her all the more determined to keep Papa's true legacy alive as far as the coolies were concerned. But lately she had begun to hope—for, with the nearing of completion of the uprooting David was once again exhibiting traces of what she told herself was his former self. He had been strangely subdued, almost as if he was privy to secrets denied to her, and accepted her actions with good grace. And, strangely enough, he had displayed the same liberalness with regards to the basti feast, and the dinner invitation to Bapu babu and Kamal. He had made only one stipulation—the bormohori and the assistant should spend the night at the dispensary. They could not be permitted to sleep in the bungalow, for that would infringe on the kind of discipline he was trying to instill at Dhanboa. Cordelia, somewhat overwhelmed by his uncarping acceptance, agreed readily.

Her affection for David had something of the maternal in it, thereby denying her clarity of discernment, inducing too quick a spirit of forgiveness. During the uprooting, when he was totally obsessed with

Dhanboa, he had exhibited a streak of self-centredness making him insensate to any other point of view but his own. His treatment of the simple-minded, innocuous Bapu babu, particularly, had been atrocious. And then came this abrupt change; lately he had become the old David again, the change coinciding with the decreasing pressures on him as the uprooting neared completion. With true motherly instinct Cordelia forgave him each earlier lapse; quickly forgot the pain and hurt she herself had been subjected to, viewing David's past behaviour as a transient aberration brought about by stupendous pressures on an unfledged mind. Ironically, she took upon herself much of the blame; after all, Christmas lay round the corner, and the spirit of charity pervaded the universe!

Bapu babu returned in the evening. He imparted the trader's message for David—the horses would be delivered only towards late January. Much to Cordelia's delight the bormohori also handed a parcel containing their first dak at Dhanboa.

There were only three letters in that packet: a fat obese envelope addressed to David Esscombe, Esquire; two slim envelopes for Miss Cordelia Esscombe. The brother and sister read the letters together. The packet for David was from Swinnerton-Dyer. On a single sheet was recorded the merchant's sorrow at Henry's death. The agreement drawn up with Henry, unfortunately, had to be redrawn now in the light of his death; the merchant was sending two copies of the rephrased document; David must sign both in the presence of witnesses, retain one copy and mail the other to Calcutta. The merchant asked David not to hesitate to write if he required any assistance, to keep his accounts correctly and religiously, not to spend beyond his means and to let him know well in advance the date when the new season's produce would reach Calcutta. As for Cordi, she had written the strangest of letters to her aunt, filled with outlandish notions. Swinnerton-Dyer would have none of it! Cordi must journey back to Calcutta immediately and come and live with them. A postscript informed that the headstone for Henry's grave had been ordered, and would be sent by steamer to reach Kokilamukh by the third or fourth week of January.

The two letters for Cordelia were from the Reverend Garry Swanson and Aunt Patricia. Cordelia opened the Reverend's letter first. He had met Michael in Sivasagar, by accident rather than design. Bad luck had dogged the footsteps of that unfortunate young man. As the Reverend suspected at the very beginning, the Lieutenant had been swindled. Adding injury to insult, he had been struck by cholera and almost perished. His visit to Sivasagar had been to lodge a complaint with the Principal Assistant, the fire-emitting dragon whom David and Cordelia and encountered on the *Ultaganga*. The Sivasagar visit had brought the Lieutenant the first slice of good news—he was the rightful proprietor of over a hundred acres of virgin land, which he intended to plant on.

Michael had been under the illusion that Cordelia had left with her father for Calcutta. He was unaware that her father was dead. The Reverend had pressed upon him the need to visit Dhanboa. Has he paid that visit? If he has not, which meant he was still enmeshed in self-created webs of doubt and hesitations, would not Cordelia find it in her heart to pity him, and herself seek him out?

Cordelia folded up the letter. An involuntary sigh escaped from her, causing David to wince and look away. 'You don't really intend to seek him out, sis?' he asked with transparent anxiety. Cordelia said nothing. She opened Aunt Patricia's letter and read it out aloud—a long, rambling missive, communicating her deep distress at 'poor Henry's' death, and her inability to comprehend the 'nonsense' she had written about staying back at Dhanboa and taking care of the 'native labourers.'

'If Henry had played the doctor to the coolies,' Aunt Patricia had written, 'it was because he wanted to cut down on costs. But David must not count the pices. Alexander will always help him out if he were ever in want of money. He can employ a doctor and his uncle will pay for it. A native quack should be good enough for the coolies. As for your doing the doctoring, why, I've never heard anything so preposterous in my life! We certainly shan't send you medical treatises!

'Alexander and I are one on this at least, though he is so perversely contradictory on most issues. There can be no question of your staying on in Dhanboa, now that poor Henry is dead. I really feel strongly on this, Cordi darling. Your youth and your beauty must not be permitted to be frittered away. So, pack your bags, Cordi dear, and come back to Calcutta. I'm having the blue room redecorated to welcome you in. I'll leave the draperies to your choice, for one's taste in such things do matter, don't they, to make one feel at home?

'Oh yes, although poor Henry is dead and buried, and your poor mama died long ago, you must not say you and David are all alone in the world. I shall be like a mother to you, Cordi dear. You can look upon Alexander as your father, although, of course, he makes a poor substitute for Henry. You unburdened your heart in your letter, so let me unburden mine. I have always, always, wanted a daughter just like you. It was the will of God which left me barren—the same divine will now bring you to me. You can't imagine, darling Cordi, how much I've missed having children of my own. Now, at last, I can show you around as my very own daughter; plan out your future—there's so much enjoyment to be derived from the Calcutta society—then there are those eligible young men who'll flock to you; with your beauty and natural grace you have just to move your little finger to make them dance to your tune. I shall fill up my life with you, dear daughter. You'll, I hope, not begrudge me that. You'll want for nothing—neither will David. If Alexander does not squander money on his own son and daughter, what on earth will he do with it?

'David can run Dhanboa if he wishes; but it is you who I want, dear daughter. You must immediately arrange passage aboard the next steamer ...'

The cessation of the letter heralded a thickened silence, punctuated by the sound of the mist coagulating on the cool thatch-roof into dew drops and dripping down the eves to the ground. It was Cordelia who tore the silence, her voice angry and bitter.

'It was my fault, I suppose! Aunt Patricia was not the ideal recipient of my confidences!'

'Her affection for you is genuine, sis,' David said, trying not to sound too eager.

'She's a dear old thing ... neither equipped with Uncle Alex's intelligence, nor his guile. But it will take more than an aged aunt's affections to pull me away from Dhanboa.'

'She has a point, you must concede that. Dhanboa holds nothing for you.'

'It holds a great deal for me, David. For one, it holds you.'

'You know my views are exactly those of Uncle Alex and Aunt Patricia. I don't want to be a cause for any contrary decision on your part.'

Cordelia felt the tears come to her eyes. 'You do not wish me to be near you, David? You'd rather I go to live with strangers; amongst people I have come to detest?'

'Now sis, don't go about twisting my words! Of course, I want you near me! But what I want is of little account. I'm perfectly willing to forgo it, if it be for your welfare.'

'Can't you see, David, that there's no conflict between what you want and what I want.'

'Not at this moment, perhaps. Nor a year later. But you can't spend an eternity in Dhanboa! Looking after the coolies … looking after me … these might fill up your life for a while. But your crusading zeal will dry up. You'll rue the day you turned down Aunt Patricia's generous offer.'

'I know what you're thinking, David. A life of comfort for Cordi, even if it be in someone else's nest. High tea with the Brooke-Smiths and dinner with the Douglases! Evening balls in silk and chiffon and diamond necklace! Gossip and scandal and back-biting! Flutter my eyelashes or my fan and the beaus come trooping in!'

'Am I being unbrotherly conjuring up such a vision for my sister? You socialized in Delhi, if I recall correctly! I didn't hear this sarcastic note in your voice then!'

'That's because I've grown since, David! I wish you would do the same!'

It was the repetitive pattern all over again. One of them irate, inducing anger in the other—the heated words, and the lonely spell of repentance. But this evening David backed off with surprising charity. 'Let's not quarrel, sis. I'm just pointing out your options. Uncle Alex is a rich man, after all. Aunt Patricia desires you desperately. They can give you the life you deserve. What *I* think you deserve.'

'I'm sorry, David,' Cordelia said. 'I know it's your love for me which makes you insist I return to Calcutta. But I've no fascination for Uncle Alex's riches, nor wish Aunt Patricia to play the surrogate mother to me. There're other things in life which will offer me more gratification. Your love, for instance, and the genuine affection of the coolies.'

'And Michael?'

The question caught Cordelia by surprise. When she spoke again, David caught the sorrow in her voice.

'Michael? No matter what you think, David, but Michael's not the primary reason why I want to stay on in Dhanboa. I want to stay because this is Papa's garden … everything in it carries his memories. I want to stay because you are here. And the coolies are here. Yes, I grieve for Michael. Sometimes I stay awake in the night grieving. His leaving the *Ultaganga* was not a betrayal, but a sacrifice. That too I know.'

Safe within the shadows, David silently waited, his ears alert for further words.

'The Reverend wants me to seek him out. But how would that help, David? If the sentiments which impelled him to leave the *Ultaganga* still exist in him, what difference would it make if he's at Chahpuli and I at Dhanboa? He must come to terms with himself and see his past in another light.'

'You're right, sis,' David said, carefully erasing the relief from his voice. 'He knows you're here, yet has made no move to get in touch with you. Indication enough that he hasn't come to terms with himself. But let a few months elapse. Maybe we'll seek him out after that.'

'No, Michael must come to me. Oh, I'll give him time, all right. Time to sort out his feelings and come to me. No, David, I'll not seek him out. But I'll not shut him out of my heart either. There can be no usurper to Michael in my heart!'

The words rang out in the cold night with the clarity of a gong and their adamantine finality put a chill into David's heart. He tried to sound casual. 'Well, it's settled then. You'll write, of course, to Aunt Patricia. Try to soften the blow, sis. She's a good woman.'

On that note they parted. David tarried a moment before the door of his room, cocked his ears to catch the sound as Cordi shut hers. Then he entered in a feverish hurry, picked up the candle, and began a frantic search. Michael's letter! Where the devil had he put it? Ah, there it was, under a pile of paper!

He picked up the letter and put it to the flame. Though he was in his own room his heart harboured a feeling of trespass as he watched the paper burst into flame and reduce to ashes Michael's words.

The Christmas dinner was an unqualified success. Bapu babu, moved by the spirit of 'Do in Roma as the Roman sahibs do,' despite being a teetotaler, imbibed a great deal of wine, and became a veritable torrent of incoherence before passing out, and had to be carried off to his bed in the dispensary. The coolies enjoyed the burrakhana hugely, supplementing the food provide by the management with mod and rice beer of their own. The feast, begun in the afternoon, carried on till late in the evening, when a bonfire was lit and there was much singing and dancing in the basti.

Three days later a visitor arrived, the Cinnamora assistant, Nicholls. He carried a gift from that garden's superintendent, George Williamson, and an invitation. The gift was an Alsatian puppy, black and male, a couple of months old. A card, signed by George Williamson, was strung to the basket. 'To Miss Cordelia Esscombe—a belated Christmas gift', it read.

Cordelia fell in love with the puppy at first sight. It was a frisky little thing. Released from the cramped confines of the basket, it pranced around the bungalow. 'You must give the tyke a name, Miss Esscombe,' Nicholls said as he lowered his lanky body into the cane chair.

'Of course, I shall. Thank you so much, Mr Nicholls. And thank Mr Williamson too, on behalf of both of us.'

Nicholls flushed with pleasure. He turned his boyish face towards David. 'The Soup's resigning, Mr Esscombe. Dashed tragic, what?'

'The Soup?'

'Oh, I mean the Super. Old George, you know. The Superintendent. Bit of a cock-up with the Board. But he aims to go out in style. Throwing a big binge on the first of Jan.'

'I see,' David said, not quite seeing.

'I've come to invite you both … to the big binge at Cinnamora … on the first of Jan.' Nicholls appeared ill at ease in Cordelia's proximity. 'The Soup gave me an invitation letter. I was holding it in my hand. It fell into the ruddy stream, ha, ha!'

David and Cordelia laughed politely. 'You won't tell the Soup that, would you now? Or I would be in the soup, ha, ha! Oh, he's a grand old bloke. Best in the business. Taught me all I know about tea … which is precious little, ha, ha! You'll come, of course?'

'A one-day affair, Mr Nicholls?' David asked.

'Well, we expect you the evening of thirty first. Every bloke hereabouts who's who in tea is coming. So, we've put up tents. You'll have to rough it out, Mr Esscombe. But the whisky's going to flow so you won't know if you're sleeping in a tent or a castle, ha, ha!'

'I am not really sure …' Cordelia began.

'Oh, not you, Miss Esscombe. You'll get a room in Soup's bungalow, never fear. That's your privilege for being born different from the likes of us, ha, ha!'

'No, it's not what you imagine, Mr Nicholls. We're still in mourning for Papa.'

'Oh, but you must come, Miss Esscombe. There's going to be a bonfire in the evening, and dinner under the stars. A greener-shoot early next morning, the first of Jan.'

'A greener-shoot?' David asked.

'Oh, green pigeons, don't you know? We shall have at least a dozen guns between us. Do you possess a gun, Mr Esscombe?'

'Yes. A Martini Henry musket. Our father's rifle. Bit rusty with disuse, I daresay.'

'Great fun, Miss Esscombe,' Nicholls chipped in. 'Our last chance this season to let our hair down a bit.'

'It does sound tempting,' David said, looking at Cordelia. 'Now that the uprooting's completed, I suppose we can go.'

Cordelia smiled. 'Mr Williamson has been very gracious to have gifted us the puppy, although we haven't made acquaintance with him. I suppose it'll be churlish to turn down an invitation from him. We'll go.'

Nicholls's boyish features exploded into a broad smile. 'That's corking news, Miss Esscombe.' He pushed himself out of the chair. 'So, we'll expect you on the thirty first eve. Goodbye.'

'Come, David. Think up a name for him.' Cordelia urged, pointing at the puppy.

David pondered for a while. 'Call him Pekoe,' he suggested at last.

'What a divine name! Oh, thank you, David. Does it have a meaning?'

'Good heavens, sis! A planter's daughter and you don't know what Pekoe is! A grade of tea … that's what it is. Derives from Pei Hao in Chinese, I believe, meaning white hair or white down. Refers to the very fine hair on young tea leaves.'

'Well, our Pekoe is black all over! But doesn't matter a whit, does it?' She picked up the warm little bundle. 'Come, Pekoe. We must make you feel at home.'

They set off for Cinnamora by boat on the afternoon of the thirty-first. A veritable flotilla of boats was moored at that garden's jetty, and a large number of individuals were present to receive them. As they made their way through a maze of narrow garden paths to the burrasahib's bungalow, David was struck by Cinnamora's sheer size. It could comfortably accommodate three Bihguris within its perimeters, with enough area left over for a Dhanboa or two! But I'll change that, David thought. Dhanboa shall be the best yielding plantation, acre for acre, before I'm through with it!

The burrasahib's bungalow was a giant of a structure, with a huge roof of thatch, set like their tiny one at Dhanboa on tree-stem stilts. A large, open space fronted the bungalow; now it was dotted with tents. Dozens of coolies were busy in diverse activities, setting up chairs and tables, piling logs into a stack for the bonfire, mowing the grass and sweeping clean the area and, in general, making preparations for the evening's entertainment.

As they stopped to take in the scene of activity, four men descended the bungalow's staircase, Nicholls among them. But it was an elderly, bearded gentleman, of medium height and solid build, who came up with outstretched hands to shake David's. 'Mr Esscombe, I presume? I'm so glad you could come.' He turned towards Cordelia and took her hands.

'Absolutely delighted, Miss Esscombe!' the eyes, set under bushy eyebrows, were filled with genuine pleasure. 'I'm George Williamson. To my friends I'm George … To my assistants, I'm the Soup!'

He laughed good-humouredly and introduced the trio accompanying him: McDonald and Lumsdaine Junior, both astonishingly young, and Nicholls, whom they already knew. All three were apparently in awe of their superior, and could barely utter their welcomes. But they seemed to be in greater awe of Cordelia!

'See, they're infatuated already!' the Superintendent said. 'I don't blame them, though, Miss Esscombe. You make me wish I were four decades younger. But let me introduce you to our guests.'

He led them up the stairs. A number of Europeans were strewn upon the verandah. With a sinking heart Cordelia realized she was the sole woman in the group. The ritual of introductions followed; she already knew three among the company—Major Gosselin, who had journeyed all the way from Sivasagar; Captain Hewitt of Jorehaut, whom they had fleetingly met at Kokilamukh ghat; and, of course, Christopher James Buckingham. But the others came up, one by one; she and David stood at one end of the verandah, shaking hands and exchanging a few words.

A chair was drawn for Cordelia between the Major and their host, while David plonked down on an empty cane chair beside Buckingham. A uniformed bearer brought a tea tray to Cordelia.

'Tea for you, David?' Williamson called out.

David looked about him, saw his compatriots were into whisky, and replied, 'Whisky for me, George.' A quick glance towards Cordelia to assess her reaction and he looked as quickly away.

'So how are you, Miss Esscombe?' Major Gosselin asked.

'Papa's death was a shock, Major Gosselin. But we've got over it.' She had intentionally brought Papa's demise into the conversation; both she and David and been conscious of the absolute lack of response from the European fraternity to Papa's death.

'You'll be returning to Calcutta, I presume, Cordelia,' Williamson put in.

'Oh, no! I shall stay on.'

'But that's admirable!' her host said, surprised. Incredulity too was visible on the faces of these planters close enough to overhear the conversation. 'Takes a great deal of courage for a woman, my dear, to confront the rigours of plantation life!'

'You'll tire of it soon enough,' said Hay Arthur of Amgoorie, a planter with greying hair and a carefully clipped goatee.

'She has her reasons,' Gosselin said, maintaining an air of confidentiality.

'Your father's dead, Miss Esscombe,' said Lyell, picking up the cue. 'Then, perhaps, there's someone else in Assam to keep you here?'

Cordelia, offended at this crude probe, said nothing. But Gosselin, willfully and with great guile, cleared the air of ambiguity. 'I met Michael Bailin in Sivasagar,' he said, loud enough for neighbouring ears to prick up. 'He seemed somewhat distraught. He had been sold a non-existent garden.' The officer looked hard at the girl before him, his gaze sharp as a butcher's knife.

'I know about it,' Cordelia said with simulated unconcern. 'The Reverend Swanson wrote about it in his letter.'

'Poor fellow,' commented Turner of Sookolatenga. 'Lots of that going around here nowadays, isn't that so, Major? Tea's drawing some awfully rotten eggs!'

'Who's this Michael Bailin?' enquired Birch of Gotoonga.

'A fellow passenger aboard the steamer. Miss Esscombe was on it, so was I. He came down with us till Gowhatty and then abruptly jumped ship.'

'An oddball?' asked Lyell.

'Not really. He called himself Lieutenant Michael Bailin. We discovered he had been court martialled at Ambala and dishonourably discharged. He could no longer face us.'

'Oh, a deserter, eh? Deserves to be horse whipped!' commented Hay Arthur.

'Miss Esscombe developed some intimacy with this chap. He had approached her under false pretences, you see. But her guardian angel showed a spot of alertness. She had not known the fellow's antecedents.'

'A lucky escape, Miss Esscombe!' said Lyell of Kaliabor. 'Shows you can't trust your own kind. But the world is not without justice. The scoundrel was duped, eh!'

'That's true,' said Major Gosselin, rubbing his hands in satisfaction. 'But he has a land grant and is bent on planting it. Calls his garden Chahpuli.'

'Bailin? Chahpuli?' said Hay Arthur. 'Must remember that. Let me meet the bloke some day. Give him a piece of my mind, I will!'

'So, this fellow's not tying you down to Assam, Miss Esscombe?' Lyell of Kaliabor took up the probe once again. 'Then what is?'

Williamson seemed to sense Cordelia's discomfort at the persistent personal queries. 'It's her own damned business. Robert!'

'Just curious, George. Miss Esscombe is young and pretty. Her place is in Calcutta, not in this jungle! She'll have a job keeping herself occupied.'

'Oh, but I have a great deal to occupy me,' Cordelia said. 'You see, Mr Lyell, I've discovered how coolies are being treated in tea plantations. I plan to ensure the ones in Dhanboa are not given the same treatment.'

The men around her fell into a shocked silence. Her host rose abruptly and held out an arm to her. 'Come, my dear. You'll wish to freshen up for the evening. I'll show you to your room.'

At the door to her room he said, 'You hit them where it hurts most, young lady. I daresay they deserved it.'

'Oh, Mr Williamson,' Cordelia cried, her face flushed. 'I hadn't expected that I would be the only woman here. If I had known, I may not have come at all!'

'I'm glad you came, my dear. Don't mind the chaps. They are all, without exception, bachelors. Not many European women have ventured into Assam thus far. The presence of a young and beautiful girl has made them curious, that's all.'

'Does it give them a right to be offensive, Mr Williamson?'

'Certainly not. Worse than a roomful of society matrons, weren't they? But tell me, my dear, did you love that fellow very much?'

Cordelia entered the room and turned around. 'You use the wrong tense, Mr Williamson!' she said as she shut the door.

At the evening's dinner, the young assistants milled around her, eager to obey her slightest command. She found them a gay and carefree lot who spoke with refreshing candour, and made her laugh with humorous narration of their travails in Assam. Just the right ambience had been created for the alfresco revelry; a fierce blaze had been lit at the clearing; the stars twinkled up above and fireflies glowed in the darkness around; hundreds of earthen chakis and candles illuminated the bungalow, magic lanterns were strung on trees and bushes. Both nature and human hands combined to evoke a fairy-tale setting, its timeless ethereality accentuated by the slow-thickening, smoky winter mist which the blaze attempted unsuccessfully to keep at bay. And Cordelia sat on her wooden throne, at a comfortable distance from the blaze, for a brief moment the eternal princess, surrounded by her Prince Charmings, who plied her with wine and the delicacies of the Orient, sang and serenaded her, made her laugh and momentarily lightened the burdens of mundanity. For too longhad she been deprived of such moments of uncaring happiness, made more pronounced by the fact that Buckingham, Gosselin and their ilk kept themselves well out of the way. Of David too there was no sight; but she knew he must be around somewhere, desperately playing out his role, that of a veteran tea planter who could drink and curse and burst into bawdy doggerel.

And then the bearded host came up to her again to bid her good night; it was his well-intentioned signal that she should depart; he had timed it to perfection, for bacchanal tensions were beginning to creep in. The young assistants escorted her to her room, marching up the stairs like a band of inebriated soldiers, singing 'she is a jolly good fellow.' She bade them all good night and shut the door to the boisterous sounds filling the night's air.

At 6 a.m. a bearer brought chota hazri. He informed her that all the sahibs had left on elephants for the greener shoot and would return at around ten for breakfast.

She had the whole place to herself! When the light grew sufficiently strong, she unfurled her parasol, tripped down the staircase and began walking across the open ground towards the tea bushes. She strolled slowly along, camouflaging her true objective, pausing here and there to watch the coolies, already at work with hoes, kodalis and daos.

A little later she hastened her pace and moved in a direction she judged would take her to the labour basti. However, she had not allowed for the plantation's extraordinary size and had to walk for over half an hour through lonely sections of plantings before she perceived unmistakable indications that the basti was nigh. Five minutes later she walked into one of them. She had wanted to see a basti other than the one at Dhanboa; learn if anything more could be done for her garden's coolies in ameliorative imitation. But the very moment she reached the fringes of this basti she realized there was nothing new she could learn. She caught the stench immediately—a mixture of excrement and urine, human as well as animal; the mildewed, dank smell of moist earth and stagnant effluvia; the treacly sweet odour of fermenting rice beer and mod. Above all was the fetid reek of human sweat a basti seemed to exude even when, like now, it was devoid of human presence.

Her reaction too was a contradictory admixture. There was anger at the sight of those empty, squalid hutments, strung together with reeds and grasses, roofs and walls sooty black with smoke from fireplaces. Yet there was joy in recalling the Dhanboa dwellings, sturdy on earthen terraces, roofs thickly thatched and walls mud-caked, able to keep the rain and the harsh fingers of winter out.

She left the basti and, for a while, walked on full of thought. Suddenly she came to a stop. She had reached the place with instinctive, yet unerring precision, like a bee reaching a pollen-laden flower; but she had not mentally marked her way. Consequently, she now found herself lost. Nothing but tea bushes lay around her; the sections were deserted and there was not a solitary creature to ask for directions. Half hour of meandering, and she was close to panic.

Finally, she came to what turned out to be a dead end, for a deep nullah bisected the path, to be crossed only by means of a thin betel nut stem laid across it, a feat she dared not attempt. Wearily Cordelia turned back the way she had come and then stopped abruptly, her hand automatically rising to her mouth to stifle a scream.

Christopher James Buckingham stood on the path, barely ten yards away!

It was not the man himself but the unanticipated abruptness of his appearance which had caused her heart to leap. His presence on the lonely, deserted path hinted that he had been stalking her for some time. He now stood casually blocking the narrow path, long, dark brown hair awash with sunshine, the face dissolutely handsome as ever.

'Did I give you a fright, dear girl?' he called out. The voice was infuriatingly intimate, though civil, and without its customary arrogance. 'Oh, come on! You're behaving as if you'd seen a ghost! Lost, aren't you? These garden paths are a ruddy maze! Come, come, I'll see you home.'

She did not move, but found her voice. 'What are you doing here, Buckingham?'

'The same as you, dear lady!' the insolence was slithering into his voice. 'I'm prying into Cinnamora's secrets. George has been doing a lot of experimentation. Thought I could pick up a trick or two!'

'Didn't you go out with the shooting party?'

'Greener shoots are such a drag! I had more important things to do so I feigned a tummy. Spent the whole morning in a stealthy scan of the garden.

But let's not waste any more time on futile explanations. Have to get back before the company returns.' He held out an arm.

Cordelia ignored the proffered arm and sought to edge past him. The arm streaked out, barring the way.

'You hate me, don't you, Cordelia?'

The words came at her like the slash of a cane! She sensed the explosion of anger in him and became conscious ofthe solitude and her vulnerability. And also, curiously, of David's dependence on him. Yet she could not sway away the distrust distorting her features as she stood waiting for him to remove the arm.

'Yes, you hate me!' he repeated. 'But you hate that bogus Lieutenant too, don't you? Now that you know the truth about him? Now that he's bolted from your life?'

Her nerves were on alert now, as she heard the man spit out the words. Infuriated, this man before her was capable of the grossest violence. She had seen it before—on Garo, and Michael. She stood transfixed and mute, fearful of instigating him any further.

Then, as abruptly, the choleric heat subsided, and she heard the taunting note once more, now ironically comforting. 'That's progress for you, dear girl! You hate Bailin as you hate me. So, you might learn to love me yet! David would like that, eh? I await the day!' He turned on his heels and, without further words, strode off.

Deeply shaken, Cordelia hurried after her saviour. They reached the bungalow within fifteen minutes. The hunting party had not yet returned. Only when she saw the planter enter a tent and close the flaps after him did she walk casually up to the bungalow and hurry to the safety of her room.

During lunch that afternoon David came up to her, guiding an elderly gentleman along. He was a sober-visaged individual, of the same build and girth as the Reverend Garry Swanson, the same grey hair and bushy beard, but dressed formally in a three-piece suit. He had been a late arrival, having reached Cinnamora only this morning, and had not had the opportunity to meet Cordelia. 'Mr Goodchild, sis. One of the Assam Company's Superintendents … Buckingham's superior. Stays in the company's Hatteoah plantation. Wished to meet you.'

Goodchild shook her hand, bowing stiffly. Cordelia saw the same good humour in his eyes as she had seen in the Reverend's. Her smile brightened.

'David has told me about what you both are attempting at Dhanboa,' Goodchild's voice was gentle, with an elegance of tone lacking in his compatriots. 'For the coolies, I mean. He tells me you're the one who keeps twisting his arms to bring improvement to their way of life. I fully support you, my dear.'

'I'm glad, Mr Goodchild,' she said.

'My colleagues in general will not subscribe to my viewpoint. They fail to learn from experience. It costs money to bring these coolies to Assam. Yet every year each garden loses scores of them to various maladies. Sound business sense to keep them healthy, I should think.'

'Oh, Mr Goodchild, one mustn't always think business! It's a matter of basic humanity.'

'You are a woman, young lady! But your planter's a creature of commerce. One must talk in terms of profit and loss to convince a planter.'

'I am no crusader, Mr Goodchild. I've no desire to convince others.'

'You underestimate yourself. Practice is always preferable to precept. Continue your good work in Dhanboa. Keep the coolies happy and healthy. Let Dhanboa thrive. Others will see and learn. I see no other plantation which can set an example. No, not even the ones I've to oversee. Take Bihguri, for instance … it makes profit for the company, despite the atrocious treatment meted out to its coolies. Buckingham will argue me down if I were to suggest changes. My board will support him.'

'Mr Goodchild,' David intruded. 'Sometimes circumstances compel one to work the coolies hard, however one might desire not to. So one can't always lay the blame at the planter's door.'

'You've had such moments, David?' Goodchild queried with a gentle note of irony.

David told him about Papa's blunder, how he had to uproot two-thirds of the plantation within a specific time, and make his depleted workforce labour that much harder.

'You say Buckingham advised this?' Goodchild asked.

'Yes.'

'It does not serve to raise him in my estimation. That was wrong advice, young man. Those bushes would've yielded some crop … kept your production above last year. They're in their third year, mind you. Thrice the previous amount, at least.'

Cordelia looked at David, a glance of anxiety rather than triumph. But David's eyes were cast down upon the earth.

'The sensible course would've been to open up more land and plant it with superior seeds and saplings. Your China plants and hybrids would have continued to yield in increasing amounts till the new plantings matured. You could have uprooted them phase by phase while extending your planted area each year.'

'There was no time to open out the jungles and mulch the area!' David exclaimed.

'You don't need to mulch a fresh jungle clearing, young man. Only used ground needs to be rehabilitated and replenished. Buckingham, by the way, is getting jungles cleared in his personal holdings. He would have it planted before March end, believe me.'

David's mind flashed back to his Bihguri visit. Why the devil hadn't he thought about it? What was that man at? Clearing jungle land while advising him not to do so!

Goodchild, seeing David silent, said quickly, 'What's done is done. Tell you what … next time I'm on a visit to Bihguri, I'll drop in at Dhanboa. Take a look at your plantings and see if I can give you a tip or two. How have the saplings in your nursery come up?'

David told him of his dependence on Bihguri for supply of seeds and plants.

'A new nursery, eh? And Buckingham's going to supply you with tea plants free of cost! Uncharacteristically generous of him!'

'You don't like him, isn't that so, Mr Goodchild?' Cordelia asked.

'Not much. Free seeds and saplings, eh! Makes me wonder, it does!'

David being present, it was as good a moment as any to press her enquiries and elicit the cause of Goodchild's 'wonder.' But the opportunity was lost with the advent of the Cinnamora superintendent, accompanied by Major Gosselin. The conversation veered off in another direction, with Williamson attempting to persuade them to stay on for one more night rather than leave after luncheon. David appeared tempted, but Cordelia firmly declined the invitation.

Finally, long after luncheon was over, came the formal farewells, much handshaking and expressions of gratitude. The return journey took far longer, but finally they were at Dhanboa, to a smiling welcome from Bapu babu, Kamal and Mongla, and a rapturous, throaty, tail-wagging, tongue-licking reception from Pekoe. Cordelia allowed the joyful ambience of Papa's garden to wrap her as she hugged the puppy to her bosom.

Goodchild's words had served to increase David's anxiety about Dhanboa's future; now he began to act the skinflint, to count each pice, talk of cutting down on expenditure, avoiding wastage. As if in coincidence there was a sudden rise in prices of foodstuff, especially rice, salt and cooking oil. David wanted to deduct eight annas from the coolies' pay to compensate for the rise in price of these items which had to be given to them free of cost, but Cordelia vehemently opposed it. What David considered recalcitrance on Cordelia's part led to greater friction between brother and sisters; minor points of disagreement being magnified out of proportion till they assumed the shapes of major battles.

All this filled Cordelia with disquietude. Her unease was enhanced by the recurrent nightmare she had been having ever since the return from Cinnamora. Perhaps nightmare was not the proper word for this dream; the horror and loathing were sensed only on awakening. But, asleep, while those shifting images slithered out from the psyche's substratum, and took on the shape of the dream, the sensations unleashed were of physical pleasure, an inner explosion which flooded her body with rapture. Her recallment of the dream was imperfect; on each occasion, upon awakening, she hazily remembered the coiling, rippling serpent which was central to it, the body of a cobra but flat-headed like a python. It shone in the dream with a weird iridescence. She herself was naked in the dream, floating softly on an ocean of ether, as those throbbing coils twirled around her, not cold and clammy to the touch but palpitating and warm and enkindling a strange bodily joy. She would feel the blunt head touch her lips and breasts and thighs, inducing ecstasy, and then suddenly would come a cataclysmic explosion, and she would awaken. The shift from the unconscious to the conscious was always accompanied by a feeling of heavy sin, making her cry out in bleak despair.

As the eerie dream continued to recur, she mentioned it to David. But he laughed at her apprehensions. Bapu babu, however, reacted with seriousness. One morning he brought with him an old man from his village, who had bright, mystical eyes, a wispy white beard and a grave air. He was the village sarabjan or soothsayer. He would carry out an age-old ritual and tell her if any significance was to be attached to her dream.

At the end of his rituals, he talked about his findings. 'Two snakes have made their dwelling beneath your bungalow. That is an ill-omen. You must have them removed.'

'I'll have it done today itself,' Bapu babu said. 'There are a couple of coolies who are adept at catching snakes.'

A gang of coolies were fetched—two among them were expert snake-catchers. Surrounded by a host of curious onlookers, the experts, armed with cleft sticks, began probing the numerous holes underneath the bungalow. Suddenly, one of them gave an animated yell; there was a universal gasp of fear as a cobra slithered out of a hole and made a frantic attempt at escape. Confronted with the stick wielding coolies the reptile raised its head, unfurling its hood in an aggressive posture. But a pronged stick streaked down, pinning it to the earth.

Its mate emerged barely half a minute later, hissing and furious, brought out by some secret summons. It streaked straight for a coolie, but the pronged stick was quicker, and in the wink of an eye it too was pinned to the ground, helpless as its mate. The two triumphant coolies, teeth bared in elation, bent down, each taking on one snake, grabbing the backs of the heads with their right hands, the bodies with the left. They straightened and held up the trophies for the admiring throng to behold.

David's smug grin withered on his features. 'Kill them!' he shrieked. 'Dash them against the ground! Maaro! Maaro!'

'No, sahib,' said the aged Assamese. 'That would be needless killing. Have the men take them out into the jungle and release them.'

'All right. *Che lao*! Take them as far inside as possible and let them go.'

The experts nodded and left, followed by a raucous procession. 'That was a nifty bit of work,' David said. 'Bloody cobras under the bungalow! Who would have thought it! Thank heavens we got wind of them.'

'We have this gentleman to thank for it,' Cordelia reminded.

David offered a couple of rupee coins to the wispy-bearded native. The old man shook his head. 'It was my duty. I can take no reward for my pains. My powers are for social good. The very moment I use them for personal gain, I will lose them.' He looked at Cordelia. 'You can sleep well, memsahib.'

Cordelia took the withered hands in her own. 'Thank you for coming.'

The man smiled, nodded to Bapu babu and Kamal, and the trio left. Their absence brought the smugness back into David. 'Clear as daylight to me, sis! That chap was hand in glove with Bapu babu!'

'What do you mean, David?'

'You told Bapu babu about your dream. He must've seen snakes beneath the bungalow sometime or the other. So, the two rigged up all this hocus-pocus to impress you.'

'For what purpose, David? He didn't take the money you offered.'

'I daresay the bormohori is fearful of losing his job. Now that he's been sidelined, he's buttering us up.'

'No, David,' Cordelia said emphatically. 'There are things that cannot be explained away in a rational way. I was witness to everything. There was nothing fraudulent in it.'

David refused to be convinced, though he expressed his relief that the venomous reptiles had been removed. Yet, with the irrationality of a miracle, from that night onward Cordelia was no longer troubled by the reptilian dream.

The days passed, one not much different from the other. David felt the monotony the most; now that the uprooting was over the pressure was temporarily off; the coolies were engaged in hoeing and clearing the planted sections which yet remained. The work on the nursery too had been completed. David waited with nervous anticipation for intimations from Bihguri that the saplings were ready to be replanted.

In the third week of January the horse trader came bearing news that two ponies had been dispatched on the paddle-wheel steamer *Madras*, scheduled to touch Kokilamukh on the twenty-seventh of the month, so a boat must be sent with adequate men to fetch them from the ghat. Coincidentally, Papa's headstone was being transported by the same steamer.

Cordelia fell in love with the walers, although she was not as pleased with the headstone. She told David that Uncle Alex could have sent something bigger and of better quality. However, there was no help for it, and on the morning of the following Sunday, the headstone was solemnly affixed to the head of Papa's grave, in the presence of the entire Dhanboa population. The flower garden around the grave, so lovingly tended to by Cordelia and Mongla, was in full bloom, and some of the girl's displeasure at uncle Alex's parsimony evaporated at the comforting sight of a solid, tangible reminder of the fact that a man called Henry David Esscombe had lived once, and lay buried in the soil of his beloved tea garden.

For the horses a simple stable, of bamboo and thatch, had been constructed, with two separate compartments. David promptly christened the newcomers Congou and Souchong, after two grades of tea, the former for himself, the latter for his sister. Two coolie chokras were given permanent assignment of looking after the horses at one rupee per month, David himself training them. He and Cordelia regularly exercised the animals so they would get acclimatized to the Assam air. The creatures were gentle, obedient and intelligent, making the task of breaking them in and mounting them all the more easier. They had come fully equipped with saddle, rein and stirrup, so no additional expenses were incurred on that score.

Congou and Souchong turned out to be worth every rupee spent on them. Not only did Congou increase David's mobility, but also boosted his confidence in no little measure. Now he could trot across the garden taller than the rest; he could come upon a tea section with unexpectedness, catching the workers unawares. This brought about general alertness and imbued into the coolies greater awe of the young sahib, who would swoop down on them out of the blue, riding crop in his hand as he bawled out someone who had been shirking.

Her steed, Souchong, had a different effect on Cordelia. Along with Pekoe, Souchong provided another outlet to Cordelia's affections. They provided her with the warmth of companionship and lessened the feeling of loneliness and isolation gripping her of late. It was sheer pleasure to sally forth on Souchong, with Pekoe trotting at their heels, over the garden paths, into the labour basti, where the coolie children would try to match the waler's speed by racing behind with wild shrieks of glee. Lately she had begun to leave the perimeters of Dhanboa and ride along the thin jungle-track which led to Bihguri, extending the distance day by day. She would have preferred to have taken another direction, but the stream which flowed along the northern perimeter of Dhanboa and the untamed jungles beyond made that impossible. David had voiced his fears of her riding over that narrow, hazardous track through jungle-land but Cordelia told him that she felt safer with Souchong and Pekoe than she might have in human company.

February came, the tribal coolies did not. Though he himself had been responsible for the loss of twenty of his finest coolies, he refused to concede it. Instead, he lay the blame on Bapu babu for not providing him with advance warning and enjoined him to take steps to make up the shortfall. Bapu babu's efforts proved futile; however, the bormohori's services proved invaluable in other ways, which made David realize why Papa had depended so much on this man. When the rains would come, and the bushes in the thirty odd acres of plantings yet remaining start to flush, the manufacturing season would commence. Dhanboa had to be readied for that season and he had to rely more and more upon Bapu babu's experience. The entire burden of purchasing the required items for manufacturing the teas, requisitioning trees in the jungle for the tea chests and having them felled, cut and planed into the required size, ensuring that the tea houses were in good repair and the roofs did not leak, and a hundred other tasks, fell to the lot of the ever-willing Bapu babu. The Assamese man made not the slightest complaint, something which even David had to acknowledge; he worked indefatigably, often spending the nights at the dispensary.

The garden was being geared up for the onset of the rains; Cordelia too was involved in the essay. She was at the basti almost every afternoon, after her stint at the dispensary was over, supervising the construction of bamboo beds in every hutment—now she exhorted the laggards to search out bamboo groves in the jungle and complete the beds in quick time, warning that she did not wish to find any coolie man, woman or child sleeping on the floor again. She made the men construct bamboo walls and thatch roofs around what had previously been open air lavatories; she had read that one of the causes of ailments connected with the stomach, including cholera, was the pollution of drinking water by human and animal excrement. Her exhortations to the coolies to boil the water which they used for drinking had had effect; as far as she was aware, each coolie family was drinking boiled water, which she hoped explained the low incidence of stomach ailments thus far at Dhanboa.

A light shower, lasting just an hour or so, fell towards February middle. The very same morning Captain Ralph Hewitt paid them a surprise visit. He was in full uniform, thereby denoting that the visit was official. 'A kind of tour,' he explained to Cordelia and David, as he made himself comfortable on the bungalow verandah. 'Part of my official duties. Got to see where our blokes are before the rains cut off all communications. By the by, I've brought some tabloids for you. They're somewhat out of date, no doubt. But will give you a general picture of what's been happening elsewhere.'

Cordelia picked them up and quickly looked at the inside cover of each. They were old copies of *The Englishman*, *Friend of India* and *The Courier*, neatly bound together.

'Oh, thank you so much, Mr Hewitt,' Cordelia cried.

'It's my pleasure,' said the captain. 'New don't get me wrong, Miss Esscombe. I don't go about carrying bound copies of *The Englishman* everywhere! But Dhanboa's a special place.'

'You must stay the night with us,' David said.

'Thank you, but no. Can't upset my schedule. Must push on towards Titabar. Fellow called Gokuldeva Barua will be my host tonight.'

'You'll breakfast with us, of course?' Cordelia asked.

Captain Hewitt pulled out his chronometer and took a peek at it. 'Time enough for that, certainly. Perhaps you could spare a bite for my men too?'

Cordelia went downstairs to the kitchen to give Mongla the necessary instructions. By the time she returned upstairs, David had brought out a bottle of Johnnie Walker, and the two men were engaged in animated discussion on the present situation in Assam. She was against David indulging himself so early in the morning, but since the visitor had apparently not demurred, she said nothing.

'As I was telling your brother, Miss Esscombe,' Hewitt said, breaking off at her approach, 'there's not much going on in the valley proper. We had a spot of trouble at few months back at a place called Phulaguri. But that has been contained. They sent a fine chap ... a Colonel, no less, named

Saunders. He did a splendid job—put out the spark before it could burst into a blaze. We don't want that kind of a thing again, certainly not.'

Cordelia's lips twisted into a bitter grimace at the mention of Colonel Saunders. Captain Hewitt, whose eyes were on her, did not fail to perceive it. 'Anything the matter?' he said, looking first to her, and then David, for enlightenment. 'Do you know Colonel Saunders?'

'No,' Cordelia said. She quickly turned her face away and reached down to stroke Pekoe. But David broke in.

'Colonel Saunders? Tim Saunders? Oh, we don't exactly know him. But we'd met him briefly once … a most accidental encounter. While we were enroute to Assam. Upon a sandbank, of all places! If my memory serves me right, he was a Lt Colonel then?'

'He's been promoted to Colonel. At the moment he's busy tackling Naga insurgency. Not too distant from our district. Major Gosselin dispatched me an urgent message, asking me to warn plantations in my area.'

'Do you anticipate any danger to Dhanboa, Captain Hewitt?' Cordelia asked.

'No, no, Miss Esscombe, no cause for alarm! At least not hereabouts. Plantations around Titabar are more vulnerable. But no harm in being alert, is there?'

'Please do us a favour, Captain Hewitt,' Cordelia said.

'Anything for you, Miss Esscombe.'

'There's a small garden there, called Chahpuli. It might be too tiny to merit a visit from you. It's being opened up by a gentleman called Lieutenant Michael Bailin.'

'Lieutenant Michael Bailin? A relation of yours, Miss Esscombe?'

It was David who answered, quickly, 'No, no. We met the chap on the steamer.'

'Now that I recall, Major Gosselin did mention Michael Bailin once, although I did not pay attention then. The Major did not appear to hold much of an opinion of him.'

'Major Gosselin's opinions are his own business,' Cordelia said. 'You'll be meeting the Assamese nobleman, Gokuldeva Barua. Please find out from him where Chahpuli is located and alert the Lieutenant of this possible danger.'

Hewitt valiantly retained his smile. 'Good you mentioned it, Miss Esscombe. Chahpuli wasn't in my schedule. But I'll pay him a visit, don't you worry.'

'Thank you so much,' Cordelia said. Then, before anything further could be elicited from her, she put in quickly, 'The breakfast table has been set. If you'll finish your drinks, we can move on.'

Captain Hewitt proved to be an excellent companion. What endeared him most to Cordelia was his unassuming amiability, the total absence of officious airs. On his part he was clearly smitten by Cordelia's soft beauty, and made no attempt to conceal the fact that the pleasure he was deriving from the visit was occasioned solely by her.

Among other matters, he had a word of caution for David. Despite large-scale importation of coolies, labour in the plantations was still in short supply, and poaching on one another's territory among planters was assuming endemic proportions. David must, therefore, hoard his coolies as through his life depended on it, and keep careful watch on them. He also warned against the coming rains—they must stock up with provisions to last at least four months.

David let out a chuckle. 'You speak of the rains as if they were the enemy and we're on the battlefield!'

Hewitt's eyebrows lifted. 'Don't take the rains too lightly. A worse enemy you'll never find! Utterly cut off, that's how you'll find yourself. For months on end, you'll have to remain cooped up at Dhanboa, making and packing your teas, but unable to dispatch them because of flooded rivers and plains. Make no mistake. The rains can wreak disaster, unless you're prepared for them. They might sustain your tea garden, but they also bring malady and death. So, dig your trenches and keep your powder dry!'

He looked at his chronometer again and sighed with genuine regret. 'Well, it was pleasant while it lasted. But one must earn one's salary, I suppose. Goodbye, Miss Esscombe. A happy morning … not many such come my way, I'm afraid.'

'Please feel free to drop in any time,' Cordelia said, taking his outstretched hand and shaking it with warmth.

'That may be many months away. But I'll keep your invitation in mind, I promise.'

'I'll see you off at the ghat,' David said. He, Hewitt and his men set off towards the stream.

'You aren't seriously thinking of going to Chahpuli, are you, Captain?' David asked, keeping his voice as casual as he could.

'Well, now that your sister has asked me to, I suppose I must.'

'May I make a request?'

'Certainly.'

'If you meet this man, Michael Bailin, please do not mention us. Neither me nor my sister. Don't let him know my sister had asked you to contact him.'

The captain cocked one enquiring eye at David. 'Don't like this chap much, do you? But your sister seemed to harbour some degree of warmth for him.'

'No, captain. Just Christian charity. We met the man in question on the steamer. A shipboard acquaintance, that's all.'

Captain Hewitt nodded. A smile of delight lit up his face. 'All kinds of rascals are taking to tea. You must be on your guard, Mr Esscombe ... about your sister, I mean. She has too soft a heart.'

'Then I can take it you wouldn't mention us?'

The uniformed man shot out his hand and shook David's with a firm grip. 'My pledge on it, I won't.'

David watched the party leave and then wended his way back, a thoughtful frown on his features.

Christopher James Buckingham, atop his steed, looked on as his coolies deep-hoed the newly cleared grounds in preparation for replanting the tea seedlings from the nursery.

The planter was in a black mood. The sirdars and the coolies were aware of it. They knew such a mood demanded a human sacrifice; some unfortunate coolie or the other would be marked out before the morning was over and sent to the whipping post. None of them wished to be chosen as a sacrificial bakra; they, therefore, displayed a desperate alacrity at their work.

His smouldering anger was not without cause. He had chosen this day to start planting out the forty acres of clearing his coolies had hacked out of the jungles. But, no sooner had work commenced there was a sharp shower, heavy enough to drench the earth and render the soil sticky and cloying—he had been forced to defer the operation till the morrow. Then Chotu had informed that a sahib named How-it sat at the bungalow, having arrived with three policemen. The man, who wore uniform, wished Buckingham sahib's immediate presence before him.

Captain Hewitt, the bloody mandarin at Jorehaut! Buckingham would have preferred to let the bastard cool his heels for a while, but dared not. He represented the official arm of the Empire and reported directly to Major Gosselin! They knew their powers, these bloody sons of bitches! Unless their whims were pandered to, they could make things pretty thorny for a planter.

Putting Luthra in charge, he rode off straight for the bungalow. Hewitt's curt, unfriendly behaviour did nothing to salve the anger within him. The officer queried him closely on the plantation's preparedness to face the rains. He had the damned effrontery to lecture Buckingham on the necessity of hoarding his coolies! All this the planter had borne with a charming smile and easy graciousness of manner; retaining his obsequiousness till the officious shrimp left along with his entourage.

Yes, the morning had been a disaster. Now, as he surveyed his workers strung along the open ground, he was suffused with a savage, sadistic impulsee—he wanted to pluck the whip from Gandru and ride among those semi-naked brutes, slashing right and left till their blood wetted the ground like raindrops. Yet, this morning, he let his anger smoulder on, not translating it into action; instead, he called Luthra over.

'Put Gandru in charge and follow me to the nursery,'

Being on horseback, he reached the nursery area much ahead of Luthra. When the head sirdar arrived, he instructed: 'Listen. The saplings which grow tallest and strongest go to my garden. You understand that, don't you?'

'*Ji huzoor.*'

'What do you do with the ones which are weak and sickly?'

'We uproot them, huzoor, and destroy them.'

Buckingham's eyes burned like twin flares. 'Not this time. We dig them up and send them to Dhanboa!'

'But they will not grow well, sahib,' Luthra said.

'I know that! But I've my reasons. I shall send you to Dhanboa this afternoon with a message for the sahib there. He must dispatch his elephants and men tomorrow morning to collect the saplings for his garden. You will ensure that only the weakest saplings are sent to Dhanboa.'

A foxy gleam appeared in Luthra's eyes. I know what he imagines, Buckingham thought. Our sahib is a crafty one! He wishes to destroy Dhanboa and drive its sahib to ruin, so he can get the property cheap. The dumb beast does not suspect the truth!

'I shall make sure of that, sahib,' Luthra said.

'Good. This is for your ears only. And those of the other sirdars and duffadars. No one else must know.'

'*Ji huzoor.*'

'Also, the company's sending a dozen coolies to Bihguri. They arrive this afternoon. Send Meghu and Bircha to the ghat to escort them to the basti and put them up at the shed for new arrivals. Then report to me.'

Buckingham did not return Luthra's acknowledging salute. Mounting his horse, he rode off towards the bungalow.

'He's the son of the Shaitan, isn't he, Bircha-bhaiya?' Meghu said, as the two of them walked to the Bihguri jetty.

'No, not the son, but the very Shaitan himself,' said Bircha.

'Just imagine! Swindling his own kind!' There could be nothing more heinous in Meghu's scheme of values! This too was what he held against Luthra, Gandru, Puran, Budhu and their ilk. Not the ingrained brutality in their character, for both he and Bircha were capable of similar violence. That their savagery had been directed against individuals of the same blood and background was what roused his ire.

'The young sahib is at Dhanboa, isn't it?' Bircha asked. 'And the white woman with the shining hair. The one we saw on the steamer. She looks like a farishta.'

'He once rode up with our sahib, don't you remember?'

'Yes. The day we *were* made duffadars. Our lucky day! He seemed rather soft. Not at all like our shaitan.'

'Don't trust a firanghee,' Meghu said. 'They're all the same, like bamboos in a grove.'

'Oh, what's he to me and I to him? Let them swindle each other. Let them kill each other. I'll dance on their graves! It rained this morning, Meghu-bhaiya. Has our time come?'

'Not yet. Don't get taken in by the early rains, Sanatan says. Wait for the real rains ... when it will pour day in and day out. Then we shall turn our backs on this plague hole.'

Two boats, small and of shallow draught, rounded a bend of the stream and made for the jetty. A man, not a coolie, jumped off a boat the moment it touched the pier, a sheaf of papers in his hand. 'Where's the sahib?' he asked the two waiting coolies.

'In his bungalow,' said Meghu. 'Come, I'll take you to him.'

Bircha was left alone with the boats and their occupants. '*Che lao*!' he shouted. 'Come off the boats and be counted.' Twelve coolies disembarked, four men and eight women, each carrying their possessions wrapped in bundles, and stood stiffly on the narrow bank.

Bircha looked over the ragged group with commiserating eyes. Travelling over their faces, his gaze suddenly alighted upon a chokri, and adhered to her as if stuck with resin.

She was a small thing, dark as the night of a new moon, not tall. She could not have been much past puberty; the body under the red sari was unfledged. Her features were regular, eyes like those of a doe, a pert nose, and lips dark red and full. There was a vibrancy in the face which Bircha found appealing, especially in the eyes and the lips, a refusal to slide towards stoic acceptance, a heroic resoluteness to cock a snook at kismet. Her raven-black hair was well-oiled and neatly combed, the strands plaited and tucked into a bun at the back. A wild orchid was wound around the bun like an ornament.

Bircha did not know what caused the unaccustomed flutter in his heart. Could it have been her spruce appearance, the neatly braided hair and the orchid? The other coolie women wore their straggling hair loose as though in perpetual mourning. This slip of a girl certainly was different!

He swaggered up to the girl, his pronounced limp detracting somewhat from the effect. '*Aarey chokri, tera naam kya re*?' he asked.

The girl looked boldly at him, eyes flashing. '*Tu kaun hein re, naam puchne*?' Who the devil was he to ask her name?

'I'm a sirdar, chokri! Watch how you use your tongue with me!' Bircha, taken aback by the girl's spirited reply, spoke with heat.

'Oh, forgive her, huzoor,' said the grey-haired woman beside the girl in great agitation.

A bad beginning, Bircha realized too late! He turned to the grey-haired woman, startled that she too was relatively young, though her lined face and peppered hair made her look positively aged. 'I'm no huzoor,' he said softly. 'You can call me Bircha. That's my name.'

The woman reacted with a wan smile. 'Her name's Saoni. I'm her mother.'

'And what might be your name?'

'Baisakhi. I'm a widow.'

'Well, tell your chokri to keep a civil tongue in her head,' Bircha said, mustering up as much brusqueness into his voice as he could. He turned and limped back to his original perch on the bank till the babu returned and left on his boat.

Then, herding the coolies into a line, they set off over the winding track that snaked into Bihguri, making straight for the shed at the basti where new arrivals were temporarily bivouacked before being allotted land for building hutments of their own.

Bircha limped up to Baisakhi. 'You have no man in your family,' he said with concern. 'It'll be difficult for you and your chokri to put up a hutment. But you needn't worry. I'll help you, and so will my companion, Meghu. If you require anything else, just tell me.'

The woman nodded. Bircha stole a glance at Saoni. The chokri was looking at him. There was no disdain in her eyes now. In fact, they were smiling impishly.

Bircha limped out of the shed, walking on air.

The message Luthra brought from Buckingham galvanized David into action. He called a coolie durbar that evening and insisted Cordelia also should be present.

Bapu babu explained why the durbar had been called. From the morrow tea saplings would pour into Dhanboa like the rains during the monsoons. The moment they arrived they had to be planted. It would be a hard, back-breaking grind, without rest from first light to sundown. But the coolielog must not complain or neglect to handle and plant the saplings carefully, for they contained in them the soul of Dhanboa.

With a final appeal Bapu babu ended his oration. The ensuing silence was broken by the cacophony of a dozen voices speaking simultaneously as the elder coolies discussed the matter between themselves. Complaints against the behaviour of Harua, Ajam and Robiya, the absence of the tribal coolies, the long hours they had had to put in during the uprooting, floated through the air and reached David's ears. The young man sat tight, keeping his anger on leash. He would not make the same mistake twice.

Suddenly Cordelia stood up and raised her hand for silence. In the wink of an eye the babble of voices stilled and an attentive hush fell over the throng. Cordelia began to speak, in their dialect, in a simple, matter of fact manner. Dhanboa, she said, was not only her father's garden, nor only David sahib's or hers. It was the garden of every man, woman and child who dwelt within it. So, each of them must help to keep the plantation alive even if it meant extra hours of toil for a short while. They must work with their hearts as well as their hands.

David looked up at his sister in admiration. Just a few sentences! Yet what a difference these made on the attitude of the coolies! The sullen faces were suddenly wreathed in smiles. The buggers simply adored her! The eldest among the coolies stood up. The memsahib was right, he said. Dhanboa was their plantation too. They would heed the babu's advice, as well as the sahib's. But most of all they would heed the advice of Cordelia memsahib. From the morrow they would toil unceasingly till every sapling was planted.

David's gratitude towards his sister was genuine. As the durbar broke up, he hugged her. 'You were a marvel, sis! And, for once, you were on my side, not theirs.'

'You're wrong, David,' Cordelia said with affection. 'They're our allies, not opponents. And I've always been on your side, though you might see it differently.'

But, in the subsequent days, Cordelia almost regretted her impulsive appeal to the coolies. Men and elephants shuttled constantly between Dhanboa and Bihguri, bringing in thousands of saplings in the outsize, bamboo baskets ordinarily carried by the pluckers. The faster they dug holes and put saplings in, the faster they came. Overriding David's objections, Cordelia borrowed a pair of old trousers from her brother, rolled up the sleeves of her shirt, shod herself in the stoutest of her shoes, and squatted, digging, inserting, filling up.

David was the odd man out; but he worked harder than the rest, yelling, cajoling, threatening, showering curses upon laggards in coolie dialect which Cordelia had not conceived to be a part of his vocabulary and which he must have picked up from his sirdars. At times he was on foot, whacking his crop against the riding breeches as he wove in and out of the coolie rows, making sudden checks to see if one was digging deep enough, and another keeping the stalk straight enough. At other times he was on Congou, galloping out to meet the sapling-bearing party, or trotting over to the stacks to judge if the planting of the importation thus far could be completed before dusk. Cordelia had never beheld such anxiety and nervous frenzy in her brother, nor the obsessed, maniacal gleam of determination in his eyes.

As he expected, Buckingham dropped in at the end of a week. The boy watched the astonishment on his visitor's face, not only at the fact that the replanting had been completed on schedule, but also at the spruce appearance now presented by Dhanboa.

'Terrific, old chap! I don't know how you did it, with your sixty odd coolies, but did it you have!'

David, naturally, knew how he did it. The ever-willing Bapu babu had cajoled young men of his village to help out with the replanting! But Christopher James Buckingham was the last person in the world to whom he would tell this.

Chahpuli was his prison. Here he had immured himself, he his own keeper, turned the key in the lock and thrown it away. Chahpuli was a refuge, the final hole for the fugitive and outcast, the safe niche where the past could catch up no longer. Chahpuli was the hermitage, the soul's monastery, where undisturbed dhyan was possible, and moksha a matter of aeons away.

He had till then envied Garo, who existed for the moment, as serene in adversity as in moments of bountiful fortune. But now, gradually and almost unconsciously, Bailin himself slid into the stoicism which sustained his companion. Thus, as day followed day, his spells of contemplation lessened, to be replaced by calm reconciliation. Garo's impassivity strengthened his own and enabled him to overcome fits of depression. It brought to existence a strange, reclusive serenity; and, as a reward, its own pleasure.

Their days were ones of unruffled placidity; simple tasks performed with languid deliberateness.

The constant exposure to the outdoors, the feel of the sun as they worked on the grounds, had tanned Bailin's skin to almost a tawny brown. While Garo did a tolerably good job of cutting his hair, Bailin had given up shaving altogether which lent to his features a weird degeneracy very much in keeping with his new style of life and heightened the intense blue of his eyes.

The line between master and servant had been erased. The rapport between the two of them was such that each seemed intuitively to know what the other thought or felt, and react accordingly. Nothing in Bailin's background had prepared him for a bond such as this! With a black man in a loincloth, a patois of English, Hindustani and Assamese the tool of communication! None among his own kind had ever succeeded in coming half as close as Garo had done. And only Cordelia had roused emotions in his breasts, though of a different kind, as powerful as Garo had.

But Cordelia was lost to him. Even if Gokuldeva had been right, and Buckingham's invisible hand had written David's letter for him, Cordelia was lost. In a moment of madness, persuaded by the Reverend's mesmeric voice, he had sought to renew the ties. But good old kismet was at work again; David's snub had been a blessing! Now that he had has ample time to reflect, he realized the truth of this.

Only on two occasions was the unvarying placidity of their life at Chahpuli disturbed. One was the visit of the officer named Hewitt which left a bitter taste in his mouth and momentarily stoked the embers of anger which he thought were extinguished. Hewitt had been unreasonably hostile; he had come of his own accord after having discovered the location of Chahpuli from Gokuldeva Barua. His behaviour had been terribly rude; he had hinted he knew something of Bailin's inglorious past though nothing explicit was mentioned. It, apparently, was an official visit; Hewitt asserted that he was under no obligation to seek out Bailin, but had been persuaded to do so by an individual dear to his heart. There had been some raids by rebellious Nagas near Sivasagar. Since Chahpuli was quite close to the Naga hill ranges, Hewitt had thought it his duty to warn him. But if Bailin, an Englishman, chose to live like a half-breed with a coolie for companion, in such a vulnerable and exposed spot, without defences, Hewitt suspected that his visit had been purely a waste of time.

The second occasion was, however, gratifyingly pleasant and fruitful. Early one morning towards February end, as Bailin and Garo worked in Chahpuli's clearing, a curious procession arrived, six elephants and two score men on foot, bearing baskets stuffed with tea saplings. The elephants were offloaded, the baskets of saplings carried to strategic points, and the men began digging and planting at a furious pace.

Gokuldeva's men completed the replanting of Chahpuli well before sundown. The tiny clearing was now carpeted like an untended lawn with hundreds of tea saplings. A curious medley of joy and hope, impatience and gratitude, played within the Lieutenant's heart as he watched the saplings weave sinuous patterns in the evening breeze. No, his kismet had not deserted him totally! When the rains arrived and nurtured the seedlings, they would grow into tea bushes. Chahpuli then would no longer be a mock-garden.

The onset of March brought expectancy, a primordial thirst for regeneration, the renewal after death and decay, to complete the cycle of existence. In Assam the earth could never be described as parched; even in winter the blades of grass and leaves of trees were wetted with dew. Nevertheless, the earth thirsted for water, for it needed the nourishing touch of raindrops for new stalks to emerge, tendrils to extend their fingers, buds to unfurl into blossoms. The rain would revitalize the inert earth and bring about the miracle called spring, welcome the sweet-voiced cuckoo, and the insistently raucous make-more-pekoe bird.

The first showers would be comparatively light, sporadic bursts of rain alternating with spells of sunshine. This would continue till end April when a brief dry spell would prevail. But, toward the middle of May, thick and sable clouds would gather overhead, the floodgates of the sky would burst open and the rain would cascade down in sheets, day after day, week after week. Towards September the rains would taper off with a few post-monsoon showers of autumn, and then would arrive the chill of winter.

Thus, March had the earth expectant. Everywhere in Assam farmers looked at the sky, tea planters kept their fingers crossed, hoping that the rain-gods would not fail them. At Dhanboa David waited for the rains, looking up at the sky each morning. Cordelia too waited for the rains, not with feverish anticipation like David, more with a sense of foreboding. Although she had done everything possible with the coolies and in the basti, one could never be certain if diseases would be averted. A single death in Dhanboa, Cordelia knew, would also be a death-blow to her soul.

Gokuldeva at Titabar, Phukan and the Chinese tea makers at Mohoniya, waited for the rains. At work among the Chahpuli plantings, Michael Bailin and Garo too occasionally looked up at the sky. In Bihguri Buckingham waited. In Bihguri's coolie basti men, women and children waited, not in anticipation, but with trepidation. The rains might bring regeneration to the earth; for them it brought only death and misery. For the next few months, they would not have a minute of respite; Buckingham's hounds would not be their sole tormentors—dampness, rot, leeches, dahs, mosquitoes, snakes—there would be no end to the list. Maladies would increase; diarrhea, dysentery, malarial fever, cold and cough. And if they had incurred the wrath of the gods, then the scourge would visit them, and carry many away.

In a shack in Bihguri coolie basti, Meghu and Bircha waited. The elder coolie's voice was filled with reproach. 'So, Bircha-bhaiya, changed your ambitions, have you? Planning to renege on me?'

His companion, hurt and surprised by the tone, flared up. 'What bakwas are you talking, Meghu-bhaiya?'

'You seem to me to be very happy these days. Less impatient too. You haven't asked me once these past few weeks if the rains were coming or not?'

'Oh, they would be coming soon. You yourself said so.'

'But it doesn't matter to you if the rains come, isn't it so?'

'What makes you say that?' It was Bircha's turn to speak with reproach.

'I've been watching you. You're taken up with that new chokri, aren't you? What's her name … Baisakhi's daughter? Oh yes, Saoni?'

Bircha grew defensive. 'That's my own business. What's it to you?'

'You stupid fool!' Meghu said, reproof changing into anger. 'We're going to make a bolt for it as soon as it starts pouring. Have you forgotten that? Or has that chokri changed your mind? You follow her around like a starving mongrel after a child eating roti. She has just to smile at you and you prance about like a Hanuman langur. So, what do you expect me to think?'

Bircha turned his face towards his companion. Meghu's anger drained out as he saw Bircha's eyes. They were blurred with confusion, dulled with anguish.

'For bhagwan's sake, Meghu-bhaiya, tell me what to do! I've never felt like this for anyone else before. That chokri makes my heart dance! She's so thin and wispy … even more delicate than the flowers she puts in her hair. But there's fire in her. Her fire has lit a fire in me too! When I'm with her, I feel as if I would never let her go. Such a feeling is eating me inside, it's driving me mad!'

'It's the madness of spring,' Meghu said. 'It happens sometimes. What advice can I give to one who is touched by the madness of spring? But this puts me in a quandary. We'd planned to leave Bihguri together. But now I suppose I'll have to go alone.'

'No, no, don't say that.'

'But what else can I say? Can I ask you to go with me against your will?'

'Can't we take her along, Meghu-bhaiya?' Bircha asked in a plaintive voice.

The anger inside Meghu flared anew. Then he saw the anguished bafflement on Bircha's features and relented. When he spoke, his voice was gentle.

'We can't do that. You know it very well. The girl will be a burden … slow us down. If we take her, we'll have to take the mother along. Otherwise, with her daughter gone even if it be without her knowledge, the shaitans would flog her without mercy.'

Bircha nodded his head mutely.

'So, you must make a decision, Bircha-bhaiya. On one side is your chokri; on the other freedom from these shaitans. It's your choice. I can't help you.'

Bircha stayed quiet for so long that Meghu thought he had gone to sleep. He blew out the earthen lamp and was preparing to sleep when

Bircha's voice abruptly cut through the air. 'I'll go with you, Meghu-bhaiya. You and I have been in this through thick and thin. We planned this escape together. I cannot desert you at the last moment.'

'In that case you must stop seeing the chokri. Cut off relations with her and the mother, do you understand? That would be fair to them. Do it even if it breaks your heart.'

'It will break my heart,' Bircha said simply. 'But I'll do it.'

The first clash of thunder caught Cordelia by surprise. The door and the windows, of solid wood and without glass panes, had shut out her vision of the outside world, so she had not seen the streaks of lightning to forewarn her. It was a deafening clap, followed by a reverberating rumble, rolling across the sky like the beats of a gigantic drum. A pause later came another mighty thunderclap, then another, and yet another, each more strident than the one before as the storm neared. Cordelia sat tight on the bed, feeling her heart lurch at every resounding peal. Pekoe's nervous whine reached her ears through the darkness.

Then she heard the wind—a shrill moan at first as it caught the hollows beneath the roof, rising to a mighty whoosh as a wall of cold air rushed in and slammed against the bungalow. The entire structure tottered and swayed as the gale hammered at it with the force of a battering ram; the wind savagely pummelled the roof and the walls, and the doors and windows shook and rattled. It seemed to her that at any moment the mighty wind would pluck the bungalow from the stilts, carry it through the tempestuous air and dash it to pieces against the jungle walls.

Never in her life, not in Calcutta nor Delhi, had she experienced nature's frenzy such as this. The thunder crashed repeatedly, exploding again and again like a thousand cannons. The wind shrieked and howled with demented fury. Then the raindrops began to fall; at first, they dropped warily, as if to test if the earth was hot enough. A pause, and the deluge came, thick, heavy rain, descending not in drops but sheets, hitting the thatch with a thud, giant fingers drumming an incessant tattoo upon the ground. The wind began to shriek again, banshees wailing and howling, and once more the thunder boomed out its vituperations at a cowed earth.

The tempest raged for a long time. The thunder was the first to depart; a little later the gale dropped. But the rain continued to fall in a straight descent. Cordelia pussyfooted to a window, opened it tentatively, not knowing what to expect. The fresh, rain-laden air that rushed into the room cooled her body and snuffed out the candle.

Cordelia stepped out of the door, a subdued Pekoe beside her. She looked along the verandah towards her right and suddenly froze, her heart in her mouth.

A flash of lightning had momentarily revealed a white figure at the other end, standing close to the balustrade!

Another continuous streak lit up the firmament for a longer span, long enough for her to see that it was David on the verandah, night dress soaked in the rain, hands stretched out towards the heavens as though in the midst of some mystic, pagan rite.

For the next week it rained every evening. The tea house activities began. David, constrained by ignorance, left it to Bapu babu to manage that end. The bormohori brought in the services of a dozen native tea makers and, along with some of the experienced Dhanboa hands, commenced manufacture, while David went to Bihguri for an overnight stay to learn the secrets of tea making.

The very moment his pachyderm entered Buckingham's garden, he caught a whiff of Bihguri's transformed air, the animated vivacity of a full-fledged tea plantation in the throes of the manufacturing season. Whip-wielding sirdars marched up and down among the pluckers, shouting and gesticulating and slashing whips in the air, urging them to make haste. Often a whip would slash down on some unfortunate laggard's back and bring a smile to David's face. Buckingham had been right. He certainly did not mollycoddle his coolies!

This is the garden of my dreams, David thought, these acres and acres of leafy bushes, in abundant flush, growing in neat rows. This is what Papa's garden—*my* garden—will look like a decade hence. This is how I wish my coolies to work, disciplined and well trained, responsive to the exigencies of the situation, sweating to make the garden pay. The saplings I have planted will grow into bushes such as these. Each year I shall clear new ground and plant them with saplings from my own nursery. I shall instill greater discipline into my coolies, make them work just that much harder, no matter how vehemently Cordi whines and complains. Without the blood and sweat of the coolies, no tea garden can thrive.

As always with David, Buckingham was a gracious host, the charming elder companion, the knowledgeable guru. 'How are the saplings doing?' he asked.

'Looks fine, Chris … to my inexperienced eyes.'

A sly smile lit up Buckingham's features. 'Watch them a year hence, old chap! But let's not waste time in small talk. You have a lot to catch up on.'

They rode across Bihguri. Pluckers were at work. The two riders, on reaching them, dismounted. Buckingham made an experienced hand demonstrate to David how a tea bush needed to be plucked. With a practiced twirl of her fingers, he snipped off a stalk and held it towards David.

'Take a look, old chap,' Buckingham said. 'Just two leaves and a bud. The bud's not a bud at all, but a young leaf which hasn't yet unfurled.'

David had previously watched his own pluckers at work in Dhanboa. They had snipped off a greater length of the stalk, often with four, five leaves on it. But here was Buckingham making his pluckers pick only two leaves and a bud.

'This is a new plucking technique. At the very beginning Bruce and company, misled by their pigtailed Chinese, used to strip the entire stalk. Just imagine that! Ten, twelve leaves at a go! No wonder they got poor tea. Our chaps, in due course, reduced it to half that number.'

'Yes. That's what we are doing at Dhanboa.'

'Oh, you might make more tea that way, but the prices obtained would be nothing to crow about. Some of us have discovered that two leaves and a bud get you the best tea. Now give me a minute, will you? The section at the other end … I'll just take a look at it and return.'

He strode off towards another batch of coolies some two hundred yards away. More to pass the time than anything else, David strolled towards a tea bush to take a closer look. His eyes widened with surprise. The saplings here looked taller than the ones in Dhanboa and their stems were thicker. These plants looked healthier than the ones in his own garden and the leaves were broader and of greater length. He bent down to examine one closely and take measurements.

'Looking for something, old chap?'

He had been concentrating so closely on the saplings that he had not heard Buckingham return. He started guiltily and rose to his feet.

'Yes, Chris,' he said. 'Taking some measurements. Your saplings have grown much better than mine. I dare say you planted them a bit earlier, what?'

Buckingham's searching gaze flitted away from David's face and came to rest on his plantings. 'That's right, old chap,' he said easily. 'At least a week ahead of you. Saplings grow pretty fast …'

'But Chris, you advised me to plant mine a foot apart. Here you've kept at least a foot and a half between one sapling and its neighbour?'

'Experiment, old chap, nothing but an experiment! A foot's the current practice. With four hundred acres in my kitty, I can afford to try out new methods. However, I won't advise you to do the same.'

David was satisfied.

'Come along,' Buckingham said. 'We'll go over to the other side. I've a great deal to show you, especially in pruning …'

Over the day, Buckingham tutored David through the process of tea manufacture—exposing the green leaves to the sun to remove moisture, withering them in 'withering machines', heating them in kwalies, or earthenware pans, over a brick oven of charcoal fire in the panning house, hand-rolling by a group of coolies, and finally sending the macerated leaves to the firing house where they were roasted in cast iron pans. David followed the entire process with dogged interest, missing nothing, constantly posing questions to Buckingham.

'You trip up at any stage, and you get bad tea,' his tutor warned. 'So, you've got to make damn certain no one shirks.'

'I understand, Chris,' David said, grimly determined.

Buckingham showed him around the sorting house, where the teas were cleansed of unwanted fibres, graded according to the different leaf sizes and carefully packed into chests lined with paper, the edges sealed with lead. When there was nothing more to be learnt they returned to the bungalow.

'I've let down my hair a bit today, old chap,' Buckingham said, as Chotu laid out the whisky bottles and tumblers. 'That's because I've you as a guest. Otherwise, I don't have the time to breathe, let alone sit like this and sip whisky.'

'You're clearly understaffed, Chris. I don't see any babus around. I understand company gardens maintain quite a few ... burrababu for the office, garden mohurer for the fields, hazira mohurer for the coolies and so on. Even Dhanboa has a bormohori.'

'It's by design, rather than compulsion. The company would provide assistants and babus ... I've only to ask for them. But, instead, I've trained up my sirdars to do supervisory work. Two assistants, both coolies, help me at the dispensary. The company likes it this way. Lesser employees mean lesser wages.'

'But without assistants and babus the pressure on you must be enormous.'

'No doubt about that, old chap. But I prefer it this way. The presence of assistants and babus would deprive me of the freedom I enjoy now. Let me put it this way ... I prefer to look upon Bihguri as my own fiefdom; within it, I'm the king of all I survey!'

'With only the company above you?'

Buckingham's handsome features broke into a smile. 'Let's invest the company with the status of divinity, shall we? As long as I perform my rituals of worship, place before it incense and offerings, it remains neutral, impersonal.'

'But you're paying the price, Chris. Alone most of the year among a bunch of coolies, immersed in your work, with little means of relaxation.'

'Oh, I've my own way of relaxing,' Buckingham said cryptically. 'You'll find that out soon enough! But such conventional modes of relaxation ... sitting on the verandah with a bottle of whisky, going out wild boar hunting, talking shop with a bunch of sozzled planters ... these don't satisfy inner cravings.'

'I understand the feeling,' David said with an intensity which secretly amused Buckingham. 'It's an obsessive desire to succeed on your own, isn't it?'

'You understand nothing,' Buckingham said, almost with contempt. 'One needs more than the smell of success to satisfy the ego. Success without potency is flat and tasteless. The ego craves power, old chap, not success … to mould other souls like bits of putty, squeezing and smoothening and reshaping to one's desires. Ascendant, preponderate, dominant power … to play a demigod!'

'But such power vests only with absolute monarchs, Chris!' David said.

'Right. And since Providence hasn't thought it fit to provide us with a throne, we must do with what we have.'

'But Chris, it's just a few acres! And a handful of coolies!'

'Come now, dear old chap! The ego's not that demanding! It doesn't need an empire for sustenance. A cat, a dog, one human being, a million … how does it matter? As long as you can break and mould. As long as you command ascendancy. Crushing the soul of a single recalcitrant bugger, so that he'll cringe and grovel and dance the way you pull the strings! These are the things that satisfy and relax. You talked of success, old chap. Well, making an acre of tea bushes yield two hundred pounds of tea … that's not success. But absolute ascendency over even a single individual … that's success!'

David sensed the narcissism overlaid with sadism underlying his host's words; and while a part of him rejected every contention, another greedily lapped them up. Outside it grew dark; an overcast sky blacked out the moon and stars. Chotu brought out a lantern and hung it up on a side pillar. It was immediately surrounded by a swarm of moths. The whisky was getting to David now; he was no longer able to keep track of his host's line of argument—Chris was muttering something to the effect that it was better to rule in hell than serve in heaven. Now, where the devil had he read those lines?

Prolonged silence on his part alerted his host to his state of intoxication, and he pulled the bell cord and told Chotu to lay out dinner. While they were at the table the sky opened up, instantly dispelling the stuffy heat of the atmosphere. This, as well as the intake of food, reduced the whisky-induced befuddlement in David's mind, so that he was in a relatively sober state as they spent some more time on the verandah, brandy goblets in hand, watching the raindrops fall.

It was refreshingly pleasant now as they lounged on the verandah, feet up on the table. David would have liked a longer sojourn, but abruptly Buckingham stood up and bid good night. 'Have to do a round of the tea houses,' he explained. 'I'll advise you to go to your room at the earliest. A surprise awaits you there. A gift from me, old chap.'

A gift? A surprise? David was curious. He gave up his intentions of sitting on the verandah and walked to his room on unsteady feet.

He caught the scent the very moment he entered the lamp-lit room and tensed. It was not the fragrance of myrrh, used to dispel insects. Rather, it was the smell of perfume, the kind Cordi sometimes wore, but of greater insistence, redolent, enticing and sensuous. It raised uneasy memories, of a time that seemingly lay in the hoary past. After his twentieth birthday, Papa at Dhanboa, Cordi spending a night with a friend, an empty house and ennui. Irfan had been with him; the aristocratic, worldly-wise Irfan. At his suggestion they had made a surreptitious visit to native quarters near Ajmeri Gate. Blurred memories of dingy staircases and shaded corridors, the tawdry brilliance of a chandeliered room, the whirl of skirts, and the rhythmic jingle of *jhumkas*. But it had not been the atmosphere or the jaded beauty of the nautch girl which had fired him up, it was the redolent fragrance that had lain suspended in the air.

The same sensations now coursed through his veins as the seductive, nauseous fragrance wafted up to him. So, this was Buckingham's surprise, the gift to the guest by the generous host? It was coming out of the shadows now, naked, golden-dusky and voluptuous. The inebriating fumes swept out of his mind and he grew rigidly sober. The apparition's arms were twirled around him now, its soft, cold body pressed against his. There was a sudden pause, an unuttered gasp of surprise at the coldness of his body; then a sudden burst of activity as the fingers furiously stripped the clothes off him. He stood with the same stiffness, though he too was naked now, as the thing entwined itself around him, caressing, touching, whispering words he did not understand, endeavouring with pathetic desperation to rouse heat in him. Then, in a last, frantic effort, it slithered down and did things that were moist and delicious and his body burst into a blaze.

The prim, dissenting murmurs in his mind were inexorably silenced after that, the abhorrent sensations stilled. There was only exquisite titillation now, and a blinding sensory explosion never experienced before. Yet he had been a passive participant, the inexperienced acolyte, initiated phase by phase into a ritual of delight. Later he threw off his passivity, sought to arm himself with greater knowledge, to attain higher flights of sensuality. Then, in the dead of the night, as he lay exhausted and satiated, the high priestess of the carnal rites left, leaving him alone with his newfound manhood, the poison in his loins and the burden of guilt in his heart.

The welcome accorded by Lieutenant Michael Bailin and Garo Munda to the spring rains proved premature. It had been wishful thinking on his part, the Lieutenant now realized, to have imagined he and Garo alone could build up Chahpuli bush by bush, acre by acre. Everything was ranged against them; like a body rejecting an object intruding into its system, nature herself seemed to be engaged in a conspiracy to obliterate Chahpuli.

Slowly, the jungle triumphed. Chahpuli's defences crumbled; at places mikania and kindred creepers curled around tea saplings; grasses, weeds and thorny brambles greened the earth. But then, when all seemed lost, the rain suddenly stopped and a spell of dry weather set in. The earth dried up rapidly, the evenings turned warm and crisp. The jungle ceased its advance.

Their limbs infused with some of the sun's energy, Bailin and Garo cleared the ground around the tea saplings, and when that was done, recovered the area on the fringes of Chahpuli which the jungle had overrun. They made trip to Titabar and replenished their supplies. Gokuldeva Barua insisted they spend a night with him, and even introduced them to his new and latest bride. The return trip to Chahpuli was made on one of Gokuldeva's elephants, laden with the sacks of provisions purchased at Titabar.

But the interlude was another illusion. Spring would come to a swift and inglorious end. Far from being the Garden of Eden, with the onset of the monsoons, Chahpuli would turn into a dank and soggy purgatory. Alerted by the experience of the spring showers, Bailin and Garo prepared themselves to confront the imminent ordeal.

The two coolie women had been in the fields with the others since morning—twelve hours of non-stop plucking! Except for the periodic visits to the weighing shed to empty their tokris, their fingers had been at work throughout the day, growing so numb with exertion that there was no more pain in them. But the pain was in the wrists, elbows and shoulders; their legs were swollen with having to stand continuously for hours; although they had rubbed their limbs with lemon grass oil to ward off insects and leeches, yet their faces, legs and arms bore innumerable marks of insect bite. Above all was the fatigue which made the body mutiny against the mind's commands or the belly's cravings.

But the bodies had to be fed; the belly's hunger satiated, before they could throw themselves onto the floor and sink into dead slumber. As they drew water from the pond and washed their arms and legs, the younger one said,

'You go rest, mago. I'll light the fire and set the pot. Drink the mod which I bought last week. It'll make you feel less tired.'

The mother took her daughter's advice, while the latter cooked. She placed half the food on a tin platter before her mago, and squatted beside her with her own dish. They shared the koloh of mod between them as they completed the meal in silence. When the food was eaten, she collected the dishes and washed them in the backyard. She returned and sat down once more beside the mother.

'Mago?' She spoke in a pensive voice.

'Yes, Saoni?'

'What's the matter with Bircha? He talks to us no more. He used to come here every evening. He doesn't come any more.'

'He's a bastard!' Baisakhi hissed. The mod was making its impact. 'All men are bastards!'

'No,' Saoni said, her voice, in contrast, was weary but gentle. 'He's a good man. Not like the other sirdars.'

'A good bastard,'said Baisakhi, nodding sagely. 'But a bastard all the same!'

'No,' said Saoni, in the same insistent voice. 'Bircha is good. So is his friend, Meghu. You saw what they did when the leaves were being weighed. That old woman, Janoki, was short-weight every time. They pretended not to notice.'

Baisakhi was suffused with compassionate enlightenment, but she kept her voice hard for her daughter's sake. She was just a slip of a girl, naive and innocent, unacquainted with the harsh bestiality the world was capable of. She herself had seen the infatuation in Bircha's eyes, and the responding love light in the eyes of her daughter. She had said nothing, done nothing to wipe the hangdog look from the young man's features. He was a duffadar at so young an age and would become a sirdar for sure. With that badge of authority, he would be able to make their life a little more bearable; also, being the sirdar's chokri, no one would be able to touch her daughter. Saoni was already flowering into womanhood and possessed the beauty which was sure to attract those bastards as insects are to flowers.

So, she had let the relationship develop, and nursed a secret happiness watching it blossom. Then, without warning, Bircha had suddenly cut them off. He stopped coming in the evening to their hovel. He was stiffly formal when he had to converse with them in the line of duty. Baisakhi had wondered what had prompted Bircha to behave as if they were strangers. But he must have his reason.

'If he's such a good man, why does he behave so, Saoni? We've done nothing to hurt or anger him. Have you said anything to offend him?'

'No,' Saoni replied. 'But a reason must be there, mago. Will you ask him?'

'It's not something good you ask me to do, daughter. Have you no self-respect that you pursue a man who has tired of you? These men want your body, that's all.'

'You're wrong. Bircha talked sweet words but he never tried to touch me.'

'He's moved your heart, hasn't he, this Bircha, this lame duffadar? But beware, Saoni, the thing called pyaar is not for the likes of us. Bhagwan has created us to work like beasts and live like them. Beasts can afford to have no pyaar, daughter.'

'Oh, mago 'Saoni cried out as if her heart would burst. 'He has indeed moved my heart! I cannot live without him!'

The mod induced euphoria in Baisakhi's mind wafted away like mist cleared by the breeze. Fear, like a knife, cut into her heart, and she dreaded for her daughter's future.

'All right, daughter. I'll talk to this lame bastard tomorrow, and find out why he has stopped seeing us.'

The very next evening, just after they had finished their meal and Saoni was washing the plates in the backyard, Bircha arrived at the hutment in response to Baisakhi's summons. Hearing his voice Saoni did not reenter the hutment, but stood behind the rear door, and listened.

'You have a lot of explaining to do, duffadar Bircha!' Baisakhi launched into the visitor. 'Are we earthenware mugs which you can throw away after drinking?'

The nagging fear in her had made her indiscreetly angry. But the frustration in her voice was not her own but her daughter's. Bircha seemed to realize this, for he curbed his own impetuous anger. When he spoke, his voice was sombre with sorrow.

'You have every right to rebuke me, mago. I've behaved shamefully with you and your daughter. These past days I've intentionally tried to avoid you.'

Baisakhi's voice softened. 'But why, Bircha? What has my little Saoni done or said that you break her poor heart so?'

'It's I who have to shoulder the entire blame, mago. When I saw your daughter, I forgot everything else. She made my mind dance. She made me forget who I am, where I was and what I had been planning to do. I'm sorry, mago. But Saoni can never be mine.'

Too late Saoni slapped her palms across her ears. They rang with the force of the blast, her mind could no longer wield control over her body, and she dropped to the ground like a wounded bird. She cringed upon the earth in a posture of despair. But her ears, in masochistic curiosity, remained glued to what was being said inside.

Baisakhi's ebony features twisted into a savage mask. 'You bastard!' she hissed with rabid anger. 'You unfeeling, wretched bastard!' She lifted the half empty bottle as if she would strike, but Bircha raised his hands in an appeasing gesture.

'Wait, mago. When I explain the reason, you'll no longer despise me. You'll pity me, for what I do I do for the good of Saoni and you.'

It was the same recurrent melancholy in his voice which subdued her maternal fury. 'Talk!' she cried. 'Tell me what makes you behave so.'

'We're leaving Bihguri,' Bircha said quietly.

The fury drained out of Baisakhi's heart, to be replaced by fear. Outside, Saoni tensed and lifted herself up so as not to miss a single word.

'Leaving?' Baisakhi could not believe her ears.

'Yes, mago. Meghu and I. We're running away. We had planned to abscond the very moment we were conscripted by those cunning bastards, who induced us with money and mod. We tried to get away at Calcutta itself, but were caught and flogged.'

'Run away?' the woman could not reconcile herself to the fact. 'With that lame leg of yours?'

'It's all pretence, mago, this lameness of mine. It has fooled the sahib; it has fooled the bastard sirdars. When we were first brought here, they beat us without mercy. Meghu-bhaiya's face was kicked out of shape. That's when I thought of this pretence. It'll come handy when we escape from this hell hole. See, I'm not lame.'

He walked the floor twice to show her that he was not lame. The woman laughed.

'You are clever, Bircha!'

Bircha squatted down and clasped Baisakhi's hands. 'We have plotted our escape all these months. Then Saoni came and drove me mad. She made me forget everything else. But Meghu-bhaiya reminded me. I desire freedom, mago.'

'And poor Saoni must suffer for your thoughtlessness?'

'I'm truly sorry. What else can I say? I should have stayed away from your daughter.'

'Can't you take her along?'

'No, mago. There's great peril in absconding. The bastards will kill us if we're caught. I'll never expose Saoni to such risks. Even if we succeed, they'll wreak vengeance on you.'

The girl's ears caught each word. She was weeping silently now, tears of acceptance flowing down her cheeks like the showers of spring.

'I understand. But that is as it always has been. We dream and then wake up harshly. You filled us with a dream, you know that, Bircha? You filled Saoni with pyaar, you know that Bircha? You're taking our dream away.' Baisakhi too was weeping.

'I'm sorry. But Saoni is young. She's beautiful. She'll find someone who'll cherish her as I do. But I have to escape, mago. You must understand. And forgive me.'

Baisakhi dried her eyes with the end of her sari. 'I understand. And forgive. Does anyone know about this? I mean, apart from me?'

'Sanatan. And his wife Lachmi. When the rains grow heavy, we'll leave. Sanatan will spread a rumour of a bagh he saw in the garden. He'll make his animal as fearsome as he can, so the bastard sirdars will not prowl about at night, but stay safely in their huts. That's how Sanatan will help us.'

'That will be the signal?'

'Yes, that will be the signal. When you hear of a bagh in the garden you'll know we're ready to leave. I must go now. Please explain to Saoni. She has my pyaar. But my pyaar for freedom is stronger.'

Bircha gave Baisakhi's hands a squeeze and was gone. Saoni entered.

'You heard, Saoni?' Baisakhi called out softly.

But Saoni remained mute. She spread the sheet of hessian and lay down on it. Her eyes were dry nowbut her mind was in a whirl. Despite the fatigue in her body, her mind would not let it sleep. She lay awake for a long time, consciously cajoling her rebellious mind to accept a future without Bircha.

What was it that her mago had told Bircha? That he had filled them with a dream, which he was now taking away. But did she not have it in her power to make the dream a reality? All she needed to do was to tell Luthra about Bircha's confession. They would inform the sahib. Perhaps he would have them flogged. But seeing the man who had put pyaar inside her being flogged would be less agonizing than losing him forever.

One word! Just one word to Luthra! Yet, even as she planned and plotted in the dark of the night, Saoni knew the very pyaar which had made her so desperate to keep Bircha to herself would never allow her to betray him.

The sudden cessation of the rains and the spring interlude should have filled Cordelia with joy, but it had not. The cause was David. Hardly seven months had elapsed since their arrival in Assam! Could an individual change so much in such a brief span? An individual who had been a life-long companion; tied to her with bonds that went beyond accidental ones of blood or parentage; a being who, in the absence of Papa, had become the sun around which her life revolved? Yet it was the same David who now seemed bent on sending her headlong down into an abyss of alienated loneliness; the warmth of companionship had petered away like the embers of a dying fire.

The germ of egocentricity must have lain dormant in some hidden crevice of his soul, not visible to her unsuspecting eyes, to germinate and flush like the camellia bushes at the touch of rain. The germ had proliferated under pressure: Papa's death, the obsessive desire to make Dhanboa profitable, and spread a corruptive canker which covered his soul like a fungal sheath over a fallen fruit. Ironically, it was David who now shied away from her as if she were the one afflicted; no longer would he admit that it was his soul which had grown diseased.

They had received another letter from Uncle Alex. It was addressed to David. Aunt Patricia had not bothered to write after Cordi's rejection of her offer. Uncle Alex had pointed out that Henry, when he summoned David to Dhanboa, had specifically asked Cordelia to remain at Calcutta with the Swinnerton-Dyers. David used the letter as a peg upon which to hang his own fears and frustrations. They had had another of their rows; no longer was he willing to make concessions on this point. Cowed by the hostility emanating from her brother, Cordelia had retreated to her room, and there, in Pekoe's company, she had impartially weighed her own actions since their arrival at Dhanboa. But she was unable to discover any shortcomings on her part which could be held responsible for the vulnerable position which David thought he found himself in vis-à-vis Dhanboa.

Yet, was it his growing unease with Dhanboa's affairs which had made David so hostile? As usual the last visit to Bihguri seemed to have raised more problems than it had solved. He had gone straight to the fields after his return, his brows creased with anxiety, to look at the newly planted saplings. The inspection had failed to satisfy him and he had returned to the bungalow worried and angered, only to be confronted with Uncle Alex's letter. But the hostility radiating from him after its perusal had not been directed solely at Cordelia. He appeared angry at himself too. What had happened at Bihguri to arouse the hostility and self-loathing?

No longer did David make secret of the fact that he would have preferred her elsewhere; had she not been armed with recollections of how Papa had run Dhanboa—his treatment of the coolies—she might have been tempted to give in. But Papa's invisible presence lent her the strength to endure the unendurable, as did memories of the Reverend Swanson and his words of compassion and wisdom. Above all, it was the coolies who filled her with a passionate determination not to yield.

But David had succeeded in making a dent in their love and trust in her! He had assured her that once the uprooting and replanting were over, the overworked coolies would have a period of rest. She had taken him on trust, had even spoken to the coolies asking them to cooperate. Yet, the moment the replanting was over and the rains arrived, he had set his men, Harua, Ajam and Robiya, after the coolies. There was no promised break from toil. Instead, they had had to drudge their hearts out, often on chores which had no urgency to warrant such furious labour.

Cordelia's objections had been summarily dismissed. The coolies of Dhanboa, like their brethren in other plantations, must earn their wages, David had said. He meant to train them up into the kind of efficiency and discipline he had witnessed at Bihguri. They had to be hammered into efficient working machines if Dhanboa was to become profitable. It was bad enough that she had alienated their godparents; now, if David fell into pecuniary difficulties, how would he go to Uncle Alex for help? She seemed to be bent on taking Dhanboa on the path of destruction and bring ruination to herself and him!

The terrifying thing was that all this was said in a dispassionate, matter-of-fact voice. Nothing would move him now from his self-appointed objectives; clearly Papa had been relegated to the dung heap of memory. Desperate and unmindful of the consequences, Cordelia fought and argued with David on behalf of his workforce, but to no avail. The reward for her pains had been reproachful glances from the hard-pressed coolies, who were awakening to the realization that though the memsahib was good and kind and concerned about their welfare, she no longer had the ears of the sahib. If David took the coolies away, there would be nothing left for her in Dhanboa.

Slowly, but surely, David was stamping the authority of his presence upon Dhanboa and its denizens, shutting her off from the ambit of that authority. Previously he had left it entirely to her to handle the affairs of the dispensary. Now he began to make morning visits there, checking up on the workers who came with complaints. He urged her to keep a dossier on each case of illness, which he could peruse at the end of the week. It would enable him to make an estimate of the workforce available to him at any given point of time, he had explained, for he wanted to run Dhanboa scientifically and systematically, not with Papa's haphazard arbitrariness. But Cordelia suspected it was more to find out if any coolie was malingering, and to take it out on him later.

'Don't you trust me anymore, David?' she had despairingly asked. 'Will I knowingly keep a healthy worker from going to the fields?' David had turned away without replying. But his silence was a resounding answer.

The traits she so detested in her own kind—arrogance and egocentricity—were being revealed in his actions. Her brother was emulating individuals like Buckingham and moulding himself into his stereotype.

Insulation seemed to have become an obsession with David. He had lately been seeking to keep villagers out of the plantation; and, this spring, when Bapu babu as before extended the invitation from his village to visit it during the *Rongali Bihu* festival, he had flatly refused. The bormohori tried to impress upon David that it would be wise to be on good terms with the villagers, for one never knew when their services might be required.

But David would not be moved. In desperation Bapu babu turned to Cordelia for help. Her own pleadings falling on deaf ears, she announced that David might do as he pleased, but she herself would go to the village.

And go she did, to a grand, memorable reception! True, Esscombe sahib had been to that village; but she was the first white woman to have set foot in it, and thus was an object of great curiosity and wonder. Bapu babu had been in constant praise of her and the manner in which she comported herself during the visit did nothing to diminish the regard with which the villagers held her. They marvelled at the creamy softness of her skin, the wondrous colour of her hair and eyes. Her easy manners and radiant smile dissolved any hesitations or qualms in the village women folk, who flocked around her, gazing at her with adoring eyes as if she were a temple idol. And how proud did Bapu babu look as he introduced her to all the village elders!

She, on her part, was struck by the cultured gentleness of these simple villagers, their generous, hospitable nature which neither persecution nor barbarism had been able to warp. They put no price on their hospitality—their love was not for barter. Yet David, the fool, had disdained their invitation, although the adoration bordering on reverence would have been grist to his bloated ego! In her it evoked humility, a feeling of unworthiness and a desire to do something in return. Thus, when a village patriarch solemnly made a request, she was most happy to oblige.

The request was a small one. During Esscombe sahib's time the village *huchari* or bihu-dance party always paid a visit to Dhanboa and gave a performance. They would like to continue the tradition. Would she talk to her brother and secure permission from him?

But, of course, they could come to Dhanboa! Not only could, they must! There was no need to seek David sahib's permission. Her word was enough.

She secured David's capitulation in a wordy duel, her rapier being Papa's name. The huchari arrived on a Sunday morning—the entire garden had come to watch; grinning coolie men, noisy children, coolie women carrying babies and toddlers in their arms, formed a ring around the huchari. David and Cordelia watched the huchari from the bungalow verandah. Such was the magical throb in the music that Cordelia caught even David tapping his fingers to it.

For over two hours the villagers sang and danced, one group replacing another. And finally, with a pulsating climax in which the entire contingent joined in, the huchari ended its performance. Now it was time for the benedictions, and the offer of gifts. Cordelia had kept ten seers of salt packed, and prepared a horai with betel-nut and paan, a single gamocha covering it. At her signal Mongla brought the horai and the packets of salt out and placed them before the huchari party.

'Come, David,' she urged her brother. 'They'll confer blessings on the household now. We must go down and join them in prayer.'

The boyish, smiling look which had unconsciously appeared in David's features vanished in an instance, to be replaced by the one she so detested.

'Join them? What for?'

'They're going to bless us, David.' she repeated, keeping her voice low. 'We must go down and kneel before them.'

David's features grew rigid with disbelief. 'You must be out of your mind! Kneel and bow before them? The very idea!'

He turned on his heels and strode off to his room.

She descended the stairs alone, shame and humiliation writ over her features, knelt and bowed before the congregation as an aged Assamese patriarch uttered the blessings in a high voice. He blessed the inmates of the bungalow, wished them continuous and growing prosperity, invoked the gods in the heavens to keep them happy and contented, to fill their hearths with many children, and to ensure that the Esscombe lineage would continue to thrive and flourish.

As she knelt on the earth to receive the benedictions, her mind went back to the noon when a patriarch, perhaps the same one, had welcomed them to Dhanboa with similar blessings. Happiness and contentment, Cordelia wryly wondered! The blessings of that first afternoon had wrought no miracle—would these be able to affect one?

Coming towards the end of May, the monsoons ruthlessly snuffed out the spring. It was the monsoon, and not winter, which was the season of death in Assam—the days of continuous downpour were sufficient to make Cordelia aware of this truth!

With the onset of the first heavy showers Bapu babu, Kamal and the Assamese tea makers moved bag and baggage into the tea house used to store the first-flush tea chests. The number of coolies dropping in at the dispensary for treatment marked a dramatic rise; she was relieved to find that almost all had needed treatment of sores and carbuncles. None so far had been afflicted with dysentery or diarrhoea. But trouble suddenly came from the most unexpected quarters. Early one morning, a week after the rain had started, Mongla tapped at her door. She opened it to find the servant almost incoherent with fear. He did not have the chota hazri tray in his hand, he had stutteringly explained, because there was a dead body lying beneath the bungalow!

Watching the monsoon showers pour down, Lieutenant Michael Bailin experienced a sinking sensation in the pit of his belly. 'The battle,' he told an uncomprehending Garo, 'is lost even before it has begun!'

'The battle, sahib? What battle?'

'Our battle to save Chahpuli, Garo. It's impossible, can't you see? We were in a state of opium intoxication when we even contemplated it! Just the two of us … it can't be done!'

'We agreed to keep on trying, remember sahib? We mustn't give up trying.'

Try they did, for a week, against desperate odds, for hours on end hacking away at the suddenly resurgent jungle which sought to smother their minuscule tea garden. Then, towards the evening of the seventh day, the thin, ankle-high sheet of water continually flowing across the Chahpuli clearing lost its flow and became stagnant. Bailin realized something was dreadfully wrong.

But the gathering dusk made investigations impossible. The duo retreated to the dry safety of their hutment for food and sleep. Around midnight Bailin found himself being violently shaken, and bolted upright.

'Baanpaani, sahib! We must get up. There's no telling how high the waters will rise.'

Baanpaani! Floods! So that was the significance his tired brain had missed the previous evening. The unexpected stoppage in the flow, the sluggishness he had felt around the ankles? Something had caused this stoppage; the water had begun to accumulate in the clearing; the level had risen. If Garo was correct, the waters were rising still.

There was not a moment to be lost. The water had climbed above the elevated, terraced floor of their hutment and was pouring through the gap beneath the bamboo door. They made haste to save their possessions, their stock of foodstuff, and his trunk containing the medicines. Guided by the lantern's light they staggered out of the front door towards the bamboo ladder leading to the roof. Bailin climbed up and Garo soon joined him at the top. They half-slithered, half-hopped frog-like to the middle of the thatch, and sat there, legs straddling the two sides of the sloping roof like a mahout on an elephant.

'Our kismet has turned sour again, Garo,' Bailin said.

'The water will go away, sahib. The rain will stop. The sun will come out again. Talk about that, sahib. How we'll build up Chahpuli. These flood waters will enrich the soil. The saplings will endure. They'll grow stronger.'

'Do you think so, Garo? Do you think we can yet make something of our mock garden?'

'Of course, we can, sahib. You promised to make me the head sirdar, didn't you?'

They chatted on, two voices in the dark, endeavouring to strengthen each other with hope. The light of the morning leapt at them with bewildering suddenness, and the landscape swiftly fell into focus. To coincide with the break of day the rains first slackened to a drizzle, and then tapered off. The effect was of a curtain being pulled away, and the two of them looked on open mouthed at the sight surrounding them.

All around was a vast sheet of water, coloured a muddy brown, the hutment an island precariously poised at the very centre. The tea saplings were totally submerged, not a solitary stalk protruding out to show they were there at all. The surrounding jungles threw a ring around this gargantuan pool, imbuing finiteness to what would otherwise have loomed to the vision as a boundless, unmoving, ocean. But the seeming lack of motion was false, for the waters, slowly but certainly, were flowing in a northerly direction—one which led to what had previously been a dry streambed.

'So, what do we do now? Return to our rooms?'

'No, sahib. That would be unwise. The water is falling. We'd better wait for it to drain out completely. Who knows what creatures infest our rooms?'

But it was written on their foreheads that they were in for another dunking! Garo's eyes detected the piece of driftwood first; a large, gnarly branch. Draped over it was the naked body of a man—dead or alive they had no means of knowing—fingers fiercely twirled around the branches.

A rumour began to circulate in the basti of Bihguri almost as soon as the monsoons arrived. A tiger had been sighted; the animal had entered the basti and attacked a hutment. The rumour proved contagious; others saw the creature on the second night and the third and the fourth! Other houses were attacked! The outcome was an epidemic of terror—neither vituperations nor whiplashes could induce the pluckers to enter the bushes until coolie drummers had first beat a tattoo through tea sections earmarked for plucking to ensure they contained no striped or spotted threat. Workers in the fields, ignoring dire warnings of sirdars, downed their implements well before sundown and made a beeline for the basti, so they could finish their domestic chores and bar their doors before twilight. Tea makers and tea house hands baulked at going out of the tea houses at night—the fear entered the hearts of the sirdars too; now they showed a distinct aversion to patrolling the plantation at night and found it more comfortable to remain in the safety of the tea houses or their dwellings.

Luthra duly informed the sahib of this four-legged apparition that stalked the Bihguri nights. Buckingham did not react with customary anger. A tiger in the plantation could spell disaster; he was endowed with enough insight into the coolies' minds to appreciate that. He could not be certain the tiger existed only in the imagination of the timid bastards. A single assault on a coolie and the season might turn into a fiasco!

The thing to do was to verify what till now had been just a wild rumour. This would entail armed patrolling at night. He summoned Luthra.

'You, Budhu and I will take up patrolling the next couple of nights,' he informed his head sirdar. 'Puran and Gandru will take up tea house supervision. Put Meghu and Bircha in the fields.'

He noticed the lack of enthusiasm on the part of his henchman. 'Ho, Luthra, petrified, are you?'

'No sahib. But just the three of us? It might be a tiger after all!'

'You needn't worry, Luthra,' his master said with a mocking chuckle. 'My rifle will be with me. *Hum saale bagh ka bachcha ko goli se ura denge*!'

There were four people were inside Sanatan's hut: Lachmi, Bircha, Meghu and Sanatan himself. Six days of continuous rain had the nullahs and rivulets overflowing and made garden paths slushy and slippery. The roads leading to Bihguri were heaped with mud, making them impassable except on elephant back. The moment was opportune.

'All is ready, Meghu?' Sanatan asked in a tense whisper.

'All is ready, Sanatan bhaiya. You did well to spread those lies about the bagh. Now the sirdars don't venture out at night.'

'Even then you must take the greatest care,' Sanatan said with gravity. 'Row upstream in the boat. A difficult thing to do, but safer. They would expect you to row downstream. It's time now. You must leave.'

Bircha had remained mutely sullen all the while, a hangdog look on his features. He now reached for Lachmi's hands, grasped them and said,

'Take Saoni under your wings, Lachmi bahen. Her mago too.'

Lachmi's voice was suffused with undisguised sorrow. 'Your pain is my pain, Bircha-bhaiya. If my assurance will lessen your pain, I give it to you.'

'Saoni is growing. With each full moon she will grow more pretty. Then the vultures will come!'

'I'll shield her!' The words were suddenly bereft of sorrow. They burned like embers with inner fury. 'I've powers of my own, Bircha-bhaiya.'

'Thank you, Lachmi bahen. Thank you, Sanatan bhaiya. Maybe we'll meet again, maybe we'll not. But I go with a lighter heart ... and filled with gratitude.'

Lachmi blew out the earthen lamp. Without further words of parting, Meghu pushed open the bamboo door and the two of them slipped into the wet, dark night.

The ground was treacherous, doubly so because the pitch darkness reduced visibility. Meghu led, Bircha followed close behind. Soon they were among the tea bushes, on the narrow path leading towards the jungle on Bihguri's eastern extremity. They would not enter it, but move along the arc of the inner perimeter, past the seed-barrie and nursery, till they reached the plantation's entry gate through which they would make their exit. That would be the tricky part, for the open ground near the gate provided no cover. But there would be no one there now; the tiger conjured up by Sanatan had ensured that.

The darkness was their ally as well as their enemy. with no landmark visible, they had to progress by instinct. Tea bushes rose like ghostly shadows around them as they groped towards the garden's edge. Suddenly they were at the seed-barrie and Meghu stopped. Bircha bumped into him from behind.

'*Kya ho gaya*?' Bircha asked angrily.

'Shh! Not so loud. I thought I heard voices.'

'Voices? Out here? You must be crazy!'

Meghu chuckled softly. 'Yes, you're right. It's the fear, bhaiya. One imagines things!' He turned a bend on the path and rammed straight into Christopher James Buckingham.

The planter, startled by the totally unexpected collision, tottered back a pace, slipped and tumbled to the ground, the rifle falling away with a thud. Behind him Luthra and Budhu screeched out in terror and alarm, unaware that it was a man and not a tiger which had pounced upon the sahib!

'*Bhago*! *Bhago*!' Meghu, recovering quickly, yelled out. He swivelled and dived straight into the bushes to his right. Once inside them, he began a frantic crawl on all fours through the narrow gaps separating the tea plants.

Bircha blundered. Instead of screening himself behind the bushes, he turned and half-ran, half-slid across the path by which they had come. Buckingham, recovering from his fall with amazing speed, groped about for his rifle, found it, picked it up and put it to his shoulder. Aiming blindly in the direction of the path, he fired.

Bircha let out an agonized scream as the bullet slammed into his back, just below the left shoulder, plunging him headlong into the mire. For a few moments he thrashed about in the slush, writhing in agony. Then, like a wounded animal instinctively seeking shelter, he rolled away from the path, crawled a few yards into the tea bushes, and lay there, teeth clamped to stifle the groans threatening to emerge from his throat.

'Got one of the bastards!' Buckingham cried out in triumph. 'Budhu, double back to the gate and cover it. Luthra, fetch men from the tea houses. And flares. *Jaldi*! *Doro*!'

The terrible pain sharpened the senses of the man crouching in the bushes. The shaitan was there on the path, cradling his rifle, ears cocked for the slightest of sounds. Soon men would arrive with flares. Wound or no wound, pain or no pain, he must move!

Slowly, testing each inch of the ground ahead for fallen branches which might snap under his weight, Bircha began to creep in a direction he judged would take him towards the nursery. The pain in his left shoulder had subsided. It had become numb and senseless; the warm flow of blood too had dwindled to a trickle.

After what seemed an eternity, he judged he was far enough from the rifle-wielding man to risk rising to his feet. At a distance he could hear clamouring voices rapidly gathering volume. Bulbous lights appeared like will-o'-the-wisps in the darkness. There was not a moment to waste. Bircha fled.

Abruptly he was at the nursery. He stopped, cocked his ears once again. A babble of sounds carried to him. Where was Meghu? Had he been able to reach the main gate before it was covered, as the shaitan had ordered? Or was he still crouching among the bushes, all exits closed to him?

As for himself, attempting to cross the main gate and reach the ghat was out of the question now. But there was another egress close by, the thinnest of jungle-tracks. Bircha knew it led to another garden, the one owned by the sahib who frequently came to Bihguri that way.

Another garden! Another trap! He might be jumping off the frying pan into the fire! But there was no choice. Pausing for a moment to fix his direction, Bircha set off towards the patch of thatch and cane he must cross before he could hit the track.

Hitting the trail, he sank to the ground and rested for a while. The fatigue was seeping into his mind; he could not allow that! There was death behind him, though he could no longer hear shouts. Perhaps there was death ahead, but the terrors of the unknown could be faced with greater fortitude than those of the moment.

Bircha got up slowly, willed his tired mind once more to issue commands to his battered body, and set off in a blind stagger. But soon there was no coordination between body and brain. His mind grew blank; his legs moved of their own volition, step by lumbering step. Abruptly, he found himself among tea bushes again. No, these were not the poisonous bushes of Bihguri, but of the garden belonging to the young sahib. Fear was a stimulant, enabling him to take the final steps which brought him to a weird hutment set on stilts.

There was nothing left in him—no strength, no sensations. Bircha dropped to the ground in a heavy fall, crawled into the emptiness beneath the hutment, and slipped gratefully into unconsciousness.

Meghu scuttled through the bushes in panic till the rifle's bang and the pain-racked shriek jolted him to a stop. *Hai Bhagwan*! The shaitan had shot Bircha dead! He heard the bastard's voice instruct Budhu to cover the gate. He had to move fast if he were not to be trapped!

He resumed his frantic, rodent crawl till he reached the end of the plantings. The small expanse of open ground leading to the gate lay before him. He saw Budhu, close to the gate, a deeper shadow within shadows, nervously pacing up and down.

Meghu groped for, and found, a fist sized rock. He fell on his belly, unmindful of the muddy ground and slithered with reptilian stealth towards the sentinel. Closing in on him, he rose noiselessly to his feet and brought the rock crashing down on the man's head.

The fellow's skull split open and he crumpled to the ground. One—for Bircha! Meghu paused to deliver a kick to the bastard's groin before flitting out through the gate, and onto the path that led to the ghat. The light, dugout canoe was there, as he had known it would be. Meghu jumped down the bank and into the skiff.

He was tempted to change the original plan and glide downstream. But safety lay in irrationality, Sanatan had advised! No, he must push on upstream, even though it might break his back.

The going was slow. He rowed on and on, unable to rest for even a split of a second, for the currents would sweep the skiff downstream at the barest pause. But the constant push against the currents took its toll upon his body; the terror-inspired strength was ebbing fast and Meghu realized he could not continue wielding the oars for much longer. With a cry of futility, he laid down his oars and stopped rowing.

Suddenly, a strange change occurred in the surroundings; the blurry banks which had given tangible direction to his progress disappeared! The very moment he stopped rowing, the boat should have floated downstream. Yet, as soon as he laid down the oars, the boat made a half turn on its own and slid off in an entirely different direction. Meghu was bewildered.

Then he understood. His upstream journey had carried the boat into a wider rivulet which had overflowed its banks and flooded the countryside. It had passed over a bank into the open countryside.

Meghu did not pick up the oars again, allowing his over-strained muscles to relax. It did not matter where his kismet carried him, as long as it was not back to that hellhole called Bihguri. He held on to the skiff's side, luxuriating in the pleasure of relaxation which succeeds hard toil, and closed his eyes.

He remained in that state of drowsy wakefulness till a harsh bump against the side of the boat jolted him aware. Shadowy columns had sprung up all around him—trees! He had entered jungle land! He heard the crunching sound as the prow cracked and splintered with repeated impact against the tree-trunks. Utterly helpless, Meghu flung himself flat on the skiff's belly, clinging desperately to a transverse beam. There was one, final clash; the prow heaved up into the air and the skiff turned turtle. Meghu was flung into the foaming waters and dashed from tree to tree.

He reached out in the blackness for something, anything, which might offer him the barest chance to live. His outstretched fingers scraped against the claw-like branch of a drifting log. He grasped it with all the strength he could muster. The huge chunk of driftwood pulled him along; renewed hope flooded his breast as he discovered that the protruding branches acted as effective buffers against the violent blows.

His dhoti had been ripped away and the pitifully small hoard of money along with it. He was naked now and his body a welter of pain. But he was alive!

A corpse? Underneath the bungalow? The blood drained from Cordelia's features. Could it be that of a Dhanboa coolie? Had the scourge struck?

She wrapped a robe around her nightclothes and emerged onto the verandah, signalling to Mongla to follow. Pekoe came up, tail wagging. It was brighter outside. The rains which had been failing continually for a week had stopped.

She descended the staircase in nervous agitation. A stifled scream escaped from her throat at the sight confronting her. A man lay sprawled on the soggy ground, face down, his broad back a mosaic of gore and mud. A tall man, dusky and strong limbed, naked except for a tattered bit of loin cloth clinging to the waist. Cuts and bruises covered the entire body.

Pekoe growled. Cordelia shushed him into silence.

She paused to control the trembling of her limbs, took a deep breath and, kneeling beside the man, picked up a limp wrist to feel the pulse. Weak, but indubitably there.

She shifted his head slightly for a glance at the face. A curious admixture of relief and astonishment flooded her mind as she recognized the mud-caked features. It was one of Buckingham's coolies, the one with fire in his eyes!

Catching Mongla by the arm she whispered urgently, 'Fetch Bapu babu. And Kamal. Ask them to bring the stretcher from the dispensary. Hurry!'

As Mongla raced away, she listened for any sound from the floor overhead. There was none. David, thank heavens was still in bed! She knelt once more beside the coolie; her eyes widened with horror as they caught the pulpy, blood-encrusted bullet wound below the left shoulder.

The wait seemed to be never ending. Almost twenty minutes elapsed before Bapu babu and Kamal arrived with the stretcher. They lifted the limp body onto it. The coolie groaned, but did not regain consciousness.

They carried the injured man to the dispensary and transferred him onto a bamboo bed in one of the rooms at the back. 'Boil some water,' she instructed Kamal. 'Put some arnica into it and cleanse every cut on his body. Be careful with that shoulder. That's a bullet wound. This must remain a secret between the four of us. The presence of this man must be known to no one else. Not even David sahib must know. Is that clear?'

Three heads dipped in unison. 'I and Mongla must return to the bungalow. Or David sahib will grow suspicious. Bapu babu must also go to his duties. So, it's up to you, Kamal. But don't worry. I'll be back at the usual time.'

Cordelia paused briefly near David's door. Her brother was still asleep. A piece of good fortune for that wretched coolie! The heavy rains had brought about the second flush in the tea bushes. David had been at the tea houses till midnight, supervising the tea makers. Had it been otherwise, he would have been awake by now!

Mongla brought chota hazri, and woke her brother up. Within half hour he was ready for the fields. Cordelia heard him depart with Harua. She recalled the first few months in Dhanboa. He would never leave for the fields before bidding her goodbye. Now he had stopped doing that.

She came out to the verandah and watched her brother disappear among the tea bushes. Then she hurried to the dispensary, Pekoe trotting at her heels. Dispatching Kamal to take care of the coolies who had come with complaints, she once more examined the runaway.

Kamal had done a good job. No longer did the man emit the foul stink of slime and sweat, but the pungent odour of the lotion. She peered closely at the bullet wound. Kamal had cleaned away the congealed blood; the puncture which the bullet had made as it entered the back glared back at her, red and snarling. A tinge of white was already flecking the frayed, ragged, crimson edges of the wound. Putrefaction was setting in! She went to the outer medicine room, picked up Dr Goodeve's medical handbook, and returned to her patient. Sitting on a murrah, she looked up the section dealing with treatment of bullet wounds. Finding it, for the next half hour she perused the pages minutely, overcome by a sense of futility as the truth dawned on her.

The man recumbent on the bamboo bed was as good as dead! Much of the medical terminology was Greek to her, but she understood the import. Sepsis or putrefaction could be combated with the disinfectants she possessed, but the wound of a bullet, if the said bullet was lodged in the flesh, was a different matter altogether. The intruding mass of lead would gradually poison the flesh, making it rot away; pernicious gangrene would set in, spread and finally infect the entire body till the patient died a painful death. To prevent this, the bullet lodged in the flesh must be surgically extracted as expeditiously as possible, and the putrefaction contained.

Surgical extraction! Cordelia knew in her heart she neither had the requisite knowledge nor the temperament to undertake surgical extraction.

The man on the bed stirred and groaned. A mumbled stream of incoherence emerged out of his lips before he drifted back into a faint. Cordelia caught a single word—Saoni! She did not know what it meant. Shot like a rabid dog! Cordelia could guess where that shot had come from! If the man died, she would not remain silent. David or no David, she would rouse the very heavens with her cries for justice.

But her concern must be with life, not death. And life could be endowed to this poor creature if only she could overcome the shortcomings in herself, her abhorrence of blood, her fears and qualms, and pick up the surgeon's scalpel. Pushing herself off the murrah, Cordelia put aside the manual and knelt beside the dying coolie. Her folded hands rested on the bamboo frame as she closed her eyes and prayed. On the screen of her darkened vision loomed an image; not one endowed with the mystic radiance of divinity, but of the bearded, half-forgotten face of Reverend Garry Swanson; and his voice, warm and compassionate, floated clearly to her ears. But it was the voice of the Lord which spoke through His apostle. 'My child,' the voice said. 'You have more strength … more resilience … in you than I could have ever imagined. Be brave and strong, my child. Never give in to despair, but draw on your inner strength.'

Cordelia opened her eyes and stood purposefully up. She felt suffused with nascent power as she took a final look at the unconscious man on the bed and strode out of the room.

With the same determined attitude of having arrived at a decision, she left the dispensary for the tea house where Bapu babu was. Drawing the bormohori away, she said, 'The bullet is still inside the man's back. I'll have to take it out.'

'When do it, Cordelia memsahib?' Bapu babu asked.

'I wish we could've done it right now. Delay increases the risks of gangrene. But I'm afraid it cannot be. David drops in at the dispensary every morning. He mustn't know.'

'Yes, yes. We hide, no? Evening best time. Dear David sahib, bery, bery busy tea house. Can't come sniffing, no, yes?'

'No alternative to that, Bapu babu. I'll need certain things.'

'Yes, yes,' the bormohori said eagerly. 'You tell. I get.'

'A bottle of phatika. Perhaps two.'

Bapu babu was aghast. 'You drink phatika, darling Cordelia memsahib? To keep hands from shaking, no? You not do that. Get vilayati paani. Not tear up intestines, yes, no.'

Despite her anxiety Cordelia could not help but smile.

'Not for me, you dolt! For the coolie! It'll be a painful business, for I have no morphine in our stock to put him to deep sleep. We must put enough phatika inside him if he's to endure the pain.'

'Oh,' said the relieved bormohori. 'I get you phatika. What else you want?'

'Two trusted men who can keep a secret. You'll have to choose them yourself.'

'That difficult, but possible. Why you need such fellows?'

'To hold the coolie while I cut him up. You, Kamal and Mongla must be there too. Get hold of two lanterns and bring them along.'

Cordelia returned to the dispensary. She rummaged through Papa's medicine shelves till she found what she had been looking for: a small, leather bag containing surgical implements. Collecting some large rolls of cotton wool, a couple of tin-trays, a bed-pan and a few other assorted items, she carried and deposited them in the room where the coolie lay. She touched the man's forehead. It was reassuringly cool.

She called out to Kamal who hurried in. 'Soak some cotton wool in water and wet his lips.' Her assistant complied. The man greedily sucked at the wet blobs of cotton.

'You're hurt,' Cordelia spoke with gentleness. 'Someone shot you. But we'll take care of you. Do you feel hungry? Nod your head if yes.'

The injured man dipped his head. Clearly, the action caused him intense pain, for his eyes blurred.

'I'll have Mongla prepare some broth and send it here. Feed it to him with a spoon.'

David's visit to the dispensary was due soon. That would be a tricky moment. She attempted to erase the anxiety from her features and act natural as she and Kamal repaired to the medicine room.

Her brother came, along with the ever-present Harua. She need not have worried at all. David was too triumphantly conscious of the deserted state of the dispensary for probing. A single look through the morning entries in the register and he departed. Cordelia, relieved, stood at the window of the medicine room and watched him go. But her brother came to a sudden stop a few yards outside the dispensary and stood there, as though awaiting the arrival of someone. Cordelia peered through the ribs of the window for a better look, her heart leaping with renewed fear.

Three men on an elephant were coming through Dhanboa's front entrance. Even from that distance she recognized the man who sat behind the mahout: Christopher James Buckingham!

The elephant lumbered up to David. Buckingham jumped lithely down, followed by a sirdar. Cordelia remained beside the window; ears glued to the conversation taking place outside.

'Surprised, old chap?' Buckingham was asking. 'Sorry for dropping in without warning. But I've had a spot of trouble. Two coolies absconded from Bihguri last night.'

'Why, that's terrible!' Trust David to be genuinely concerned!

'Potted one with my rifle. Could've sworn I killed him. But we scoured the concerned tea sections last night and all of this morning. The corpse is nowhere to be found.'

'And the other?'

'Got clean away, I'm afraid. Bashed one of my sirdars on the head with a rock. Damn nearly killed him. Stole a boat and pushed off! I've sent my men to alert the villages around Bihguri. The word will spread from village to village, right up to Kokilamukh.'

'So why come to Dhanboa, Chris?'

'It's the other bastard. The one I potted. Maybe my shot wasn't lethal. He was close to the track leading to Dhanboa when I shot him … there's a chance he may have headed this way. Mind if we take a look around?'

'Leave that to me, Chris.' There was iron in David's voice. Her brother was learning fast! 'I'll have my sirdars do that.'

'Suit yourself, my dear fellow.' Buckingham could not quite erase the displeasure from his voice. 'I've put a reward on the fellow's head. Fifty rupees alive, twenty dead. Spread the word around.'

'Fifty rupees? That's a great deal of money.'

'Worth every pice, if it helps me lay hands on him. I'll make such an example of the bastard that there will be no more absconders from Bihguri for another hundred years!'

'What sort of a chap my men must look for?'

Cordelia sensed hesitation in Buckingham. The information was given grudgingly.

'You've seen him. On your first visit to Bihguri. The one I made a duffadar ... the bugger with the limp. Only he wasn't limping much when I last saw him!'

David sounded smug. 'But I thought you'd tamed him?'

'I daresay I was mistaken.' Buckingham remounted the elephant. Then, as a rejoinder to David's smugness, he said, 'You won't be tempted to keep him, will you, old chap? In case you do find him?'

'Don't be asinine, Chris,' David retorted heatedly. 'The very moment I discover he's actually at Dhanboa, I'll let you know.'

Garo and Bailin quickly slid down the ladder and grabbed the log just as it was about to float past. Careful to keep it steady, they dragged the unlikely raft, the body still draped across it, towards the foot of the ladder and secured it.

Garo touched the body and found it warm. 'He's alive, sahib,' he cried out in delight.

'Took a buffeting, by the looks of him,' Bailin said. 'Well, we can't do a thing until the waters recede.'

The two climbed up once more to the roof and waited. Finally, the waters seeped completely away, leaving behind a layer of slimy mud which covered the ground like a huge, grey-white carpet.

An hour later, the sun exploded into the open. The mud around them began to steam, as did the roof on which they straddled, and the wet, swampy jungles. The last vestiges of life in the mud disappeared, throttled to death by the hardening slime. To be on the safe side they waited an hour more, and then cautiously descended the bamboo ladder.

The log had gone down with the failing waters and now lay at the foot of the wall, shadowed by the projecting roof. The man continued to lie in the same inert posture.

They spattered some water on his face; the fellow groaned, and opened his eyes. One of Buckingham's coolies! The man too recognized them, and his eyes became two pools of impotent fear. He tried to rise, but Garo held him down.

'*Dhire dhire, dost*! You're in safe hands. You have nothing to fear.'

The softness in Garo's words acted as a sedative; the fear slid off the eyes. The man closed them, his naked body relaxed and he lay recumbent.

'How are you feeling, bhaiya?' Garo asked.

'Pain all over my body. My head aches. Apart from that, no problems. No bones broken, see?' The man stood up and walked a few clumsy steps to convince them.

'You're from Bihguri, aren't you?'

'Yes. My name's Meghu.'

'Tell us what happened. Speak slowly so the sahib might understand.'

The man related his harrowing experience. 'I should've been ten times a dead man,' he concluded. 'But I'm not dead. Instead, my brother Bircha lies dead, shot through the heart by the Bihguri sahib.'

'You'll be safe with us,' Bailin said. The coolie looked at him with skeptical eyes.

'You'll let me stay here, sahib? You'll not send me to Bihguri?'

It was Garo who answered. 'My sahib hates that bastard even more than you, Meghu-bhaiya. He would rather go to *narak* himself than send you back.'

'Thank you, sahib. I'll serve you as best as I can. You'll have no regrets.'

'I'll get you a dhoti the very moment we enter our hut,' Garo said. 'But first I've a task to perform.'

Collecting some firewood, he piled them just inside the front room of the cottage and, with the tinderbox, built a small fire, and heaped green and sappy twigs upon it. The moisture laden branches emitted whitish grey smoke which soon filled up the entire cottage, pouring out from windows and gaps beneath the roof, so that the hutment appeared to be on fire.

'Watch, sahib!' he cried with childlike excitement. 'If there are snakes inside, this'll smoke them out!'

Bailin watched in fascinated horror as a long, black reptile slid out of an open window. He had a quick glimpse of the whitish underside as the cobra, tail entwined around a bamboo rib, slithered down the mud wall, tongue flicking out of its evil mouth. Once it reached flat ground, it streaked off at an incredible pace towards the jungle. More was to come—a banded krait this time, sluggish but deadly. It rippled slowly out of a window, the yellow and black pigmentation brilliant in the sunlight.

'Another hour, sahib,' Garo said. 'Then it should be safe to enter.'

Even after the wait was over, Garo did not allow his master to enter the hut till, armed with a stick, he had inspected every inch of the interior. The floods had not caused any irreparable damage; their stock of food was safe, as were their personal effects. While Garo, assisted by Meghu, set about preparing food, Bailin embarked on a reconnaissance of the terrain, viewing it with a different eye. After they had eaten, they sat underneath the bel-tree.

'So, the mandarin was right!' Bailin said with feeling. 'He told me he suspected Leach sahib had attempted planting here and then gave it up as a bad job. Now we know why! He discovered that the land is subject to inundation during heavy rains.'

'What do we do, sahib?' Garo asked. 'We can't spend our time on the roof every night it rains!'

'We'll have to cut a ditch to the nearby stream, Garo, to provide another outlet from our clearing. How long might it take the three of us to dig a nullah? If we start this afternoon?'

'Two days, sahib … at the most.'

'Then Garo, pray for two more days of sunshine.'

David was as good as his word. He alerted his workers to be on the lookout for any stranger in Dhanboa. However, no stranger—dead or alive—was sighted. David communicated this to a sirdar from Bihguri who came that afternoon.

No one contemplated a search of the dispensary for the fugitive. That was memsahib's domain. Even David was not man enough to push his sister too far!

That evening Cordelia marched to the dispensary, the houseboy carrying a lantern. Kamal opened the backdoor in response to her thumps, shutting it as soon as they entered. They made their way to the room where the injured coolie lay.

Three other men were inside the room—Bapu babu and two coolies, Tuilu and Deba, both trustworthy garden hands. With the windows barred and the door shut, it was suffocatingly hot inside. The room reeked of disinfectant, sweat, urine and kerosene from the lanterns. Cordelia caught another smell—of stale wine!

The Bihguri runaway lay face down on the bed in an inebriated stupor. Bapu babu and the two coolies tied the man's legs and arms to the bed with ropes. Kamal fetched the pan of boiling water in which the surgical instruments lay.

'Clamp a towel between his teeth, Kamal,' Cordelia said.

The man shook his head slightly as Kamal forcibly opened his jaws and thrust a wad of towel material between the teeth. Cordelia picked up a pair of surgical scissors from the pan and cut away the bandage protecting the wound. She lifted the wad of cotton which lay like a lid upon the bullet hole and threw it into an empty cane basket. The wound had festered rapidly. The snarling, red-edged mouth was replaced by a white circle of suppuration. Cordelia probed the circle's centre with a finger. The body beneath her grew rigid.

She took a deep breath. 'All right, hold him tight,' she hissed. Four of them took grip over each limb, while Kamal clutched the man's head. Cordelia picked up a scalpel and, gritting her teeth, plunged the sharp edge into the flesh, cutting deep, an incision around two inches in length, bisecting the white circle at the centre.

The man's body tautened; pus mixed with blood erupted. Quickly she made a second incision, crosswise from the first. The man shrieked but the sound was muted by the gag. He was in the throes of a convulsion, body twisting and turning to escape the agony, muscles straining against the tethers. The others threw themselves upon him to hold him immobile.

Kamal gripped his hair tight and thrust the side of the head deep into the pillow.

Closing her eyes, stifling the nausea rising up inside her, Cordelia thrust her thumb and forefinger into the oozy orifice, probing. The body thrashed and squirmed under her, emitting hoarse, choking, piteous sounds. Panic overtook her as the searching fingers failed to find what it sought. Then she touched it—the lethal intruder—securely lodged in a mass of tissues. She would have to cut deeper to get at it!

'Oh God!' her mind shrieked silently. 'It's not a living thing under me…but a chunk of mutton, hacked out by a butcher from the carcass of a creature long dead! Using the fingers of her left hand to part the flesh, she made two deeper incisions around the hard, unyielding mass. The man's tortured body went into a final spasm; what sounded like a sigh of futility emerged through the nostrils, and suddenly he went limp. For one dreadful moment Cordelia thought he was dead. But a stentorian nasal snore reassured her. Some mysterious mechanism of the mind had blanked out the pain from his consciousness.

Once more Cordelia's fingers clasped the cold ball of lead and forcibly pulled it out. It emerged with a plop, encrusted with gore and pus. Five pairs of eyes watched horrified as she held it up in the lamplight before throwing it into the waste basket.

The wound continued to exude purulent blood that trickled down and stained the mattress below. Liberally dousing a swab of cotton wool with arnica, Cordelia scrubbed the incisions. She picked up the threaded needle from the pan, pulled together the skin around the cuts and stitched them close. The heavy bleeding lessened perceptibly, though some blood did ooze out through the stitches. She covered them with a large, flat spread of cotton wetted in disinfectant, placed some more cotton padding to soak in the drops, and wrapped up the back with a roll of bandages. The man lay limp and unconscious all through.

The others removed the fetters. The foul stench of defecation touched Cordelia's nostrils! The violent spasms of the body had caused the coolie's bowels to empty, soiling the loincloth around his waist.

'Clean him up, Kamal,' she said in a small, tired voice. 'We've done what we could. Now it's all in the hand of God. You'll have to stay with the patient all through the night.'

'I stay,' Kamal said.

They dug a hole behind the dispensary and buried the blood-drenched cotton and the soiled loincloth. The coolies left. Cordelia took one last look at the unconscious man on the bed and then, bidding goodnight to Bapu babu and Kamal, accompanied by Mongla and Pekoe, returned to the bungalow.

David was still at the tea houses.

Two days of continuous sunshine, that was what they required. The weather-gods gave them three. Labouring in the harsh glare of the summer sun, they hacked away at the rain-softened earth with long handled kodalis, cutting a nullah to the stream. Meghu was a godsend and, by the third morning, the job was completed.

The skies opened up once again on the third evening. The cascades descending from the sky loosened the silt stranglehold on the saplings and swept away all the rotting matter. The three were out of bed at first light the next morning. They stepped out of the door together, prepared to see the worst.

The thin film of water was there, no doubt. But there was no stagnant accumulation!

'We've won, sahib,' said Garo.

'It's too early yet. Let it rain for a few days more, then we'll see what happens.'

It rained continuously for three more days. But nothing happened. The thin flow of water did not cease. No flotsam glided down the swirling currents into Chahpuli.

They had won indeed, Bailin thought with elation. They had thwarted kismet's insidious designs and managed to breathe renewed life into Chahpuli tea garden.

Her joy at the successful extraction of the bullet from the coolie's back was reinforced by the bright sunshine which greeted Cordelia the next morning. Excessive dampness induced by continuous rain was detrimental to vigorous healing of wounds. A few days of sunshine would prove invaluable to the stricken man. Thus, it was in an optimistic frame of mind the she repaired to the dispensary after chota hazri.

Her optimism was not misplaced. Cordelia cut away the dressing, peeled off the wad of cotton covering the stitched incisions. The sallow, puffy appearance of the suppurated flesh had disappeared, and the skin had become creased and flaccid. Though the greenish tinge remained, it was far less pronounced. The reek of decaying flesh had also decreased considerably. Applying arnica to wound, she wrapped him up once more. Hope perched on her soul as Cordelia finally left the dispensary.

The escape of two of the inmates fired up the imagination of the coolies of Bihguri. Where there had been dark despair now filtered in the barest glimmer of hope. The victory of Meghu and Bircha was their own.

No one was more aware of this sudden surge of hope in them than Buckingham. The planter smelled danger. A rent now in the chrysalis of fear which cocooned them might grow into a fissure tomorrow, unless he took corrective measures. He summoned his henchmen for an urgent conference.

'One whole week without the slightest information about the bastards. This is not good.' He told them. 'The coolies are smug and full of insolence. The time has come to stamp our authority. Herd them up at the open ground before the tea houses this evening. I'll speak to them.'

At six in the evening the entire Bihguri workforce stood assembled before the tea houses. Seated upon his horse, with a rifle in one hand and a whip in the other, Bihguri's Lord and Master confronted seemed as the scourge to them.

'*Coolielog, suno!*' his voice rolled over the heads of his audience like thunder among the clouds. 'Two traitors, not knowing my power, forgot where their duty lay and attempted to leave Bihguri some nights ago. Do you wish to know that happened to those traitors, coolielog?'

Except for the muted fall of the light drizzle, there was no sound. Not a soul moved. Not a suckling baby let out a cry.

'I was out that night among the Bihguri bushes, looking for the bagh which was terrorizing you. Now I know there was no bagh. It was a ruse to keep me and the sirdars to our quarters. I was there amongst the bushes, my rifle in hand, searching for a bagh which did not exist. It was then, in the darkness, that one of the two traitors attacked me. But no coward traitor can harm a single hair on my body. I am invincible, do you understand, coolielog? I shot the traitor through his heart. He crawled away into the jungles to die, to become food for scavengers, who stripped him to the bones. We have found his bones!'

A collective gasp of horror rose from a hundred throats. A woman screamed and collapsed in a dead faint onto the ground. The babies and toddlers, frightened by the reaction of their elders, began a clamorous wail.

'That, coolielog, is the fruit of defiance ... death without the rites of purification, the spirit condemned to wander in the jungles, to terrorize wayfarers and coolies. The other thug, Meghu, has been caught at Kokilamukh, trying to cross the Brahmaputra on a stolen boat. Right now, he is in the hands of the policelog, who pull out his nails and burn his testicles with red hot iron so none may again defy me, the company and the sarkar.

'But the traitor who has been caught is no longer our concern. What is of our concern is that the traitor made confession before the Laltopiwallahs. He told them there were coolies who aided their escape. If this is so, then it is bad.

'So coolielog, by the time the sun sets again, I want those who aided the two traitors to come to me and beg forgiveness. I'll forgive them. But if they do not come; it is another matter. Then shall we know there are traitors amongst us. The loyal amongst you must then point out to me who the traitors are amidst us. I will keep everything secret. And, if the information is valuable, I will reward the informant with baksheesh of ten silver coins. So now go, coolielog. But keep this in mind ... ten silver coins await him who gives information of value.'

Buckingham wheeled his mount around and trotted back to the bungalow.

Lachmi and Baisakhi supported the dazed Saoni as they walked to the basti. Such was the shock to the poor girl on hearing that Bircha was dead, she had fainted. In the nick of time, before the sirdars could take note of her reaction, the two women had pulled her up and kept her propped on her feet till she regained consciousness. Once inside their hut they released her and she dropped to the ground, sobbing her heart out.

'She's a foolish little girl,' Baisakhi said apologetically to Sanatan and Lachmi. 'But she had love in her heart for poor Bircha.'

'We understand, Baisakhi bahen,' Lachmi said. 'But the danger is real. After what the sahib said. If any one suspects she had pyaar for Bircha, she would be in grave trouble.'

'What can I do?' Baisakhi said. 'I tell her to forget Bircha. I tell her to look for some other man. A sirdar, a duffadar, anyone! But she's a wilful, headstrong girl. She says there can be no other man for her but Bircha. Even if Bircha is dead!'

'No, Bircha is not dead. It's all a pack of lies,' Sanatan said.

The two women threw him puzzled glances. Saoni ceased her sobs, sat up and looked hopefully at the elderly coolie. Sanatan smiled—a tired, wan grimace. 'A pack of lies, I tell you … what the sahib said. They have searched and searched, but they could not find Bircha, neither dead nor alive. The sahib must pluck out the fear from his own heart, like lice from a woman's hair, and put it into the hearts of the coolielog. That is why he claimed Bircha was dead. But Bircha is not dead, you can be certain.'

'And Meghu? Was that another lie?'

'Another lie! Meghu is not stupid. He would not change his plan, whatever be the circumstances. Caught at Kokilamukh? Bah … it's all a pack of lies!'

Saoni's mind, however, was only filled with Bircha. 'He is alive!' She cried out happily. 'My pyaar is alive! That is all that matters. Even if he's not here.'

'Hold your tongue, you stupid girl!' Baisakhi admonished, more in exasperation than anger. 'He may be alive. But for you he's dead, understand?'

'Your mago is right, Saoni,' Lachmi said, not unkindly. 'Bircha has left for good. Only his shadow falls on your heart and mind. You cannot have pyaar for a shadow, chokri.'

'There can be no room for another in my heart. I shall hold Bircha in my bosom … even if it be only his shadow!'

Baisakhi was about to say something when Sanatan intervened. 'Let her be, Baisakhi bahen. Words do not sweep away a fever. Time does.'

'But her willfulness will put her into danger. Put us all to danger. What'll happen if those rakhshas come to know of her love for Bircha?'

'Yes, Saoni,' Sanatan continued in a gentle voice. 'None of us want to invite needless trouble. For a while we must maintain low profiles; do nothing which might single us out. So put your love away. For your own sake. For your mago's sake. For our sake.'

'I'll do that.' Saoni seemed as if she would burst into tears again. 'But what kind of a life is this, in which we cannot proclaim our love to the whole world? When will all this change …?'

Sanatan's eyes were directed far away. 'It'll all change one day, Saoni. There'll come a time when the heavens will belch out fire and skies will pour down blood. Then shall we rid the world of these oppressors, these evil men who chain and make slaves of us. We all await that day. But till it comes learn to be crafty, and keep your love out of sight.'

Day after day Cordelia dressed Bircha's wound, exulting as the signs of healing grew stronger. On the sixth day after the extraction of the bullet he could sit up without help, and remain unflinching as she cut away the sutures and plucked out the strands. The flesh around the incisions and the bullet hole had distended into ridges shaped into a four-fingered star. The man would carry a brand for the rest of his life, but that was a trifling inconvenience considering what he had been through. He would live.

Sheer joy seemed to explode in her heart like one of those wondrous firecrackers during *Diwali*, the Hindu festival of light, which burst and threw out red-blue-silver-gold stars that lit up the firmament in a dazzling glow. The gamut of her entire existence seemed to her to have been directed towards this single action—imparting to this poor soul a new lease of life. Nothing else seemed to matter—neither Michael's disappearance nor Papa's death or David's abandonment. It was as though by giving life to the coolie she had infused new life into herself.

Cordelia was one of those creatures in whom joy and gratitude induced blinding compassion, a naive eagerness to forgive. Her happiness enkindled resurgent optimism, a hope that the slate of the past could be wiped clean; that bonds of affection could be re-forged. She made it a point to join David for dinner that evening and engage him in vivacious conversation, unconcerned that it might be interpreted as a humiliating retreat, wanting only to show him through words and gestures the love she cherished for him. David, at first, was perplexed by her amiability, and then overwhelmed. His words were couched with touching gentleness, his manners with love.

For the first time in many months, they sat together on the verandah as of old. The heavy curtain of rain shut out everything else from their vision and reinforced the feeling of togetherness. Her brother did most of the talking, unburdening his heart of his fears and frustration. The truncated area of older bushes had yielded far less during the first flush than he had hoped. Thank heavens the local tea makers whom Bapu babu had engaged were proving their worth—David had induced them to train up a few more of the garden coolies—'those endowed with a modicum of intelligence, a faculty they seemed woefully short of.' The bloody tea makers had been reluctant to do this at first, but agreed to it when David pointed out that as the years passed the volume of leaf would increase and more trained tea makers would be required to handle the increased yield. The stupid bastards had been fearful they would not be hired the next season if they trained up more garden coolies, which explained their initial aversion. The funny thing was that they were perfectly right in their surmise; once sufficient garden hands were trained in the art of making quality teas and grew proficient at it, David proposed to dispense with the services of the locals, which would bring about great savings.

Cordi might not realize it, but it was becoming day by day an uphill task keeping the plantation free of unwanted vegetation, particularly the sections containing the new planted saplings. With almost half the workforce engaged in the tea houses and the other half engaged in plucking, where the devil could he find hands to do the ruddy cheeling and hoeing? The ruddy tribal coolies had let him down; Cordi must try and understand his problems! It was not that David was incognizant of the additional workload upon the coolies—but the pressures in this busiest of seasons required every man, woman and child be conscripted to work. There must be no shirking, no laziness, no false complaints of ailments just to secure a few hours off work. That was why he had taken to visiting the dispensary on the lookout for any bugger doing a bunk. They could pull the wool over her eyes, but not his. The pressures on him or the coolies might have lessened if he could have augmented his depleted coolies through fresh recruitment. He would write to Uncle Alex after he had dispatched this season's produce, and request him to arrange for reinforcements to Dhanboa's workforce. Of course, once the second flush was over the pressures would ease. Once winter dormancy sets in, apart from a bit of skiffing, pruning and hoeing, the coolies would have hardly anything to do. As for now, they had to be driven hard; he hoped she would see the necessity.

But what was worrying him most and giving him sleepless nights were the newly planted saplings. He was not sure he had planted them right for they were not growing at the rate he had hoped. In fact, some of them wore a woefully stunted look. If the fresh plantings did not grow well, it could lead to Dhanboa's ruination! Their finances had dipped seriously—oh, they were not bankrupt yet, ha, ha,—but if the new plantings did not turn out well there would be a crisis of funds. After Cordi's refusal to their offer, he was not sure he could ask Uncle Alex to bail him out. That last letter from him was a real stinker—oh, the words were civil enough, but he could read between the lines! It was all such a muck up and why the devil he had had to face it when his own plans had been otherwise …

All this David spouted, sitting in the damp darkness, in a querulous whine. Cordelia listened patiently. The ceaseless litany, especially when he hinted of selfishness in her actions, threatened to dampen the effervescent mood she was in, but she held onto her euphoria, rekindling it with the thought that one of Buckingham's coolies lay in the dispensary, unknown to Dhanboa's master, a creature to whom she had given a new lease of life!

The evening's conversation seemed to do good to David too. He mellowed as he talked and, when it was time for her to retire, and he to go to the tea house detail, accepted Cordelia's good night kiss with surprising gratitude. Back in her room, bolstered with strength and optimism, Cordelia dropped to her knees in prayer, thanking the Lord for all that He had done for her, entreating Him to look after David and the coolies of Dhanboa, and to safeguard the Bihguri coolie who had suffered so much. She slept that night without her burden of imagined guilt, her mind rendered tranquil by a sense of achievement.

The Bihguri absconder was seated upon the bed, wolfing down doubleroti, eggs and milk, when she visited the dispensary the following morning. Pekoe, who had accompanied her, greeted the man with a bark, tail wagging furiously.

When the coolie finished eating, Cordelia undid his bandage. The man grew warily stiff at her touch. His pulse raced and there was deep fear in his eyes. However, his wound was healing rapidly. Taking over the duties of the dispensary, she allowed Kamal, who had spent the night at the dispensary, to sleep. Bapu babu arrived just as she had finished off with the last of the visitors to the dispensary. She told him about the tensions and fear in the patient and his failure to respond to her queries. 'Me speak him,' Bapu babu said grimly. 'Put sense in head.'

Speak he did, in a curious language, a patois of English, Assamese and Hindustani liberally peppered with invectives. 'You are an ungrateful wretch, you mangy mongrel,' was the sum and substance of Bapu babu's harangue. 'You do not show respect to the woman who saved your worthless life. She has taken out the bullet from your body. She has sweated and wept and prayed for you. Is this how you reward her, you ill-bred gutter snipe, you half-baked biscuit?'

Strangely enough, what Cordelia's gentleness could not achieve, the severity in which Bapu babu's words were phrased, did.

The coolie pushed himself to a sitting position and said sullenly, 'What good will all this do, brother? She'll send me back to Bihguri. The shaitan there will skin me alive. It would have been better if I'd died.'

'And what makes you think she'll send you back to Bihguri, you worthless lump of cattle-dung?'

'She's a white bitch! They're all the same, these firanghees!'

Cordelia recoiled at the venom and loathing with which the crude words were uttered.

Bapu babu blushed. 'Hold a civil tongue before our memsahib, you jackass! She'll not send you back to Bihguri.' He turned to Cordelia. 'You not despatch him to that blasted place, do you, darling Cordelia memsahib?'

Cordelia spoke in Hindustani directly at the coolie. 'Under no circumstance will I ever send you back to Bihguri. *Mein tumhe Bihguri kabhi nahi bhejuga, jo kuch ho*!'

The softness and sincerity with which she spoke struck a chord in the coolie. He raised his sullen face and looked for the first time into her eyes. What he saw seemed to soothe and reassure him. The fear slid away from his features.

'*Mujhe maaf karo,* memsahib. *Mein jaanta nahi thaa.*' He bowed his head and waited, as if seeking her benedictions.

'What is your name? I knew, but have forgotten it.'

'Bircha. You have saved my life. I'm grateful.'

'Was it a hard life at Bihguri, Bircha?'

'Narak is a better place, memsahib. The sahib is worse than a shaitan and the sirdars are bastards. We are no better than animals at Bihguri.'

'So, you ran away?'

'Yes, memsahib. I ran away. I and my dost Meghu. We tried to run away before … in Calcutta. They caught and flogged us. On our first day at Bihguri the sirdars beat me and Meghu. They called us rangkukurs. Said we needed taming. They broke Meghu's jaw.'

The man paused, tired by the effort of speaking. But the growing anger gave him strength to continue.

'We pretended to be tamed, memsahib. We licked the sirdars' arses. The sahib was pleased. He made us duffadars. Thought that would keep us tied to Bihguri. But we ran away again. That sahib must indeed be a shaitan, else how could he know we would make the attempt to escape that particular night and lie in wait for us? He shot me as I fled, memsahib. I do not know what happened to my dost Meghu, the one with the broken face. I dragged myself here. The rest you know.'

'You kept calling out a word when the fever was upon you … Saoni! What does it mean?'

Bircha's face crumpled with grief as he told her, with innocent simplicity, who Saoni was. Cordelia felt the tears spring to her eyes. Bircha was perplexed. How could a white woman cry at the love story of a wretched coolie, one who was no better than a mongrel?

'I am sorry, memsahib,' he said with genuine concern, 'if my words cause you pain.'

Cordelia held back her tears. She turned to Bapu babu, who stood sad and silent beside her. 'What's to be done with him? He is in great danger here. We must arrange to send him to a safer place as soon as he's sufficiently recovered.'

'I'll leave soon, memsahib,' Bircha said. 'I'll not make trouble for you and the young sahib who is your husband.'

Cordelia smiled despite her grief and anxiety. 'He's not my husband, but my bhaiya. He doesn't know you are here. It is better he doesn't know. You cannot leave for another week or so. You must eat well, sleep well and get back strength into your limbs. Then we can plan your escape.'

Bircha would not be reassured. 'You do not understand, memsahib. I must leave this night. The bastards will come for me soon. I feel it in my bones.'

'Where will you go, Bircha?'

'Anywhere, as long as it is away from your garden. I wish no trouble to befall you.'

'You need not worry about us. But the heavens are bursting with rain. Everywhere there is ankle deep mud. You are ill and weak. How far can you go under these conditions, Bircha? No, they'll catch you and drag you back to Bihguri. It's safer to stay here.'

'But, memsahib, the rains will pour on and on for many moons. I cannot stay in hiding for so long. Someone or the other will find out.'

'I realize that. No, you'll not have to spend many more days here. I have a plan. Let the rains abet, even if for a day, and sunshine dry the paths. Then Bapu babu will take you to his village … You'll do that, won't you, Bapu babu?'

The bormohori tried hard to keep the dismay from his visage. He was well versed with the Workman's Breach of Contract Act of 1859, which made aiding and abetting an absconder a cognizable offence. If anything went wrong, he would be in 'boiling hot water'!

'Of course I do that, Cordelia memsahib,' he said valiantly. 'He safe in village. My villagers not open their bloody traps!'

'Then, Bircha, when the rains depart, we'll help you to get to a place called Sivasagar. There's a wonderful man there. He'll find a place for you where you can live in peace.'

For the first time since she set eyes on him, the coolie smiled. The hope lighting up his face transformed it. In his own way, he was a handsome man. 'I told Meghu you looked like a farishta, memsahib,' he spoke with complete seriousness. 'You indeed are a farishta!'

Bapu babu nodded in complete agreement. A sudden thought struck Cordelia and she cried out, 'Good heavens! David will be here any moment now!'

Bapu babu shot out of the room like a bullet through the back door and, unfurling his umbrella and hitching his dhoti up to his knees, bolted for the tea houses. Cordelia hurried out of the sick room, barring the bamboo door carefully after her, and was in the outer medicine room just as David, accompanied by Harua, swept into view through the open window.

But he did not tarry long. Heonly smiled at her and walked out into the rain.

David had impotently watched the gradual loosening of the bonds tying him to Cordi. Her recent attempt at rapprochement induced triumph within him, although he was charitable enough not to let it show. But, as day followed day, his feel of personal victory evaporated as a germ of suspicion entered his mind. Nowadays, she seemed to be strangely happy. Something had caused the transformation in Cordi.

He pondered deeply in his bed before going to sleep. A sudden thought struck him. In the days prior to the rapprochement Cordi had been in a contradictory mood to what she was now. She had seemed anxious; this anxiety had appeared on her features on the same day Buckingham had come looking for his absconders. Then, with amazing abruptness, the wonderful change towards joy had come over her. Was there some hidden link between her transformation and Buckingham's visit?

It was the ruthless logicality of his deductions, and the inexorable inference, which made his blood run cold. Buckingham had shot one of the absconders. What if the injured bugger had actually made his way to this garden, and sought shelter here?

David's men had assiduously searched the garden for the absconder. But there had been one part of Dhanboa no one had thought for searching. The dispensary! It held the key! He must search it. But he must do so without alerting Cordi and endangering the joyous mood she was in. If it were merely a wild goose chase, there would be no fallouts then.

The following night, returning from the tea houses, Harua and David made a detour towards the dispensary. Once inside, taking care not to make a sound, they searched the rooms by the light from a lantern. The doors of the rooms were ajar, all except one at the rear. David cautiously unbarred the door, heart lurching as the bamboo frame creaked open. Harua raised the lamp high to light up the entire room.

A man lay asleep on the bed, on his stomach, snoring gently, head turned away towards the wall. But there was no need for David to look at the face to know who it was.

He retreated slowly, pulled shut and barred the door. The two men pussyfooted over the earthen floor and reached the outer room. David tore off the last sheet of paper from the dispensary ledger. Picking up a quill, he dipped it into the inkwell on the table and scribbled a hasty note to Buckingham. He folded the paper and handed it to Harua.

'Go to Bihguri before sunrise,' he instructed. 'Give this to Buckingham sahib.'

He was angry and suffused with shame and humiliation. As far as he was concerned, it was not a man but a viper that lay asleep on the bamboo bed of the dispensary!

Cordelia leant on the balustrade of the bungalow and gazed happily at the clear sky. The sun, this day, would be a saviour. It would dry the slush-heaped earth; the paths would grow passable. Then Bapu babu and Kamal would guide the runaway coolie through the concealing cover of darkness to the village where he would hide till the time grew opportune for further flight.

David's behaviour at the breakfast table, inexplicable though it was, could not blank out the light inside her. He did not visit the dispensary in the morning and breakfasted early without waiting for her to join him. He had not responded to her smiling good morning, but got up brusquely and departed for the fields. So suffused had she been with her own radiant glow that the extraordinary behaviour of her brother had failed to fill her with qualms or subdue her happiness.

The sun being out, there were a hundred chores to be completed! Thus, even while she heard feet running up the stairs and watched a bewildered

Kamal burst into view, no alarm bells pealed in her mind. She looked on uncomprehendingly as the dispensary assistant cried out, '*Memsahib, memsahib*, they've come!'

'They? Who's come, Kamal?'

'The Bihguri sahib! With elephants and men!'

Comprehension slithered into her consciousness and she rushed to the verandah. 'Oh, God!' she cried as she sighted the intruders. She could see them across the tea bushes separating the dispensary from the bungalow. Two elephants, eight men! The glint of rifle-barrels reflecting the sunrays caught her eyes. There was no mistaking their objectives, no solace in self-delusion. But how had they found out? She recalled the expression on her brother's face this morning and knew. David!

The men were dismounting and surrounding the dispensary. 'Mongla, Kamal, come!' she cried, and flew down the stairs and over the path to the hutment where the fugitive lay trapped.

Buckingham's men, strung around the dispensary, were alert and waiting. The planter, accompanied by the giant coolie whom she recognized from previous visits, stood a little away from the front door, apparently awaiting the arrival of someone from Dhanboa to authorize their entry. His delicate eyebrows went up in surprise as Cordelia and her assistants raced up to the entrance, lips curling into an amused, insolent grin.

Flanked by Mongla and Kamal, Cordelia stood at the front door. Pekoe too stood by her side. The Alsatian had sensed danger to his mistress. His ears were straight, his brown eyes watchful. Buckingham shifted his rifle to the left hand and walked up to them.

'Good morning, Cordelia,' he said. 'I received a missive from your brother early this morning. It appears he discovered one of my runaway coolies hiding inside this cottage. The coolie in question is my property. He has breached the contract he had made with me and attempted to abscond. I shall be beholden to you if you'll permit me and my men to enter this cottage and apprehend him.'

'This is our property, Buckingham,' Cordelia retorted. 'Unless you have a warrant from the authorities, I shall not permit you to enter its precincts.'

'Don't make things more difficult, Cordelia. Perhaps you are conversant with the law which makes aiding and abetting an absconder a criminal offence?'

'No, I am not,' Cordelia said fiercely. 'But I do know of the law against trespassing!'

'Very well,' the planter bowed stiffly. 'We shall wait for your brother to arrive.'

He strolled languidly back and said something to his henchman. The coolie sirdar left, apparently in quest of David.

Buckingham turned his back on the trio at the door and began a conversation with one of the mahouts. Cordelia, Mongla, Kamal and Pekoe stood at their posts—powerless defenders of a flimsy citadel.

Bircha had been asleep when the Bihguri party arrived. He awoke abruptly, springing up on his haunches like a resting chital when it scents danger. He heard a babble of voices outside, stridently delivered commands, and the squashy tread of feet running over slushy ground. Shafts of fear tingled down his spine as he recognized one of the voices. The dreaded voice of the shaitan, the sahib of Bihguri!

A trap! A trap! Something inside him screamed out. With one bound he was at a window. He slid it open—he could not see the shaitan. But he saw another equally hated creature—Budhu, his head wrapped in a bandage, guarding the flank of the hutment.

He had been betrayed! The white woman was no farishta! Rather she was a treacherous whore, one who fed him with lies and false hopes even while she had plotted to send him to his doom.

Bircha was confused. Then why all this toil to save his life? She could have betrayed him the very first morning itself. Why lavish so much time and care on him?

He stumbled across the floor on weak and rubbery legs and slid out of the room into the corridor. Here he abruptly stopped. He could see the open door at the end of the narrow corridor. Three figures were outlined against the framed rectangle of light. All three he intuitively recognized—the white woman, with her hair shining like gold in the sunlight, Kamal and Mongla. He saw another man approach the front door; though his body was obscured by the other three, his head and face could be seen—it was the Bihguri shaitan! Bircha waited. The shaitan spoke to the woman in the language of the firanghees. Though he understood nothing he understood it all.

The white woman was no betraying whore! She and the other two were guarding the door. No. Betrayal, for betrayal it certainly was, had come from other quarters!

There was no escape. Death lurked everywhere. Bircha retreated once more, drowned in hopelessness. Unconsciously, his hands flitted over his chest and thighs and limbs. His poor, tortured body! Now condemned to greater torment! He flung himself down on the mud floor in a foetal crouch and began to cry. Then Bircha crawled on all fours under the bamboo bed.

Despair, similar to Bircha's, had overwhelmed Cordelia too. She sensed that the transient truce with David would end now.

'Go and get Bapu babu, Kamal,' she quietly told her assistant.

Kamal left and returned ten minutes later with the bormohori. Bapu babu surveyed the situation with grave eyes and silently took up position beside the garden's mistress.

David arrived, features forbiddingly stern. Luthra had apparently apprised him of the stalemate, for he did not go to Buckingham, who stood some distance away under the shadow of one of his elephants, but strode straight up to the front door. Catching sight of him, Buckingham hurried up.

'What's all this, sis?' David asked unsmilingly.

'I was about to ask that of you, David!' Cordelia said.

'You know very well why Buckingham has come.'

'No, I do not. He arrives at our garden with armed men … says me that he wishes to search the dispensary. Where's the warrant, David? Where're the officials?'

David hesitated. It was Buckingham who answered. 'I came at your express invitation, David, to claim my property. I have no intention of searching the premises. Hand over my chattel to me … that's all I ask.'

'He's right, sis,' David said placatingly. 'One of his fugitive coolies is inside the dispensary. He has simply come to take him back to the garden.'

'With armed men and elephants? Who does he think he is, David … trying to cow you down with such blatant show of force? This is Papa's cottage … the one in which he breathed his last. It is a sacred shrine, hallowed by Papa's memories. Under no circumstance will I allow its sanctity to be desecrated by unwelcome intrusion of strangers.'

She was using every weapon in her armoury. 'It's me or him, David!' her eyes screamed out the words at him. David could not but be moved by the force of her unuttered plea. His hesitation grew more pronounced. Buckingham sensed this, and spoke up.

'I repeat, David. I came at your express invitation. That's no trespass. So why this delay, old chap? I have no inclination to enter the hutment. I respect your Papa's memory too deeply for that. Hand over the fugitive, and I'll be on my way.'

'Give me a moment, will you, Chris?' He turned towards Cordelia. 'Please sis, I beg of you. Don't make things more difficult for me. It's a bit of an embarrassment, as it is.'

'An embarrassment, David?' Cordelia's bitter query was in fact a statement of disillusionment.

David flushed, but kept his exasperation in check. 'Yes, an embarrassment! Look sis, you're being fair neither to me not to Chris. It's the principle of the thing. The ... the ethics of it all! That coolie inside is Chris's property. We have neither the legal right nor the moral authority to retain what does not belong to us. We have to abide by the rules of the game, sis. We have to .. to play fair.'

Her defeat was inevitable, Cordelia had known that from the very beginning! Yet she refused to concede and played her final card.

'How do we know the man inside is from Bihguri?' she asked. 'Has your friend branded his flanks with the name of his garden? Or his own name? No, I'll not hand the poor fellow over to your friend. Let him bring someone who represents British officialdom. Let him bring Hewitt. Then, and only then, will I back down.'

Buckingham's patience was running out. 'Hewitt? In this season?' he cried out. 'She's procrastinating, old chap. Trying to buy time for the nigger. I have his contract at Bihguri … his thumb-print is upon it.'

'A coolie-catcher's contract, David! Remember what the Reverend had said. Not worth the paper it's written on!'

There was not the slightest doubt in David's mind that the Bihguri absconder must be returned to his rightful owner. Yet he hesitated, as though aware that something more than the fate of a wretched coolie was at stake this morning.

'How much more of this will I have to take, old chap?' Buckingham said with a flash of anger. 'My behaviour towards you has been impeccable. I have assisted you in every possible manner. Is this how you repay my generosity?'

David abruptly squared his shoulders. His voice was hoarse with strain. 'Get out of the way, sis, for God's sake! The coolie belongs to Bihguri. There's no help for it. We must hand him over. Go inside, Harua. *Usko pakar le ao.* Drag the man out.'

Clearly David had underestimated the hold his sister had over the Dhanboa coolies. Harua did not move. He stood where he was, eyes downcast, silent and morose.

'Still wearing the corset laces, old chap?' Buckingham's sarcastic goading drilled into his ears. 'They don't consider you the master, is that it?'

David took two steps forward. 'Damn you, sis, get out of the way!' he cried, as she continued to stand blocking the door. There was madness in him now. He took the third decisive step, thrust out his right arm, and gave her a violent shove. She fell heavily on the floor, but David had no eyes for her, nor for Pekoe, who let out a bewildered growl. He strode into the dispensary and marched straight for the room in which he had seen the Bihguri coolie. He opened the door and found the room empty.

He heard a sobbing emerge from beneath the bed. It was a terrible sound, that of a grown man crying like a child. But David remained unmoved. He reached down, grabbed the cringing man by his hair, dragged him out and thrust him in the direction of Buckingham.

Only then did he look towards Cordelia. She was still on the floor, though she had been helped up to a sitting position by her three acolytes, who squatted around her, filled with concern. There were no tears in her eyes. Instead, her face held a mix of emotions shock, horror and rage. Without another word David turned his back on the whole lot and walked off towards the fields.

As soon as the sobbing, staggering coolie was brought out, Buckingham's hounds pounced on him. They tethered his wrists in front. One end of a long rope was tied around his waist, the other end being thrown up to the mahout atop one of the pachyderms. Buckingham gathered in his troops, all of them climbed aboard, and the two elephants sailed out of Dhanboa, towing the trophy of the expedition, who slipped and skidded along behind them.

Bapu babu and Kamal helped Cordelia to her feet. They had never seen her as angry as she was now. The fierce expression of hate and wrath subdued even the loquacious bormohori into silence.

'It's been a severe shock to me, Bapu babu. I had never imagined my brother could stoop so low. But what do we do now? We can't allow the Bihguri sahib to achieve such an easy win.'

'He win, Cordelia memsahib. We can do nothing!'

'Do nothing to save the poor wretch?'

'No, darling Cordelia memsahib. That poor wretch coolie fellow, he dead. He finished. Buckingham sahib peel his skin like monkey peel banana.'

'Not if I can help it,' Cordelia cried out. 'I must go to Jorehaut, Bapu babu. Summon a mahout and have the elephant readied.'

'Go to Jorehaut? You mad, darling Cordelia memsahib? No road to Jorehaut. All water and mud. Elephant stuck. Mahout stuck. You stuck. All stuck.'

'The sun is out, so I must try. Or the guilt will tear me up inside, Bapu babu! It will destroy me!'

Bapu babu saw the despairing guilt in her eyes. He nodded solemnly.

'I understand. I get mahout and elephant. But there's bery bery much danger. You not go alone. I go with you.'

'No, Bapu babu. You've rubbed David the wrong way too much already. The mahout will be with me. The elephant is well trained. No harm will befall me.'

Cordelia went to the bungalow to change into a pair of drill Jodhpurs, a full shirt with buttoned up cuffs, walking shoes and stockings. By the time she returned, her hair tucked under a sola toupee and armed with her parasol and a jerry-can of drinking water, the animal had been readied. Soon they were off.

The pagal ghanta sounded in Bihguri. The string of clangs vibrated through the plantation, echoed off walls and rooftops and set off corresponding palpitations in the hearts of the coolies. For one moment time itself stood still; each living creature in Bihguri froze into stony immobility, ears cocked, trying to fathom the insidious significance in the ringing of that infernal gong. Hardly had the sound weakened into silence when the sirdars were once more with them, rounding them up and herding them towards the open square before the tea houses. A bound and mud-caked creature, a rope around its waist, lay sprawled on the slush. Beside him stood an elephant upon which sat Bihguri's Lord and Master.

Soon those at the van of the throng knew who it was. Bircha! They communicated this to those at the back, and the air grew thick with the unfortunate fugitive's name.

But wasn't Bircha dead, shot by the sahib in the dark of the night, his body consumed by jackals and hyenas? By what magic had the sahib restored the runway to life? How was it that Bircha now sprawled on the ground, tethered like a pig to the slaughterhouse?

Saoni, flanked by Baisakhi and Lachmi, stood at the rear of the throng. The wall of coolies before them had screened off Bircha from their sight. But the wave of wondering whispers carried his name to them and Saoni cried out, 'He's alive, mago! My Bircha is alive!'

She tried to power her way through the human wall, but Baisakhi caught her arm in a vise-like grip. 'Keep quiet, chokri,' she hissed viciously. 'Stay where you are. You'll be the death of all of us.'

Heads had turned at Saoni's outburst. 'Yes,' Baisakhi said aloud to Lachmi, 'that wretched duffadar is alive. Then why did the sahib tell us he's dead?'

'The sahib lied,' Lachmi spoke out equally loudly. She turned towards Sanatan and whispered, 'Spread the word. Bircha is alive. The sahib lied. The sahib is a liar!'

Sanatan caught the words, looked around him for a face he could trust, and passed them on. The refrain hissed through the air like steam from a kettle. Bircha is alive. The sahib lied. The sahib is a liar!

High up on the elephant's back Buckingham picked up the import of the words and stiffened. If he were not quick about it, Bircha might turn out to be more a liability than an asset!

He signalled to his henchmen; they moved around the babbling throng, whips crackling in the air, calling for silence. But a mass hysteria seemed to have suddenly gripped the coolies. The whispers, fuelled by hidden presences, intensified into jeers. Bircha is alive. The sahib lied. The sahib is a liar!

Buckingham let out a suppressed oath, sprang up to his feet on the howdah, raised his rifle, and fired into the air. The shot boomed out as a thunderclap, shocking the coolies into abrupt silence.

'Coolielog, *suno*,' the planter spoke, voice hard and stentorian. '*Kaan khulke suno*. I was wrongly informed. Bircha is very much alive. There he is, coolielog, cowering on the ground, his heart bursting with terror at the fate which awaits him. I'll use him as an example to all of you, coolielog. *Dekho, aankhe khulke dekho!* Open your eyes and look at what befalls a renegade who tried to throw dust in our eyes.'

The transient hostility in which the coolies were steeped bare moments ago vapourised into nothingness at that voice. The coolies shuffled uneasily on their feet and looked fearfully at one another.

Buckingham signalled once more to hishenchmen. They hauled Bircha up on his feet, untied the rope around his waist and dragged and strung him to the whipping post.

'Twenty lashes, Budhu,' Buckingham called out.

Budhu nodded. He twirled the whip in the air with practiced ease, swivelled on his toes, and brought the lash curling around the man. A thin streak of red encircled Bircha's body. He let out a scream of agony.

But the pain-wracked scream was drowned out by the collective groan which emerged from a hundred throats—a weird and terrible sound, pregnant with fear and pain and anger and humiliation. Again, and again, Budhu whipped the lash around the wretched captive—again, and again, the coolies groaned. Halfway through the whipping Bircha, already weakened by his injury and the frog-march to Bihguri, lost consciousness. His head lolled forward and his body slumped against the fetters.

Buckingham, aware that Budhu could not count up to twenty, had kept score. The moment the twenty strokes were delivered, he called out to his sirdar to stop and looked at the coolies to gauge the impact. He had achieved his desire.

'Coolielog,' he shouted, 'this is the fruit of betrayal. This renegade will stay tied to his post, day and night, sun and rain. He shall be fed with twenty strokes of the whip each day. Each evening you all will come from your work and watch him eat that meal. He shall be given no other food to eat. Not a drop of water shall wet his lips save the ones he can scour out of the rain. He shall hang here till his flesh rots. He shall hang here till his traitorous soul departs from his whipped body. He who attempts to give him food to eat and water to drink shall suffer the fate of this wretched traitor who had sought to betray me. Now get back to your work.'

The coolies dispersed in heavy silence. None dared speak; none dared look back at the man slumped at the whipping-post. For a few minutes Buckingham continued to gaze at Bircha, a thoughtful frown on his forehead. Things had degenerated even more than he had conceived. He had not been quite prepared for the wave of hostility which had emanated from the coolies. Bircha, indeed, had been a godsend!

Cordelia climbed the staircase of Captain Ralph Hewitt's bungalow at Jorhat with great difficulty, her body stiff and aching, and sank gratefully into one of the cushioned wicker-chairs on the verandah.

Ten minutes later the captain emerged, hands outstretched in welcome, his features a mosaic of pleasure, anxiety and apprehension. Cordelia stood up. Hewitt took her gloved hands and said, 'What a delightful surprise, Miss Esscombe! I only hope you've not brought unhappy tidings. Is anything the matter at Dhanboa?'

'Something *has* happened, Captain Hewitt, but not at Dhanboa. It's a matter of life and death. Only I don't really know how to go about telling it.'

'Well, do try, Miss Esscombe.'

Collecting her thoughts and arranging them into a sequential pattern, Cordelia told him of the past events as they had occurred. The strong passions kindled in her by the recapitulation swept away the tiredness from her voice.

'You've undertaken such a hazardous journey for the sake of a mere coolie?' Hewitt intruded.

Well, there it was: the flat rejection even before the appeal could be made! But she would not give up the fight.

'A mere coolie, Captain Hewitt?' She could not keep the acetous note out of her voice. 'To you, perhaps. But for me the wretched creature is a human being. A thing of flesh and blood who feels and suffers as you or I might. Make no mistake. Buckingham will kill the poor soul unless we intervene!'

'You misconstrue my astonishment,' the officer said hastily. 'You misread my words, Miss Esscombe. I'm not an unfeeling monster. It was my admiration at your action which made me burst out like that. At your ... your courage and humanity. To have braved a journey to Jorehaut in this season! You're a unique lady, Miss Esscombe!'

Cordelia's tired eyes brightened at his words. 'You ... you'll help?'

'Of course, I'll help. Not only because the appeal comes from you. But on the urgings of my own soul. I'll do all in my power to save that coolie ... as an officer of Her Majesty's Government and a human being.'

Cordelia stood up. 'Oh, thank you, Captain Hewitt. You don't know how happy you've made me. But we have not a moment to lose. We must set off at once.'

Captain Hewitt smiled at her earnestness, but did not get up. 'We'll leave for Bihguri,' he said firmly. 'But not this evening. To travel at night would be sheer madness. Your elephant is fatigued from the long journey. It must rest. And so must you.'

Her host sensed her disappointment. 'We'll set off at dawn, my pledge on it, Miss Esscombe. There's no alternative. We'll be at Bihguri by noon. We can only hope and pray we will not be too late.'

Cordelia bowed her head. Now that the decision had been made for her, she felt the strength which had sustained her through the eventful day drain away. A uniformed bearer brought a tea tray and placed it before them. Cordelia thankfully sipped the brew as she watched the man light up the long-chimneyed lamps pegged to the walls, and move around the verandah waving an incense pot.

'I almost made up my mind to return when I saw the conditions. Only my concern for the poor soul kept me going. I'm glad I made the attempt though, Captain Hewitt. You have put hope in my heart.'

'I too am glad you've come. And since you're here, I must not neglect my duties as a host. My bungalow, you can see, is large. Well, Miss Esscombe, tonight you'll sleep in the best of our guest rooms. But it must first be readied to be worthy of your presence. So, you must excuse me for a while.'

For the better part of half an hour she was left alone. Then Captain Hewitt returned and escorted her to the door of her room. 'The bath is ready, Miss Esscombe. And afterwards, when you're done, dinner too will be ready. Please pull the bell-cord if you require anything.'

David had walked away from the dispensary enveloped in self-righteous anger. He was angry with Buckingham, with his sister, with Harua and the blasted bormohori. But though he would not admit it, he was most angry with himself for the momentary weakness which had made him hesitant in carrying out what he believed was the proper thing to do. The dispensary fiasco should never have been allowed to take place.

Buckingham's mocking smile had followed him all the way to the fields. Harua's intransigence had been utterly humiliating, though he could appreciate the fellow's reluctance to displease the memsahib. Then he had seen the look in Cordi's eyes. It had filled him with self-loathing, and angry despair.

He did not return to the bungalow till it was time for the evening meal. Mongla had set the table for one only. 'Where's memsahib?' he asked the houseboy.

The youngster's customary pleasant face wore an unsmiling frown this evening. '*Jorehaut gaya hai, sahib. Haathi mein.*'

David was dumbfounded. What was happening to Cordi? Were her obsessions driving her mad? She had gone without letting him know … and taken an elephant and a mahout without his permission?

'Who else has gone along with her?'

'I do not know, sahib.'

'*Bapu babu ko bulake lao*. He ought to know.'

Yes, the bloody bormohori would know! He knew more about what went on in Dhanboa than the sahib himself!

Mongla returned ten minutes later without the bormohori. 'He's eating food, sahib. Says he will come after meal is over.'

This delay further infuriated David. Suddenly he discovered that his appetite had deserted him. 'I won't have dinner this evening, Mongla. Put a glass and a couple of sodas on the verandah, will you?' He unlocked the almirah in which he hoarded his stock of liquor and brought out a bottle of Johnnie Walker. He sat in the lonely verandah and allowed the heat of the whisky to fuel the fears and anxieties and anger in his mind.

Bapu babu hurried up half-hour later, profusely apologetic. 'Me berry, berry sad, dear David sahib. But Mongla catch me eating. Too many thorns in fish. Takes bery, bery long time, yes, no?'

As was his habit, Bapu babu drew up one of the murrahs and was about to sit upon it when David exploded.

'Keep standing, damn you, when I'm talking to you!'

Bapu babu shot up from the stool, eyeing the whisky bottle as he would a snake.

'Where's Cordelia memsahib?'

'She go Jorehaut.'

'So why wasn't I told about it? She has taken an elephant and a mahout. You're the bormohori here. You're responsible for garden property. You jolly well knew that the elephants cannot be used without my consent. So why didn't you tell me about it?'

'You, sahib. I simple bormohori. I stand when sahib talk to me. I answer only when sahib ask me.'

David was on his feet in an instant, the chair crashing to the floor as he caught the spindly figure by the collar. 'How dare you, you bloody nigger!' he shouted, his left hand raised as though he would strike.

'What you do, you evil man … you killer of coolies?' Bapu babu cried out fearfully as he struggled to get out of David's grip. A speck of sanity pierced the young man's inebriated consciousness, warning him that he was reaching the point of no return. With a grunt of contempt, he let the bormohori go and stumbled back to a chair.

'I no bloody nigger. You no Papa Esscombe sahib,' the bormohori said in a quavering voice before turning on his heels and scampering down the stairs.

David sat heavily down, striving to get a hold on himself. It had been a mistake, drinking whisky on an empty stomach. It was all Cordi's fault! Where the hell had she gone go? To Jorehaut. But what the devil for? She had never been to that place before. She knew no one there. Then why had she made such a hazardous journey to that place? The stupid bormohori was sure to be in the know. But he had frightened the fellow away. Now he wouldn't tell even if he knew.

Then it came drunkenly upon him, the answer to the mystery of Cordi's visit to Jorehaut. His assumption that she knew no one at that place was false. She did know someone there. The bloody mandarin—what was his name—Hewitt! She had gone there to complain to the bloke against Buckingham. On God, why couldn't Cordi leave things alone?

He stumbled to the balustrade and gazed up. Beyond the edge of the thatch lay the rain-scrubbed firmament, brilliant with a million stars, the light of the full moon unable to lessen their lustre. So that was why there was so much light outside? 'Yes, that's bloody why there's so much light outside,' he yelled to no one in particular. By God, how tired he was! He must shut out the moonlight, the stars. He must close his eyes and seek the quietude of sleep.

He tottered to the door of his bedroom, roughly thrusting aside the houseboy who had come to his aid. At the door he stopped. Something was wrong. He should not be sleeping now. He had duties to perform! He must make Dhanboa pay. he cried out. He must get to the tea houses. He had a pledge to fulfill.

He stumbled across the verandah, down the staircase and out into the moonlit open. The verandah had been cooler. It was hot outside, a bloody steam-bath. He felt the sweat soak out the whisky vapours. Hundreds of fireflies flitted around; stars come down from the sky. They said if fireflies filled up the night, it would rain. Who said that? Who the devil were they? He looked up at the cloudless sky. The Milky Way arched across it. The natives called it Haatipoti. Elephant trail! If it appeared clearly in the heavens, there would be sunshine. Bloody contradicting niggers! Let there be no sunshine. Let it pour and pour till Dhanboa became a bloody island. It would keep Cordi away from Dhanboa—Cordi with her accusing eyes!

Where the devil were the tea houses? Ah, he could see them ahead, lit up like a bonfire in the darkness. The tea house air touched his face, heated by a dozen charcoal fires. Coolies were at work, panning, rolling and firing the leaves. Robiya was in charge. As the sahib stumbled in, grabbing the door post to keep balance, the sirdar grew brisker, and barked out commands. What would he do without his sirdars? At least *they* gave him respect!

But something was wrong! Dhanboa coolies were at the charcoal fires, handling the final firing. The Assamese tea makers should have been at those fires. The coolies were not experienced enough for this delicate operation. Where the hell were those tea makers? The bastards, where were they?

'Robiya, *yaha ao*.'

The sirdar hurried up. A knowing look appeared in his eyes as he saw the state the sahib was in. *Ji, huzoor*.'

'Where are the tea makers? Why are our men at the fires?'

'*Woh chala gaya,* huzoor. They've left. Back to their village, they said. *Bapu babu bhi chala gaya. Kamal bhi*.'

'*Unhe pakar ke le ao*! Set the dogs after them, you fool! Get them back here this minute!'

'They left when it was light, sahib. Spoke evil things about you. Made threats. Warned that if you make trouble for them, they make trouble for you.'

'I've paid them. They have to be here. I'll have them arrested, the bloody bastards!'

'They said the month ended yesterday. The month's advance you paid them ended yesterday too, that's what they said.'

The heated air was burning him now. The coolie bastards were drenched in sweat. He was tired. He must get back to the bungalow. He must sleep. He would tackle those bastards tomorrow. Show them who he was.

Robiya left him, but returned with a small, paper-wrapped packet. 'Bapu babu asked me to give you this, sahib,' he said, thrusting the packet at him.

With unsteady hands David tore the wrapping. He gazed stupidly at what lay inside the paper: a moth-eaten half coat, greasy and stained, with all the buttons plucked away—Bapu babu's insignia of office!

Dinner was by candlelight. Dinner over, they sat on the verandah. 'To be honest with you, Miss Esscombe,' Captain Hewitt was saying, 'When I was informed about your arrival this evening, I thought you had come to report an outbreak of cholera among your coolies. Since the rains started, reports of cholera outbreaks have been pouring in from tea plantations. And frantic pleas for medical assistance!'

'I thank the Lord we haven't been touched yet, Captain Hewitt.'

'You have been lucky, indeed!'

'Luck had nothing to do with it,' Cordelia said with some warmth.

'Yes, yes,' Hewitt conceded. 'A matter of cleanliness, I suppose. The coolies are so incorrigibly dirty. No sense of hygiene at all!'

'It's for us to educate them and show them how to live. We make them slave away morn to eve, giving them no respite. We roast them in the sun, drench them in the rain, whip them and starve them, but not arm them to fight the scourge. Oh, Captain Hewitt, it's a terrible thing that we do!'

'You've endeavoured to set things right at Dhanboa?' Hewitt asked gently.

The question was enough for the stream to break its banks. She talked at length about all she had striven to do for the Dhanboa coolies—the fixed wages and a day off each week, the bamboo beds, the potassium permanganate footbaths and carbon tetrachloride dosages, and a score of similar ameliorative acts, which any planter was capable of, if only he had a mind to. She spoke candidly about the perpetual struggle with her brother, who had looked at the whole thing from the viewpoint of a planter. As he listened to her outpourings his own heart was overwhelmed by the radiance which poured out from her inner self, as it had already been by her external beauty. He drank in her words, yet thirsted for more.

'I can appreciate the point you are trying to make, Miss Esscombe. Good sense to keep the workers healthy and happy. Can't for the life of me say why planters don't see the same.'

'Cupidity, Captain Hewitt! It's their greed which makes them so blind and unfeeling! It's all avarice and exploitation!'

'A hundred and odd coolies have perished already in plantations this month, from the reports received so far. Merely the tip of the iceberg, I suppose. I've scanned past records too, Miss Esscombe. These have convinced me that, by the time the heavy rains end, in my subdivision alone there would be over a thousand deaths. We can only conjecture the loss in all the tea planting districts. It's queer logic, no doubt, but such colossal losses give rise to hope.'

'Hope?' Cordelia exclaimed in amazement.

'Viewed dispassionately, Miss Esscombe. As more jungles fall to the planter's axe, the demand for coolies is far outstripping the catchers' ability to supply them. Thus, the cost of conscripting and transporting them here is mounting day by day. Last year steamer services increased rates for coolie transportation to 17 rupees per head from rupees 12. As I said, it's queer logic, yet all this might induce your planter to take better care of his workforce someday.'

'But at what cost? How many of these wretched creatures must be sacrificed before there is a change of heart? No, Captain Hewitt, the authorities must step in to stop this barbarism. Tea planters must be coerced into benevolence through the force of law.'

'As things stand, that's not possible. Our job in Assam is to maintain law and order and collect revenue. We are here merely to make it safe for British commercial enterprise to consolidate and expand.'

'But you agreed to go to Bihguri, Captain Hewitt!'

'Of course, I did, Miss Esscombe. And go I shall. The issue in question involves law and order, and invokes provisions of our civil penal code. Absconding is a criminal offence. The Workman's Breach of Contract Act specifically lays down that if a coolie absconds, the planter must inform the authorities. He must not attempt to hunt down the absconder but must leave it to us to trace him. The absconder would remain in our custody and be tried by a civil judicial court. In this particular case the planter has infringed the existing laws by not reporting the absconder to me.'

'It's a wise law,' Cordelia said. 'A just law, for it protects the Birchas of this world from the vengeful wrath of its Buckinghams. Whatever your mandate might be, Captain Hewitt, such laws do exist. Can a law not be enacted which offers more protection to the coolies? Appointment of a 'Coolie Protector', for instance. To ensure that the garden hands are treated more humanely.'

'I'm an insignificant mandarin, dear Miss Esscombe ... a small cog in the gargantuan machine that is the British Civil Service. I acknowledge, from my limited experience, that there's a dire need for the kind of functionary you've suggested. But it's for the powers that be in Calcutta to change existing statutes. May I make a suggestion, Miss Esscombe? Why don't you visit Sivasagar and speak to Major Gosselin. As a senior covenanted officer, based in a tea district, his words carry greater weight.'

'Yes, I must do that. I strongly doubt anything will come out of it. But, as an individual very close to my heart once said, we've to justify our existence.'

The officer stood up and said, 'Come, Miss Esscombe. You've had a tiring day.'

He led her to her room. 'A coolie protector, Miss Esscombe?' he said in parting. 'Tell you what, I'll be your personal coolie protector … absolutely unofficial, of course!'

She heard his happy laughter even after she shut the door.

They were eight in Baisakhi's hutment that evening: five men and three women. Three of the men were in their late teens: Pahar, Bihuti and Tuvuk. The fourth man was the oldest among the Bihguri coolies. His name was Dudhu. Despite his long white hair and furrowed face, he could not be over fifty. His age made him an exception; not many coolies could ever hope to live as long as he had done.

Baisakhi and Lachmi were there. Saoni was crouched in one corner, stupefied with grief.

The naked terror which the nature of Bircha's chastisement had inserted into the collective consciousness of the coolies had not touched these young men. Their hearts were filled with hatred and anger rather than fear.

Sanatan enjoyed a reputation for possessing a wise head on his shoulders. The three young men had come to him, asking what they could do to assist the wretched coolie strung up in front of the tea houses. Sanatan could provide no answer.

'A slow, miserable, painful death, Sanatan bhaiya,' Pahar said. 'How can we bear to watch it? We can set him free in the dark! Give him a second chance at escape.'

'Escape, Pahar? How can he escape, weaker than a doddering man that he is?'

'You're right, Sanatan,' Dudhu said. 'Bircha's in no shape to escape. On the other hand, helping Bircha would bring down the sahib's vengeance on all of us. Greater suffering for the many to save one from suffering. That does not add up right.'

'Then why not end it all for the poor fellow?' This came from Tuvuk. 'Give me the word and I'll drive a knife through his heart.'

In the shadowy corner of the room, where the flickering light of the small, earthen diya could not get at her, Saoni listened.

'Kill him, Tuvuk?' Sanatan spoke in the same tired voice. 'Deprive the man-eater of his meal? He'll eat us raw.'

'You're all the same, you old men!' Bihuti spoke angrily. 'You teach us not to act. You teach us to whine and cringe before these sons of bitches.'

'Haven't you seen the terror on the coolielog's faces?' Lachmi spat out. 'If you do not blow the way the wind blows, you'll stick out like a solitary tree among tea bushes. They'll cut you down as they have Bircha-bhaiya.'

'Can we not do a thing?' Pahar cried out.

Sanatan spoke, 'You can nurse your hatred and anger. Drain away the fear from the minds of other young people like yourselves. Light the fires of defiance into them as you would light an earthen diya.'

'But,' added Lachmi, introducing a note of caution, 'do so with guile and stealth. Do not allow the shaitans to suspect that you have hatred in your hearts.'

'Right,' agreed Dudhu. 'We can light the flame of hate and anger in the coolies and burn away the fear from their bellies.'

'We'll do that,' Bihuti said fervently. 'We promise you. We'll light a hundred diyas!'

They all left. 'Saoni, it's time to sleep,' Baisakhi called out. There was no response. The poor girl must have fallen asleep already, fatigued by her grief and her weeping. Baisakhi put out the earthen lamp and stretched out on the floor.

But Saoni was not asleep. She huddled in the corner, arms hugging her legs, head resting on her knees. She was no longer crying. Either the wells in her skull from which these tears streamed out had dried up. Or the burning rage within her had dried those tears away, like the charcoal ovens in the tea houses dried the tea leaves, so that only the sting of brine in her eyes and tongue and throat remained. The words of her elders had ignited fury in her. The treacherous bastards! They only thought of themselves. How to save their own lice-bitten skins! They've given up on Bircha. The bastards!

She continued to sit hunched in the dark, allowing the blaze within her to feed upon her breasts and heart and intestines. She hated the whole lot of them. They would do nothing to ease the torment wracking Bircha's body. But she must do something. She would. To hell with them!

She heard her mago snore, as if she had not a care in the world. There was no fatigue in her own body. The blaze had burnt away the tiredness form her limbs too. The fire had singed off her eyelids, driving off sleep. So, she waited, in the same posture, uncrying and unsleeping, for the hours to pass, for the dark of the night to thicken.

Two hours later she arose and tiptoed out of the hut. She glided over the dirt track, unconcerned that someone might see, her thoughts centred round her love and his deliverance.

The knife in her hand gleamed dully in the moonlight.

There was no use cutting off Bircha's bonds and setting him free. She agreed with the bastard Sanatan on that. Bircha did not have the strength to escape his captors. But he would escape all the same. Escape to an unseen world where there would be no drudgery, no sahibs and their sirdars, no lashes of whip on bare back. Just a single slash at the wrist! Swift and painless! She had seen it done once, when she was a child, many years ago.

This night too another knife would slash. Twice—for the sahib and his dogs must know who had wielded that knife! The bastards in the *basti* would not feel the backlash of the sahib's wrath then. She would lie on the ground on Bircha's chest.

Without hesitation she streaked across the open ground and reached the crumpled figure of Bircha. His head was slumped against his chest, the limp body was straining against the bonds. Tenderly she placed her left hand under his chin and lifted up the head. She felt the touch of his exhalation on her palm. Her love was unconscious, but alive.

Fierce emotions welled up inside her as she gazed at the haggard features; deep seated, womanly instinct of the mother and the lover made her tarry despite her urgency—to stroke the stubbled face with one hand. Her touch evoked no response. With a choking cry she let go the head. It lolled once more onto his chest. Stifling her sobs, she hugged him in a possessive embrace, her arms curving across his raw, flagellated back. The violence of her passion had made her forget the whip-cuts! Piercing pain thrust into Bircha's consciousness. He stirred. His neck straightened. His eyelids fluttered open. She stood before him, rendered mute, mortified at having caused him pain. Her gaze was fixed on the pair of sightless eyes, mesmerized by the glint of reflected moonlight which made them twinkle like stars.

His eyes focused. 'Saoni, is that you?'

'Hush, my love. It is me. I've come to set you free, my Bircha.'

'My body burns, Saoni!'

She held his face in her hands. He saw the knife.

'Have you come to cut me down? To set me free? *Kuch phaida nahin*! My legs are numb. There's no strength left in me.'

'I'll set you free, my love. I'll take you away with me. Soon there will be no pain. We'll go to a place with no pain.'

He saw the look on her face and, all of a sudden, understood the depth and desperation of her love. But it could not be. He had no illusions about his own fate. But Saoni! In the flush of her youth! He must not allow it. It would be an act of betrayal which would keep him eternally wrapped in pain, even after death.

'Thehro, Saoni!' He was frightened. Not for himself, but for her.

'What is it, my Bircha?'

'I don't want to die like this, Saoni. I am afraid to die like this.'

She smiled. A reassuring smile; of a mother hushing her fearful child to sleep. 'Do not be afraid. There'll be no pain. We'll slip away together, Bircha my love.'

'I'll not die like this, Saoni,' he reiterated, his voice firmer. 'If we die by our hands the spirit which dwells within us will reach neither hell nor heaven. Would you condemn my spirit to forever float in a limbo, Saoni? Finding no rest, no relief from pain?'

With guile he had talked about his own deliverance, his simulated fear overtly for himself. The words were right. The resolute fire in her eyes was snuffed out instantly. He could see hesitation in them now.

'Do you show your pyaar in this way, Saoni?' he pressed on relentlessly. 'Condemning me to eternal pain? No, Saoni, we will not float away to another world. We will not smile in our death.'

She started to sob. Each grief-filled sob was a whiplash on his back. But he would not allow the hardness in his voice to soften, for her sake.

'Go away, Saoni. Let me accept the death the shaitans have planned for me. I shall then find peace. Go away, Saoni. Leave me to my fate.'

She nodded, touched his cheeks in a fleeting caress, and was gone.

Much of the travails of the previous afternoon's journey to Jorehaut were absent the following morning when Cordelia, along with Captain Hewitt and his men, retraced the route. Never would she forget their triumphant entry though the main gate of Bihguri, the bewilderment on the faces of the coolies, the confused consternation among the sirdars as they sprinted furiously to apprise their master of this invasion, and the anger and apprehension on Buckingham's features as he rode back from supervisory work among the pluckers. But the sight which would remain imprinted upon her mind was that of Bircha dangling limply against the stakes, not a human being but a marionette!

Behind her, Hewitt let out a stifled oath, steeped in disgust. They reached Bircha much ahead of Buckingham. Hewitt was on the ground even before the elephant had completed kneeling, the mahout's dao in his hands. He raced up to the tethered coolie, severed the leg fetters, grabbed him with his left hand to keep him from sinking, and cut away the ropes binding the wrists. Bircha sagged into the captain's arms and Hewitt gently laid him upon the ground.

Meanwhile Buckingham had hurried up. 'What's the meaning of this, Captain Hewitt?' he thundered, the voice raised for the benefit of a rapidly enlarging audience. The officer ignored him and continued rubbing the atrophied limbs of the prostrate man, urging the constable to do the same.

Cordelia looked up. The news of their arrival had spread. Unmindful of threats and slashes, the coolies dropped whatever they had been doing and converged from all corners of the garden to that spot. They stood at a distance and quietly watched the scene.

For the split of a second her eyes met those of Buckingham. She had seen that venom-filled gleam before, in a gaze directed at Michael, and at the Reverend.

The officer stood up and looked around, continuing to ignore the planter. He saw Luthra and barked, 'Hey, you there! Go and get a stretcher ... and medicines and bandages. *Che lao*! On the double!'

The stupid menial backed away in sullen refusal. A policeman stepped out and brought his baton on Luthra with a resounding thwack. '*Saala kukur poali*!' he roared. 'Do as the sahib says!'

That mighty thwack cracked the shell of the coolies' fear and a hubbub of approving sounds erupted from them. Buckingham's head turned sharply around for a look, and a change came over his visage. The choleric lustre disappeared, to be replaced by a smile of nonchalance. 'Go and get the stretcher,' he told Luthra. 'Bring the medicine bag along.'

As they were lifting Bircha onto it, the planter turned to Captain Hewitt. 'We'd better take him to my bungalow. You can wrap him up there.'

The officer guessed why the planter wanted Bircha to be shifted. 'No,' he said shortly.

'Suit yourself.' Buckingham shrugged his shoulders. 'I'll be in my bungalow. At least have the courtesy to call on me before you depart.'

'I'll do that,' Hewitt said with intensity. 'I have a great deal to say to you, Buckingham. Yes, I shall certainly call on you.'

The planter walked away with a negligent air, followed closely by his henchmen. Emboldened by the absence of the sirdars, a number of coolies came up to assist the sahib. They carried Bircha to the shade of a tree. Someone fetched a koloh of water and thrust it at Cordelia. She looked up from her ministrations to see who it was. A young coolie damsel. On the girl's face was a brightness she had never seen in a coolie, not even in those of Dhanboa!

It took half hour more for Bircha's wounds to be treated. He lay supine on the stretcher, a swath of bandages covering his upper torso. Cordelia stood up and addressed the girl, still beside her, the rapture-filled eyes fixed on the recumbent coolie.

'Where can we take him?' she asked.

But it was the captain who replied. 'We'd better take him to the bungalow and put him under Buckingham's charge. He'll be in need of medicines and nursing for some time.'

'No, Captain Hewitt,' Cordelia said. 'He'll be safer among his own people. Once Buckingham has him alone, there's no telling what he might do.'

'Oh, you needn't worry on that score, Miss Esscombe. Leave it to me to ensure Bircha's safety. But I daresay you're right. He'll get better care amongst the coolies.' He spoke to the coolie girl standing beside Cordelia. '*Aarey chokri, Bircha ko kahan ley ja sakta hoon? Uska apna jhopri hein kya?*'

'Yes, yes,' the girl said eagerly. 'But he and Meghu lived together. Now that Meghu is in your lockup, sahib, there'll be no one to take care of him.'

'Meghu? Lockup? *Kaun sa* Meghu? *Kaun sa* lockup?'

'Meghu? Bircha's dost! They ran away together. You caught Meghu and put him in your lockup. That's what the sahib told us.'

'Your sahib is a liar! I know no Meghu ... don't have him in the lockup. Anyway, chokri, can you suggest someone who can take care of Bircha?'

'I'll take care of him.'

Cordelia caught the possessive tenor in her voice and was suddenly blessed with insight. 'What's your name, chokri?' she asked.

'Saoni, memsahib.'

Cordelia sighed with relief. 'She's the best person to take care of Bircha. Believe me, Captain Hewitt, I know!'

A dozen young men helped carry the stretcher in a procession to the basti and deposit Bircha in Baisakhi's hutment. Cordelia took out three shiny coins from the money-bag at her waist and gave them to Baisakhi. 'Here, buy whatever you need for Bircha. Make sure he gets well.'

The woman took the coins with reluctance. 'Don't be afraid,' Cordelia told her. 'No harm will come to you. This sahib here is the sarkar. He'll ensure that no one harms you for providing shelter to Bircha.'

'Give me a couple of minutes, will you, Miss Esscombe. I have a pleasant task to complete before we can depart,' Hewitt said and strode purposefully towards the bungalow.

'What the devil are you up to, Hewitt?' the planter launched into the officer as soon as he was within earshot. 'Make me look a damn fool before my coolies! Who the hell do you imagine you are?'

Hewitt's deceptively boyish features remained impassive. 'I'm Captain Ralph Hewitt,' he said laconically. 'Assistant to Major Gosselin for the Jorehaut sadar.'

'That's not what I meant, goddamn you! You appear in my garden un-summoned. Meddle into its affairs without being asked to. Humiliate me before my coolies. You are exceeding your authority, Captain Ralph Hewitt!'

'Is that all you hold against me?' Hewitt retorted. 'Humiliating you before the coolies? Exceeding my authority? But I've come with motive of greater import. I've come to charge you with willful violation of the laws of the land. I have come to charge you with attempt at manslaughter, Christopher James Buckingham.'

The planter looked thunderstruck. 'Have you gone mad, Captain?' he asked.

Hewitt was at his officious best. 'Do you deny you shot a man, sir? Do you deny that, having failed to kill him, you strove to starve and flog him to death? Attempted manslaughter, may I remind you, is a cognizable offence.'

'You can't be serious, Hewitt? Attempted manslaughter? For potting a ruddy nigger? Why, old chap, the man assaulted me. He tried to kill me. I *had* to fire in self-defence.'

'My observations do not bear out your claim. The man was shot in the back. He was, clearly, running away when you shot him. My *daroga* and constable will bear witness to that. Also, charges have been brought against you from other quarters.'

'That bloody bitch! She aided and abetted an absconder! Or didn't she tell you that?'

For the first time since the exchanges the phlegmatic exterior presented by the captain suffered a change. Buckingham saw the face flush with anger. But, with great effort, the officer retained the calmness of tone.

'Nursing a wounded human being, Buckingham ... giving him back his life ... that's not aiding and abetting in the eyes of justice. You, on the other hand, flouted the law by endeavouring to take it into your own hands. You didn't alert us of the absconders. On the contrary, you hunted the runaways on your own, apprehended one of them, and attempted to end his life.'

'Alert you, Captain? Surely you jest! In this season? With every outlet closed?'

'Don't be fatuous, Buckingham, Miss Esscombe reached Jorehaut last evening despite the condition of the terrain. If a woman can do it, I'm sure you are man enough to have attempted the same?'

Buckingham flinched. He had caught the tenor of the officer's arguments and was aware that, with the attitude of hostility the man was displaying, the dice was loaded against him. But this sally of his was too much to bear! Against his better judgement, he lapsed into insolent sarcasm.

'She's woven her tresses around you, hasn't she? You're a covenanted officer, Hewitt. You have a fine career ahead of you. Leave that bitch alone, do you hear? She'll scuttle your ship. She'll destroy your career. Let her sink her claws into you, she'll destroy your sanity!'

'You're contemptible!' Hewitt spat out. 'You're scum! To speak such words against a woman whom your very shadow would sully! Which gutter were you spawned in, Buckingham?'

'How dare you?' Buckingham shouted, his anger bringing him a step forward.

'If you so much as take another step, Buckingham, I'll put you under arrest.'

Hewitt appeared enraged enough to carry out his threat. The planter stopped.

'Now look here, Hewitt ...' he began.

But the officer cut him short. 'I've wasted enough time on you,' he said, the cold rage in him icing the words. 'I am no coolie who you can browbeat into submission. I'm an officer of the Imperial Crown. I invite you to taste a little of my power, Buckingham.'

The planter wilted. 'I apologize,' he said hastily.

'No apology on your part would lessen the heinous nature of your offence,' Hewitt said testily. 'Unfortunately, you're an Englishman. So, I'll not proceed against you, but let you off with a warning. The coolie whom you sought to kill is under my protection from now on. If you as much as touch a hair on his head, you'll be answerable to me. Let the rains cease, I'll be back in Bihguri. Till then guard him as you would guard your own despicable self. If anything happens to that coolie, you'll live to regret it. By heavens, I'll make you pay, Buckingham!'

'Is this official, Captain?'

'Don't test whether it is or not, Buckingham!'

'Well, Major Gosselin shall hear of it,' the planter said. 'Perhaps you underestimate me, Captain. I might carry the issue right up to the Viceroy. Our company is not without resources.'

Hewitt laughed. 'You are welcome to do so, Buckingham. But before you embark on any steps towards that let me ask you something. Have you ever heard of a gentleman named Anthony Cuthbert Hewitt?'

'Yes. He's the Personal Assistant to the Viceroy.'

'Right. He also happens to be my father, Buckingham.'

With a final look of contempt, Hewitt turned his back on the planter and strode out.

He made straight for the elephants. His bureaucratic training enabled him to regain his composure the minute he stepped out of the bungalow. Cordelia, therefore, remained clueless as to what had transpired between him and Buckingham. Nor was he very forthcoming on the subject. 'Buckingham is convinced I'm in dead earnest about Bircha,' he said shortly. 'He'll not touch him again. You can rest assured on that, Miss Esscombe.'

He thrust out a hand as if to take hers before departing. 'But surely, Captain Hewitt,' Cordelia cried out, 'you're not contemplating a departure for Jorehaut straight away?'

The officer lowered his hand. 'I was doing precisely that, Miss Esscombe. We've to leave immediately if we are to reach my headquarters before dark.'

'Oh Captain, I can't allow you to leave! It'll tax you as well as your mount. No, you must come and spend the night at Dhanboa.'

'Well yes, we can stay the night, I suppose,' Hewitt said, grinning with delight.

Buckingham watched the two elephants depart. So, Cordelia had found a powerful ally, and Bircha a protector! He had met the captain a couple of times before. The bloody fellow had given no hint that he was the son of the Assistant to the Viceroy.

But these government bastards were never kept in the same position for too long. Till Hewitt was posted elsewhere, he must bow to the fellow's caprice. For the time being, he could not touch Bircha, though it was because of that mongrel he had been humiliated before the coolies.

Buckingham stepped out of the bungalow, determined to salvage something out of the day's fiasco. His henchmen stood in a cluster. Some of their sahib's discomfiture had rubbed on to them too. They could not face him squarely and shifted uneasily on their feet as he approached.

'Where have they taken Bircha?'

'To the basti, sahib. Baisakhi *ki jhopri mein*. The memsahib gave Baisakhi money.'

'Now that the other sahib has left, we can bring him out.' This was from Budhu.

'No!' Buckingham said. 'Bircha is not to be touched! Leave him alone, understand?'

The others looked blankly at him, puzzled. Buckingham realized this, and sought to explain.

'Bircha has come under the protection of the *raani sahiba's* sarkar. So, leave him alone. But the other coolies have not come under its protection. We are free to do with them as we wish.'

If he had thought this would be a tempting bone before his pack, he was mistaken. Luthra said, 'This morning's happenings have caused them to be gripped with a new madness. I don't like it, sahib.'

'Neither do I,' Gandru said. 'We tried to get them back to work but they won't listen.'

'Where are they now?' Buckingham asked, the anger stirring in him. His sirdars were pleased with that anger. Somehow it reassured them.

'In the basti. Jabbering like a pack of monkeys.'

'Follow my instructions closely. True, we cannot touch Bircha. But we can whip the rest raw. So, every time you chastise a coolie, tell him or her that it was Bircha who had caused the chastisement. Every time you use your whip, call out Bircha's name. That way they will begin to think it was Bircha who has brought misfortune on them. They'll start to hate him. No more will he put fire in their bellies.'

The sirdars dipped their heads in approval. This was their old master talking!

'Good. Now go and plough into them, all of you. I don't care how you do it, but I want them back at work in half an hour.'

The alacrity with which they departed to carry out his hukum rearmed the planter with confidence. The extraordinary happenings at his plantation this morning had been an aberration. They must not be allowed to disturb the placidity of Bihguri's atmosphere!

Their party reached Dhanboa within the hour. As the elephants neared the bungalow, Pekoe burst out in vocal welcome and rushed down, followed by a joyous Mongla. David was nowhere to be seen.

'Sahib left for the fields after breakfast,' Mongla informed her.

That was a blessing! She busied herself preparing for the guests' stay. Captain Hewitt would spend the night in the bungalow, his men would be accommodated in the dispensary. Having had their breakfast, and seen Hewitt to his room for a bath and rest, she summoned Mongla. 'Go and fetch Kamal. He has to prepare three beds in the dispensary for the visitors.'

'Memsahib, *woh to chala gaya*!'

'Gone? Gone where?'

'Back to the village. Last evening.'

'All right. Go and get Bapu babu.'

'*Par woh bhi chala gaya, memsahib*. Back to the village. And so have the Assamese tea makers. They took away all their belongings.'

What? Cordelia felt fear raise its hood in her heart.

'*Par kiun*, Mongla? Why have they all left?'

'Sahib was angry at Bapu babu. Called him names. I was listening, memsahib. Caught him by the throat. I watched in secret. Sahib had taken too much vilayati paani. Full one bottle. Bapu babu shook like the earth shakes sometimes. Then they all left.'

Cordelia tottered to a chair and sat heavily.

'Are you all right, memsahib?' Mongla's voice was full of concern.

She got a hold on herself, and stood determinedly up. 'I'm fine, Mongla. But come, we have work to do.'

Collecting linen from the almirah and with Mongla in tow, she went to the dispensary and prepared the beds. Then she slept for a while. Captain Hewitt was seated on the verandah, the tea tray before him. She greeted him with a cheery smile, determined to conceal her shock and sorrow. She took the captain to the coolie basti, proudly pointing out to him the deep nullahs which drained away effluence, the bamboo framed beds which kept the coolies safe from the malaria inducing miasma, the elevated mud terraces, the thick, mud layered walls and thatched roofs which screened them from damp and cold. Every month she had punctiliously dropped bags of lime in the community pond from which the coolies drew water, she informed him, and had ensured that the coolies boil the water before drinking it, which explained the low incidences of stomach ailments among them. Captain Hewitt was more than impressed.

She took him around the dispensary, showed him Papa's grave and the garden around it, now bereft of flowers and looking untended. They brought Congou and Souchong out and exercised them in a slow canter round and round the bungalow. Cordelia was loath to take Hewitt towards the fields or the tea houses in fear of chancing upon David. Her brother must have been aware of her return by now, and the presence of the visitors. Yet he had not made an appearance. She could guess why!

'I'm afraid that's all the entertainment Dhanboa has to offer,' she said lightly as they led the horses back to their paddock.

'Your presence yields pleasure enough, Miss Esscombe,' the officer replied in all seriousness.

As they sat on the verandah watching the daylight fade, she heard David reach the stairs and give parting instructions to his sirdars. Hurriedly she excused herself with the plea that she had to oversee preparations for dinner and, retreating to her room, listened as David walked up to the visitor.

Her brother greeted Captain Hewitt cordially, exchanged a few pleasantries and then said, 'Give me ten minutes to clean up, will you? I'll join you for a sundowner.'

Crossing the verandah on the other side, out of sight of the visitor, she went down to the kitchen. Mongla was dispatched to the dispensary with the evening meal for Hewitt's men. On his return she asked him to set the table. Only when that had been completed did she go to where David and Hewitt sat, whisky glasses in hand, to inform them that dinner was ready.

Even had he not had an inkling of the events which led the girl to go to Jorehaut, Hewitt would not have failed to feel the tension between brother and sister. They tried to act and sound casual, in deference to his presence, but the tell-tale signs were there, the sudden silences and frowns. He, therefore, completed his dinner as speedily as he could, keeping small talk to a bare minimum. David sat with him over an after-dinner brandy and then excused himself. He had to be in the tea houses earlier than usual, he explained, because the blasted Assamese tea makers had left him in the lurch. He would see Hewitt only the next morning.

The officer was not really sorry to see him depart, for, as he expected, Cordelia reappeared as soon as her brother left. Seated on the verandah, they chatted on.

'Captain Hewitt,' Cordelia suddenly asked. 'Do you believe in miracles?'

He was taken by surprise at the abrupt query. 'Well,' he said hesitantly, 'it depends upon the nature of the miracles.'

'I refer to the weather … the sunshine in the past two days. Just think of it. If it had rained, Bircha might be dead by now.'

'Well, I would prefer to call it a coincidence,' Hewitt said. 'But there was a miracle involved in Bircha's resuscitation … so you're right in a way. You, Miss Esscombe, were that miracle!'

Cordelia blushed.

'Truly, Miss Esscombe,' Hewitt continued. 'If Bircha had been endowed with the miracle of a second, nay, a third life, it was entirely due to you. Your brother, by the way, conceded this.'

'You told David about it?' Cordelia asked, perturbed.

'Yes. I had to. Your departure to Jorehaut and my equally unexpected arrival entailed some explanation. He took it very well. In fact, I sensed a marked relief in him at the news that Bircha was safe.'

'I know why he felt relieved, Captain Hewitt,' she said, unable to keep the bitterness from her voice. 'It was he who restored the fugitive to Buckingham. That Bircha is alive and under your protection is a load off his conscience.'

'You shouldn't judge him too severely. You both travel on different paths. His priorities must necessarily differ from your own.'

'I suppose that's true,' Cordelia admitted with a sigh. 'Our priorities change as we grow up, don't they? It was foolish of me to yearn for the uncomplicated relationship of childhood.'

'You're not happy in Dhanboa, are you, Miss Esscombe?'

The question was put softly, almost in a tender whisper. Yet it touched her ears like a cannon shot, momentarily deafening her. The officer took her silence to be affirmation.

'Miss Esscombe, what I'm about to say to you is not out of a sense of pity,' he continued. 'Although I've not had the pleasure of a knowing you for long, the little I've seen of you fills me with deep regard. You are outwardly beautiful; but from the background whence I spring, physical beauty is not a scarce commodity. I speak of the beauty of your soul. Your outward beauty pales into insignificance before the beauty of your soul.'

The bungalow was no longer a bungalow but a steamer floating on a river. The verandah was not a verandah but the forward upper saloon deck.

Those were not tea bushes painted with moonbeams but watery waves glistening in the night.

'You have enkindled emotions which I never suspected had existed in me,' Hewitt, unaware that he had transported her to another world and another time, continued in the same whispery voice. 'Till not long ago you were a total stranger to me. So why does it hurt me so much to find you hurting? Why do I feel your pain as my own?'

Different time, different place, but the same tone—the inflections, the hesitations, the earnestness and the intensity. She would never forget the words uttered in a different time, at a different place. 'But ever since I beheld you first on the deck you've meant more to me than I am capable of ever expressing ... your presence was a gentle breeze which swept away all the noxious exhalations poisoning the horizons of my mind. That night, as you sat fanning my head, it was not only the fever that had been cleansed from my body. The deep wound in my soul, which was slowly but surely killing me, you've healed. You've given me new life, Miss Esscombe, and for that I'm deeply grateful.'

Those words had burnt into her soul. It was the voice of memory which was uttering them in her mind now, drowning out those emerging from the man who sat beside her.

'Yes, Miss Esscombe,' Hewitt continued. 'Your unhappiness makes me unhappy. Let me take you away. My life too is a lonely one. You were at Jorehaut just last evening. You could see for yourself the loneliness of my existence, placed as I am, like you, amongst strangers, in a land not my own. We can fill each other's lives, Miss Esscombe! Fill up the empty loneliness with our love. Also, my father is the Personal Assistant to the Viceroy. One of the top bureaucrats in Hindustan. I had withheld this from you ... I wished you to weigh me as I am. If I mention him now, it's only to show you that though a petty mandarin, I'm not totally without power or influence. He can be of invaluable help in your ... and now mine ... crusade.'

'My crusade, Captain Hewitt?'

'Our crusade, Miss Esscombe! I'm on your side. To bring about amelioration in the lot of the coolies. Come away with me ... we'll do it together.'

'But you'll not do it alone? Should charity be conditional, Captain Hewitt?'

'Don't misjudge me, Miss Esscombe. Whether you accept me or not. I'll not back away, for that would be a gross betrayal of the fine feelings you've aroused in me. But if you can find it in your heart to accept me ... accept my offer ... it would empower me, infuse in me a greater will. Be mine and we'll embark on our crusade together.'

The storm which had been building up in the past couple of hours had neared now, the lightning flashes were more frequent and vivid. She could hear the distant rumblings of thunder.

'I'm sorry, Captain Hewitt. It cannot be.'

She heard the sharp intake of breath in the man at her flat refusal. He was silent for some time, grappling with his emotions. When he spoke, his voice was composed.

'I understand, Miss Esscombe. You have pledged yourself to another. It's Michael Bailin who has laid claim to your affections, is it not?'

'Yes.' Cordelia spoke with anxiety. 'Have I caused you offence, Captain Hewitt?'

'How can you cause me offence when it is I who unasked thrust my pleas on you? I must confess I was cognizant of your attachment to the Lieutenant. I suspected it in my last visit itself, when you asked me to go to Chahpuli to warn him. But those suspicions were lulled by what your brother told me.'

'David? What did he say?'

'That the Lieutenant was a mere shipboard acquaintance. That, having come to know of his background, you harboured no affection for him. Your brother appeared somewhat apprehensive that the Lieutenant might attempt to renew the relationship built up aboard the steamer. He was very anxious to prevent that at any cost.'

The storm was no longer far away. It raged within her brain and pounded savagely at her skull. Cordelia gripped the arms of the chair, fearful that the tempest would blow her sanity away.

Unconscious of the turmoil in her, the officer asked, 'You are completely aware of the Lieutenant's background, aren't you, Miss Esscombe?'

'Yes, I'm aware of his background.' She spoke with great difficulty. 'He has kept nothing from me.'

Hewitt sensed the powerful emotions his words had evoked in her, but he could not resist asking, 'And yet you give your heart to him, Miss Esscombe?'

'I love him, Captain Hewitt,' she said simply. 'They've fed you malicious lies. Michael is not the kind of man these petty people make him out to be. Please believe me, I know.'

'If you have weighed his actions and found them irreproachable, I bow to your judgement. But your brother seems to think otherwise.'

'David knows the truth too. If he has suddenly changed his opinion of Michael, you can be sure there are extraneous reasons for it.'

'It that case it's only fair that I enlighten you about Lieutenant Bailin's circumstances at the moment. From what I could make out during my visit to Chahpuli, he is at the end of his resources. He has a small landholding, no doubt; but not the money to convert it into a tea concern. He lives in a tiny hutment no better than the ones we saw at the coolie basti. A small tract of land has been cleared, but he employs no workers. He appears to be attempting to work the clearing by himself and a native assistant ... that way it'll take him a decade to make something of it.'

'I'll wait,' Cordelia said softly.

'Well, I can only apologize, Miss Esscombe. I had no idea you were so strongly attached!'

'You're a good man, Captain Hewitt,' Cordelia said with warmth. 'A gentleman. I shall harbour nothing but the deepest regards for you.'

Those words lessened the pangs of disappointment in the officer. 'I too will wait, Miss Esscombe ... and help you in every way I can. But you must meet Major Gosselin and place your views before him. He's my superior officer. It would be wrong of me to go over his head.'

Hewitt rose.

'I'll do that,' Cordelia said, rising and escorting him to his room. At the door she held out her hands. He caught them in a grip so strong that it hurt. 'Goodnight, Captain Hewitt. And thank you for all you've done.'

Gently disengaging her hands, she walked away, leaving him staring after her.

The tiredness was not in her body only. Her mind too had been overwhelmed by fatigue, the kind of exhaustion that breeds despair. But sleep would not come. Oh God, how tired she felt! It was this tiredness which made Hewitt's offer so enticing. He could arm her with incredible powers to pursue her cause. No longer would her ambit of influence be confined to Dhanboa; there would be no need to beg and cajole and fight her brother to wrest for the coolies their minimal dues. An affirmative answer to the officer may truly transform her into an instrument which brought forth general good—the Reverend's instrument! Hewitt's father had the power and influence to effect far reaching improvements, enact laws which would protect the coolies from the sadistic rapacity of their employers. She could, with the officer and his father's help, usher in a better life for the coolies. With her acceptance of his offer, she could bid farewell to the fatigue overwhelming her mind and body.

Then what had made her resist? A face which hovered in her imagination even as Hewitt was making the offer? Eyes racked in pain and self-doubt, which her smile had rendered lustrous? A soul blackened by the terrible consequences of its own unsullied goodness, which she had cleansed with her love? A betrayal which in reality was the supreme sacrifice a man can make for a woman?

Was she chasing a chimera? Almost ten months had elapsed since she last looked into those blue eyes, caressed those handsome features. Oh, Michael, where are you? Was our love so fragile to be shattered by whispered innuendos? No letter, no news, not a word, despite the Reverend's urgings? Would you fill me with the self-doubts and hesitations which you yourself are filled with? I am tired, Michael, and weighed down with uncertainties about my own future!

Outside, the tempest broke. The sky rumbled; the rain came down once again in cascading sheets. Cordelia lay sleepless in the bed, her unuttered shrieks drowned by the shrieking wind in the rafters.

It took Lieutenant Michael Bailin just a fortnight to realize the incontrovertible truth that kismet could not be thwarted by a mere ditch!

The disaster had struck without forewarning.

The hawk-eyed Garo was the first to point it out to the sahib. One of the saplings had developed a sickly, wilting look. They examined each leaf, every inch of the stem and stalk. He saw nothing to explain the droopy appearance of the sapling—there was no grub or pest or fungal growth.

Worse was to follow the next morning. Scores of other saplings developed similar symptoms of debility. Bailin plucked one, wondering at the lack of resistance it offered as it emerged. 'Oh, my God!' he cried out as the truth hit him. The sapling's roots were a rotting, pulpy mass!

Despite his inexperience, he guessed what was happening to the tea plants of Chahpuli. With the rain constantly seeping into the porous soil the underground water table had risen abnormally, causing the entire root system of the saplings to rot.

This was proved in the days which followed. The saplings sagged, drooped and fell, one by one, until Chahpuli was a mock-garden again.

xxxxxxx

BOOK THREE

LEAVES NO LONGER GREEN

'A functionary has been appointed to look after the welfare and inquire into the treatment of the labourer in Assam, who delights in the appellation of Coolie Protector. *Amongst a certain section of the rough and ready fraternity, men who value a coolie on the principle that the immortal Mr Grandgrind did his "hands", this gentleman's services are very desirable, and without doubt, the improvement in the coolie's condition, from a humanitarian point of view, tends to raise his working capabilities for the benefit of his taskmaster. That a* Protector *is really required now that a different class of men has taken the place of the old planter is another question, but the powers that be, viewing the state of things through maternal spectacles, see in the present race of planters only the successors of planters that have gone before, inheritors of all their faults and vices (for they had a very had name). Quite enough that we shall be tarred with the same brush. Now, is it not ridiculous to suppose that owners would willfully maltreat their servants, knowing that everything depends upon their being in a good state of health, coupled with an amount of willingness, sufficient, at any rate, to complete a Governmentally prescribed day's work?'*

—George M. Barker, tea planter of the 1870s

For five long years Christopher James Buckingham had ruled his microcosmic kingdom with an iron hand. Nothing had occurred in these years to disturb the realm's fearful tranquillity. But now alien actors had suddenly walked onto the stage, evicting the one who had been playing the stellar role.

Christopher James Buckingha had never felt as vulnerable!

Things were not going as planned. The cause was Bircha—a constant reminder to the coolies that their master's presumed omnipotence was bound by finite limits. The Bihguri sahib could not touch Bircha! So, the coolies converted him into a beacon of hope.

To add salt to his wounds, Buckingham had to pay the bugger his wages! As soon as he was sufficiently recovered Bircha had approached him to request he be given work. Inwardly, Buckingham had exploded at the coolie's effrontery; it took all his self-control to hold himself back and not throttle the twerp. Nevertheless, circumstances dictated that he yields to the request. Though, under no circumstances would he allow Bircha to work in the garden, he would be paid as if he were engaged in regular chores.

This, in the minds of the coolies, was another feather in Bircha's cap! As long as he remained in the garden, Buckingham's unchallenged supremacy would always be under threat. Buckingham summoned Bircha and told him he was relieved of his contractual obligations. He was free to leave Bihguri and go where he pleased. His master would pay him a handsome amount to begin a new life somewhere else.

The nigger had rejected his offer!

Then, in the second week of June, an incident occurred which further deepened his concern. The early morning roll-call of a plucking detail had revealed the absence of a coolie by the name of Dudhu. Puran, the sirdar in charge of that detail, made enquiries among the coolies and discovered that Dudhu was still in bed, apparently ill with fever. Puran had been conditioned to act in a set pattern in such a situation. He did not, therefore, come to his master, but acted on his own. Having set the other coolies to work, he marched to the basti, dragged Dudhu to the field, and put him in one of the most difficult sections of the plantings.

An hour of work in the pouring rain proved too much for Dudhu. Suddenly, without making a sound, the elderly coolie crumpled and fell face down in the mire.

Puran had been trained to act in such a situation too! He threaded his way through the pluckers to where the man lay and delivered a vicious kick on the prostrate body. The very next moment he felt strong hands around his own limbs, pulling him down, pummelling him in the belly and groin, tearing his hair and clawing at his flesh. They were like a pack of wild dogs upon a prey, snarling and savage. Certain his end was near, Puran fought the animals with all his might, shrieking for help.

Fortunately for him the planted section happened to be adjacent to the sahib's bungalow. Buckingham, dressed in his nightwear, was at his chota hazri when the screams reached his ears. Without another thought he clutched his rifle and raced in the direction from where the cries had come. His timely arrival saved Puran from certain death. At the approach of their master, the coolies backed off.

Then something inconceivable happened. Instead of returning to plucking, the coolies picked up the aged Dudhu and marched off towards the basti. Buckingham fired in the air to bring them back, but to no avail. In some inscrutable manner the news spread with astounding rapidity and, within the hour, coolies all over the garden downed tools and trooped back to the basti. The tea house detail followed the others soon after and operations in Bihguri grounded to a halt.

Such a show of collective defiance was unprecedented! Buckingham realized he had to tread warily. Though aware that a day lost entailed a sizeable loss of production, he took no immediate action. But, in the dead of the night, he struck. His army moved stealthily through the basti like a python through a colony of monkeys, battering open doors of pre-targeted hutments, grabbing and pulling away young men. In the inky darkness of the wet night, amidst the wails and shouts, Buckingham's raiding party snatched six hostages and tied them to whipping posts erected before the tea houses.

At the first flush of the following dawn the coolies, who had spent a dread-ridden night, gathered in the open ground before the tea houses to find the young men guarded by the sirdars. Buckingham made a short speech. He had not so far punished the youths who had made a cowardly attack on Puran the previous morning. But unless the coolielog tendered an abject apology for their wicked attack and promised to resume work, he would shoot each man one by one before their very eyes.

Renewed wailing broke out from the womenfolk, while the men shuffled their feet. Suddenly an elderly coolie stepped out. The planter recognized him—it was Sanatan, Lachmi's husband. Looking Buckingham straight in the eye the coolie spoke. On behalf of the coolielog he was making abject apologies to the sahib for yesterday's incident. He also pledged on behalf of the coolielog that such a thing would never take place again. He had only one request to make to the sahib. Dudhu, whom Puran had so thoughtlessly dragged away from his sick-bed, was terribly ill. Would the sahib take a look at him and administer medicines?

Buckingham's smile was triumphant. He ordered the hostages to be freed. He announced that he forgave his rebellious subjects and no fine would be imposed. Also, he himself would go with his medicine bag and take a look at Dudhu.

The coolies went back to their tasks. Production commenced one more. True to his words, Buckingham paid Dudhu a visit. It was nothing but a malarial attack which a few days of rest and a few dosages of Edward's Tonic would not cure.

Soon, however, Buckingham grew to realize that what he had conceived to be an outright victory was in reality more of a fragile truce. Virulent undercurrents continued to flow amongst the coolies, especially the youthful ones, revealing themselves in the growing incidents of petty insubordination which he would ordinarily have overlooked and left to his henchmen to tackle. That his sirdars had become more wary while tackling the coolies was of equal concern. Recent events had unnerved them. Now they always moved in pairs and were cautious while returning to the basti after dusk. They no longer shouted obscenities at coolies and firmly barred the doors of their hutments from the inside at night.

Things were getting out of hand. But then, Providence itself came to his aid! It came towards the end of July, when the rains were slackening, in the guise of an epidemic of black-death: the scourge!

Its first victim was a toddler who had been well enough till one evening when he developed a high fever and began passing rice-watery stool. A few hours later he was dead. By the next evening a dozen coolies in the basti where the baby had died were taken till, and seven perished within the night. Wails of despair once again rent the Bihguri air.

Buckingham went into action to contain the scourge. He distributed boxes of cholera-pills, one pill to be taken per day by every coolie. Apart from cholera pills, salt and jaggery, bottles of potassium permanganate and sacks of quicklime etcetera were supplied to the collies. Also provided was a stack of hessian-sacks to pack the corpses in so they could be conveniently carried for cremation.

The scourge arrived and departed quickly. Thirty-nine inmates had been stricken of which thirty-one perished, including fourteen adults. Within a week the scourge left as mysteriously as it had arrived. By the first week of August, it became obvious that there would be no further casualties. By the second week of August Bihguri's tears had dried and the epidemic became just another minor episode in the garden's chequered history.

For Christopher James Buckingham, however, the cholera epidemic had arrived none too soon. The scourge killed something more than those fourteen buggers and seventeen brats! It had, at the same time, killed the defiance which recent events had sparked off in the bastards. Visitation by the black death had hammered home into their stupid minds the reality of their absolute dependence on him for sustenance, and snuffed out hostility. Once again, he loomed in their imagination as the mai-baap, one who bestowed not only food and medicine, but the very breath in their bodies. The scourge also effectively destroyed the sense of vulnerability as well as the indecisiveness which plagued the planter.

The stirring events of Bihguri had touched Bircha but lightly, like the soft autumn breeze which fans the cheeks without leaving its imprint behind. The ordeal he had undergone cleansed his soul of the hellfire which had previously burnt inside and threatened to consume it. Strong passions yet burned within the coolie youth. But, unlike former days, these were not the fires of hate, but of love. They gave his thoughts maturity, his bearings a dignity and his movements an infinite gentleness. That a mere slip of a girl whose body had not yet filled out, whose eyes yet retained an elfin innocence, could work such a change in him seemed to Bircha to be the biggest wonder of all. Never before had such powerful emotions throbbed in him; not even the recollection of Meghu could arouse such sensations. And she had reciprocated; not with silly infatuation, but with a fierce, possessive passion worthy of his own turbulent love.

Bircha had refused to leave Bihguri; he felt that if he left now he might be betraying the memsahib who had given him renewed life, and the sarkari sahib who had thrown a shield of protection around him. Had not the sarkari sahib said that he would visit Bihguri again?

Let the sarkari sahib pay his visit. Bircha would thank him for his kindness and concern. He would talk about Saoni and request him to convince the shaitan to let the girl leave Bihguri with him. Then, and only then, would he depart and go straight to the farishta memsahib in the other garden. She had spoken of a wonderful man who lived in another place called Sivasagar. Bircha would request her to send the two of them of that wonderful man who would help them start a new life.

Thus, as the days were on, Bircha wove his dreams. Most of the coolies were by now aware of the relationship between him and Saoni. But, apart from Sanatan and Lachmi, and of course mago herself, none knew of the fever which burned in the two, the hunger that perpetually lay in them. Yet, despite their cravings, each had shown the other their pyaar through words and gestures, not with the body. That would come, but only after they were wedded. Yes, after he received permission to take Saoni away with him he would marry her. And then they would turn their backs on Bihguri.

The death of the saplings had atrophied not only Bailin's hopes, but also his will. He had shied away from working in the fields. 'What's the damn use, Garo?' he had asked. 'Let our kismet clean up the muck, while we rest for a change!'

With tenacious loyalty Garo had endeavoured to pull his master out of this melancholia, playing down the disaster, encouraging him to make one more effort, keenly aware that only unthinking physical toil could keep the sahib afloat. His persistence paid off, and the sahib had reluctantly agreed. Through those rain-filled days they had continued to toil, the empty garden taunting at the futility of their labours. As the rains lessened in intensity and spells of sunshine lengthened, the jungle's onslaught grew less strong. The clearing had been preserved—but to what purpose? Perhaps to preserve their sanity, Garo thought.

'Can't you ask Barua dangoriya for money, sahib?' It was less a question, more of a suggestion. 'He's a rich man. He can lend you five thousand rupees.'

'I'm my worst enemy, Garo,' Bailin said. 'I don't know what's inside me. Pride, perhaps? Or shall we call it vanity? Whatever it is, it makes me baulk at asking Barua dangoriya for money.'

'There are others who can lend you money, sahib,' Garo insisted. 'I've heard Marwari traders at Jorehaut lend money.'

'May be. But they'll demand heavy interest. And collaterals.'

'How about the land-deed, sahib? Can that not be given as collateral?'

'I suppose I can do that. Let the rains cease altogether. Then I'll go to Titabar and speak to Barua dangoriya about it.'

They had all departed, one by one, from her life. No sooner was she drawn to an individual in a meaningful relationship—even such innocuous beings as Bapu babu or Kamal—he or she departed, leaving her defenceless against the solitude.

David had pleaded with her to try to get Bapu babu and the tea makers back to the garden but she did not heed his pleas. Rather, she derived satisfaction from the innumerable problems he was beginning to face in Bapu babu's absence. Let him realize for himself how indispensable that thin little Assamese had been to the smooth running of Dhanboa! Let him sink into the quagmire of his egocentric ingratitude! Cordelia would not throw him as much as a straw!

Apart from maintaining the garden records and expense sheet, Bapu babu had carried out scores of chores. It had been Bapu babu who had fetched provisions for the coolies from Jorehaut. It had been he who had doled out their weekly rations, punctiliously keeping records of the amount which had to be deducted from the cumulative pay of each household. Fetching the mail, going to Kokilamukh for purchase of European goods from steamers in transit, arranging for import of medicine, keeping a strict watch on garden property to prevent theft—David had so much to be grateful for! When the dry season set in her brother was sure to try and get another bormohori. But no matter who he acquired, the new entrant would be a poor substitute for the loquacious, honest, Bapu babu.

She felt Kamal's absence equally keenly. The boy had been quiet and intelligent, a quick learner, eager to please. She missed his cheerful 'good morning' and his warm smile. To David he and Bapu babu may have been mere employees of the garden. To her they were much more. They had played a vital role in filling up her life with their affection and goodwill. David had thoughtlessly put paid to that!

As for her work in the dispensary, Kamal's absence had not inconvenienced her unduly. Though David had stopped his morning visits since the day Bircha was taken away, his invisible presence in the dispensary continued to haunt the workers, and not many turned up. She periodically inspected the basti and was satisfied with what she saw. The surroundings had become slushy, but that was inevitable. The hutments, however, remained comparatively dry and healthy. But, most pertinent, her efforts at educating the coolies into hygienic living had paid off.

The workers of Dhanboa had become extremely health conscious. All through the rains there had been only two cases which merited some anxiety, both malarial attacks, quickly cured with quinine. Also, youngsters continued to have attacks of diarrhoea, but none of a severe nature.

Yet, both physically and emotionally, she was drifting away from the coolies. Here too David was the cause. He had not kept his pledge to drive them less hard after the replanting ended. Once the rains came heavily down, he had set them to work with even greater vengeance. These days they were at the fields or the tea houses from dawn to dusk. She hardly got to see them, let alone mix and talk with them. No more Sunday breaks, when they could turn to petty domestic chores, or sit around her talking of their hopes and fears, or dance the jhumur in the evening. David had not only erected a wall between himself and her; by denying her contact with the coolies he had effectively cut her off from them. This, in turn, had lessened the faith and trust she had forged.

Yes, one by one they had left, leaving her defenceless. She too was wilting as Papa had wilted, though only in mind and soul. After Papa's death she had built up her defences layer by layer against this hopeless loneliness but David had taken her meanings away. He had destroyed the barriers she had built, till nothing remained to shield her.

David had a powerful ally in the rains which poured and poured, hour after hour, day after day, week after week. There was nowhere to go and no one to talk to. The euphoria of her success with Bircha was sucked into nothingness by the immense void of futility made more unbearable by David's tormenting presence.

Sitting alone on the verandah, she would summon Mongla to sit beside her on a murrah and let him tell her of the goings on in the basti. She talked at length to Pekoe—of her childhood, of Papa and Khan, Tulsi and Putlibai, of her friends of yesteryears, of Mildred and Catherine who had disappeared on the very day of the sepoy assault on Delhi, cut down in the first flush of youth and thrown into some nullah; of Constance, Marianne and others who had survived; of Mr Darley, who tutored her and David in Delhi; of Samrat, her very first pony and Puffy, her very first puppy. Pekoe was an attentive listener, ears alert and tongue lolling out of his mouth, looking at her with eyes full of understanding. Sometimes, when Mongla could not be disturbed and Pekoe slumbered, she talked to herself, telling out loudly not to forget to perform some task or the other as though such utterances would help memory, wondering aloud if the rains would ever stop. Occasionally she talked to inanimate things like her dress when taken out for airing or the flower vase which almost slipped out of her hands while being cleaned. And, without fail, alone in her room at night after the candle had been put out and the mosquito curtain draped, she talked to God, asking him for guidance and strength.

The lessening of the rains brought about renewed optimism; spells of sunshine made her believe the worst was over. Autumn would ensure the dissipation of despair and winter would become the season of hope! On the morning of the second of August David left for Kokilamukh. The tea chests were carried out from the tea house, loaded onto two *maar-naos* and covered over with waterproof sheets. By mid-morning the loading of the boats was completed and they had set off, David leaving in a smaller boat laden with tents and other paraphernalia for camping out. Cordelia donned her Jodhpurs, brought Souchong out and, with Pekoe alongside, rode out into the fields.

The coolies were at work. Heads turned quizzically as she rode by, like cattle on riverbank looking up at a passing boat; the men offered salutations, the women shy smiles. She summoned Robiya. The sirdar came running up.

'I'm countermanding the sahib's order,' she told him. 'The coolielog will have chutti for this afternoon and the next two days.' She did not wait for the sirdar's response and addressed the coolies. '*Coolielog, Tum kaam chor sakte ho*. Go back to your basti. I've given you chutti for today and the next two days.'

But the coolies stood unmoving, confusion pasted upon their features. Though the prospect of chutti was welcome, they were not too sure whether to take up the memsahib's offer. She meant well, no doubt. But she no longer had the ears of the sahib. And, in truth, they had grown afraid of the young sahib.

But the confusion on their faces was nothing compared to that on Robiya's young visage! He was a picture of utter dismay.

'Memsahib, what are you saying? Sahib will be very angry. He … he will eat me alive, memsahib!'

'Your sahib can go rot in hell, Robiya,' Cordelia cried. 'I'm giving you a command. Don't you dare disobey me.'

Cordelia spoke again, her voice high pitched. '*Suno*, coolielog. You've been working too hard the past few months. I am giving you chutti now. Go back to your basti. Do not worry. No evil will befall you.'

Her words made up the coolies' minds for them. They picked up their tokris and other implements and departed. Soon work at the tea houses also stopped.

She rode to the basti that evening and watched the coolies prepare to celebrate their unexpected reprieve. The salutations she received had the cheer as of old. The drums, pipes and cymbals, which had ceased to fill up Dhanboa's air with lilting melodies, were unstrung from walls and dusted. Coolie chokris tried on their jhumkas around delicate ankles. Men folk counted their stock of mod and replenished it if required from the brewer. The children were infected with the gaiety that touched their elders. They frolicked in the mud and dust without a care in the world.

It was a scene reminiscent of her very first visit to the basti. Not one to cheat herself, Cordelia tried to analyse her unrestrained delight at the sight. There was an element of ambiguity to the happiness which overwhelmed her—it was not the unsullied offspring of altruistic goodness. There was a negative triumph to her emotions; her happiness sprang out of a sense of hurt, the feelings of a suppressed creature when an opportunity to hit back comes. She was truthful enough to concede that she was happy not only because she had snatched for the coolies some moments of respite, but also because she had cocked a snook at her brother. But her awareness induced no compunction in her—that too was an index of the extent to which she herself had changed.

The maar-naos returned that very evening. The following morning the crafts were loaded with the remaining tea chests. Sure enough, Robiya made the trip to Kokilamukh to apprise the sahib of the goings on at Dhanboa. Cordelia was not bothered. Let David come. He would find she was more than a match for him.

David reached Kokilamukh in the afternoon and made enquiries at the sizeable godown of the Jorehaut Tea Company for space to store his tea chests. He was gratified to find that the Cinnamora assistant, Nicholls, had arrived an hour before with boatloads of his plantation's produce. Nicholls was glad to help out—a corner of the vast shed of corrugated iron was allotted to David. The maar-naos were unloaded and the tea chests transported safely. While David stayed back at the ghat, his boats set out on their return journey to Dhanboa for a second trip.

Tents were pitched on a sandy clearing a little away from the Brahmaputra, swollen with the rains in this season. The same afternoon two more planters arrived and the area, with tents set up and fires got going, began to resemble an army encampment. The arrival of the planters made the evening a pleasant occasion—whisky was downed, notes exchanged and off-season activities discussed.

As was to be expected, the conversation soon veered round to Cordelia. The planters, particularly Nicholls, were very interested in knowing how the young girl was taking to Assam. They were astonished to learn that she was doing the doctoring in the garden, and even more astounded that Dhanboa did not have a solitary coolie death during the monsoons.

His stunning revelation that Dhanboa had been untouched by what was universally deemed as the inevitable monsoon deaths pricked the curiosity of the others; they were eager to learn if such an unusual phenomenon was coincidence or had something more substantial behind it. David, gratified at being listened to by planters of greater experience, was more than pleased to enumerate what 'he' had attempted at his plantation.

Five more planters arrived the next morning, each escorting a fleet of boats, and set up camp. Soon the boats of the four who had arrived the previous day returned with tea loads; the maar-naos of David were the last to reach. If David was surprised at the presence of Robiya among the crew of his boats, he gave no indication to the fellow planters. But, at the first opportunity, he drew his sirdar aside and asked him why he had left his post. Robiya apprised him of the state of things at Dhanboa. David concealed his fury and asked Robiya to return to the garden on the maarnaos but to do nothing till he got back.

The *Ultaganga* hove into view early on the afternoon of the fourth. By then more planters, coolies and tea chests had poured into the spot and these, along with the locals who had arrived on hearing the steamer's blaring siren, lent it the appearance of a crowded mela. There was much confusion, and it required the appearance of the tall and stately Salim Ali and his stentorian appeal for calm to restore some semblance of order. Finally, Captain McClintock made his appearance, face creased and rubicund as ever, the ubiquitous briar emitting foul smoke. He was accompanied by two bowler-hatted gentlemen who turned out to be agents of the insurance firm affiliated to the Indian General Navigation Steam Company.

A table and chairs were arranged for the agents beneath the shamiana and the paperwork commenced, the planters displaying some urgency to have their tea chests registered and insured.

For the next hour David remained engaged in completing these formalities and supervising the loading of the tea chests. There were more convivalities in the evening. When David awoke the following morning, the *Ultaganga* was gone. There being nothing to keep him at Kokilamukh any longer so he left for Dhanboa.

Nothing had changed in the garden. The coolies were in the fields, the tea house fires were alight, the air filled with the pleasant aroma of freshly made tea. Knowing, as she did, he would return that day, Cordelia had put the coolies back to work. David did not react in the manner she had presumed he would and accordingly prepared herself to confront him. He carried on as if nothing had happened. He totally ignored Cordelia and did not allow her the luxury of a quarrel.

Only when the week came to an end did Cordelia discover that her brother, with guile which would have done Buckingham proud, had deftly out-manoeuvred her. At the weekly payment of wages, he announced that since the coolies had taken unauthorised chutti for three days, he was deducting six annas from the wages they would receive for the week.

With the same air of munificence, he further announced that in future the coolielog were free to take chutti whenever the memsahib felt like giving it to them, but two annas per day would be deducted from their wages. If they felt this was unfair, they could complain to the memsahib, and ask her to recompense them!

Finally, towards end August, Bailin left in the company of Garo and Meghu for Titabar. Whatever misgivings the Lieutenant had harboured were swept away by the warmth of Barua dangoriya's welcome. And, indeed, his host could help out with a loan.

'There's a merchant at Jorehaut … a Marwari trader by the name of Hazarimal. A word from me and he'll give as much loan as you might seek.'

Then, much to the Lieutenant's surprise, Gokuldeva Barua added: 'But, Michael, I do not give my aid freely. I must set a price on my generosity. You've a commodity which I am desperate to make my own.'

'Name it, and it shall be yours.'

'Meghu! I must have Meghu!'

Bailin laughed. 'But, my dear Barua dangoriya, I was going to request you to keep him! He's an absconder from Bihguri. Basic humanity dictates that he be not repatriated to the inferno whence he made good his escape.'

'I am in complete agreement with you on that, Michael. But there's something in my mind … a nebulous notion. The esteem I hold for you requires I tell you of my scheme. After that you can decide whether to put Meghu in my hands.'

Gokuldeva's features turned hard, his voice grew animated. The Lieutenant listened.

'Enormous impediments were placed on my path when I opened out Mohoniya. The European planters were up in arms against me. I continue to be a thorn in their flesh. Major Gosselin has quite a few memoranda and petitions against me. But recently they've begun to concoct lies. A few days back I had a missive from Captain Hewitt. I realize you do not like him … but trust my judgement, he's a decent individual … far better than Major Gosselin. Hewitt informs me that European planters have brought charges against me. They have accused me of luring away coolies from their plantations to serve in mine. Inciting neighbouring villagers to destroy seedlings in their nurseries … half a dozen similar, dastardly lies! I shall be paying a visit to Jorehaut to refute these charges.'

'You feel there's more than meets the eye?'

'Yes. A stridently fresh offensive! No more memorandums filled with solicitations to the administration. They're sharpening their knives. They mean business this time!'

'Is Buckingham behind all this?' Bailin spat.

'He's not alone. European planters in this region, with very few exceptions, have lent voice to the campaign. But Buckingham's the prime mover. He is the strategist.'

'For heaven's sake, Barua dangoriya!' the Lieutenant cried out. 'You must back off! You're a well-to-do man, respected in your society, trusted by the administration. Mohoniya would neither add to your stature, nor to your wealth. Don't fight the might of British commerce for something you have no need for.'

'Knowing me as you do, would you advise me thus, Michael?'

It was not the implied reproof in the words but the tone in which they were uttered that chilled Bailin's blood. It was the ton of a man who had made an irrevocable decision, and had strengthened himself to face the consequences. The Lieutenant could already see the rope-marks around his throat!

He lunged out of his chair, stepped closer to the seated nobleman, knelt and took his gnarled, bony hands. 'Think again, Barua dangoriya, I beseech you! For God's sake, don't let this evening be a prelude to the making of a martyr!'

The old man's hands tightened around his. There was nothing frail about the grip; some of the unfathomable strength which lay in Gokuldeva flowed into his own heart.

'Have no fear for me, Michael,' Gokuldeva said softly. 'When I strike, I shall do so with the stealth and swiftness of a jungle cat. But strike I must. The planters have to be warned where to draw the line.'

'Will Meghu be a part of your scheme?'

'A vital part, Michael. I'll not burden your conscience any more by divulging my plan. But rest assured that without Meghu it will not be possible to carry it out. Well, after having learnt why I want Meghu, would you still trust him in my hands?'

Lieutenant Michael Bailin hesitated, then laughed uneasily. 'To be candid, I feel no revulsion at what you contemplate. On the contrary, I detect pleasure inside me, tinged with anxiety.'

'At possible danger to myself? Rest easy, dear Michael. I shall proceed with great caution. Now, can I take it that you give Meghu without a prick of conscience?'

'Certainly. May he prove to be Mohoniya's saviour!'

'A sentiment I whole-heartedly share with you. So, you see, Michael, I am obligated to you for bringing him here and wish to do something for you to return the favour.'

The Lieutenant laughed. 'The Marwari trader?' he asked.

'Yes. Hazarimal. I'll put you in touch with him. A week from now I depart for Jorehaut to face my inquisitor. I shall call on you at Chahpuli and take you along. Will that suit you?'

'That would suit me nicely, Barua dangoriya. But do take care how you tread. I am most anxious for you.'

'I told you I am a survivor. I have survived the Burmese barbarians … I have survived the British. So, you needn't worry. I'll survive Christopher James Buckingham and his breed!'

In the afternoon, after his guest had departed, Gokuldeva Barua summoned Meghu and questioned him closely about the plantation from which he had made such a dramatic escape. He learnt of Buckingham's ruthless treatment of his sizeable workforce and the intense disaffection bordering on naked hatred which lay in the coolies. But helpless as they were against the power and resources of their Lord and Master, they could do nothing to translate the hatred into action.

What if they were assured of outside help? Would that put some fire into them—enough to make them defy their oppressors and secure concessions for themselves?

Meghu was cautions. What did the *devta ishwar* have in mind? Disobedience? Refusal to work unless meted out more humane treatment? Meghu could not assure him on that. As he had said, the coolielog were a castrated lot. But there was more to it than that. The coolielog were the poorest of the poor. Even a week of idleness would entail starvation. How could they refuse to work and starve to death?

Suppose the coolielog received adequate money to see each household through a month of not being paid wages? Suppose Meghu himself took the money to them? Would they then have courage to shy away from work?

A sly look appeared on Meghu's awry visage. Yes, if assured that the needs of the belly would be taken care of, the coolielog might summon up the gumption to defy their master. But unless one talked it out with them, nothing could be guaranteed.

Would Meghu himself steal back to the hell hole and discuss the matter with the coolielog?

To Gokuldeva's amazement, Meghu wasted not a moment in replying. Why Bihguri? Meghu was willing to enter *jahannam* if it would harm the Bihguri sahib! But he must be sure of two things—that his going to Bihguri would cause incalculable harm to the shaitan. And, at the same time, would not bring further misery upon the wretched coolielog.

Could Meghu keep a secret close to his chest? Meghu insisted he could.

Gokuldeva's scheme was shrewd and simple. Meghu must pay a visit to Bihguri to sound out a few trusted coolies about the offer. On no account must he intimate where the offer came from. Meghu must tell the coolielog that a benefactor, who wishes to remain nameless, horrified at the brutal treatment being meted out to them and wanting to better their lot, was making them an offer. They must strike work for a prolonged period till the Bihguri sahib promised to mend his ways. In return the benefactor would pay them two weeks' wages in advance, and weekly advances thereafter as long as the idleness lasts. Meghu must go to Bihguri and return to make his report. If his report was positive, he must hie once again to Bihguri at the opportune moment with the money to organize things at that end.

The fixed smile on the absconder's face widened into a lopsided grin as he listened, and nodded.

Meghu was put up in the servants' quarters. The very next day a Mohammedan bonesetter arrived at the mansion in response to Gokuldeva's summons. The man pushed his fingers into Meghu's mouth, grabbed the upper denture with an upraised left palm and the lower with his right, and gave a mighty twirl. There was an audible crack. Meghu grunted in agony and would most certainly have bitten off the bonesetter's fingers had his grip not been firm enough. But the pain lasted just a fraction of a second; when the man withdrew his fingers from the mouth, Meghu's features had undergone a wondrous transformation. The jaws were aligned once more, though the nose remained bent and flattened. Someone brought a small looking glass. Meghu took one look at the mirror, saw his face restored, and scampered around the courtyard, whooping in joy.

On the third night he was transported in a small canoe to Bihguri. He had expected difficulty in arousing Sanatan. But, surprisingly, his first taps on the bamboo door of Sanatan's hut evoked a response. 'Lachmi, is it you? Why do you tap on the door? It's open.' There was no sleepiness in the voice, though the words were tired.

'Sanatan bhaiya! It's me, Meghu! I've returned. Light a diya. I've important things to discuss with you.'

Sanatan lit the earthen lamp. Meghu entered, shutting the door behind him. Sanatan's two children lay fast asleep on the floor. He fixed Meghu with a puzzled, fearful look.

'Your face? What has happened to your face?'

'It has been set right. It's really me. Here, feel my arms. I'm truly alive.'

Sanatan rose to his feet and hugged Meghu in a fiercely loving embrace.

'Where's Lachmi bahen?'

'The bastard has summoned her tonight. That's why I'm awake.'

Meghu put an arm across the elder man's shoulders. 'We'll bring all this to an end, Sanatan bhaiya. Listen to what I have to say. I won't be staying long.'

Quickly he recapitulated the sequence of events which began the night he and Bircha made their bid for freedom. Now he had found a patron, a rich and powerful man. Meghu had vowed to keep the individual's identity a secret. This man has offered to help the coolielog of Bihguri. Meghu explained what the coolielog were expected to do.

'Is this man to be trusted?'

'I'll trust him with my life, Sanatan bhaiya. He tells me he is moved by the suffering of Bihguri's coolies. But I think there is more to it. I feel he hates the sahib as much as you and I … that he wishes to strike at the bastard through us.'

'He's trying to use us. You must realize that.'

'Perhaps so. But does it matter? We too can use him to finish off the shaitan!'

'From what you tell me, your rich and influential benefactor wants us to stop working. Bihguri will suffer loss, no doubt. But the shaitan will not be finished.'

'Ah!' exclaimed the visitor, a craftiness entering into his voice. 'Here our aims differ, Sanatan bhaiya … our benefactor's, and yours and mine. He wishes us to stop working. From what I could make out, that is to be a warning. But our objective goes beyond that … when the coolielog stops working, lots of things will happen. There will be great excitement. There will be violence. Perhaps, who knows, in the violence and the excitement, we might find the opportunity to finish the bastard off?'

Some time elapsed before Sanatan spoke again. 'The consequences will be severe, you realize that?'

'That is true. *Par socho*, Sanatan *bhaiya*. Is the life the coolielog lead now worth living? Yes, there'll be great suffering. But aren't the coolielog suffering now? If we can finish off the bastard, would we not ourselves be serving a warning? Ill-treat the coolielog, and your life is not worth a lump of cow-dung! Might not the suffering of a few bring about salvation for the many?'

Sanatan nodded. 'Perhaps greater good might come out of what you contemplate. Too long have we borne the sahib's cruelty. We must strike back. But this is not the proper time.'

'I know that. But these things have to be well thought out in advance. I'll carry back my report to my patron. We'll plan out everything and strike when the time is ripe. Now tell me, how are things at Bihguri?'

Sanatan related what had transpired in Bihguri the past few months. The lot of the coolielog had deteriorated further. The scourge had paid its annual visit, taking its quota of human sacrifice. The sahib had succeeded in instilling the deepest dread in the hearts of the coolielog. 'They shift between despair and defiance, Meghu-bhaiya.'

'But can we not use that despair to strengthen the defiance? Especially with outside help?'

'It can be done. But for that they need a person they can rally around. Someone to lead them.'

'Is there such a man amongst the coolielog?'

'Yes. Bircha. Perhaps you can persuade him.'

Meghu looked hard at the elderly coolie, utterly bewildered. 'But … but, Bircha is dead!' he stuttered.

'Huh! *Tum jaante nahin ho*?' Oh, of course you wouldn't know. Bircha is not dead. He lives. He's in Bihguri right now.'

'Bircha! My dost! Bircha! Alive!' He gripped Sanatan by the shoulders. 'Take me to him. Oh, Sanatan bhaiya, I've lain awake many a night thinking of Bircha. I believed he was dead. He was in two minds about escape since he saw that chokri … Saoni. It's I who persuaded him to abscond. I thought I'd killed him! We must go to him at once.'

'Wait,' said Sanatan, restraining the excited Meghu. 'Bircha lives. But he has suffered more than any man can withstand. That has completely changed him. He's not the same Bircha you knew.'

Sanatan told Meghu the Bircha's story and how his ordeal had made him a bahadur amongst the coolielog. If anyone could instill courage into the coolielog and rid them of their dread of the sahib, it was Bircha. But, twice on the brink of death, Bircha's attitudes had changed completely. All he was interested in was Saoni. He doubted whether even Meghu could persuade him to take up the coolielog's cause.

'Nothing has changed,' Meghu said with confidence. 'He'll listen to me. I'm his friend … his brother. Come, we must go to him.'

The two stole out to Bircha's hutment. He expressed neither surprise nor asked questions on seeing Meghu. He stepped up and caught his former companion in a fierce hug. They had a great deal to talk about. Sanatan squatted patiently on the floor and heard them chatter away. Meghu was weeping openly in his joy, but Bircha's eyes were dry.

Sanatan was right. This was not the Bircha of yore, the impulsive, headstrong, impatient Bircha, filled with fire and hatred. There was a gentle passivity in his words, an innocent wisdom, which Meghu found appealing yet somewhat daunting. In earlier times Meghu had been the dominant partner and Bircha had looked to him for guidance. But now Meghu found himself listening to Bircha, as if he were an acolyte before a guru. As they talked, his confidence of being able to persuade Bircha evaporated.

'You'll have to leave me out of it,' was Bircha's response when Meghu finally put it up to him. '*Dekho*, Meghu-bhaiya, do I not deserve my moment of contentment? Nothing seems to matter anymore but Saoni's love. I have emerged unburned form the fires of narak. Would you, my friend, ask me to plunge into those fires again?'

'The joys of vengeance are far greater than the joys of pyaar,' Meghu said with all the intensity he could muster. 'Think of the coolielog, Bircha-bhaiya. Think of how much they've suffered at the hands of the sahib. Believe me, the joy you shall feel when your fingers are around the white bastard's neck will be a thousand times greater than can be provided by many Saonis.'

'You feel that way because you haven't felt the force of love, Meghu-bhaiya. I've made up my mind. Let the sarkari sahib come. I'll have him persuade the Bihguri sahib to let Saoni leave with me. We two will then travel far away to a better life. For god's sake, Meghu-bhaiya … if you love me, do not try to rob me of this dream!'

'Where will you go? As long as the Bihguri sahib is alive, he'll seek you out … no matter where you are or how far you are … and sink his deadly fangs into you and Saoni.'

'He cannot,' Bircha said with complete conviction. 'The memsahib at Dhanboa has promised to send me to such a place where the Bihguri sahib cannot touch me.'

'They are both white! All white-skinned log are bastards. Their promises are not worth a cowry-shell!'

'No. You're wrong. There are good people among them, just as there are evil people among us.'

Meghu finally conceded defeat. 'Sanatan bhaiya spoke the truth. You've changed.'

'You're not angry with me?'

'*Arey, nahin dost*! I'm happy for you.'

He hugged Bircha, a brief but fierce embrace. Then he and Sanatan slipped quietly out of the hutment, leaving Bircha alone with his dreams.

The two stopped in front of Sanatan's cottage. 'I'm sorry I cannot wait for Lachmi bahen's return,' Meghu said in parting. 'Tell her what I've told you. Now that Bircha is out, you'll have to do the job. Handpick some trusted coolielog and tell them of the plan. Through them fuel the hatred in the coolies till it overrides their fear. Prepare the ground well, so we can sow the seeds of revenge!'

'I'll do that, Meghu-bhaiya. When will you return?'

'I cannot tell. But I shall return, never fear.' The two embraced and Meghu was gone.

Gokuldeva Barua arrived at Chahpuli early in the morning of 7 September, at the head of a huge elephant-caravan, accompanied by a score of retainers. Bailin was offered the seat beside the nobleman, Garo was accommodated on another elephant, and the party left for Jorehaut.

The Assamese nobleman conversed animatedly with the Lieutenant. He was travelling in such a grand procession, he explained, to remind all and sundry that he was a man to be reckoned with. Let those who see his caravan know that he was no resourceless coolie or timid yokel. If someone sought to antagonize him without cause, he did so at his own peril.

Bailin asked the old man about Meghu. But, apart from an enigmatic reply that Meghu was well, the nobleman vouchsafed nothing, and quickly changed the subject towards the loan which the Lieutenant sought. He had already sent a messenger to the Marwari trader named Hazarimal requesting a loan of four thousand rupees for Michael at an annual interest of eight hundred rupees. Michael must visit the Marwari's shop and collect the money.

They were at Jorehaut by three in the afternoon. The caravan paused at the crossroad beside the bazaar for Bailin and Garo to disembark before continuing on its way. Thanks to Gokuldeva Barua, the loan was given without any hassle.

'How are you going to convey the bags to your garden, huzoor?' Hazarimal Babu asked. 'They weigh quite a lot. Also, it's dangerous to travel unescorted with so much money.'

'Barua dangoriya's haathi is being sent to fetch us. Kindly see if it has arrived.'

Hazarimal bawled to a shop assistant to step out and see if an elephant had arrived for the sahib. The youth returned and answered in the affirmative. The leather bags were lifted up and Bailin and Garo mounted. As the beast set off the mahout handed over a slip of paper to Bailin. It was a note from Captain Hewitt. 'Much obliged if you can come over to my place,' it read.

'An apology is called for on my part,' Captain Ralph Hewitt said.

The Lieutenant was surprised, and greatly relieved. The officer's greeting had been cordial. And now here was an apology—the last thing Bailin expected!

'I'm conscious I behaved somewhat officiously when I met you at Chahpuli,' Hewitt continued. 'My plea is I was misinformed about you.'

'And now you're better informed?' Bailin asked with asperity.

The captain took no offence. 'You must forgive me, dear fellow. What I'd heard about you put notions in my mind.'

'Since you've condescended to apologize, captain, apparently something has occurred to change those perceptions. May I enquire as to what did occur?'

They were seated on the verandah of Hewitt's bungalow. Gokuldeva Barua was in another chair, unobtrusively, as though a mere spectator, with no role in the exchanges.

'I had the good fortune of encountering an individual for whom I've developed the highest regards. A lady in the truest sense of the term.'

'Miss Esscombe?' A wariness crept involuntarily into the Lieutenant. He stiffened.

'Yes. Her faith in you is irrefragable. At first, I presumed womanly sympathy to be the cause. But her attachment to you turned out to be deeper. Nor was she ignorant of your past, though she didn't enlighten me as to what exactly you'd done. She, however, left me in no doubt of the depth of emotion she cherished for you.'

A wave of bewildered yearning swept through the Lieutenant, reflecting in his eyes. Hewitt saw it and sighed.

'Well, Lieutenant Bailin, I've come to learn of the secret of your past only today. Yes, from Barua dangoriya. Believe me, Lieutenant, had I been in your shoes I would've acted as you'd done. That's why I must apologise.'

'No need, no need,' Bailin said distractedly, his mind not concentrated on the officer.

'Tell me, Lieutenant Bailin, why have you not attempted to renew acquaintance with Miss Esscombe? She cherishes you deeply. By your strong reaction to my words, you've shown you regard her as someone much more than a mere acquaintance. Yet you do not make the slightest endeavour to get in touch?'

'Didn't Barua dangoriya tell you?' The words emerged with difficulty.

'Tell me? Tell me what?'

'That I wrote to Dhanboa. A letter sent through my personal messenger. I wished to visit Dhanboa... David sent a written reply. It wouldn't be convenient for some time, was what the letter said. It wouldn't be convenient for eternity, was what the letter implied!'

'She never saw that letter!'

'I told you so, Michael,' Gokuldeva, for the first time, intruded into the conversation.

'Yes, Barua dangoriya. I misinterpreted, didn't I? Miss Esscombe may not have been present when Garo delivered the letter to David. But I took for granted that he showed it to her when she returned. Are you telling me, captain, that David did not show her my letter at all?'

'Does look so, doesn't it? Also, Miss Esscombe had asked me to drop in at Chahpuli and warn you about Naga rebels. But, while seeing me off at the ghat, her brother told me you were a mere shipboard companion and not to mention him or her to you.'

'David is not behind such skullduggery.' Gokuldeva insisted. 'Buckingham's somehow involved. Take my word for it.'

'Perhaps so,' Bailin said. 'I imagined she had read my letter. When no further communications were made, I considered myself unwelcome. Tell me, Captain Hewitt, how is ... is ... Miss Esscombe?'

'I wish I could say she was fine, Lieutenant Bailin. But the truth is she's desperately unhappy at Dhanboa. And extremely lonely.' The intensity with which the officer spoke alerted Bailin that more than compassionate disinterestedness lay in the man.

'Her father's death must have been a crushing blow.'

'Undoubtedly. Also, her brother's indifference.'

'David! Oh, but that cannot be, Captain Hewitt. I spent a month with them aboard the *Ultaganga*. The two of them were welded with unbreakable bonds.'

'Those bonds have loosened. She and her brother tread different paths.'

'If we can't change the system, the system will change us,' said Bailin bleakly.

'I do not understand, Lieutenant.'

'Nothing. Just a phrase uttered by a wise and perspicacious individual a long time ago. Poor girl! Her father dead, her brother estranged! Not a friend in whom she can confide!' He attempted to keep his voice neutral.

'An extraordinary lady … Miss Esscombe! She willfully chose the lonely environs of a plantation because she had set objectives before her. I've been privileged to assist her in a humble way.'

He told Bailin of Cordelia's attempts to better the lot of Dhanboa's coolies and how she had saved the life of one, an absconder from Bihguri. The Lieutenant, once more the master of his emotions, listened, his blue eyes shutting out from the others' view the love and longing coursing through each vein, each sinew of his body.

'The magic of Miss Esscombe's personality lies in the undeviating passion which she puts into what she believes is right, just and humane. Should such an individual be subjected to pain, Lieutenant Bailin? She is hurting, I tell you! Her brother … beset by his own compulsions … not only refuses to concede the validity of her objectives, but is putting hindrances in her way. Is it not the duty of those who understand and cherish her to take her away from the lonely futility of her existence?'

The officer paused, weighing the effect of his appeal on the man before him.

'You're in love with her, aren't you, Captain Hewitt?'

The question, unexpected, made Hewitt snap his head back as though Bailin had jabbed at him. But he recovered quickly.

'If I am, it's immaterial. She has given her heart to you, Lieutenant Bailin. You, and you alone, can end her misery. For God's sake, Lieutenant, if you have a spark of compassion in you, claim her as your own and make her happy.'

'There're realities, Captain Hewitt, which cannot be ignored.' Bailin's voice was cold and emotionless. 'My life too is barren if Miss Esscombe is evicted from it. Yet I must evict her. My present circumstances leave me with no choice.'

'Don't say that, Michael!' Gokuldeva cried out. 'I will help. We all will.'

'Yes. Lieutenant,' Hewitt spoke with equal conviction. 'I shall do all in my power to assist you. For her sake … as well as yours.'

'No, Captain Hewitt.' Bailin's features retained their inflexibility. 'Do not forget … I left Miss Esscombe before I knew Chahpuli was not the thriving plantation I'd thought it was. I ran away from her not because I was a pauper, but because I'd become a pariah in the eyes of fellow Englishmen. It's to her interest to stay as far away from me as possible.'

'She's a lady of strong attachments. Would you, knowingly, condemn her to lifelong solitude? That would be a betrayal beyond forgiveness!'

'I too am a man of strong attachments, Captain Hewitt. No other woman will occupy the seat where Miss Esscombe lies ensconced in my heart. But betrayal? Would it not be a betrayal of my love if I entice her into my arms again?'

'Trust me, Lieutenant. I'm fully cognizant of your dilemma. My concern for Miss Esscombe made me frame my appeal to you. I appreciate the qualms you harbour. Yet something needs to be done! But I can't for the life of me think what we can do.'

'Is there any possibility you might meet Miss Esscombe in the near future?'

'Oh, yes,' the officer said eagerly. 'I have a visit to make to Bihguri … to ensure Bircha is all right. Then to Miss Esscombe to reassure her. I'd promised her that.'

'I beg you to tell her of the constraints which shackle me. Convince her I can never be hers.'

'Thereby enhancing her torment, Lieutenant?'

'Anguish is not only the child of despair, Captain Hewitt. It can also be the offspring of hope. If she suffers, it is because she harbours vain hopes. Cauterize those hopes, and she'll suffer no longer. Time will heal the wound. Perhaps someone else will fill up the emptiness in her … someone such as you!'

'Me?' The officer, incapable of dissimulation, could not conceal the hope surging in his own bosom.

'Yes, you! You've everything I cannot offer. You can provide her with a secure future. She is delicate … like a tea seedling. You have the strength of character which will prop her up. More important, you possess the capacity to love and cherish her as I've done.'

'I regret I misjudged you, Lieutenant,' Hewitt said with feeling.

Bailin attempted a laugh. 'That's been my fate all along … being misjudged! I have no idea what has happened to David. Or why Miss Esscombe is so unhappy. But promise me you'll get her out of Dhanboa. Give her the life she deserves.'

'My pledge on it,' the officer said, offering his hand. Bailin shook it warmly.

'Strange, Captain Hewitt! But I feel happy today as I've never felt for a long time.' Not waiting for a reply from the officer, or from the nobleman, he descended the stairs, to await Barua dangoriya on the lawn in front of the bungalow.

The manufacturing season's closure did not mean an end to the drudgery of the coolies of Dhanboa. David ensured they no longer fell into the idle ways of Papa's days. With the assistance of Harua, Ajam and Robiya, he instilled greater discipline into his workforce. True, he had not hardened enough to mete out the kind of corporal punishment most planters used to deal with 'continued laziness or malingering'. But he had an equally effective instrument in the punitive pay cuts which he regularly imposed on those who failed to complete their allotted tasks on time.

More than ever, he needed a visit from his mentor, Christopher James Buckingham, to reassure him on the anxieties which plagued his inexperienced mind. Over six months had elapsed, but the newly planted saplings had not grown the way he had imagined they would. On the contrary, quite a few of them had withered away, leaving vacant spaces in the rows. But the events concerning the Bihguri absconder had put paid to any possibility that he might get further assistance from Buckingham!

Also, David was determined that at least forty-fifty acres must be opened up and planted this winter, and had planned out his nursery with this in mind. But, without Bapu babu, he found it impossible to find a reliable Naga or Assamese contractor who could do the job for him on the basis of *ticca* hazira or contract work. Therefore, David had perforce to throw his coolies against Dhanboa's eastern flank to hack out additional acres of cultivable land. Not only were the coolies physically unsuited for the task, they also lacked the expertise and experience it required. Cutting down and uprooting the stumps of the huge trees in the jungles was a particularly difficult job. The going was slow and exhausting and David and his sirdars had their hands full keeping the coolies at the job.

He too tried finding a replacement for Bapu babu, but there were no takers. Word had got around the nearby Assamese villages that the management of Dhanboa was not to be trusted and that the plantation's young proprietor was a sadistic savage who enjoyed inflicting fancy tortures on his employees. David could well guess where these rumours sprang from. Clearly, Bapu babu was wreaking revenge!

Slowly, but inexorably, experience was beginning to teach David a thing or two. The coolies now appeared to him to be even more precious than he had ever viewed them. He shuddered to think what might have happened had an epidemic struck Dhanboa and carried some coolies away, as had been the case in most plantations!

He soon conceded he had made a serious mistake in pitting the coolies against the jungles. The realization had come by itself, without Cordi's nagging! Ever since the affair of that Bihguri absconder she had exhibited total unconcern as to what he did; she could not be ignorant that the coolies were being put to the taxing task of jungle clearance, but had not uttered a word. David, of his own volition, back-tracked. He cut down the clearing target by half, telling his sirdars that not more than twenty-five acres needed to be opened up that winter, so they could go easy on the coolies. He reduced the work shift by as much as two hours, but made it clear that this applied only to the 'off season' period. Simultaneously, he declared Sunday to be a chutti day. He also began to take a personal interest in the health of the coolies, especially the toddlers and young ones, whom he considered to be investments for the future.

The nascent reawakening of his concern was not utterly utilitarian. It too was a movement towards rapprochement, for just as his sister had sensed the desolate loneliness of the Assam tea plantation during the rains, he too had been touched by the absence of warmth and companionship. He took particular care to let Cordi know the change in his approach. For a start he refunded the wage cuts inflicted upon his workers and had Mongla communicate the information to her.

But Mongla played the go-between in vain. David discovered in his sister a stone-hard obduracy which brooked no compassion. Formerly a simple sorry was enough to move her into tenderness, but now his indirect approaches were snubbed. This hardened his own stance; he gave up seeking rapprochement and descended into self-pitying anger. Time and again she found him seated on the verandah, a glass of whisky in his hand, a half-empty bottle before him, on his face a darkened scowl of mute fury. She ignored him. Strangely, her indifference seemed to affect him more than her antipathy!

Nicholls dropped in at Dhanboa in the last week of September to invite David for a greener shoot on the fourth of October. He should be at Cinnamora by the third evening. David accepted the invitation with pathetic alacrity. That, Cordelia thought, was a measure of her brother's transformation. In his eagerness he had totally forgotten the significance of the date. It was on the night of October the fourth, a year ago, that Papa had died!

Ralph Hewitt, accompanied by a posse of policemen, journeyed to Bihguri in the first week of October. Once there, he made straight for the basti. As he expected Buckingham arrived on horseback just as he reached Bircha's hutment. He made the planter cool his heels outside while he engaged in a personal conversation with the coolie.

He discovered an unearthly equanimity in the man over whom he had thrown his protective mantle. Bircha did not overwhelm his saviour with expressions of servile gratitude, nor was there arrogance in his demeanour as he answered his queries. Yes, he was content with the life he was leading. No, the sahib had neither touched nor threatened him.

The coolie asked about the farishta memsahib who lived in the other garden. Would the sahib please inform the memsahib that Bircha was well and happy? Hewitt assured him he would. Then, with the candour of a child, Bircha made his request. Now that the sarkari sahib had met Bircha, could he leave the garden?

He could, if he wished to!

However, there was one solicitation Bircha must make to the sarkari sahib. He had pyaar for a garden chokri, the one who had nursed him back to health. Her name was Saoni. He wanted to marry her and take her away with him. But the chokri was contracted to the Bihguri sahib. Would the sarkari sahib talk to the Bihguri sahib and arrange things so that Saoni could leave with him?

Hewitt hesitated. A difficult thing, he told Bircha. He would make the request, but it was up to the sahib to grant or not grant it. The sarkar had no authority to terminate privately made contracts.

Hewitt emerged out of the hut and, without a word to Buckingham, began a fast walk to the planter's bungalow. Only when they were seated on the wicker-chairs of the bungalow verandah did they converse.

'You realize you've put me in a spot, dear fellow,' Buckingham said, but seemingly without rancour. 'By acting the godfather to an absconder, you've encouraged lawlessness. There was an incident in Bihguri when the buggers turned on one of my sirdars and almost killed him. I have a large workforce. More and more it is becoming difficult to keep them under rein. For all you know, tomorrow they might turn on me? I'll know who to blame, then!'

'Terminate his contract, Buckingham. Give him some money and let him leave.'

'I tried it. The bugger wouldn't take the bait. Why should he? He's leading a cozy life, no work, full pay!'

'It's your fault! He wanted work … you wouldn't let him.'

'A matter of principle with me, captain. I'd rather chop down the tea bushes than have that nigger work in my garden!'

'I can provide you a way out of this impasse, if you're willing.'

'Get the bastard out of Bihguri?'

'Well, certainly, if you put it that way. Your bastard will get out of Bihguri on one condition. He fancies a garden chokri named Saoni. The girl is the reason why he had chosen to remain at Bihguri.'

The planter's face remained bland, though his mind raced. A chokri named Saoni? Why the devil hadn't his sirdars passed on this vital piece of information to him?

'I see.'

'He wants to marry her and take her away with him. He'll gladly leave this garden if you agree to terminate her contract and allow her to go with him.'

'The devil I will!' Buckingham cried out. 'It's bloody blackmail, can't you see? You can't make me do it!'

'I shan't try to,' Hewitt said with dignity. 'The law is with you all the way. I simply repeat what Bircha has proposed to me. Whether you accept it or not is entirely up to your conscience. A loss of a chokri will not tax your resources unduly. You'll get Bircha out. That's what you desire, isn't it?'

'My concern is for the pernicious effect it might have on the coolies. Abscond from Bihguri … and get paid for it in the bargain! Then get married and take your wife away! Why, , I'll soon have half my workforce decamping bag and baggage!'

'You'll not concede Bircha's proposal?'

'Certainly not! Let him leave and I'll bid him good riddance. But alone, Captain Hewitt! Not with another coolie contracted to me!'

The officer got to his feet. 'I'll tell Bircha of your decision. As for my personal opinion, I think you've made a mistake, Buckingham.'

The mocking tone was back in the planter's voice. 'On the contrary, Captain Hewitt, I believe I've found a way out of my predicament!'

Hewitt did not fail to catch the significance of the planter's words. He spoke with all the authority he could muster, 'I'm cautioning you, Buckingham. If he can't take the chokri away Bircha might decide to stay on. He'll continue to enjoy my protection.'

'Don't worry, dear fellow,' Buckingham said. 'I'll not as much as touch a hair on the bastard's head!'

His smile lingered on his lips as he watched the mandarin stride out of the verandah.

Saoni? One who was born in the month of Savan? Oh yes, Captain Hewitt, I shall have to rewrite the script again. And Saoni shall have a stellar role in it!

The monsoon months had seen Cordelia confined mostly to the bungalow and the dispensary. That she could now move about freely gave her a feeling of infinite boundlessness. She loved to mount Souchong and, with Pekoe alongside, trot over the gloomy, shadow-filled jungle-track leading to Bihguri. Each day she would travel further and further, gripped with the excitement of an adventurer traversing untrod paths.

When not at the dispensary she spent time in the open, tending the kitchen garden, feeding the chicken, trying her hand at milking the cows, making a round of the basti. She and Mongla worked many afternoons on Papa's grave, setting the headstone aright, piling up fresh earth on the mound and replanting flowering shrubs.

Such activities once again filled up her days. At the same time, they lessened the hours of futile self-introspection yet nothing she did could erase the emptiness. She might have found succour in the Dhanboa coolies, but David had effectively denied her this. As soon as the rain ceased, she had begun work in the basti. With what devious intent she could not fathom, but lately David had begun to intrude into her domain. Sundays were off, a reduction of two hours in their toil, wage cuts refunded. But she was not taken in. If he had been genuinely sincere about their well-being, he would not have set them against the jungles, but found a Naga or Assamese contractor for the job, as Papa had done. Oh yes, she could see through his game! The real motive behind his new found concern was to make the coolies absolutely dependent on him and deprive her of a share of their love and trust!

The coolies, too, had responded to his gesture of hypocrisy with touching faith. From being the stern taskmaster, he had overnight metamorphosed into their mai-baap. His simulated concern had evoked deeper gratitude than her unalloyed commitment. She did not blame them. David's, after all, was the hand which fed them. What pained her was the certainty of betrayal. They would not have to wait for the monsoons to see the viciousness which lay behind the benign mask. It would be revealed sooner, when the new cleared ground would require to be planted. Then David and his handpicked sirdars would be at them again, transmuting them into mindless tools of profit!

Even then, despite David's indifference and his endeavour to usurp her role in Dhanboa, the daily chores and companionship provided by Mongla, Pekoe and Souchong may have sufficed to keep her content, if not altogether happy, had she not sensed a change in herself. And changed she had! It was an inner change, a hardening coarseness, the coarseness of implacable hatred and the concomitant urge to hit back at the one who aroused that hatred—David. She had fought this desire for retribution, for it terrified her, and also brought in its wake a consciousness of harbouring un-Christian thoughts. Her terror lay in the recognition that she had failed to eradicate this incipient hatred. Even amidst routine, everyday work it clung to her heart, mind and soul, and fatalistic sadness, which the end of the rains should have extirpated, had become her constant companion.

On the morning of the fourth of October, she conducted a memorial service at Papa's grave. David had left the previous afternoon for the greener shoot at Cinnamora, so she had only Mongla's company. The service over, she visited the basti, but had to return sooner than intended because Robiya informed her that Hewitt sahib had arrived.

She was inexpressibly glad to see him. The officer was visibly affected by the joy with which she greeted him.

'I have come directly from Bihguri, Miss Esscombe,' he said. 'I bear glad tidings. Bircha's fit as a fiddle. My warning to Buckingham has served the purpose.'

Only one aspect of the visit held a discordant note. Bircha wished to leave Bihguri with Saoni but Hewitt could not persuade the planter to part with her.

'But his pettiness will be disadvantageous,' Hewitt asserted. 'If Bircha can't leave with Saoni, he won't leave Bihguri at all. Bircha is proving a thorn in his flesh and inspiring the other coolies to resist oppression. So, perhaps, it's just as well he stays on.'

'Will he not be in perpetual danger, Captain Hewitt?'

'On the contrary, it is he who will be a perpetual danger to Buckingham! Don't worry, Miss Esscombe. No harm will come to Bircha as long as I'm alive. Bircha will marry Saoni and be happy with her, even though at Bihguri.'

The captain's eyes dazzled with his own joy. She looked beautiful seated on the verandah; her features radiated ecstasy as the sun's rays melted her auburn hair into gold and refracted into a halo. He had another piece of information to impart, but withheld it, fearful of disturbing her happiness.

'It's given me immense satisfaction,' he acknowledged. 'I would never have thought saving the life of an insignificant human being, a native at that, could yield pleasure. Upon my soul, Miss Esscombe, your concept of a coolie protector was not as Utopian as I'd initially envisaged. I should know, for have I not been an unofficial one to Bircha?'

'A single life, Captain! How gratifying then would it be to save thousands?'

'Yes, indeed! Your concept must certainly be endowed with legal shape. If you recall, Miss Esscombe, I'd suggested you go to Sivasagar to talk about it to Major Gosselin. Have you contemplated a trip?'

'Oh yes, in a vague sort of way. But your visit today has made me decide. I shall leave in a day or two.'

'May I suggest you defer it for a week? On the eleventh of this month, shall we say? I require sufficient time to make arrangements for your stay at Sivasagar.'

'That's kind of you, Captain Hewitt. It'll be of great help if I can leave the planning to you.'

'If you depart by boat at daybreak on the eleventh morning, you should be there before nightfall. I'll arrange for someone to meet you at the ghat. I shall also ensure that you have an undisturbed stay at the dak-bungalow.'

'I'm grateful, Captain Hewitt. But aren't I being selfish? You must be famished. And your men. But where are they? I can't see them anywhere.'

'Well, I didn't wish to impose on your hospitality over much,' the officer said. 'Thought I would just drop by and let you know about Bircha. So I left my men on the boat.'

'But you must spend the night at our garden, Captain Hewitt. I insist.'

The officer chuckled delightedly. 'Your brother won't mind, Miss Esscombe?'

'Oh, David's not here right now. He left yesterday for Cinnamora on a greener shoot. He is expected back this evening.'

Later in the afternoon the two mounted Congou and Souchong and headed for the jungle track to Bihguri, so narrow that the two walers could barely progress side by side. Cordelia had been using it almost every afternoon the last few weeks, so the overgrown grass had been flattened by the horse's hooves. Soon they had crossed the red-flowering simul tree which marked the distance Cordelia had travelled on the path thus far; but this afternoon she pushed Souchong on, and twenty minutes of slow canter saw them reach the end of the path, beyond which lay the boggy stretch of cane and thatch separating the two plantations.

As they were turning back Hewitt's sharp eyes caught something among within the shrub-strewn flatland and he abruptly reined Congou.

'My goodness!' he cried out. 'Do you see that, Miss Esscombe?'

It was a mound of leaves, about a foot high and three feet in diameter, with a crater shaped depression at the top. The weird structure resembled a miniature volcano, or the nest of some gigantic bird.

'Oh, what is it, Captain Hewitt?'

'A king cobra's nest, Miss Esscombe!'

'But the king cobra's a snake, Captain Hewitt! Snakes don't build nests!'

'Oh, female king cobras do. Trust me on this, Miss Esscombe. It's the only species of snake to build a nest such as the one we see over there … mostly of bamboo leaves. She lays her eggs in that depression on top and sits over them for near two months. She doesn't stir from her perch in this period, not even to feed herself! Leaves her absolutely weakened by the time the eggs hatch.'

Cordelia felt her skin crinkle at the images conjured up by the captain's words. She stood on the stirrups and craned her neck for a better look. 'There's nothing on top of this one, Captain Hewitt.'

'Not the season for it … But thank goodness we spotted it! Indicates the presence of king cobras around. It should serve as a warning to you. This jungle path is none too safe for solitary rides. Other snakes might make a run for it, but not the king cobra. Fiercely aggressive, Miss Esscombe … attacks without provocation.'

'I've been told so. But please be assured I never ride up alone this far.'

They retraced their route and, leaving the animals with the young *syces*, walked to the bungalow.

David returned before dusk, dusty, bleary-eyed from lack of sleep, his mouth reeking of beer. He bathed and changed, talked with Harua about the progress of the clearing operation, joined Hewitt briefly for a couple of sundowners, had his meal with him and his sister, and then excused himself, pleading exhaustion. Cordelia and the Captain were left alone on the verandah.

The officer grasped at the opportunity to introduce Lieutenant Michael Bailin into the conversation. 'By the way,' he said, speaking as casually as he could. 'I met Lieutenanct Bailin a few weeks back. At Jorehaut.'

The darkness within the verandah was unrelieved. No taper or lamp, which could attract insects, was laid on the wicker-table, so he could not see her grow rigid.

'He met me at my request. I had to know why he didn't seek you out. He made a startling disclosure. He did attempt rapprochement, and sent his man to Dhanboa along with a letter. Did your brother not show you that letter?'

'No, he didn't.'

'Your brother wrote back. He did not wish the Lieutenant to come to Dhanboa for the time being, his reply said. Bailin, naturally, assumed the letter had your approval. He took it that you were offended with him for leaving the steamer as he did. That, and the straitened circumstances in which he found himself, forestalled him from making another approach.'

Cordelia made no comment. Strange how this act of treachery on David's part failed to arouse anger in her! It almost seemed to her that she had known it all along!

'I had misjudged him gravely, Miss Esscombe. Bailin is a decent man. Bad fortune has dogged him. An English thug sold him a non-existent garden. He spent whatever money he had trying to make something of the few acres his land deed entitled him to. He was at Jorehaut to borrow money from a usurer and have another go.'

Cordelia felt nothing. She urged her heart to grieve for poor Michael but there was no grief. She tried to find words to respond to the man who sat beside her but there were no words. There was nothing, no anger, no feelings, no words. Hewitt could not know about this. He wished he could have said something to lessen her hurt. But he had made a pledge. He must go through it, right to the bitter end.

'The Lieutenant wished me to convey a message to you, Miss Esscombe. But I hesitate to utter it, fearing it might cause you inconsolable grief.'

She found her voice. 'Please go on, Captain Hewitt.' It was a stranger speaking.

'He wants you to know there can be no place for you in his life. I've phrased it badly, Miss Esscombe. What he implied was that, given both his past and present, he feels it unjust to maintain any links with you. He has decided that he'll no more attempt rapprochement. I'm sorry, Miss Esscombe, if my words have caused you anguish. But I promised the Lieutenant.'

'No, Captain Hewitt, I'm neither hurt not angry.' The officer searched for the tremor which might belie her statement. But her voice held a curious dispassion that gave nothing away. This made him hope.

'I'm glad, Miss Esscombe, that you take it so well. Perhaps you've come to realize it is for the best. I admire the Lieutenant for his honesty. He cares too deeply for you to expose you to shame or misery.'

'We can't always have what we crave. Isn't it so, Captain Hewitt?'

'I shan't blame you if you consider it churlish of me to speak of myself at such a moment. But, Miss Esscombe, you must keep in mind what I had earlier told you. I'm in a position to take you away. This plantation holds no future for you. I realize the depth of your feelings for the coolies. But here they're just a handful. If you condescend to accept my offer, you'll have a far greater scope for indulging the charitable instinct which is an integral aspect of your beauty. I shall not demand an answer from you tonight, Miss Esscombe. But I'll wait. If you ever come to a decision, please remember I'm waiting.'

'I will, Captain Hewitt. I promise you.'

'Thank you, Miss Esscombe.' He got up from his chair. 'I have to leave early tomorrow morning so I'll bid you goodnight.'

She remained seated. He stood hesitantly for a moment more, and then strode across to his room, leaving her alone upon the verandah gazing vacantly at the firefly-lit darkness.

Her craft reached Sivasagar a little before sundown and moored at Dikhow ghat. She was surprised to find a welcome party awaiting her on the bank. To her delight, it was led by the Reverend Garry Swanson, who swept her into an unabashed embrace the very moment she set foot upon terra firma.

The padre held her by the shoulders at arm's length and gazed up admiringly through his horn-rimmed bifocals. 'My, my, you grow lovelier each day! The horrendous Assam climate has been kind to you.'

He helped her up to where a motley group waited at the top of the bank and introduced each in turn. Mrs Hodges, the wife of a Baptist missionary who had recently arrived from a mission in Moulmein; Dr Crombie, portly and pompous, who took care of the health of the white residents and the planters of the area as well as the few natives who had money to pay his fees; Captain Fordyce, the official presence in the party, who was Major Gosselin's deputy, and had been personally instructed by his superior to offer Cordelia all courtesy and hospitality; and Ebenezer Darby, a native convert to Christianity.

After the introductions, the bamboo-thin and supercilious Fordyce took charge of her with a vengeance, and it was only the next morning that she could meet Major Gosselin, who had invited her to breakfast with him. The Major lived alone. He greeted her with an effusiveness which surprised her. She was not left guessing long as to the cause.

Having dismissed Fordyce and guided her to the dining table, he began without preamble, 'It's a wise decision you've made, Miss Esscombe. Ralph gave me an inkling of it. Mind you, he didn't spell it out in black and white. But I'm astute enough to read between the lines!'

'I do not understand. What decision do you refer to?'

'Oh Miss Esscombe, you needn't be coy with me. I'm like a father to young Ralph. And I thoroughly approve. He's a far better catch than that mad Lieutenant you'd the misfortune of encountering.'

Cordelia flushed and was about to embark on a rebuttal when a cautioning impulse checked her. Let the pompous ass think what he might! If she could use his misconceptions to her advantage, let it be so.

The Major mistook her flush for feminine modesty, a trait which he thoroughly approved of. 'A lucky escape, thank heavens! By the way, I have had words from my superiors at Calcutta. They checked with the military authorities at Ambala. The same Lieutenant, no doubt about it.'

Cordelia concentrated fiercely on the food before her rather than the Major's words. She dared not look up, for one glance at her eyes and Gosselin would know!

'But Ralph is a different proposition altogether, Miss Esscombe,' the Major continued. 'I don't know if you're aware of it, but he comes from one of the finest families. His father is Tony Hewitt ... Personal Assistant to the Viceroy!'

Which makes all the difference to you! She valiantly maintained a slight smile on her lips, but her heart was filled with contempt. She had heard the Major address his Sivasagar deputy as Captain Fordyce, not by his first name. But with Captain Hewitt it was 'Ralph' all the way!

'Mark my words, Miss Esscombe … Ralph has nowhere to go but up! He's young, bright and dynamic. Has the proper background and just the right connections to help him along. The only thing he lacked was a wife, one who would keep him away from the follies of youth. I'm dashed pleased that you aim to fill the hiatus. Not that I'm surprised. You're a delightfully beautiful creature, Miss Esscombe.'

Cordelia felt grossly demeaned. Yet she carefully modulated her voice to the same neutrality as she said, 'There's something else I wish to discuss. Perhaps Captain Hewitt … Ralph … gave you a hint.'

'No, He didn't mention any such thing in his letter. But, Miss Esscombe, you can speak freely to me. I'll help in any way I can.'

'Recently I and Captain Hewitt … Ralph … had a rather uncommon experience. It put a notion into my head, one I wish to discuss.'

'Please go ahead.'

She told him of the incident involving the Bihguri absconder and how Captain Hewitt had saved the fellow by throwing a protective cover around him. Major Gosselin was vastly amused.

'So that's what drew you and Ralph close… But what's the purpose of telling me all this?'

'It set me thinking. If the administration takes interest in the coolies … appoints coolie protectors, for instance … much could be done to safeguard these wretches from the brutalities committed by planters. Captain Hewitt … Ralph … agrees with me. It was he who suggested I approach you with the idea.'

'He did, did he?' A frown of perplexity creased the officer's imperious brows. 'But he's young, and perhaps not aware of our mandate in this region. It's a hands-off policy for us, Miss Esscombe, as far as the tea industry is concerned. We assist them whenever approached. We intervene only when a law-and-order problem manifests itself. As for policy decisions, however, it is the authorities in Calcutta who make them.'

'Oh, he's aware of it,' Cordelia said. 'In fact, he proposes to talk to his father about it. But he has a great deal of regard for you, Major Gosselin. He thinks it would be discourteous of him to approach his father without first putting you in the picture.'

Gosselin looked pleased. 'He thinks that, does he? Rather handsome of him! Well, Miss Esscombe, I do suppose something needs to be done for the coolies. Far too many deaths around here. A coolie protector? Why, that's not such a bad idea, after all. But it must be known to come from you. On no account should it appear that it is I who made the suggestion, or I would be the laughing stock of my associates, ha, ha!'

'Can you instruct me on how I can go about it, Major Gosselin?'

'You can, I suppose, couch your ideas in the form of a petition. The authorities are not insensible of the mortality among the coolies. In fact, early last year, the Government of Bengal set up an Enquiry Commission to investigate the cause of abnormal mortality amongst immigrant coolies. The Commission, I believe, has pursued its investigations with admirable vigour and is all set to submit its report by the first half of next year. If you address your petition to them, I'll certainly pass it on.'

'Oh, thank you! I shall do that.'

'If we're earnest about this, we might as well go the whole hog,' said the Major reflectively. 'I suggest you make a second copy of the petition. Just after Christmas the Commissioner for Assam is paying a visit. Ralph will play the host to him at Jorehaut. I suggest you personally hand him the copy and discuss it with him.'

Cordelia's gratitude shone in her eyes. The officious Major softened before her joy. As the house bearer began to clear the breakfast things, he stood up.

'It was pleasant talking to you, Miss Esscombe,' he said. 'But now I must hand you over to my deputy and get back to my own work. Take your time. Go back to your garden and put your thoughts to paper.'

'No, Major Gosselin. The petition shall be ready before I depart from Sivasagar. The Reverend Swanson shall help me frame it.'

There was a distinct cooling of the officer's warmth, but his smile was bland. 'Well, just as you wish. I'll keep my pledge of forwarding it to the Commission. Goodbye for now, Miss Esscombe. You'll find Captain Fordyce in the outer chamber.'

Cordelia was about to step out of the door when he said something that sounded to her ears as a caution. 'Try not to be too impulsive, Miss Esscombe, for Ralph's sake. A woman who marries a British officer must not be too altruistic.'

Brother Garry Swanson replaced the quill on the inkstand and leant back in his chair. 'That's ended at last,' he said.

Cordelia sat on the wooden bed. The two were in the padre's room at the Baptist mission—little more than a cubicle, cluttered with books and papers.

The padre was referring to the petition they had painstakingly drafted out the whole of the afternoon and which the Reverend had copied out—two copies, one to be handed over to Major Gosselin, the other carried by Cordelia to be given to Captain Hewitt so it could be passed on to the Commissioner. The words of the petition were those of the Reverend, Cordelia's own contribution being the concept of 'coolie protector'.

'I have my reservations about the amount of good it'll do,' Swanson, unable to share her enthusiasm, said.

'By itself, perhaps not. But, Father, if Captain Hewitt follows it up as he promised, something might come of it.'

'Ah, Captain Hewitt! I have developed a strong curiosity about the gentleman. You haven't been very forthcoming about him, my dear.'

'Later, Father,' Cordelia said with a smile. 'It's time for me to bid goodbye to the others at the mission. Then you and I shall walk to the dak-bungalow. I've a lot to tell you, Father.'

Indeed, she had! At the dak-bungalow, seated upon the verandha, Cordelia began to bare her soul. Words poured out of her mouth, and tears from her eyes. The Reverend sat silent, not endeavouring to stem the flow of her words or tears. But there was pain in him as he listened; even had she not shed those tears he would have sensed her pain, for her words were bloated with sadness. She took a long time to retrace the experience of the past year—David's betrayal, Michael's aloofness; she talked of her dispensary, and Dhanboa's coolies, of Bapu babu, Kamal, Mongla, Pekoe and Souchong. She spoke of Bircha and Captain Hewitt, of the latter's proposal and Michael's final message. Somewhere along the way, at some point of time, her tears lessened and finally dried up altogether; but her words continued to be soaked in sorrow.

And finally, like her tears, her words too were spent. She stumbled into silence, as though the failing strength of her soul, rather than having nothing more to say, had rendered her mute.

He waited for her to speak again and then, when she would not, broke the silence, his voice strong. 'I do not pity you, my child. You have suffered through no fault of your own, yet I do not pity you. You've been true to your convictions … true to yourself. You've acted as you believed a human being should act. You'll recall what Michael told us once … the consequence of action can be frightful. He spoke of himself, but his was the voice of all who act and suffer consequences. Such suffering denies pity, it evokes admiration. At no point of time have you compromised with your beliefs. But this milieu is not conducive to uncompromising goodness. Michael discovered it earlier; you now.'

He paused to wave away a huge moth which was repeatedly flinging itself at the heated chimney of the lamp; a futile gesture, for the moth flitted away only to return and dash itself against the glass. Soon it lay belly upwards on the table, its legs furiously fluttering before stiffening into the rigor of death.

'Selflessness is suicidal in such a milieu, my child.' Cordelia could feel harsh cynicism in his voice, an inward anger. 'To survive in it one must compromise with the urgings of the soul. Self-centred compromise, that is the path to salvation. The change in David has hurt you most, hasn't it? Ah, but David in his own way has unlocked the secret of survival! He has allowed himself to be moulded by the milieu. He has compromised with his conscience. You say he talks of his compulsions, but those are mere pretexts for compromise. Since your goodness would not allow you to compromise, you cannot align your actions to correspond with David's so-called compulsions. It would be foolish to feed you false hopes. David is lost to you … to us.'

Her eyes were starting to fill up with tears again. 'First Michael! Then Papa and David! Oh, Father, when will this ever end?'

'It must end!' the Reverend cried out, almost involuntarily, as if surprising himself. The anger had flared out of him like a ball of fire. But a little later his face relaxed, the creases which had been so vividly chiselled upon it smoothed away. He opened his eyes. Once again, they were illuminated b the customary benevolence.

'Forgive me … I have not been myself lately. It's these coolie deaths. Gosselin strives to shield things away from me, but a friendly clerk in his office keeps me well informed. Over eight thousand deaths in this region due to pestilence and other causes … three thousand in this district alone! Yet no one is bothered. You and I, dear girl, are exceptions. And we're the ones who do not matter. Those who matter are blind and deaf. The germ of doubt has now infected my soul. I lie awake at night mulling over the state of things. The more the doubt, the greater is my self-loathing.'

He smiled in a bitter grimace. 'But my doubts last but a moment. They pass, and I'm strong again. It's not in us to question the ways of the Lord. It's not in us to seek meanings to this mélange of hope and despair. It is for us to believe. And act. From what I've learnt of your circumstances, so must you. You must escape before it's too late!'

'I've burnt my bridges, Father. I can't crawl back to Uncle Alex and Aunt Patricia. Michael will not come to take me away. Oh, where can I escape to, Father?'

'Captain Ralph Hewitt!' the Reverend spoke in urgent tones. 'The mandarin is clearly infatuated with you. He appears to be a decent individual. You tell me he propositioned to you. Listen to me, my child. Allow him to take you away to safety.'

'Michael! Shall I cut Michael out from my life forever? Father, what are you saying?'

The padre winced at her recrimination. But the eerie forebodings were strong within him, and he hardened himself to say to words. 'Michael has clearly decided to chart his destined path without you. You must accept that and learn to live with it.'

'Captain Ralph Hewitt?' She was fighting on two fronts now, against him, and her own feelings. 'I admire him. But I don't love him as I do Michael. He too realizes this.'

'Strong passions do not make for good marriages, my child. Parity of sensibility and objectives do. Attachment with the Captain will take you away from Michael, but not from your commitments. With the officer's powers strengthening you, just imagine the good you might do. In advising this, I'm not being as cynical as I might appear to be.'

'Pragmatic, yes. Cynical, no. You can never be cynical with me, Father.'

'If you marry Captain Hewitt, you will have to fight the system no more. You will indirectly be a part of it and achieve much more than what you might have had through fighting it. Yes, my child, accept Ralph

Hewitt as your own. That'll take you away from Dhanboa. It'll arm you in your struggle on behalf of the coolies. Above all, it'll absolve me of my burden of guilt.'

Cordelia was startled. 'Your burden of guilt, Father?'

'Yes, it was I who set you on this course! If it had not been for me, perhaps you might have returned to Calcutta to another life.'

Cordelia's voice was shrill. 'No! You are not to blame for the circumstances I find myself in. A voice raised against injustice should never be ridden with guilt ... you yourself had once said this to me, Father!'

The stocky figure seemed to shrink before her eyes, looking aged and defeated. A laugh emerged from his throat, cutting sabre-like through the cool, autumn air.

'There come moments in our life, my child,' he said, looking not at her, but at the twinkling lights of the boats moored on the river-bank, 'when we have to eat our own words!'

The return to Papa's garden no longer seemed like a homecoming.

Night had fallen by the time they reached the Dhanboa jetty. Ajam, who was on *chowkidar* duty that night, wore a surprised, fearful look on his face.

'You, memsahib?' he stuttered out in agitation. 'So late at night? When darkness fell the sahib decided you weren't coming this day.' She was puzzled. Ajam appeared to be panic-stricken!

As she waited outside Papa's cottage, a black shape came hurtling through the darkness and lunged at her, almost toppling her off her feet. Pekoe! The dog was demented with joy. He danced frantically around her, letting out short, welcoming yelps.

A little away from the bungalow she thanked the accompanying coolies and told them to go to their own homes. She bent down and put her fingers to her lips. 'No sound, Pekoe,' she whispered. 'We mustn't wake Mongla up. Or the master.' At the foot of the stairs, she took off her shoes and ascended as quietly as the creaking planks allowed. She reached the top and was pussy-footing across the verandah abutting David's bedchamber when she abruptly froze.

An alien smell hung in the air—the cloying odour of the cheap perfume which coolie women daubed upon themselves at festivals. Yet she might have missed the scent, ascribing it to some unseen source, had not undisguised sounds emanating from David's bedroom made misunderstanding impossible.

Titillating feminine laughter was followed by throaty sighs of ecstasy! Cordelia wanted to clap her palms to her ears to shut off those bestial sounds, but could not. She wanted to rush away to the oblivion of her bedroom, but her legs would not move. Her mind went blank. She wanted to leaveand bury her head under her pillow but her legs would not move. The woman uttered a subdued shriek of pleasure, David grunted loudly, and then there was deathly silence.

The stark end of sound was the blow which shocked her into awareness. Like a thief she stole to her room, cautiously bolted the door, and flung herself onto the bed.

'Meghu-bhaiya came again last night,' Saoni said to Bircha, as she brought the evening's meal to him.

'Let Meghu-bhaiya come and go as he pleases. What's it to you or me?'

Saoni's face wore a grave, grown-up look. It made her even more endearing to his eyes.

'Seriously, Bircha, I'm frightened. *Bihguri me kuch ho raha hai*!'

Bircha said nothing, but concentrated on finishing his meal. Having finished, he washed his hands, sat next to her, and put his arm across her shoulders. She snuggled unreservedly up to him. There was nothing lascivious in the way he held the half child, half woman; it was the protective embrace of a father rather than the grasp of a lover.

'Listen, Saoni,' he said. 'Nothing else matters but you and me. Let Meghu-bhaiya come and go. Let the coolielog plot and plan. They don't matter. Only you and I matter. We've suffered a great deal. We deserve the joy we feel in each other.'

But the fear in her would not go away. 'Oh, Bircha, we must not shut our eyes. We must not shut our ears. It would have been all right if the white sahib had allowed us to leave. Since we have to stay, we must be alert to what is happening in Bihguri. We must not lose ourselves in a dream world. Bircha, I'm afraid!'

His arm around her tightened. '*Arey pagli*! Who can touch us now? Did you not see the sarkari sahib come? Did I not tell you what he said?'

'Even then I'm afraid. I sense a new mood in the young coolielog. The way they look at the sirdars. The angry comments they make about the white sahib. How I wish we were away someplace else! The white sahib allowed you to leave. You wouldn't go. There's time yet. You can still leave.'

'I cannot even think of leaving without you, my Saoni.'

'It was a mistake ... your staying behind. Even for my sake. I have bad dreams. I see dead bodies. And blood. Oh Bircha, my own blood runs cold. Here, feel my heart. How fast it beats!'

She caught his free hand and drew it to her bosom. The feel of her taut, unripe breasts sparked sudden, violent desire in him. Her heart pulsated against his palm. He withdrew it hastily.

'There's nothing to fear, my Saoni, my love!' he cried out, his voice suddenly hoarse and filled with desire. 'Once we are married all your fears will go away. I have waited too long. I'll go tomorrow itself to your mago. We shall fix a date for the marriage.'

'*Sach*? *Kal hi*?' It did not require much to make her happy. She was almost laughing now. Then her voice grew less animated as she said, 'But I must warn you, Bircha. You will need to please mago ...'

The next evening, a little after the work-gang returned, Bircha went to Baisakhi's hut.

'I've come to seek your daughter's hand,' he told her. 'I've saved a great deal of money. If you have me as a son-in-law, neither you nor your daughter would want for anything.'

Baisakhi said amiably, 'That's all very well, Bircha. But Saoni is all I have. Take her away and I'll be alone. Can you not wait a while longer?'

'Oh, mago, you'll not lose a daughter but gain a son. I shan't take her away from you. On the contrary, it is I who shall come into your house. Together we will take care of you in your old age.'

The offer swept away Baisakhi's resistance. The date for the marriage was fixed. It would take place in the beginning of the month of Magha, on the day of Tusu Parab.

'Give us the word, sahib. We will take care of it.' Luthra said. Puran, Gandru and Budhu nodded. They squatted upon the floor. Buckingham sat on the verandah chair.

'The time's not ripe,' he said.

Luthra was not convinced. 'If we wait much longer, sahib, things will get out of hand.'

'The bastard's getting married, sahib!' Budhu added. 'On Tusu Parab. The whole garden is talking about it.'

'*Woh chokri ke saath*? Saoni?'

'You know of it, sahib? Yet you do not act?'

'The blasted sarkari sahib, Luthra! He always pays a visit in the month of Phagun.'

'But after the coming of Phagun, sahib?' Gandru queried. 'After the sarkari sahib paid his visit? We can get at him then, sahib.'

'Jaroor! The rains will come. Bihguri will be cut off. We shall have the garden to ourselves. Then you can get at him!'

Gandru, endowed with the slight trace of intelligence which marked him out from his brainless compatriots, pointed out the fallacy in the sahib's reasoning. 'But the rains will end! The sarkari sahib will come again, asking for Bircha. What then?'

Buckingham smiled 'Ah, Gandru, you're not going to touch Bircha … physically, I mean. We aren't going to hurt his body. But we'll destroy his mind. Then, even if the sarkari sahib comes, he'll have no cause for complaint. Listen to me, all of you. Bircha attempted to leave when he couldn't. Now he doesn't when he can. It's the chokri who keeps him in the garden. He's planning to marry her in Magha. Doesn't all this tell you something?'

Luthra's stupid mien relaxed and he broke into a smile. 'He has fire in his balls for her, sahib,' he said, grinning lewdly.

'Your words are crude, Luthra, but you've got the point. So let them get married. When the time comes, and the rains begin to fall heavily, you four can have her. Show her what real men are like, huh, Luthra?'

'Put the fear of Bhagwan into the coolielog too,' Gandru said.

Luthra's grin widened, revealing bared teeth. His three companions too were grinning. 'Till Phagun, sahib? We'll count the days.'

The days shortened and grew chilly and misty. David sat on the verandah of the bungalow, allowing the rays of the enfeebled wintry sun to slant across his body and warm the outer frame. The sun did not need to warm the inner man. The glass of whisky in his hands was doing that quite well!

Today was a chutti day, one of the myriad festivals of his coolies, but an important one that deserved a day off—Durga puja, the worship of the goddess Durga, the slayer of asuras. Cordi had been at the basti since daybreak, involved with their pagan rites.

There was nothing he needed to prove to Cordi. Nothing he needed to prove to anyone—not even Uncle Alex. But he had a great deal to prove to himself! And prove it he would, Cordi or no Cordi! Had he not, despite being hemmed in with constraints right from the start, made a creditable job of it so far? Had he not tightened up the management of the garden, brought a semblance of discipline into his workforce and moulded it into an efficient body without suffering the losses other plantations experienced? He had uprooted the China bushes and replanted the area, opened out a nursery, produced and dispatched the teas, and compensated for the loss of Bapu babu and the tea makers. Another headache would be over when the fresh batch of coolies arrived from Calcutta. Uncle Alex's letter specifying the date of their arrival should be with him any day now.

Yet inadequacies continued to shackle him; not of self-confidence, but of knowledge. He was like a man groping his way amidst foggy darkness, with no one, nothing, to guide him to his goal. How much hoeing must the freshly cleared grounds undergo before being considered fit for planting? Should he stick to the spacing charted out by Buckingham, or should he experiment on his own? Were his nursery seedlings quite ready to be transferred? Should he set about pruning the replanted sections? Had he incised too deep with the mature bushes? Questions, questions and more questions in each stage, at every step!

Yes, ignorance implies impuissance! His situation now was that of Papa's; he himself had to answer the questions his ignorance had posed! One false step, a trifling omission, and he would make mistakes as Papa had. Papa's mistakes had delayed his dreams for Dhanboa as also of his own future. He could not afford to make another blunder. This spectre of possible blunder and consequent failure, more than Cordi's indifference, was driving him to distraction. What if he was plunging headlong into failure?

Damn Cordi! Damn that runaway coolie bastard! One miserable nigger had knocked out the crutch which would have propped up Dhanboa! Dhanboa would have continued to thrive under Buckingham's guidance. Now there were no answers to questions. Now there was only blind groping!

Abruptly the sound of horses' hooves disturbed his thoughts. David sprang up and strode to the balustrade. Two riders were trotting in through the main gate. It was Luthra, accompanying a short, squat, thickset and hirsute man. Goodchild, the Superintendent of the Assam Company, Buckingham's superior and David's possible saviour! Placing his glass on the table and calling out to Mongla, he raced down the staircase.

The riders dismounted and Goodchild warmly shook hands. David escorted the visitor upstairs. He had arrived a few days ago on the annual inspection of Bihguri, the Superintendent explained. 'Promised you a visit, didn't I … when we last met at Cinnamora? Let it not be said that Goodchild doesn't keep his pledge.'

His eyebrows shot up half an inch as he saw the whisky bottle on the table. 'Bit early for that, isn't it, young man?'

'An exception, sir,' David said, signalling to Mongla to take the drinks tray away. 'I normally don't get the time for a morning snifter. But chutti today. Durga puja.'

Goodchild's demeanour retained its pleasantness, but his voice grew sombre. 'Keep it an exception, young man. Many a good man in Assam has gone under the earth because they couldn't.' He looked around before taking a seat. 'Where's your sister?'

'At the basti, Mr Goodchild.'

'An excellent girl. Durga puja, eh? You're a sensible planter, young man. The dumb brutes at Bihguri were slaving away when I left.'

'You can't imagine how pleased I'm to see you, sir,' David said eagerly. 'Must take you round the garden. I have a thousand and one questions to ask of you.'

Goodchild looked hard at David, alerted by the unctuousness. 'What's wrong, young fellow? I was under the impression Buckingham's your tutor.'

David turned red in the face. 'Chris is a busy man,' he said lamely. 'Moreover, he has been having some coolie problems lately.'

'Oh, I know all about it … straight from the horse's mouth, ha, ha! Hewitt stitched him up so tight the poor chap can't move. Egged on by your sister, of course. Don't get me wrong. I don't blame your sister one bit. Nor Hewitt. Buckingham's a blackguard in the most comprehensive sense of the word. No longer the Good Samaritan, is he now?'

'He hasn't been to Dhanboa since that episode.'

'And you're at a loose end?'

'Yes, sir.'

'I shall certainly help you out. You and your excellent sister deserve all the assistance you may get. When do you expect her back?'

'In an hour or so, Mr Goodchild. She should be home for breakfast.'

'Well, if the mountain doesn't come to Mahomet, Mahomet must go to the mountain. So, what says you, young fellow? Shall we ride into the basti and meet this sister of yours? And take a peek at the festivities?'

The basti was inspirited with festal fervour as they rode into it. A coolie artisan had fashioned a rude idol of the mother goddess with clay, thatch and bamboo. Yet, clearly, the external from was less important than the inherent idea; the coolie women who sat a little away from the pedestal upon which the deity was placed radiated piety; the young men who danced before her with bizarre, near comical steps, large pots of smoking incense in their hands, were inebriated as much with adoration as with mod.

Cordelia sat with the womenfolk, on a murrah, as expectant as the rest, delicately white against the pool of duskiness. The babble of voices sank into a timorous hush as the coolies saw the two sahibs ride up on their horses. The dancers came to an abrupt stop. David forced his features into a broad smile and with an opulent gesture of his hand ordained that the rituals be carried on. Voices broke out again; the dancers recommenced their invocatory genuflexions. Coolie man ran smilingly up to help the sahibs dismount and take the horses to the tree where Souchong stood tethered.

Cordelia hastened up to accord the visitor a warm welcome. Though her smile ignored David, Goodchild was too entranced by the scene around him to notice. She led them to two murrahs and sat with them, explaining some of the details of the ritual to Goodchild, who laughingly confessed that though he had been in plantation life for a long time, he had never seen puja being performed at a basti.

'But we can't stay for very long,' the visitor said.

'It's all right, Mr Goodchild. You needn't stay long. See how grateful the coolies are. That you've dropped in here is more than enough.'

'We must leave now, Mr Goodchild,' David cried impatiently into his guest's ears a few minutes later. The three of them moved away to their horses.

'I mustn't draw you away from here, young lady,' Goodchild protested.

'It's fine, Mr Goodchild,' Cordelia said with a smile. 'They'll be at it for hours. You'll not deprive me of my duties as a hostess, I hope.'

David was not the best of hosts at breakfast, being restless and impatient. As soon as the meal was over, he suggested they make for the plantings. Goodchild agreed, on the condition, stated jestingly, that Cordelia accompanied them.

David led them to the mature bushes, which had suffered drastic pruning, and thereby lost almost all the foliage, except the bigger and older leaves upon the lower branches.

'Have I cut too low, Mr Goodchild?' he asked in trepidation.

Goodchild laughed. 'On the contrary, young man, you've done a first-rate job. Set your mind at rest. Come the spring showers, they'll throw out new stalks and flush as profusely as ever.'

'That's a load off my mind.' David cried out happily. 'The fresh plantings are just ahead. Shall we move on to them, Mr Goodchild?'

Riding single file over the narrow path which meandered through the mature bushes they emerged into the replanted sections. These were closer to the basti, thus the drumbeats issuing from the puja site were clearly audible. The beats had attained a feverish tempo and were accompanied by sporadic, frenzied shrieks.

David, being in the lead, was the first to enter the sections. He did not stop, but trotted on further ahead. Only when they were well inside did he turn and look straight into Goodchild's eyes.

Those black orbs were two dolorous pools of dismay. David knew all was lost!

Dismounting, the visitor closely inspected the saplings. 'You planted these in February?'

'Yes.' David found his voice choked. He did not dismount.

'Were the saplings from Bihguri?'

'Yes.'

'Buckingham's a perfect bastard!'

The profanity, though emerging from an elderly man who was ordinarily courteous to a fault, did not sound incongruous, despite Cordelia's presence.

It was the girl who put the question. 'Is something wrong, Mr Goodchild?'

The elderly man said nothing. He strode to his steed, mounted it and rode determinedly back to the bungalow. David and Cordelia had no option but to follow.

As they reached the bungalow, Buckingham's head sirdar came hurrying up.

'*Mein kaun hoon tum jaante ho*?' Goodchild asked angrily. Luthra looked up, surprised by the question, and the fierce anger with which it was flung.

'*Haan, huzoor. Aap bara sahib ho.*'

'*Phir suno. Tumhe sach bolna hoga.* If you don't speak the truth, not even your master can save you from my fury. Do you understand? What kind of seedlings did your sahib send to Dhanboa?'

Sudden alarm darted into Luthra's eyes. The man's gaze broke away from Goodchild's and remained fixed to the ground. He did not speak.

'*Suno*! I know you're afraid of your master. But you needn't be afraid. I shan't say a word to him, nor will this sahib and memsahib. On the other hand, if you decline to speak, I shall come down so heavily you'll wish your mother never begot you. So, speak! What kind of seedlings were sent from Bihguri?'

'The worst seedlings, sahib! The ones we always discard. The ones which never grow well. We talked about it between us sirdars. We were sure that our sahib was out to destroy the Dhanboa sahib.'

'All right. You can go, Luthra.' He turned towards David. 'I'm sorry, young man. A mistake … taking the fellow's help! Speaking for myself, I'd rather trust a king cobra than Buckingham!'

David only half heard the man. His eyes were upon his sister's. Hers radiated neither sorrow nor pity. Rather, an odious blend of arrogance and exultation lit them up. He had seen that look in another pair of eyes this morning—in those of the clay idol fashioned by a coolie artisan!

He sat on the verandah, in the same posture as in the morning, holding the glass of whisky in his hand as though an instrument of defence. Defence? Defence against what? Against Buckingham's tendentious designs? Against the guilty prods of conscience? Or against Cordi's contemptuous indifference?

The hours between morn and eve had seen a complete turnaround in his expectations. He had been cradled in the blissful lap of ignorance this morning. The helplessness he had experienced then was nothing compared to what he experienced now. Goodchild had not lived up to his name; far from being Dhanboa's saviour he had turned out to be a nemesis of delusions. In ignorance lay bliss. In knowledge lay dashed expectations, scattered mirages and the despairing end of innocence.

Goodchild, seer-like, had lifted the veil of ignorance and thereby locked on the manacles. There was no escaping that reality. Sixty acres of land filled once again with unproductive bushes! A whole year's effort—so much sweat, such agonies—and Dhanboa had not taken as much as half-step towards the garden of his dreams. On the contrary, it had skidded backwards. Goodchild had insisted he do not undertake uprooting and replanting exercise immediately. The elderly planter had inspected the nursery and expressed satisfaction at the seedlings being raised there. He had advised David to continue clearing more land and plant it with these seedlings.

Perhaps, in years to come, after more land had been cleared and fresh sapling raised, prosperity would come to Dhanboa. The thought, far from exciting hope, dampened the mind into despondency. There was no escape! He could, of course, dispose it off and sail away in quest of his own dreams. But David knew that could never be. If he ran away, he would be haunted with the failure throughout his life!

The throbbing drums from the basti could be heard clearly. The beat was different. The rituals were over. The feasting and dancing had commenced. The bastards were singing and dancing and feasting while he sat crushed and crippled, seeking courage in whisky.

Cordi had warned him against Buckingham. How blind he himself had been! Yet, with Papa dead and he unversed in tea craft, had there really been another choice? And wasn't Cordi the nodal cause of Buckingham's perfidy? If only she had left for Calcutta after Papa's death! That might have made Buckingham indifferent to the fate of Dhanboa; his indifference would have been far better than pretended help! But now the truth had to be confronted. The truth was the look in Cordi's eyes when Goodchild had uncovered Buckingham's perfidy. The truth was the manacles around his wrists.

He must pull himself together. Forget his personal dreams and confront reality. Twenty-five acres! Only twenty-five acres of jungle clearing so far! He had been a fool to have eased up on his workforce. At least fifty, sixty acres this winter—though time was short he could still do it if he squeezed the blood out of them. Perhaps even a hundred acres if he shoved the coolies Uncle Alex would be sending straight to the task.

With a half-uttered oath David sprang out of the chair. He had almost forgotten. A letter had arrived from Uncle Alex that morning which he hadn't yet read.

He walked unsteadily to his room. The letter was on his work table where he had placed it. Returning to the verandah, he tore open the envelope and extracted the paper.

My Dear David,

Received your letter on September the third instant. Intimation of the Dhanboa tea dispatch lying in the Indian General Navigation Steam Company's godown on the strand reached me a day later. I have since forwarded the consignment to the London Auctions aboard the *S.S. City of Cashmere*. I am expecting the results as well as proceeds of sale of the first tea dispatch sent by Henry to reach me within a month. I shall forward the amount to you after deducting expenses and my share.

According to the terms of the contract made between Henry and I, the onus on me was initial financing and to act as a conduit between Dhanboa and the London Auctions. You will, therefore, appreciate that the provisions and terms of the contract do not in any way bind me to assist Dhanboa in other matters. My advanced years also preclude the same. I, therefore, do not find myself in a position to comply favourably with your request to make arrangements for the dispatch of a batch of coolies to Dhanboa.

Cordelia's attitude towards us has not the slightest bearing on what you rightly perceive as a purely business matter. You may rest assured on that score.

I trust everything is well with you and your sister. Patricia sends her regards.

Alexander Swinnerton-Dyer, Esquire,
Calcutta,
September the Twenty-first

The letter fluttered gently from his nerveless fingers on to the wooden floor. David reached out for the glass of whisky.

Since his return from Jorehaut it had been incessant work for Lieutenant Michael Bailin. Gokuldeva Barua assisted him in acquiring the manpower to dig an intricate system of ditches to drain away all water from Chahpuli and render the land fit for growing tea. By the time the work was completed, the open area resembled a gigantic spider web. The dug-up earth was used to lay elevated terraces on which hutments would later be erected.

By the middle of November, the clearing and drainage operations had been executed. Bailin engaged an Assamese contractor to carry out the seeding. Planting of the seeds took a week. By end November the first phase of the endeavour to resurrect Chahpuli was complete. On tenth December Gokuldeva's man Phukan arrived at Chahpuli and delivered a packet of sweetmeats as well as a letter from Gokuldeva.

My Dear Michael,

Do you remember I had told you I desperately desired a son. My young wife, at last, has fulfilled my desire. Day before yesterday she gave birth to a healthy boy-child. You cannot comprehend how happy it has made me. All my other achievements pale before the fulfillment I derive from this event.

I had promised a celebration to outclass all celebrations, did I not? On the seventeenth of this month, I propose to give a feast.

Can I hope you will honour me by being present at my house on that day? With Garo, of course.

Barua dangoriya

Bailin whooped in delight. Garo, who was at work clearing the chicken-coop, came running and found himself enfolded into the arms of his master.

'Oh Garo, the dangoriya has been presented with a son,' Bailin cried out in joy. 'At his age? A bloody marvel! Come, we'll not wait till seventeenth, but set out today itself.'

Gokuldeva Barua's mansion was cluttered with workers engaged in clearing, beautifying and, in general, preparing the mansion for the celebrations. Bailin counted a dozen elephants lugging in bamboo, betel-nut stems, thatch, cane and other requirements for a gigantic pandal designed to seat a thousand people at a time.

The nobleman chatted with Bailin over a cup of tea. Two menials appeared carrying a wicker crib on which lay a tiny, gurgling baby, dressed in fine muslin.

Gokuldeva's eyes flashed with pride. 'I'm sorry the mother can't come to greet you,' he said. 'She's convalescent at the moment.'

'Perfectly all right with me,' Bailin said as the crib was ceremoniously carried away.

'You'll not be coming on the seventeenth,' Gokuldeva said softly. 'I can guess from your demeanour. Instead, you will conceal yourself in Chahpuli, like a brat who has committed mischief and is fearful of being discovered.'

Bailin chuckled without mirth. 'You know me more than I do myself, Barua dangoriya. I trust you'll appreciate the cause and forgive me.'

'Oh, this place would be filled with *boga bongals* on that day, to be sure. With people you love to hate! I have sent out invitations to each and every one of them in this district.'

'Major Gosselin and the rest?'

'Certainly. The good Major will be coming, as will all the British officers of the district. They in turn will draw in quite a few European planters, but not all, naturally. Buckingham, for instance! I doubt he'll accept my invitation.'

'Buckingham? You've invited Buckingham?'

'I'm simply being politic. Buckingham's the type who is quick to misread courtesy as cowardice. My invitation to him is not extended in the spirit it should be. He will not accept it in the spirit he should. You get my meaning, Michael?'

'Holding out the olive branch … is that what he'll imagine?'

'Absolutely. That's how he'll read my seeming act of courtesy. It'll induce complacency. A man who makes it a habit to create enemies cannot afford to be complacent. He's in for a surprise, our Buckingham! Oh sure, when the blow lands, he'll guess the source it came from. But by then it'll be too late to forestall the inexorable march of events.'

'You're a crafty old fox, Barua dangoriya!'

Gokuldeva smiled. 'The invitation is also another item in my repertoire of camouflage. I shall certainly make it a point to let everyone know I'd invited Buckingham.'

'Determined to go through it, aren't you, Barua dangoriya?'

'Oh, I've already set the wheels in motion. Meghu has made two trips to Bihguri. He brings back favourable reports. Buckingham drives his coolies brutally. They hate but fear him too. Meghu's mandate is to increase the hatred and neutralise the fear.'

'Tread with care, Barua dangoriya. Buckingham's not a man to be trifled with!'

'Nor am I, Michael. I sense no compunction. From what Meghu tells me, the Bihguri coolies lead the life of the living dead. Things can't get any worse for them, only better.'

'My concern is not for them, but for you. I fear for your safety.'

'That's because you see shadows where there are none. I haven't fully told you of my plans, have I? Quite uncomplicated, really. In the start of the manufacturing season, when Buckingham can ill afford it, Bihguri coolies will strike work. My unseen role will be to recompense the loss in pay suffered during the period of idleness. Buckingham will, naturally, make all efforts to get them back to work. The Bihguri coolies will resist till he pledges better working conditions and more humanitarian treatment.'

'Suppose the coolies can't resist for long?'

'No matter. It's a warning … that's all. He'll soon know where the trouble originated.'

'What if he preempts you by accepting your invitation?' Bailin asked lightly, though his apprehensions were in no way assuaged.

'No earthly chance of that!' Gokuldeva laughed. 'However, there are two who might attend … individuals of your direct concern.'

Bailin caught on instantly. 'David? And Miss Esscombe?'

'Miss Esscombe, eh? Oh Michael, when'll you ever stop deceiving yourself?'

'Quite the opposite, Barua dangoriya. It's my inability to deceive myself any longer which is at the root of my misfortunes.'

'You view things from your own perspective. What you imagine is reality might not be so. Change your position, view it from a less egocentric angle, and your eyes might perceive another reality. Have you seen a glass paperweight, Michael? One of those round things with a many coloured pattern in the centre? Shift the angle, let the light fall from another direction, and the pattern changes.'

Bailin laughed bitterly. 'The Reverend Swanson … you sound just like him! Not long ago he tried to coerce me into self-delusion, just as you do now. But I shall no longer be coerced. I have forever shut Miss Esscombe out from my mind and heart.'

'That's unimportant. The question to be asked, Michael, is whether she's shut you out from hers!'

'Time will do that, Barua dangoriya.'

'No longer blind, are you?' The old man was not being taunting. 'Then I must be turning so, for my experience and instincts tell me otherwise. You heard what Captain Hewitt said? She is desperately unhappy at Dhanboa.'

'And you heard what I said to Captain Hewitt! He's in a far better position to pull her away.'

'There's nothing he desires more, if only she would have him. I haven't met Miss Esscombe overmuch … but the little I saw of her convinces me that she's a woman of irreversible attachment. Such strong passions breed danger.'

'It's you who're seeing shadows, Barua dangoriya!'

'No, Michael. I say it in all gravity. An isolated existence, an indifferent brother, an estranged paramour! It's an explosive recipe!'

The Lieutenant said nothing and turned his face away so it could not be seen.

'Listen, Michael,' Gokuldeva spoke in earnest tones. 'Time will not erase you from Miss Esscombe's heart. Instead, it will breed a melancholic bitterness. There's no telling where such a state of mind can lead to. For her you are irreplaceable. She will not compromise, not even if the suitor is one such as Captain Hewitt. I'll prove to you this is so. David might or might not accept my invitation. But all my instincts tell me that Miss Esscombe will come to Titabar. She'll come secretly hoping that some coincidence of fate will place you face to face with her.'

The Mohoniya tea garden seemed deserted. Gokuldeva had taken his entire workforce to Titabar to assist with the preparations for the feast. But Garo knew it was not quite deserted. There was a man in one of those hutments, the man whom he had come to meet.

Meghu! He was not amongst those working at devta ishwar's house. The devta ishwar had wisely ensured that not many see Meghu around his house. Garo knew why. Meghu was to be the destroyer of the shaitan, the one who had once whipped Garo's back raw, the one who had beaten his sahib to a pulp. The one who almost ended Meghu's life.

But he did not know the precise details, the extent to which the devta ishwar would go. Nor had he the opportunity to discuss the new developments with Meghu. But this morning was as opportune as any. Sahib would be staying the night at Titabar, leaving Garo free to seek out Meghu.

As he neared the first group of hutments Garo began calling out Meghu's name. Meghu stepped out from a hutment and embraced the visitor.

'I'm terribly lonely,' he confessed. 'Devta ishwar shuts me away from the world. But I understand. It'll all be worth it in the end.'

'That is why I've come, Meghu-bhaiya. How are the preparations? What are the plans?'

Meghu sat cross-legged on the floor and told him. Sanatan and others at Bihguri were stirring up the coolies to rise against their master. The devta ishwar had already sent some money to them. When the rains come the coolielog will go on strike. The devta ishwar will make good the loss in wages.

'Pah!' scoffed Garo, his features screwing up in contempt. 'Go on strike! What good will it do to us, Meghu-bhaiya? The shaitan will lose some tea. But how will it heal the cuts in my soul? Or the pain in yours?'

Meghu grinned slyly. 'Would I have risked entering that hell hole had I not other plans of my own? Listen with closed mouth, Garo bhaiya. When the coolielog go on strike the shaitan will hit back through his sirdars. There will be chaos and confusion. We shall take advantage of the chaos and confusion to hack the bastards to pieces. The shaitan and his dogs!'

'He'll be killed? You guarantee that?'

'*Woh aur unke kutte.* I guarantee.'

Meghu bounded up and, striding to the chang-bed, pulled out a covered bamboo basket from underneath it. With the panache of a roadside conjuror opening his bag of tricks, Meghu flicked the cover away. Inside lay an assortment of daos, iron spearheads and axe-blades, all of them new, edges sharp.

'I've already smuggled one such basket in,' Meghu said in triumph. 'By the time it all starts, every household in Bihguri will be armed.'

Pushing back the basket he stood up and slapped Garo on the shoulder. '*Daro mat*, Garo bhaiya.' he said with confidence. 'The bastard is as good as dead!'

The twelfth of December proved unusual, for two individuals arrived at Dhanboa that day, each bearing an invitation for Mr David and Miss Cordelia Esscombe.

A policeman had been the first to arrive, carrying a formal invitation and a personal letter for Cordelia. The invitation stated that His Excellency, Commissioner to the Viceroy for the Province of Assam, would be visiting Jorehaut from the twenty-seventh to the thirtieth of December. A public reception was slated for the twenty eighth, a luncheon the same afternoon, and a shikar on the twenty ninth. The administration would arrange for accommodation of invitees who were unable to arrange it on their own, and transportation for the shikar. However, those invited to join the hunt must provide their own weapons and ammunition.

Captain Hewitt's note to Cordelia was an extension of the formal invitation. He would be delighted if she would come with her brother for the reception and the shikar. The visit would also provide her an opportunity to hand over the memorandum to the Commissioner. Moreover, she could personally discuss the issue with the senior most covenanted officer in Assam and impress upon him the urgency of the measures suggested.

Commonsense dictated that she accepts the invitation. Yet something inside her issued an obdurate denial; each beat of her fluttering heart warned that a visit to Jorehaut would be fraught with pitfalls. She wrote out the reply to the captain declining his invitation, penning each word with caution, unwilling to cause hurt. She did not fabricate excuses, simply stating that she was in no frame of mind to attend the reception or the shikar. Her brother, David, however, was sure to go.

A little later another party arrived, a group of natives led by a man who introduced himself as Phukan. David, meanwhile, had returned from the fields and listened with aggravating hauteur as the native stated the reason for his visit. On the seventeenth of the month, Gokuldeva Barua dangoriya was hosting a luncheon at his mansion in Titabar to celebrate the birth of his son. Phukan had been sent to Dhanboa specifically to invite the sahib and the memsahib to the celebration.

'A son!' David cried, revealing to her how grossly callow he had grown. 'Why, the chap is old enough to be a grandfather! We don't know him well enough for that. I certainly shan't go.'

But Cordelia had made her own decision. 'Dhanyabad, Phukan dangoriya,' she said, ignoring David. 'I shall attend.'

And gone she had, a parched traveller in search of water. But there had been no oasis at the end of the quest as she secretly knew there would not be. Her courteous host had been overwhelmed to see her and treated her as if she were royalty. Never in her life, neither in Delhi nor Calcutta, had she seen so many people congregated in one place. The majority were natives, but at least a dozen white men were present, seated in the 'Europeans only' section of the pandal. Major Gosselin was there, as also Captain Fordyce, though no one attended form the Sivasagar Mission. Ralph Hewitt had been both astonished and hurt to see her. Cordelia made no attempt to explain her presence, but he instinctively he knew and understood.

And all the while her eyes had poked and probed at the native sections and the stream of people coming and going. Shunning white company, could it be that he was seated with the natives? Many a time she almost put the question to her host, but backed out at the last moment. Once she imagined she saw his servant's face in the crowd, looking towards her and grinning. But in the span of a moment that mirage too had vanished.

She returned that evening to Dhanboa's solitude, tense and unfulfilled. She had never expected him to be there in the first place. She could not understand why, then, she felt so desolate and afraid.

'She did come, sahib! I saw her with my own eyes!'

Michael Bailin's features, tanned and stubbled, remained phlegmatic. There was no hint in the blue eyes of the almost physical pain at the words. Garo thought the sahib had not heard what he had said.

'Sahib, sahib! She did come! I'd have gone up to her and talked. But she was with the other sahibs.'

'It's all right, Garo. What else did you see?'

'She kept looking here, there and everywhere, sahib. I know for whom she was searching. She was searching for you, sahib.'

For a brief moment it seemed that his master would speak again. But there was only a slight twitching at the edges of his lips. He remained mute, unable to trust his voice.

'She looked lonely, sahib. I could feel her loneliness. For Bhagwan's sake, sahib, go to her. Why do you hurt yourself like this? Why do you hurt her so?'

Bailin's gaze swivelled swiftly towards Garo. The native quailed. There was madness in that gaze. The Lieutenant's arms shot out and caught his in a vicious grip. There was iron in those arms.

'Listen, Garo,' he shouted. 'You are not to mention the memsahib to me again, do you hear? Cordelia memsahib is dead to me. Dead, Garo, do you understand?'

Bailin released him and strode into the hutment. It was the very first time, Garo thought sadly, that his master had used words of anger with him.

⁂

David reached Jorehaut on the afternoon of the twenty-seventh. A room in an adjacent dak-bungalow had been reserved for him, and an elephant put solely at his disposal for the shikar. He was secretly overwhelmed when he learned that though almost all European tea planters had been invited to the reception and luncheon for the Commissioner, the shikar would be an extremely elitist bash, the party in attendance to the Commissioner to comprise of covenanted officers and a few of the topmost tea planters.

David mulled over it in bed that night. If he had been enfolded into that exclusive shikar company, the credit belonged to Cordi! Infinite possibilities loomed up at the prospect. It wouldn't be a bad thing at all if the mandarin could get Cordi out of his hair!

Sequestered as he had been at Dhanboa, David had not conceived there could be so many Europeans, primarily tea planters, in the district. The introductions to new acquaintances and the back slapping bonhomie of the old imbued in him the comforting feeling of belonging to a community. He could not see Buckingham anywhere, which was a relief.

All in all, that trip to Jorehaut was a memorable experience. He was at Hewitt's place for the luncheon, his clannish comfort strengthening as he mingled with the others. The Commissioner personally shook hands with each planter and posed intelligent questions about the state of the fledgling industry. During the course of the meal, he made a brief speech, wherein he expressed gratitude to the planting community for hazarding the unfavorable Assam conditions so that the pennant of British industry could be kept fluttering. A burst of patriotic cheering greeted these pronouncements, with David, his fraternal instincts now totally dominant, joining throatily in.

The shikar too was an out of the world experience! The party had set out to Pekar chapori, a vast stretch of alluvium running to thousands of acres, which lay at the mouth of the Dehong tributary. It contained an astonishingly diverse variety of wild fauna: barking deer, hog deer, swamp deer, sambars, wild buffaloes, wild boars, mithuns, elephants, rhinoceroses, tigers, leopards and black panthers, as well as a mind-boggling diversity of birds, which made the chapori a paradise for sportsmen.

It was conceded by all that the hunting expedition was an unqualified success. A satisfying number of animals had been shot—rhinos, buffaloes and mithun—and the trophies collected. The Commissioner bade them goodbye at the chapori itself, departing with his retinue for Lakhimpur on the opposite bank, Major Gosselin in accompaniment. The rest of the company crossed the Brahmaputra soon afterwards and were at Jorehaut by late noon.

The past few days had proved a purgative for the soul. It was in a mood of reconciled acceptance that David left Jorehaut for Papa's garden.

Christopher James Buckingham was not invited to the luncheon with the Commissioner but he didn't give a damn! The mandarin had sought to drive home his displeasure. Little did the officious twerp know that he was least bothered whether he was invited or not. He had rather remain in his own realm, within the gratifying ambit of his own prepotency, than trudge down to Jorehaut to be a member of the fawning, sycophantic crowd!

In ironic compensation, other invitations had come his way. A hand-delivered letter from Gokuldeva Barua intimating the birth of his son and heir; inviting him to a luncheon on the seventeenth. The planter well knew the motive behind the invitation. With all European planters arrayed against him, how long could Gosselin protect the nigger? An ultimatum had already been issued by the planter-lobby along with charges against the nobleman. Either the native close down his garden, or the administration confiscate it. The planters had impressed upon Gosselin the urgent necessity for action.

And the bastard was feeling the pressure! The letter in Buckingham's hand was not a piece of paper—it was a white flag waved by an old native desperate to save his estate.

But the greatest surprise, one which filled him with such fiery wrath that he could barely resist the impulse to bring down the cat-o'-nine-tails hanging on his bedroom wall, was the invitation extended by Bircha. The coolie's behaviour had been without arrogance; polite, suffused with humility. Yet the very fact that he had had the temerity to invite his Lord and Master to his wedding was an affront which brooked no mercy. But he could not physically touch the son of a bitch! He had watched with baffled fury as the impudent bastard mouthed his invitation and walked away.

In some inconspicuous nook within his skull lay awareness as to why Bircha aroused such maniacal fury in him. Though he would not admit it, the violent anger Bircha evoked was because the man had assumed a divinity of his own in the coolies' imagination. Time and again his sirdars had told him how greatly Bircha was influencing the attitudes of the coolielog. Uncaring and invulnerable, he had exposed his master's own fallibility!

And Christopher James Buckingham, undisputed Lord and Master of his realm, could not strip the usurper of his divinity, divest him of his hollow godhood. This had sparked anger—this too had induced disquietude in his mind. An instinctive feeling, like of a creature of the wild sensing approaching peril. Buckingham did not know what brought about this unease.

Were there darker undercurrents running in his garden he had no knowledge of? Try as he might, he could not shake off the feel of danger. He had asked his sirdars to be on the alert. Apart from reporting that the coolies were becoming intransigent, they had mentioned nothing out of the ordinary. He, however, took no chances. Four new rifles had been purchased for his sirdars and he spent a week training them. Previously he moved freely about the garden atop his mount, alone or with Luthra. But now he always kept another sirdar along with Luthra by his side. The bungalow looked to him to be too open and unsafe; he put some coolies to lay a tall bamboo fence enclosing it from all sides except the opening in front, where a wooden gate, which could be padlocked during the night, was erected. He had another two-roomed hutment built inside this enclosure, to be occupied by Luthra and Gandru, so they would be at a hearing distance at night and come to him whenever he beckoned.

An incident occurred in the second week of January which set alarm bells ringing in his mind. At the end of the day, as he relaxed on the verandah with a gin and tonic, three coolies came to the bungalow. They were led by an elderly native called Sanatan who made a request on behalf of the coolielog. Ever since they had left their native villages, they had not been given opportunity to perform puja and propitiate the gods. Perhaps that was why the scourge visited the basti every year. Tusu Parab was due three days hence. The coolielog would like to perform puja on that auspicious day. Would the sahib give permission and declare the day as chutti?

Buckingham, instantly, was on the alert. Previously no coolie would dare to approach the sahib directly, even less to come to his bungalow unbeckoned and ask for chutti. That the trio had broken this strict convention made him smell a rat. Were these bastards testing the waters? Were they willfully exposing themselves to punishment?

The planter did not reprimand them. On the contrary, he put on a casual smile and gave permission. The fourteenth of January, the day of Tusu Parab, the day Bircha was to be married, would be a chutti day, the first in Bihguri during his reign!

That smile concealed the sudden dread which shot into his heart. Unconsciously Buckingham looked at the sky as if wondering when the rains would arrive.

'The shaitan suspects something,' Sanatan said.

'How can he suspect? You worry needlessly, Sanatan bhaiya,' Meghu countered.

'No. Upon my dead mother! He suspects. He's a cunning devil. Maybe he knows.'

Meghu chuckled nervously. Sanatan was shrewd. If something made him anxious it needed to be his own anxiety too.

'Suspect? Know? How can it be so? Is there a traitor among the coolielog?'

' I don't think so. Only the trusted few are privy to our plans. But the sahib is the very devil incarnate. I cannot tell you how, but I can swear he suspects! We sought a day's chutti for Tusu Parab. A calculated gamble. We wished to push him a bit harder. Provoke him. See which way the wind blew.'

'And he did not punish you? That's unusual.'

'He didn't punish us. Just the opposite … he smiled and gave us chutti.'

'The shaitan has never done so before. But perhaps because we never asked?'

'No, Meghu-bhaiya. I was watching his eyes as we put in our request. You can tell what a man is thinking by watching the eyes.'

'And what did you see in the bastard's eyes?'

'Alarm! I saw fear dart into his eyes. His smile was on his lips, not in the eyes.'

'Not anger? Fear, eh? That's bad.'

'He suspects something is brewing. He has even put up a fence around the bungalow.'

'Perhaps something has alerted him? Some action on the part of the coolielog?'

'I wouldn't know. But this I can tell you. The sirdars are behaving oddly. All of a sudden, they seem to have lost their sting. The coolielog are having it relatively easy now. Lighter jobs and less working hours. I don't like it at all.'

'May be the son of a bitch is changing,' Meghu said, but without conviction.

'Does the sun shine at night, Meghu-bhaiya?'

'*Jo hoga, so hoga*,' Meghu said philosophically. 'There's no point in speculations. And no turning back.'

'Certainly not,' Sanatan said. 'But if he's on alert it'll be doubly difficult to get at him.'

'We'll get at him, never fear. If they can shoot us from far, we too can kill from far. Let me show you what I've brought tonight.'

He un-wrapped a small bundle to reveal a few pieces of a fibrous root. The pieces looked so harmless that Sanatan and Lachmi could not conceal their disappointment.

'*Yeh kyaa cheej hai*?' Sanatan asked.

'Looks harmless, does it not? But it is deadly. I acquired it from a Naga man with great difficulty and a considerable amount of money.'

Sanatan had stretched out a hand to pick up a piece. At Meghu's words his hand shot back as if the piece was a live snake. Meghu chuckled.

'Oh, it is harmless to the touch. The Naga told me that this root is used by a tribe called the Abor. Like the Nagas they too live in the mountains. They use it to kill haathi and other wild creatures.'

'Haathi? This tiny little thing?' Sanatan was sceptical.

'Yes, haathi! But it must be prepared first. You've to pound it to a powder and mix it into a paste with the juice of the outenga. Then put a bit of it on the tip of your arrow or spear. The outenga juice makes it stick fast. The Naga tells me a scratch from such an arrow can cause instant death.'

Sanatan gingerly picked up a piece of the root and scanned it. 'Poisoned arrowhead, eh? That should even out things a little. Their bandooks and our arrows.'

'We come from a land where even toddlers know how to use bows and arrows. Our skills may have grown rusty with disuse but the bows and arrows have to be made. And in secret. Maybe, we should ask Bircha-bhaiya to make them for us.'

'Bircha is out,' Sanatan said. 'I had asked him to take up my burden. He'll have none of it. He's getting married the day after tomorrow.'

'Is Bircha getting married?' Meghu asked excitedly and then his face fell. 'Only I will not be present. But I'll meet him before I leave.'

'You don't need to worry about the bows and arrows. There's enough bamboo around. We've more time in our hands these days.'

Meghu retied the bundle and handed it to Sanatan. 'I leave now. To Bircha's hutment and then to the boat. I'll not return till the rains start. Then I'll come and stay. I'll bring more money. And together we'll slit that shaitan's throat!'

January fourteenth was a balmy day, dry and bright with wintry sunshine. The coolielog were up at the very first flush of dawn, preparing for the Parab. Oh, what a transformation had come over the basti as the innate joi de vivre of the coolielog, cruelly suppressed for so long, burst out in full measure! The elderly workers, who normally slouched about with cowed looks, seemed suddenly to swell out with dignity as they prepared for the puja, walking straight and throwing out instructions to the younger folk. Coolie women put on bangles on their normally bare arms, vermilion on their foreheads. The young men, dressed in clean garbs, pranced about cock a hoop, making eyes at the colourfully decked young belles, who giggled shyly in response.

However, not all the young men were making eyes at the young girls, or all the young girls sizing them up. Some of the young men and women were at Bircha's hutment, helping in the preparations for the feast. Some were at Baisakhi's house, helping the mago have everything organised for the nuptial ceremony.

And, with the permission of the sirdars, some young men were in the jungles, cutting shrubs to decorate the altar and bamboo stems to affix to the palanquin. Yet what a lot of bamboo they had brought in! Enough for a hundred palanquins! And strands of dwarf bamboo? What were those for?

Bircha was in his hutment, as euphoric as the rest. The chutti had been an unexpected boon, a propitious omen. The gods were pleased with him. He and Saoni were going to have a prosperous wedded life. They were going to be happy.

He had embarked on the preparations for this day well in advance, not forgetting to invite everyone, including the sahib and the sirdars. He had retraced that fateful route to the neighbouring garden to invite the farishta memsahib. He had requested her to send words to the sarkari sahib of his wedding and invite him on his behalf, which she had promised to do. She herself, for obvious reasons, could not come. She offered him a few rupee coins. He had refused with dignity, as was the proper thing to do. But she had pressed the coins into his hand, calling it a *shaadi buksheesh*, and asking him to buy something for Saoni with the money.

Everything was ready now. After the rituals for the Tusu parab were over, a huge marriage party set out for the bride's house in the afternoon. He found himself seated beside a heavily draped Saoni. Dudhu was invested with the honour of solemnising the union. He did so with priestly gravity, the women who were in the bride's party appropriately wailed on behalf of a dry-eyed Baisakhi, and Bircha, the handsome prince, finally carried off the beautiful princess to his castle.

Then the feasting started. A large bonfire was lit in the open and buckets of steaming, spice-smelling food brought. Mod flowed like the nullahs flow during heavy rains. The moon and stars lit a million candles in the sky, fireflies lit diyas on the earth. Ribald jokes were bandied, snatches of song rose above the din, men and women broke out in spontaneous, inebriated dancing. The coming dawn might bring back the fog of perpetual despair wrapping the Bihguri basti. But for tonight at least the fog had lifted and joyous sunshine had lit up the lives of the coolielog. Far into the night the celebrations carried on, till the bottles were empty, the pots scraped for the last morsel of food, and the final embers of the bonfire flared out. The coolielog trooped back one by one to their hutments, hoarding in their hearts the glow enkindled that day, to fuel their hopes for many moons to come.

Saoni awaited Bircha in his hutment. She had excused herself early from the revelry, while courtesy demanded the host had to tarry till the last guest had departed. No longer did she wear her bridal finery; she was dressed instead in an old sari. But the enticing aroma of perfume lingered on her body. Bircha saw that she had removed the flowers form the nuptial bed and those in her hair.

She came to him the very moment he entered through the door, clasping him in an embrace which belied her outward fragility. 'I am ready, my Bircha,' she whispered in all seriousness. 'Mago has instructed me as to what I must do.'

The earnestness of the tone amused him no end and he began to laugh even as he held her, till she cried out in exasperation. 'Oh, you're worse than ever! Don't treat me as a chokri, my Bircha. I'm your wife.'

That made him laugh all the more and he was laughing as he picked her up and laid her gently down on the nuptial bed. It was just a sheet of hessian laid on the floor. But no emperor's featherbed could yield the soft joys and ecstatic delights of this rude sheet of hessian, for theirs was the consummation of their pyaar. He was tender and caring, she strong and fiercely insistent, suffused with a continuous drive to drown him in pleasure. Later they lay face upwards on the bed, fulfilled and happy, listening to the subdued sounds of the night.

'Will it be like this always, my Bircha?'

'Yes, my love. It will be like this always. For ever and ever.'

'You will love me like this always?'

'Yes. Always. For ever and ever.'

Saoni sighed. 'To think I almost lost you! *Kasam khao*, my Bircha, you will never leave me.'

Bircha placed a hand over her heart. '*Mein kasam khata hoon*. In life or in death, I'll never leave you.'

Pekoe's deep throated growls jolted her into awakening. Hurriedly she thrust aside the mosquito curtain, and tiptoed to the window, pushing it open. Outside it was pitch black.

Someone was calling out. 'Memsahib! Memsahib!'

'*Kaun hai*?' she called out.

'Me, memsahib. Bamni. I'm on chowkidari duty tonight.'

'*Kya baat hai*?'

'Mrigal's wife ... Chameli. She's in great pain.'

'Wait. I'm coming.' She dressed quickly and emerged from the room.

The noise had awakened David too. His door opened and he came out. He was startled to see her dressed for leaving.

'What's up, sis?' he said, trying to sound casual. She ignored him and went down the stairs, Pekoe by her side. Three men awaited her. Chameli's husband, Mrigal, was deeply agitated. His wife was heavy with child. She had returned from the fields in the evening and complained of great pain. Now she lay in the basti, writhing and groaning.

'*Saala bewkuf*!' David said angrily. 'You woke us up in the middle of the night just for that? Don't you know a woman with child writhes and groans when she's about to bring it into this world?'

The men quailed at David's outburst, but Cordelia said. 'Has a woman of the coolielog examined her?'

'*Ji* memsahib. The old woman, Sukhmati. She says it's bad.'

'All right,' Cordelia said. 'Let me get the medicine bag. I'll go with you.'

'At a time like this? You must be out of your mind!' David cried out.

Once more she ignored him and strode towards the dispensary to get the medicine bag, the chowkidar and the two coolies in attendance. David followed a little behind. Mrigal's wife, Chameli, was just a slip of a girl, seventeen years at most. Coolie chokris married early, just as they died early. She lay on a bamboo chang, the bulge under the blanket covering her tell-tale sign of her advanced stage of pregnancy. She was in a very bad state, twisting and turning and shrieking in such great agony that the two women who held her arms had difficulty maintaining their grip.

'Boil some water,' she directed Sukhmati. She turned to Mrigal, whose face was screwed up in grief. 'You knew she was so large with child,' she said accusingly. 'Why did you let her go to work?'

'I did not, memsahib, Bhagwan be witness! I wouldn't allow her. But Harua and Ajam wouldn't listen. I begged and pleaded, but they wouldn't listen. The cleared land must be readied within this month, they said. Sahib wants every hand in the field, they said. It was the sirdars who took her away, memsahib.' Mrigal was close to weeping.

David quietly slipped out of the door and stood outside.

The boiled water was brought in an earthen jug. Cordelia dropped some disinfectant into it and dipped her hands. The men in the room went out. With a woman holding Mongla's lantern to give her light, she pushed her warm hands under the blanket and probed with exploring fingers. The hessian serving as mattress was clotted with blood and mucus. Good Lord, how much blood was there! She felt vomit rise to her throat but fought it down as her slippery fingers reached deeper inside.

On the bed the woman uttered a shriek as her body heaved and thrashed, struggling to eject the lump of flesh and blood which obdurately would not be ejected. Cordelia knew Dr Goodeve's utterances on childbirth by heart. Something was dreadfully wrong here! The baby was not emerging as it should. Her fingers touched soft, mucous-lined flesh instead of the hard roundness of the head. An ominous lifelessness to the touch, as though it was an inert tumour rather than a living presence! Cordelia understood. She could do nothing for the child. But the mother must be saved.

Taking as firm a grip with fingers of both hands as she could, she pulled with increasing strength as the woman continually shrieked in diminishing intensity. Some resistance at first and then, mercifully, there was none, and Cordelia found herself staring with shocked eyes at the lump of gore and mucus which made no movement, uttered no protesting wail. Sukhmati was at hand with a knife heated in fire. Cordelia handed the stillborn infant to her and turned to the woman on the bed.

Her struggles to bring the baby out had pushed away the blanket covering Chameli so that the girl lay with bare legs outstretched in pathetic obscenity. Cordelia cried out as she saw the blood continue to ooze and tried frantically to stem its flow with bandage padding. But the cloying, dark liquid would not be stemmed. It stained the hessian bedding and when that could absorb no more, dropped through the bamboo chang, creating a pool of red on the floor. The woman on the bed made no sound now. The end of her agony had instead brought a strange half smile, half grimace to her lips. The smile clung to her features as the life drained out of her body. She was smiling even as she shuddered and lay still, staring at the thatched roof with eyes of death.

It took the women in the room a few moments to realize what had happened. They set up a high-pitched, choric wail which shuddered off the mud walls and fell with deafening numbness against Cordelia's ears. She stood up, dazed and unbelieving, as Mrigal and the others rushed into the room. The duality of his loss sank into the young coolie—he flung himself upon his dead wife and began to sob in asthmatic gasps.

Cordelia stepped forward to hold the grieving husband and soothe him with her balmy touch. Her gaze fell on her hands. They were a fiery red with the blood of the dead woman. She lurched back and stared around her. The men seemed to stare back at her with accusing eyes! Cordelia staggered out of the hutment and ran into the mist-filled night.

Footsteps sounded behind her, hands gripped her roughly, bringing her to an abrupt, painful stop. 'Where the devil are you going, sis?' her brother's voice came to her. She struggled to release herself, but he held on with fierce strength.

'For God's sake, sis, come to your senses!' he was shouting in panic, shaking her violently into submission. She stopped struggling as the strength ebbed out of her body. Like a small, obedient child she allowed herself to be led back to the bungalow.

'I didn't know,' David kept saying, his voice panting and hoarse. 'I swear on Papa's name I didn't know! If I'd known, I'd never have let her go to work.'

At the foot of the staircase, she shook herself off from her brother. The wailing in her skull was silent. 'You know very well you killed her, David,' she said, her voice cold with contempt. Turning sharply round, she walked steadily up the stairs and into her room.

A little later, having cleaned herself, she stood on the verandah railings and looked through the wall of darkness towards the basti. The continuous wailing floated to her ears. Was David listening too? Or had he buried himself inside his quilt to shut out the howls? Had he muffled the ears of his soul to shut out the howling of his conscience?

Had not Dhanboa been free of death the past one and a half years? Even during Papa's days, despite his liberal concern for the coolies, more than a dozen garden hands had died. Over a thousand deaths in the plantations of this subdivision last season! Not one in Dhanboa! Had she not through her unswerving will kept Yamadut, messenger of the Lord of Death, from plucking away the souls of Dhanboa's coolies?

So futile, this death! So stupidly futile! Protest as David might, Chameli's death lay at his door. To put a woman big with child as Chameli had been to labour in the fields! Tonight, David had taken refuge in profession of ignorance. Tomorrow, he would cheat his conscience by talking of his compulsions. Goodchild's revelations had knocked the wind out of him. The same day Uncle Alex's letter had come. The twin blows had devastated him. For days on end, he had moved about in a baffled daze. Not all of his dazed distractedness was due to his misfortunes. Inordinate consumption of whisky had something to do with it. Her weak-kneed brother, he had been fatally struck. She had exulted in the knowledge.

But then David had returned from Jorehaut a rejuvenated creature. Something had happened there to put renewed resolve in him. He had turned his attention to preparing the newly cleared ground for replanting. If Uncle Alex would not send reinforcements, he would get the job done with whatever resources he commanded. And poor Chameli had been the sacrificial goat at the altar of David's resolve!

So futile, the death of the woman and thc child! The logs would be piled up, the fire lit. Nothing else to do but watch memories fade. Then what was she doing on the balcony in this bewitched hour of the night, peering into the sooty blackness? No, it was not a black and foggy wall she faced. It was a dark mirror reflecting the charred bleakness of her soul. And she could see it laid bare—the guilt and hypocrisy—for her eyes to see and recognize.

Yes, the image of her own guilt loomed clearly upon that black mirror, her culpability no less than that of David, even more heinous, for she had not been blinded by illusory compulsions as he had been. Previously she had kept watch over the coolies like a shepherd's dog guarding the flock. Chameli's advanced stage of pregnancy would never have escaped her noticc. Prcviously she had fought and argued with David, wresting out of him concessions for the coolies. But the repeated buffeting upon her sensibility had made her withdraw turtle-like into a carapace of egocentricity. In the past few months, the coolies had slid away towards the fringe of her concerns. Had it not been so Chameli would not have died. The coolies who had looked so accusingly at her this night had not done so without reason. In her hysteria lay her guilt—the darkness mirrored the truth.

She willed herself to turn away from that stark, all-revealing mirror, but her legs would not move. Her eyes continued to strip the image, peeling away the shell, flagellating her soul in masochistic delight. But soon the focus shifted, for pinpricks of illumination filtered through the fog. Flares!

The dead woman and the baby were being carried towards the burning ground. A while later a single flower bloomed out, a distant, tiny bud magnified by the fog.

That solitary bloom unleashed a pack of ravenous images which fed on her brain and her heart. A cluster of blooms upon a sandbank! The steamer's deck a ringside seat. So long ago, oh, so long ago! She had agonized then. But there had been Michael's protective arm, David's comforting presence, the Reverend's consoling voice. Every one of them had been taken away from her.

The fiery flower loomed bigger and bigger till it filled up the entire screen of her vision. The wavering edges reshaped into a spectral, human form. For one demented moment Cordelia thought it was Chameli's face she saw in that hallucination. But the blurry outline congealed into a death's head and she cried out in terror. Not Chameli's but Dorothy Winterbotham's skeletal features grinned at her from that dreadful, glassy blackness.

The grotesque, grinning face filled her consciousness. Of her own volition she raised her arm and touched the crinkled, leathery cheeks. 'Leave that place, do you understand? Put it forever behind you, unless you want your firm flesh to rot and your soft skin to wither!'

Leave that place? But where could she go to? The answer was there the very moment her heart posed the question—provided by the rational mind which could apply cold logic to situations, ignoring the yearnings of the soul. Even the Reverend, despite his deep understanding of her character, had suggested she make a compromise with herself and take that egress. For David it would be removal of a thorn from the flesh. To the Reverend it would be a turning away from the ravagery of change.

Yes, cold logic dictated she accept Captain Ralph Hewitt's offer of marriage. Yet she knew in her heart that she would never accept the good and decent captain as her husband. She would not take recourse to escape but wait like a toad on a rain filled afternoon for the venomous fangs of her destiny to strike. She would live on in Dhanboa, oscillating between hatred and insanity, poised for an eternity on the edge of a precipice.

With the onset of March, the air heated up once again. Once more farmers and tea planters looked up at the sky for dark clouds to gather, the showers to slake the parched earth.

At Dhanboa David waited with resolve. Nothing could now shake that tenacious certainty. If need be, he would throw out his roots deep in Dhanboa as the tea bushes had done and foliate here for an eternity. On no account would he allow Buckingham's saplings to bleed Papa's garden dry. If that bag of pomposity in Calcutta chose not to aid him, he would make his niggers toil till the last man dropped. But he would make Dhanboa pay!

At Chahpuli Lieutenant Michael Bailin waited for the rains with stoicism. The trick was to live for the moment and let kismet do all the planning and plotting on his behalf.

At his Titabar mansion Gokuldeva Barua awaited the rains with vengeful eagerness, as did Meghu in the solitude of his hutment in Mohoniya; and Sanatan, Lachmi, Dudhu and others in Bihguri's coolie basti. The daos and axe blades were buried underground, the bamboo bows, arrows and spears cleverly hidden inside the rafters. The forces of retribution were ready, each player in his appointed place.

And, at Bihguri, Christopher James Buckingham awaited the rains, holding his dogs on a tight leash, cursing the mandarin for delaying his visit. What was keeping that bastard? Ordinarily he paid his annual visit around end February. It was well into March now, and he had not come. His dogs, their nostrils quivering with the smell of prey, were getting restless. But he could not unleash them. No, not yet. The spring showers would peter out into a spell of dryness. The bastard might well decide to drop in then!

The heavy but sporadic downpours heralding spring's graceful advent arrived at the appointed time. Winter's immobility dispelled, Dhanboa was prodded once again into continuous movement. Neither David nor his sirdars and coolies had a moment to rest between daybreak and sundown. With the mature bushes flushing, the newly cleared area replanted and the tea house fires blazing, each coolie man and woman, chokra and chokri, was goaded on by dint of threats and blows to perform the work of two. David himself was equal to ten—now in the fields, flaying his riding crop in the air as he yelled '*Che lao, che lao*' as lustily as his sirdars; now in the weighing shed overseeing the storage of plucked leaves; in the tea houses ensuring that none of his tea makers shirked, in his room at night meticulously putting down figures in ledgers by the light of a taper. Gone was the indecisiveness, the vacillations wrought by ignorance. Now he was fired by a demonic energy as white-hot as a tea house blaze; a snarling, angry fire that singed his coolies into a submissive terror.

Only one creature in Dhanboa remained impervious to this universal eruption. No longer was work an anodyne to pain, for there was no pain but a dulled weariness. Nothing could shake away this nerveless lethargy—though she continued to work in the dispensary it was but in a mechanical way. In the same mechanical manner, she continued her work in the basti preparing the coolies for the onslaught of the heavy rains. She nursed her hatred for David; but this too proved an inadequate stimulus. Not only was David engrossed with the garden's activities, he had also armoured himself with an indifference which nothing short of a violent assault would pierce.

Towards the middle of April, the spring showers waned and once more a spell of dryness prevailed. It permitted Cordelia to take Souchong out for rides.

The day was the fourteenth of April. The first of Baisakh according to the Hindu calendar, called Bohag in Assamese. It was the day when the natives celebrated the Rongali Bihu festival. The previous year, Cordelia remembered, she had visited Bapu babu's village on this day. But there had been no invitation this year. Nor would the garden reverberate with the lilt of buffalo-horn pipes and the pounding of huchari dancers' feet. No village elder would shower benediction over the Esscombe household. Where had Bapu babu and Kamal gone, she wondered. And where had captain Hewitt gone? She had expected him to drop in at Dhanboa in February itself. Had she offended him by refusing his invitation? Had her action angered him into forsaking Bircha?

In the afternoon, having taken her post-siesta cup of the brew, she summoned Mongla and gave him instructions for the evening meal. Then, donning her Jodhpurs and riding boots, she went to the stables, accompanied by the ever-vigilant Pekoe. The caretaker chokra was nowhere in sight. Perhaps he had wearied of having nothing to do and gone into the jungles in search of edible fruits. Cordelia brought Souchong out, saddled and mounted it, and urged it on to a slow trot.

She did not delay long at the empty coolie basti, but pulled Souchong around and headed for the mud track leading to Bihguri. Disuse had narrowed the track further; the trees and bushes on either side had flung out leafy branches so that she had to progress with care. The track was carpeted with thick grass which muted Souchong's hoof-beats and camouflaged slushy patches. Clearly it was not as dry as she had assumed and for a moment she contemplated turning back. But the pervasive gloom seemed to blend well with her mood and she pressed ahead. On her right Pekoe let out a whining complaint. The mud thrown up by Souchong's hooves had spattered the dog, giving him such a comically mottled appearance that Cordelia laughed.

'Now Pekoe, don't be grouchy,' she called out, marvelling at how loud and hollow her voice sounded. 'I shall give you a bath the minute we get back.'

As they neared the invisible line demarcating Dhanboa's boundary the woody jungles gave way to scrub and grass. Unscreened sunlight made her squint her eyes as they sought to adjust to the brightness. Cordelia paused at the edge of the patch of thatch and cane and gazed across it towards Bihguri's vast enclave. At a distance she could see the sheds of that plantation's nurseries, and tiny, beetle-like figures busy among them. The sight of the nurseries and the thatch and cane patch evoked memories of Bircha. It was by this route the man had come into her life and reshaped her destiny.

Where was Bircha now? Waiting in his hutment for Saoni to return from the fields? Filling her days with fervour and her nights with passion? Her own love may have faded away, but she had at least given Saoni back hers.

Cordelia sighed, pulled Souchong around and urged him into the slowest of trot. Had she not been so rapt in her own thought she might have observed it earlier—the sinuous parting of the grass a few yards ahead, as though an invisible hand was tracing a pattern upon it. But the time the wavy ripple caught her eye, it was too late!

With Souchong a few feet away, the king cobra shot up from the grass. A hiss like that of escaping air sounded a daring challenge. The horse let out a terrified whinny and reared up on its hind legs.

Cordelia had been riding slack rein, or she might have saved herself. The abrupt upward movement of Souchong caught her by surprise. Even as the horse's forelegs thumped back onto the ground and it swiftly wheeled away, she found herself flung into the air. A bushy growth softened her fall so that she sprawled unhurt.

There she lay, petrified with horror, as the king cobra, hissing and infuriated, streaked towards her. For one ghastly moment Cordelia stared into the beady eyes of death. The head swayed back, enticingly graceful, to deliver the fatal strike. Cordelia screamed.

The jungle took up the sound in an affrighted echo! Yet the stinging pain of those lethal fangs was not felt, for Pekoe flung himself between them and their intended target. The powerful head-blow momentarily knocked the dog off his feet. But he was up in the split of a second and at the reptile's white-grey throat, digging his teeth into the cold flesh. Cordelia screamed and screamed again as the cobra thrashed about, its tail flailing the grass, seeking to dislodge the canine's grip. Though mortally wounded, Pekoe hung desperately on till the thrashing eased, the coils around his body relaxed their strangling hold and the king cobra was dead.

But Cordelia had not tarried to witness the end of reptile and beast. Her nerves and sinews were screaming now. She staggered up and ran in blind panic, unseeing as to where she was headed, unmindful of the thorns and sharp, reedy blades tearing at her clothes and flesh. And suddenly there were faces around her; brown visages with mouths agape and eyes staring, unnerved by the screams rising from her throat. She saw all this and yet did not see. She heard her screams and yet did not hear. And suddenly he was there confronting her, hands outstretched to stall her panicked rush. She felt the power of his embrace as his arms coiled around her violently trembling body and his words came to her as if from a distance. 'Easy now, girl! Easy, easy!'

But the hysteria would not subside, the trembling not cease. She was fighting him now, thrashing and wriggling. His right hand uncoiled itself from her body, swayed back like the dilated hood of a cobra, and hit her full across the face.

Cordelia slumped unconscious in Christopher James Buckingham's arms.

'Sahib! Sahib!'

David was in the field amongst his pluckers when he heard Mongla's worried call. The young servant boy came running up. 'Sahib! Sahib!' he shouted. '*Memsahib ko kuch hua hai*! She rode off on the ghora. Pekoe went with her. The ghora has returned. The memsahib is not on it. Pekoe *bhi wapas nahin aya*.'

Summoning Robiya to take charge of the pluckers, David rode off towards the bungalow, Mongla racing after him. Souchong stood at the stable door, held by his youthful syce, saddled and with reins trailing. Only when David reached closer did he notice that the horse was sweating profusely and trembling now and again. The horse had suffered a severe shock. David's anxiety deepened into alarm.

He pushed Congou towards the coolie basti. Souchong's hoof marks were clearly visible on the soft earth. David followed them to the basti, and thence towards the jungle track. He was in a funk now. Damn Cordi! How many times had he warned her not to take that trail! David raced towards and sounded the pagal ghanta.

The summons brought forth his sirdars and other coolies. A rescue party was quickly mustered: within twenty-five minutes from the sounding of the pagal ghanta it was on its way, David in the lead upon Congou, the others on foot.

The deeper they went into the gloomy, shadow-filled jungles the more apprehensive David grew. Gone was the pretence of haughty indifference. They passed the red flaming simul tree marking the midway point of that track and heard incoherent voices filtering through the foliage. Quickening their pace, they emerged out of the gloom. A group of Bihguri coolies were at the other end of the track, babbling in frenzied excitement. David recognized the tall figure of Luthra. The coolies looked up as they heard the rescue party approach and instantly fell silent. David jumped down and hastened towards Buckingham's minion. 'My sister,' he shouted. 'Has something happened to her?'

Luthra pointed to the ground. 'Look, sahib!' he said.

David gasped in horror. Even in death Pekoe had not released his grip on the reptile!

'We measured it, sahib,' Luthra spoke again, awe in his voice. 'Almost ten hands!'

'Damn the snake! Where's my sister? What's happened to her?'

'She's safe, sahib. But frightened to death. Screamed and ran to Bihguri and swooned in our master's arms. Now she rests in his bungalow.'

'She's not hurt?'

'*Nahi, sahib*. But the shock was severe.'

Thank heavens Cordi was safe! That was a vast weight off his mind. The decent thing for him to do was to carry on into Bihguri and get her back. But he baulked at setting foot in that garden once again or meeting Buckingham. He called out to Robiya.

'Go with these men to Buckingham sahib's bungalow. I'll despatch the two elephants the minute I get back. Escort the memsahib to Dhanboa as soon as you can. You there, Harua, get Pekoe. He saved the memsahib's life. Deserves a decent burial.'

'And the snake? What do we do with it, sahib?'

It was Luthra who answered. 'Let it be where it is, sahib. The *kaala naag* moves in pairs. Most likely its mate is nearby, warming eggs in her nest. If you take this kaala naag to your garden the mate will come seeking revenge. Leave it here, and she'll not know who killed her mate.'

David thought of contending the stupid bugger's superstition, but then wisely held his tongue and nodded. 'We'll let it lie. But Pekoe must be taken away.'

His coolies cut a bamboo staff and strands of cane, pulled the stiff body of the dog away from the snake, and tied him to the staff. While Ajam and Robiya crossed over to Bihguri the rest of their party returned to Dhanboa. Pekoe was deposited on the bungalow verandah—he must not be buried before Cordi had an opportunity to bid him final farewell. Having made arrangements for the elephants to be sent, David sat on the verandah awaiting his sister's return.

Cordelia lay on the bed, face chalky-white, the rise and fall of her breasts the sole indicator of life in her. The imprint of Buckingham's fingers stood out in ruddy contrast upon one bloodless cheek.

The planter stood close by; features flushed with triumph as he looked down at her. The score had been evened this afternoon—as he had never doubted it would be!

She moaned, stirred and opened her eyes. The hungry blaze in his eye died out and a look of concern took its place. He said nothing, permitting her time to orient herself to her surroundings, watching the shadowy fear wash over her as the terrible images came flooding into her memory. His words were layered with predesigned gentleness.

'You're safe now, Cordelia. Here, drink this.'

He sat sidewise on the bed, put his arm around her shoulders and helped her up to a sitting posture. She responded meekly to this intimate gesture. He held the brandy goblet to her lips. She lapped up the libation. But neither the brandy nor his own body heat could thaw the cold numbness, and kindle her flesh into renewed warmth.

'Oh, it was awful!' she said as though talking to herself. There was no self-consciousness in her at his proximity.

'Try not to remember. Let your mind and body relax.'

'Pekoe? Souchong? How are they?'

'The horse is safe. But Pekoe, I'm afraid, is dead.'

She shuddered violently, but just once. He thought she would burst out crying, but her eyes remained dry. Her body continued to be infuriatingly cold and unresponsive.

'Does David know?'

'Yes. Two of his sirdars are waiting outside to take you back to Dhanboa.'

'I shan't be going.'

The words were uttered tiredly, so weakened as to be almost a whisper. Yet they fell upon his cars with the irrevocable clang of a hammer on an anvil.

'You'll have to tell them yourself. Your brother might otherwise misconstrue the situation. Are you sure you can walk?'

She tried to raise herself on the bed. Once again, his powerful arms were around her, helping her onto her feet.

'Paper. I must have pen and paper to list the things I need from Dhanboa.'

Wordlessly he left the room, returning moments later. She sat down at the writing table set against a mud wall and penned out the list. She waved him away as he sought to help her rise and walked out of the room.

The worry and excitement, as well as exhaustion, induced in David an intense yearning for a restorative. But he fought down the urge to bring out the whisky bottle. This evening Cordi must not catch him drinking. A bloody miraculous escape, that's what she had had! He recalled his own horror at the sight of the dead kaala naag. What a nerve-wrenching shock it must have been for the poor girl! A shock which made her rush blindly towards Bihguri. To a man she hated with every fibre of her body.

The last of the lingering, summer light faded into darkness. How lonely the bungalow loomed in his imagination this evening! Mongla came up to ask about dinner. David asked him to set the table for two and wait. Ah, there they were finally! Two flares upon two mounts wafting across the darkness like will-o'-the-wisps. The coolies preferred flares to lanterns. Creatures of the dark seemed to fear the naked fire of flares than the shielded light of lanterns. David bounded up eagerly and raced down the stairs, Mongla, equally eager, at his heels.

'Cordi? Cordi? Are you all right now?'

But it was Ajam who answered. 'The memsahib will not come, sahib.'

'*Kya hua*? Is something the matter? Has she not recovered yet?'

Ajam and Robiya hopped off the kneeling brutes. Once again Ajam spoke. 'She has recovered, sahib. She seems to be well enough.' The sirdar's voice held a slight note of reproof and shame.

Fear seeped in through the folds of his flesh to clutch at his heart. She was well! But she had not come! That perfidious bastard was behind all this! He was restraining Cordi against her will!

'What the devil do you mean?' he shouted. 'She is well but wouldn't come? Was it the sahib who told you this? Did you speak to the memsahib yourself?'

'*Haan, sahib*. The memsahib come out and talked to us. Asked us to return to Dhanboa, for she would not be coming with us.'

The truth was there before him. But even then, he refused to acknowledge it.

'*Achcha*! Too much of a shock for her, was it? But she'll come tomorrow morning? Will the Bihguri sahib arrange for an elephant? Or do we send our own animals to Bihguri?'

The shame and sadness in Ajam's voice grew more pronounced. 'You don't understand, sahib,' he said, his head lowered. 'Memsahib told us she would never again come to Dhanboa. Gave us a paper to give you. Said it contained a list of things which must be sent tomorrow morning to Bihguri.'

David's world exploded. A despair-filled wail welled up inside him, but he stifled it. The final act of treachery! But deep inside him he knew it was neither treachery nor betrayal but a hurt creature striking back. Savagely he fought down his emotions, the perpetual need to maintain a phlegmatic exterior before his coolies aiding him. He took the paper which Ajam held out. Nothing was addressed directly to him. But the paper contained a list of her personal affects to be sent to Bihguri.

The scrutiny of the paper gave him the pause required to regain control. '*Theek hai*,' he said with attempted nonchalance. 'We'll do that. But Pekoe can't wait. It must be buried immediately. Dig a hole, you two, and get it over with.'

He walked up the stairs, back erect, master of his emotions. But, on reaching his room, he made straight for the liquor cabinet and reached out for a fresh bottle of whisky.

The pallor did not leave her face despite the bath with steaming, medicated water. The lethargic indifference in her speech, movement and gait too remained. Apparently, the trauma of her ordeal had not worn off. Yet there was something more to her listlessness; a hint of surrender; of sacrifice. He had given her one of his nightgowns to wear and a robe too large for her. The outsize garbs accentuated the waifish image; of a lost and lonely child far away from home. The image evoked no pity in him. But the vacant stare dampened his ardour. Once or twice, in the guise of assisting, he had thrown his arms around her. He had been repelled by her iciness.

But there was time enough for that!

At his bidding she joined him for dinner, but barely touched a thing. Later, while a bed was readied for her in the guest room, she sat with him on the verandah. Though complacent, his ego yet demanded confirmation and, despite the fact that she had not quite recovered from the terror-induced stupor, he could not help but speak.

'Cordelia?'

'Yes, Christopher?' The 'Christopher' had come out on its own, without prompting.

'It's a rummy thing, you know. But I'd never doubted you would be mine. Ever since I first saw you on that steamer's deck, I knew you would come to me someday.'

She said nothing but stared vacantly at the speckled darkness.

He could have taken her silence for acquiescence, but that would not satisfy the ego. His exulting soul demanded words.

'Let me tell you, dear girl, when I saw you come running towards me, I wasn't at all surprised. You could've run back to your brother. But you came to me!'

Still, she remained silent. 'Come, Cordelia, why don't you say something?'

'Christopher, you poor fool,' she said tiredly. 'It wasn't you who brought me to Bihguri. It was David!'

His eager desire to meet Cordelia once more had made Captain Ralph Hewitt chafe at the recurrent postponement of his annual, pre-monsoon tour of the sadar. He had received a letter from her, courteous and noncommittal, wherein she had mentioned that Bircha was getting married, and had requested her to invite him on his behalf to the shaadi. Much as he would have liked to use that as a pretext for a visit to Dhanboa, there had been no help for it. His presence in Jorehaut during the Bohag bihu festivities being considered vital, only on the twentieth of April was he finally able to set out on his tour.

He had quite a few stops to make before he would be able to reach Bihguri on the morning of the twenty third, meet Bircha and proceed to Dhanboa, where he would spend the night. And what wonderful tidings he was carrying to Cordelia! The news had arrived almost a month back, contained in a letter from his father, who congratulated him on his efforts to do something for the coolies 'who were being transported wholesale by those amoral purveyors of death and misery', the coolie-catchers. The Commission of Enquiry constituted by the Government of Bengal to look into the matter of coolie conscription was in the process of finalizing its report. His father had had a preview of the preliminary draft and was glad to intimate to him that his suggestion of appointing 'Coolie Protectors' had been incorporated in the report.

He could visualize the happiness this news would bring to Cordelia. Happiness induced generosity, melted resolve. Perhaps her joy would change her attitude, make her more receptive to the overtures he was determined to make. He could propose again to her with a clear conscience—had not Michael himself invested him with this sacred trust? There had been, apparently, no change in the Lieutenant's stance, for he had been absent from Gokuldeva Barua's celebrations to which the girl had gone.

Early on the morning of the twenty-third Hewitt reached Bihguri and made straight for the coolie basti along with the posse of policemen. Unlike on previous occasions, Buckingham did not arrive immediately on the scene, but Hewitt read no significance in this. Bircha was in the otherwise deserted basti in the front-yard of Baisakhi's hut, weaving strands of bamboo into baskets. He brought out a murrah for the sarkari sahib. Hewitt seated himself and began questioning him about his affairs.

Oh yes, the wedding had gone well. No, the Bihguri sahib has created no problems. Yes, he was getting his wages regularly without having to toil for them. Very soon he would need as much money as he could earn. Saoni was with child. When the chokra arrived all their suffering would be worth the while. His and Saoni's life would be complete then.

'I'm happy for you, Bircha,' Hewitt said, rising to his feet. 'I leave now for Dhanboa to tell the farishta memsahib about your good fortune.'

Bircha frowned in perplexity. 'But sahib, you do not know?'

'Know? Know what?'

'The farishta memsahib is at Bihguri … in the sahib's bungalow!'

The captain's bewilderment evoked in him a foolish reiteration of Bircha's words. 'At Bihguri? In the sahib's bungalow? What're you talking about, man?'

'*Haan, sahib*. It's true. She came some days ago.'

Had David and Cordelia made up with Buckingham? Were they paying him a neighbourly visit? At this time of the year, with the season already started?

'David sahib is with her, of course?' he said as casually he could.

'No, sahib. She is alone with the Bihguri sahib. We know not what to think. How can she bear to put up with that shaitan? But then the ways of the heart are not for us to know. Perhaps she discovered love for the Bihguri sahib.'

The blood drained away from Hewitt's visage. Seeing his strong reaction, Bircha hastened to explain.

'It was all the doing of the kaala naag, sahib. She's not to blame.'

'Kaala naag?' Hewitt, legs weak and rubbery, sat down again on the murrah.

Bircha told him about the incident and the consensus amongst the labourers that before dying the kaala naag had cast an evil spell on her. Why else would she farishta memsahib rush into Bihguri screaming like she was demented? Why else would she choose to live with the shaitan who ruled Bihguri?

Hewitt smelt a rat! Suspicion gave rise to hope, and hope took away angry bitterness. Dangerous creature that Buckingham was, he could be capable of the blackest dastardly. A terrible thing, to be attacked by a king cobra! Could it not be that the fellow was restraining her against her will, with David not giving a damn! He must not waste another moment. He must seek out Buckingham and wrest out the truth, even if he had to throttle him in the process.

But he did not have to seek out Buckingham—the latter awaited him at the basti's entrance, the insufferable smile adorning his face. He was in a buoyant mood, and eager to impart information, for he called out, 'I've a secret to share with you, Captain Hewitt.'

'Miss Esscombe is here?'

'Ah, our good Bircha has spoken,' Buckingham, unfazed by the hostility, replied with humour.

'Yes. Bircha has spoken. What are you up to, Buckingham? Miss Esscombe has had a dreadful experience. Will you take advantage of it?'

Buckingham raised a delicate eyebrow. 'Take advantage? Surely not! She and I shall be man and wife soon. In truth we would've been at Sivasagar this day itself to have one of those Baptist padres tie the nuptial knot … only she doesn't wish to go to Sivasagar. So, the moment I can lure a padre to Bihguri, we shall be wedded!'

The planter spoke with confidence. Hewitt kept his emotions in check, his face in no way betraying the tempest raging within.

'Are you claiming Miss Esscombe is in Bihguri of her own free will?'

'Asserting it, old chap! Not claiming! Maybe you would like to talk to her?'

'Yes. I must satisfy myself.'

Without another word Buckingham led the way to the bungalow. Cordelia was seated on the verandah, her eyes resting on a volume. She looked up at the sound of the gate being opened; though she could not have failed to recognize him she did not rise or make the slightest gesture of welcome.

'Go ahead and talk to her,' Buckingham said.

Hewitt approached. She was looking at him now, yet seemed to look through him. Not a twinge of recognition in her lovely features let alone a smile. As he reached her, she closed the book and placed it on the table. He saw her eyes, two pools of sadness and compassion, yet with an obdurate solidity to them, as though her suffering had congealed into opaque spheres of glassy marble. There were dark pouches underneath, from crying or insomnia he could not tell. On one delicate cheek, in stark contrast to the pallid skin, was visible a dark, red-rimmed welt. Her entire aspect was a mingle of helplessness and resolve, violent sorrow and secret satisfaction, which wrapped her in an enigmatic sanctitude, an indefinable air of hallowed martyrdom.

Agitatedly he knelt beside her on the mud floor and took her hands in his. The fingers were cold.

'Are you all right, Miss Esscombe?' he asked, his gaze square on her in close observance.

He watched the resolve well up in her eyes, erasing the compassion and helplessness. She nodded, and struggled to muster up a smile for him. Her failure told him all.

'I've come to help you, Miss Esscombe. To take you away.' for the briefest of instance the light of resolution wavered in her eyes, like a candle-flame shifted by a draught, but then grew firm again.

'Please go away, Captain Hewitt. No one can help me now. No one can take me away from myself.'

His grip on her hands tightened. 'For God's sake, Miss Esscombe, come, leave with me. You've had a terrible shock. I entreat you, Miss Esscombe, let me take you away from this blackguard!'

She shook her hands free from his clasp, turned her face away. Her body stiffened and harshness crept into her tone. 'Please go away, Captain Hewitt.' She spoke no more, but picked up the book and leafed through its pages.

The officer stood up, turned and walked down the stairs.

'Leaving so soon, Captain Hewitt?'

The officer flushed, but said nothing. He passed through the gate which the planter held open for him with exaggerated courtesy and strode on ahead. From his rear came Buckingham's thorn-sharp voice. 'The best man won, Hewitt! But you didn't congratulate me!'

Captain Ralph Hewitt kept walking.

A pair of smouldering, black eyes watched through a crack in the bamboo door as the sarkari sahib left the basti. After a while, when he was certain the sahib would not return, Meghu emerged through the door of Sanatan's hutment. He looked cautiously around and then darted across to Baisakhi's dwelling.

Bircha had resumed working on his basket. So absorbed was he at the task that he did not sense his friend's presence till Meghu called out softly to him. His features betrayed neither surprise nor alarm but he was not unconscious of the danger to Meghu, and quickly pulled him into the hut.

'You take grave risks, Meghu-bhaiya, coming and going like this.'

'Yes. The danger is great. But I care not for myself. Only for the cause.'

'And I care not for your cause. Only for you.'

'No, Bircha-bhaiya. I no longer matter. One burns wood to light a fire. The wood is insignificant. The fire matters. I'm like a piece of wood to light a fire! The fire will be lit! The time is not far.'

'I repeat, Meghu-bhaiya. I care not for the fire, but only for you. I do not wish you to suffer as I have.'

'But I do suffer, Bircha-bhaiya! Not the physical suffering you went through, but the suffering of the mind. The fire inside me has eaten up my soul. I am no longer Meghu ... just a ball of fire!'

'Such a fire would be terrible. It'll devour everything, including you. Can you not back off, even now?'

'There can be no backing off! The weapons are in the basti. I arrived last night with the final lot. The tinder is dry. All it needs is a spark to set it ablaze. We await that spark.'

'The spark, Meghu-bhaiya?' Bircha asked in perplexity.

'Yes, the spark! Just one incident which will give us a pretext.'

'What happens if the spark comes when you're not here?'

'You do not understand, Bircha-bhaiya. You live in the basti yet you're no longer one of the coolielog. You do not sense their mood. You're too immersed in yourself. Your aloofness makes you ignorant. As I said, you're not aware of the new mood in the basti. There are a hundred Meghus in it now.'

'And the same fire blazes in each?'

'Haan. The same fire! So even if I'm not here it doesn't make any difference. But then we talk in emptiness. There's no question of my not being here. From now on I'll be here till my mission is fulfilled. Till the hated bastards have been razed to ashes. Sanatan bhaiya and the others are sheltering me.'

'Your staying here is even more dangerous. They might come to know. Someone might babble. I hardly dare to think what they'll do to you if they catch you.'

Meghu grinned. 'Not a bad thing, now that I think on it. If they catch and torture me, I mean. The spark, eh, Bircha-bhaiya?'

The implication of his friend's words sank into Bircha. 'Would you allow yourself to be caught?' he cried out agitatedly.

'Ah, now you understand!' The grin remained on Meghu's face. 'We need a spark. But if the spark doesn't come of its own, what then, Bircha-bhaiya? We've to provide the spark, don't we?'

'You'll sacrifice yourself for the cause?' Bircha said in wonder.

'I'll do anything to destroy the shaitans,' Meghu said fiercely. 'Even if it calls for my own destruction. The cause, Bircha-bhaiya, goes beyond Bihguri. It extends to all the wretches who have been lured away from their native lands to work in these chai-bagans. It extends to all the coolielog … everywhere!'

'I can only hope and pray that the spark comes from some other direction.'

'Oh, you might get your wish after all, Bircha-bhaiya. We're in no hurry. We must wait for the heavy rains to come. So, there's time enough for something else to happen.'

'But if the spark comes before the heavy rains?'

'We'll not wait. We'll seize the chance.'

'We always wait for the heavy rains, is it not so, Meghu-bhaiya?'

The grin was back on Meghu's face. 'Yes,' he said softly. 'We always wait for the heavy rains.'

Buckingham's eyes followed the captain and his entourage till they made their exit through Bihguri's main gate. Then he turned for another look at the verandah. Cordelia Esscombe was still there, seemingly absorbed in her book, unaffected by the visit of the mandarin who had loved and lost her.

The girl's cold reception of Hewitt sharpened his own feeling of triumph and invested him with renewed confidence. There were other triumphs to be achieved! He remained at the wooden gate, secure in the knowledge that his henchmen would come to him the very moment they saw the visitors depart.

Nor was he wrong. Minutes later Luthra and Gandru arrived, with knowing looks and expectant eyes.

'The time has come, sahib?' the head sirdar asked.

'Yes. The time has come.'

'*Kab, huzoor*?'

'This evening. Tell the others.'

The two salammed happily and lumbered on towards the fields where the other sirdars were on duty. Buckingham headed back to the bungalow.

Captain Hewitt, understandably, did not go on to Dhanboa after leaving Bihguri. Instead, he directed his boatmen to take the river-route to Titabar. He maintained a stiff upper lip, not letting out his inner turmoil before his men.

At Titabar the officer requested Gokuldeva Barua for the temporary use of an elephant and, leaving the policemen behind for food and rest, set off alone for Chahpuli. He reached the tiny plantation a little before sunset.

One look at the officer's downcast features and Bailin's welcoming smile withered.

'You bring bad tidings, Captain Hewitt?'

'I'm afraid I do, Lieutenant Bailin. A beastly piece of news. I … I can hardly believe it myself, though I met and talked to her.'

'Miss Esscombe?'

'Oh, sorry, my dear fellow,' the officer said. 'Took quite a jump there, didn't I? It's been such a severe shock! I ... I don't quite know how to phrase it!'

Bailin saw the confused hesitation in the officer, the deep hurt flickering in his eyes, and was gripped by foreboding. 'For God's sake, captain!' he cried out. 'Has something happened to Miss Esscombe?'

Ralph Hewitt pulled himself together and said, 'She's at Bihguri … with Buckingham!'

Bailin heard the words, but comprehension eluded him. He stared stupidly at the officer.

Each word of the captain was soggy with sadness and revulsion as he told the Lieutenant of his visit to Bihguri and the bewildering jolt awaiting him in that benighted garden. 'Utterly inexplicable, I tell you. They aim to get married as soon as a Christian priest can be procured. Miss Esscombe! To that scoundrel! I simply don't know what to think! Perhaps the trauma of the cobra's assault … or the shock of the fall! But she seemed normal enough when she spoke to me.'

The shutters were back upon the Lieutenant's eyes. He said nothing.

'You can't imagine how hurt I am,' Captain Hewitt said. 'I realize that all is not what it seems. Some maleficent force is behind all this … you can take my word on it. Something black and evil. But for the life of me I can't fathom what it might be. I try to make allowances. But one can't cheat one's heart!'

The Lieutenant continued to stand rigidly immobile. But his face mocked his simulated impassivity. Captain Hewitt, though equally affected, seemed to find relief in words.

'I understood when it was you, Lieutenant Bailin. You're a gentleman. But Buckingham's such a rotten egg! A rogue and villain! To have turned down my fervent pleas for that knave! I feel betrayed. And violently demeaned, as though her actions question my manhood. What incomprehensible motive actuated her to take this atrocious step? What accursed spell had that despicable blackguard cast over her that she must fling me aside and rush into his embrace? A man whom she had despised with all her heart! Absolutely unbelievable, I tell you. Why do you remain silent, Lieutenant? Why don't you say something?'

Michael Bailin gave a start, like one awakened from a trance. 'What is there for me to say?' he asked in a low voice. 'It's not for us to speak. Nor to act. We can only exist. And watch and suffer.'

'Watch and suffer? I can't watch and suffer, Lieutenant Bailin. There's some mischief afoot! We must get to the bottom of the thing!'

'No. We cannot act. You've spoken to her. She had chosen to stay with him of her own volition. It's not for us to question her actions. Or pass judgement. We have no claims on her will. Yes, Captain Hewitt, all we can do is watch and suffer.'

The officer stared incredulously at the man before him. 'She loved you, Lieutenant Bailin!' he cried out, angry and contemptuous. 'I'm certain she loves you even now. How then can you view her situation with such passivity? I dashed hither with a desperate notion that knowing the facts, you would stir into action. But I misjudged you badly. You're not half the man I thought you were. Your love for her was a pretence, Lieutenant Michael Bailin. You may drown yourself in self-pity, but I care no longer. You can continue to rot in the selfish morass of your own making … I don't give a damn!'

With a last angry, bitter look, the officer remounted his elephant and urged the mahout onto a quick departure.

Garo had stood beside the Lieutenant all through the exchange. Though he did not understand what was being said, he could guess that some serious accident had befallen Cordelia memsahib, and the sarkari sahib had been angered at his master's lack of initiative. He had observed with growing consternation the opaque sheath cover his sahib's eyes, and a look appear upon his face, one which Garo had seen long ago, upon a country boat as it was being pulled upstream on the Brahmaputra, self-accusing, bleak with destructive despair. But Garo held his peace, even after the sarkari sahib had departed, instinctively aware that this was not the right moment for intrusion. He remained rooted to the spot while his master stumbled towards their hut and entered it.

Only after the sun disappeared below the skyline did he enter the hutment. His master lay face upwards on the bed, eyes fixed onto the ceiling rafters.

'Is something the matter, sahib? Something to do with Cordelia memsahib, isn't it, sahib?'

But his master seemed not to have heard, for he veered off at a tangent. 'What's this demon inside me, Garo? Why does it pull me back when all my instincts call out that I must go to her? Hewitt said I'm not half the man he had thought I was. How right he is, Garo! A self-pitying, contemptible mongrel, that's what I am.'

'I do not understand, sahib. What has happened to Cordelia memsahib? Why are you so perturbed? Why was the sarkari sahib so angry?'

'She's at Bihguri now, on the brink of marrying a man she despises. A man you and I despise.'

'At Bihguri, sahib? But that's terrible! She is in great danger. I fear for her life.'

'You might fear for her soul, Garo,' Bailin said, lips twisting in a sardonic grimace. 'Not for her life. Buckingham's sure to take good care of that.'

' I speak of the Meghu business, sahib. Barua dangoriya had sent him to Bihguri, you remember?'

'Of course I do. But the affair will not touch her. The coolies will go on strike. Production in that plantation will come to a halt. Maybe the coolies will secure for themselves a better deal. Provided they can hang on. Most likely Buckingham will let loose his dogs and cow them into submission. But Barua dangoriya's purpose will be served. A warning … that's what he wishes for.'

'No, sahib! Buckingham sahib is slated to be killed. The coolies will butcher him.'

Bailin sprang up from the bed, ashen-faced and trembling. He caught Garo in a fierce grip. 'What the devil are you saying, Garo?'

'It is true, sahib. There are people who hate the Bihguri sahib more than you or I. More than Barua dangoriya. They hate him enough to slit his throat. Barua dangoriya doesn't know about this. But Meghu and others will carry the scheme beyond what he had planned. They're arming themselves to attack the Bihguri sahib and his sirdars. Make no mistake, sahib. Meghu and his cohorts will kill them as they would dogs which froth at the mouth.'

The Lieutenant released his grip on Garo and fell back onto the bamboo bed, unnerved.

'You must go immediately to Bihguri, sahib,' Garo urged. 'For the memsahib's sake! Ask the sarkari sahib to accompany you along with his policemen. There's no telling when trouble might break out there. Meghu and the others are like hungry tigers. They thirst for blood. Crazed as they are for vengeance, they might not wait for the heavy rains. If you care for the memsahib, you must set off now. Get her out of the garden before it's too late. Otherwise, her life's not worth a blade of grass, sahib!'

'But can't you see, Garo? If we tell the sarkari sahib of the danger to the memsahib, we expose Barua dangoriya to him!'

The native blanched. Concerned as he had been for the safety of the memsahib, he had not given thought to the peril which faced the Assamese nobleman. Hewitt sahib would be sure to enquire how they could know that trouble would break out in Bihguri. Even if they prevaricated, the shrewd officer would put two and two together and arrive at the answer. Conspiracy against an angrez was a serious offence. One could never tell how the officer would take it. And not only would Barua dangoriya be endangered, Meghu and his fellow conspirators would find themselves in serious trouble too.

'Yes, I see it now,' Garo nodded. Some of the Lieutenant's irresolution rubbed on to him. But he manfully threw up a suggestion. 'We tell the sarkari sahib absolutely nothing. Just ask for his assistance in persuading the memsahib to leave Bihguri. That way nothing is changed. There is no betrayal.'

'No, Garo. The silence you advocate might not be a betrayal of Barua dangoriya, but it would be betrayal of myself. His initial scheme aroused no moral repugnance because no violence was involved. But violence is a different matter altogether, Garo. Violence which might lead to a massacre! Our conscience can be silenced no longer. Captain Hewitt must be informed.'

Garo did not venture a rebuttal. The Lieutenant stood up. 'I don't know what to think, Garo. But I'll place the issue squarely before Barua dangoriya. We'll abide by his judgement and advice. So, let's leave for Titabar.'

Spring was Saoni's season, even though she had been born in the month of Savan and thus named Saoni. It had been her mago who was born in the month of Baisakh, the month when spring comes to full fruition. But Baisakhi was heavy-built and plodding. Saoni, on the other hand, like a child of spring, light of movement and frisky. Her restless exuberance and inquisitive vitality, her overt delight at simply being alive, her doe-like steps, blended exquisitely with the spirit of spring. But to Bircha, more than anything else, what made spring Saoni's season was her passion for flowers. She adored the blossoms thrown out with such gay abandon during that season and, had she only had the time for it, might have been content to while away her existence flitting from flower to flower, savoring their pollen-laden fragrance.

In a corner of their unkempt backyard grew a bushy togor plant which exploded into a dazzling globe of blossomy white each spring. Saoni had not planted that togor bush; it had been standing there when they first arrived at Bihguri. But she had made the plant her very own and cherished it as she would some precious earthly possession. She knew it even better than she knew Bircha's body and could tell which bud had unfurled on any one morning, although the bush blossomed with myriad flowers. She made garlands from the perfumed, white flowers and wreathed them around the bun of hair at the back of her head. Bircha recalled with amusement that it had been a flower-band in her hair which had first drawn his attention to her. An orchid, he yet remembered—the long, snake-like, brilliant-hued blossom which the locals called kapouphul.

Bircha never ceased to tease his chokri-wife about her penchant for talking to the togor bush, or decking her hair with flowers. '*Aarey*, Saoni,' he would cry out, his lips bared in a toothy smile. 'What basti gossip are you two exchanging now?' Or, 'Why do you preen yourself up so with flowers, Saoni? And in the morning too, when you're merely going to the fields to work? Trying to entice a sirdar, are you now?' But, while entering the jungles in search of fruits or edible shrubs, he would always keep an eye open for exotic flowers he could take as a gift to her. Her delighted amazement at the sight of some unique blossom never ceased to thrill him. Occasionally, she would wear his gift in her hair to show off before the other women; more often than not she would try to prolong the beauty of the blossom by placing it in a clay pot half-filled with water.

To Bircha's eyes she appeared as delicate and helpless as the flowers she loved. Deep inside Bircha was aware of the falsity of the image his love for her had wrought. She was, he knew, neither delicate nor weak-willed; though so slightly built that she seemed a girl who remained perpetually on the verge of fledging into adulthood, yet she possessed strength and resilience of body and mind. Previously it had been she who had cooked and washed and kept the hutment spick and span, sparing her mother the burden of household chores after a day's harsh labour. After the marriage he had suggested that he do some of the chores around the house, and prepare the evening meal, but Saoni would have none of it. To work the whole day in the fields, then do cooking and washing, and finally satiate his hunger late into the night—no, certainly, there was nothing remotely weak and helpless about his wife!

Recently, however, Bircha had put his foot down, and begun cooking the evening meal, so she could have an additional half hour of rest after returning from work. She was with child, he had reminded her. She must give her body as much rest as she could; the child within her must be allowed to sleep in comfort. She must also eat as much as she could, despite the bouts of nausea, and ensure that the baby grew healthy. The Bihguri sahib would not give her a break from work even during the final weeks when she would be big with the child. Just as other coolie women she too would have to toil on almost till the moment of birth. Miscarriages in the garden were frequent. It was imperative, therefore, that she grab any opportunity for additional rest and eat much more than she normally did. He did not want anything to happen to the child within her.

Saoni had argued about it with him. But he would not be deterred. Let others think or say what they will. They did not matter. Only Saoni mattered. Only the chokra yet to be born mattered.

This evening, when Baisakhi and Saoni returned from the plucking detail, their meal was cooked and ready. These days the coolielog had a little more of daylight to spend in the basti. No one knew why, but the Bihguri sahib had reduced their hours of toil. Thus, the light was sufficiently strong when mago took her bath and, while Saoni cleaned away the day's grime from her body in the backyard, brought out a koloh of mod and sat with Bircha exchanging news of the day. Suddenly footsteps sounded outside and someone called out to him.

'Bircha-bhaiya? Bircha-bhaiya?'

Bircha went to the door. Gandru stood outside. The contemptuous bravado with which the squat, powerfully built sirdar normally comported himself was absent from his demeanour. He had even addressed Bircha as bhaiya!

'Huh! Gandru! Why do you call for me?'

'I have come for Saoni. She is wanted in the bungalow.'

Bircha, taken by surprise, could only gape. But not Baisakhi. The mod she had consumed instilled courage into her. She rushed to the door, the empty koloh in her hand, ready to clobber the sirdar on the head with it if he so much as ventured to step into her hutment.

'Saoni? Wanted at the bungalow? You filthy bastard! How dare you come to my house?'

Bircha caught hold of the inebriated woman and steadied her. 'Let me tackle this, mago. *Daro mat*! Nothing will happen to Saoni.' Pushing her behind him, he stepped out of the threshold to confront the sirdar. He had expected Gandru to flare up at mago's challenge; but, to his astonishment, the man continued to be conciliatory. He held up a hand, and said,

'I haven't come for what you think. It's the memsahib, the one our sahib maintains as his mistress. She's the one who sends for Saoni.'

'The farishta memsahib?'

'Huh? Farishta memsahib? Oh well, I suppose you can call her that.'

'Don't listen to him, Bircha,' mago's voice slurred out from behind. '*Yama ka bachcha hai, saala*!'

Gandru could take it no longer. 'Why, you vixen,' he shouted. 'Any more of your lip and I'll take it out on you at the plucking!'

Gandru's rage, strangely, was more reassuring than the assumed meekness with which he had made his initial approach. Bircha hushed Saoni's mother. He turned to Gandru. 'Don't mind her, bhaiya. She's drunk, that's all. Why does the farishta memsahib send for Saoni?'

The sirdar had been tutored well. He spoke without batting an eyelid. 'The memsahib wishes to have a maid of her own at the bungalow. You should be pleased, Bircha-bhaiya. It was she who suggested Saoni's name to the sahib.'

A plausible explanation! Bircha, indeed, was pleased. A god-given opportunity, the ideal solution to his dilemma. Fear for the unborn child's safety had nagged him ever since he learned Saoni was with child. The work at the bungalow would be light. Saoni would not have to toil towards the final months of pregnancy, drenched in the rains or roasted by the sun. Bircha trusted the farishta memsahib with his life; nay, with the life of his wife and his chokra.

The coolie smiled warmly at the man before him, the one whom he had once hated enough to kill. But his love had burnt away all the hatred from his soul as a fire burns away a heap of festering garbage. If he had been less innocent, more cynical and suspicious as Baisakhi was, his gaze might have penetrated the veil of bland nonchalance covering Gandru's face and seen the evil beneath. But the thought for Saoni's welfare clouded insight; the mention of the farishta memsahib lulled forebodings. And mago, who had always protected her daughter as a tigress her cub, was too full of mod for rational protest.

'Why don't you come in and be seated, Gandru bhaiya?' Bircha invited, moving sideways to allow passage. 'Saoni's at her bath. It'll take a while for her to get ready.'

'No. I'll wait outside. There's no hurry. Let her take her time. Make her dress well. Have her put some attar on her body. She must make a good impression before the memsahib.'

Saoni, back from her bath, was excited enough by the news to hug Bircha in front of her *mago*. '*Bari khush khabri hai*, Bircha!' she cried out in enthused joy. '*Ma Tusu* is looking after our child!'

'I don't like it,' mumbled Baisakhi. 'I'll go along with her.' But the fatigue in her body and the mod robbed the words of their words of their cautionary sting.

'With your breath reeking of mod, mago?' Saoni said laughingly. 'What would the memsahib think?'

'You worry needlessly, mago,' Bircha said with complete conviction. 'Remember, me and all mine enjoy the sarkari sahib's protection. The farishta memsahib is the finest of human beings. She will not let any harm come to your daughter. Now, Saoni, go and dress with care. Put on the sari which you wore on the shaadi day. Dab yourself with the perfume I bought for you. Wear togor flowers upon your hair.'

'Am I to be housemaid, Bircha? Or a bride again?' But there was no plaintive mockery in her words; only happy banter.

'Arey Saoni, you aren't a housemaid yet! You must impress the memsahib with your cleanliness and your manners. Don't be saucy with her as you always her with me … be demure and polite as befits your job. Now off with you. Be quick, for Gandru is waiting.'

Saoni put out her tongue at him and darted out to their room. But she returned soon afterwards, looking like a farishta herself! She had put on earrings and bangles; there were white flowers in her hair and her body exuded an enticing fragrance. She was so divinely beautiful that Bircha felt a lump in his throat just looking at her.

He started to lay out the tin-plates on the floor for the evening meal. But Saoni said, 'No. You and mago eat. I'll have my *khaana* after I return. I don't like to keep the memsahib waiting.'

'*Theek hai*. Let mago eat. We'll have ours together after you are back. *Phir chelo, jaldi*. We've kept Gandru waiting long enough.'

The sirdar was outside, patient and noncommittal. Bircha accompanied them up to the edge of the basti. 'Come back soon,' he shouted in parting as they disappeared around a bend in the path.

'Thank you, Michael. I'm grateful.'

'Grateful, Barua dangoriya? What for?'

'For coming to me first. Someone dear to your heart is in danger. You could've run straight to Hewitt, leaving me in the lurch.'

'I couldn't have done that! You too are dear to my heart, Barua dangoriya. Where's Captain Hewitt?'

'In one of my cottages. He dines with me at eight. I presume he's dressing for the occasion.'

'Then we don't have much time. What's to be done, Barua dangoriya?'

'Do we have a choice, Michael?'

'The thing has blown up in your face, hasn't it? A temporary suspension of garden work in one thing … but murder's a far more serious matter. Meghu has proved treacherous.'

'Oh, I half expected something like this to happen. Perhaps unconsciously wished for it.'

'Wished for Buckingham's murder? I can't believe it, Barua dangoriya!'

'But it's true, Michael! Remember what I told you once … if anyone volunteers to rid the world of Buckingham, I would render him all assistance. If Bihguri coolies put an end to that pestilence, it shan't lie too heavily on my conscience, you can be sure of that.'

'It shall lie on mine.'

'You possess a most quirky sensibility, Michael! How can the death of a man like Buckingham fill me with remorse? Or prick my conscience? On the other hand, if my actions bring harm to innocent goodness, my conscience would drive me insane.'

'Miss Esscombe?'

'Yes, Miss Esscombe! I do not know by what devious means Buckingham enticed her into his arms. From Garo's revelations it is clear she's in great danger. I shall never be able to forgive myself should anything happen to her. So go and alert Hewitt about the situation in Bihguri. Leave immediately with him and his policemen and disarm the coolies.'

'That'll be throwing you to the wolves, Barua dangoriya! I'll not divulge your role in this to the captain, nor will Garo. But Meghu will talk.'

Gokuldeva Barua chuckled in his throat. 'I'm an old man, Michael. I've lived out a full life. Throughout its span I've faced every situation with courage and dignity. Would you make a coward of me yet?'

The Lieutenant spoke no more. The two stood up and embraced. Bailin walked out with Garo, a menial guiding the way with a hand-lantern.

In the guest house Captain Ralph Hewitt listened with incredulous concern as Bailin told him about the explosive state of affairs at Bihguri and the danger Miss Esscombe and Buckingham faced.

'How do you know all this, Lieutenant?' he finally asked.

'I'd rather not tell,' Bailin replied obdurately.

The officer raised his eyebrows. For a moment it seemed he was about to pursue the matter, but then he said, 'Let's leave that for later, shall we, Lieutenant? Miss Esscombe's safety must be our primary concern for the time being. The sooner we can get to Bihguri, the better.'

'We must go within the hour, Captain Hewitt!'

'True. But we've first to get to Jorehaut. What you tell me calls for more policemen than I have with me. We can be at Bihguri only in the morning.'

'I and Garo shall accompany you.'

'But, of course!' The captain held out his hand to Bailin. 'Sorry about this afternoon, my dear fellow. The unforeseen encounter with Miss Esscombe at Bihguri had thoroughly upset me.'

Bailin grabbed the outstretched hand. 'Let's not waste precious minutes in needless apologies. Miss Esscombe must be brought out of Bihguri. We'll do it together, won't we, Captain Hewitt?'

The scream tore apart the evening's dusky stillness, silencing the song of cicadas.

A single shriek, abruptly stifled, as though some unseen hand had suddenly clamped the mouth which gave it birth. It had emanated from close by, just behind the bungalow.

Buckingham froze the very moment his ears caught it. He shot a quick glance at Cordelia, sitting at the other end of the dining table. But the girl appeared not to have heard it. She continued eating with the same forbearing indifference she had displayed throughout her sojourn at Bihguri.

Buckingham could not explain to himself why he felt so relieved she had not heard the scream.

The meal over, Cordelia retired to the guest room. Buckingham came out to the verandah and sat there in tense anticipation. The wicker gate creaked open and four shadows materialized out of the darkness. The planter stood up and strode ahead to meet them halfway.

'She's dead, sahib!' Luthra said.

'Dead? But that was not part of the scheme?'

'It's all Luthra's fault, huzoor.' The petulant voice belonged to Puran.

'She was a hell-cat, kicking and punching! So, our Luthra hits her on the face,' Gandru spat. 'Our Luthra doesn't know his own strength. Our Luthra doesn't know she is not a man. Her neck snaps … crack, just like that!'

'Even before the rest of us could have a go,' whined Budhu.

Buckingham chuckled. 'Did you try to, Budhu?'

'Of course not, huzoor!' Budhu spoke in sullen earnestness.

'I'm sorry Luthra spoilt everything for you,' Buckingham said, growing serious. 'Too bad the chokri is dead. I don't blame you, Luthra. I understand.'

'*Ab kya kare,* huzoor?' the head sirdar asked.

'First, call off the tea house detail. Send them back to the basti. I want them all to be there when the body is discovered.'

'*Ji,* huzoor.'

'Then dump her body on the path coming out of the basti. They will be searching for her soon. Make sure she's naked.'

'She already is, sahib.'

'*Phir che lao*. Budhu and Puran, you two stay away from the basti. Sleep with Luthra and Gandru in their shack. Get as much rest tonight as you can. You'll have your work cut out for you tomorrow. *Ab che lao. Jaldi.*'

The sirdars hurried off to do his bidding. Buckingham retired to the bungalow.

Saoni's terrified scream had carried to the coolies in the tea houses. None of them, however, read any significance to it, mistaking it to be the screech of a nightjar.

The scream had not carried to the far off basti where Bircha waited with growing trepidation. Overtaken by fatigue and mod, mago lay asleep on her bamboo bed.

As the moments passed and Saoni did not return, doubts began to assail Bircha. What was taking his wife so long? Was the memsahib lonely in the

Bihguri bungalow and longed for someone to talk to? After all, now that the spring rains had awakened the tea bushes, the sahib was out most of the time. Was that the reason she kept Saoni with her, although day was speedily turning into night? Couldn't Saoni point out to the memsahib that her food was growing cold? Had she not been able to convey how late it was and that her Bircha awaited her in their hutment?

As Bircha walked up and down in nervous agitation, he heard voices. Relieved, he hurried out of the hut to greet his wife and fold her into a loving embrace.

But it was only a part of the tea house detail returning to the basti. He hailed the men. 'Back from tea making?'

The men replied in the affirmative. 'Something's going on out there,' one of them said. 'A lot of green leaves are still to be rolled and fired. Yet the sirdars have doused the fires for the night and let us leave much before we were due.'

Bircha thanked the men for the information and enquired if they had seen anything of Saoni. Learning they had not, he bade them go on, not letting out the fear which wrung his entrails. What could be going on out there which did not involve Saoni? What a blind, unthinking fool he had been! Suppose they had used the farishta memsahib's name just to lull his misgivings? Suppose the memsahib had not summoned Saoni at all?

Bircha raced into the hutment and tried to arouse Baisakhi. The old woman mumbled incoherently and went back to sleep. On the verge of panic now, Bircha raced out again and hastened through the rude, dusty path towards the basti's entrance. The moon, low in the clear night-sky, cast a pale, alabaster light which enabled him to see his way. How deathly silent the basti was! Not a diya to be seen in any hutment, not a sound to be heard! A soft breeze, pungent with the smells of spring, gently swept away the heated air and soothed the hot, sun-baked earth. But the breeze could not sweep away the terror inside him, or the fragrances overpower the smell of disaster touching his nostrils.

He paused at the fringe of the basti for a moment, unsure as to what he should do. Should he go back and rouse Sanatan bhaiya and others? Or should he go on to the bungalow, despite it being so late, and enquire with the memsahib about the whereabouts of his wife? He came to decision.

Waking up the others would mean that much delay. No, he must press on alone in his search for Saoni.

He set off at a furious run towards the bungalow, oblivious of anything else but his fear that Saoni might be in danger. A little further ahead his feet caught onto something and he came tumbling down. Picking himself up quickly he instinctively turned for a cursory look at what had caused him to trip and was petrified with shocked disbelief.

The naked body of a woman lay face down on the bare earth—a body so familiar that he did not need the wilted *togorphul* still clinging to her hair to tell him who it was. The ones who had placed that body on the path possessed a malignant humour, for they had pillowed her head with her neatly folded sari.

He thought he knew the nature of her ordeal, but he did not know she was dead. 'Saoni?' he called out with perplexed tenderness. She did not stir with his call. He bent down and placed his hand on her naked back. The flesh was stiff as leather, the skin gelid to the touch.

Bircha's cries of despair rent the Bihguri night.

The half-human, half-animal cries were loud enough to wake up the dead! Frightened eyes peered out through barred windows as the inmates sought to locate the source of the sound.

Those furtive eyes beheld the strangest of sights—of Bircha howling with grief as he carried Saoni's limp, naked body into the basti; of Bircha throwing out challenges in the wind to those who had robbed him of his love as he laid the corpse gently on the front-yard of Baisakhi's hutment, and covered it with the silken wedding sari. Bamboo doors creaked open; men and women emerged, cowed and silenced by the force of Bircha's grief. The women squatted around the draped figure and began their hysterical wailing. The men huddled together in groups, wondering how Saoni's death had come about, and if Bircha was really as invincible as he had loomed.

The clamour and the wailing roused Baisakhi from her stupor. She lumbered out of the hut with dread in her eyes. For a fractional moment she took on the scene before her and then, when memories of the evening's summon flooded her drowsy consciousness and realization jolted her into sharper awareness, she went into a paroxysm of hysteria, and flung herself onto Bircha, and beat him with her fists, as if he were the one who had killed her daughter. Bircha made no effort to ward off her blows and she might have inflicted damage had not other hands pulled her away and held her off till the tempest within her subsided. Then she squatted on the ground and took Saoni's head on her lap and, beating her chest with her fists, wailed louder than the rest.

Soon more and more coolies came up till the wailing reached a crescendo and the space before the hutment grew so crowded that one could hardly move. No one knew what exactly had happened; though, from the disjointed remarks let out by the sobbing Baisakhi, they could glean that somehow it was murder, and the Bihguri shaitan and his gang of cutthroats were involved. Neither Bircha nor Saoni's mago were in any condition to give details. While mago cradled the dead body and continued to voice her lamentations, Bircha had fallen silent and sat unmoving beside his wife, gazing at her with unflinching eyes.

Some of the young men were already at the cremation ground building a wooden pyre, while others were fashioning a bamboo changi to carry the corpse. Sanatan and Lachmi had come out of their hut, but Meghu stayed inside. He had imparted instructions; Sanatan shuffled through the packed crowd, picking out his men and whispering into the ears of each, 'After the cremation. At my house.'

The changi was ready, as was the funeral pyre. But when the young men sought to place the corpse upon it, Bircha emerged from his trance and stopped them. He picked up the dead body of his wife, as easily as a twig or a leaf, and walked with measured steps down the path towards the cremation ground, followed by the voiceless men-folk, many of whom carried flaming torches of thickly bound twigs. The women continued to sit in the front-yard around Baisakhi; none, however, tried to comfort her, sensibly allowing the old woman to dissipate her grief.

Reaching the heap of firewood which would soon consume the corporeal frame of his pyaar Bircha lifted her up as though an offering to the gods in heaven and shouted aloud, '*Dekho,* coolielog, *aankh khul kar dekho*! See how they have dealt with my young and innocent child-wife. See how they have dealt with the chokra in her womb now destined never to see the light of day.'

There was sorrow and anger in Bircha's voice. But more, there was a wondrous power in it, which seeped into the hearts and minds of the coolielog, and strengthened their spines so that they no longer moved about stooping and fearful, but squared their shoulders and held their heads up. A few shouted out aloud at the terrible injustice of it all.

'You all know how joyful and inoffensive my child wife was. Never in her life had she harmed anyone, least of all the shaitans who have caused her death. Yet have they taken away her life, and the life of the chokra within her.'

A wave of contentious muttering rippled through the men-folk. Bircha's voice dropped a pitch. 'I was wrong, coolielog. I'd thought the world of love could keep me away from the harsh reality of our existence. I'd selfishly shut my mind to the pain and suffering of you all, and sought to build a heaven out of my love. The brutal killing of my child-wife and the chokra within her has opened my eyes. The world of love is not for the coolielog. Ours is a hell of treachery and suffering, hatred and revenge.'

Bircha raised his voice. 'I swear by *Ma Kaali*, coolielog! I swear by *Ma Tusu* on whose parab day I married my child-wife. I swear by my child-wife and the chokra within her. I swear revenge for this vile killing, coolielog. I've left the world of love, coolielog. Now I have entered the world of hatred and revenge!'

He gently placed Saoni's body onto the pile of wood. Plucking out the wilted togorphul still valiantly clinging to her hair, he tucked it into the folds of his dhoti. Then, taking a burning flare from Sanatan who stood close beside him, he set fire to the wood.

The flames lit up Bircha's face and those of the others. Sanatan looked at those faces and gloated with secret triumph. There was anger on those faces. And, above all, a hatred which would empower the most timorous of them with the strength to kill!

The demise of the will had not destroyed the mind's delicate sentience, the intuitive feel for evil when it pervaded the air. And, without doubt, evil did stalk Bihguri this night, though her skin tingled at its touch her mind retained its callous indifference. She had sensed it the very moment Captain Ralph Hewitt departed from Bihguri. With the onset of dusk and thickened darkness it had congealed like a wintry fog and draped itself over the plantation. The scream had drifted through this fog to reach her ears; she had seen Buckingham stiffen at the scream, but in her it had evoked no reaction. Nothing, neither fear nor pity. That night as she lay prostrate in bed other sounds buffeted the spongy pall of evil; the familiar, despairing wails of humans giving vent to grief. The waves of sound had echoed off the empty shell that was her mind, striking no responding chord. Cordelia had simply turned over and gone to sleep.

They were all there in Sanatan's hutment. 'We should attack now,' Pahar cried out. 'No more nonsense about striking work. *Hame budla lena hein.* Those who killed Saoni bahen must be punished.'

'Blood for blood,' spat out Bihuti. 'Attack now, I say. The bungalow, while they're asleep.'

A murmur of assent arose from others squatting on the mud floor.

'And how do we know they're asleep?' asked Sanatan, voice gentle and grave. The question quelled the murmuring voices as the coolie youths pondered over the answer.

'On the contrary,' Meghu said, lending his voice to Sanatan's, 'in all probability they are wide awake and watchful. Saoni's murder was planned … its aim was to cow the coolielog. The shaitans can't be unaware of the stir it has created in the basti. They'll be on full alert.'

'So, what do we do?' Tuvuk asked. 'The minds of the coolielog are as fickle as the moon. Now they are angry and filled with thoughts of revenge. But then the fire will cool and fear overwhelm their anger.'

'Better to attack the bungalow,' Bihuti reiterated. 'Even though they may be awake and alert.'

'That would be foolish,' Sanatan spoke again. 'They're five. They have guns. The bungalow is fenced in. They can cover it from all directions.'

'*Sach hai*,' said Meghu. 'So, we will wait in the basti. The sons of bitches are not aware we're armed. When we do not stir out of the basti they'll come for us. Draw them out into the open … that should be our plan of attack.'

'Listen to Sanatan, you young sucklings,' Dudhu put in. 'Listen to Meghu. Attack the bungalow and there will be a massacre of coolielog. But out in the open our arrows would be as good as their guns.'

'All right,' Pahar said. 'We'll listen to them. But what if they don't come out? What if they sit on their arses in the bungalow … do we sit on ours at the basti?'

'I know the white bastard,' Meghu was confident. 'Come daybreak, and he'll be here.'

'However, we've to take precautions,' Sanatan said. 'The Bihguri sahib might have second thoughts and decide to get in touch with the sarkar. So, the front gate should be guarded. Pahar and Tuvuk, take a dozen men and guard the gate. But stay out of sight. Bihuti and Phagu … you and others must watch the path to Dhanboa. The shaitan must not be allowed to slip out of the garden.'

Meghu turned to Bircha, who had been sitting quietly in the background. 'Have you nothing to say, Bircha-bhaiya?'

Bircha stood up, towering over the seated coolies. 'I've only one request to make, Meghu-bhaiya,' he said with deceptive mildness. 'We kill each and every son of a bitch who murdered Saoni. But we do not touch the memsahib.'

Though he spoke softly, none dared challenge him. 'Yes, coolielog,' he repeated, the ominous undertones more pronounced. 'We leave her unscathed. She had nothing to do with this. If anyone harms her, I shall throttle him with my bare hands.'

'*Kya baat hein,* Baisakhi bahen?' Meghu, perplexed, asked. The others had filed out of the room. But Baisakhi remained, her arms barring his way.

She drew him further inside, her grip on him hard as a hawk's talons. Her face, ravaged with grief, did not startle him—her eyes did! They were not her own, but the blood-red eyes of Ma Kaali, devourer of demons, nemesis of the wicked. Like a cat's eyes they glowed in the dark.

'The bastard Bircha!' she hissed. 'He wants to spare the white woman … that shameless whore. But she too must be slain, do you hear, Meghu? Only then will vengeance be complete.'

'We're of the same mind, Baisakhi bahen,' Meghu said gently. '*Phikar mat karo*! They'll all die … the white bitch too! I shall see to it myself!'

The querulous chirping of birds pealed out the alarm bells of the mind. Buckingham's eyes jerked open.

The light in the room was unacceptably bright. Automatically his hand reached out for his time-piece on the side table. Six o'clock! Good heavens! He bounded out of bed, ears pricked, listening for sounds other than those of birds. There were none.

Chotu? Where the bloody hell was he? The houseboy had not brought his chota hazri, due an hour ago. Stupid bastard! A momentous morning! And he had overslept!

Dressing quickly, he stepped out of the room. Silence in the bungalow—no sound from the guest-room. Cordelia was still asleep.

Exiting through the backdoor, he traversed the corridor to the kitchen. Chotu was nowhere to be seen.

'Chotu?' he called out. But, instead of the houseboy, his sirdars came running, faces flush. They could not have slept at all the previous night!

'Where's Chotu?'

Luthra answered. 'No idea, sahib. He's not in his jhopri. Most likely he has run to the basti. Great excitement there last night. Much shouting and wailing.'

'As expected, Luthra? Have things quietened down now?'

'*Haan,* sahib, *sab chup chaap hai*. But we don't like it, sahib. The new sirdars and duffadars haven't come.'

'Phagu, Dalama? They haven't come? And the coolies yet in the basti? Defiance, huh Luthra?'

'*Haan*, sahib.'

'All going as we had hoped, Luthra?'

'*Haan*, sahib.' The head sirdar did not sound quite convinced.

'So, what're we waiting for? Saddle up the horses … yes, both of them. You shall ride to the basti along with me this morning.'

'What about us, sahib?' Puran asked.

'You three will be on foot. We each carry rifles. And ropes. Phagu and Dalama … they'll be our targets for now. Oh yes, I almost forgot … and Chotu, if he's in there.'

The chattering of magpies had roused Cordelia too. Unlike in the past the sound did not bring the pleasure of anticipation on another spring-scented day. She heard sounds within the bungalow, the master of the house preparing to depart. Chotu would be coming soon with chota hazri. She did not get up from the bed.

But Chotu did not come. She rose and washed and dressed languidly, only once pausing to listen to horses' hoof-beats. Then she walked through the hushed, empty cottage to the kitchen. There was no one there. The chula was unlit. Retracing her steps to the outer verandah, she sat on a wicker-chair. The putrid reek of evil was strong; far stronger than the smells of spring. In her it kindled no sensation, neither fear nor revulsion.

The area just behind the entry of the basti was deserted. Empty hutments, empty courtyards; tattered loincloths and saris hung out to dry dancing in the breeze. But no voices, no smell of cooking or flurry of domestic activity.

Buckingham swore.

'There's more to this than meets the eye, sahib!' Gandru cried out. 'Where could the bastards have gone to?'

The planter glanced at his henchmen. The empty basti had unnerved them.

'We'll find them gathered at one place further ahead, for sure,' he spoke assuredly, attempting to instill confidence into the others. 'Making things easier for us, aren't they, Gandru?'

'*Daal mein kuch kaala hai,* sahib,' Luthra sounded anxious. 'Should we not return to the bungalow? Think about what to do?'

'Scared, Luthra? We have five guns between us!'

He urged his mount on, the three on foot running to keep up.

Then, suddenly, they heard it, the sound of a hundred hearts simultaneously beating up ahead—the tick ticking of a gigantic timepiece! Buckingham pulled his mount to a stop, eyes hooded against the glare. Two figures stood at the other end of the dusty path which bisected the basti. Bircha! And Meghu!

Cordelia stood up and walked out of the cottage. What quirky impulse from deep inside had prodded her into moving, to saunter with unerring precision in the direction of the nurseries? Was it for a final glimpse of the tea garden Papa had built? To rekindle memories of a lost home, a lost brother, a lost innocence? Or was it for another look at beady eyes which atrophied the will and incinerated the conscience?

She crossed the wide path which fronted the bungalow and was amongst the tea bushes, moving over the narrowest of tracks, unaware that others were following her progress with anxious gazes.

The men hiding amongst the tea bushes near the entrance gate could have killed her there and then. But it was Bircha's order that she be spared.

Meghu? Were his eyes deceiving him? Shading them with his free palm, Buckingham scanned the sunlit path in a sharp appraisal, nerves taut, all instincts fully alert. No doubt about it! It was Meghu standing side by side with Bircha, both unarmed, waiting for him to make the first move!

Had it been Bircha alone Buckingham would not have hesitated. He would have ordered his dogs to search each hutment, kick open doors, crack open skulls with their rifle butts, if need be, to seek out Phagu, Dalama and the ingrate Chotu.

But Meghu? What perfidious intent had brought the escapee back to Bihguri?

The sight of Meghu sparked cautionary impulses. Could it be that the niggers were not as intimidated and helpless as he had thought? Otherwise, how was it that Meghu and Bircha stood barely three hundred yards away, very much within range of a rifle-shot, with such casual disdain?

Those ticking hutments, with doors closed but windows open! Could it be a well-laid ambush? They would expect him and his men to ride right up to where they stood, thereby encircled on all sides.

'*Kuch garbar hai*!' he spoke in a tense whisper. 'Something's wrong! Do you sense it, Luthra?'

'*Haan,* sahib. I smell danger!'

'Let's find out, shall we?' Raising his rifle to his shoulder, Buckingham fired.

The mirage vanished. The two coolies were there one moment and gone the next. The shot raised dust at the spot where Meghu had stood. But the shafts, thin and deadly as bamboo-snakes, which suddenly hissed through the air, were no mirages. Puran cried out as one pierced his arm.

Lips curling into a sneer of contempt, Buckingham let loose another shot at a hutment. His minions began firing blindly, bullets ploughing into mud walls. The arrows stopped coming.

Suddenly it happened! He was pausing to reload when he saw Puran lurch and fall. The sirdar writhed upon the ground as though a pack of wolves were tearing him up. All at once he went limp, stone-dead!

The arrow! A mere flesh wound—Puran had plucked out the shaft and thrown it away. Yet a bare minute later he was dead! Tipped with lethal poison!

Buckingham's blood ran cold as the implication hit him.

'*Bhago*! Run! To the jetty!' he yelled, pulling his horse around as more arrows whistled through the air. His men needed no second urging, for they too were now aware of the venomous sting in those shafts.

At their inglorious retreat the basti came obstreperously alive as doors burst open and the coolielog poured out, daos, improvised spears and axes flashing in the sunrays. They fell upon Puran, hacking at the inert cadaver, dismembering the limbs and head from the torso, plucking out the sightless eyes.

Sanatan, Meghu and Bircha stood apart, surveying the scene with satisfaction. The bastards had called them rangkukurs! The coolielog this morning were indeed wild dogs. Rangkukurs who had tasted blood!

Cordelia was well inside the tea bushes, moving in the same mechanical manner, when the sound of the rifle shot reached her. It unleashed bewildered ripples inside her mind, jolting her to a stop.

More gunshots. Then the drumming of horses' hooves and wild shrieks. In response shrieks and hoops sounded ahead from the nurseries.

Primordial instincts churned within her, countering the mind's lassitude. She turned, hesitated for a moment, and began walking back towards Buckingham's bungalow.

The horses thundered over the dusty path towards the main gate. Gandru and Budhu, running for their lives, were left behind. But Buckingham had no thought for them, or for the girl who must still be inside the bungalow. His thoughts were centred entirely upon himself. He must get to the jetty and a boat!

The instant they crossed the bungalow, and were within reach of the front entrance, arrows showered once more upon them. From the front this time, one piercing Buckingham's mount and bringing it down.

Luthra turned and rode hard for the safety of the bungalow.

The planter was thrown clear as the horse toppled in midstride, the rifle flung from him. Unhurt, he rolled over and over till he reached his weapon and fired off two quick shots at the niggers who had popped out of hiding. They dived inside the tea bushes.

Flat upon the ground, he commenced a frantic backward crawl to his bungalow, conscious that the clamour from the basti was gradually increasing in volume. The craven bastards at the gate remained well-hidden, all except the one who sprawled face downwards on the path, shot through his head.

As soon as he judged he was far enough, he raced towards the gate. One mighty bound and he was inside the compound with Luthra. Minutes later Gandru came into view, running as fast as his legs could carry him, pursued by a horde of demented coolies.

A fusillade of shots saved Gandru from certain death. The coolies halted in their tracks, , while Gandru scampered into the fenced-in compound.

'Budhu? Where's he?'

'They got him, sahib. Chopped him to pieces!'

'Poison-tipped arrows? Daos and axes? Why the devil didn't you warn me?'

'We didn't know, sahib,' Gandru stuttered. 'We swear on Bhagwan we didn't know!'

'We must hold them at bay till nightfall! That way we stand a chance … slip out of Bihguri in the darkness.' Gone was the assumed nonchalance, the thespian posturing! Their sahib's face, like their own, was a mask of terror.

'Only three of us, sahib,' Luthra cried. 'Three flanks … that's all we can cover. But we leave the rear open. They can rush us, sahib!'

'The memsahib … perhaps she can help,' Gandru said.

Cordelia! He had completely forgotten all about her! If he provided her with his spare rifle, she could cover one wing. Long enough till the sun set for the day.

But where was she? Covering in her room? 'Keep careful watch, you two,' he shouted. 'They may attempt a rush. I'll get the memsahib.'

He ran to her room. It was empty. Where the devil was that goddamn bitch? He called out to her. No answer. She was not in the bungalow.

'She's not to be found,' he said, emerging. 'Luthra and I will cover the front and sides. Gandru takes charge of the back. Shoot at anything which moves.'

Now it was merely a matter of waiting. Buckingham took a look at his chronometer. Not yet seven. The wait for the sun to set would be a long one.

The uproar in the basti had taken on jubilant overtones. The air was scorched with the heat of violence.

Sound of running footsteps. Cordelia dropped to her haunches below the height of the tea bushes. A dozen coolies raced past barely ten yards away from the direction of the nurseries, towards the bungalow. Each carried a weapon, a bow, a dao or a bamboo spear with iron head. Savage cries, steeped in hate and fury, emerged from each throat.

Even then she did not fully understand. Her dropping down behind the screen of tea bushes had been instinctive. She stood up and sauntered on without urgency towards the bungalow.

Almost at the end of the planted section she stopped. There were coolies among the bushes ahead of her, strung out around the bungalow, as though laying siege to it. Not only men but women, chokras and chokris, all armed like those she had seen run past her. Yet, though their features were monstrous with bloodlust, and they screamed out words of wrath, the evil which had been constantly touching her skin since last evening did not emanate from them but the seemingly deserted bungalow.

Cordelia crouched among the tea bushes and watched.

Had the wild dogs not tasted blood Meghu, Bircha, Sanatan and Dudhu might have advised the coolielog to be patient. There were three bandooks in the bungalow, capable of snuffing out a dozen lives before the coolielog could reach the sons of bitches. The wiser course would be to wait for the sun to set and close in when the shaitans could not see them.

But the coolielog had tasted blood! Two of the shaitans had been slain, their bodies cut to pieces. But the biggest shaitan of them all was still alive, holed up behind the bungalow fencing. The coolielog were shrieking for the signal to be given so they could move in for the kill.

Bircha was compelled to give the signal. 'Victory to the coolie people!' he yelled, his voice carrying to the furthest edge of the plantation.

'Victory to the coolie people!' the demented mob took up the refrain as, weapons upraised, it hurtled in a solid mass towards the bungalow.

There was no stopping that remorseless surge of retribution. Time and again firearms spoke and time and again a coolie staggered and fell. And then they were at the fencing, hacking at it with daos and axes and ramming it with shoulders till it toppled. The shaitans had retreated into the bungalow; but that was no impediment to the soldiers of vengeance. Gandru was the first to be killed, wielding his rifle like a club in the medicine room, breaking limbs and cracking skulls before his hands and legs were chopped off, the eyes pierced with knives and the torso left to bleed itself out. Luthra, caught climbing the rafters, was brought down with spears which filled him with more holes than a sieve. And the white shaitan was found cringing in his bedroom, too petrified to ward off the talons which clawed at his flesh, tore his hair, gouged out his eyes, crushed his testicles and slit his throat.

The sight of those ghoulish creatures baying for blood retrieved from the depths of the psyche buried images of that summer night in Delhi, of blazing houses and shrieking darkness, of Papa and Khan and Tulsi, of evil and terror and death and gore. Perhaps only those stark and terrible images could liberate the mind from its passivity. Cordelia turned around and fled.

She ran on and on till the shrieks diminished, the shots no longer sounded like cannonades to the ears. Emerging out of the plantings and onto the nurseries, lungs bursting, legs weak and rubbery, she tumbled to the ground and lay there gasping, waiting for another wave of terror to impart strength to her limbs.

But the physical terror had spent itself. The strength did not return to her limbs and the mind slid back again into uncaring lethargy. Cordelia dragged her stiff and weary frame to the shade of a neem tree, rested her back against its mottled trunk and gazed into nothingness.

'The white woman? Where's she?'

The dao in Baisakhi's hand was rusty-red. There was blood on her hands and clothes.

'Shh! not so loud, Baisakhi bahen!' Meghu cautioned.

'You promised me her head!'

'So, I did! But I can't find her. I've searched. She's not here.'

'Ask Tuvuk. Or Pahar. They were near the gate. They will know.'

Meghu's eyes scanned the anarchic throng and glimpsed Pahar. He ran up to the youth, pulled him aside and asked about the white woman.

'The farishta memsahib? We saw her walk out into the plantings. She was headed for the nurseries.'

'And you did nothing?' Meghu whispered fiercely.

'Bircha-bhaiya did not want her harmed!' Pahar muttered in his own defence, taken aback by the vehemence of Meghu's anger.

Meghu wasted no time on remonstrations. Tightly gripping the long, sharp dagger in his hand, he raced away from the bungalow and into the tea bushes.

'Good heavens! What's that!' Captain Hewitt cried. His forces, upon two longboats, were a mile downstream from the Bihguri jetty when the gunfire and riotous din reached them.

The blood drained from Michael Bailin's face. 'Gunshots! Pray God we're not late!'

The officer exhorted his boatmen to push on faster. But the upstream course and heavy boats rendered the pace agonizingly slow.

There was an intensification of firing, and the tumult appeared to be on the rise. But sometime later the noises died away and then nothing remained but an ominous silence. The Lieutenant, who had risen to his feet at the sounds, sat heavily down on a crossbeam, his head in his hands.

'If anything happens to Miss Esscombe,' he said brokenly, 'I'll never be able to forgive myself, Captain Hewitt.'

The bewilderment which had gripped Meghu was in Bircha too. All around him the coolielog were whooping and dancing. He had jostled his way through them searching for the farishta memsahib. But she was nowhere to be found, neither alive nor dead.

As he stood at the rear of the cottage wondering where she could be, Pahar ran up to him, shouting, 'Bircha-bhaiya! Bircha-bhaiya! Meghu-bhaiya spoke to me just now … asking for your farishta memsahib.'

'Do you know where she is?'

'We saw her leave the bungalow, Bircha-bhaiya … headed for the nurseries.'

'And Meghu-bhaiya was asking about her?'

'Yes, Bircha-bhaiya. There was madness in his eyes … and a knife in his hands!'

There was a sinuous rustle among the tea bushes, as though some invisible presence slithered through them. And once again she was on the ground, immobilized with terror, as the king cobra, hissing and infuriated, streaked towards her. The reptilian head shot up and the hood unfurled. For one ghastly moment Cordelia stared into the beady eyes of death.

The hood swayed back, ready to deliver the fatal strike. Cordelia screamed.

But, once again, the slashing pain of those lethal fangs did not fall. There was the vibrating whine of a spear hurtling through the air. Cordelia saw the surprise on Meghu's face as it plunged into his back, heard the pain-racked grunt. The knife dropped from his hands; the coolie staggered on drunken feet and toppled heavily. Bircha was there to catch him, pluck out the spear puncturing his heart, and lay him gently on to the ground. By then Meghu was dead.

The coolie to whom she had breathed life knelt beside his dead friend and stroked the stubbled features. Cordelia could not move. All she could do was watch the tall and broad-backed man weep like a child over the body of his departed friend.

Abruptly the man stood up and turned towards her. 'Are you all right, memsahib?' he asked.

Her frozen tongue would not allow her to make answer. The man saw the horror and revulsion in her shocked gaze and winced as if it were a spear-thrust on his own back.

'My love gone … my friend gone,' he said. 'Are you too lost to me, memsahib?'

If, perhaps, she had been able to reply she might have bestowed another life to the man. Had she screened away her fear and revulsion he may not have picked up Meghu's knife. If only she had been able to coerce her stony limbs to move, he may not have plunged the sharp blade to his chest.

An hour later, Lieutenant Michael Bailin and Captain Ralph Hewitt found her, still under the shade of the neem tree, cradling Bircha's head on her lap.

EPILOGUE

The Bihguri massacre created less of a flutter then it might have amongst the tea planting fraternity. The tardy speed with which news travelled in the region ensured that quite some time elapsed before the gory details filtered through to the ears of the planters. Moreover, the manufacturing season, when planters forsook socializing and remained ensconced in their plantations, had commenced. In fact, many a planter in the district, not to speak of those in other parts of Assam, stayed uninformed about the grisly fate of Christopher James Buckingham till the end of the monsoon rains.

The administration kept the affair on a low key. It knew from experience that such incidents could escalate into similar conflagrations elsewhere. The Assam Company, on its part, was anxious to avoid inordinate administrative scrutiny directed at its affairs.

Not that anyone treated it lightly but Major Gosselin himself visited Jorehaut and Bihguri to take stock of the situation. Mr Goodchild was at the plantation soon after he was informed of the violent happenings, accompanied by Doctor William Gordon and other company personnel. There was universal praise of the manner in which young Captain Hewitt had handled things after his forces landed at the Bihguri jetty. On seeing the sarkari sahib and his sepoys the coolies offered no resistance, but retreated quietly to their basti, carrying their dead and wounded. Apart from Buckingham and four coolies who were identified as his sirdars, seven garden hands had been killed and twice that number wounded, a few severely.

Hewitt instructed his policemen to make certain none of the coolies could leave the basti. However, the coolies were allowed to cremate the dead, and Hewitt had first-aid administered to those with minor injuries, the more grievously injured being dispatched by boat to Jorehaut.

Buckingham's festering cadaver had to await the arrival of personnel of a government-approved physician to undertake postmortem. The corpse, therefore, remained for the whole of a day and night wrapped in a sheet, its reek filling up the bungalow and attracting flies. However, after the postmortem was finally concluded, the doctor having handed over his report to Captain Hewitt, the tea planter's corpse was placed in the coffin, wrapped and sealed, and put on a boat to be taken to company-headquarters at Nazira.

Meanwhile Major Gosselin reached Bihguri along with additional police reinforcement. He immediately invested Captain Hewitt with the responsibility of conducting an official enquiry into the incident and submitting a report. The Major was aware of the difficulty of identifying the true culprits in a riotous offence such as this one in Bihguri and subjecting them to judicial scrutiny supported by cognizable evidence. It was, therefore, decided that the enquiry would be conducted within the precincts of Bihguri and only those against whom sufficient grounds for trial and possible conviction existed were to be arrested and sent to the lockup at Jorehaut. The police then launched an operation to disarm the coolies, the quantity of weapons discovered in the process astounding even the normally unflappable Major.

Captain Hewitt spent two additional days at Bihguri cross-examining the coolies and shifting through the mass of statements. On the basis of the available evidence four coolies were put in handcuffs to be taken to Jorehaut and tried. His report to his superior was an admirably factual and unbiased document which identified brutal treatment of coolies by Buckingham and his minions to be the general, and rape and murder of a coolie woman by the name of Saoni to be the specific cause of the riot and mayhem. One passage of the lengthy report made interesting reading:

'On searching the coolie basti a large number of weapons were unearthed, including knives, daos, axes, spears and arrows tipped with lethal poison. This gives rise to suspicion that an extraneous and invisible force was behind the riot, for it was physically as well as financially impossible for the workers of the garden to procure the same. My investigations into this aspect led to the conclusion that Meghu, the above mentioned Bihguri Coolie who had successfully absconded from the garden a few months back and had mysteriously returned and who, as stated, was the chief architect of the affair, was also responsible for smuggling weapons into the basti. However, it also appears that Meghu, if he was aided and abetted by extraneous force or forces, kept their identity close to his chest. Detailed and repeated questioning of Bihguri hands leads to the inescapable conclusion that none in that plantation possesses an inkling of who aided Meghu in procuring the weapons. The said Meghu having been killed during the violence, any endeavour at identifying the extraneous force or forces can be only conjectural and hypothetic and, from a pragmatic and legal perspective, an exercise in futility.'

Captain Hewitt's report contained no mention of Miss Cordelia Esscombe and her presence in Bihguri during the rioting and violence.

The mortal and mutilated remains of Christopher James Buckingham were laid to rest at the Sivasagar cemetery. A memorial service was conducted at the Baptist Mission chapel which was attended by a few functionaries of the Assam Company.

Though there was none to shed tears at Christopher James Buckingham's demise, the planter had not died in vain! The coolies of Bihguri, despite the fact that seven amongst them had perished, and Sanatan, Tuvuk and Bihuti tried for incitement to rioting and murder and lodged for seven years in the Central Jail at Sivasagar–Dhudhu having been let off due to lack of evidence—gained substantially from the death of their former Lord and Master. The company, in order to propitiate them, increased their pay and brought about improvements to their living conditions and the new manager, the shadow of his predecessor's fate hanging over him, handled them with kid gloves. The company's Board of Directors had nothing to grouse about—they had lost an outstanding manager but gained two hundred acres of land, three-fourths cleared and planted, which with a bit of clever paperwork was in due course transferred from their servant's account to that of the company's and added onto the Bihguri holdings. The coolies of Assam in general too benefitted—with the passage of time news of Buckingham's violent end percolated to the remotest plantation and induced fear of God and coolies into many a planters' hearts, thereby effecting tangible reshaping of attitudes. Buckingham's end also brought about an end to Gokuldeva Barua's travails concerning his tiny tea plantation, Mohoniya. Captain Hewitt's report had not indicted the Assamese nobleman nor was there the ghost of evidence that the dangoriya was involved with the Bihguri happenings; yet planters had a nose for such things and aired their own suspicions in private conversations. The campaign against competition from natives petered out!

And a few months later two individuals in London received a windfall in the form of a letter intimating the tragic death of their son and expressing condolence. The letter also stated that as the next of kin they were entitled to receive the former planter's personal effects as well as the not inconsiderable amount of money saved by him, from the company's London office, whenever it was convenient for them to call at the same.

At Gokuldeva Barua's mansion in Titabar, to where Lieutenant Michael Bailin had brought her after her refusal to go to Dhanboa, Cordelia recovered remarkably quickly and was well enough to be married to him just a month after the Bihguri massacre. Apart from the Lieutenant four individuals with their care and concern contributed to her emergence from the dazed stupor in which he and Captain Hewitt had discovered her on that fateful morning. All four—Brother Garry Swanson, Captain Ralph Hewitt, David Esscombe and Gokuldeva Barua, were present at the nuptial ceremony, with the Reverend undertaking the priestly duties.

Ironically, her brother and the padre, perhaps even more than the Lieutenant himself, were instrumental in helping Cordelia overcome the melancholia which had in the initial days kept her to bed. David's arrival had spurred her on the road to recovery. Her brother, after learning of the happenings at Bihguri and her whereabouts from Captain Hewitt, had come to Titabar penitent and remorseful—the hours he spent with her, the genuineness of his contrition and plea for forgiveness, had made Cordelia cry, something which she had not been able to do for some time. This was good, avowed Gokuldeva Barua, for her tears indicated that her brother had penetrated through her sheathed mind and aroused feelings which were more natural to her.

Close on David's visit came the Reverend's; only he could have pulled the girl out of bed and taken her on a ramble around the nobleman's estate. They sat on a rustic bench beneath a takou-palm and talked. He probed into her mind with the incisive dexterity of an inquisitor, prised out constricting guilts and fears and, in the process, extirpated the dark and smoggy vapours befogging her psyche. And though he suffered with her in her agonized reappraisal, he did not allow it to decant the humour from his words or obfuscate the twinkle in his eyes.

She was happy when he gave her the news Captain Hewitt had wished to be communicated to her—that the Commission of Enquiry constituted by the Government of Bengal had recommended the appointment of 'Coolie Protectors' to safeguard the interests of immigrant tea workers in Assam. 'Your refusal to compromise, and suffer because of it, has brought Michael back to you … and David who I thought you'd lost. The good Lord does not forsake His own. Consequences of action might appear fearful in this depraved milieu, and the route to felicity might be tortuous … but there is a rainbow at the end. No longer will I compromise. I'll carry on with the struggle.'

'But Bircha, Father?' The tears were back in her eyes. 'And Saoni? Was it necessary they be destroyed?'

'Sacrifice is not destruction, dear child. Some innocent blood needs be spilt … that's inevitable. How else can the pervasive potency of evil be combated? The sacrifice of Bircha and Saoni would forestall the future destruction of a thousand Birchas and Saonis … you can take heart from it.'

Both David and the Reverend returned to Titabar for the wedding. Captain Hewitt too was able to frame and submit his report and reach Gokuldeva's mansion well in time to be Michael's best man. That evening, in the European sitting room surrounded by individuals who mattered to them, the Lieutenant and his bride divulged before Captain Hewitt and David their plans for the future.

He was selling off Chahpuli, Michael told them. This would fetch him enough to repay the loan taken from the Marwari usurer, and adequate amount remaining with which to make a fresh start in life. But that start would not be made in Assam, or for that matter in Hindustan. The Reverend had suggested that as soon as the monsoons were over—they were due any day now—he and Cordelia should set out for the New World, America, a land in which, so the father told them, there was no past but only a future.

But would he be able to find a buyer immediately? Oh, he had already found one, none other than Barua dangoriya, who had offered to pay an exorbitantly generous amount. The Assamese nobleman interposed to say that Michael had made it sound as though he were doing the Lieutenant a favour whereas in reality it was a business transaction beneficial to both parties. His own garden being close to Chahpuli, the latter could be added on to Mohoniya provided, of course, he could persuade Major Gosselin to allow him to buy the jungle land separating the two. Captain Hewitt advised him to lay a claim to that piece of land—he himself would ensure that the claim was upheld by the Major so that it could be procured at a reasonable price.

In the first week of September Lieutenant Michael Bailin, Cordelia Bailin and Garo Munda paid a visit to Dhanboa where they laid two wreaths, one on Papa's grave and the other at the spot where Pekoe lay buried. They spent an hour with the coolielog before bidding a final farewell to Papa's garden.

On the eleventh of October, eighteen sixty-three, Lieutenant Michael Bailin, Cordelia Bailin and Garo Munda boarded the *Ultaganga* at Kokilamukh on the first stage of their journey to the new world. Brother Garry Swanson, Captain Ralph Hewitt and David Esscombe were at the ghat to wave them off to the land where there was no past, only a future.

ABOUT THE AUTHOR

Arup Kumar Dutta is an author, freelancejournalist and social commentator based in Assam. Acknowledged as a pioneer of English writing in the North-East, he writes short-fiction, long-fiction, non-fiction, newspaper editorials, articles and columns, satirical pieces, etc. for adults and adventure novels for young people. In a career spanning half a century, he has authored forty books, including *The Anagarika's Swansong*, *The Bag*, *The Brahmaputra*, *Unicornis*, *Cha Garam—The Tea Story*, *The Roving Minstrel*, *The Ahoms*, *Saint; Saviour; Soul; Society*, *The Kaziranga Trail* and *The Blind Witness*. He is a recipient of the Padma Shri, the Madhavdev Award and the Rongmon Award, among others, and was bestowed with D. Litt. (Honoris Causa) degrees by Dibrugarh University and Gauhati University. His official website is www.arupkumardutta.com.

ALSO BY THE AUTHOR

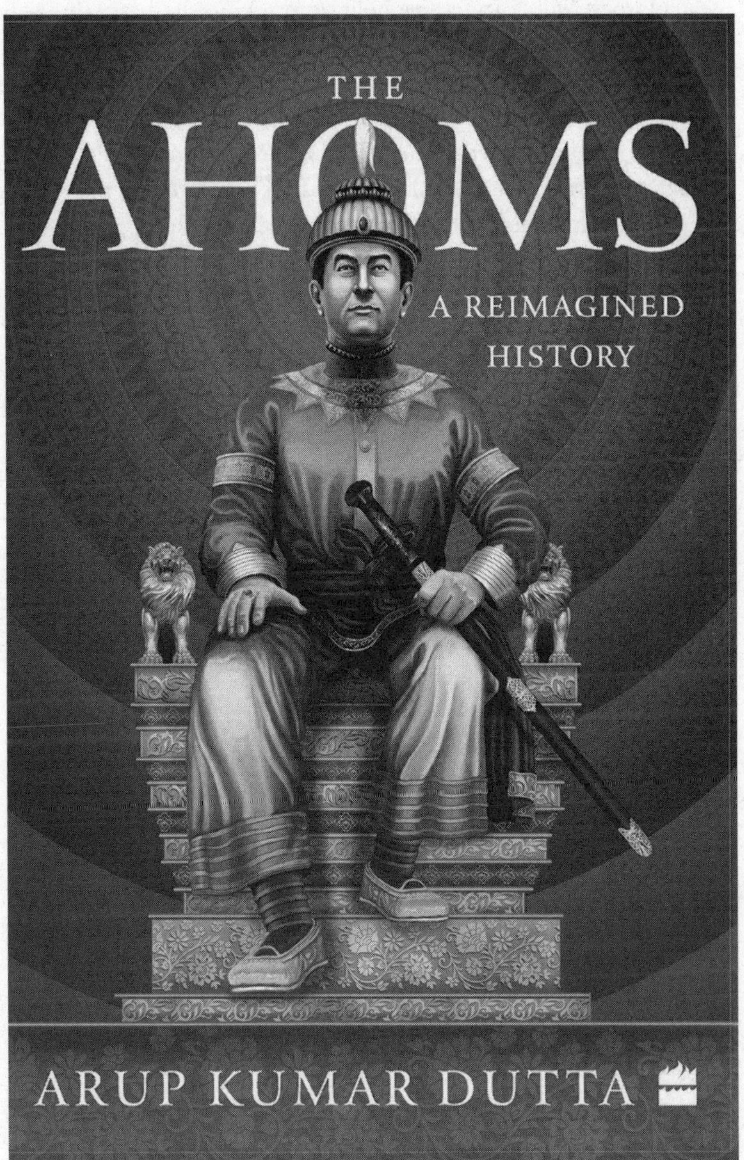

Harper
Collins

Harper
Sport

HARPER
FICTION

HARPER
NON-FICTION

हार्पर
हिन्दी
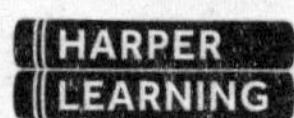
HARPER
LEARNING

HARPER
VANTAGE

HCCB
HARPERCOLLINS
CHILDREN'S BOOKS

4th

HARPER
PERENNIAL

HARPER
DESIGN

BOOKTOPUS

HARPER
BUSINESS